Just Before Midnight

A Tale of Love, Romance, Treachery and Treason

Charles S. Viar
CENTER FOR INTELLIGENCE STUDIES PRESS
WASHINGTON, DC

This is a work of fiction. Most of the characters and events are fictitious, although some historical figures appear under their own names. All rights reserved.

Cover Art by: Debra Miller, of DMR-ArtandDesign.com
Edited by: Janet Ruegg Wynne
Prepared for publication by: Janet Ruegg Wynne
Copyright © 2012 Charles S. Viar

ISBN-10: 1480142360
ISBN-13: 978-1480142367
CENTER FOR INTELLIGENCE STUDIES PRESS
WASHINGTON, DC

All rights reserved.

*Dedicated to my daughter, Anastasia.
Like Alicia, a kindred soul.*

JUST BEFORE MIDNIGHT

PROLOGUE

Suddenly aware, the Marine looked down at his body. Suspended six or seven feet above the operating table, he watched as doctors and nurses frantically struggled to revive his lifeless form.

A bit late for that, he thought. *But I appreciate the effort...*

His surroundings grew dim as the darkness closed in around him. But there was a light, far off in the distance. More curious than afraid, he began walking toward it.

He was almost halfway there when he heard the clip-clop of women's shoes behind him, and then the voice of a young girl calling after him. "Hey, Mister, wait!"

Halting in mid-stride, the Marine turned around and peered in the direction of the voice. A girl of 10 or so was running after him. Dressed in one of her mother's dresses and wearing a straw hat with artificial flowers arranged along the brim, she was hugging a Raggedy Ann Doll against her chest with one hand and holding up her skirt with the other, to avoid tripping over the hem in her mother's shoes.

Careening to a halt a few feet from him, she lost her balance and almost fell over. But she recovered, and then she looked up and smiled. She was missing a tooth.

Puzzled, but pleasantly surprised, the Marine greeted her. "Well, hello there."

The little girl smiled again, and said "hi" in return. Then after leaning over to glance around him, she pointed at the light. "You can't go there," she said.

"Really?" said the Marine as he knelt down on one knee. "And why not?"

Suddenly very serious, the little girl shook her head back and forth emphatically. "You can't go there, because you have to come back with me!"

Smiling gently, the Marine asked her why.

"Well," she said. "So I can grow up and we can get married, and live in a big house with three kids and some dogs!"

Amused, the Marine smiled again. "Really?"

Nodding again with extra emphasis, the little girl said, "Really!"

Humoring her, the Marine pretended excitement. "Wow!" he said. "That sounds great!"

Smiling from ear to ear, the little girl extended her tiny hand. "It's gonna be fantastic!"

Then after tugging on his hand with hers, she said "Come on!"

The Marine smiled, and rose to his feet. "Alright," he said. "But just for you."

As they started back into the darkness, the Marine asked the little girl her name. "I'm Alicia McAllister, from Glen Meadows," she said proudly. "It's in Connecticut."

Glancing down, the Marine nodded. "It's nice to meet you, Alicia. I'm Alex…Alexander de Vris."

Stopping suddenly, the little girl looked up and raised her index finger to her lip. "I think I knew that," she said.

Then after a long pause, she smiled again. "I have to go home now, and you have to go back to that hospital…

"But remember," she said emphatically. "You have to wait for me to grow up, OK?"

Releasing her hand, the Marine smiled down at her. "I will."

As her smile turned into a grin, the little girl laid her head over on her shoulder. "You promise?"

The Marine nodded. "I promise!"

Stepping back, the little girl pointed a tiny index finger at the Marine and pretended to be stern. "Now, don't forget!"

Then she gave him an excited, open-handed wave, and disappeared into the shadows. "See ya!"

INTRODUCTION

I turned the last page of my husband's photo album, and closed it. After savoring a memory for a long moment, I finally pushed it away and reached for a tissue. There were tears in my eyes, and I didn't want to ruin my makeup.

Even after all these years, I missed him more than words could possibly convey.

Mai Ling knocked on my bedroom door, and opened it slightly. She peered around the dark oak, just long enough to tell me in badly broken English that they were ready for me downstairs. I got up, and took one last look in the mirror. After tugging at my vest and smoothing my skirt, I turned ever so slightly to glimpse my profile.

Not bad for an old woman, I thought.

I strode across the room and exited into the upstairs hallway where Mai Ling and the Secret Service agents were waiting for me. Mai Ling took the lead, and with two agents in front of me and one behind, I started down the long steps.

I had objected to the Secret Service agents after leaving Washington, but the government had insisted. Rules were rules, they said, and they were going to protect me whether I liked it or not. But in time I had reconciled myself to their constant presence. They were such nice young men, and in truth I had come to adore them. They were always willing to talk with me, and on many a windswept night we had shared whispered secrets before a raging fire in the den. They were always up for a hand of gin rummy or hearts. Fools that they were, they would even play a little poker with me on payday, even though I'd cleaned their clocks time and time again.

But they were good-natured about it. Years ago, one of them told me that the head of the Protective Division had started an office pool with a $100 contribution, and each new agent assigned to me had contributed a like amount ever since. They knew I was cheating, but they couldn't figure out how. So the first agent who caught me – and could prove it – was going to hit the jackpot.

According to rumor, the prize had passed the $20,000 mark, and they all wanted to win.

Fat chance, I thought. *Alex taught me better than that.*

We reached the bottom of the steps, and turned right into the enormous living room. Waiting for me was Suzanne Hernandez.

She was the brightest star in a new galaxy of journalists, or so I was told. But I really had no way of knowing. I hadn't granted an interview in more than 15 years, and I had long since given up on TV. Or whatever it is they call it these days.

Ms. Hernandez rushed forward, and extended her hand. "Mrs. de Vris, thank you so much for meeting with me today. I'm a great admirer of yours, and I can't begin to tell you how thrilled I am to meet you in person. You're a national hero."

She seemed sincere, so I smiled graciously as she went on.

"I am so sorry to have kept you waiting. There was a great deal of unexpected solar activity this morning, and the flares played havoc with the satellite feeds. And then we have had problems with the lighting...I am so sorry."

I smiled at her indulgently. "It's quite alright, dear. It gave me a chance to look through my husband's photo album. It made me realize how anxious I am to see him again."

Taken aback, she looked at me with concern. "In the next life, perhaps?"

The look on her face made me laugh. Obviously worried that I had become a religious nut in my old age, I decided to toy with her a bit. "In this world or the next, Ms. Hernandez. Frankly, it wouldn't surprise me if he turned up at the door one day."

With that she turned ashen, so I quickly explained. "My husband was a most remarkable man, Ms. Hernandez. He cheated death a thousand times, so I wouldn't be the least bit surprised if he did it again."

I looked at her with a wry smile. "I don't know if God has him or the Devil, but there is one thing I'm sure of: The instant he knew he was dead, he started hatching an escape plan. And if there is anyone who can pull that off, it's Alex...

"As I said, he was a most remarkable man."

She stared at me, dumbfounded.

"I understand you wanted to talk with me about my career in politics and power." I shook my head in disapproval. "Mere icing on the cake."

She started to protest, but I cut her off with a wave of my hand. "What your viewers would really like to hear about is my husband, and the years we spent together."

"I have never once discussed our relationship in public, so this will be an exclusive. And you will be grateful for it, my dear."

I looked at her and smiled with mischievous rue. "It's one *hell* of a story."

From behind a bank of monitors, the crew chief was gesturing frantically. "Got the uplink, Suzanne. 68 seconds to feed."

Facing certain defeat, Ms. Hernandez conceded. "Very well, Mrs. de Vris. It will be about your husband."

I gestured towards the overstuffed chairs that had been rearranged for the interview and waited for her to be seated. She was, after all, a guest in my house.

The makeup man rushed around and dabbed her face, and then mine. Getting a thumbs-up from the lead cameraman, he retreated into the background while Suzanne stared into the lens. From somewhere a voice called "On my mark...five, four, three, two, we are *ON THE AIR*."

Ms. Hernandez smiled, and began addressing the audience. "Good morning, and thank you for joining us. I am Suzanne Hernandez with Global News Network, and we are broadcasting live from the living room of one of our great national heroes, Alicia de Vris. A living legend, Mrs. de Vris has never before discussed her relationship with her late husband, Alexander de Vris, and we are here today to bring you this Global News exclusive."

She leaned forward, and looked at me intently. "Mrs. de Vris, your relationship with your late husband has been discussed endlessly in books and articles. In fact, it is often said that yours was one of the greatest love affairs of all time…

"Tell us, please. How did it begin?"

I leaned back in my chair, as a smile of delight danced upon my face. "It was, Suzanne, it was. And believe it or not, it began one miserably hot morning in front of the old bus station in Washington, DC."

CHAPTER ONE

Dragging my oversized suitcase behind me, I worked my way through the milling crowd toward the front of the bus station. Stopping every three or four feet to get a better grip on the handle, or to apologize for having run over someone's foot, or bumped them with the carry-on bag slung across my shoulder, it took me ten minutes to cover the two hundred feet from my bus to the big glass doors. When I finally emerged into the sunlight to look on R Street, I was exhausted, exhilarated, and happy.

I had been planning the move ever since my junior year at Township College, when my boyfriend took a job in suburban Virginia. A year older than I, James had majored in business administration. The country was just emerging from a deep recession, and his prospects didn't look good. Very few companies were hiring, and so we assumed he would stay on at Township for another year of graduate study. But just before graduation he had received an offer from a management-consulting firm based in Arlington, Virginia. It was an exciting opportunity, and he had accepted it on the spot. Two days later, he was gone.

It was all so sudden that we didn't have time to talk about it, or our future together. But in the midst of a tearful goodbye, he asked me to join him in Washington as soon as I finished my senior year. And in the almost daily long distance calls, hundreds of cards and letters and occasional visits home he had never wavered. He wanted me to be with him, here in the nation's capital.

The idea had thrilled me for an entire year, and now it had finally arrived. As I stood in the hot sun and searched the crowd outside for James, a welcome feeling of triumph possessed me. Getting from Glen Meadows, Connecticut, to Washington, D.C., had not been easy. It had taken an enormous amount of planning and preparation, financial sacrifice and – of course – parental disapproval. When I had first broached the idea with my Mom, she had laughed. Chasing after James was a damned stupid idea, she'd said, and in the months that followed she had done everything she could to talk me out of it. But that had only hardened my determination.

It wasn't just that she disapproved of James. She had never liked him very much, and even though she had tried to hide it from me, it still showed in unguarded moments. But the real issue was that she wanted me to stay close to home. We had been on our own ever since Dad died when I was four, and she dreaded being alone. Whenever things were hard, or frightening, she had always reassured me that we were a team. We'd always be together, she said, and as a little girl growing up in a fatherless world, those words had comforted me. But as I got older I realized that she had said them to comfort herself as well. Being a single mother was hard and sometimes scary, and at times it must have been as frightening as being a little girl without a dad.

But childhood always ends, and as I moved into my teens new traits took hold. I had always been stubborn, like my Dad, but by the time I turned 16, a restless curiosity had seized me. There was more to the world than the small town I was growing up in, and I wanted to know more about it. I wanted to experience it, and to make it my own.

I knew it would be hard to leave my Mom, but I also knew it was the right thing to do.

I felt like I owed her that. Throughout the 18 long years since my Dad died – years that had often been filled with hardship and struggle – she had been the perfect Mom. Now it was time for her to have a life of her own. She was only 42, and she was stunning. When we went out together, the men didn't just look. The ones with proper manners stared, and the others gawked.

She was a beautiful woman, and I knew the men would beat a path to her door. Or at least they would, once I was out on my own.

So as I dragged my big suitcase up to the retaining wall that ran beside the bus station's entranceway, I congratulated myself. *Ya done good, Alicia.*

The retaining wall seemed a bit dirty, so I sat down on my suitcase and pulled the carry-on off my shoulder. As it hit the ground with a dull thud, I glanced at my watch. *9:18 am. Where is he?*

James was a complex guy, a fact that had intrigued and often delighted me. But punctuality had never been one of his strong points, and if I hadn't been there to roust him out of bed at

Township, he probably would have slept through half his classes. So I shrugged, and watched the traffic pass by.

James had warned me about Washington's weather, but I hadn't really believed him. Who would be stupid enough to put the nation's capital in a swamp? But by now it was 9:30, and it was already hot and humid enough to persuade me. Making a mess out of history, I began to wonder if the Founders weren't so smart after all.

By that time I was bored. Knowing that James had probably overslept, I figured he wouldn't be up until about noon. I thought about calling him, but the way he slept it wouldn't make any difference. He wouldn't hear the phone even if I yelled in the answering machine. So to pass the time, I started making up stories about the people passing by. The longhaired man in the brightly painted Volkswagen was obviously a leftover hippy, or at least a wannabe. But the guy in the Mercedes looked rich and distinguished, and I wondered if he was a big shot in the government.

Maybe a cabinet member?

I was almost lost in the thought when I noticed a guy in a pickup truck, piled high with furniture. He had been by before, or at least I thought he had. It looked to me like he was moving, and I wondered where he was going, and why.

There had been a minor fender-bender at the light, and traffic had backed up while a motorcycle cop inspected the damage and talked to the drivers. From where I was sitting, I couldn't see what had actually happened, but the drivers stalled in front of the bus station were getting a bit irritated. From somewhere back down the line, impatient horns were blowing.

The guy in the pickup rolled down his window and leaned his head out in a vain attempt to see what was going on. Back in the truck, he looked down at his watch with unmistakable irritation. Obviously he had better things to do than sit in Washington traffic on a Saturday morning. *He must not be getting paid by the hour*, I thought.

Or maybe his boss would get mad at him for being late...

He was handsome, ruggedly handsome, like the guy in the Marlboro commercials. With his dark brown hair and mustache, I could see him galloping a horse across the plains. Distance and a pair of aviator sunglasses hid his eyes from me, but I imagined them to be a piercing blue. And I wondered how old he was...

Although I could see him plainly, it was impossible to tell. His face had a certain indeterminacy about it, and he could have been 25, I thought, or 35 or maybe even 40.

By then the long line of backed-up cars finally began to creep forward, and I lost sight of him. Disappointed, I went back to my game.

This time it was a girl in a Toyota. She was wearing a gorgeous dress that was thoroughly rumpled, and as she waited for the light to change again, she tilted the rear view mirror so she could see and began brushing her hair with long, fast strokes. *Someone had a good time last night...*

Snickering, I looked down at my watch. *10:30! It can't be!*

More cars passed, and then a score of kids on bikes. Careening through the traffic like madmen, they seemed to be having fun annoying the adults. *Oh God*, I thought. Convinced that one of the kids was going to get run over, I looked the other way.

And there he was again, the guy in the pickup truck.

I looked away quickly so he wouldn't see me, and crossed my fingers. *Come on light, turn red!*

But it didn't, and he drove past again. This time there wasn't any furniture, so I guessed he had dropped it off someplace close by. *But where?* The bus station was in an awful neighborhood, and I couldn't imagine him living anyplace like that.

Do you suppose he's really poor? Maybe he's just helping a friend who's down on his luck.

I didn't like those thoughts, so I pushed them from my consciousness. There was a perfectly reasonable explanation, I told myself.

By now it was hot. *Really hot...*

I pulled my cotton headband down on my forehead to wipe away the moisture, but things were more problematic inside my blouse. Beads of perspiration were forming on my chest, and starting to trickle into my bra. It was an awful feeling, one that made me long for a shower. I had ridden the bus all night from Glen Meadows, Connecticut, and I was beginning to feel a bit grimy. *God, I must look terrible!*

I grasped the top button of my blouse and fanned it to and fro to cool myself. A police officer who had been standing by the doorway laughed and smiled knowingly. "Welcome to D.C., Miss. You're going to love it here."

He was big, black and powerfully built. I smiled and nodded. Happy to have someone to talk to, I asked him if it was always this hot.

He shook his head sadly. "You ain't seen nothing yet, Miss. By August it will be 100 degrees in the shade, with 90 percent humidity. It's awful."

He rolled his eyes and shook his head again. "If I had known about the weather, I would have found a police force someplace else. Criminal justice majors were in short supply when I graduated from college and I could have gone anywhere."

Then he laughed. "Like maybe Alaska."

I couldn't help but laugh, too. Under the circumstances, it was pretty funny. But then he turned very serious, and asked what I was doing sitting in the sun all alone. Did I have friends or relatives who might pick me up?

I shook my head no, and explained the situation. The officer nodded, and suggested that I try calling James. The weather was brutal, and the last thing he needed was a heat stroke victim on his hands. He was supposed to get off in a few minutes, and if I passed out the paperwork would take him at least another hour. He volunteered to watch my bags for me, so I got up and went inside.

There was a bank of pay phones against the wall, so I picked up the handset of one, dropped a quarter in the slot and dialed the number from memory. It rang once, then twice. There was a click, and suddenly a recording. The number I had dialed was not in service.

Darn! I opened my purse and began fishing in the bottom. There were four or five quarters in there, someplace. *This always happens!* Irritated, I wondered why James couldn't just get up on time.

I finally found a coin, and dropped it in the slot. This time I punched in the numbers more carefully. It rang, and rang again. And then the click, and the mechanical voice.

His phone is out of order? This can't be happening...

As I slumped against the wall, my mind raced, turning over one awful possibility after another. What could have happened? I had just talked to him two days before, and everything was fine. *I bet the dummy forgot to pay his phone bill again.*

I hung up the phone, and took a deep breath. Shaking my head, I walked back outside and smiled weakly at the police officer. "Thanks for watching my bags. He'll be here in a few minutes."

I was lying, and he knew it. He hesitated a moment, and I could see that he was calculating the possibilities. He looked at me closely, then nodded. "Glad to hear it, Miss." Then he turned, and walked back into the building.

I sat down hard on my bag. My mind was racing again, and I was desperately trying to shut it off. *It's just a glitch, he's done this before. He just forgot to pay the phone bill again, that's all. He'll wake up anytime now, and come for me. He won't leave me sitting on the sidewalk. I know he won't.*

After reassuring myself over and over again, I began to calm down. *The game*, I thought. *I'll play my game again.*

Hey! I looked down at my watch. It had been an hour or more. *Where's the guy in the pickup?*

By then it was almost noon, and I had to make a trip to the ladies' room – no ifs, ands or buts about it. So I slung my carry-on over my shoulder again, and tugged on the big bag. It had gotten a lot heavier.

I dragged it through the automatic doors, and began looking around for the restrooms. The crowd had thinned out quite a bit by now, and I caught a glimpse of the sign off to my left. I jerked the bag hard, bouncing it up on the little back wheels, and then made my way inside.

I reemerged ten minutes later, much refreshed. The bathroom had been deserted, and I had taken advantage of that fact. After locking myself in an empty stall, I peeled off my top and jeans and used moistened paper towels to wipe down my body. It was a far cry from a shower, but under the circumstances it was the best I could do. After dressing once again, I had tied my hair up and washed my face. I even thought about putting on some makeup, but it was just too darned hot.

I had just emerged from the double exit doors when I heard a terrific crash. And there was The Mystery Man, at long last.

He had hit one of the potholes that Washington had become famous for, and a large wooden table had somehow come free and bounced off the truck. It had hit the road hard, and shattered into a half dozen pieces. But before the rubble had finished bouncing, he'd stopped the truck and jumped out. There was a rueful look on his face, and from where I was standing I could almost make out the muted swearing.

After surveying the damage, he shrugged and began picking up the pieces. He had almost finished loading the debris back onto the truck when he noticed me staring. He was down on one knee, gathering up pieces of kindling when he looked up and saw me. Our eyes met for the briefest of moments, and before he could look away an embarrassed smile flickered across his face. Blushing badly, he retrieved the last shattered stick and climbed back into the cab. A moment later he was gone.

I felt badly for him. It wasn't his fault that the table fell off, or at least I didn't think it was. But still, I knew that it must have been humiliating.

And of course, my staring made it all the worse...

Dejected, I sat down on my suitcase again and rested my chin on two balled fists. I knew that if past experience was any guide, I'd never see him again and that depressed me. Male egos being what they are, I was pretty sure he would be taking another route on the next trip.

Over the past couple of hours I had grown sort of attached to him in a curious kind of way, and the thought that he wouldn't be back saddened me for some reason. *Oh well*, I thought, *it's not like I was going to marry him or anything...*

By then it was well past one o'clock, and I was hot, tired, and hungry. I wanted to go inside to get something to eat, but I just couldn't afford it. I had begun the trip with exactly $100, and I had $98 and some change left. It was all the money I had in the world, and if I spent it now I might end up in real trouble later. If anything went wrong – and deep down inside, I was beginning to suspect it had – I'd have to call my Mom and ask her to wire me money. I desperately wanted to avoid that, because I knew I'd never hear the end of it. So I sat on my suitcase and sweltered, as my feelings cycled between self-pity and livid anger with James.

After a while I stopped feeling sorry for myself and started plotting my revenge. I was going to read him the riot act when he finally showed up. And after that, I was going to make his life a living hell for three, maybe four days.

And if he thinks there is going to be any sex in his future, he'd better think again...

Because trust me on this – I was gonna make that boy grovel!

Pleasantly distracted, I almost didn't notice the guy in the pickup as he pulled to a halt across the street. When it came to a stop, he turned around to look through the rear window, and whistled. A moment later, a huge black dog jumped out of the back and trotted around to the cab.

Curious and puzzled, I watched as he opened the door and handed him a big white sack. The dog grasped it in its mouth, turned, and stopped. After checking the traffic both ways, he trotted across the street and up the tarmac to where I was sitting. He stopped in front of me and sat down, wagging his tail.

Incredulous, I looked up at the guy in the pickup. I pointed at myself, and mouthed the words: *For me?*

He smiled and nodded. Curious and flattered, and a bit hesitant, I reached out and took the bag. Nestled inside was a smaller bag, from Wendy's, and inside that one I could see a bacon cheeseburger, french fries, packets of salt, pepper and catsup, and a Coke. Next to it all was a small bottle of Evian water, and curled around it was a note. *How cool*, I thought.

Holding the bag from the bottom with my left hand, I pulled out the note with my right. After snapping my wrist three or four times to flick it open, I read the words scrawled on it: *Hope you like Wendy's!*

With a huge smile on my face, I looked up to thank him. But by then the pickup was already disappearing down the street. The dog's head was sticking up over the tailgate, so I waved him goodbye. He acknowledged my gesture with a friendly bark, and disappeared around the corner.

I was flattered, and delighted. It was a class act from start to finish, and it made my spirits soar.

I ate the cheeseburger happily, and started nibbling on the fries. As I reached into the bag for another couple, I found myself wondering about the mysterious man in the pickup, and his well-trained dog. I wondered when he'd first noticed me, and how he'd known how hungry I was. The thought that he was a mind reader briefly flickered through my consciousness, before I dismissed it as silly. But I soon found myself thinking about the strange bonds that sometimes connect people through time and space, so strongly that they know what one another is thinking and even feeling in times of stress or anxiety. I had read about that in Psychology, and I remembered that for some reason the people it happens to are always connected on some really deep level. Most of the time it happened with twins, or with couples who had been married for years and years. But sometimes it just happened with people who hardly even knew one another, and I couldn't help but wonder if we hadn't made some sort of connection. It didn't seem very likely — after all, we hadn't even met — but the thought intrigued me.

After finishing off the fries, I went back to my game. But the traffic was even less than before, and I soon became bored. As hard as I tried to concentrate, I kept thinking about *him*. And hoping he would come by again soon.

But I was cruelly disappointed. Thousands of cars passed as the sun made its way slowly across the sky; and as it began to settle in the far west, I finally realized that he would not return. And at long last, I admitted to myself that James would not be coming either.

I was lost, alone and abandoned. My courage exhausted, I broke down and wept.

CHAPTER TWO

I'm not sure how long I cried. It might have been for a half-hour, or maybe even an hour. Oblivious to the people who occasionally walked through the bus station's doors, I sat on my suitcase and wept until I choked on my tears. It was only then that I noticed someone was standing there. Startled, I looked up through grief-stained eyes.

It was him, the guy in the pickup. Aghast, I burst into tears again. But by now he wasn't wearing jeans and a T-shirt. He had changed into a double-breasted navy blue blazer, and razor-creased khaki trousers. A pale blue button-down shirt subtly contrasted a regimental tie, and from just beneath the cuff of his shirt came the gleam of a Rolex watch. Horrified that he would see me this way, I turned away in shame.

He knelt down on one knee beside me, and without saying a word offered me his handkerchief. Afraid to face him, I took it and turned away. I dabbed my eyes, and then gently blew my nose. Looking down at the ground, I slowly folded his handkerchief and handed it back to him. "I'm sorry," was all I could say.

He smiled softly, and reached up to touch my face. Guiding it gently around, he looked into my eyes and smiled again. "Hey, I've had some pretty bad days myself."

His voice was soft and gentle, but it conveyed an unmistakable sense of power. Wiping my eyes, I nodded again and again. "It's been a really bad day for me."

I thought he smiled, but through my bloodshot eyes I couldn't be sure. "Mine wasn't so great either," he said. "Not only did I have to move about ten tons of accumulated junk, but I broke an antique table into a million pieces...

"So I think we're about tied."

I was incredulous. "That was an antique? Oh, my gosh, it must have been worth a fortune!"

He smiled and rolled his eyes. "Leave it to Alex to make a mess out of moving...

"Oh, by the way...I'm Alex. Alexander de Vris."

Sniffling, I said, hi. "It's nice to meet you, Alex. I'm Alicia McAllister, from Glen Meadows. It's in Connecticut."

I felt like a complete idiot. I hadn't introduced myself to anyone like that since I was ten years old. But thankfully, he didn't seem to notice. Or if he did, he was too much of a gentleman to show it. Instead he stretched out his hand. "It's nice to meet you, too, Alicia."

We shook hands, but he didn't let go immediately. Still kneeling, he pivoted slightly on his heel and gestured behind him at an Asian couple. "And these are my friends, Nguyen and Mai Ling Tranh."

I looked up, noticing them for the first time. Nguyen smiled and said "hi" in perfect English. His wife – at least I assumed it was his wife – smiled as she placed her hands together, and bowed slightly.

I tried hard to smile, and said hello.

Alex cocked his head to the side, and asked me if he could be of assistance. He had watched me bake in the hot sun all day, and he was concerned.

With that, I burst into tears again. After sobbing for a few moments, I blurted out my predicament. For whatever reason, James wasn't coming, and I had less than a hundred dollars to my name. Lost and alone, I was stranded in D.C. I had no place to go, and no one to turn to. I didn't even think I could afford a hotel room, even if I could find one.

Too embarrassed to even look at him, I broke down and wept again. He remained motionless for a moment, then gently touched my knee. "Please don't cry."

He paused for a moment, suddenly thoughtful. "You know, I keep a suite at the National Hotel for business purposes. I hardly ever use it, but it comes in handy now and then…"

I looked up at him incredulously. "A whole suite?"

Even in the dim light, I could see he was embarrassed. "Just for business purposes. Every now and then someone important comes into town on short notice, so we put them up there. And once in a while we use it for a reception or an open house…

"No one's using it now, but I have to pay for it anyway. So why don't you stay there tonight?"

I was mortified. "Oh, no, I couldn't. I can't possibly impose on you like that."

Alex smiled. "It's no imposition at all, Alicia. It would be my pleasure."

I didn't know what to do. Alex and his friends seemed really nice, but I didn't know anything about them. They could be serial killers — or even worse, for all I knew.

But if I didn't accept his offer, I'd have to call my mom to come bail me out, and she'd never let me forget it. I'd be hearing about it for the rest of my life.

Not to mention the fact that I'd never see him again…

Looking back on it now, it all seems pretty crazy. But at the time, risking life and limb seemed a whole lot more appealing than the alternatives. So I reached out and took his handkerchief again. Then after taking a moment to mull it over, I wiped my nose again and nodded. "Thank you," was all I could say.

Alex smiled. "I have a couple of things I have to attend to, but Mai Ling will get you checked in. I'll be along in a half-hour or so, and we can get something to eat in the restaurant, OK?"

With that he stood up, and said something in what I thought was Vietnamese. Mai Ling swept forward, and put her arms around me. "We go now," she said in broken English.

Stunned by my good fortune — and still more than a little bit fearful — I nodded silently and let her steer me to a BMW parked across the street. Nguyen followed behind us, carrying my bags.

He opened the rear door for me, and then walked around and opened the opposite door for his wife. After maneuvering my bags into the trunk, he got in himself and started the car.

Mai Ling put her hand on my knee. "Poor dear," she said. "But not worry. You fine now."

I was embarrassed, and a little bit ashamed, so I didn't say anything. I nodded and smiled instead.

Nguyen started the engine and pulled out into traffic. Glancing in the rear mirror, he asked me if this was my first time in D.C. When I told him it was, he grinned. "It can be kind of intimidating at first. I remember the first time I saw Washington…I was blown away."

Feeling a little better, I asked him where he was from. "Oh, I was born in Hue, but I grew up in Saigon. That's in the Republic of Vietnam."

He stopped abruptly. "Or at least it was. Anyway, my father was a member of the diplomatic service, and we were posted here when I was 14."

He laughed to himself. "You know it's really kinda funny. Saigon was a lot bigger than D.C., but for some reason this place really cowed me. I was scared to death when I first got off the plane."

Interested, I asked Mai Ling if she was from Saigon too. Yes, she said, Cholon. She went on to explain that was Saigon's equivalent of Chinatown. Her family were expatriate Chinese, and had lived in Vietnam for generations.

I wondered if they had been able to escape the war here, but I was afraid to ask. Saigon had fallen to the Communists only a few years before, and I didn't want to raise a painful issue.

Curious, I asked Mai Ling how they knew Alex. Before she could answer, Nguyen informed me that he and Alex had been classmates at St. Alban's Preparatory School in Northwest D.C. He laughed and said that was where all the spoiled rich kids went to high school.

They'd been the new kids in their class that year, and in such a cliquish environment they had become friends of necessity. But strangely enough, they'd found they had a lot in common. In addition to being social outcasts, they shared a love for fast cars, science fiction, horror movies, pinball and – especially – oldies music.

Then he glanced over his shoulder and grinned. "And pretty girls, of course."

With that, Mai Ling lashed out with incredible speed, cracking him on the back of his head with her purse. A torrent of Vietnamese followed.

Grimacing, Nguyen apologized. "My wife says that I shouldn't talk that way in front of a proper young lady." He looked over his shoulder and said, "I am sorry."

I laughed. "Oh, that's OK. Boys will be boys."

Mai Ling rolled her eyes. "Dat right, dose two boys," she exclaimed in a voice filled with exasperation. "Keep dem out of trouble make hair gray!"

Nguyen laughed easily. He glanced over his shoulder at his wife and smiled. "It's all part of my charm, darlin."

Mai Ling shrieked in horror as Nguyen suddenly hit the brakes and swerved hard, barely missing a kid on a skateboard who had shot out in front of him. In the process, he almost took out a police car parked on the side of the street. Glancing guiltily in the rear mirror, he apologized to us both. The hotel was only a block away, and he promised to get us there in one piece.

My heart was still stuck in my throat when he pulled the Beemer into the shallow circular drive in front of the hotel.

Through the windshield, I could see the Capitol Building just blocks away, its dome illuminated by spotlights. For a girl from Glen Meadows, it was a breathtaking sight.

A liveried doorman stepped forward and opened my door. Extending a white-gloved hand to help me out of the car, he wished me a good evening.

Needless to say, I was impressed. I thanked him, and took his hand.

Nguyen had already opened the door for Mai Ling, and was struggling with my bags. Although he was clearly in excellent shape, he was slight and slender like most Vietnamese. Standing only a bit taller than me – he couldn't have been much more than 5'5" – I didn't think he could possibly lift my oversized bag. But somehow or another, he managed to get it out of the trunk and up on its wheels.

Mai Ling took my hand, and led me into the lobby with Nguyen tagging behind. As I glanced around, all I could think was, *Wow!*

It was huge, ornate, and richly furnished. Suddenly conscious of the fact that my mouth was hanging open, I turned crimson. Mai Ling saw my expression out of the corner of her eye, and smiled. "It nice."

"Yes," I said. "It's more than nice." Glancing around again, I whispered, "It's gorgeous."

Nguyen dragged my bags over to the check-in desk, and said something to the concierge. After the man gestured, two members of the staff scurried over and picked them up. Then with my luggage in hand, they vanished into an elevator as the concierge walked over to greet me. As he approached, it suddenly occurred to me that I was badly underdressed for such an elegant establishment.

The concierge extended his hand. "My name is Antoine, and I am the night concierge. I understand you will be staying in Mr. de Vris' suite?" His accent was French, and apparently genuine.

I took his hand, and nodded dumbly. He shook my hand and apologized with a practiced smile. "I am sorry, *Mademoiselle*, I did not get your name."

Letting go of his hand, I introduced myself. He bowed slightly, and said "*Enchanté*".

Glancing around at the desk clerk, he snapped his fingers. The clerk removed a key from one of the mahogany boxes behind him, and hurried over. Antoine took the key from him and handed it to me ceremoniously. *"Monsieur* de Vris is our honored guest, as you shall also be...

"I understand that you wish to be served dinner. Please follow me and I will rouse the Chef."

He turned stiffly on his heel and led us across the lobby and through a beautifully carved doorway. "Mr. de Vris' table is this way."

Nguyen had vanished, but Mai Ling was still holding onto my hand as we followed Antoine across the deserted room to a table in the far corner. There he pulled out a chair on the left and seated me, then a chair on the right for Mai Ling. He said something to her in French, and listened attentively as she replied. He nodded. "But of course, *Madame*."

Antoine disappeared into the shadows of the partially lit room, returning a few moments later with the wine steward and the chef. The wine steward showed Mai Ling the bottle, opened it ceremoniously and handed her the cork. She sniffed it, and smiled with delight. "Excellen!"

The steward poured her glass, and waited while she tasted it. With a puzzled look on her face, she asked the steward something in French. She sat in rapt attention, apparently fascinated by his lengthy answer. Then she smiled broadly, and gestured for him to pour me a glass. All eyes were on me as I raised it to my lips.

My God, I thought. *This is incredible!* I'd tasted wine before, but never anything like this. "It's wonderful," I said.

With that the steward smiled broadly, and retired. The chef stepped forward, and graciously apologized. The kitchen had closed sometime before and most of the help had been let go for the night. But for Mr. de Vris' friends, he would do his very best. He switched into French, and began reciting a lengthy list of delicacies that he could prepare unaided.

Mai Ling raised her hand to silence him. She would be staying until Alex arrived, and then collect her wayward husband and depart. But she was sure that Alex would like his usual, a strip steak covered in Béarnaise sauce. And of course, a mountain of french fries. She turned to me and asked me what I would have. Dumbfounded, I said that would be fine for me as well.

And a small salad, if it wasn't too much trouble...

The chef clapped his hands together in obvious relief. "Of course, *Mademoiselle.* Immediately." Then he turned and disappeared into the kitchen.

Antoine asked Mai Ling something in French, but I couldn't follow it. I had taken two semesters of Modern French in college, and I could read it reasonably well. But I was far from fluent, so I couldn't keep up with their rapid-fire speech. After Mai Ling finished speaking, Antoine nodded. "Certainly, *Madame*. I will see to it."

Turning to me, he expressed his delight that I would be staying at the National and informed me that he and the staff were at my service. I need only ask for anything I wanted. I smiled nervously, and thanked him. Since I hadn't seen the bill of fare, I couldn't be certain – but I was pretty sure I couldn't even afford a cup of their coffee, so there wasn't much chance I'd be asking for anything.

Just as Antoine turned to go, Alex walked in. He smiled and waved.

He stopped for a moment to talk to the concierge. They were too far away for me to overhear what they were saying, but after a few moments of discreet conversation Alex reached into his pocket and handed him a folded bill. Then he smiled and thanked him again before turning away.

He strode across the room, and stopped before the table. Smiling, he pulled out a chair and turned it around before sitting down casually. "Have you ordered?"

For the first time, I caught the faintest hint of a southern accent, and for some reason it surprised me.

Mai Ling said something to him in Vietnamese. Alex looked disappointed, but he shrugged before nodding. "That's OK. Maybe tomorrow afternoon?" Mai Ling said she would check with Nguyen, and leave a note on the nightstand.

That piqued my curiosity, but I knew it would be rude to inquire. Mai Ling pushed back her chair and stood up. She extended her hand across the table, and told me what a pleasure it had been.

I thanked her in turn, and I meant it. She had been gracious to a fault, and she had made me feel at ease in very difficult circumstances. I really appreciated it.

She smiled as she turned to go, and asked me to look after Alex. Then she bent over and kissed him on the cheek, and hurried out the door.

Alex got up and turned his chair around so that it faced properly, and sat down. Reaching for the bottle of wine, he grinned. "Hell of a day."

I'm not sure if it was the wine or the expression on his face, but I cracked up. Less than an hour ago I had been sitting on my bag crying, lost, alone and broke – and now I was sitting at a private table in the deserted dining room of some fantastically expensive hotel, sipping wine with a guy I had been fantasizing about all day. It was, in fact, one hell of a day.

Alex grinned sheepishly, as though he had said something wrong. He raised his glass and said, "To you, Alicia McAllister, of..."

He paused and looked at me quizzically. "Where did you say you were from?"

Flushing badly, I reminded him. "Glen Meadows," I said. "It's in Connecticut."

"Glen Meadows, it is." He clinked his glass against mine, and downed the entire contents. His elbows propped on the table, he held the empty glass before him with both hands and looked at me. "So tell me about yourself."

He was looking at me intently, but I thought there was a mischievous look in his eyes. I didn't know if he was flirting with me, or just putting me on the spot. As I felt my face flush yet again, I fell back in my chair and looked at the ceiling. I was smiling, involuntarily, and trying hard not to laugh in embarrassment. As unsettling as it was, I liked his attention.

In fact, I liked it a lot. But I had no idea what to say to him. He was handsome, obviously rich and probably powerful. And I was just a kid fresh out of college. A state college, no less. In Glen Meadows, Connecticut.

What could be more boring?

I just couldn't believe there was anything about my life he would find interesting. In contrast, he was charming and sophisticated – and if there was a certain shyness about him, there was also an intensity that whispered of danger. For beneath the practiced charm and polished manners, I could sense roiling emotions. Like an ocean storm, they were frightening and exciting and all too erotic.

Made suddenly uncomfortable by my sensual response, I pushed it out of mind. Then after summoning up my courage, I looked into his deep green eyes and tried to smile. "Well..."

But just then, the Chef arrived with our salads.

Alex thanked him and unrolled his silverware from the starched linen napkin, and began eating. After he had taken a few bites, he looked up at me and smiled. "You were saying?"

So at last I began talking, and to my surprise he seemed genuinely interested as I told him about my life. And as he encouraged me with an occasional word, or question, my halting sentences began to flow more smoothly. By the time our steaks arrived, I had shared with him the joys of my tree house in the backyard and the Raggedy Ann doll I had implausibly named Skinnard, and the awful fights I used to have with my mom over dresses. As a little girl I had hated wearing them, more than anything else in the world.

Alex laughed softly. "You must have been quite the tomboy."

Blushing badly, I admitted that it was true. If Skinnard was my best friend and constant companion, I had no time for other dolls or tea parties like the other little girls on my street. I was far more interested in climbing trees, and chasing balls, and exploring the mud puddles that formed in the backyard after a hard rain. And I told him about the big woods that backed up to our property, and how Skinnard and I had set out to explore every inch of it, and gotten hopelessly lost in the process.

And I shared with him the agony of losing my Dad, and the painful years that followed. I told him about what a geek I had been in high school, and how ugly I had been with braces and glasses, and straggly blonde hair. And then in a moment of terrible indiscretion, I told him about my first kiss – my first real kiss – when Tommy Jurgensen walked me home after a basketball game that had gone late into overtime my junior year. I had just finished telling him about Township College when he looked at his watch.

It was very late, he said, we really should go.

Terribly embarrassed, I apologized for rambling on and on. Alex shook his head, and said there was no need. It had been his pleasure.

As he escorted me to my room, he explained that he hadn't any plans for the morning. He would pick me up at nine, if that was OK, and run me out to James' apartment in the suburbs. I didn't have a clue as to where Alexandria was, but Alex assured me that it was adjacent to Arlington, just across the river.

When we reached my door, he held out his hand and thanked me for a lovely evening. I couldn't believe that he was thanking me, but he seemed so completely sincere. I was thrilled, and I didn't care if it showed. I took his hand in both of mine, and thanked him instead.

Then with glistening eyes, I stood up on my tiptoes and kissed him on the cheek before disappearing inside.

It was only after the door had closed and locked behind me that I realized I had spent the whole night talking about myself. Throughout the long evening we had spent together, he'd deftly kept the focus of conversation on me. After a long dinner, two bottles of wine and three hours of conversation, he remained as mysterious as the moment I'd first laid eyes upon him.

As I drifted off to sleep that night, I wondered why.

CHAPTER THREE

I was awakened by a courtesy call from the front desk. It was eight o'clock, as I had requested. Vaguely conscious, I thanked them and hung up the phone.

I crawled to the edge of the bed, and pulled myself upright. I stretched and yawned, and with sleepy eyes, looked about me. *So it wasn't a dream after all...*

I sat there for a moment, taking it all in. The suite was not merely enormous, but luxurious as well. The entrance from the outer hallway led into a large living room, with several overstuffed chairs, two couches, a huge table and a fully stocked bar. To the left were the double doors that opened into a study, perhaps half the size of the main room, and to the right another pair of doors that opened into a hallway that led to the bedroom where I was sitting. In between was a small galley equipped with a full sized refrigerator, stove, microwave, dishwasher and coffee pot; and of course the bathroom, which opened onto both the hallway and into the bedroom. Half the size of the sleeping chamber, it was divided into three sections: a dressing area, and then to the left, a separate room for the toilet, and to the right, another room with a traditional shower bath, a whirlpool, and a sauna.

Definitely not Holiday Inn, I thought. Delighted by my circumstances, and suddenly awake, I stood up and headed for the shower. Thinking that my good fortune was somehow deserved, I was in the midst of congratulating myself when I tripped over the smaller of my two bags and launched into space.

I hit hard, halfway across the room.

Being a good Catholic girl, I knew a sign when I saw one. Face down in the luxurious carpeting, there could be no doubt. *God's punishing me for that...*

More than a little irritated, I had just started to wonder what else the Almighty had in mind for me when I saw my watch. *Holy Cow!*

Ten minutes had somehow slipped away. If I was going to meet Alex in the lobby at 9:00, I would have to fly. Anxious, I jumped to my feet and ran for the shower.

Five minutes later, I emerged with one towel wrapped around my head and another around my body. Grabbing my oversized bag, I dragged it up on the bed and dumped it out.

Frantically rooting through the contents, I found a pair of jeans and a top. It took another minute of furious searching to come up with a bra, and another after that to find a pair of matching panties. Not that it mattered...

Shoes...

I tore through the pile of clothes before suddenly realizing I had shipped most of them ahead, along with my winter clothes. I had exactly one pair of flats – the wrong color – and one pair of heels. I was going to have to wear my sneakers again.

I pulled on my clothes and ripped open my smaller bag. *Makeup, lipstick, comb, blow dryer, brush...*

Hurrying back to the bathroom, I plugged in the hair dryer and began combing out my hair. It was long – just below my shoulders – and thick. Thinking that it would never get dry, I dropped my head to my knees and began combing it furiously.

But it did dry, and just in time. Leaning into the mirror, I put on a bare minimum of makeup. Satisfied I wouldn't scare any small children, I applied a thin coat of lip gloss and blotted it before glancing at my watch. *8:50 am!*

Pack...

I ran back to the bedroom and began throwing my clothes back into the overstuffed suitcase. They were going to get wrinkled, but it couldn't be helped.

With the last of my things crammed inside, I pushed the top down as hard as I could. It wouldn't close.

Darn it!

Uncertain, I looked around the room. *Something, anything for an idea...*

But nothing came.

Scowling, I dragged it off the bed and onto the floor, and kneeled upon it. Pushing down as hard as I could, I got the first latch closed, then the second.

I ran back into the bathroom and scooped up the things I had left there, and raced back to the bedroom. I crammed them into the carry-on, zipped it shut and slung it over my shoulder.

Purse...

I looked around frantically before locating it on the floor. I snatched it up, and grabbed hold of the oversized suitcase. After jerking it up on its wheels, I began tugging it down the hallway.

Key...

Darn it! I dropped both bags and ran back into the bedroom. Grabbing it off the nightstand next to the bed, I raced back to my bags. Repeating the whole process, I got the carry-on over my shoulder and the oversized up on end. I dragged them down the hall to the door, and yanked it open. As I was backing out into the hallway, I saw the bouquet of fresh cut flowers on the table.

Wow!

The door slammed shut before I could catch it, and I knew I didn't have time to go back to look at the beautiful arrangement. Disappointed, I stared at the polished oak door for just a moment. Then I jerked the oversized bag hard, and dragged it to the elevator.

I jabbed the button once, twice, then three or four times more. When the elevator finally opened, I dragged my bags inside and punched the button marked Lobby. For an interminable moment it stood completely still. Then it suddenly jerked and began the long descent. Out of breath, I fell back against the brass railing in the rear.

By the time the door finally opened, I had regained some of my composure. I hoisted the carry-on up on my shoulder and jerked the oversized bag back up on its wheels. Dragging it behind me, I backed out into the lobby.

As luck would have it, an alert bellhop spotted me and bounded over. He grabbed my oversized bag and was carrying it toward the desk when I saw Alex out of the corner of my eye. He was wearing sneakers, a starched pair of jeans and a polo shirt.

"Mr. de Vris! I hope I haven't kept you waiting."

He was smiling, and for the slightest moment I wondered if he'd been laughing at me. I knew I must have looked pretty stupid backing out into the lobby like that, but a pair of aviator sunglasses hid his eyes so I couldn't tell. Flustered, I looked at him expectantly.

"No, I just got here. And please – call me Alex."

He was lying about the first and sincere about the second, so I flipped my hair and smiled. "Alex it is."

Although I didn't realize it at the time, I was already starting to imitate his speech and mannerisms.

He took my carry-on off my shoulder, and gestured towards the door. "Shall we?"

I walked beside him through the ornate entranceway, with the bellhop trailing behind. Outside was a cherry red 1964 Mustang convertible with a white racing stripe running the length of the driver's side. I recognized the car because my father had one, and after his death my mom had kept it for years and years.

The top was down, and as we approached a dog poked his head up and barked. An instant later, another slightly smaller dog appeared beside him.

I recognized the first as the dog who had brought me lunch the day before, so I reached out and rubbed his head. Turning to Alex, I asked him their names.

"Oh, let me introduce you. This is Big Minh, and the one next to him is Lady Godiva." Grinning, he told me that she was a chocoholic.

I reached over to give her a pat on the head too. "Well hello, Lady Godiva. We've got a lot in common!"

Having never had a dog of my own, I was curious about their breed. So after politely asking, Alex smiled. They were mostly Rottweiler, he said, with just enough German Shepherd thrown in to give them their long hair. An acquaintance in downstate Virginia was crossing unusually large specimens of the breeds in the hope of coming up with a new kind of guard dog – intelligent, friendly, and gentle, but ferociously protective at the same time.

Then as Alex walked around to open the trunk, I asked him about Big Minh's name. He laughed as he hoisted my bags in the trunk, and explained that had been the nickname of a flamboyant Vietnamese general-turned-politician. Gen. Minh had been unusually large for a Vietnamese, and frequently went unshaven – so with his enormous paws and a little wisp of white fur on his chin, the overly large puppy had reminded Alex of him.

After closing the trunk, Alex opened the door for me and waited until I was seated. He turned to tip the bellhop, then walked around and climbed in the driver's side. After fastening his seatbelt, he asked me for James' address.

I finally found it after fumbling in my purse. "Let's see…"

I opened it and handed it to him. He glanced at it and said, "No problem. I know exactly where it is." He put the car in gear, and as he pulled out into traffic, the radio came alive. *Tan Shoes and Pink Shoe Laces* was playing, so I guessed he was listening to an oldies station.

Alex grinned and turned the volume up slightly. "I love this song."

I smiled indulgently. *So does my Mom…*

I still didn't know how old he was – in fact, I didn't have a clue. In the restaurant the night before, he had sometimes seemed much older and more mature. But just when I was about to guess he was thirty-five or so, he would grin and the years would melt away. At times like that he barely looked eighteen.

I was stealing a glance at him when he suddenly asked me if I had called James.

Oh God, I thought, *I forgot all about it…*

Grimacing, I told him I'd been too busy tripping over my luggage. But it was OK, I said. If I knew James, he would still be in bed sound asleep when we got there.

Alex nodded, and suggested we stop at a pay phone along the way. I nodded and agreed, but deep down inside I was gripped by an awful feeling. I wasn't quite sure what it was, but all of a sudden I desperately wanted to go back to the hotel and start over again. Fearful and confused, I bit my lip and rode along in silence.

It was a beautiful day, and Alex was clearly enjoying it. Apologizing for his forgetfulness, he asked if I had ever been to D.C. before. He had asked me that last night, but somehow the memory had slipped away.

Shaking my head, I reminded him that I hadn't. The sun was in my eyes, so I opened my purse and got out my sunglasses.

He glanced at his watch, and asked me if I had time to take the scenic route. It would add 15 or 20 minutes to the drive, he said.

Excited, I practically begged him. "Don't worry about James," I said. "He'll be lying in bed until noon, at least." Although I didn't say so, I thought he was probably sleeping off a hangover.

Alex looked at me quizzically. "You're sure?"

I nodded emphatically. "Absolutely. He likes to sleep in on weekends." I paused for a moment, somewhat hesitant. "I'll probably end up sitting on his doorstep for a couple of hours before he wakes up. He's a really heavy sleeper."

A hint of concern crept across Alex's face, but he didn't say anything. He turned left at the next light, and as we proceeded up a hill, he explained that Capitol Hill was divided into sides. We were on the Senate side, and in just a few moments the Capitol would appear on the right and then Senate office buildings a bit farther up on the left. Sure enough, through a parting of the trees I caught sight of the Capitol again.

For someone who had never seen it before, it was a majestic sight. And for a girl from Glen Meadows, it was positively overwhelming. Awestruck, I asked if we would see any important Congressmen or Senators.

Alex said he didn't think so. It was Saturday morning, and in any event, most of the members were out of town. The House of Representatives had adjourned early, and the Senate had followed suit, so they wouldn't be back until late August. Disappointed, I asked him if he knew any politicians.

Alex laughed wryly. A few, he said. Washington was a small town, and they were always underfoot.

Puzzled, I asked him what he meant. But he dodged the question and changed the subject as we turned right onto 1st Street, and then right again onto the long circular drive in front of the Capitol building. He slowed the car to a crawl as he pointed out various features.

Completing the circle, he turned back onto 1st Street, and pulled over to the curb. He pointed to the massive building behind and to the left, and identified it as the Library of Congress. The one just beyond it was the Supreme Court.

Unbuckling my seatbelt, I turned around in my seat. Then as I began raising myself up on my right knee to get a better view, Big Minh poked his head up and licked my nose. Alex saw it and whacked him on the snout. The dog yelped, and ducked down behind the seat.

Taken by surprise, I had recoiled backwards against the dashboard and lost my balance. Laughing, I held out my hand and let Alex pull me back upright. After wiping my nose with my hand, I reached between the bucket seats and scratched Big Minh behind his ears.

Alex apologized for the dog's behavior. Clearly flustered, he told me that Big Minh usually had better manners. "He must like you."

That really pleased me, although I wasn't sure why. So as I re-fastened my seat belt, I told Alex that Big Minh was a sweetie.

The long ride down Independence Avenue was incredible. I had no idea where we were, so it wasn't until Alex turned right on 14th Street and then left on Pennsylvania that I had the slightest inkling. He pulled the car over against the curb, and gestured over his shoulder. "The White House."

"Wow" was all I could say. I sat and stared, my mouth agape. "You don't think…"

Alex grinned. "That we'll see the President? Not today, he's out in California giving a speech. But if you stay in Washington for any length of time, you're bound to run into him at some point or another."

With eyes opened wide, I asked him if he had seen the President. Alex laughed and nodded. "Yeah, his motorcade cut me off Thursday morning." Pointing at the intersection just ahead, he showed me where the Secret Service had stopped traffic for ten minutes. "Made me late for my 11:30 appointment."

Suddenly curious, I asked if he had ever *met* the President. Alex smiled softly and nodded, before changing the subject.

By now excited, I wanted to ask him all about it. But my instincts warned me not to – I'd asked him about the politically powerful twice already, and both times he had evaded the subject. It was as though I had crossed an invisible line, and for reasons I did not understand, trespassed on grounds that were closed to me.

Embarrassed by my *faux pas*, I fell into an uncomfortable silence.

As we turned left around the corner, he pointed to the layer-cake building immediately adjacent to the White House and identified it as The Old Executive Office Building. It had been built after the Civil War, when Rococo architecture was in style, and it had once housed the State and War Departments. The majority of the White House offices were located there now, and most of the 2200 or so presidential employees worked within. Fascinated, I stared at it until Alex turned left again into a winding drive behind it. A moment later, he pulled the car over to the curb so I could get a better look at the South Lawn.

Even though I had seen this exact same view a thousand times in photographs, I was totally unprepared for its breathtaking beauty. And all of a sudden, it hit me: I was in Washington, D.C. It was not only the nation's capital, but also the First City of the Free World. It was the place where important decisions were made, decisions that affected the lives of billions of people all over the world.

It was awesome and inspiring, and I suddenly knew that I wanted to be a part of it.

Alex asked me if I would like to get out of the car and take a closer look. Nodding dumbly, I opened the door and climbed out. He walked silently behind me as we crossed the street onto the sidewalk, and stood there as I walked up to the ornate iron fence and grasped the bars with both hands. Leaning my face between them, I stared for a long time. Finally, I stepped back and looked at Alex. He had been standing on the sidewalk, silently observing me. Caught in an unguarded moment, all I could do was look at him and smile.

"Impressive, isn't it?"

I nodded, almost reverently. "Yes, it is."

We walked back to the car and he opened the door for me. After I was seated, he closed the door and walked around to the driver's side. He got in and started the engine and in a moment the radio came back to life. The oldies station was playing Diana Ross's *The Happening*, and as I listened to the refrain, I was struck by how apropos it was. Alex gunned the engine and nosed the car back into traffic. In a moment of presumption, I reached over and turned up the volume.

By now the sun was high in the heavens, so I leaned back in my seat enjoying the breeze as it played across my face. As we turned right onto 15th Street, my spirits soared. Coming to D.C. had been the right move after all.

As we passed the Washington Monument I couldn't help but snicker at the polished granite pun. After glancing at me, Alex broke up laughing. *Oh, my God*, I thought. *He read my mind!*

Mortified, I covered my face in my hands.

We turned left, then right onto 14th Street. Still grinning, Alex glanced over at me a second time, and made me blush all over again. Hoping to divert his attention, I pointed at the building across the street and asked him what it was.

He looked at it and tilted his head quizzically, but after a long while he finally admitted he didn't know. The only thing that saved him was the light, which changed from red to green. He gunned the engine, and a moment later we were crossing the 14th Street Bridge.

The cherry trees planted along the banks of the Potomac River had already blossomed, but it was a beautiful sight nonetheless. In the distance I could see Arlington National Cemetery, and just ahead, the Pentagon. Somehow, it wasn't quite as big as I had imagined.

After about five minutes on I-395, we passed the Army-Navy Country Club and then exited a mile or two later onto Glebe Road. Alex turned left down the hill, then bore right across an ugly concrete bridge. We had just passed a Pizza Hut on the left when Alex suddenly swung the car across the road onto the parking lot of an adjacent 7-11. After pulling to a stop, he suggested that I use the pay phone on the wall to call ahead.

I clambered out of the car and walked up to the phone. Digging through the bottom of my purse, I found a quarter and dropped it in the slot. I waited for the dial tone, then punched in the number. On the fourth ring, the mechanical voice kicked in. *Still out of service...*

Not yet in a panic, I turned back to the car. I climbed in and explained that James' phone still wasn't working. Alex put the Mustang in reverse and backed out just enough to turn it around. The 7-11 was perched on a steep hill, and the incline leading back down to the road looked treacherous. I wondered how many people had wrecked their cars exiting back out on the road.

Alex didn't say anything. He was studying the traffic, looking for an opening. After a long minute or two, he put it in gear and turned left up the hill. We were only a couple of minutes away, he said.

We passed the local power company and a couple of sets of dilapidated apartments before being stopped by a red light at Russell Road. Alex pulled the paper out of his shirt pocket and looked at it, then turned to look over his shoulder. "Sorry, I overshot."

When the light turned green, he turned left. Halfway down the street he made a U-turn, and when he reached the intersection again he turned right. An instant later, he made another right onto Executive Drive and slowed the car to a crawl. A few feet onward, he spotted an empty parking space and turned into it. "This is it."

The complex seemed huge – quaint little apartments stretched down the hill as far as I could see. A big sign out in front of the manager's office informed me that they were being remodeled, and it promised luxurious living for only $800 a month. I gasped at the price; in Glen Meadows, this kind of apartment went for $300 a month, or maybe $350 if it was close to the business district. With those kinds of prices, I was going to have to find a really good job.

Alex opened the door for me, then went around to the trunk. He lifted my bags out, and checked the address. "Apartment 114."

I nodded and grabbed my carry-on, and started up the steps. Alex followed along behind, lugging the big bag.

I pushed open the entryway door, and held it open for Alex. Apartment 114 was the first door on the right, so I turned to him to thank him for everything. I stood up on my tiptoes again and kissed him on the cheek, and told him there was no need for him to wait. I'd be fine now.

Alex smiled, and said he would wait until I was safely inside. I thanked him, and knocked on the door.

It was only 10:30 in the morning, so I didn't expect James to be up. Embarrassed, I mumbled an excuse to Alex and knocked again much louder. I waited a minute and banged on it again. Frustrated, I reached down to try the knob. It wasn't locked, so I turned it and opened the door.

The apartment was empty. Except for a few unused packing boxes and the debris on the floor, everything was gone.

CHAPTER FOUR

I stood in the doorway, staring incomprehensibly at the barren apartment. Unwilling to admit the truth, I heard myself mumble that there had to be some mistake.

But there wasn't. The apartment was empty and James was gone. It seemed as though my heart had stopped beating. Suddenly very weak, I grasped the door jamb and turned into it. *That bastard!*

Shaking violently, I began to cry.

It was several minutes before I felt Alex's hand on my shoulder. In a voice that was reassuring in its soft calm, he suggested we check with the manager. Perhaps there *had* been some kind of mistake...

Although I knew it wasn't true, I nodded and let him lead me back outside. We walked back to his car, and put the bags into his trunk. Still crying, I leaned against the rear fender for a few moments while I pulled myself together. Then I followed Alex across the street to the management office.

The door was open, so we went inside. An elderly woman behind the counter looked up and welcomed us to Executive Park.

Alex explained that we were in search of a friend, who we had thought lived in Apartment 114. The woman smiled and said oh yes, Mr. Winton. She was sorry, she said, but he had moved out on Friday. He had come in early that morning and informed the manager that he was being transferred to the West Coast, and had to leave that day. He'd paid off the balance of his lease and turned in his keys, and the movers had come almost immediately thereafter. He was packed up and gone within a few hours.

Alex asked her if he had left a forwarding address. She said she didn't think so, but she would have to call the manager to be sure. Alex asked her if she would be so kind, and she smiled and said "Of course." She disappeared into the back room, and after a few moments of muted conversation, she reappeared. She was sorry, she said, but Mr. Winton had not left a forwarding address, and because he had paid off his lease with cash, they had not required one. Perhaps we could check with the post office?

In a weepy voice, I asked her if he had left any packages behind, and described the two big cardboard boxes I had sent ahead. She looked at me quizzically, then shook her head no. She was quite sure that Mr. Winton hadn't left anything at all.

I had managed to maintain my composure up to then, but the loss of all my things – my winter clothes, my sweaters, and all my shoes – was unbearable. I buried my face in Alex's chest, and burst into tears.

Thanking the lady, he handed her his business card. If the boxes should turn up somehow, would she give him a call?

He put his arm around my shoulder and steered me towards the door. By then I was shaking so badly that I could barely walk.

There was a small wooden bench just outside the doorway, and Alex led me to it. With my face pressed against his chest, I sat there and sobbed.

Alex didn't say anything. He put his arm around me, and held me in another uncomfortable silence.

I have no idea how long I cried. But the tears slowed and eventually stopped, replaced by a dull ache in my chest. After a while I pushed my hair back away from my face and rested my forehead against his shoulder. "I'm sorry" was all I could say.

He lifted my chin with his index finger, so that I had to look into his eyes. It was okay, he said. He understood.

Wiping away my tears, I let go of him and stood up. Looking away down the street, I told him that I should have known better. Coming to Washington for James had been a damned stupid idea.

Alex stood up and glanced at his watch. It was almost noon, he said, and he thought we should get something to eat. He knew of a quiet place nearby, something of a neighborhood tavern. It wasn't a particularly fancy place, he said, but it was favored by the Pentagon brass for its excellent menu and reasonable prices. Would I join him?

Sniffling, I nodded numbly and started back towards his car.

Alex opened the door for me, and after he had gotten in himself, he started the engine and backed into the street. He turned the car right onto Glebe and then left after a few blocks. After winding through a succession of tree-lined neighborhoods, we emerged at a small commercial strip. Alex turned left and then right into a back parking lot.

By then it had become hot again, so after I got out, he put up the convertible top to shade the dogs. He leaned in the passenger's side window and told them to stay put. Big Minh didn't seem very happy about it, but Lady Godiva seemed content. She lay down on the back seat and seemed to go to sleep.

Alex patted Big Minh on the head and told him to stay out of trouble, then he opened the glove compartment and reached in. He pulled a pack of Marlboro 100s out from under a mountain of folded papers that had hidden them, and put them in his shirt pocket.

Darn, I thought. *I didn't know he smoked.*

Alex smiled and told me that the restaurant – *Ramparts*, he called it – was just around the corner. So I walked alongside him, past a TV repair shop and a Baskin Robbins, up the street and to the almost hidden entrance.

It was cool inside, and dark, and much nicer than I had thought. It was a tavern, to be sure, but it was tastefully furnished. A waitress that had been adding up checks saw us and waved to Alex. "Well, hey, stranger, where've ya been?"

Alex escorted me towards the bar where she stood. He grinned and told her he had been busy saving the Free World, but seeing as how it was Sunday and all, he'd decided to take the day off. Then he turned to me and introduced me as his friend.

The waitress laughed at Alex, and smiled at me. Her name was Betty, she said, and she would be our waitress. Would we like a booth or a table?

Alex asked her for a booth, off in the far corner. Betty picked up two menus and told him to consider it done. Along the way she informed him that he had just missed General Thompson.

I crawled into my side of the high-backed booth and after an uncomfortable silence apologized again. "I'm really sorry, Alex. I didn't mean to break down like that…

"It's just…I've never been so humiliated in my life. He lied to me, and he lured me here and he just dumped me…

"I don't understand."

Tears were rolling down my cheeks again, so I looked down at the table.

Alex pulled the Marlboros from his shirt pocket and shook one free. He offered it to me, but I shook my head no. So he picked up the pack of promotional matches that had been placed in the ashtray and lit it for himself. He inhaled deeply, and shook his head.

"I know you must feel awful. But I think you are being too hard on yourself." Then he looked at me, sympathetically. "Washington isn't like Glen Meadows, or anyplace else for that matter. It's cold, and it's cruel…

"It changes people, and usually for the worse." Resting his elbows on the table, he looked straight at me. "You had no way of knowing."

I wiped the tears from my eyes with my napkin, and excused myself. After washing my face in the ladies' room, I returned to the booth and sat down. By that time Betty arrived to take our order.

"Oh, gee, I haven't even looked at the menu." I asked Alex what was good.

"Like Eggs Benedict?"

I nodded. "That would be fine."

Alex looked up and told Betty that we would like the eggs benedict, with french fries. And a couple of Cokes. She nodded, and took our menus.

After she walked away, Alex asked me what I was going to do. I shrugged, and told him I'd have to call my Mom. She'd give me her credit card number for a hotel tonight, and arrange for a bus ticket home. So I guessed I was going back to Glen Meadows, to look for a job. Not that I could find anything in international finance in a two-stoplight town.

Alex nodded, and asked me about my studies. So I explained to him again that I had taken a double major in international finance and economics. I had hoped to find a job here in Washington with a big bank, but since that wasn't going to happen I supposed I could find something with a much smaller bank at home. Maybe with a couple of years' experience, I could find something better in a big city.

Alex nodded and told me that seemed sensible, and then asked me what I thought about President Reagan's economic policies. They had initially been greeted with derision – no one had ever cut taxes and increased deficit spending in the middle of a recession before – and even though it seemed to be working, his concept of "supply-side" economics still drew snickers from the press.

At that I perked up. Not only did I know a lot about Reagan's economic policies, they fascinated me. I had put a lot of time and effort into mastering the Administration's approach to the economy, and I was delighted to talk about it.

Fumbling in my purse, I finally found a pen. I turned over the paper placemat in front of me and began sketching out some quick graphs. Pointing to the first, I explained that this was where Reagan had found the economy in January of 1981. Wages and consumer demand were either flat or falling, depending on the economic sector, and prices were skyrocketing. Inflation was running at 20 percent per annum, which meant that workers were being priced out of the market.

Housing was becoming impossibly expensive for the average American, and even automobiles were moving beyond his reach. Given that consumer spending drove the economy, we were headed for a train wreck.

I pointed at the other graph, which depicted the current situation. It was little short of miraculous, I said, because Reagan had pulled it off by manipulating perceptions. By proclaiming a new era of American power and influence, he had restored confidence in America abroad. Foreign capital was flooding into the United States, and it wasn't just the high interest rates that were attracting it.

Sketching out another quick diagram, I showed him how the Administration had financed a succession of staggering deficits with foreign capital. It was a neat trick, I said, and as long as foreign investors *believed* in the United States, it would work. In my view, Reagan was one heck of a salesman.

Alex interjected. He didn't know a great deal about international finance or even economics, he said, but it seemed to him a house of cards. If for any reason the foreign investors lost confidence in America, it would all come tumbling down.

"Exactly," I said. "But how likely was that?" It would take a major disaster to shake their faith in the U.S., and in any event, I was pretty sure it would hit somewhere else first – like Japan.

In my view the Japanese had climbed way out on a limb by investing so heavily in real estate all around the world, and the day of reckoning couldn't be all that far off. But if the Japanese economy tanked, the American bond market would look even better. And the same was true of Europe.

The bottom line – at least in my opinion – was "refuge." Due to the twin factors of deregulation and financial innovation, the world was awash in capital, and for the first time in history it had become a relatively simple matter to move it from one country to another. There were amazing investment opportunities opening up all over the world, but most of them were in high-risk Third World countries.

The only place where an investor could find a high rate of return and a reasonable assurance against loss was in the United States. In this new era of internationalized capital, political stability was the key. And that, I said, was a matter of perception – which meant image is as important as reality.

Alex leaned back in the booth, and toyed with his cigarette. "*That* was impressive."

"*Really?*"

He nodded emphatically. "Yes, *really*."

As he stubbed out his cigarette, he told me that I wouldn't have any problems finding a job.

I was beaming when Betty arrived with our eggs benedict. Thoroughly pleased with myself, I turned my placemat over again, and arranged my tableware.

I hadn't realized how hungry I was, so as soon as Alex picked up his fork I began eating. I was halfway through my meal when I suddenly realized that I didn't even know what Alex did for a living. He had a company, or so he said, but I didn't have a clue as to what kind.

I cocked my head, and asked him. "Alex...what exactly do you do?"

He put down his fork and wiped his mouth with his napkin. "Public education, primarily. I run a 'think tank,' so-called...a non-profit, non-partisan educational foundation...

"We do reports, studies and analyses concerning international security issues."

Intrigued, I asked him the name.

"The Center for Strategic Studies," he said. "I founded it back in '78."

"Wow," was all I could say. Alex looked up at me quizzically. "Wow?"

I nodded. "You must be really important."

Alex smiled softly, and took a sip of his Coke. "Sometimes I like to humor myself and think so. But the truth of the matter is that I'm just a small fish in a very big pond."

That didn't seem very likely, but it would have been rude of me to have said so.

He was swishing his Coke around in the glass when he suddenly looked up. "I don't know if you would be interested in something like this, but if I'm not mistaken Scotty MacLaughlin is looking for someone like you."

It was my turn to be puzzled. "Scotty MacLaughlin?"

Alex nodded. "Yeah, Dr. MacLaughlin. He used to run the CIA's Econ shop. Taught a little too...

"After he retired from the Agency we hired him to run our international economics division, and he's just started a rather specialized project. He's been looking for a research assistant, and I'm pretty sure he has an ad in the paper right now."

Alex excused himself and walked out the door. A minute later he returned, carrying a Sunday newspaper under his arm. He sat back down and began peeling away the sections until he found the help wanted advertisements. Pushing his plate to one side, he opened it up and started scanning the columns.

"Here it is." He folded it over, and then in half and handed it to me across the table. It was halfway down on the left column:

NON-PROFIT, NON-PARTISAN PUBLIC POLICY CENTER HAS AN IMMEDIATE OPENING FOR AN INTERNATIONAL FINANCE SPECIALIST TO ASSIST WITH A DEFENSE-RELATED ANALYTICAL PROJECT. MUST HAVE A DEGREE IN INTERNATIONAL FINANCE; TWO YEARS' EXPERIENCE IN THIS OR RELATED FIELD PREFERRED

Qualified applicants were requested to send their resumes to the CSS, addressed to the attention of C. L. MacLaughlin, PhD.

Downcast, I handed it back to Alex. "He's looking for someone with two years' experience. I just graduated from college and the only job I've ever had was in a drug store, part-time after school."

Alex took the paper from me and re-read the ad. "Look, I know what Scotty's working on and it's just number crunching. I can't believe that experience is all that important."

Putting the paper aside, he said that he'd call him. Before I could stop him, he got up and disappeared down the hall at the end of the bar.

By this point, I didn't know what to think. On the one hand I was up the proverbial creek without a paddle. On the other, I was sitting in a quaint neighborhood tavern having lunch with a man that was handsome, rich and unquestionably important.

And he's calling the former head of the CIA's Economics Division to see if I'm qualified for a job???

The whole thing was overwhelming, so I turned back to my lunch. *That* I could deal with.

I had just finished the last french fry when Alex returned. "Scotty – Dr. MacLaughlin – is on the phone and he'd like to talk to you." He pointed down the hallway, and told me he had left the phone off the hook.

I was stunned. "You're kidding?"

Alex laughed, and shook his head. "Not at all. I just told him what you told me about Reagan's economic policy and he wanted to talk to you."

Reluctantly, I got up and walked down the hall to the phone. I picked up the dangling handset and said hello.

An intense voice replied in a think Scottish brogue. "Good afternoon, Scotty MacLaughlin here...

"Alex tells me you are quite an expert on the political aspects of supply-side economics!"

Oh, God, I thought, *I've really put my foot in it this time...*

Stammering, I told him that it had been one of my areas of interest in school. But I quickly added that I was hardly an expert. After all, I had just graduated from college.

Dr. MacLaughlin sternly brushed aside my protest. "Nonsense, Lass. Just tell me what you told Alex, and I'll be the judge of it."

So I crossed my fingers and took a deep breath, and began an impromptu presentation.

Fifteen minutes later, I found myself standing back in front of the booth trembling with excitement. Engrossed in the international section, Alex didn't notice me until he turned the page.

When he finally looked up, I told him. "Dr. MacLaughlin wants to see me in his office tomorrow at 9:00 am."

CHAPTER FIVE

At precisely 8:50 am the next morning, I sat down in a chair outside Dr. MacLaughlin's office at the Center for Strategic Studies. Had I not already been seized by nervous anticipation, I would have been overwhelmed by my surroundings.

His secretary had offered me a cup of coffee, which I had gratefully accepted. After stirring in a packet of Sweet N Low, I settled in my chair to wait. But for some reason, my mind refused to focus on the interview. Instead, it drifted back to the day before.

After finishing lunch, Alex had driven me back to the hotel. He smoked another cigarette on the way back, then carefully hid the remainder in the bottom of the glove compartment. Turning to me with a conspiratorial grin, he made me promise not to rat on him. Mai Ling was a physician, and when it came to smoking she was a real nag.

"A doctor? I had no idea!"

Alex nodded, and told me she had graduated from medical school in '74. And like most physicians, she was really down on smoking. Unable to convince either Alex or Nguyen to quit altogether, she had put them on a ration of five cigarettes a day – and if she found out he was cheating, he was a dead man.

Laughing, I asked him what kind of medicine she practiced and if Nguyen was a doctor too. Alex said she did research – she had specialized in geriatrics, but her real interest was in comparative medicine. She had thus far published two well-received books comparing traditional Chinese healing practices with Western medicine, and had a third in progress.

Nguyen was a different story, he said. Having come from a prominent Vietnamese family, he had been expected to follow his father's footsteps in government service. Instead, he had enrolled in the U.S. Marine Corps Platoon Leaders Class as a foreign officer candidate, and after graduating from Georgetown he'd been commissioned as an officer in the South Vietnamese Marines.

He had risen to the rank of major, and had been the executive officer of an elite battalion when the war unraveled. According to Alex, he had been one hell of field commander –

but these days he made his living as a stockbroker. He owned a small investment house that catered to a select clientele.

His statement seemed to imply that he had seen Nguyen in action, and I wondered if they had served together in Vietnam. Fascinated – and by now thoroughly impressed – I wanted to ask him to tell me more. But I hesitated, because I didn't want him to think I was prying. So as he turned the Mustang into the circular drive outside of the hotel, I made a mental note to follow up on the conversation at a more auspicious time.

He told the dogs to stay put, and unloaded my bags again. Then after instructing the bellhop to take them back up to the suite, he informed the concierge that I would be staying after all. With that taken care of, he had escorted me to the coffee shop and guided me to a table in the far corner. We ordered and made small talk until the waiter arrived with cups and saucers, sugar, cream, and an overly large pot of coffee.

Alex poured an amazing amount of cream and sugar into his cup before topping it off with the coffee. Astounded that anyone could drink such a concoction, I poured a small cup for myself with just a smidgen of cream and a single packet of sweetener.

After he finished blending his, he laid down his spoon and took a sip. Satisfied, he put the cup down and told me that he would have to leave in a few minutes. He had to catch a flight for Paris first thing in the morning, and he hadn't even packed yet.

"Paris!" Gasping with envy, I told him how much I wanted to go there. I had decided years ago that I would take my very first foreign vacation there, and I couldn't wait until I could finally afford it. I was dying to see the Eiffel Tower, and the palace at Versailles, and all the famous museums.

And do a little shopping, of course...

I must have sounded like a country bumpkin, because Alex turned away laughing. After a few moments he looked back at me and smiled indulgently. Paris was nice, he said, but the trip was strictly business and he wasn't looking forward to it. He hated flying, and he hated living out of a suitcase even more. But he had to do both quite a bit, and he had resigned himself to three weeks of lousy food and uncomfortable beds.

Three weeks! Trying hard to hide my disappointment, I mumbled something about how important the trip must be.

Alex nodded and said it was. The CSS had maintained a small liaison office in Paris for the past several years, and he'd recently decided to expand it into a full-scale branch office. He had to find new office space and a new executive director for the Paris operation, and mend a few fences while he was at it. He had ruffled some feathers the last time he had been in town, and the trip presented the best opportunity to date to smooth things over with his French counterparts. After that, he had to fly to London to check in on the office there.

Oh, my gosh! Offices in Paris and London?

Alex pulled out his checkbook and tore a check from the pad within. After slashing an X across the face of it, he turned it over and wrote down a series of phone numbers. The first was his home telephone. He shared a house with Nguyen and Mai Ling, and he wanted to make sure I could reach them in the event of an emergency. The second was a contact number for Paris, the third for London. He would be hard to get a hold of, but I could leave a message at either number and he would get back to me in a matter of hours.

Hesitant and more than a bit nervous, I took the paper and put it in my purse. My hands had begun to shake a little, so I folded them in my lap and hoped he hadn't noticed.

As far as the suite went, I was welcome to stay there until I found a job. Congress was adjourned, and summers were traditionally very slow. It would be at least a month and probably more before it was needed for business purposes. I started to protest, but he grinned and told me not to worry – he'd throw me out on my ear if anyone important showed up.

I made him promise, and after he swore a solemn oath to send me back to the bus station if any VIPs arrived, he became quite serious. The suite cost him a fortune, he said, and he had to pay for it whether anyone used it or not. Under the terms of the contract, everything the hotel offered was covered by a flat rate monthly fee and that included the pool, the sauna, the health club, the restaurant, the bar, valet service, limousine service, the gift shop and even the beauty salon on the second floor. I started to protest, but he cut me off. He had to pay for it one way or another, and he hoped I would take advantage of it.

I understood the logic of the situation, but it just didn't seem right. But there was no graceful exit to be found, so I offered him a reasoned compromise instead: I would use the facilities, but only when I really had to. *Deal?*

Alex smiled and said "Fair enough." Draining his coffee cup, he turned to the last item on his agenda. He hoped things went well with Dr. MacLaughlin, but even though he was Chairman of the Board and Chief Executive Officer, he wanted me to understand that he didn't get involved in personnel matters at the department level. It was up to Scotty, he said, but he thought that it would go well. He had been impressed by my analysis of

Reagan's economic policy, and he was sure that Dr. MacLaughlin had been too. He wanted me to call him in Paris to let him know how the interview turned out.

I assured him that I understood his position, and promised him that I would call him as soon as the interview ended...

Provided I could find it, of course. I didn't know where the office was.

Alex winced and apologized. The CSS was located in the building next door to the hotel, he said. All I had to do was walk out the main entrance and turn right. The reception area was on the Sixth Floor; Dr. MacLaughlin's office was on the Seventh and his own was on the Eighth. All I had to do was check in with the receptionist, and she would make sure I was escorted to the proper place.

With everything settled, he signaled for the check.

He walked me to the elevator, and I thanked him for everything. Unable to resist any longer, I asked him why he was being so good to me. He paused for a long moment, and then explained that it was a matter of character. He had watched me bake in the hot sun for hours upon end outside of the bus station, and he had admired my fortitude. After that, he had been impressed by the way I had handled adversity. It took a great deal of courage to endure the humiliation I had been subjected to, and he commended me for it. And finally, he was impressed by my impromptu presentation at *Ramparts*. It had been truly exceptional.

I started to thank him, but he cut me off. In a quiet and very matter-of-fact voice, he told me that I had displayed virtues he admired, and he strongly believed they should be rewarded. He was in a position to do so, and for that he felt fortunate.

I was speechless. In my whole life I had never heard anyone say they felt fortunate for being able to help someone else. To me, at least, that implied a profound sense of humility – despite his wealth and his power, his rugged good looks and his mischievous charm, he possessed a rare decency.

I liked that. In fact, I liked it *a lot*.

I stood there and searched his eyes until the elevator doors opened. When they did, I reached up to kiss him.

He put an index finger to my lips as I reached up, as if to quiet me. So I kissed his finger instead, and said goodbye.

By the time I got back to the suite I was walking on air. The fact that my boyfriend of three years had cruelly betrayed me had somehow receded into a far distant past. In fact, I wouldn't have even thought about it if reality hadn't forced itself upon me.

My Mom!

I suddenly realized that I had been in Washington for almost two full days and I hadn't even called her. She would have called James by now, and gotten the mechanical voice.

She's probably sick from worry...

I had to call her, but I had no idea what to say. I didn't want to lie to her, but there was no way I could tell her the truth. If I did, she'd go through the ceiling.

I walked back in the bedroom and sat down on the bed by the nightstand and phone, trying to think of something that would mollify her.

I looked at the clock. It was almost 4 pm, which gave me an idea. *If I wait another 45 minutes, she'll probably leave for 5 o'clock Mass.*

I can leave a message on the answering machine...

I'll tell her I'm calling from a pay phone, because dummy forgot to pay the phone bill again and his phone was disconnected, and I'll promise to call her again in a couple of days...

That'll keep her happy for a while.

With 40 minutes on my hands, I went back down to the Lobby to buy a newspaper. I had been completely out of touch for the past two days, and I wanted to get caught up with the world. Especially with the interview in the morning. The last thing I needed was for Dr. MacLaughlin to ask me what I thought about the *coup d'etat* in Gondowondoland when I hadn't even read the Sunday paper.

It was a great plan, or so it seemed at the time. Then I passed the coffee shop and noticed the chocolates and fresh baked pastries they had placed under glass by the door.

Chocolate is my undoing. Followed closely by whipped cream, with fresh baked pastries coming in a close third. I stopped – and like a child staring through the window of a candy store, I stood there and stared with my mouth half open. I didn't even notice the waiter.

Oh, I can't...

I won't...

But my finger had taken on a life of its own. It jabbed at the chocolate mousse near the center of the tray, and as it did I heard a little girl say, "I want that one..."

Then it pointed at the oversized éclair just to the right of it. "And that one too, please."

Having turned a thousand shades of red, I was thankful that the waiter pretended not to see. "Would you like these here, Miss, or shall I have them sent to your room?"

Decisions. Awful, horrible decisions...

I didn't realize it but I was shifting from one foot to another, trying to make up my mind. With my index finger pressed hard against my lip, I finally asked him to put the goodies on a paper plate for me.

Oh yes, and a Diet Pepsi in a cup...

I rushed over to the newsstand and bought a *Washington Post*, then hurried back to the coffee shop to claim my treasure. I scribbled my name and room number on the check, and ran for the elevator. The éclair vanished somewhere between the Second and Third floors, but the mousse lasted a bit longer. I finished off the last spoonful as I was opening the door. Overwhelmed by guilt, I promised to starve myself for a week.

But I got a *diet* Pepsi, I thought. *That should count for something...*

With that, I lay down on the bed and opened up the paper before me. *The usual stuff*, I thought, as I glanced through the front section. The Russians were raising hell about President Reagan's plan to place intermediate-range ballistic missiles in Europe, and the Democrats were accusing him of bankrupting the treasury. Senator Mondale had just about locked up the Democrat nomination, Jesse Jackson was organizing a boycott in Chicago, and former President Jimmy Carter was building low-income housing for the poor...

Bored, I pulled out the help wanted section and re-read the ad. I was lying there fantasizing about how cool it would be to work at the CSS when I suddenly remembered to call my Mom. Startled, I looked at the clock. It was five o'clock, straight up.

Crossing my fingers, I lifted the handset and dialed "9." When I heard the dial tone, I punched in the number and quickly reviewed the message I was going to leave.

No such luck. My mother picked up the phone on the second ring. Wincing, I said 'hi.'

I could hear the relief in her voice. She had been frantic when I hadn't called, and had been pacing the floor for two days. Bracing for the inevitable lecture, I apologized and tried to change the subject. But after twenty-two years, she was wise to my tricks, and there was no way she was going to let me wriggle off the hook. So I dangled my legs over the bed, half-listening as she read me the riot act.

After she calmed down a bit, I apologized again and launched into my cover story. Dummy that he was, James had forgotten to pay the phone bill again and his line had been disconnected. I was really sorry that I hadn't called earlier, but I had been so busy that I just hadn't had a chance.

"Yes, Mom, busy. Really."

"Job hunting. And I already have an interview lined up for tomorrow morning..."

"Yes, tomorrow morning. At a big think tank..."

"No, Mom, I am NOT making that up!"

Irritated, I couldn't resist jerking her chain a bit. "Dr. MacLaughlin – you know, the former head of the CIA's Economics Division – wants to see me in his office at 9 am sharp."

"You've never heard of Dr. MacLaughlin? *The* Dr. MacLaughlin?"

"Well, you should have. He's a *very* famous economist!"

"As a research assistant..."

"No, Mom, I'm *serious!* I wouldn't make up a story like that!"

"Oh, networking...last night, at an Alumni party. There are a lot of Township grads in Washington, you know..."

"Yes, Mom, it's a good job...

"Uh-huh, I'll call you tomorrow just as soon as I finish the interview...

"Who???

Oh, James!" Cringing, I wanted to kick myself. "Yes, Mom, he's fine. Everything's fine. Great little apartment, in a nice area..."

"Mother!"

I growled indignantly. *She ought to know better than to ask me a question like that!*

"OK, OK, OK...I love you too. I'll call you tomorrow, I promise."

I hung up the phone, seething. *I'm 22, for God's sake! When is she going to stop treating me like a baby?*

I didn't belabor the point, because I already knew the answer. As her only child, I'd be her little girl forever. *Even if I live to be a hundred and ten...*

Resigned to my fate, I turned to the more urgent business at hand. Dragging my oversized suitcase to the little folding stand by the closet, I hoisted it up. After a lengthy struggle I finally got it open, and started pulling out my clothes. I hadn't packed very well, so they weren't in any particular order, but I finally found my new interview suit down at the very bottom. I pulled it out and hung it up, hoping it wasn't too badly wrinkled.

I stood there for a few moments and admired it. I had never owned a suit before – and frankly, I had never even wanted one. But Mom had insisted I had to have one, and she had even driven me all the way to New Haven so I could have a better selection.

It really hadn't been much fun, and for the first time in my life I had found shopping to be a real chore. But after spending all day and most of the evening traipsing from store to store, I finally found it. Hidden away on a sale rack, I almost didn't see it. But when I did, I knew it was perfect.

It was a three-piece suit – which was really unusual for the times – made of lightweight summer wool. Charcoal gray in color, it had vertical red pinstripes that were so thin that they were almost invisible. The skirt was slit on the side, just a little higher than usual, and it had a matching vest and jacket. It was the last one, and as luck would have it, a Size 6. With a white blouse, it would look incredible.

Even my Mom was impressed, so after trying it on to make sure it fit, I bought it. Happy and exhausted, we made our way for the nearest exit. Passing through the men's department, I was struck by a red silk tie on a mannequin. *Whoa...*

I stopped for a moment to look at it, then pulled up the hem of the plastic garment bag so I could see how they looked together.

Perfect! I thought. *Annie Hall goes to Washington!*

That of course necessitated a trip to the boy's section for a white oxford cloth button-down shirt and, naturally, a minor skirmish with my Mom. Which was par for the course, since we had been fighting about clothes for as long as I could remember. I *liked* guy stuff – and besides, men's shirts were cheaper and far better made. A white button-down shirt was perfect for the suit, and wearing a man's tie beneath the vest was really quite chic.

Facing certain defeat, she finally relented. "Just don't grow a mustache," she said.

I *loved* that suit. Wrinkled or not, it was gorgeous.

Which was a good thing for me, because it was *really* wrinkled. So after a moment's thought, I put each piece on a separate hanger and carried them into the bathroom. Hoping for the best, I turned on the hot water in the shower and closed the door. Back in the bedroom, I started laying out all my other things for the morning. I found the tie in the little side compartment, still wrapped in fine paper.

Thankfully, I had brought the shoes that went with the suit in my bag rather than sending them on to James.

Oh Lord...my shoes!

The sudden realization that I had lost all my shoes – not to mention my winter clothes – shocked me back to the present. And as fate would have it, Dr. MacLaughlin strode through the door just as I was reminding myself to strangle James if I ever saw him again.

From where I was sitting, he looked enormous. He was at least 6' 2" tall, with broad shoulders and full head of hair, and a neatly trimmed beard that still retained a bit of red. Dressed in a beautifully tailored three-piece Scottish wool suit, an off-white shirt and a tie that accentuated his bright blue eyes, he made me feel small and insignificant.

Shrinking down in my chair as he breezed past me, I couldn't tell if he was oblivious to my presence, or merely indifferent. But as he stopped at his secretary's desk to pick up his messages, she reminded him of his 9 o'clock appointment.

"Miss McAllister is here to see you, sir."

CHAPTER SIX

He glanced around and waved in my direction, before turning back to his messages. He pulled four of them from the stack and laid them on her desk. "Yes, yes, no, I'll call him back tomorrow." Nodding, she said, "Yes, Sir," and reached for the phone.

Dr. MacLaughlin stuffed the rest of the pink slips into his vest pocket and gestured for me to follow. So I jumped up and scurried after him, resume in hand.

He rounded the door into his office and strode across the room to a large table piled high with boxes. Taking out a pocketknife, he carefully slit the tape on the first one and looked inside. "Right. These are supposed to be a complete record of the Soviet Union's hard currency earnings from 1919 through 1983…

"And let's see …oh yes, and those of the satellite states from 1947 onward."

Pushing the box aside, he slit open another. "Wrong box." He lifted it off the table and dropped it on the floor beside me. It hit with a heavy thud, shaking the picture frames on the wall.

He opened another and looked inside. "Good. These are the complete records – supposedly – of the Soviets' borrowings from Western banks. Same time frame, satellites included." Pushing it aside, he began rummaging through the next. "Nope." It followed the other to the floor, but this time the box split open.

Dr. MacLaughlin was rummaging through another. "Here we are! This contains – again, supposedly – a complete record of the Soviets' hard currency purchases, dates specified, and those of the satellites after 1947." He turned around and handed it to me, then scooped the other two up under his arms. "This way, Lass."

The box was heavy. *Really heavy*. Staggering along behind him, I hoped that we weren't going very far.

He led me back through the secretarial area and across the hall. Pushing a door open with his foot, he turned the lights on with his elbow. Then after putting the two boxes he was carrying on an empty desk, he told me to put mine there as well.

As he brushed off his hands, he told me that he wanted the materials checked to make sure that the data for each year had been enclosed. Everything was clearly marked, and if anything was missing, I should write it down – legibly – on a legal pad. If I needed any supplies, all I had to do was ask Jennifer, his secretary. *Understand?*

He must have seen the confusion on my face, because he asked me what was troubling me. Nervous and more than a little bit intimidated, I cleared my throat before answering. "Yes, Sir, I understand what you want done. It's just that I thought you wanted to interview me?"

He looked puzzled for a moment, then reached into his coat pocket and withdrew a small notebook. He thumbed through the pages, before stopping somewhere near the middle.

"Ah yes...an interview."

He pursed his lips and looked at me. "Ever heard of Adam Smith?" I nodded and started to recite a brief biographical sketch from memory, but he cut me off with the wave of his hand. "Know the difference between a supply curve and a demand curve?"

Flustered, I said, "Yes Sir."

Seeming very pleased with himself, he nodded his head and told me I'd do. "Try to get this sorted out by tomorrow morning." Looking in his book again, he said to meet him in his office at 10 am. With that he thrust the book back into his pocket and strode out the door, leaving me thoroughly confused.

Did he just hire me?

A moment later there was a knock, and Jennifer stuck her head in the door. "Get the job?"

I shrugged, and told her I didn't know. "He said 'I'd do,' and he told me to get all this stuff sorted out. Then he just left."

Jennifer squealed in excitement. *"Oh good, oh good, oh good!"*

After she finished jumping up and down, she said "Finally! Someone to talk to!"

She went on to explain that she was the only girl on this end of the hallway. The next closest female was Susan Thompson, but Susan was six doors down and she rarely had a chance to say anything to her except for an occasional "hi" in the hallway.

I didn't know what to say, so I smiled to be polite. Jennifer was running on and on about how bored she had been when she suddenly stopped. "I'd better take you up to see Christine. Dr. MacLaughlin really isn't very detail oriented, and if I don't take you upstairs no one will know you're here."

I started to ask her who Christine was, but she cut me off.

"Would you believe I worked here for almost a month, and no one even knew about it? After going for weeks without a paycheck, I finally said something to Dr. MacLaughlin...

"He'd forgotten all about it! Can you imagine?"

"Anyway, I had to go up and introduce myself as the 'new hire' – after almost a whole month on the job!"

Without waiting for a reply, she said "Come on. We have to get you checked in." So I followed her down the hall and up the stairs to the Eighth Floor. En route, she explained the stairs were a lot quicker because the elevator was on the other side of the building. That was important when you wanted to sneak out for a soda.

As we emerged out into the hallway of the Eighth Floor, she explained that this is where all the "brass" worked. Turning around to face the far end of the building, Jennifer pointed down the hall.

"Admiral Taylor is there on the right...he was Chief of Naval Operations...

"And General Thomas' office is the next one down...he was Army Chief of Staff." Off to the left was General Lloyd's office – he had run the Pentagon's Science and Technology shop – and next on the right was General McGreggor's office. Jennifer wasn't quite sure what he had done, but she thought he had been in charge of the Defense Intelligence Agency.

After turning around and leading me up the hall and around the corner, Jennifer pointed to the left and informed me that was where Mr. de Vris and Mrs. O'Connell had their offices. Pushing through the polished double doors, she stopped in front of a secretarial desk.

The reception room was large, but not overly so. To my immediate right was the secretarial desk where we stood, and to the left, another identical desk. Both were manned by exceptionally well-dressed young women, and for the first time I realized that *all* the women I had seen at CSS had been extremely fashionable. Especially Jennifer, my new hall mate and guide.

There was an upholstered couch at the far end of the suite, and a half dozen intricately carved chairs distributed evenly on either side. I stole a glance over my shoulder at Alex's office, but was disappointed to find that the doors were closed shut.

The girl was on the phone, listening intently. "Yes, Sir, of course. I'll make sure she gets the message." She was scribbling furiously on one of the pink slips.

After putting down the phone, she looked up and said "Hi" to Jennifer. They exchanged small talk for a few minutes, until Jennifer finally introduced me. "This is Alicia McAllister, the new hire. She's going to be Dr. MacLaughlin's research assistant."

She looked up at me and smiled, and extended her hand. "Well, congratulations! I'm Linda, Mrs. O'Connell's secretary." I shook her hand and told her I was pleased to meet her as well.

Jennifer turned and pointed behind her. "And this is Mr. de Vris' secretary. Her name is Jennifer too, but since I was hired first, everyone calls her Two – as in T-W-O. That way nobody gets confused."

I wanted to strangle her the moment I laid eyes upon her. Slowly. *Very slowly...*

She was a lot prettier than I was, and she saw Alex every day. But I forced a thin smile instead, and waved hello.

As I turned back, Linda addressed me. "I guess you want to see Christine, huh? Hold on, let me buzz her." She picked up the phone and pushed the intercom button. After holding for a moment, she spoke into the mouthpiece. "Jennifer just brought up the new hire. Do you have time to see her now?"

She smiled and put down the phone. "Follow me."

Jennifer One excused herself, and I followed Linda to the doors on the right. She knocked twice before pushing the doors open. "Mrs. O'Connell? This is Alicia McAllister."

I was stunned by her office. It was large, airy, and beautifully furnished. An Oriental rug lay upon the wall-to-wall carpet, and impressionist paintings hung on the walls. I couldn't be sure, but I thought they looked very much like originals.

Linda turned to leave as Mrs. O'Connell got up to greet me. She was very tall, very blonde and very beautiful. She rounded her desk with practiced grace, and as she extended her hand I couldn't help but think that she looked more like a supermodel than an executive.

She was wearing a dark blue skirt, slit high on the side, which she had accessorized with a brightly colored batik sash that fell almost to her hem, and a sheer white blouse. It was pinned rather daringly, just below the third button.

My God, she is gorgeous!

"I'm Christine O'Connell, the Center's Executive Vice President."

I shook her hand, and followed her to the large leather couch on my left. "I really like your office, Mrs. O'Connell."

She smiled and thanked me as she sat down. Crossing her legs with incredible grace, she rested her hands on her knees and congratulated me on joining the CSS. Asking me to call her Christine, she told me that the Center was a remarkable institution, and that the work it did was critically important to the nation's future. She said that she understood I would be working with Dr. MacLaughlin on a major project, and expressed the hope that I would find it interesting.

Oh yes, I said. I wasn't quite sure that I understood it as yet, but from what I had seen of it so far it appeared fascinating. I had double-majored in economics and international finance, and working for Dr. MacLaughlin was a really great opportunity.

Christine nodded and said that was what she had understood. Alex had called her yesterday, and told her I was quite remarkable. He was a good judge of character, she said, so she was sure I would do well.

Explaining that there were some things we needed to go over, she got up and walked to her desk. Leaning over she opened up a drawer, and pulled out a half dozen forms and what looked like a manual. Returning to the couch, she placed the materials on the coffee table and sat down again. She sorted through them for a moment, before pulling out a chart.

Laughing softly, she said, "I don't suppose Dr. MacLaughlin informed you of pay or benefits?"

I shook my head. "No, Ma'am." Flushing badly, I corrected myself. "Christine."

"In fact, I'm not entirely sure that he's hired me. I thought he was going to interview me, but instead he gave me a bunch of boxes and told me to sort out the contents."

Christine smiled. "Well, you have to understand that our Dr. MacLaughlin is...

"Uhhh...a bit eccentric, shall we say?"

Then after pursing her lips, she explained he was a brilliant economist and that many of his colleagues considered him a genius. But he was something of an Ivory Tower type, with no interest in administration.

"You won't believe this," she said, "but the last time he hired someone he forgot all about it, and the poor girl ended up working down there for almost a month before he remembered to put her on the payroll."

She shook her head and shrugged. "Well, anyway. You will be starting at $36,000, with full medical and dental benefits provided by the Center...

My jaw dropped. "Thirty six thousand dollars?"

Then I heard my voice squeak. *"Me? Make thirty six thousand dollars???"*

For that time and place, it was *a lot* of money.

Christine laughed. "Yes, you! The starting salary for a research assistant in the Econ Department is $36,000 per annum, with full medical and dental benefits."

She looked at me wryly. "Is that too much?"

I shook my head in disbelief. "No, no, it's not that at all. I just didn't think someone with a degree in international finance/economics could make that much to start."

"My boyfriend – my *ex*-boyfriend, that is – majored in business, and he started at almost half that!"

Christine frowned. "That would be James?" She leaned forward and looked at me intently. "He's really a jerk, you know."

Oh God! I covered my face in my hands in embarrassment. "Is there anyone who *doesn't* know about that?"

Christine reached out, and put her hand on my knee. "Your secret is safe. Alex had hoped that you would be hired, and in the course of conversation I asked him about your background…

"I assure you that everything said was spoken in the context of your employment. There was nothing personal about it, and it certainly will not be discussed with other members of the staff."

Having thus comforted me, she shook her head and chuckled. "But one girl to another…that guy's a *schmuck!*"

There was no point in denying it. It was true: James was truly and undeniably a schmuck, and all of a sudden that seemed really funny. Emboldened by my sudden change in fortune, I told Christine that he was a loser to boot. He didn't deserve *me* – and one of these days, the jerk was gonna realize it.

It was just that I had spent three years with that guy. *What was I thinking?*

Christine brushed it off. If she had a dollar for every loser she had dated, she and her husband could retire to Tahiti. Laughing, she said there really ought to be a law about that: jerks should have to pay you a buck every time they dump you. "That way," she said, "we'd all be rich."

That cracked me up, and all of a sudden I realized that I liked her. She had a great sense of humor, and she made me feel so at ease. No longer intimidated by her beauty, I wondered if I might ask her a question.

"Be my guest," she said.

"Well, it might be a little bit personal…but from what you said, it seems like you married a really great guy. So I was just wondering where you found him?"

Christine laughed softly. "Let's just say I kissed a lot of frogs before I stumbled across him. And I mean a *lot* of frogs!"

Still laughing, she told me it was a numbers game: keep kissing them, and eventually one of 'em will turn into a prince…

"I guess I'd better pucker up, huh?"

She nodded. "You know, dating really isn't much fun in Washington. This town is full of guys with little tiny brains and great big, oversized egos."

She shuddered. "I can't imagine going through *that* again." She glanced down at the enormous diamond ring she was wearing. "But you know, it all worked out. I found a really great guy, and I'm very happy now."

She smiled. "You'll find one too, in time..."

Already have, I thought.

"But right now we'd best get back to business," she said.

Suddenly aware of my intentions – and to tell you the truth, awed by them – I quickly corrected myself. *Or at least I hope so...*

But since I was brand new at the CSS, I thought I should probably keep that to myself.

Christine pointed to the chart on the table. "Your base salary will be $36,000 to start. But that's not what you will be taking home...

"Fifteen percent will be withheld and invested in an individual investment account, and one fourth of that fifteen percent will be released at Christmas time as part of a matching bonus. In other words, you will receive $30,600 in gross salary, while $5400 will be invested in your name. On the fifteenth of December, $1350 will be withdrawn from your account and presented to you as a Christmas bonus. The CSS will match that $1350, so your bonus will actually amount to $2700. With me so far?"

I nodded. "Except that I will have only been here about seven months."

"Right," she said. "This is just an illustration. In the actual event, you will get a little more than half that."

"OK...as I said, the 15 percent that is deducted each year is invested. If you are dismissed for cause or quit at any time before you become fully vested in the program – that takes eight continuous years of employment – you walk away with half. But after eight years of service, you can leave at any time and take it all with you, or leave and keep whatever portion you like in the investment fund...

"Which would be a really good idea. Nguyen Tranh manages the fund, and so far he has never turned in a per annum growth of less than six percent over the rate of inflation. His overall rate of growth has been close to 11 percent."

Christine looked up at me intently. "That's one hell of a performance, and if he keeps it up he's going to make us all rich."

I nodded my head in amazement. *The guy must be a genius,* I thought.

"Now, as I said you will start at $36,000, but you will be reviewed at six month intervals." Then she looked at me rather sternly. "I want you to know that Alex is rather liberal in granting raises, and I want you to know why...

"The work we do here is important, and highly specialized. Only rarely can we hire someone off the street, such as yourself, and even then we have to invest a great deal in training. Maintaining a highly specialized staff is mission-critical, and so is maintaining their morale...

"Alex calls the pay schedule his 'Golden Handcuffs.' If you are hired here, it's because we're impressed with your ability and we want to keep you...

"Understand?"

I nodded.

"Good. Because that ties into our image policy."

I looked at her quizzically. "Image policy?"

"Image. It's critically important to the organization's success. You must understand that in politics, the distinction between image and reality is blurry at best."

She gestured at her office. "Look around you. We have spent a literal fortune decorating these offices, and for good reason. They reek of money, success and power, and deliberately so...

"Politicians find these things all but irresistible. For the most part they are very bright individuals, but they tend to be exceedingly shallow and their horizon extends only so far as the next election...

"Our offices were purposefully designed to convey a sense of permanence – which in their minds, is the highest form of success...

"You have to understand that they want to stay in power forever, and the aura of permanency we project makes subtle reference to that fact...

"Our mission is fundamentally one of public education, and our primary task is to educate and inform the general public as to the nature and the severity of the threats that confront the United States today...

"But we also devote a great deal of effort to influencing the Executive and the Legislative branches. You must understand that Washington is not merely the capital of the United States – it is the capital of the Free World...

"The decisions that are made here are consequential. They affect the lives of every man, woman and child in America and far beyond.

"We attempt to influence these decisions in various ways. One of them is through personal contact, which brings me back to my original point: in Washington, image matters...

"We have two or three congressmen or senators visiting our offices each and every day, and we try hard to impress them...

"You may have noted, for example, that CSS personnel are exceptionally well dressed. That is a matter of deliberate policy. The men are required to wear classic three-piece suits, and the women are expected to dress well....

"High maintenance, in other words. A girl doesn't have to be beautiful to work here, but I expect her to do her very best. That means careful attention to personal grooming: well-cut hair, manicured nails, and tasteful makeup. It also means jewelry and expensive, fashionable clothes."

Despite my best effort, there was just no way I could suppress my smile. Glancing up as it crept across my face, Christine chuckled. "I know what you're thinking...

"Terrible, isn't it? Having to go out and buy all those gorgeous new clothes? Spend all that time getting your hair and nails done?"

"Scandalous," I said.

Smiling mischievously, she agreed. "And I tell that to my husband every time I come home with a new outfit."

We were both laughing when she sat up rather suddenly, and cocked her head. "You know...you probably won't believe this, but Alex honestly thinks the effort we make is a big sacrifice. That's one of the reasons the pay scale is pegged so high."

She winked slyly, and warned me not to spill the beans.

"Not a *word*, I promise!"

"OK. Now all of this was supposed to be serious, and it really is. I want to emphasize that, because it's hard to keep a straight face when I give this little lecture of mine."

She sat back and held out her hands, palms up. "This is my style. Alex calls it 'refined sensuality' and I think that's an apt description...

"A lot of the congressmen and senators that come in here get a big thrill out of looking down my blouse...

She paused for a moment, and knitted her eyebrows. "Well, the really tall ones anyway...

"But as long as they return my business calls, that's just fine."

She shifted on the couch slightly, before looking up. "But there is one thing I want to make clear: I'm not a Fashion Nazi, and I certainly don't insist that you or any of the other girls follow my lead...

"I used to do a bit of modeling, and it taught me that style is very much a matter of individual expression. So figure out what works for you, and perfect it...

"Understand?"

I couldn't have agreed more, and I told her so.

"OK, so much for the lecture. You have a bunch of paper work to fill out – a W-2 form, insurance forms, individual investment plan enrollment, emergency contact information, and all that. Take them back down to your office."

A look of concern flickered across her face. "Dr. MacLaughlin *did* give you an office, didn't he?"

"Yes, Ma'am. The one across the hall."

She looked relieved as she picked up where she had left off. "OK, so take these back to your office and fill them out. When you're finished, bring them back up and give them to Linda."

I picked up the personnel manual, and put the loose papers inside it. Then just as I was about to stand up, Christine told me that payday was on Friday – but since I was a new hire, my check would have to be processed separately. She'd have accounting send it to her, and I could come by any time that afternoon and pick it up. Smiling, she said she would have a list of the better stores in Washington to go along with it.

I stood up, and shook her hand. It had been a pleasure I said, and I meant it.

I'm gonna like it here...

CHAPTER SEVEN

I was walking on air all the way back to my new office. I filled out the forms as quickly and neatly as I could, and took them upstairs to Linda. Then I hurried back, to get started on the boxes.

All three of them were stacked on my desk. But since Dr. MacLaughlin wanted me to inventory their contents, it didn't seem to matter where I started. So I lugged two of them across the room and stacked them in the corner. Returning to my desk, I pulled open the flaps of the one remaining and started removing the contents.

It was filled with bundles of standard sized papers. Most of them were clipped together with binder clips, but some of the smaller ones were stapled. I was pulling the second batch out of the box when I saw the bright red stamp that sprawled across the cover sheet.

I did a double take, just to make sure I wasn't seeing things. *Holy Cow*, I thought. *This stuff's Top Secret!*

It was only then that I noticed the masthead, which read Central Intelligence Agency. Flipping through it, I found the TOP SECRET stamp on every page. I was about to panic when I finally saw the much smaller stamp that angled across the bold red lettering. Inside the faded green ink border was the word DECLASSIFIED, and just below it was scrawled a handwritten date followed by an illegible signature.

Relieved – and more than a little bit intrigued – I sat down on the straight-backed chair that was placed against the wall, and began looking it over. The cover sheet identified it as a summary of the Soviet Union's hard currency earnings for calendar year 1954. I flipped it over and began scanning the columns on the first page. There were some forty or so line item entries, ranging from the sale of gold on the international market to interest income from Soviet accounts in various banks around the world. *Wow...*

It was my first glimpse into a secret world, and it intrigued me. Wondering how the CIA managed to get hold of information like this, I got up and pulled another batch from the box. More hard currency earnings, this time from 1921. Putting it aside, I reached in and pulled out a third batch. It was from 1944.

By now fascinated, I began stacking the batches on the desk. Once the box was empty, I put it on top of the two cases stacked in the corner and returned to my desk. I sat down, and began thumbing through them one by one. I didn't know a great deal about Soviet finances – just the smattering I had picked up in my Socialist Economics class – but the line item listings looked pretty standard, and the bottom line figure seemed about right. So I stacked them in a neat pile, and began sorting them by date for the inventory. Some of the cover sheets had apparently torn off and others were missing entirely, so it took more than an hour just to get them in chronological order. Still uncertain as to whether all the dates were accounted for, I decided I had better heed Dr. MacLaughlin's advice and ask Jennifer for some supplies.

Five minutes later, I returned with a fourth box filled with basic office necessities: Rolodex, post-it-notes, a pencil holder, a mechanical pencil, two pens, rubber bands, binder clips, a stapler, scotch tape, an eraser, an X-acto knife, a box of magic markers, a desktop calendar, a pack of legal pads and – naturally – an adding machine. She had put it all together for me while I was meeting with Christine.

I put the calendar in the center of my desk, and the Rolodex and pencil holder off to the right by the phone. I used the X-acto knife to slit open the package of legal pads before pulling one free, and then I put the rest of the stuff in the top drawer. Picking up a pen, I began making up a complete list of the contents. Everything was there.

I put the export earnings summaries back in the box, and taped the inventory to its top. Then I repeated the process with the second box, which contained calendar year summaries of the Soviet Union's borrowings from, and loan payments to, Western banks. This one took a lot less time, and I had just finished it when Jennifer poked her head in the door to tell me it was 5:30. She pointed to the photo ID badge she had clipped to the pocket of her skirt, and apologized. She had forgotten to take me down to the print shop to have mine made, and if security found me here after hours without a badge they would make a big deal out of it. It was only then that I realized I had worked straight through lunch without even knowing it.

Jennifer apologized again, but I shook my head. I'd come in early tomorrow, and I'd have the inventory done well before ten.

Jennifer winced, and confessed that she had forgotten to get me a key to my office. But it was OK, she said. She had a lot of work to catch up on, so she'd be coming in early. After promising to be there bright eyed and bushy tailed, at seven o'clock sharp, I laughed and told her that I'd be there too – but I warned her not to count on the bright eyed and bushy tailed part. Mornings and I just didn't get along.

No problem, she said. She'd have a fresh pot of coffee waiting.

I picked up my purse and the employee handbook Christine had given me, and turned off the lights. After Jennifer locked the door, I thanked her for all of her help and encouragement. Suddenly excited, I ran down the hallway in search of the elevator. I had promised to call Alex after the interview, and I couldn't wait to tell him that I'd been hired.

I had promised to call my Mom, too, and the thought of telling her about my new job was almost as exciting as the prospect of talking to Alex. She was going to have a cow when she found out how much I would be making – and in fact, the whole thing was so incredible I wondered if she was going to believe me at all.

By the time I got back to the suite I had calmed down, but only slightly. I had stopped at the coffee shop to pick up a Diet Pepsi, and I was pulling on the straw as I dialed the contact number Alex had given me for France. I knew he probably wouldn't be there, but I was hoping that by some miracle he'd pick up the phone anyway. I didn't realize it was almost midnight in Paris.

After dialing the number I waited through the half-dozen mechanical clicks as my call was routed through the international system, and then through three maddeningly long rings. Just as it had begun to ring for the fourth time I heard someone lift the receiver, and then a moment later a deep male voice said "'Allo." Struggling with my imperfectly learned and half-forgotten words of the foreign language, I identified myself and asked to speak with Alex. I must have made a mess of it, for the voice replied in heavily accented English. He was sorry, he said, but Monsieur de Vris was unavailable. Would I care to leave a message?

I said yes, of course, and gave him my name and number.

Disappointed, I hung up the phone. Dangling my legs over the side of the bed, I bounced them off the heavy bedspread as I figured out what to do next. Suddenly cognizant of the time difference, I realized that Alex probably wouldn't get my message until sometime the next day. There was no point in waiting around for him to call me back, I thought, and my Mom wouldn't be home for another half-hour or so. After checking my watch just to make sure, I decided to go down to the coffee shop and get something to eat.

But since the last thing I wanted to do was spill something on my brand new suit, I changed into a pair of cuts offs and a red cotton T-shirt. As I pulled it over my head I realized that it must have shrunk in the wash, for it had suddenly become awfully tight. Concerned that it might be *too* tight, I walked over to the full-length mirror to see how it looked. After studying myself from various angles, I finally concluded that it would be okay. I might get a look or two but hey, that might not be all bad. *Maybe some really cute guy will notice me?*

From somewhere deep inside, a little voice challenged me, saying *Yeah, that'll be the day.* But I was in no mood for sarcasm, so I chased it back into the shadows of my mind where it belonged. Indignant, I insisted to myself that it could happen...

Maybe. Someday...

At that point, The Ghost of Experience Past butted in, just to let me know I was dreaming. But by then I'd had quite enough of my self-doubt, so I snarled at him illogically. *He could be really cute and blind too, ya know!*

More than a little irritated, I shoved the shirttail down in my cutoffs and pulled my wallet out of my purse. I folded some money around my driver's license and stuffed them into my back pocket, then grabbed the key off the nightstand. Just as I was about to head out the door, I glimpsed the CSS employee handbook lying on the bed, and as an afterthought, I decided to take it with me so I could look through it while I ate.

Forty-five minutes later I plopped back down on the bed, happy, sated, and at least ten pounds heavier. The coffee shop had the best burgers in the world, and probably the largest as well. And then there was the cheesecake...

As per usual, I insisted that that the cheesecake shouldn't count. I had my very own system for counting calories, and according to my House Rules, a Diet Pepsi cancelled out whatever was most fattening.

Having struck at least 1500 calories from my Guilt List, I happily checked my watch. It was time to call my Mom, and the prospect of playing a little *Gotcha!* with her cheered me up immensely. So I opened the handbook to the pay and benefits section, and dialed the number.

She must have been waiting by the phone for me to call, because she picked it up on the second ring. I gave her a cheery 'hi,' and casually asked her how she was.

"Oh, good...I'm fine...I'm sorry. But after I got off work I was really hungry so I went out to get something to eat. That's right, work. They hired me on the spot.

"Uh-huh...research assistant to Dr. Charles L. MacLaughlin, world famous economist."

"How much?"

Grinning from ear to ear, I told her. "Thirty six *thousand*."

I jerked the handset away from my ear to escape the shriek. After she calmed down a little, I put it back on my shoulder.

"Yup. $36,000 to start, plus benefits...

"Uh-huh. Full medical and dental, plus life insurance. Not to mention a free health club membership at this really elegant hotel next door, and some huge discounts on everything they offer."

Flattening the handbook out on the bed, I started reading.

"50% off breakfast, 35% off lunch, 25% off dinner. 50% off drinks at the bar during weekdays, and 25% off on weekends...
"And Ladies Night is free altogether. For the girls, anyway...

"Let's see...Oh yeah, 15% off at the gift shop, boutique and beauty salon...

"And 20 % off valet service. We can drop our dry cleaning off on the way to work, so that's really convenient...

"And the pool. They have an indoor-outdoor pool up on the roof, and that's included in the health club membership.

"Pretty cool, huh?"

Trying hard to suppress my laughter, I listened as she went on and on about how I was going to be making as much as she did, right out of college! Had I been a bit more cynical, I would have thought – well, suspected at least – that she was hinting around about my student loans, but I knew her better than that. She was just amazed and really, really happy.

I was too, but there was no way I was going to let her know it. That would have ruined a really good game of *Gotcha!* So I just held the handset to my ear and said *Uh-huh* from time to time until she calmed down.

"Who?

"Oh, right. James...

"Well, Mom, we kinda split up. So I'm not staying at his place."

Although she tried really hard to hide it, the relief in her voice was unmistakable. *Bet she breaks out the champagne tonight*, I thought.

"The company is putting me up in a hotel until I find a place."

"No, Mom, that's not so weird. Lots of big companies do that."

"The National Hotel."

I pulled open the drawer of the nightstand, and pulled out the brochure. I read her the address, and then gave her the phone number.

"Suite 807...

"That's right," I said *"Suite.* And I'm not just a-whistling Dixie, Mom. You should see this place." Glancing around, I described it down to the last luxurious detail.

Finally she got around to asking me about the organization. So I read her the history and the mission statement from the handbook, and told her a little bit about what it did. She had heard about the CSS on the evening news, she said, and I could tell she was really impressed.

Since when does she watch the news???

"Huh?" She had asked me if Mr. de Vris was in charge.

"Right. Alexander de Vris. He's a big wheel here in Washington...

"I think he's one of the President's top advisors."

I kicked off my sneakers and tucked my legs underneath myself, Indian style. "Yup. I've met him. He even took me out to lunch."

"Swear to God, Mom...

"Oh come on! I wouldn't lie to you about a thing like that!"

"What's he like?" I flopped backwards on the bed with my legs still crossed, and grinned. "He's incredible, Mom. He has the *most* gorgeous green eyes you have ever seen. And he is just *soooooooooo* good looking."

Then I growled a little bit, just to make sure she got the message.

"How old? I have no idea. Thirty or maybe thirty-five or something...

"Mother!"

Untangling my legs, I rolled over on my side and pouted. "I'll have you know he was a *perfect* gentleman!"

It was entirely true, and I was about to press the point home when it suddenly occurred to me that the Perfect Gentleman thing might be something of a mixed blessing. Acutely conscious of the fact that Alex had stopped me from kissing him in the hotel lobby the night before, I began wondering if chivalry was all it was cracked up to be.

The whole point of the exercise is to drive the boy wild, right? But how the heck do you do that if he's gonna be a Perfect Gentleman?

There was clearly something wrong with that picture, and I had just begun wrestling with the conundrum when my mother's voice jerked me back to reality. "Sorry, Mom, I was just thinking...

"Uh-huh. Thinking. I do that now and then, you know...

"Oh *very* funny, Mom! Do I make jokes about *your* intellect?"

Sitting up with one leg crossed underneath me, I reminded her that she was the original Space Cadet. "Uh-huh, that's what I said. *Space Cadet!"*

"I suppose you've forgotten about the time you took me to the emergency room for swollen glands, and accidentally took that other little girl home with you? It would have served you right if you'd been busted for kidnapping!

"And what about the time your heel got stuck on the floor mat and you drove the car all the way through the garage? If there hadn't been that big tree in the back yard, you would have ended up in Wisconsin!"

Chortling, I warned her that she was playing a dangerous game. She'd better go to Sears and get herself a new IQ before she started picking on *me* again.

"Yeah, Mom, sure. You've told me that a thousand times and I still don't believe it." I stuck my nose up in the air and told her there was no way in the world she was ever going to convince me that she had graduated *Magna Cum Laude*. "Come on Mom, fess up. You stole that Phi Beta Kappa Key, didn't you?"

Laughing, I looked down at my watch. We'd been on the phone for half an hour, so I told her I had to go. But first I demanded that she congratulate me.

"That's right, congratulate me...

"Why??? 'Cause I done good!"

By now we were both laughing so hard we could barely talk, so I promised to call her again in a couple of days and stammered out a goodbye.

After I hung up the phone I lay back on the bed and chuckled for a long time. Mom cracked me up, and she was never funnier than when we were teasing each other. She had her fair share of faults, but I was really lucky to have her and I never let myself forget it. Space Cadet or not — and trust me, she was just what Star Fleet was looking for — she was a really wonderful mother, and for that I was truly grateful.

Still lying on the bed, I turned and glanced out the window. It was only a little after 7:30 and it was still light outside. Suddenly enthusiastic, I decided to go exploring.

After checking my back pocket to make sure my money and driver's license were still there, I grabbed my room key and bounded out the door. Energized, I took the staircase down to the lobby, two steps at a time. I got a lot of looks when I burst through the door into the lobby, but they weren't directed at my too-tight-T-shirt. It was more like, "Who's the crazy girl running through the lobby?"

As I zoomed out the door I waved to Antoine, and to his everlasting credit, he didn't even cringe. He smiled instead with practiced grace, and as I emerged out onto the street a decorous, "Good evening, *Mademoiselle*" wafted after me.

With no plan or destination in mind, I set off walking in the general direction of the Capitol. I could see its dome rising up from behind a forest of trees, a half mile or so away. Retracing the path Alex had taken me on the previous morning, I started down to Constitution Avenue. But rather than follow the exact same route, I decided to strike out on my own. So I followed a little unmarked street down in front of the Capitol building, which led to an ellipse that arced in front of the reflecting pool. Although it was almost 8 pm by then, the sun still hung high above the horizon, and for a long moment I watched its rays dance across the surface of the water. Then I was off again on my grand adventure.

I passed the Botanical Garden off on my right and continued around the elliptical path until it turned uphill. Pausing for a moment to take my bearings, I decided to cut across the grass to Independence Avenue and take the sidewalk up the long incline. That put me in front of the Rayburn House Office Building – which I learned from reading the big brass plaque outside the door. As I trudged up the hill, I marveled at the huge glass and polished marble structure. Like so many of the other buildings I had seen in Washington, it was truly imposing.

I crossed over South Capitol Street and passed the Longworth House Office Building; after crossing over New Jersey, I saw the Cannon House Office Building. Finally crossing over First Street, I stopped in front of the new Jefferson Building, right across from the Library of Congress. The big sign in front of the main entrance told me that it was a part of the Library, and listed a series of public displays inside. For someone who had been born and raised in a two-stoplight town like Glen Meadows, it was exhilarating and almost overwhelming. *So this is my new home,* I thought.

Independence Avenue mysteriously morphed into Pennsylvania Avenue as I crossed over Second Street, and broad tree-lined medians appeared in its center. A whole row of quaint little shops and restaurants appeared on my right, and as I looked up the street I could see a street kiosk and a half dozen sidewalk cafes, replete with multicolored awnings. Despite the hour – and the heat – I could count thirty or forty patrons amongst them.

It reminded me of Paris – or at least the Paris I knew from books and travel brochures – and I fell hopelessly in love with it. Making a mental note to come back for dinner as soon as I could afford it, I made my way past the tables and chairs of the outdoor cafes before stopping to look in the window of a bookstore.

From the titles in the window it was clear that this was no ordinary bookshop. All but one or two books dealt with military strategy, geopolitics or international economics. Some of them were marked with small handwritten signs, recommending them to various House and Senate committee staffers. It was all serious and weighty stuff, and amazingly expensive: one of the books on global economics was priced at $110; all of the rest were well over $50.

Along with chocolate and cheesecake and pastries – well, let's face it, just about anything that's fattening – I have a special weakness for books. So it took a real act of will to pull myself away from the window. With a last mournful glance at the tome on global economics, I resumed my journey.

I crossed over one last street, and walked to the end of the block. It was pretty much the same as the one I had just trod, but with fewer restaurants, more bars and no bookstore at all. But at the very end of it was a small grocery store, and through the window I could see a clerk stocking a refrigerator case with soft drinks in the back. Hot, tired and thirsty, I pushed open the door and went inside.

It was so small I couldn't see how it qualified as a grocery, but the shelves were a lot higher than usual, and they were packed with goods. As I walked down the aisle to the refrigerator case, I was amazed to see a tiny meat counter on the other side, complete with a glass case and scales.

When I finally reached the refrigerator, the clerk was down on both knees pushing six packs of Coke into the far recesses, so I asked him to excuse me as I reached over him and took a Diet Pepsi. I was just about to turn away when I thought twice, and put it back. I took a bottle of Evian water instead.

I walked back to the front of the store, and put my bottle of water on the counter. The guy in the back was apparently the only one working that night, so I glanced around as I waited for him. Right by the door was a newspaper stand, and beside it was a revolving carousel filled with paperbacks. Unable to resist the temptation, I walked over and started turning it.

On the second turn, I caught sight of *Murder in the White House*, which had just come out in paperback. It was a who-done-it written by President Truman's daughter, Margaret, and according to all the reviews, it was a real thriller. I had wanted a copy when it first came out in hardback in 1980, but as a college freshman I just couldn't afford $20 for recreational reading. So I made a mental note to get it just as soon as it came out in paperback – and now all of a sudden, it was right there in front of me.

I hesitated for a moment, because it was priced at $4.95, and after buying a copy of the Sunday Washington Post last night, I had a grand total of $96.40 to my name – and that had to last all the way to Friday. But after landing the job at CSS, it didn't take much to persuade me. I felt that I deserved a special treat, so I decided to splurge a little. Not only did I break down and buy the book, I got a banana Popsicle as well. It had been beckoning me from the glass freezer case that supported the cash register, and under the circumstances it didn't seem fair to refuse it.

Happy and content, I emerged onto the sidewalk with the book in a plastic bag, the water in my hand and the Popsicle in my mouth. I must have looked like a 12-year old as I strolled back down the street, because people were staring at me. But I didn't care. *What's the point of living if you can't enjoy a Popsicle once in a while?*

By now the sun was sinking in the far west, and the light had begun to fade. I decided to take the same route back to the hotel, in part because I didn't want to get lost on Capitol Hill at night. But I really wanted to get back as fast as possible so I could start on my book, and I thought that was probably the fastest way.

There was a lot less traffic now, and the crowds at the sidewalk cafes had thinned out considerably. By the time I passed the Jefferson Building again it seemed as though I had Washington all to myself. There wasn't a car or pedestrian in sight.

After depositing my Popsicle stick in an ornate, wrought iron trash can, I headed down the hill. Then as I passed into the lengthening shadows cast by the House office buildings, the silence became almost eerie. All I could hear was the gentle padding of my sneakers on the concrete sidewalk.

That might have scared most girls, but I wasn't concerned. To compensate for my non-existent social life in high school, I had not only immersed myself in academics, but sports as well. I had gone to the state championship with the girls' track team my senior year, and I had continued with athletics in college. Having just won my brown belt in Tae Kwon Do the week before graduation, I was pretty sure I could outfight anyone who was even close to me in size. And if they were a lot bigger, I could always outrun them.

That's why it came as such a surprise when I began feeling frightened as I retraced my steps through the ellipse. Just as I approached the reflecting pool, I shivered involuntarily as the hair on the back of my neck stood up. I had checked behind me periodically along the way, and I was sure no one had followed me into the pathway. But even so, I couldn't escape the really creepy feeling that someone was watching me. By now more than a little bit scared, I decided to jog the rest of the way. So with my book in one hand and my water bottle in the other, I picked up the pace.

Although the sun had by now settled below the horizon, I was jogging out in the open. There were scattered trees to my right, but to my left was open field – grass for the most part, with an empty parking lot at the far end. It was hardly the place for an ambush, but as I trotted through darkness I was gripped by fear. In the very depths of my soul I was sure that someone – or some *thing* – was out there, and the fact that I couldn't see it made it even scarier.

As I hit the little unmarked street that led back to Constitution Avenue, I broke into a dead run. The hotel was only a few more blocks, and I was fast – *very* fast – and I was sure I could make it to the bright lights of the entranceway before they – or *it* – could catch me.

The thought consoled me as I pounded down the pavement, but it also confused me. Because if there were a Miss Boring USA Pageant, I'd win that sucker hands down.

So why would anyone be after me?

CHAPTER EIGHT

As luck would have it, I made it back to the hotel alive, well and entirely unharmed. But the strangeness of it all had put a real damper on my mood, and by the time I got back to the suite, the murder mystery in my bag had lost its allure. So after making sure I had double-locked the door, I took a quick shower and crawled into bed.

I must have been really tired, for I fell asleep almost immediately. I had forgotten to call the desk for a wake-up call, but the morning sun awakened me a little after 6:00. I showered and dressed, and ate a quick breakfast in the coffee shop. Arriving at the office just a few minutes after seven, I was pleased to find that Jennifer had already opened up.

She was in the process of making a pot of coffee when I walked through the door, so we chatted for a few minutes until the coffee was done. After searching through the credenza, she found me a mug, so after pouring myself a cup I thanked her, and walked across the hall to my office. I had just sat down when Jennifer poked her head in the door to tell me that she was going down to security to get me a key, and to remind me we had to go down to the print shop to get my ID badge.

The best time, she said, would probably be right after lunch, so she'd come get me about 1:00. I told her that would be fine, and thanked her. Then I turned to the task at hand, which was inventorying the last box containing summaries of Soviet hard-currency purchases.

I finished up just after nine, and taped the inventory to the box. With nothing else to do, I went over and asked Jennifer if there was anything I could help her with until Dr. MacLaughlin arrived. I had assumed that he would be there first thing in the morning, but Jennifer checked his schedule and said no. He was out at CIA headquarters for something or another, and he wasn't supposed to be back until ten.

But given the way those guys did business – and the traffic on the George Washington Parkway – she figured he wouldn't be in until eleven at the earliest. Since she was catching up on some typing, there really wasn't anything I could help with. Uncertain as to what I should do, I went back to my office and reopened the boxes.

Although I couldn't be sure what Dr. MacLaughlin had in mind, I decided to take a guess. Since the only logical reason to have that sort of data organized chronologically was for comparisons across time, I inferred that he was looking for possible discrepancies in the relationship between Soviet hard currency earnings and expenditures. So I reorganized the boxes by setting them in a neat row against the far wall, and retrieved the first year's data for hard currency earnings, hard currency borrowings, and hard currency expenditures, and spread them out on my desk. The first question, obviously, was how they lined up. So I plugged in my adding machine and set to work crunching numbers.

For most people, calculations of that sort are the stuff of nightmares. But I was a born number cruncher, and I could bang away on an adding machine for hours and hours on end. Solving standard mathematical problems gave me a sense of mastery and control, but financial analysis had a more mischievous appeal.

Comparisons of income to expenditures tells you as much about nations as it does about people, and if the data is broken down properly you can not only observe their behavior but deduce their priorities and infer their motivations as well. It's a lot like peeking through someone's bedroom window, except that it's legal and it pays really well.

Three and a half hours later I was still at it. I was peering through the Kremlin's window *circa* August of 1949, when Dr. MacLaughlin appeared in the doorway. I was so deeply engrossed in what I was doing that I didn't notice him at first, and when I finally did, I almost jumped out of my skin. He apologized for having frightened me and sat down. While I was recovering my wits, he pulled a pipe out of his coat pocket, and began stuffing it with tobacco.

After a lengthy search through all of his pockets, he finally found a lighter. Then after he'd taken a few puffs, he asked me to bring him up to speed. I told him I had sorted through all the boxes, and with the exception of the Soviet's hard currency purchases for 1964, everything was there. Since I hadn't anything else to do, I'd started a preliminary analysis of hard currency income to expenditures – assuming that the Soviet's borrowings abroad were intended to finance imports from the West – and I had been looking for possible discrepancies. Rather self-consciously, I told him that I hoped he didn't mind.

Dr. MacLaughlin chuckled again. I was a clever girl, he said. That was *exactly* the point of the exercise. The Soviets had been up to their ears in shady financial dealings from Day One, but no one had ever called them on it. He suspected that the data I was working with would reveal a significant discrepancy between their hard currency income and expenditures that could not be explained in terms of hard currency borrowings abroad. If that turned out to be the case, he and Alex were reasonably confident they could persuade Congress to initiate an investigation into that fact.

I was puzzled and confused. Surely the CIA had already done that.

Dr. MacLaughlin puffed on his pipe for a few moments, then shook his head. He had spent most of the past decade trying to obtain authorization for just such a study, but he had been blocked at every turn. For reasons that weren't immediately apparent, The Powers That Be didn't want him poking his nose into that particularly dark crevice. Admiral Stansfield Turner – Jimmy Carter's handpicked CIA Director – had threatened to fire him over the issue, and since he had no doubt that Turner intended to carry out that threat, he'd opted for early retirement instead. Which was fortunate, for if he hadn't resigned, he would have been booted out the door just like Jim Angleton. For my information, he explained that Angleton had been Chief of Counterintelligence until Turner's predecessor had thrown him out on his ear for raising uncomfortable questions about the Agency's analytical approach.

"That's incredible," I said. "People get fired for *that*?"

Still pulling on his pipe, Dr. MacLaughlin nodded his head. As much as one would prefer it otherwise, the CIA was a government agency, and it was subject to the same faults and failings as every other. During the early years of the Cold War, the CIA had generally managed to avoid the sort of political pressures that were brought to bear against the other parts of the bureaucracy, but after Watergate all that had changed. Congress had asserted its oversight authority to an unprecedented degree, and as a result, the Agency's activities had been sharply circumscribed. The Congress didn't like the CIA raising uncomfortable questions about illegal exports – especially when they involved big campaign contributors – and the Carter Administration had supported Capitol Hill. As a result, inquiries into Soviet finances had been ruled out of bounds.

But the Reagan Administration had taken a different view of the matter, and we had that to thank for the boxes of data sitting on my floor. When Carter was voted out of office, Admiral Turner had resigned and President Reagan replaced him with Bill Casey. Dr. MacLaughlin had known Casey since their days together in the Office of Strategic Services – the World War Two forerunner of the CIA – and when he had approached him with the idea of taking a hard look at the Soviet's finances, Casey had been enthusiastic. Grinning, Dr. MacLaughlin said that with any luck at all, our little research project might shake a skeleton or two out of the Soviet's closet – and if it did, the Reagan White House was prepared to make an issue out of it. Mixing his metaphors with evident glee, he smiled and said we might even chase a rat or two out of our own cupboard.

Rather tentatively, I asked him if that wouldn't mean stepping on some powerful toes. Suddenly serious, Dr. MacLaughlin knitted his eyebrows together and nodded. What we were engaged in was politically consequential – potentially, at least – and for that reason it should be held in strict confidence. Knowledge of the project had been deliberately limited to a select few, and he warned me that it must stay that way for the duration. Aside from those immediately involved in it – which included himself, Jennifer, Alex, Christine, and now me – only Director Casey and President Reagan knew of its existence.

I was incredulous. *"President Reagan?"*

Dr. MacLaughlin nodded and smiled. "Bill Casey ran it by the President before signing off on it, and after talking it over with Alex, the President gave it his full support."

My jaw dropped. *"He talked it over with Alex?"*

Dr. MacLaughlin nodded. "They have an unusual rapport. Alex, of course, was the President's foreign policy advisor during the campaign, and even though he declined an appointment with the Administration, he carries a lot of weight at the White House..."

Dr. MacLaughlin's voice faded off, and he stared off into the distance for a while as he puffed on his pipe.

"Despite the age difference – which is quite significant, you know – I would have to say that they are friends. They share a common vision of America, and that vision binds them together."

I was speechless. I had known that Alex was politically influential – after all, the chairman of the CSS simply had to carry some weight around town – but when I'd told Mom he was one of the President's top advisors, it had just been part of my game of *Gotcha!* I had no idea he was *that* important...

Dr. MacLaughlin's pipe had gone out, so he rapped it on my desk a couple of times and then stuffed some more tobacco in it. After lighting it again, he became serious once more and explained that while the documents in my possession had been declassified, they remained proprietary, and for that reason confidential. I should not leave them unattended, and he instructed me to make sure that I locked my door whenever I left my office, even for brief periods of time. Overwhelmed by the seriousness of the endeavor, I nodded and assured him that I would guard them carefully.

Dr. MacLaughlin nodded, and proceeded. He wanted me to continue exactly as I was doing, and to provide him with an interim summary report at close of business each week – typed, single spaced and no more than one page in length, listing the materials analyzed during the preceding period and any points of interest that may have emerged. To make sure Jennifer had time to type it up before leaving, he suggested that I give her the summary no later than 2:00 pm on Friday.

I nodded and said "of course," and with that, he got up and excused himself. He was halfway out the door when I called after him. "Dr. MacLaughlin?"

He turned and looked back at me.

"Sir, I was just kinda wondering...

I shifted uncomfortably in my seat as I struggled to find the right words. "I guess...

"Well, I'm kinda surprised that I was hired for such a sensitive project. No one here at CSS really knows me or anything, and Alex didn't even ask me anything about politics."

I could feel my cheeks flushing as I looked up at him.

Dr. MacLaughlin smiled and shook his head. "I've known Alex for a great many years now, and I have to say that his ability to judge character is simply uncanny. It only takes him a matter of moments to size someone up, and I can't recall a single instance in which he has ever been wrong..."

He knitted his eyebrows together, and pursed his lips. "If I didn't know better I'd attribute it to sorcery...

"But having said that, I would hasten to add that while this project is confidential it will not remain so indefinitely...

"Secrets have a short shelf-life in Washington. Almost everything leaks eventually, and this will too. Our sole concern is to keep it under wraps until such time as we have something to show for our efforts. After all, we intend to give it a great deal of publicity at the appropriate time."

Dr. MacLaughlin stopped abruptly, and grinned. "In any event, you don't impress me as being much of a spy. You're far too taken with Alex to betray him, so I think we can trust you."

Oh, God! I hid my face in my hands.

"Is it that obvious?" I asked plaintively.

Hiding behind my hands I couldn't see his face, but from the tone of his voice I was quite sure that he was grinning from ear to ear. "Let's just say that whenever I've mentioned his name, your face lit up like a young lass in love…

"But that's not such a bad thing, now is it?" Chuckling, he turned and walked out the door.

I had never been so embarrassed in my life. If I hadn't been wearing heels I would have got up and kicked myself. But I knew if I tried that, I'd fall flat on my face, so I banged my head on the desk instead.

Way to go, dummy! Why don't you just wear a big sign that says, "I've got the hots for Alex?"

Feeling like a complete idiot, I banged my head again for good measure. *It'd serve me right if he never talked to me again…*

I sat there with my face buried in my hands for a good fifteen minutes, feeling all the while the fool. After the flush finally faded, I shook my head in disbelief.

I've got to get back to work…

I was alternating between crunching numbers and berating myself when Jennifer showed up an hour later, to give me a key to my office and an electronic pass card for the building. She was grinning like the Cheshire Cat, so I was pretty sure she had overheard my conversation with Dr. MacLaughlin. Resigning myself to eternal humiliation, I followed her down to the print shop to get my picture taken for my ID card, and a half-hour later I emerged back into the hallway with my photo ID clipped to my waist, an employee in good standing at the Center for Strategic Studies. An idiot of an employee, no doubt, but in good standing nonetheless.

After that, it seemed as though my life went into hyperdrive.

As it turned out, Alex had called while we were down in the print shop and I was furious for having missed him. Unable to find either me or Jennifer, he had left a message with Jennifer Two upstairs congratulating me on the job. He would be back in a couple of weeks, and said that he'd look in on me then.

Sorely disappointed, I went back to my office, and immersed myself in the project. Now that I knew for sure what it was all about, it was a whole lot more interesting. On most days I'd arrive at the office early, and if Jennifer didn't come across the hall to remind me that it was time for lunch, I'd usually forget and work straight through. But it wasn't just work that kept me busy. Aside from living down my embarrassment, I had to find a place to live and do something about my wardrobe.

I spent the next two weeks scouring the real estate ads for an apartment. So far, at least, there hadn't been any visiting dignitaries, and in fact no one had mentioned the suite to me at all. I probably could have stayed there for the rest of the summer, but now that I had a job I wanted to find a place of my own as quickly as possible. The problem, of course, was the Washington housing market.

For most of its history, Washington had been a sleepy little river town, distinguished only by the fact that it was the seat of government. For the first hundred years of its existence, Washington had been so small that there hadn't even been a need for a fence around the White House. Local farmers had supposedly grazed their cattle on the South Lawn, and the neighborhood children had commandeered the front lawn for a playground. Although historians still disputed the number of White House windows that had been shattered by errant baseballs, they generally agreed that it was in the high hundreds.

But all that changed with the New Deal. In an effort to cope with the Great Depression, Franklin Delano Roosevelt had dramatically expanded the size and scope of government and a host of new agencies had sprung up in Washington. Government had expanded again during the Second World War, and yet again during the early stages of the Cold War. But according to local historians, Washington had really taken off with Lyndon Johnson's Great Society.

The problem was that Washington was located in a small valley formed by the intersection of the Potomac and Anacostia rivers, and there was a limit to how many buildings it could hold. Priority had gone to government and commercial buildings, and for that reason residential properties were generally small, always scarce and extremely expensive.

Even though Washington had spilled across both rivers and beyond the formal boundaries of the District of Columbia, the housing situation remained critical. This unfortunate fact had been seized upon by rapacious landlords, who often divided and subdivided dwellings that were tiny to begin with. After traipsing all over Washington for ten consecutive nights in a row, all I had found were overpriced cracker boxes. A typical basement efficiency in a dubious neighborhood was going for well over $800 a month, rats and roaches included.

There were nicer apartments available in the Northwest section of Washington, and across the river in Arlington and Alexandria. But since I didn't have a car I had to stick with the Metro, and apartments along the Metro line were way out of my price range. Disheartened and discouraged, I finally concluded that I would have to find a couple of roommates and share an apartment at the far end of the subway line. It wasn't an appealing prospect, but as luck would have it, I stumbled into a really good situation at the end of my second week.

The CSS occupied the top four floors of the eight-story building. The print shop, production, and mail room were all on the Fifth Floor, along with security, accounting and supply; reception was on the Sixth Floor, along with the library, two conference rooms and the auditorium; the Econ shop was on the Seventh Floor, along with most of the area specialists; and the military and intelligence types were on the Eighth Floor, along with management – meaning Alex and Christine. Every floor had a small employee lounge with a microwave, refrigerator and vending machines of various sorts, but the girls almost always used the one on the Eighth Floor. It was a little bigger and the vending machines had a better selection, and there was always the chance of running into Alex. And needless to say, that irritated me to no end.

The Eighth Floor lounge also had a bulletin board, and employees posted various messages and announcements on it. I had gone up there for a Diet Pepsi, and on my way out I happened to see an ad posted by a girl named Julia Shurga down in accounting. She had an overly large apartment in the Dupont Circle area, a block and a half from the metro stop, and she was looking for a roommate. By that time I had figured out most of the local landmarks, and I knew that Dupont Circle was a reasonably good neighborhood. The apartment she described seemed really nice, and she only wanted $400 a month, so I wrote down her extension and called her when I got back to my office.

After talking for a few minutes, we agreed to meet after close of business, so at 5:30 sharp I emerged from the stairwell onto the Fifth Floor. For some reason or another, the girls always took the stairs at CSS and I had started doing it too. It was kinda like our secret passageway, with no men allowed.

After searching about the accounting section, I finally found Julia in a cube at the far end. She processed payroll checks, which made her everyone's favorite. As a clerk she didn't quite merit an office, but she had used her status to wrangle a window with a view. *Not bad*, I thought.

We hit it off right away. Like me, she had come from a small town in New England and had moved to DC after she'd graduated from college. She had stayed with her older brother for the first couple of weeks she had been here, but had moved out as soon as she found a job. Her big bro was a sweetheart, but he was a hopeless slob. And in any event, she couldn't stand his girlfriend – a first class you-know-what, she said.

To make a long story short, her brother had a friend in the Air Force who had been transferred to Greenland on short notice, and she had taken over his lease. The apartment was in an old commercial building that had been gutted and remodeled for residential use, and although it was technically an efficiency, it was huge and it had a gigantic loft. The lower part measured 25' x 40' with an 18-foot ceiling, and the loft covered almost half of that. It had a small but fully equipped kitchen tucked away in one corner, a large bathroom, and a really cool spiral staircase that led upstairs. As an additional bonus, there was already a bed, a sofa, chest of drawers, and a table with four chairs up in the loft so I wouldn't have to worry about furniture. But the walls were brick and the floors were finished concrete, so I'd want a couple of throw rugs and some really warm slippers.

The whole thing sounded really great, so I rode the Metro home with her to take a look. We talked the whole way there, and found we had a lot in common aside from our New England origins. She had been a social reject in high school too, and an academic superstar in college. To top it all off, she was really funny. Her sense of humor was a little on the weird side, but she cracked me up with a running series of one-liners about life in Washington.

Not counting the walk to Union Station Metro, it took less than twenty minutes to reach her place, and when she opened the door I was really impressed. It was even bigger than I imagined, and I really liked the open space. She had organized it functionally, and divided it with freestanding partitions.

It took less than a minute to work out the deal. Since I had just started, she knew I couldn't afford to give her a security deposit or an advance payment on the rent, so she agreed to let me pay $125 a week for the first four months, and a hundred a week thereafter. We'd split the utilities, but buy our food separately. She had a boyfriend and she stayed at his place two or three nights a week, so she rarely kept anything in the refrigerator except ice cream – and some chocolate, of course.

We decided that I would move in the following week, at my convenience. Since it was Friday, she promised to get a set of keys made for me over the weekend, and then she walked me back to the Metro to make sure I got on the right train. They were running a bit slower by now, so it took me almost an hour to get back to Union Station. But from there it was only a couple of blocks back to the hotel.

I didn't have much to pack, but as soon as I got back to the suite I made a quick inventory and sorted everything out. Since most of my clothes happened to be at the hotel's laundry, I wouldn't have much to carry.

I still didn't know anyone in Washington, so I spent most of the weekend in the office crunching numbers. It wasn't a whole lot of fun working all by myself, but I had nowhere else to go, and in any event, I couldn't afford going anywhere. I had spent my entire income to date on clothes.

True to her word, Christine had included a list of the nicer shops in Washington with my first paycheck. Since I didn't know my way around at first, I drafted Jennifer as my guide on my first two expeditions, and she was a big help. Not only did she know where all the stores were, she knew which ones had sales and when.

Thanks to James, my most pressing problem was shoes. Aside from my sneakers, I had just one pair of flats and one pair of heels. But my heels were only two inches, and as per Christine's example, the girls at CSS never wore less than two and a half.

That posed two entirely separate problems. The first was that clothes were incredibly expensive in Washington, and that was especially true of shoes. On a good day, you could find a decent pair of flats for under $50, but heels were something else altogether. It was impossible to find a pair of two and a half inch heels for less than $75, and most of them were well over $100.

The second problem was I didn't know how to walk in them. Until I bought my interview suit, I had never even owned a pair of heels, and even though they were just two inches, I felt like I was walking on stilts. I was pretty sure it was just a matter of time before I tripped and broke my neck, but Jennifer assured me that it was just a matter of practice.

Besides, I only had to wear them in the office. Girls in Washington wore sneakers on the way to and from work, and carried their heels in a little tote bag. And sure enough, all the stores sold them as accessories – for just $19.95 a piece…

My first two forays with Jennifer netted just four pairs of heels, a suit, two skirts, and three blouses – all of which were expensive, fashionable, and appropriate for the office. But as nice as they were, they just didn't excite me. Something was missing, but I couldn't quite put my finger on it. So as payday approached, *The Big Question* was very much on my mind.

I'd been thinking about it ever since my talk with Christine. She had been right, of course: fashion is very much a matter of individual expression. But therein lay the problem: I wasn't sure which aspect of my personality I wanted to express. Just before I moved out of the suite to Julia's place, I bought a copy of every fashion magazine I could lay my hands on, and I had studied them intently. I found a lot of good ideas, but nothing that really thrilled me. To tell the truth, I really wanted to emulate Christine but I wasn't sure if I had the figure – or the nerve – to pull it off.

Both questions were answered definitively the next Saturday. Jennifer, Julia and I met at the Dupont Circle Metro at ten o'clock, and piled into a cab for Georgetown. Jennifer and Julia hadn't known each other until I introduced them, but they hit it off right away.

After talking it over for a few minutes, we had made a solemn oath to shop-until-we-dropped, and we were determined to uphold it.

During my search for an apartment, I had been through Georgetown several times. But these had always been in the late evenings when I was already tired and cranky, and for that reason I hadn't had a chance to appreciate it.

But this morning I did, and as I stood at the corner of 22nd and M Street, the hundreds of little shops and restaurants that stretched ahead reminded me of the three-block shopping area on Capitol Hill. It was quaint, colorful, and ever so old. I knew that the travel guides often compared Georgetown to the French Quarter in New Orleans, but as the late morning breeze blew through my hair the comparison faltered. Shimmering in the sunlight, Georgetown exuded an indefinable energy and I was sure that it could not be matched. This was Washington, after all, the most important city in the world...

We started at a boutique about halfway down the block, and began working our way down to Wisconsin Avenue. After stopping at Nathan's for a riotous lunch, we began working our way up the hill. I finally struck gold in a little shop called *Enchanté*. It was on the left hand side of the street, and to my surprise it occupied both floors of what had once been a townhouse. It was expensive – *really expensive* – but the clothes were gorgeous, and they had everything in my size.

Christine encouraged the women to wear suits at CSS, but skirts were permissible as long as they were accompanied by a fashionable blouse and properly accessorized. Having already bought one suit – which I'd left for alterations – I was thinking along the lines of a slit skirt when I found one on the second rack.

A deep emerald green, it was made from finely woven light wool, and it reminded me of the skirt that Christine had worn when I had first met her – except that the side-slit was cut a full two inches higher.

Jennifer and Julia had wandered off by then, and all the sales clerks were helping other customers, and for a few moments at least it seemed as though I was entirely alone. So as I twirled in front of the three-way mirror I let my fantasy take hold, and for the very first time in my life I imagined myself a *femme fatale*. After rummaging through my purse, I pinned my hair up on my head and turned around slowly.

Beyond any shadow of a doubt, the slit was daring. But the skirt itself was *elegant* – it simply reeked of refined taste and cultured sensibility – and as I looked on myself in the mirror, my face began to glow hot as I indulged my dreams. Since my collar was already open I unbuttoned the second button on my blouse, and then the third before pinning it midway to the fourth. By the time I finally got the safety pin closed, my hands were shaking.

I had hoped to find a goddess in the mirror when I looked up, but I found a badly flushed young girl instead. She looked at me with plaintive eyes, as I turned first to the left and then to the right, to no avail. The skirt was stunning, but even with a diamond necklace the open blouse just wouldn't work.

Guess there won't be anyone looking down my shirt, I thought, as I watched my dreams of glamour abandon me.

Consumed by a terrible sense of loss, I hadn't noticed the owner of the shop standing just outside my view. She was perhaps 30, tall, and incredibly beautiful. And she must have read my mind, for as I undid the safety pin just above the fourth button, she assured me that it would be OK. Give it another couple of years, she said, and I'd fill out just fine.

I knew that she meant well, but her words cut deep. For the first time in my life I really *wanted* men to look at me – including one very special man, in particular – but I knew they weren't going to. Not like they looked at Christine, anyway.

Fighting back the tears, I nodded and turned back into to the dressing room.

She must have realized how badly I felt, for when I reemerged I found her there waiting. "You have your eye on someone really special, don't you?"

I nodded glumly, and bent over to pick up my purse. She stopped me with a touch to my arm, and explained that her figure had been much like mine when she was younger. She had been forced to learn all the tricks the hard way, and she thought that I might benefit from her painful experience. Smiling, she held out a cream colored pullover made of sheer silk, and the merest wisp of a bra. She urged me to try them on with the skirt and if I didn't like the blouse, the bra was mine to keep anyway. Curious and impressed by her kindness, I hurried back into the dressing room. A minute later, I was back in front of the mirror.

As I turned to the right and then to the left, all I could think was, *Whoa...*

Grinning from ear to ear, I told her I wanted the skirt, the blouse and the bra. Not to mention everything else in the store...

Two hours later I emerged back on the sidewalk with two skirts, three blouses, the non-existent bra, two pairs of heels and a ton of accessories. I was flat broke, but happy as a clam. *Come Monday, I'm gonna knock 'em dead.*

Which in fact, I did.

On the way to work, Julia and I had become separated on the Metro and I had to walk from Union Station to the office alone. There was a really good-looking guy standing at the bus stop in front of the Old Post Office, and as I approached, I could tell he was trying to make eye contact. Pretending hard not to notice, I walked past him, and just as soon as I did, he whistled at me. Thoroughly pleased with myself, I walked the rest of the way to the office with my nose stuck *way* up in the air.

But it got better. I had already had a cup of coffee before leaving the apartment, so I went straight to the Eighth Floor lounge to get a Diet Pepsi. General Thompson was sitting at the table, reading the morning newspaper when I walked in. He did a double take, and spilled his coffee all over the place.

It had cost me $450 bucks, but I have to tell you – between the whistle and the look on General Thompson's face, it was worth every penny!

More than a little bit pleased with myself, I spent the lunch hour chatting with Jennifer in Dr. MacLaughlin's outer office. I was sitting on the edge of her desk with my legs crossed, wearing my new cut-oh-so-high skirt when Christine walked in. Chuckling, she made me get up and walk an imaginary runway she had drawn through the outer office into the hall. That wasn't easy in my new three-inch heels, but I managed to pull it off.

After I had finished walking up and down, she warned me to stay off the Eighth Floor. Grinning from ear to ear, she explained that the generals and admirals were getting along in years, and she didn't want any heart attacks up there. Or any more spilled coffee, for that matter...

On the way out the door, she gave me a sly wink and whispered "well done."

CHAPTER NINE

It was the end of August by the time I wrapped up my preliminary report. Alex had finally turned up in late June, just long enough to check in with Christine before he took off again. He'd come down to see me before he left, but as luck would have it, I was at the Library of Congress doing background research that day. I would have been really disappointed, but he left a note saying that he would be back right after Labor Day, and if I could find the time he would like to take me to lunch. That seemed like a pretty good consolation prize, so I started counting down the days instead.

With Labor Day less than a week away, I was really excited. But I had to focus, to prepare for my meeting with Dr. MacLaughlin.

I pushed a big pile of reference books to the far left-hand corner of my desk, and placed the draft copy of my report in front of me. After taking a swig of cold coffee from my mug, I took a deep breath and opened it. With only fifteen minutes left before the scheduled meeting, I wanted to go over it one last time.

It's crunch time, I thought, knowing that the report would probably make me or break me at the CSS.

I had spent the last thirteen weeks living and breathing the project. I had crunched and re-crunched the numbers a thousand times, and I was certain they were correct. I was just as sure about my analysis and conclusions, but I was concerned that Dr. MacLaughlin might not accept them. *Worried might be more accurate*, I thought.

Then I glanced up at the clock. Thirteen minutes to go. *Better make that panicked, instead...*

From 1919 through 1950, the numbers had been more or less congruent. But after 1951, they'd become increasingly weird. Year after year, the Soviets had spent a lot more hard currency than they had taken in, and I had to wonder where it was all coming from. By 1983, they were spending almost a hundred billion more than they earned abroad, which meant that there were only two possible alternatives: either the data were wrong, or they had a major source of income that wasn't showing up on the books.

I had originally suspected that the data were in error, but Dr. MacLaughlin had assured me it was rock solid. Although he couldn't tell me where the numbers had come from, he said that they were the same figures the Soviets had used in their five-year plans. If they were wrong, the Soviet economy would have fallen apart decades ago.

That left the second alternative – the Soviets had developed a source of off-the-books income, starting about 1950. *But what could it be?*

My first guess was that they were selling stuff out the backdoor; but given the money involved, that would have shown up somewhere. But even if it didn't, I would have caught it when I analyzed their Gross Domestic Product. Since I had initially thought the data was flaky, I had cross-referenced and compared it in every way I could think of. If the Soviets were selling a hundred billion dollars' worth of stuff out the back door, it would have put a real dent in their domestic consumption. But in actual fact, consumption had been steadily increasing since the late 1950s. It didn't make sense.

In fact, none of it made sense until I had a sudden epiphany on the way to work one morning. As usual, I was riding the Metro, and I was looking through the *Washington Times* when I found an article on page four that seemed interesting. According to a Justice Department report that had just been released to the media, international organized crime – that is, organized criminal activity that crossed national borders – was grossing almost a trillion dollars a year from smuggling, drug running, and illegal weapons sales world-wide. To illustrate the point, the report had a handy little graph that charted a steady increase in the estimated gross income of international organized crime over the last 15 years. I did a double take, and then a quick calculation. *What the...*

As I stared at the graph, all the pieces of the puzzle seemed to fall into place. *That explains it,* I thought. *The low-lifes are working the black market!*

By the time I got to the office, my suspicions had hardened into a near certainty. I was sure, absolutely certain. But how the heck could I prove it?

Obviously, the financial data wasn't enough. I had to figure out what they were selling and how, and then come up with a reasoned estimate of their market-share in guns, drugs or whatever. If that matched their mysterious hundred billion dollar hard currency surplus – or if it even came close – I'd have 'em. Suddenly confident, I wondered what the guys in the Kremlin were gonna think when they found out they'd been busted by a 22-year-old chick straight out of Township College!

Then more to the point, I wondered what the U.S. government was going to think.

This is gonna rate a statue, I thought. *A big bronze statue of Yours Truly, right out in front of the Justice Department!*

It was a great fantasy, but reality was bound to catch up with it sooner or later. Which it did, just as soon as I unlocked my office door. This was going to take a heck of a lot of research, and I hardly knew where to start. I knew very little about the Soviet Union, and nothing at all about black markets and organized crime.

But I had to start somewhere, so I picked up the phone and buzzed Gen. McGreggor's office. He had been the director of the Defense Intelligence Agency, and I was pretty sure he knew everything there was to know about the USSR. After identifying myself, I explained that I was working on a project for Dr. MacLaughlin and that I needed some additional background information on the Soviet Union and – especially – the Soviet government. Nuts and bolts stuff, I said, and asked him if he could recommend a couple of books to start with.

Happy to be of assistance, he rattled off the titles of a half-dozen volumes, and as soon as I had jotted them down, I thanked him and hung up. Then I called information for the number of the FBI's public affairs office.

They picked up the phone on the second ring, and I introduced myself as a research assistant from the Center for Strategic Studies. I told them pretty much what I had told Gen. McGreggor, and asked them if they could recommend any good books on international organized crime. The lady on the other end of the phone said that Public Affairs didn't really do that sort of thing, but if I would leave my name and phone number she would pass my request along to the relevant section. So I repeated my name and gave her my number, and then walked across the hall to give Jennifer the list of books Gen. McGreggor had recommended. Jennifer had purchasing authority, and as soon as I explained why I wanted them she said "no problem." She'd order them right away.

About a half-hour later, she stuck her head in my door. Special Agent Tom Rogalski was on Line 2, returning my call. I thanked her, and picked up the phone. Agent Rogalski identified himself as the senior agent in charge of the organized crime division at FBI Headquarters.

Impressed, I explained that I was working on a project for Dr. MacLaughlin and told him that I needed some basic reference materials regarding international organized crime.

I gulped hard. "Yes, sir. He's here at the Center for Strategic Studies now."

Agent Rogalski explained that they went way back, and after making me promise to give Dr. MacLaughlin his regards, he gave me three titles. All of them were still in print, he said, and I could probably pick them up at *Olsen's Books* in Georgetown. There wasn't much that he could tell me, as almost everything the Bureau had on international crime syndicates was classified. But the Justice Department had quite a bit of statistical data that were available to the public, and he would have it sent over by courier that afternoon. After thanking him, I hung up the phone.

Just my luck, I thought. Call the FBI on a hunch and what happens? They hook me up with one of Dr. MacLaughlin's old buddies from way back when...

Thinking that I had probably put my foot in it big time, I wondered if I should tell the boss what I was up to. After thinking it over for a few minutes, I decided not to. I was right – I was sure I was right – and in any event, I was well within my writ. As long as I didn't step on anyone's toes, Dr. MacLaughlin wouldn't mind. After repeating that to myself a half-a-dozen times, I actually started believing it.

But I still had a slight problem on my hands. I had promised Agent Rogalski I would remember him to Dr. MacLaughlin.

Which I did, a few hours later. Dr. MacLaughlin had been out at Langley all morning, but he breezed in for a few minutes right after lunch. He had stopped in to pick up his messages and grab a cup of coffee. He was picking through the box of doughnuts Jennifer had brought when I ambushed him at the coffee pot. "Tom Rogalski told me to tell you 'hi,'" I said.

Dr. MacLaughlin was stirring sugar into a styrofoam cup at the time. He looked up quizzically, then smiled in recognition. "How nice of him to remember me!" Then he stuffed a glazed jelly doughnut into his mouth and darted out the door, coffee in one hand and a bulging manila folder in the other.

Jennifer looked up from her typing, and rolled her eyes. "You know I love the man dearly, but he can be a complete flake at times."

Puzzled, I looked at her. "Because he didn't remember that Rogalski guy?"

Jennifer shook her head and said, *"Nooooooooo...*

"Because he stuffed an éclair in each pant pocket just before you walked in, and he's going to forget all about them by the time he gets upstairs for that senior staff meeting."

She shook her head and sighed. "Just wait till he sits down."

I scrunched my nose. *"Ewwww."*

Jennifer shrugged and went back to her typing. "It's a wonder his wife hasn't killed him by now."

Thinking I might find something up in the Library, I took the stairs up to the Eighth Floor. I was just pushing open the door when Dr. MacLaughlin came storming down the hallway, swearing like a sailor. I ducked inside the double doors so he wouldn't see me as he rushed into the men's room, and bit my lip really hard so I wouldn't laugh out loud. I felt sorry for him, but Jennifer was right. He really needed to spend a bit more time on Planet Earth.

There wasn't much in the Library on international crime syndicates, but the courier arrived from the Justice Department a little after four. I spent the rest of the day analyzing the statistics, and by the time close of business rolled around, I was more certain than ever. But statistical correlations weren't going to be enough. I had to come up with some hard evidence to prove the point.

Just after 10:00 the next morning, a delivery boy arrived with my books. Jennifer had given Olsen's her suite number so he had taken them over there first. She signed for them, and then told him to take them to my office across the hall. He seemed a bit confused when he knocked on my door, but he was really cute and I was flattered by his poorly concealed interest. At least until he called me "Ma'am."

That was a first for me, and I wasn't quite sure whether it was a compliment or an insult. But he was so well mannered that I thought I should give him the benefit of the doubt. So I dug through my purse until I found two dollars. After I handed them to him he stammered out a polite 'thank you,' and disappeared out the door. Then I got down to business.

For the next several weeks, I spent every free minute poring over the books Gen. McGreggor had recommended. One of them was a gigantic tome entitled *The Soviet Government*, and another *Soviet Covert Operations Against the West*. Both of them were impressive works of scholarship, meticulously researched and documented. The other four were general histories of Russia and the Soviet Union, all of which were excellent for background information.

Working nights and weekends, I managed to get through *The Soviet Government* in a little under ten days. It was over 1,100 pages, but length wasn't really the problem. It was understanding how their system actually worked.

On paper, the USSR was a representative democracy much like our own, and the governmental apparatus was structured in much the same way as ours. But it didn't function like our government, or for that matter, any other Western government. Despite the fact that the Soviet Constitution was among the most liberal in the world – it guaranteed Soviet citizens rights that Americans could only dream of – the Soviet Union was nonetheless a totalitarian police state. The incongruity had bothered me until I got to the chapter on "Party-State Control," which explained that the state apparatus was controlled by a Communist Party apparatus that had been constructed alongside it. For every government position, there was apparently a corresponding Communist Party position, and the Communist Party called all the shots. They even had a nifty constitutional provision that specified "the leading role of the Party" in Soviet government and society, which made the police state legal. As best I could figure it, the Soviet government functioned pretty much like any other as long as the Party wasn't involved. The problem was that the Party stuck its nose into almost everything.

By way of analogy, a Soviet peasant busted for stealing eggs from his neighbor's chicken coop was looking at pretty much the same sort of trouble that an American farmer would face for doing the same thing here in the United States – so long as the Party was out of the picture, the Soviet courts would slap him with a fine and tell him not to do it again. But if the Party decided that stealing eggs fell under the heading of "economic sabotage," he was looking at a firing squad. Millions of Soviets had been executed for such infractions in the past, and it still happened every now and then. An example of this recounted in the book was *The Great Teddy Bear Caper*, which the Party had turned into a national scandal.

It seemed that a scheming artisan had stolen some materials from the factory where he worked, and fashioned them into a half-dozen teddy bears. They had turned out so well that he had been able to persuade a manager at GUM – that was their big department store, right off Red Square – to put them in the window and sell them as examples of Russian handicrafts. Then he had his relatives rush in and buy them the moment they were put up for sale.

The manager was so pleased that he requisitioned materials for more teddy bears. But the artisan didn't actually need them – he had bought the original six teddy bears back from his relatives. He resold the bears to GUM, and brokered the raw materials on the black market for a respectable profit. He ran the scam a half-dozen times before the authorities finally caught on.

The total value of the materials he had swindled amounted to only a few hundred rubles, and under any other circumstances the judge would have given him six months in a workhouse. But the Party had decided to use the scam as a pretext for an "anti-corruption campaign." After a nationally publicized show trial, the poor guy had been stood up against a wall and shot.

The more I learned about it, the more the Soviet Union reminded me of Alice's *Wonderland*. It was a place where the rules could change in an instant, and in fact, they often did. I didn't see how the people that lived there could stand it.

But there was a larger lesson to be learned from all this: the people who ran the Soviet Union exercised their power in a manner that was arbitrary, capricious and utterly immoral. People who would shoot a petty criminal just to make a point would also murder millions as a matter of policy. As in fact, they had – between 1927 and 1953, they had murdered at least 20,000,000 of their own people, and almost all of them had been entirely innocent. By the time I finished the chapter on what they called *The Great Terror*, my skin had begun to crawl.

The books on Soviet covert operations against the West were even worse. The moment the Communists had finished consolidating power in Russia, they had launched a secret campaign of espionage, subversion, sabotage and terrorism against the West, and it continued to the present day. Their principal instrument in this was the Committee for State Security – or using the Russian initials, the KGB.

The KGB had a long and complicated history, and it had operated under a number of different names and acronyms over the years. But the thread that ran through it was political murder. The KGB called itself "The Sword and Shield of the Party," and for good reason – although it was often represented as a combined intelligence and security service, it was in fact an army and it waged war without mercy upon all who dared to oppose its masters. Its total strength came to about a million and a half, and almost a third of that number was organized into heavily armed combat divisions complete with tanks and artillery. In this sense, it was a lot like the Nazi SS.

The KGB was organized on the basis of nine Directorates, five of which were termed Chief Directorates. The organizational chart in the back of one of the books was simple and logical, but reading about it was confusing because of the way the Soviets used the terms.

It was often hard to tell the difference between a Chief Directorate and a Directorate because the Soviets themselves often failed to make the distinction. Compounding the problem was the fact that they frequently interchanged the word "direction" with "directorate." In the Russian vernacular – supposedly – they meant the same thing, even though they meant something entirely different when used in the context of the organization. Not surprisingly, whenever the books made references like "the First Direction of the Third Directorate of the Fifth Chief Directorate" I got lost.

But even though the particulars confused me now and then, I was pretty sure I had a handle on all the basics. Simply put, the KGB was the action arm of the Party and it did all of the Party's dirty work. For most of its history, it wasn't even a government organization: the government simply deputized it, and delegated to the KGB the power to arrest people and put them on trial.

More to the point, it was the Party's principal instrument in waging war against the West. In addition to espionage, it engaged in what the Soviets called "Active Measures." Active Measures was a difficult concept, compounded by the fact that it was not an exact translation from the Russian term. Russian language, I learned, is a lot more descriptive than English, and it's filled with nuanced concepts that have no exact equivalent. But a fairly accurate description of Active Measures would be the use of intelligence assets for purposes that went beyond simple espionage, but stopped just short of outright warfare. As such, it included bribery, corruption, propaganda, disinformation, blackmail, kidnapping, assassination and terrorism.

It also included peddling drugs and black market weapons sales, as I learned from an obscure reference buried in one of the innumerable footnotes in the back of one of the books. During the Korean War, the KGB had decided that it could help the Communist cause by selling drugs to the American stevedore battalions who unloaded the ships that supplied our troops, so they had gone into the heroin business with the Chinese Communists at the end of 1950. The Red Chinese obtained high-quality heroin from the so-called Golden Triangle on their southern border, and the KGB used their intelligence networks to distribute it to dockworkers. They had not been particularly successful in stopping the flow of supplies to American combat troops, but they had made a ton of money off the drug sales. More importantly, they had spread the plague of drug addiction among the mostly black stevedores. Needless to say, they took their habit with them when they finished their tour of duty and returned to the United States.

As it turned out, the KGB didn't have the sort of network that was needed to support the stevedores' habits when they returned home, but the Italian Mafia did. So the KGB promptly cut a deal with the Mafia types, and in a matter of a few short years they were up to their ears in narcotics trafficking. The Chinese obtained the heroin, the KGB brokered it, and the Mafia sold it on the streets of America's inner cities.

One big happy family, I thought. *Just like the Corleones...*

Things got even more interesting years later, when cocaine emerged as the drug of choice among America's middle-class Yuppies – that is, the young, upwardly mobile professionals who were beginning to dominate the economy. Cocaine came from South America, and most of it was produced in areas under the control or influence of Soviet-backed guerillas. Suddenly awash in profits from the drug trade, the guerillas and their friends could pay cash for the latest Soviet weaponry. Not surprisingly, a major arms race had developed between the pro-Soviet guerillas-turned-drug-lords, and the American-backed governments of South and Central America.

When I first read the footnote about the KGB's drug running in Korea, I couldn't believe my eyes. So I jotted down the citation and took off for the Library of Congress. Sure enough, they had a copy of the original text and I used its footnotes and citations in exactly the same way.

It took some serious digging through a lot of moldy texts and back-pages, but I was eventually able to tie up all the loose ends. Using newspaper accounts of French and Italian court proceedings, I was able to establish a definitive connection between the KGB and the mafia. And then with declassified documents I found in the Congressional Record, I was able to demonstrate the link between the KGB and the South American guerillas-turned-drug-lords. After that, it was a simple matter of lining up the estimated drug profits of the mafia and the druggies, guesstimating the KGB's cut as a wholesale supplier of heroin to the mafia, and factoring in CIA estimates of Soviet arms sales to the guerillas/druggies down south.

Sitting at my desk, I closed my eyes and punched the total button on my adding machine. I took a deep breath and crossed my fingers, and then opened my eyes.

Bingo! It all added up.

Thinking I had just won a major battle in the Cold War all by my lonesome, I spent the next five minutes wondering what outfit I should wear when I posed for the big statue of me they were going to put up out in front of the Justice Department. Or maybe the CIA, come to think about it. Then I got down to business and started writing up my draft report.

It had taken me almost a week to pull all the evidence together, and write it up in an acceptable form. When I'd finally completed it late the night before, I plopped it down on top of top of Jennifer's brand new IBM desktop computer with a note asking her to type it up and pull copies for myself and Dr. MacLaughlin.

Jennifer was a wizard when it came to typing, and she had it typed up, spell-checked and proofread by 10:00 that morning. She came across the hall to give me a copy, fresh off the printer, before taking another to Dr. MacLaughlin. After scheduling a one o'clock meeting, he had retreated into his office and closed the door.

I began worrying when he didn't emerge for lunch. All of a sudden it occurred to me that maybe I wasn't so smart after all.

What if I'm wrong?

Stricken by fear, I had just buried my face in my hands when Jennifer buzzed me. Dr. MacLaughlin's ready, she said.

After saying a quick prayer, I picked up my copy of the draft and walked to his office. His door was open, and I could see he was still reading. He looked up rather sternly when I knocked on the door jamb, and gestured towards a chair. So I walked in and sat down, and waited until he had finished.

He tossed the draft on his desk, and reached for his pipe. He stuffed it with tobacco and lit it, and after taking a few puffs, looked me straight in the eye. "Alright," he said, "tell me what you think of your draft." He was very professorial.

After I had crossed my legs and tugged on my skirt, I took a deep breath and looked up at him. "Well Sir..."It's my best effort, and I think it's pretty good."

"Pretty good?"

I nodded. "Yes, Sir, I think it's pretty good."

Dr. MacLaughlin shook his head. "No," he said firmly. "It's damned good..."

Then he stuck his pipe back in his mouth, and after relighting it, he leaned back in his chair and waved at the paper in front of him. "This is one of the finest analyses I have seen in years...

"In fact, it's probably the best."

Suddenly relieved, I started to thank him. But all of a sudden he started chuckling. "I'm going to have to reconsider my first impression, Lass...

"Perhaps you're a spy after all."

Flattered, I grinned and sat straight up in my chair. "Ya think?"

Dr. MacLaughlin smiled and shook his head. "No, not really. But if you ever get tired of CSS, I will be happy to recommend you to the Agency...

"This is a first rate piece of work, Ms. McAllister. It has professional written all over it, and it is everything we had hoped for...

"Perhaps more importantly, it has confirmed some very dark and long-held suspicions that some of us in the intelligence community have harbored."

He pulled on his pipe again. "I'm very pleased, and I know Alex will be as well."

I started to thank him happily, but he brushed my words aside. "I'll polish this next week and after I've finished tweaking it a bit, I'll send it off to the publisher."

Then he looked at me closely. "I had intended to list you as my research assistant, but given the caliber of your work, I will list you as co-author. It's to be published in the October edition of *The Washington Journal of Political Economy*."

My jaw dropped. "Me? As co-author?" I couldn't believe my ears.

Dr. MacLaughlin nodded, and smiled. "Now go on, girl. Take the rest of the afternoon off. It's a beautiful day outside, and you've earned it...

"A bit of shopping perhaps."

With that I felt my face light up. "Can I take Jennifer with me?"

Dr. MacLaughlin looked at me sternly. "You're pushing your luck, Lass..."

Then all of a sudden he threw up his hands and laughed. "Oh, what the bloody hell. Take the girl and be gone!"

We were halfway down the hall when Dr. MacLaughlin stuck his head out of the outer office and bellowed after me. "Ms. McAllister, I forgot to tell you...

JUST BEFORE MIDNIGHT

"Christine wants to see you, first thing in the morning."

I turned around and gave him the thumbs-up sign. Then I pushed Jennifer around the corner and raced her to the elevator. Just in case he changed his mind...

CHAPTER TEN

I was rudely awakened the next morning by a shattering crash. Julia was banging around downstairs, packing for a three and a half-day weekend camping trip with her boyfriend, and she'd knocked the downstairs floor lamp over while she was trying to hoist her bag off the table and onto the floor. The camping trip was kind of a special deal, so she had made arrangements to take off early. But she'd blown off packing the night before, and she had been frantically racing around to find everything she needed.

Thinking it was probably time to get up, I rolled over and looked at the alarm clock on the nightstand by my bed. *5:30 in the morning???*

I pulled the covers back over my head and tried to go back to sleep, but by then she was making a racket in the kitchen. Knowing it was only a matter of time before she broke something else, I sat up in bed and shook the cobwebs from my head. "Julia," I croaked. "Do you have any idea what time it is?"

Remembering that we actually had food in the fridge for once, I warned her that she'd better be fixing my breakfast.

There was a long silence as I got out of bed and put on my robe, then an awkward acknowledgement. "Uh, sure...scrambled eggs ok?"

By that time I had made my way down the spiral staircase from the loft. "With buttered toast and some of those little microwave sausages."

She made a funny face and stuck her tongue out, but by then I had found my way to the bathroom. I emerged from a hot shower ten minutes later, ready to face the world. Julia plopped a cup of fresh coffee in front of me, and told me breakfast would be ready in a minute.

I loaded my coffee up with cream and sweetner, and asked her the occasion. "Camping trip," she said. "I told you about it yesterday."

I looked at her bulging suitcase. "You need all that for a three day camping trip?"

After swearing she had packed only the bare essentials, she laughed and told me that she didn't think this was going to be just any camping trip.

I raised an eyebrow as she put a plate in front of me. "Oh, yeah?"

She nodded and grinned triumphantly. "Uh-huh. When I was straightening up Mike's place last weekend I happened across a receipt from a jeweler."

That got my attention. "And that wouldn't have been for a diamond ring by any chance, would it?"

By now she was grinning like the Cheshire Cat. "Yeah. A really big one, too!"

I reached across the table and gave her a high-five. "Way to go, girl!"

"Pretty cool," she said.

I stuffed a sausage in my mouth. "Way cool." Ignoring my manners, I asked her how she had stumbled across the receipt. "Oh, Mike and his friends had gone to a sports bar to watch the pre-season game so I decided to straighten the place up a bit."

I was half way through a piece of toast, but that didn't stop me. "So where was it?"

"In his wallet," she said. "He forgot to take it when he left."

"You went through his wallet?" Feigning incredulity, I picked up another piece of toast. "So you're a snoop, huh?"

Julia was munching on a sausage. "Am not! I was hungry and I wanted to order something to eat but I didn't have any money with me. So I figured fair was fair: I cleaned up his apartment, so he could buy me a pizza…

"And as luck would have it, there was this receipt all folded up behind the bills." Julia took another sip of coffee before deadpanning, "Couldn't have missed it if I tried." Reaching across the table, she beat me to the last sausage. "So I don't think that counts as snooping, do you?"

I was busy finishing off my eggs, so I ignored her question until I had washed them down with some more coffee. "So did you find anything else interesting?"

Julia looked disappointed. "Just the usual. Drivers' license, credit cards, pictures of his family, stuff like that…

"No phone numbers, or I would have killed him already."

"Well, that's good," I said. "No phone numbers is always a positive sign."

Julia nodded, and changed the subject. "So how's your love life? I heard Tom Andrews wants to ask you out."

"Tom Andrews?" I was aghast. Tom had just completed his doctoral coursework at Johns Hopkins, and he doing an internship with Dr. MacLaughlin part-time while he finished his dissertation. He was nice enough, and passably good looking, but the thought of going out with him sent shivers down my spine. "He's a nerd!"

After taking another sip of coffee, I reconsidered. "Actually, he's more of a geek..."

Now certain, I nodded to myself. "A geek, definitely...

"Has to be, because the nerds were picking on him in the lounge the other day, and they don't pick on each other, ya know...

"Union rules and all that."

Julia leaned back in her chair and gave me a stern look of disapproval. "Aw, come on. Tom's not that bad!"

I got up and poured another cup of coffee. "He's alright," I said. "I just wouldn't want to date him."

Julia pushed herself away from the table and smirked. "And that wouldn't have anything to do with a certain big shot by the name of Alexander M. de Vris, would it?"

"Julia!" If looks could kill, she would have been a dead one. But they don't, so I stuck my tongue out at her instead.

Ignoring my insult, Julie told me to hurry up and get dressed. "You have to help me get my bag to the office."

I was about to tell her to go to a very bad place when I caught myself. I had a bit of experience dragging big bags around, and it wasn't much fun. "Ok," I said. "Give me a few minutes. I have to figure out what to wear." I had that nine o'clock meeting with Christine, so I wanted to look good.

A hour later we emerged from our apartment building, dragging her suitcase between us. It had a big handle, so I grabbed it from one side and Julia grabbed it from the other. Between the two of us, it wasn't so heavy, and we managed to get it down the three steps to the street without dropping it.

By then it was already eight o'clock, and the guy on the radio had said we were looking at another scorcher. But it had rained the night before, so the humidity wasn't too bad.

We made it to the Metro without too much trouble, and caught the train to Union Station. Lucky for us, there was a really nice older man going in the same direction, and he carried the bag for us almost all the way to the office. I hadn't thought it was such great idea to let a guy his age carry something that heavy, but he picked it up and carried it with ease. As it turned out, he had been a linebacker for the Washington Redskins during their glory days and he even had a Super Bowl Ring to prove it. Needless to say, I was thoroughly impressed. I'd never met a Super Bowl champion before!

After he left us at the corner, I helped Julia get her bag up to the Fifth Floor. Then I ducked into the ladies' room to fix my hair and makeup and change into my heels before taking the elevator up to the Eighth Floor.

It was exactly 8:45 when I walked into the Executive Offices. Alex's secretary, Jennifer – the other Jennifer, Jennifer Two – was on the phone so I waved at her en route to Linda's desk. Linda was engrossed in a file folder, so I waited until she looked up. "Dr. MacLaughlin told me Christine wanted to see me first thing."

"Hey, I didn't see you standing there…"

"She just went down the hall. She should be back in a minute, so why don't you take a seat?"

I thanked her, and sat down. Two was still on the phone and Linda was busy with her folder, so I picked up a journal from the end table and started thumbing through it. I had just started reading the introduction to an article on Soviet naval strategy when Christine breezed in. She smiled and said good morning, and gestured for me to follow her.

Once inside her office, she sat down on the couch and signaled for me to do the same. She started to say something, then abruptly changed her mind. "Would you like some coffee?"

I had already had two cups, but after almost three months at CSS I'd become an inveterate coffee guzzler. "Oh, please!"

Christine leaned over on the couch so that Jennifer Two could see her. "Two? Would you bring us a carafe? And a couple of cups, with some cream and sugar?"

I couldn't really hear what Two said in reply, but I saw her disappear through the double doors into Alex's office. A minute or two later, I heard a door open behind me, and Two walked in carrying a tray loaded with a carafe, cups, cream, sugar and some glazed doughnuts. The latter were from Alex's private stash, she said. Since he kept them in the refrigerator, she had nuked them in the microwave. Once they cooled off, they'd be really good.

She set the tray on the coffee table in front of us, and after Christine thanked her, Two headed for the double doors. Just before she got there, Christine called after her, and asked her to close them behind her. Then she poured our coffee and picked up a doughnut.

Delight spread across her face as she bit into it. "These are *sooooo* good," she said. Then she pushed the plate across the tray and told me I had to try one. "I wish I knew where he gets these things."

I picked one up from the plate and took a bite. It was still warm from the microwave, and totally delicious. "Wow! This is great!"

Christine shook her head, and told me that Alex claimed they came from a little hole-in-the-wall doughnut shop in Southeast. She had tried to find it once, but ended up lost in one of the District's worst neighborhoods. But bad neighborhoods didn't seem to bother Alex, and every couple of weeks he'd run down to Southeast and pick up a couple of bags of their glazed doughnuts. He froze most of them in the freezer, but always kept a couple down below in the refrigerator compartment. After a couple of seconds in the microwave, they tasted like they had been fresh baked. Or boiled, or whatever it is they do with doughnuts.

"He has a kitchen in there?"

Christine shook her head. It was more of a galley, she said, much like the one in the suite at the hotel. She'd show it to me later, if I liked, but right now there were more pressing issues at hand. Such as my future with the CSS.

That sounded serious, so I finished off my doughnut and said "Yes, Ma'am."

Christine turned on the couch so that she could look at me directly. "First of all, I want you to know how pleased everyone is with your report. Dr. MacLaughlin has told me that it's a first-class piece of work, and I'm inclined to agree..."

I cocked my head in surprise. "You've read it?"

Christine took another sip of her coffee, before saying no. "Dr. MacLaughlin brought it up at close of business yesterday and we discussed it in some detail. I didn't read it in its entirety, but I did skim through it...

"It is clearly a solid, well-researched piece of work."

By that time I was beaming. "I'm really glad you liked it," I said.

Christine nodded. "Frankly, I'm fascinated. There have been rumors circulating about the Soviet Union's involvement in the black market for a long time, but to the best of my knowledge, this is the first time that anyone has ever assembled sufficient evidence to give them credence."

Hey, I thought. *I'm gonna get that statue after all!*

"Anyway, your successful completion of the project has raised the obvious question of 'what next.' Dr. MacLaughlin has assured me that the Econ shop has more than enough work to keep you busy for years to come, but we both felt that you're well suited for something more sophisticated."

I was flattered. And to tell you the truth, a little bit surprised. "Really?"

Christine picked up her coffee cup again and took a sip. "Yes, we do. If you are interested, I'd be happy to tell you about it."

Intrigued, I practically begged her to continue.

"This project is in some respects comparable to the one you just completed. It involves an analysis of classified budget figures. In effect, an audit of the Black Budget."

I looked at her quizzically. "The Black Budget? What's that?"

The faintest hint of a shadow passed across Christine's face. "The term refers to that part of the budget that is classified....

"Almost all of it involves secret military or intelligence programs – programs that are so secret that even the Congressmen and Senators who appropriate their funds don't know anything about them..."

My jaw dropped. "You mean that Congress approves funding for things they don't know anything about?"

Christine nodded, and said that was more or less the case. The senior members of the defense and intelligence committees were privy to the details, and they passed judgment upon the budgetary requests. But the rank and file members of the House and Senate were clueless. At best, they knew the approximate size of the Black Budget and no more.

"Once approved, the authorized funds are hidden in the regular federal budget and no one is the wiser."

"Wow," was all I could say.

Christine nodded and continued. "As perhaps as you have surmised, the CSS has a rather special relationship with the Intelligence Community, and at times we undertake certain types of studies of mutual interest and concern. Such as the project you have just completed...

"But having said that, I hasten to add that this is much more complex and involved."

Christine leaned forward, and looked directly into my eyes. "It is also much more sensitive. If you accept this assignment, you will be working with some of America's most carefully kept secrets."

Confused, I shook my head. "But don't you have to have some sort of security clearance to do that?"

Christine nodded. "That's true under almost any circumstances. But the law provides the President with the authority to make certain exceptions and waivers where he thinks appropriate, and the same law permits the President to delegate that authority to the Director of Central Intelligence as well...

"You see, the Director of the Central Intelligence Agency is also *the Director of Central Intelligence*, which makes him the titular head of the entire US Intelligence Community...

"In theory, at least, he is not only in charge of the CIA but also the FBI, the National Security Agency, the Defense Intelligence Agency, the National Reconnaissance Office and so on and so forth...

"In other words, he's the Big Dog."

The colloquial reference cracked me up. Christine smiled and assured me that was Director Casey's own characterization, rather than hers. Then she went on to explain that as the Director of Central Intelligence, he had the authority to issue waivers and exceptions for security clearances, and that he was prepared to do so if I was interested in undertaking the new project. An attorney from the General Counsel's office would come out and I would have to sign about 10,000 forms, but other than that it was a done deal.

Except for my new office, she explained, which we would get to later.

That perked me up. "A new office?" It wasn't as though I didn't like the one I had. I did, but it didn't have any windows and it was about to overflow with all the newspapers, magazines, journals and books I had accumulated in the course of the last project. For some really weird reason, the Econ shop was short on bookcases, and Dr. MacLaughlin hadn't given me any at all.

Christine nodded. "Yes, of course. The materials you will be working with will be very sensitive. For that reason Alex wants to move you up here with us."

Me? On the Eighth Floor? With Alex and Christine?

"Provided, of course, you want to undertake this project."
Well duh, I thought. *Who would turn down an offer like that?*

Nodding eagerly, I told Christine I wanted to take a shot at it. "When do I start?"

Christine told me it would be at least a couple of weeks. First of all, I had to get squared away with the General Counsel's office, and then she had to get my new office space prepared. She got up and asked me if I'd like to see it.

I followed her to the far end of her office, and she opened a door for me on the north wall. It was the same door that Jennifer Two had come through when she had brought the coffee and doughnuts, and it opened into a huge room. It was at least thirty feet long, and probably twenty feet deep, and it was piled high with crates and boxes. Although I couldn't see the windows from where I stood – there was just too much stuff piled up – I was pretty sure they ran the length of the room. Off to my left was a pair of double doors that had once opened up into the reception area.

Christine walked in behind me, explaining that she would have to get all the boxes and crates moved, and have the carpet replaced and the walls painted. She wasn't sure what Alex wanted to do about the double doors, since they had been sheet rocked over years ago, but she thought it would make sense to have the sheetrock torn out so I could use them again. Otherwise I'd have to cut through her office or Alex's just to get to my desk…

And of course, she'd have to order me some new furniture and drapes.

Then she pointed to the door at the far end and explained that it opened up on Alex's galley. That was technically his, but as long as they were quiet he didn't mind if she or the girls used it. He had an industrial sized coffee pot back there anyway, so they tiptoed in and out all the time to get coffee. "But God help you if you take his last glazed doughnut. Jennifer Two made that mistake once, and I thought he'd never stop ranting."

Then she shook her head in amazement. "You wouldn't believe the words that came out of that man's mouth."

Taken aback, I looked at her quizzically. "Alex was swearing?"

Christine chuckled. "He has a truly astonishing vocabulary of four letter words, but I wouldn't worry about it. Unless you swipe his last doughnut – or something similarly stupid – you'll never hear it."

I was giggling so hard I almost missed her next comment. "He's mellowed quite a bit from his days at Georgetown."

That got my full attention. "Did you go to school with Alex?"

Christine nodded, as she put her hand in the small of my back and nudged me toward the far end of the room. "We were classmates," she said. "We took a number of the same courses, and we were often in the same lectures and seminars."

This I have got to hear!

"What was he like back then?" I asked excitedly.

Christine looked down at me and chuckled. "I understand your interest in Alex's wild and misspent youth, Ms. McAllister, but right now we have other things to do." Pulling open the door at the far end, she gestured inside. "This is the galley, and if you turn left through the door it will take you into his office…

"When he's here, you'll need to keep this door shut during business hours. Alex often has distinguished visitors in his office, and discretion is an overarching concern...

"So eavesdropping is entirely out of the question."

I was aghast. "Oh, absolutely. I wouldn't even think about it!"

Christine was suddenly stern. "Good. Now please understand the nature of the project you will be undertaking. You will be handling highly classified data on a routine basis, but you will not be at liberty to discuss it with anyone other than myself, Dr. MacLaughlin and, of course, Alex...

"And then only in these offices or in the Executive Conference Room. They are swept for bugs on a regular basis, and are presumed secure."

Christine paused and looked at me very seriously. "Understand?"

Surprised – almost shocked – I nodded silently.

Christine said, "Good. Because this is so very serious, I will repeat myself. As of this moment, you are forbidden to discuss this project with anyone other than the three of us. You cannot discuss this with your roommate, or any of your friends or family...

"The mishandling of classified information is a serious criminal offense, and if you disclose any information regarding this project at all – including its existence – you will find yourself in a great deal of trouble...

"Let me emphasize *will*, as opposed to *may*."

I gulped hard. "Like what kind of trouble?"

Christine looked at me sternly. "Like about twenty years' worth of trouble."

"Oh," I said. "That kind of trouble."

She nodded. "Uh-huh. The 'Big House' kind of trouble."

I scrunched up my shoulders and winced. "Not even my Mom?"

Christine shook her head. "Not even your Mom...

"We'll provide you with a suitable cover story when the time comes, and that will suffice for friends, family and so on. But for now I want you to go back down to the Econ shop and carry on. Dr. MacLaughlin has a number of things he wants you to help him with over the next couple of weeks...

"And remember, none of the secretaries are cleared for any of this. That means you can't tell Jennifer One...

"Or Jennifer Two, or even Linda. *Comprende?*"

"Yes, Ma'am, my lips are sealed..."

Then I looked up at her and grinned. "So do I get a secret poison pill, in case I get tortured?"

Christine chuckled. "No poison pill, for now. Just be discreet, OK?"

I held up my hand and made the Girl Scouts sign. "Promise," I said. "But now you have to tell me about Alex's wild and misspent youth."

Christine rolled her head over and tried to give me her adult-authority-figure stare – Dr. MacLaughlin called it her "Nazi look" – but she couldn't pull it off. Just as soon as we made eye contact the corners of her lips started to turn up on their own. After another second or two her chest started heaving up and down, and she finally broke up laughing.

It took her several tries to form a complete sentence, and even then she had to wipe the tears from her eyes. "Alex was...."

"Alex was...

Laughing harder, she turned away and looked at the ceiling. "Let's just say that Alex was a *very* naughty boy!"

Still laughing, she wiped her eyes again and told me to get back to work...

Immediately!

CHAPTER ELEVEN

I was still floating on air when I emerged from the stairwell on the Seventh Floor. It was almost impossible to believe – just three months before I had been broke, unemployed, and abandoned. And now I had an incredible job at the most prestigious think tank in town, doing top-secret analytical work that could change the world. And more to the point, in another week or two I'd have a huge office up on the Eighth Floor right next to The Mystery Man – otherwise known as Mr. Alexander M. de Vris.

Wow, I thought. *Kinda like the Washington version of Cinderella!*

At least I hoped so – until doubt suddenly assailed my fantasy.

But that could happen! I insisted. *Cinderella was a fairy tale and all that but, hey – can't dreams come true? At least sometimes?*

Still puzzling over the question, I unlocked my office and picked my coffee cup up off my desk. There was an icky residue in the bottom from the day before, so I took it down the hall to the ladies' room to wash it out. After that, I headed back towards Dr. MacLaughlin's office. I didn't have anything to do, and Christine had said he had a lot of work piled up, so I thought I should check in with him to get my next assignment. That and the fact that I really wanted to see him. I was bursting with pride and excitement.

Much to my surprise, Jennifer wasn't at her desk. So after I poured a cup of coffee, I walked over and knocked on Dr. MacLaughlin's open door.

He was sitting at his desk reading a journal when he heard my knock. He looked up pleasantly, and invited me to take a seat. He waited until I had sat down and smoothed my skirt before asking if I would be moving upstairs.

Beaming from ear to ear I told him that I would, just as soon as Christine got my office ready. But until then, I was supposed to stick around the Econ shop and help out. Dr. MacLaughlin smiled, and said we would have to talk about it sometime. But not here, on the Seventh Floor.

I leaned forward, puzzled and confused. "Christine said that they had the Eighth Floor swept for bugs." Looking at him quizzically, I asked if that was really a problem.

Dr. MacLaughlin chuckled. "I'm afraid it is...

"This is Washington, after all, and there are almost 200 foreign intelligence services at work here...

"There are so many, in fact, they tend to trip over each other in the dark, so to speak...

"And then of course, there's the FBI nipping at their heels." He paused rather suddenly, then shrugged. "Supposedly, at least."

For a girl from Glen Meadows, all the spying and counter-spying was pretty strange stuff, so I sat there for a long moment trying to take it in.

"Wow," was all I could say.

With a wistful smile, Dr. MacLaughlin compared living in Washington to life in a fishbowl. For anyone even remotely involved in national security affairs, privacy was a fool's comfort. And then in a voice that was kind but nonetheless emphatic, he suggested that I reconcile myself to that fact. By now, he said, it was a foregone conclusion that my name had been added to the files of every intelligence service in the world.

Yikes! I thought. *I was just joking about that poison pill...*

Not quite sure what to say, I nodded silently. Then I sat up straight, and asked him if there was anything I could help with before I moved upstairs.

By then he was stuffing his pipe with tobacco, so I had to wait for his reply. After he finished, he lit it, puffed on it a few times, and then leaned back in his chair. "I have any number of things for you to do, but none of them are terribly urgent and I had planned on sneaking out early...

"Holiday weekend, and all that."

Then he leaned forward very suddenly, and asked me what I knew about geopolitics.

Surprised, I shook my head. "Next to nothing, Sir. In fact, I'm not even sure that I know what it means."

Seeming very pleased with himself, Dr. MacLaughlin smiled broadly. "Well good, let's start you on some readings. I'd hate to send you up to the Eighth Floor ill-prepared...

"There are any number of authorities you could start with, but I'm inclined to recommend Alex." Then he turned in his swivel chair, and began searching through the built-in shelves behind his desk.

"Ah! There it is." Pushing himself halfway out of his chair, he reached up and pulled a volume from the third shelf. Then he turned around, and handed it to me across his desk.

I took it from him, and turned it over in my hands. It was entitled *An Introduction to Geopolitics.* "Alex wrote this?"

Dr. MacLaughlin nodded. "He did indeed, and I recommend it highly. I think it is probably the finest introductory text ever written on the subject, and the Pentagon apparently agrees. It's required reading at the War College, you know."

I was amazed, and I told him so.

Dr. MacLaughlin cocked his head and looked at me quizzically. "Amazed?"

"Well yes, Sir. I know he's really smart and all that, but after what Christine told me, it just seems funny that Alex would write a book."

Dr. MacLaughlin chuckled. "He's written half a dozen, actually, all highly regarded."

Then he grinned, and told me that he could appreciate my point nonetheless. From the standpoint of Georgetown's faculty and administration, Alex's undergraduate career had been an unmitigated disaster, and the fact that he had eventually achieved academic and literary acclaim had been quite a surprise for them as well.

He was just about to say something else when I cut him off. "I just have to ask – was he one of your students?"

Dr. MacLaughlin snickered. "Oh, no! To be a student, Ms. McAllister, one must study. And I assure you, Young Master Alex did not."

Then he began laughing uproariously. Alex, as he was able to eventually explain, had been enrolled in several of his classes, and he'd even shown up for instruction on occasion. But in those rare instances when he had graced the classroom with his presence, he had invariably been either ill-prepared or hung over or – most often – both.

"Oh my," I said. "Was he that bad?"

Still laughing, Dr. MacLaughlin nodded. "He was the worst, absolutely the worst student I ever encountered in all my years of teaching."

By then I was laughing so hard it felt like my sides were going to split. It took me a minute or two, but I was finally able to ask him how Alex had managed to graduate. Georgetown was a pretty tough school, after all, and it was a wonder he hadn't flunked out.

Dr. MacLaughlin laughed dismissively, and shook his head. Alex had been a legacy, he said – his father had graduated from Georgetown before him – and in any event, Georgetown was a private university, heavily dependent upon the largess of their wealthy alumni.

Given the facts of financial life, private universities were not averse to bestowing a "Gentleman's C" on the sons and daughters of their larger contributors. And as painful as it was for him to admit, Georgetown was no exception.

In keeping with that tradition – and an occasional six figure check from the elder Mr. de Vris – Alex managed to squeak through, he said. "But just barely."

When he said that, I cracked up again. With tears running down my cheeks, I curled my hand into a ball and pressed it hard against my mouth. It was just so funny!

When I finally stopped laughing, I asked Dr. MacLaughlin what had happened. From all that I had heard, it seemed like Alex had been the world's biggest screw-up in college, but look at him now...

Writin' books and everything!

Dr. MacLaughlin shook his head, and begged me not to take away the wrong impression. Alex hadn't been a bad kid, by any means. He had been unfailingly polite and well mannered – with the faculty, at least – and generous to a fault with his fellow students. He had gone out of his way to help the poorer ones with a little cash now and then, and sent anonymous pizza deliveries to their late night study sessions.

But as the sole heir to the de Vris family fortune, Alex was destined to inherit more money than he could possibly spend. He needed an education no more than he needed a job, and he had enrolled at Georgetown for the sole purpose of getting his ticket punched. Given his fortunate circumstances, Dr. MacLaughlin said, one could hardly blame him for that.

I looked up quizzically. "Ticket punched? What's that mean?"

Dr. MacLaughlin smiled. "That's something of a slang expression. In this context, it refers to the fact that Alex needed a degree to receive his commission...

"He had wanted to make a career out of the military – the Marine Corps – and generally speaking, their officers are required to have a college degree.

"You do know that he and Nguyen enrolled in the Platoon Leader's Course down at Quantico?" Confused, I shook my head. "Quantico?" I'd never heard of it before.

Dr. MacLaughlin stuffed some more tobacco into his pipe, and nodded. "A Marine Corps base, about 30 miles or so down I-95...

"That's where they keep their officer candidate school."

"Oh," I said. "Alex told me that Nguyen was in the Vietnamese Marines, but he didn't say anything about himself." Crossing my legs again, I tugged on my skirt. "I had just met him then, and I didn't want to pry."

Dr. MacLaughlin nodded approvingly, and puffed on his pipe. "They went down there the summer of their junior year. Nguyen as a Foreign Officer Candidate, and Alex as regular American O.C....

"From what I understand, Marine officer candidate school is a truly miserable experience. But they both excelled...

"Alex graduated first in his class, and Nguyen second, as I recall. After they took their degrees, they were commissioned as second lieutenants in their respective services."

Intrigued, I cocked my head and asked Dr. MacLaughlin why Alex hadn't stayed in the Marines.

Dr. MacLaughlin shook his head sadly. "He had wanted to, but fate conspired against him. He was badly wounded, and after many months in the hospital he was subjected to an involuntary medical retirement."

I was on the edge of my seat, horrified. "Good God, what happened?"

Dr. MacLaughlin frowned. "I'm not sure that I remember it all that well...

"Alex has never said anything, but I do recall reading about it in *The Washington Post*...

He paused for long moment, reaching back in time. "If memory serves me correctly, it was toward the end of his second tour. He had done one 13-month rotation as a lieutenant, and had volunteered to return for another...

"He had just been promoted to captain, I think, and was commanding a Marine rifle company up on the Demilitarized Zone...

"The North Vietnamese had launched a major offensive, and another Marine unit had been cut off and surrounded. A relief force was dispatched to their rescue, and Alex's company was in the lead."

Dr. MacLaughlin cocked his head. "You know I'm not quite sure of my facts at this point, but as I recall, it was a trap. The North Vietnamese had several battalions hidden in the jungle, and when the relief force approached they leapt on it...

"Alex's company bore the brunt of their attack...

"There was a tremendous battle, and it raged all through the night. Total confusion, as I recall, and Alex's company was separated from the main force. But Alex out-maneuvered and out-fought the enemy, and when the sun finally rose, the North Vietnamese had been decimated...

"It was really quite a remarkable feat of military prowess, I must say..."

Dr. MacLaughlin lit his pipe again, and knitted his eyebrows together. "It's been such a long time that I may be mistaken, but it seems to me that Alex was leading an assault on the enemy's command post when a mortar shell landed nearby and ripped his back open..."

Horrified, I gasped out loud.

Dr. MacLaughlin puffed on his pipe again, then continued. "He barely survived..."

When he looked back up at me, it seemed as though his eyes had misted. "He was awarded the Congressional Medal of Honor, you know."

My eyes bulged. "Alex won the Medal of Honor?"

Dr. MacLaughlin laughed sadly. "It rounded out his collection quite nicely. He came back with a chest full of medals, and of course we were all very proud of him...

"It was a big story, you know. Vietnam was an awful, ugly war, and for the most part it was fought by conscripts too poor to escape the draft.

"The sons of millionaires were few and far between in Vietnam, so of course his gallantry was front page news."

Dr. MacLaughlin pulled a wire bristle cleaner out of the holder he had on his desk, and began to work it up the stem of his pipe.

"That," he said without looking up at me, "and his parents untimely death."

Stunned, I asked him what happened.

Dr. MacLaughlin played with his pipe for a few more moments, before finally withdrawing the pipe cleaner and tossing it in the general direction of the trashcan. Then he stuffed it with some more tobacco, and lit it.

"It was odd, even a bit eerie...

"But it seems that at the very moment Alex was struck down in Vietnam, a drunk driver crossed the median on the Beltway and hit his parents' car head on. They were both killed instantly."

"What?"

Dr. MacLaughlin looked up at me. "As I said, it was very odd. But as far as anyone can calculate the times, Alex's parents died at precisely the same moment he fell in battle...

Puffing on his pipe again, he turned in his chair to gaze out the window. "I'm not quite sure what to make of that."

Whoa. I felt an unnatural chill run up my spine, as goose bumps rose on my arms.

There was a long and uneasy silence before Dr. MacLaughlin began speaking again. "In any event, Alex's wartime service stood him in good stead, so when he applied to Georgetown for readmission as a graduate student, the recommendation of the Admissions Committee was unanimous."

"I happened to be on the Committee at the time, and despite his miserable undergraduate record, we were pleased to take him back."

Dr. MacLaughlin took his pipe from his mouth, and pointed it at me for emphasis. "And rightly so. He breezed through his master's and doctoral course work, and completed his dissertation in short order...

"It took him three years to the day to earn his PhD., which is something of a record."

"Wow!" I had never heard of anyone finishing a doctorate in less than four years. "What happened then?"

Dr. MacLaughlin leaned forward and propped his elbows on his desk. "I snatched him!" he said.

"Huh?"

"Georgetown was prepared to offer him a position as an associate professor in the School of Foreign Service. But I convinced him to come out to Langley."

"He joined the CIA?"

Dr. MacLaughlin smiled again, and nodded. "He did indeed. I had hoped to get him assigned to my shop, but the SB Division – the Soviet and East Bloc Division, that is – got their claws into him first. So he ended up a counterintelligence officer on the other side of the house...

"Poetic justice, I suppose. I snatched him from Georgetown, and the SB people snatched him from me."

"So you were a headhunter?"

He chuckled softly. "Indeed. That was, after all, why the Agency permitted me to teach part time...

"You see, teaching at Georgetown made it possible for me to observe the 'best and the brightest' at first hand, over an extended period of time. Whenever I came across a young man or woman I thought was particularly suited for intelligence work, I would forward their name to Langley...

"On rare occasions, I was instructed to approach them for recruitment. But for the most part, the personnel shop would ask me to keep an eye on them, and to quietly assist them with their academic careers in whatever ways I could...

"That's pretty much standard fare at most of the major universities and, indeed, at many of the smaller colleges."

My eyes bulged. "Professor Watkins? My academic advisor?"

Dr. MacLaughlin leaned back in his chair and chuckled. "You're quite the clever lass."

"You're kidding! You have *got* to be kidding!"

Eyeing me steadily, he puffed on his pipe again. "Perhaps I am. But then you will never know, one way or another."

"What?" I slammed both fists down on the arms of my chair. "That's *not* fair…

"You can't leave me hanging like this! Tell me!!!"

Suddenly stern, Dr. MacLaughlin shook his head. "I've told you quite enough for one day."

He glanced at his watch. "Now take your book and be gone, Lass. Enjoy your Labor Day weekend, and when we come back on Monday – Tuesday, that is – we'll discuss the finer points of geopolitics…

My eyes flashed as I glared at him. *"THIS IS NOT FAIR!"*

Much to my surprise, Dr. MacLaughlin nodded in agreement. "It's not at all fair, but it is entirely to the point…

"If you will recall, we began this conversation with a discussion about hostile surveillance here in Washington…

"You will also recall that I compared living in Washington to living in a fishbowl, and the analogy is apt. If you are to live and work in Washington – especially for an institution such as the CSS – you can be assured that someone has their eye on you…"

He jabbed his pipe at me again for emphasis. "But you will never know who, and only rarely will you know where or when…

"It's far more important for you to understand *that*, Ms. McAllister, than it is to know whether your suspicions about your academic advisor are correct."

I almost snarled at him, but caught myself short. Overwhelmed by sudden understanding, I collapsed back into my chair.

Good Lord, I thought. *That man is one hell of a teacher…*

CHAPTER TWELVE

I had intended to start reading Alex's book that night, but by the time I got home, I was exhausted. I'd been working really hard all summer, but it wasn't the work that had worn me out. It was the excitement.

Since I was too tired to concentrate, I promised myself that I would read the book at the pool over the long Labor Day weekend. Then, I plopped down in front of the TV and started flipping channels. There wasn't anything particularly interesting on, and had all else been equal, I would have climbed up to my loft and gone to bed. But there was a quart of Haagen-Dazs calling to me from the freezer, and I hadn't had anything for dinner. I resisted valiantly for at least 15 seconds, but in the end I was forced to concede defeat. But since it wasn't a fair fight, I didn't feel the least bit guilty about surrendering. Let's face it – an empty stomach just doesn't have a chance against Cookies 'n Cream.

So I sat on the couch cross-legged, eating the ice cream straight out of the carton. After another couple of channel flips I came across an old Fred Astaire movie, so I decided to watch that. But after a few minutes my mind started drifting, and I found myself thinking about other things. Specifically, my new bikini.

I had brought a two-piece swimming suit with me when I had moved to Washington, and it had been the height of fashion back in Glen Meadows. But you could pass a whalebone corset off as fashionable that town, and with a bit of luck, a pair of Army boots as well. Washington, however, was a different story.

I had been working on my tan all summer. The rooftop pool at the hotel was not only gorgeous, but also free for CSS employees – and given the amount of money I'd been investing in my wardrobe, free was about all I could afford. But for a girl from Glen Meadows, the pool posed something of a dilemma.

First of all, I was hopelessly out of style. If my two-piece suit bordered on the risqué in Glen Meadows, in Washington it was pure frump. On our first trip to the pool together, Julia joked that I must have ordered it from a Nun's Wear catalogue. Which wasn't all that far from the truth, come to think of it.

The second problem was that I was a complete coward. The swimming suits that were in style at the time were about as wide as a strip of Scotch tape, and almost as revealing. That might have been fine for most girls, but I just didn't have that much to reveal. Assuming, of course, that I could work up the nerve to do any revealing in the first place.

Lucky for me, Christine was there to bail me out again. After patiently listening to my sad tale of woe, modesty and embarrassment one afternoon, she had called her husband at work and told him that she would be late for dinner. After that, it was off to The Bikini Shop in Georgetown.

The Bikini Shop was a whole new experience for me. They sold tops and bottoms separately, which made it possible to get a suit that actually fit. Contrary to the opinion of fashion designers, most girls don't have perfect figures and I was no exception. Like almost every other girl my age, my rear end was too big and my top was too small, and I was perpetually at war with my waistline. Which is pretty much par for the course, you know.

But Christine knew her way around bikinis, and in less than an hour I had found three or four that looked great. Except for a slight problem with the tops.

Seeing the forlorn look on my face, Christine had laughed and reminded me of Sun Tzu's famous aphorism that "all warfare is based on deception." The same applies to fashion, she said. With a little help here and a nip and a tuck there, I'd be able to pass for a supermodel.

I didn't actually believe that, but it was awfully nice of her to say. I was about to tell her that when she disappeared in the direction of the sales counter, leaving me standing alone in front of the three way mirror. A minute later she reappeared with a little piece of tailors' chalk, some straight pins and two crescent-shaped inserts.

Which is something we really don't have to go into...

After a discreet trip back into the dressing room, and a couple of minutes of tugging and pinning, she stepped back outside the mirror.

"How's that?" Christine asked.

Wow!

I turned to the left, and then slowly back to the right. I was amazed, and I told her so. "I didn't know I could look this good."

Then I looked up at her, with a mixture of awe and incredulity. "Where did you learn that?"

Christine grinned. "Tricks of the modeling trade. They come in handy now and then." Then she looked me up and down again, and asked me if I liked it.

Well, yeah!

Needless to say, I bought the bikini. After that we made a quick trip to the back of the shop, to have the seamstress make the adjustments.

I was reveling in the thought of how gorgeous I was going to look at the pool when I fell asleep. Lucky for me, I had already polished off the last of the Cookies 'n Cream when I drifted off. 'Cause even God wouldn't have been able to save me if it had melted all over Julia's brand new couch.

I woke up about 8 o'clock the next morning, refreshed and ravenously hungry – the latter of which was totally unfair. You'd think that if you ate a million calories before going to sleep, you'd be set for a week. But for some perverse reason, it just doesn't work that way. I was so hungry that I would have eaten Julia's chocolate, but she had already beaten me to it. Except for an over-ripe melon and a jar of mayonnaise, the refrigerator was completely empty.

As I closed the insulated door, I realized that there was a definite whiff of conspiracy hovering about, and I was pretty sure the people who made ice cream were behind it. But since I knew I'd never be able to prove it, I decided to take a quick shower and eat breakfast at the hotel instead.

I had already decided that I was going to wear my bikini under a T-shirt and a pair of cut-offs, but I ran into an immediate problem. I wasn't sure if it was a case of foul treachery, or an act of revenge for some unintended slight – but by the time I pulled on the bikini, it had somehow become a whole lot skimpier. When I looked in the mirror, I was aghast.

No way, I thought.

I must have stood there for a good five minutes, cringing as I weighed the possibilities. Having already thrown out my old two-piece, I didn't have much of a choice. I could wear the new bikini to the pool, or I could spend another interminable weekend home alone.

I was still cringing in front of the mirror when I suddenly realized that this was exactly the sort of swimming suit Christine would wear. She'd even told me so...

So if she can wear a bikini just like this, why can't I?

Suddenly empowered, I was reveling in a surge of confidence when a little voice in the back of my head responded. *'Cause you're a big fat chicken, that's why!*

I was on the verge of tears when I realized that I just couldn't spend another weekend at home. I had been working a brutally hard schedule all summer, and I really needed a couple of days of rest and relaxation. During the week I had made a point to get to the office early, and I had often worked late into the night. I had spent most of my Saturdays there as well, to make sure Dr. MacLaughlin's project was completed on time.

Because of my financial circumstances, tanning at the pool had been my only real escape, and now that the project was over, I felt like I really owed myself a long, relaxing weekend before I started on my new assignment. If that meant putting up with a little embarrassment – well, actually, a whole lot of embarrassment – that was just tough. I was in Washington after all, and I really wanted to fit in.

Besides, it was Labor Day weekend. DC was a ghost town for most of the summer months, and that was especially true on holiday weekends. Anyone with a minimum of intelligence and a working set of wheels fled the heat and the humidity for the beach or the nearby mountains. Suddenly determined, I pulled on my cut-offs and a T-shirt, and laced up my sneakers. Then I stuffed Alex's book into my bag, and zoomed out the door.

The streets were almost empty, and the Metro was actually deserted. Aside from the attendant at the gate, I didn't see another soul until I emerged into the heat outside of Union Station some fifteen minutes later. It was a little after 9:00 by then and already brutally hot.

After a quick stop in the hotel's coffee shop for breakfast, I took the elevator up to the roof. It was a bit cooler up there and altogether devoid of life. That was kind of strange – almost spooky – because the hotel normally kept a lifeguard on duty whenever the pool was open. But a quick glance around reassured me: a cigarette butt was smoldering in an ashtray perched on the arm of the lifeguard's chair, so I figured he had just stepped away for a minute. So I set my bag and my Diet Pepsi down on a table, and pulled off my clothes. Then I dove into the pool.

Big mistake!

I was halfway up the ladder before I realized that my top hadn't come with me. And wouldn't you know it – at precisely that moment, three geeky-looking teenaged boys pushed through the double glass doors.

To this day, I'm not sure who was more surprised. But I can tell you I was at the bottom of the deep end in the blink of an eye, and I didn't come up until everything was *exactly* where it was supposed to be.

If I'd had a scuba tank, I probably would have spent the rest of the day down there. But since there is a finite limit to how long I can hold my breath, I was eventually forced to face the music. But as luck would have it, a set of parents had turned up while I was underwater and that kept the snickering to a bare minimum.

Climbing out of the pool with what was left of my dignity, I returned to my table. Hiding behind my sunglasses, I turned the lawn chair away from the geeks to face the sun and laid out my beach towel. Then I buried my face in Alex's book.

By the time I was halfway through the first page, my feigned fascination had become a reality. Since *An Introduction to Geopolitics* was a textbook, I had assumed that it would be as dry as the desert and twice as boring. But that was far from the case.

Alex began by recounting a Native American story of creation. According to the myth, the Great Spirit had made the Earth and the Moon and the Stars above as a gift for the Spirits he had created in Heaven. It had been a mighty labor, but when at last it was complete, it was a thing of great beauty.

> *And so the Spirits looked upon it with awe and wonder. One – a beautiful maiden named Ithwanna – was overcome with joy. Her tears of happiness fell from Heaven unto the Earth, forming the lakes and rivers and oceans. She loved the Earth so much she asked the Great Spirit if she could live there and make it her home. After promising that she would treasure it with all her heart, The Great Spirit granted her wish, and she became Mother Earth.*
>
> *Other Spirits loved the Earth as well, and asked if they could live there, too. The Great Spirit granted their requests one by one. They fell to earth to become the deer, the elk, and the mighty buffalo, and all the other animals that soar the skies, walk the land, and swim the rivers and the lakes and the seas.*
>
> *Only three Spirits remained in Heaven - three spirits that The Great Spirit had made as brothers. The first of these said that he loved the mountains and the deserts and the plains, and asked if he could live on them. The second said that he loved the rivers and the valleys, and asked if he could live within them. The third said that he loved the seas, and asked to live beside them. The Great Spirit granted their wishes as well, and they too fell to Earth.*
>
> *The descendants of the first brother became the People of the Mountains, Deserts and Plains. The descendants of the second*

> brother became the People of the Lakes and the Rivers and the Valleys. And the descendants of the third brother became the People of the Seas. And at first they lived in peace with one another, and with Mother Earth. For they had promised The Great Spirit that they would love and cherish Mother Earth, and all her bounty, and honor her with peace and goodwill.
>
> But as time passed on, their memories grew dim and they forgot the promises they had made to The Great Spirit. They demanded more and more from Mother Earth, and when she had no more to give they fought one another for the largest share. The People of the Mountains, Deserts and Plains, the People of the Lakes and the Rivers and the Valleys, and the People of the Sea began to look on one another as enemies, and from their hatred was born the cruelty and war, and the suffering and death that we endure to this very day.

It was a 'just so' story, much like the Rudyard Kipling tales that had delighted me as a little girl. But Alex had re-told the tale with serious intent, for it illustrated the influence of geography upon settlement, economic development and social organization.

According to Alex, this influence was so profound and so pervasive as to shape almost every aspect of human existence. Human societies first arose in response to environmental challenges, and because these vary greatly from place to place, the sort of societies that arose in the mountains and the deserts and the plains differed from those that arose in river valleys and around the oceans' shores.

The climactic extremes of the mountains, deserts and plains produced a tribal structure based on clans that could gather or disperse over vast areas in response to dearth or plenty. Although charismatic leaders such as Genghis Khan occasionally disrupted this pattern of assembly and dispersal, the tightly centralized empires constructed from conquest were invariably unstable and short-lived. In contrast, the seasonal ebb and flow of the great rivers – and the trade, commerce and invasions they invited – made permanent settlements possible. These most often gave rise to a more centralized monarchical structure based on feudal obligations, while the great harbors encouraged large-scale trade and commerce, which favored a moneyed economy and an oligarchical form of governance. In this way, geography gave rise to different societies that produced inherently conflicting political systems.

Geography not only shaped the external form of these early societies, but what Alex called their "inner logic" as well. By that, he meant the collage of broadly held beliefs and values, and practices and procedures, that defined their collective identity and their traditional style of relating to one another. Of these, the most important was their chosen means for resolving internal conflicts – in other words, politics.

The clan-based tribal societies of the mountains, deserts and plains are based on bloodline, birthright and a vague sense of obligation to the tribal leader. Their values are based on an intense loyalty to their immediate group, accompanied by a corresponding fear of and distrust for all others. Within and between these groups, conflict is typically resolved by bloodshed.

The agrarian societies of the valleys are based on inheritance, class, and written law enforced by a king. Their values are practical, and they are typically organized on functional lines: a peasant class to provide agricultural sustenance, a warrior class to provide military security, and a priestly class to – supposedly – ensure Divine favor. As these societies grow and develop, a small class of free artisans typically emerges to provide skilled labor and manufacturing in the fortified compounds that pass for towns and cities.

The commercial societies of the seaports are based more on financial success than lineage, birthright, obligation, class or personal loyalty. Although an aristocratic oligarchy typically controls the mechanism of government, it is generally elected to office by an enfranchised propertied class in a more or less democratic process like that which characterized ancient Athens or – more recently – imperial Britain.

In recent years, political scientists have been inclined to emphasize process at the expense of substance, defining politics as no more than "the authoritative allocation of values." Although this definition has the contemporary virtue of being value-free, Alex argued that it also deprived the subject of meaning. For politics must ultimately be understood as a quest for justice.

This quest had been the central preoccupation of philosophers from Plato to Marx, and for good reason: societies depend on government for their survival, and effective government requires the consent – or at least the acceptance – of the governed. In the Western democracies, this has been understood as a system of government in which the governed appoint their governors in free elections. But it has a deeper and more traditional meaning as well, in which a "just" government is understood to be one that governs in accordance with the core beliefs and values of its society. In this sense an absolute monarchy that respects these core beliefs and values can be understood as "just," and in an earlier era, they often were.

The limitations placed on the exercise of political power by these core beliefs and values were understood as "liberties" in earlier ages, and even the lowliest peasant possessed a form of freedom within them. In Mediaeval Europe, for example, a king could command the peasant's labor and force him to work without pay on the royal estate, but the king could not force the peasant to give up the harvest from his garden, or to surrender the eggs of his chickens, or the milk of his goats. Nor could the king prevent a peasant from entering into voluntary contracts with his peers, or force him to labor on Sunday, or prevent him from attending Church, or marrying, or having a family. Kings who impinged on these ancient liberties were considered no more than tyrants, and in accordance with the moral teachings of that time and place, fit subjects for assassination.

The problem was that different types of societies – each shaped by the environmental challenges that geography posed – had different conceptions of justice, and these different conceptions were reflected in the governments upon which the societies depended for their survival. Because the effectiveness of these separate governments ultimately required them to conform to their societies' traditional beliefs, values and expectations, the governments of the world necessarily employed different and often incompatible practices and procedures. Thus whenever they came into contact, conflict was the most likely result; the level of violence associated with the ensuing conflict depended heavily on the degree of difference between their respective systems.

The great commercial empires, for example – Britain, Spain, France, Portugal and Holland – had been involved in naval skirmishing for centuries, but their conflicts were limited by their financial objectives. Although they fought to improve their relative positions with regard to one another, the costs associated with defeating, occupying, and subjugating a rival were so enormous that they rarely sought to achieve a decisive victory. But when different systems came into conflict – for example, when an agrarian society like Rome came into conflict with a commercial society like Carthage – a war of annihilation was the most common result. And much the same was true when a clan-based tribal society came into conflict with either an agrarian society or a commercial society.

This pattern of geographically inspired systemic conflict had shaped human history throughout the ages, and according to

Alex, it continued to do so in the late Twentieth Century. For even though the United States and the Soviet Union preferred to cast their Cold War struggle in ideological terms, the majority of America's European allies were avowedly socialist – closer, ideologically, to the Soviets than to the U.S. But they had cast their lot with the United States instead, because their systems – which had been overlaid on the ancient structures of agrarian societies – were closer in practice to our commercial, maritime system. For while the Soviets professed Communism as their official ideology, and occasionally practiced it, the Soviet state had been built on a foundation first laid by the Great Khan.

This was not to say that ideological, economic and military factors were not at issue. They were, and they would remain so. But the underlying dynamic of the conflict was geopolitical – the Cold War was a coalition war, one that pitted the People of the Mountains, Deserts and Plains against the Peoples of the Rivers and Valleys and the Peoples of the Sea. American strategy must therefore be based more on geopolitical principles than force of arms.

To prevail, the United States had to defeat the Soviet system, rather than the Soviet military, and that could best be achieved by deliberately accentuating the centrifugal forces that naturally pulled on it. And to this end, Alex advocated a strategy he called "tipping," i.e., a strategy designed to shift the center of gravity within the Soviet Union from Moscow to the constituent – and subject – republics. If that could be accomplished, the USSR would fly apart.

But understanding why this was possible, and how it could be accomplished required a thorough understanding of geopolitics from the empires of antiquity to the modern day, which was – as Alex explained – his purpose in writing the book.

By now completely overwhelmed, I laid the book in my lap and stared off into the distant sky.

CHAPTER THIRTEEN

I'm not sure how long I lay there, but it must have been a half-hour or more. Then, as my wits gradually returned, I realized that I was way out of my league.

I had taken Ancient, Mediaeval and Modern History in college, along with Introduction to Political Science, World Geography and International Relations, so I was familiar with the geographical and historical facts Alex had recounted. Yet, in the entire four years I spent at Township College, not one of my professors had tied it all together. But in the six short pages of his introduction, Alex had laid out an explanatory theory of human conflict – and for the very first time, it all made sense to me. I wasn't an historian or even a political scientist, but his arguments were consistent with every fact I had ever learned, and I began to wonder why I had never been offered a course on geopolitics in college. *Shouldn't that be part of a higher education?*

Obviously, it should. But deep down inside, I had to admit that it wasn't my lack of education that bothered me. It was Alex.

I had known he was smart from the moment I met him, and that was one of the things that attracted me. But there is smart, and there is *really* smart – and after reading the introduction, I was beginning to worry that he was way over my head. And his style only made matters worse: Alex wrote as though he were an artist painting a masterpiece upon a canvas, evoking one beautifully crafted image after another until a picture emerged in the mind of the reader. Except that he used words, rather than colors.

So what's a guy like that gonna see in me?

Not wanting to know the answer, I bit my lip and brushed it all aside. Suddenly angry and more than a little bit determined, I sat up and crossed my legs underneath me, and opened the book to Chapter One. And except for a short break for a late afternoon lunch, I stayed with it until late into the evening.

It wasn't a long book – there were only 220 pages of text, and charts and maps took up about a third of that – but it was deep. And when I say deep, I mean *really* deep. Which meant that I had to go slowly, puzzling out one page at a time. But I finished it just before the sun disappeared behind the Arlington suburbs across the river, and I was back home by 10:00 – a little wiser and a whole lot browner than I had been when I left.

There was no way I could get a handle on Alex's book with just one reading, so I got up early the next morning, and after a quick stop at the corner drug store to pick up a spiral notebook, I headed back to the pool. But this time I sat at one of the waterside tables, so I could outline the chapters one by one. It was an old trick I had learned freshman year, and it had a lot to do with my nearly perfect grade point average.

This time through, I wasn't quite as intimidated. I knew I wasn't as smart as Alex, but I was thorough and methodical, and I was pretty sure I'd figure it out eventually.

I broke for lunch about 1:30, and by 2:30 or so I finished up Chapter 10. That was about the One Hundred Years War and the emergent balance of power in Western Europe. In passing, Alex had gone to considerable lengths to distinguish between the Classical West – that is, the Mediterranean world of Greece and Rome – and the Atlantic West that had eventually supplanted it. This was important because the center of gravity of Western civilization kept shifting westward with history, and with each shift, Western culture had undergone a profound transformation. It had begun in Ancient Greece, and then shifted westward to Rome, and then northwest to Aachen, and then southwest to Paris, then London some centuries later, and eventually on to New York. This sort of geographic migration was historically unprecedented, and in Alex's view, it was a critically important factor in the development of the West.

It was an interesting point, one which merited a great deal of consideration over an ice cream sundae. So as I made my way down to the coffee shop, I began to wonder where the migration would stop. *If the center of gravity keeps moving like that, it's gonna end up in the middle of the Pacific Ocean...*

A half-hour and a million calories later. I was back at my poolside table. And except for an occasional – and cautious – dip in the pool, I stayed there until almost 6:00 pm. By then I was too tired to keep going, so I stuffed the book in my bag with my notes and pulled on my T-shirt and cut-offs. Since there was still one day left to the holiday weekend, I figured I could finish up the last five chapters in the morning. Then I'd have the rest of the day to work on my tan.

Which, by the way, was coming along quite nicely.

But as fate would have it, Debbie Stevens turned up at the pool the next day and I spent most of the morning catching up on the latest gossip. Debbie worked for the generals up on the Eighth Floor, and since she was situated in an alcove between their offices, she had the northern wing totally covered. A mouse couldn't sneak by without her knowledge, and of course, being kind of out in the hallway like that, she could hear almost everything.

Now, I like to think that I'm not much for gossip, but this was clearly an exceptional situation. Given the fact that I was about to move up to the Eighth Floor, I thought it made perfect sense to find out which big wheel was up to what. So, I spent an intriguing four hours squeezing every last lurid detail out of her.

Or as Christine would put it, "intelligence gathering."

She was right in the middle of Gen. McGreggor's latest affair when her boyfriend showed up. Which was really unfortunate, because McGreggor was quite the man about town. Single and still strikingly handsome at 56, his romantic conquests were stuff of Washington legend. As the generals' secretary, Debbie had been taking his messages and routing his calls for almost three years. Grinning wickedly, she claimed that she had every one of his girlfriends' phone numbers in her rolodex, and that if she ever got fired she was going to make a fortune selling them to the tabloids.

Laughing, I waved hello to her boyfriend and retreated to an empty table to finish the remaining chapters. I would have wrapped it up by 6:00 or so, except this time I read the last chapter and the conclusion twice.

The first time through, the full implications of what Alex was saying had escaped me, but as I re-read the last two sections of the book, I began to realize how serious it all was. This may seem a bit strange for someone who grew up in the shadow of a nuclear Armageddon, but to tell you the truth, the prospect of war seemed surrealistic from the apparent safety of my childhood home. And while most of the older men in Glen Meadows had served in World War II – and quite a number of my teachers in high school and college had been in Korea or Vietnam – the tidal wave of violence that was sweeping the Third World seemed impossibly far from the safety and isolation of rural Connecticut. In fact, if it hadn't been for the evening news I probably wouldn't have thought about it at all.

But after reading *An Introduction to Geopolitics*, ignoring the world's problems ceased to be an option. I'd finally realized the United States and the Soviet Union were engaged in a global struggle of epic proportions, and when the dust eventually settled only one would be left standing.

That frightened me almost as much as the book's concluding arguments. For Alex had not only developed – but publicly advocated – a strategy that was deliberately designed to smash the

USSR into a million itty-bitty pieces. And given the weight he pulled at the White House, I was pretty sure the Reagan Administration had decided to do just that.

Bet he's popular with the Kremlin...

I was still worrying about that when I finally made it back to the apartment. With the holiday almost at an end, traffic had picked up a bit and it seemed like Washington was returning to normal. That was strangely reassuring for some reason or another, and as I walked into the dimly lit hallway I found myself hoping that Julia had returned from her trip. Thinking about the Cold War had given me the creeps, so I was really relieved to see that the door to our apartment was slightly ajar. Thinking Julia must have just walked in, I pushed it open and yelled out our standard "Hey, it's me" greeting.

Oh God...

I was halfway through the door when I saw the wreckage. The apartment had been completely trashed.

I stood there for a moment, frozen with fear. Then my instincts took hold, and I turned away and ran as fast as I could.

Out on the street, I stopped to look at the building's entranceway. I was shaking, and my face was contorted with fear and rage. *Who could have done a thing like that?*

I didn't know – but whoever it was might still be in there. So I backed away step by step, never taking my eyes off the double glass doors that opened onto the street.

My heart was still pounding by the time I reached the corner. Grateful for the traffic passing to and fro, I stopped at the edge of the curb and desperately tried to focus. My first thought was to flag down a police car, but in the five or ten minutes I stood transfixed on the curb none passed by.

Thinking there was nothing else to do but call 911 from the pay phone on the wall of the corner laundry, I began digging through the bottom of my bag for a quarter. Not an easy feat with my eyes still locked on the apartment building.

There must have been a couple of dozen coins at the bottom, but they kept slipping through my fingers. It took a while, but after balancing the bag on my right knee, I finally got a firm grip on one. I was pulling it out when my watch band caught on my checkbook, and I suddenly remembered I had Alex's phone number tucked away inside. I grabbed it and ran to the phone.

Praying that he had returned on schedule, I punched in the number. *Please be home, please!*

The phone rang twice before a female voice said, "Allo?" It was Mai Ling.

Breathing a deep sigh of relief, I told her who was calling and asked for Alex. My heart dropped when she said, "Alex still way." Then I heard her put the phone down, and say something in French. A moment later, Nguyen came on the line.

Oh, thank God...

"Nguyen? I don't know if you remember me, but this is Alicia McAllister. From the bus station?"

He must have heard the trembling in my voice, for he seemed instantly concerned. "Yes, of course, Alicia. How are you?"

With my eyes still locked on the apartment building, I blurted out what had happened. His response was immediate, and altogether profane. "Are you OK?" he asked.

I nodded into the mouthpiece, and told him I was unharmed. "But I'm scared and I didn't know who else to call."

Nguyen brushed aside my comment, and asked me where I was. I told him that I was on the corner, calling from a pay phone, and gave him the address to my building. He knew where it was.

"I have an old friend who has a restaurant a block or so from there. I'm going to call him right now, and ask him to meet you on the corner...

"His name is Dang Ho Trung.

"Expect a forty-something Vietnamese man – and maybe a couple of his sons – in a few minutes. Wait for me on the corner and don't do anything until I get there...

"I'm leaving right now, but you're over in Northwest and it's going to take me at least 10 to 15 minutes to make it across town...

"Understand?"

Nodding again, I told him I'd wait. Then after thanking him, I hung up the phone.

Looking back on it all, I may have overreacted. But I was barely 22 at the time, and I had never felt really threatened before. And by then I was scared to death that Julia might be in there, beaten senseless or even worse. Feeling frightened and sick at the same time, I wondered again about who would do such a thing...

Retreating back to the corner curb with my eyes still fixed on the apartment's entryway, I started counting the seconds...

To this day, I'm not sure what happened to the time. Two or three or maybe even four minutes must have passed, when all of a sudden I heard someone shouting "Miz Aliza, Miz Aliza!"

Startled, I turned around to see a wiry Vietnamese man in an apron racing towards me, shouting and waving. Following just behind him were two much younger Vietnamese men who might have been his sons. One was carrying a baseball bat, the other a meat cleaver.

The older man came to a sudden stop about five feet from me, and introduced himself. Bowing slightly, he said, "Miz Alizia, I Sergeant Trung...

"Major Tranh send me."

Deeply relieved, I held out my hand. "Oh, thank you so much. Someone broke into my apartment and I didn't have anyone to turn to except Alex and Nguyen."

The elder Vietnamese smiled and nodded. "Dem good men...

"Major Tranh specially. I make him good officer."

Seeing my obvious confusion, Sgt. Trung grinned again and laughed. "Young pup from OCS, they make him platoon leader. He only know war from books...

"I teach him fight Viet Cong." Then he nodded again, more thoughtfully. "He good student, make fine officer." Then he smiled again, and gave me the thumbs up sign.

Then he jerked his head over his shoulders. "Deese my sons, Dang Huu and Do Van." I smiled and said hello to both. The older one with the meat cleaver said "hi" in heavily accented English, but the younger with the baseball bat spoke flawlessly. He smiled and said, "Nice to meet you, Ma'am."

I was trying to think of something to say when I heard a car roar up behind me. Startled, I turned around just in time to see Nguyen screech to a halt alongside the curb in a beautifully restored Corvette Stingray convertible, painted in metal flake maroon. Big Minh and Lady Godiva jumped out the moment the wheels stopped rolling, with Nguyen right behind them. He was wearing jeans and a polo shirt and – for some weird reason – a windbreaker.

Nguyen bounded up and asked me if I was OK. I nodded and started to thank him, but he had already turned to his friend.

Sgt. Trung stiffened, and for a moment I thought he might salute. But instead he bowed slightly, and said "Major."

Nguyen clapped him on the shoulder before shaking his hand, and they exchanged a few words in Vietnamese before turning back to me. After a few quick questions, he turned on his heel and started marching towards the apartment building. "Let's take a look."

Sgt. Trung followed immediately behind him, his sons in tow. Not quite sure how I fit into the picture, I followed along behind them with Big Minh and Lady Godiva trotting along on either side.

Once inside the building Nguyen moved noiselessly along the wall. Stopping a few feet from my open door, he looked over his shoulder and made some sort of signal with his hand. Sgt. Trung nodded, and took the meat cleaver from his older son. Then he put a finger to his lips, and waved us all back down the hallway.

Nguyen kneeled just outside the doorway, and let out a barely audible whistle. When the dogs padded up to him, he put his arms around their necks and pulled them close. After whispering something in their ears, he turned around to look at Sgt. Trung.

When Sgt. Trung nodded, he reached behind him and pulled a handgun from underneath his windbreaker. Pulling the action back slowly, he chambered a bullet. After it clicked into place, he spat out a command in Vietnamese and the dogs surged through the doorway barking and snarling.

Nguyen followed right behind them. Diving through the entranceway, he rolled across the carpet and came up on one knee prepared to fire. As he did so, Sgt. Trung leapt through the doorway at an angle, the cleaver upraised and ready to throw. With no target in sight, he threw himself forward and rolled behind the overturned couch. Then they were both on their feet, advancing through the wreckage in a half-crouch.

Big Minh had already raced up the spiral staircase and run back and forth across the loft. By the time Lady Godiva had pawed open the bathroom door and checked the shower, he was on his way back down.

There was no one there.

Nguyen and Sgt. Trung stopped at the far end of the apartment, and looked around. I followed their glance, and as I surveyed the wreckage, my heart fell. The place had been totally wrecked. All of the furniture had been turned over and some of it had been broken, and our clothes had been torn from their hangers in the closets or pulled from our drawers, and strewn about the floor.

Whoever had done it seemed to have had a particular fascination for our intimate apparel. For while most of our outer garments were piled in a heap by the closets, our bras, panties, hose and slips had been deliberately – and prominently – scattered about. Sickened by the sight of it, my stomach began to churn. Shaking badly, I sat down on the edge of the overturned couch and wept.

After a few moments, Nguyen walked over and gently asked if he could use the phone. The break-in should be reported, he said, and the door had to be secured. Not quite sure what he meant by that, I nodded. I was deeply thankful for the fact that he and his friends had come to protect me, but I was so hurt, angry and humiliated that I couldn't find the words to express myself. So with the tears drying on my face, I turned away and started straightening up.

Nguyen picked up the phone, and after a moment began speaking in Vietnamese. Then he hung up, and called the police. He explained what had happened and asked that they send an officer to examine the premises and take a report. After a moment's pause, he gave them the address and phone number and thanked them.

After hanging up the phone, he told me that he had called a friend who owned a mobile locksmith service. Even though it was after hours, his friend had promised to send a man right away to replace the handle and deadbolt locks, and probably make some additional improvements on the apartment's security. In the meantime, the police were en route.

We had swept up most of the broken dishes and glassware and had just begun turning the couch back over onto its legs when a young Vietnamese man knocked on the door jamb. Nguyen said something in Vietnamese and gestured toward the door. Then after another brief exchange, the young man set down his tool case and began examining the deadbolt. Lost in my own thoughts, I began picking up the clothes that had been strewn all over.

A police officer and two evidence technicians showed up fifteen or twenty minutes later, followed by a detective. Since I lived in the apartment, I had to stop straightening up and tell him what had happened. So as the evidence technicians dusted for fingerprints, I recounted everything I had done that day after leaving for the pool and then described what I had found when I returned home. I left out the fact that Nguyen was armed, but only because I thought that it might get him into trouble.

As it turned out, he had a federal firearms permit and a federal concealed weapons permit, both of which he showed the detective. Which was a really good move, because those kinds of permits were so rare that the detective hadn't actually seen any before. Thoroughly impressed, he asked Nguyen only a couple of quick questions before turning to the locksmith.

Still kneeling in front of the door, the locksmith told the detective that the intruder had picked both locks. To prove the point, he held up the broken-off tip of what he called a "wiggle pick," which he had found lodged in the deadbolt's cylinder.

Whoever had done it had quality tools at his disposal, but apparently didn't have a great deal of experience. A wiggle pick was fine for a key-in-knob lock, he said, but anyone who knew the first thing about picking locks would have used a "J pick" on the deadbolt.

The detective had him drop the broken-off fragment in a plastic bag, and handed it to an evidence technician. Then he scratched his head and said it was weird. Another break-in just like this had been reported a few hours earlier, only a couple of blocks away. His guess was a semi-talented freak with an underwear fetish was on the loose, and he promised to carefully examine recent burglary reports to see if he could find a pattern. In any case, I should be angry but not unduly alarmed, because that particular kind of weirdo wasn't usually violent and hardly ever returned for a second visit. They got their kicks by doing certain disgusting things with women's underwear, and then moved on.

Now that just made my day. Although I knew the detective was trying to reassure me, I really wasn't in the mood for that sort of graphic detail. But since I wasn't in a position to mouth off to him, I gave Nguyen a disgusted look instead. But he was too busy trying to wrest one of my slippers from Big Minh to notice.

The detective said he would make sure the patrol officers kept a close watch on the apartment for the next couple of days, and gave me his business card. After making me promise to call him if I remembered anything else, he left with the street cop and the evidence technicians in tow.

After getting whacked in the head, Big Minh finally surrendered my slipper, and Nguyen handed it to me. Looking rather sheepish, he apologized for the dog's behavior. "He doesn't usually do that."

Under any other circumstances I might have been irritated. But considering what some freak had probably done with my underwear, having Big Minh slobber on one of my house shoes seemed like small change. So I laughed a little, and said so. Then I reached down and scratched him behind the ears.

At that point, the locksmith interjected. He had replaced the old locks with new ones that would be much harder to pick, and the hole he was drilling in the concrete floor was for a metal stopper. Once the door was shut and the stopper in place, he said, no one would be able to force it open.

Except for Superman, of course...

Clearly skeptical, Nguyen walked over and looked first at the hole, then at the stopper, and then finally at the locksmith. "The Lone Ranger could."

Apparently offended, the locksmith was derisive. "Ain't no way in hell," he said.

Sgt. Trung – who had been quietly standing by the wall with his two sons, passive and inscrutable in the way only Orientals can be – suddenly looked up. "You crazy boy. Lone Ranger get through door in flash."

Then all hell broke loose. In less than an instant, all five of the men were engaged in a superheated debate. Nguyen and Sgt. Trung were absolutely, positively certain that the reinforced door couldn't possibly stop the Lone Ranger, while the locksmith and Dang Huu were just as sure it would. Do Van wasn't entirely certain about the Lone Ranger, but he was damn sure The Incredible Hulk could kick it in. "Well yeah," said the locksmith, "But The Hulk is an exception." And in any event, the door would stop Spider Man, Wonder Woman and Captain America dead in their tracks.

Huh?

Crossing my arms across my chest in complete disbelief, I looked on as Sgt. Trung yelled, "Gimme break! You say Captain America can't kick in door???"

Then all of a sudden the argument turned back to the Lone Ranger, and Nguyen settled it by pointing at the locksmith and telling him he was confused. "You obviously missed the issue where the Bad Guys hit the Lone Ranger over the head, tied him up, and left him locked in the bank vault to suffocate...

"When he woke up, he pulled the pins out of the hinges of the vault door with his teeth, for God's sake!

"Then he rolled over and kicked the door down, with his hands still tied behind his back!" The locksmith looked at Nguyen, incredulous.

Nguyen nodded. "Really! That was like Number 8400 and something, and if you don't believe me, come by my house and I'll show it to you...

"It's in my collection." Meaning, as I later learned, his comic book collection.

Completely awed, the locksmith finally conceded that he might have underestimated the Lone Ranger. Looking back at the door, he thought about it a moment. "Well, maybe he could after all."

Then the whole thing about Captain America started again. But I'd had enough of that nonsense by then, so I slammed my foot down on the floor and screamed. *"BOYS!"*

You could have heard a pin drop...

Suddenly aware that they had been caught in one of those completely inane arguments that girls aren't supposed to know about, they all fell very silent.

And then they began turning bright shades of red.

Badly flushed, Nguyen winced and apologized. Although I didn't know it at the time, American comic books had been so wildly popular in Vietnam that even the Western-educated elite had become Superhero junkies.

Still looking foolish, Nguyen changed the subject by asking the locksmith if he was done. When he acknowledged that he was, Nguyen told him to send the bill to his office. Desperate to escape the scene of his humiliation, the locksmith snatched up his things, handed me the keys, and darted out the door.

Sgt. Trung and his sons – grimacing with embarrassment – bowed a couple of times and raced after him. But wouldn't you know it – just as soon as they were out in the hallway, the whole argument started up again.

Looking very much like a little boy caught raiding the cookie jar, Nguyen stuffed his hands in his pockets and scrunched up his shoulders. "Guess I kinda blew my cool, huh?"

The look on his face was priceless, and I had to try really hard not to laugh. So after clucking my tongue a couple of times, I shook my head back and forth and sighed for effect.

Mom was right, I thought. *Boys get bigger, but they never really grow up...*

Nguyen finally cleared his throat. "The door's secure, and I think you'd be safe here tonight. But the house Mai Ling and I share with Alex has a couple of guest rooms, and we'd all feel a lot better if you stayed with us tonight."

Now it was my turn to blush. I couldn't believe they would ask me to spend the night in their home. "But what would Alex say?"

Nguyen smiled and told me not to worry about it. "He's very fond of you, you know."

My jaw dropped, and I think my eyes probably bulged a little. "Alex is fond of me?"

Nguyen looked suddenly puzzled. "You didn't know?"

Almost transfixed, I shook my head back and forth slowly.

Nguyen inhaled sharply, and rolled his eyes towards the ceiling. Then he grimaced and said, "Oops!"

There was a deafening silence, and it lasted for a long and really uncomfortable moment until Nguyen cleared his throat and looked back at me. "Anyway, why don't you pack an overnight bag, and stay with us tonight?"

I would have killed to spend the night at Alex's house. But I was expecting Julia to come home at any minute, and under the circumstances, there was no way I could bail on her. Frustrated beyond belief, I wanted to bang my head against the wall and scream.

But I didn't. I put on my very best manners instead, and explained why I had to stay at the apartment. "That's so very kind of you to offer, Nguyen, but I can't. My roommate will be back soon and I just can't leave her alone tonight."

I looked around, and shook my head sadly. "Not with this mess."

Much to my surprise, Nguyen seemed disappointed. "Well, keep the dogs then. They're very protective, and you can take them to the office in the morning...

"I fed them just before you called, so all they'll need tonight is some water...

"And Alex has plenty of dog food under the counter in the galley, so you can feed them when you get to work in the morning."

Amazed and thankful, I asked him if he was sure it would be OK. After all that had happened I didn't want to spend a single second alone in that apartment, locks or no locks.

Nguyen nodded. "No problem. Alex always takes them to the office."

"That would be great," I said. "But how would I get them there? I don't think you can take dogs on the Metro."

Nguyen paused for a moment, and scrunched up his face. Then he shrugged and reached into his pocket, and pulled out the keys to the Vette. Handing them to me, he told me he would catch a cab.

"You have got to be kidding!!!"

CHAPTER FOURTEEN

He wasn't. After handing me the keys, Nguyen took me outside and showed me how to put the convertible top up and down. After that, I pulled the Vette around behind the building under his watchful eye, and parked it in the tenants' parking lot. Nguyen walked along behind, and as soon as the wheels came to a stop he placed both hands on the driver's side door and leaned forward. It was a fun car, he said, but I had to be careful with it. The Vette was equipped with a 396-cubic-inch engine, and I could end up in another dimension if I accelerated too quickly.

Although I wasn't quite sure what he meant by that, I nodded earnestly and promised to drive carefully. Nguyen searched my eyes for a long moment before finally smiling and opening the door for me. After he had helped me out, we walked back out onto the street and I waited with him until he managed to flag down a cab. Delighted with the prospect of driving the Corvette to work, I went back inside the apartment and locked the door behind me. Having already cleaned up most of the mess by then, I turned to the more urgent tasks at hand.

My biggest concern was for Julia. I had no idea when she would be back from her camping trip, or even where she would stay. Normally, she would come back to the apartment, if only for fresh clothes. But if Mike had actually proposed to her, it was a safe bet she would be staying at his place tonight. She might end up going to work looking like a street urchin, I thought, but with a brand new diamond ring on her finger, who's going to notice?

Finally concluding that she would probably stay at Mike's, I scribbled a cryptic note telling her to knock really loud, and folded it over before taping it to the outside of the door. Then, I turned to the remaining tasks at hand. The first was to find a water bowl for Big Minh and Lady Godiva, the second was to decide on an outfit for work the next day. Alex was coming back so I wanted to look good, and then of course there was the Vette to think about. Because I knew there was a law that said you have to look your very best when you drive a hot car like that, and I didn't want to get busted by the fashion police.

After about 45 minutes of rummaging through my closet, I finally settled on a new blue pinstripe suit I'd just bought. It was tight and tailored and tastefully slit on the side, and with the white button down oxford I had bought to go with my interview suit and a red silk tie, I'd have just the perfect look. Satisfied, I bounded down the spiral staircase to take the dogs outside. After they made a quick trip to the fire hydrant, I locked the door again and put the new metal stopper in place. Then I scratched them both behind the ears and turned off the downstairs lights.

Much to my surprise, they didn't follow me up to the loft. They took up positions by the door instead, and made themselves comfortable. Looking over the railing onto the floor below, I could see that they were deployed in a defensive posture, and I wondered if they had done that by instinct or by training. After puzzling over it for a moment or two, I decided it didn't matter. Although I didn't think anyone could get past the new locks and the metal stopper, the fact that Big Minh and Lady Godiva would be waiting for them on my side of the door made me feel a whole lot better. *If that creep comes back, they'll rip him to shreds…*

Comforted by the thought, I pulled off my clothes and climbed into bed.

I must have fallen asleep as soon as my head hit the pillows, because it seemed like only a moment had passed before the alarm went off. It wasn't fair because I was right in the middle of a really good dream, and just as soon as I started to come to consciousness it slipped away from me. So I whacked the snooze button and pulled the covers back over my head. But by then it was too late.

From somewhere far away there was a flurry of padded feet, and then a heavy thud as Big Minh landed on the bed. Lady Godiva pounced on my stomach a half-second later, knocking the wind out of me. Startled and gasping for breath, I did my best to hold onto the comforter. But by then, the dogs had already grasped it firmly in their mouths. Little by little, they managed to peel it back.

That left me sitting upright, half-awake, and deeply skeptical. Having a pair of well-trained dogs around had seemed like a good idea the night before, but at 6:30 in the morning it seemed a lot more questionable.

Do they do this to Alex?

Shivering from the steady stream of cold air pouring out of the duct on the far wall, I fell back on the bed and curled up into a ball. I pulled a pillow over my head, but the moment I closed my eyes, Big Minh hopped back up on the bed and forced his head beneath it. After just staring at me for a minute or two, he began licking my nose.

Facing certain defeat, I conceded. I pushed him away with the pillow and swung my legs over the side of the bed. After stuffing my feet into my slippers, I struggled into my robe. Then I stumbled down the spiral staircase to the coffee pot below, muttering all the way.

An hour later I stepped out into the morning sun and looked up into a cloudless blue sky. It must have rained a bit before dawn because the air was clear and crisp, and with a gentle breeze it didn't seem hot at all. Perfect weather for tooling around town in a fully restored Corvette classic…

After a quick trip to the bushes, Big Minh and Lady Godiva followed me around behind the building and sat patiently as I put the top down. Then they bounded in when I opened the door, one after the other. Lady Godiva made herself comfortable in the well on the passenger's side, while Big Minh took up his post in the passenger's seat. As they were getting situated, I put on my sunglasses and stuffed my purse, shoe bag, and briefcase behind the driver's seat. Then I climbed in myself, and started the engine. After it roared to life, I had to adjust the rearview mirror and, of course, the seat. Nguyen was barely an inch taller than I was, but then he didn't drive in a rather short skirt. Or at least I didn't think so…

I searched around until I found the lever, and pulled the seat forward a notch. Finally satisfied, I put the car in reverse and began backing it up ever so slowly. I was a good driver – without a ticket to my name – but even so, I was really careful. Telling Nguyen I'd wrecked his car would ruin my whole day. Assuming of course, he hadn't already found out and killed me first.

I had nosed out into traffic and pointed the car in the direction of the metro stop when I suddenly realized that I didn't have the slightest idea of how to get to the office by car. For while I had become intimately familiar with the underground transit system over the past three months, the streets of Washington remained a complete mystery. After thinking about it for a moment, I realized that my only option was to pull over at the first newsstand and buy one of the wildly overpriced maps they pawn off on the tourists. Not that it would do me a whole lot of good, since I hadn't the slightest idea of how to read one.

Lucky for me, a police car pulled up on my left at the second light. Since the officer riding shotgun had his window down, I tapped on the horn. When he looked over, I gave him my "Lost Puppy Look" and asked him how to get to Union Station.

He looked at me, and then the Vette, and then back at me. Smiling, he leaned partially out of his window and pointed ahead to the next light. If I turned right there, and then took the next right, that would take me to Massachusetts Avenue, and if I made a left turn on Mass Ave, I could follow it all the way to Union Station. After making a mental note I smiled sweetly and waved, and accelerated through the intersection when the light turned green.

Halfway through the turn at the next intersection, I suddenly realized that I had forgotten about the radio. So just as soon as it was safe, I reached down and clicked it on. An instant later the Pointer Sisters came through the speakers, singing *Jump for My Love!* Since that was one of my favorite songs, I cranked up the volume as soon as I finished turning onto Massachusetts.

Much to my surprise the traffic began to fade almost immediately after I made the turn, and that helped calm my nerves. I had never driven anything like a Vette before, but as I maneuvered in and out of the taxis and delivery trucks of early morning D.C., I started to get a feel for the car. With the radio blasting and the wind playing through my hair, it was really a lot of fun. And of course the smiles and the occasional whistles from the guys I passed only added to it.

Although I knew that Nature's Laws made cute girls in hot cars absolutely irresistible to young guys, I didn't realize that also applied to older men until I pulled up alongside a Lincoln Town Car at a stoplight. The very distinguished-looking gentleman driving it glanced over, did a double take, and then broke into a huge smile. Since it had been impossible not to notice, I waited until the light turned green. Then I beeped the horn and gave him a little wave, and floored it. As I shot up the hill I caught a glimpse of him in my rearview mirror, laughing appreciatively.

I was laughing myself when I suddenly realized that my surroundings had changed. The retail shops and office buildings that should have been there had given way to stately mansions, most of which had gigantic brass plaques on their facades identifying them as foreign embassies. *Definitely not Kansas*, I thought, as I stared at the sea of unfamiliar flags dancing ahead of me the morning breeze.

Since I was still on Massachusetts Avenue, I must have turned right onto Mass Ave rather than left like I should have. That meant all I had to do was turn around and head back the way I came. *Easy enough*, I thought.

And it should have been. But a half hour later I found myself on Washington Boulevard in Arlington – which happens to be in the State of Virginia, all the way across the Potomac River.

Frustrated, I pulled over at the first public phone and called the office. Jennifer picked up on the second ring, and before she could even finish her stock greeting, I began spilling out my tale of woe. Lucky for me, she had been driving around the Washington area for the past 18 months, so she knew the streets pretty well. When she stopped laughing, she told me to go get a pen and paper and write down her instructions word for word. I ran back to the car and pulled out my briefcase, and after I found a note pad and a mechanical pencil I went back to the phone and took down her directions. After I read them back to her, she turned suddenly serious. Rumors were flying all over CSS about the break-in, and everyone was really worried about me. Christine, Dr. MacLaughlin and Julia all wanted to see me as soon as I arrived, and of course, she just had to hear every last detail herself.

That came as an unpleasant surprise to me, and as I hung up the phone, my stomach started getting queasy all over again. I had managed to push the whole thing out of mind – and to be honest, the break-in was something I really didn't want to revisit. But as I made a U-turn on Washington Boulevard, I realized that I didn't have much of a choice in the matter. Over the past couple of months, I had become really close to a lot of people at CSS, and when I stopped to think about it, I was thankful for their concern.

I pulled into the alleyway behind the CSS just before 9:00 am. That was late for me, given my self-imposed schedule, but technically at least, I was still on time. Or at least I would have been, if Wilbur hadn't stopped me. He was the young guy with peroxide-blonde hair who sat in the little booth all day, pushing the buttons that raised and lowered the wooden blades at the entrance and exit of the underground parking garage. Now for most people that wouldn't be a particularly challenging job, but for Wilbur it was something of a stretch.

Since I had never parked in the garage before I wasn't quite sure of the procedure. But Nguyen had a CSS parking sticker glued to the windshield, and he had told me that he had a reserved parking space by the elevators. So when I pulled to a stop in front of the entranceway I just assumed that all I would have to do was hold up my CSS employee badge so Wilbur could see it. But Wilbur wasn't just slow on the draw – he was insatiably curious as well. And that makes for a really bad combination.

Wilbur had straightened up as soon as he had seen the Vette, but when I rolled to a stop and held up my badge, he just sat there and stared. After a long moment of confusion, he finally climbed out of his booth and walked over to the driver's side door. Looking down at me quizzically, he asked if that wasn't Mr. Tranh's car I was driving.

That seemed like a reasonable question, so I nodded and explained that Mr. Tranh had lent it to me. Wilbur pursed his lips and knitted his brow as he struggled with the possibilities. "Are you his girlfriend?"

At first I thought he was joking, but after a long moment of uncomfortable silence I realized that he was serious. So I gave him a withering look and corrected him. Taking his name from the patch embroidered above his left pocket I said, "Mr. Tranh is a happily married man, Wilbur, and I am most certainly *NOT* his girlfriend. He is merely a friend who kindly lent me his car after an unfortunate occurrence."

Although it took a while for my words to sink into his dense head, I could see that I had hurt his feelings. "Well, you're pretty enough to be his girlfriend."

I suppose that was a compliment, but by that point I was in no mood to hear it. In fact, I was about to bang my head against the steering wheel in frustration when Wilbur suddenly noticed Big Minh and Lady Godiva. "Say, aren't those Mr. de Vris' dogs you got there?"

Taking a deep breath, I began counting to ten. When I finished, I looked up and glared at him.

"Yes, Wilbur, those are Mr. de Vris' dogs."

Wilbur started to say something, but by then I'd had enough. I pushed the door open against him and climbed out. Then I stood up on my tiptoes with my fists pressed against my hips and stared straight into his eyes. He was a full foot taller than I was, but I wasn't about to let that intimidate me. I pointed at the car. "Mr. Tranh's Vette," I said. Then I pointed at Big Minh and Lady Godiva. "Mr. de Vris' dogs." Then I held my employee badge right up to his nose. "CSS employee."

Then I pointed at the gate and roared at him. "Now open the darn gate so I can park Mr. Tranh's car, feed Mr. de Vris' dogs, and do CSS work!"

Then I slammed my foot down on the concrete and screamed, "NOW!"

Wilbur had apparently never seen an Irish temper before. He gulped nervously, and as his eyes grew wide a look of fear flitted across his face. Then he stepped back first one pace and then another, before stammering an excuse. But his retreat turned into a rout when I jabbed my finger at the barrier again. Seeing that I was about to start screaming again, he turned and fled for the safety of his booth. Slamming the door shut behind him, he punched the button on the little console before him.

I climbed back in the car, and after tugging my skirt down, I put it in gear and drove down the ramp into the garage. I was still seething when I found Nguyen's parking space on the other side of the building, but by the time I strolled into the Executive Offices fifteen minutes later, I was the very picture of angelic calm.

The Irish have a reputation for being hot-tempered, and since both sides of my family came from the Emerald Isle, I can attest to that as fact. But what most people don't realize is that an Irish outburst is a lot like a summer storm: it may take you by surprise, but it won't last long. It will rage a while, and then it will move on.

The incident with Wilbur was pretty much par for the course. After I parked the car it had taken me a while to get the top up on the Vette. And then, as a precaution, I stopped at the First Floor so the dogs could make a quick trip to the local fire hydrant. By the time we stepped off the elevator onto the Eighth Floor, I had all but forgotten it.

Since Linda wasn't at her desk and Christine's office doors were closed, I figured the smart move was to get the dogs fed while I could. So I said "hi" to Jennifer Two, and asked if I could take the dogs into the galley. Intently focused on typing something or another, she didn't look up. Instead, she held up her index finger to signify "wait." After banging on the keyboard for another ten or fifteen seconds, she suddenly tore the sheet of paper out of the machine and said, "Sure." Then she got up from her desk, and told me to follow her.

As she opened the door into Alex's office, she said that she'd heard about the break-in and asked me if I was all right. As soon as I nodded and told her I was OK, she grabbed a hold of my arm. Dragging me through his office into the galley, she demanded that I tell her all the gory details.

Since I really wasn't in the mood to discuss it, I started to give her the short version, but she cut me off before I could say a word and asked if I had talked to Julia yet. By that time I had found the dog food, and was struggling with a hand-held can opener. Holding the lever with my left hand and twisting the crank with my right, I shook my head and told her that I had just arrived. I was explaining that I would buzz Julia just as soon as I got the dogs fed, when she cut me off again.

Julia already knew about the break-in, she said, but it didn't seem to have fazed her. She had turned up about 8:30 – looking very much like something the cat might drag in – but she was wearing a gigantic diamond ring that Mike had given her over the weekend, and all she could talk about was the wedding. They hadn't set a date yet, but Julia had said they were thinking along the lines of May or early June.

Since that was a whole lot more exciting than talking about the break-in, I ended up being the one asking all the questions while Big Minh and Lady Godiva ate their breakfast. We were speculating about what sort of dress Julia should wear when Linda stuck her head through the doorway to tell me that Christine was waiting for me in her office. Since Two said she would take care of the dogs, I followed Linda back out through Alex's office.

In terms of size and space it was identical to Christine's, but it was a lot more traditional. Built-in bookshelves ran almost the entire length of the interior wall, while a huge oaken desk with a credenza behind it stood between me and the bank of windows that opened to the outside world. Off-set to the right of the desk and perpendicular to the wall were two leather bound couches separated by a polished coffee table, and towards the end of the room stood an elegant conference table with eight chairs placed around it. Beyond them, was a single unmarked door in the center of the far wall, framed by two large paintings.

But the flags that flanked the credenza behind Alex's desk were what really caught my eye. I immediately recognized the American flag standing to the west, but I couldn't make out the red and gold one to the east, draped by streamers. Curious and a bit puzzled, I made a note to find out what it was.

After I finished glancing around, I hurried after Linda. Without looking around, she knocked on Christine's door and then opened it for me. When Christine looked up from her desk, Linda excused herself and closed the door behind her.

Christine smiled and said good morning as she got up, and gestured for me to have a seat on her couch. Looking very concerned as we sat down, she asked me how I was holding up.

I told her I was OK, and thanked her for asking. It was just some freak, I said, and with the new locks and the metal doorstopper, I'd be fine.

Christine nodded, and seemed to agree with me. Nguyen had called her after he had returned home last night, and told her what had happened. Although he was reasonably convinced that it had been a random break-in, he was nonetheless concerned, and had asked her to touch base with me this morning to make sure that I was OK.

And for good reason, unfortunately. Ever since he had left the apartment, I had been struggling to keep a tight grip on things. But as I told Christine how grateful I was for Nguyen and his friends and for all they had done for me, I began to break down.

Fighting back the tears, I told her how humiliated I felt. "And I've never been so afraid."

Christine nodded, and handed me a tissue from the box on the coffee table. As I dabbed at my eyes, she assured me that she understood. If she had been in that situation, she would have been shaking in her shoes, too. And very emphatically, she told me that I had done the right thing. "We're like a family here at CSS, and we look out for one another."

That made me feel a lot better, and I told her so. Christine smiled, and then looked down at her watch. It was time to get back to work, she said, but before I went back to the Econ shop she wanted to let me know that the attorneys from the CIA's General Counsel's office would be here tomorrow morning, and that we were scheduled to meet with them in the Eighth Floor conference room at 10:00 am. They were going to brief me on the laws governing classified documents, and after they were satisfied that I understood them, I would have to sign about a million forms. Then, I could get started on the new project.

When I asked Christine what sort of forms I'd have to sign, she laughed. "Confidentiality agreements for the most part...

"But these guys are government lawyers, and dealing with them is a bit like dealing with the Devil. So don't be surprised if they demand your firstborn as collateral."

Then she winked and smiled, and stood up. Looking down at me, she warned me to stay sharp. Alex would be in at some point that afternoon, and she wanted the staff to be squared away when he got there."

"Alex is back?" I asked hopefully.

Christine nodded as I stood up. "He called me this morning...

"He got in late last night, and he sounded pretty jet lagged when we spoke. So stay on your toes, because he may not be in the best of moods."

I nodded and said, "Yes, Ma'am." Suddenly buoyant, I snatched up my purse and my briefcase and then my shoe bag, and headed for the door.

Given the circumstances, I didn't really expect Alex to take me to lunch on his first day back. But since I was dressed to kill, I was really hoping that I'd run into him in the halls. *This outfit's gonna* set *that boy on fire*, I thought.

Or hoped, as the case may be…

Halfway through the double doors, I was slipping into the sort of fantasy I wouldn't want my mother to know about, when Christine called me back. Apologizing for having forgotten about the furniture and decorations for my new office, she told me that we still had to get together to decide on a desk, and drapes and artwork. After flipping through her appointment book, she asked me if 3 o'clock tomorrow would be OK. When I told her it would, she said we'd meet back here in her office, and she would have the furniture, art catalogues, and cloth samples ready.

That cheered me up even more, so I smiled and waved goodbye and headed for Accounting on the Fifth Floor – 'cause I just had to see that brand new ring Julia was wearing. And of course, to wring every last detail out of her. Her fiancée was something of a romantic, and I couldn't wait to find out if he had gotten down on one knee when he proposed to her.

But as luck would have it, Julia was nowhere to be found. It was only a little after ten by then, and I couldn't imagine where she would have gone off to at that hour. Sadly disappointed, I left a note on her desk asking her to buzz me just as soon as she got back, and slipped her new set of keys beneath it. Then I retraced my steps up the stairs to the Seventh Floor.

Since going up two flights of stairs is a whole lot harder than going down them, I was a little winded by the time I emerged from the stairwell at the Econ shop. I could have taken the elevators, of course, but the girls at CSS always took the stairs and I'd fallen into the habit as well. Most of the time I enjoyed it, because climbing up and down the stairs all day kept my ankles, calves and thighs tight as a drum. And if I made the extra effort of stepping high, I could give my abs a pretty good workout, too. But on that particular day, I just wasn't into it.

Halfway to my office I heard a weird noise behind me. Turning around, I saw Jennifer One elbowing her way through the staircase door. She had a Diet Pepsi in one hand, a bag of popcorn and a package of Twinkies in the other, and a piece of cherry pie hanging from her teeth, still wrapped in cellophane. Which was pretty strange, because she didn't usually raid the canteen that early in the morning.

Taking the pie from her teeth, I asked her what was up. After scrunching up her nose a bit, she licked her lips and made a nasty face. "That wrapper tastes awful!"

Well duh, I thought. "Only about a million different people handled that thing before it went in the vending machine. What did you expect?"

Jennifer shrugged. "Probably true, but not what I really wanted to hear..."

"So what happened last night?"

I shrugged. "Some creep broke into our apartment and trashed the place. Nguyen came and bailed me out."

Jennifer looked at me quizzically. "Mr. Tranh? How do you know him?"

Oops, I thought. "Long story, but he really helped me out."

"So what happened?" Jennifer demanded.

By that time we had reached my door and I was fumbling through my purse to find my key. "Just what I told you. Some creep broke in while I was at the pool, and trashed the place."

Jennifer said, "Wow" and then asked me a pointed and distinctly unappetizing question. Shocked by her words, I gave her a nasty look. "Good Lord, girl! Do you kiss your mother with that mouth?"

She flushed as her look of intense curiosity was displaced by an embarrassed grin. "That was pretty gross, wasn't it?"

But before I could answer, she told me that Dr. MacLaughlin had wanted to see me but he'd already left for a meeting out at Langley. But he'd be back about 2:00 or maybe 2:30, so just to be on the safe side I might want to be prepared. Figuring it probably had something to do with the break-in, I thanked her and pushed open my door.

Just as I was hoisting my briefcase onto my desk, I suddenly realized that I hadn't asked her about Julia. Racing back to the door, called after her. "Hey, did you hear Mike proposed to Julia this weekend?"

Jennifer turned around and grinned. "Yeah, she was up here looking for you, and man – that guy must really love her..."

"You wouldn't believe the size of the rock she's wearing!"

With eyes suddenly the size of saucers, I said: "Tell me, tell me!"

Jennifer rolled her head back towards the ceiling, and smiled deliciously. "It's incredible," she said. "It looks like something Richard Burton might give Liz, if you know what I mean."

With a conspiratorial grin, I asked her how many carats. Jennifer didn't know, but she said it had to be at least one and a half, maybe two. "It's huge!"

"Wow," I said. "Must be nice, huh?"

Jennifer rolled her head over and smiled. "Yeah, and Mike is just the sweetest guy...

"They're perfect for one another, ya know?"

Nodding in agreement, I turned back to my desk and began getting organized.

Since I really didn't have anything to do until Dr. MacLaughlin came back, I decided to catch up with the stock market. It had been closed over the holiday weekend, and since today was the start of business, the numbers wouldn't mean much until late afternoon. But the *Wall Street Journal* always had some pretty good analytical articles on opening days and I was a lot less interested in current business than overall trends anyway. So I got up and walked across the hall to see if Dr. MacLaughlin had left the department's copy in the office.

Jennifer had just finished stuffing an entire Twinkie in her mouth when I walked in. Needless to say, she turned about 15 shades of red when she realized that she'd been busted. Laughing at her embarrassment, I waited for her to swallow enough of it to answer my question. She gulped hard, and after taking a swig of Diet Pepsi, she pointed towards the coffee pot. "Over there with *The New York Times*."

I didn't normally read the *Times*, but since it looked like it was going to be a slow day I picked it up as well. Scanning the headlines, I was on my way back to my office when Jennifer asked me if I wanted to order lunch from the hotel. She had a whole bunch of stuff that had to be typed up before Dr. MacLaughlin came back, so she was going to have them send something over.

I normally skipped lunch, but since I had blown off breakfast this morning it didn't take much to convince me. The hotel had really good food, and if you got your order in by 11:00, they'd deliver it for free.

That pretty much cinched it. So I told Jennifer to order me a bacon cheeseburger with everything on it, and a side of fries. Then I made a quick trip up to the Eighth Floor lounge to get a Diet Pepsi, so I would have something to sip on while I read.

I had just put the *Times* aside and started the *Journal* when my burger showed up. It was only 11:48, but by that time I was on the verge of starvation. So, I decided to eat it while I read a rather lengthy article on the price of copper – which was exactly what I was looking for, since copper prices provide a more or less accurate indication of overall price trends. When copper prices go up, you can be pretty sure that it's the result of hidden inflationary pressures. When they go down, it's a safe bet that deflation is 12-18 months down the road.

The reason for this is the lengthy lead-time involved in mining and smelting copper ore. Because it's so long, manufacturers base their orders on projected requirements rather than present needs, and that gives economists a fairly good idea of what the economy will look like downstream. Or it least it had, up until now.

But according to the *Journal,* something really weird was going on. Despite the tremendous increase in demand brought about by the Reagan economic boom, copper prices were tanking worldwide, even though orders for future deliveries had actually increased. From the standpoint of logic, then, copper prices should be holding steady or even increasing a bit. But they weren't, and that strange fact had led the *Journal's* analytical staff to speculate that a long-term overall decline in raw materials prices may have begun.

Skeptical, I kicked my shoes off and leaned back in my chair to think it over. After taking a bite out of my burger, I leaned forward again and began thumbing through the back pages with my left hand to find the rest of the article. As I did so, my right hand drifted over the side of my desk.

Big mistake...

There was a sudden tug at my wrist, followed by the sound of claws tearing on carpet. And then there was a flash of black fur as Big Minh raced through the doorway with his quarter pound prize clasped firmly in his mouth.

I sat there for a moment in stunned disbelief, staring at the hand that had held my cheeseburger just an instant before. And then I was up on my feet chasing after him.

Nobody steals my lunch!

Big Minh was fast, and he had a head start. But I wasn't going to let that stop me. I had been the fastest member of the girl's track team at Glen Meadows High for three years in a row, so I figured the odds of catching the furry thief were better than even.

As I raced down the hall after him, it seemed as though my odds had actually improved when Big Minh screeched to a halt at the end of the east hallway and started to backtrack. Then he looked over his shoulder and saw me bearing down on him, and bolted around the corner.

He had hesitated for only a second or two, but it was enough. *That fur-ball's mine,* I thought, as I tore around the bend.

And he would have been, if I hadn't slammed into Alex.

CHPTER FIFTEEN

Alex had half-turned to look over his shoulder when Big Minh raced by. Mystified at his dog's strange behavior, he was still watching the canine's hindquarters disappear down the hallway when we collided.

Although Alex wasn't particularly tall – he stood only 5' 11" – he was powerfully built. But even so, the force of the impact staggered him. He stumbled backwards three or four steps, before finally regaining his balance. Which was a pretty impressive feat under the circumstances, because I'd tried to throw my arms around his shoulders in a desperate effort to remain upright.

I was sliding past his solar plexus when he arrested my fall by thrusting his hands under my arms and pulling me towards him. Which explains how I found myself in the CSS hallway, with my arms wrapped around the Chairman of the Board and my chin planted firmly in his upper abdomen.

Under almost any other circumstances, I might have enjoyed that. But since I had just knocked my boss halfway down the hallway – and made a complete fool of myself in the process – it was rather embarrassing. Not knowing what else to do, I looked up at him and forced a cheery smile. "Hi, Alex!"

He looked down at me quizzically, and then back over his shoulder, and then back down at me again. "Did Big Minh steal your lunch?"

Since I was still leaning against him at a thirty-degree angle, I had to push my head back to reply. "Just my cheeseburger."

Alex frowned, and shook his head. "And he chewed up one of your shoes last night?"

Pushing my head back again, I explained that he really hadn't chewed anything. "He just kinda slobbered on one of my slippers."

Alex shook his head and sighed, before lifting me up in the air and setting me back down in an upright position. "I don't know what's gotten into him...

"But for some reason or another it seems like he's always misbehaving around you." He looked down at me again, and very earnestly apologized.

Grateful for the diversion, I brushed my hair back with my hand and told him not to worry about it. Big Minh may have misbehaved a little, but he was still a sweetie. And then I made a point of letting Alex know how much I had appreciated having him and Lady Godiva stay with me the night before.

Alex nodded as a serious expression crept over his face. But after a short moment he smiled, and asked me if I had ever been to Ollie's Trolley.

"To where?"

"Ollie's Trolley…

"It's a Washington landmark. They serve fast food out of an old trolley car over in Arlington – and their burgers are by far and away the best in DC."

Now it was my turn to be surprised. "Better than the hotel's?"

Alex nodded emphatically. "Oh, yeah. And their fries are the best in the world…

"I was going there for lunch anyway, so why don't you come along?"

Grinning from ear to ear, I said sure. But first I had to go get my shoes and lock up my office.

Alex smiled, and then glanced down at himself and laughed. "Glad to hear it, because Ollie's is about the only place in town that will serve me like this."

Which was almost true because he was wearing a red pocket T-shirt, faded jeans and a pair of ancient penny loafers with no socks. He was also badly in need of a haircut, but that stood to reason. After all, he had been traveling overseas for almost three months straight.

But even with shaggy hair and dark circles under his eyes, I thought he looked really sexy. I was trying to figure out how to say something along those lines when he told me that he'd bring the car around front. "Meet me outside the lobby in 5 minutes?"

After he had turned back towards the elevators, I raced back down the hall to my office for my shoes and my purse. I was just locking the door when Jennifer One stuck her head out of the Econ shop. Leering from ear to ear she asked, "So, what that was all about."

"What was what all about?"

Jennifer jerked her head back and rolled her eyes. "Oh, don't give me that 'Little Miss Innocent' stuff. I saw you climbing all over Alex!"

I winced, and turned about twenty shades of red. "Jennifer, it's not what you think…

"I was chasing after Big Minh and I accidentally ran into him…

"As in *literally* ran into him."

Hurrying across the hall, I pointed my index finger at her nose. After looking both ways to make sure no one could hear, I ordered her not to tell anyone. Because if she did, I was going to kill her.

"Dead. As in way dead."

Jennifer smirked. "Oh, so not just a little dead?"

"Oh no," I growled. "We're talking Wicked Witch dead – as in *really, MOST* sincerely dead."

Then I glared at her for emphasis. "So don't even think about it!"

Snickering again, Jennifer asked if I was gonna drop a house on her. But before I could come up with a witty retort, she grinned and warned me her silence wouldn't come cheap. "It's gonna cost ya, girlfriend."

Then she grinned again, and asked me where I was going.

Exasperated, I gave her another nasty look. "If you must know, Big Minh stole my cheeseburger so Alex is taking me out for another."

"Now go away," I said, "And keep your big mouth shut!"

Laughing, Jennifer stuck her nose up in the air and said "maybe." Then she turned around and disappeared into the office.

Finally, I thought. Then I raced for the stairs.

I burst through the lobby doors just as Alex pulled up alongside the curb in a BMW. Although it was the same car that Nguyen had been driving the night we met, I had been expecting to see the Mustang again so I didn't recognize him until he got out to open the door for me. As I got in and thanked him, I expressed my surprise.

Alex didn't say anything until he had climbed in the driver's seat and closed the door. "Nguyen had an early morning meeting so he borrowed the Mustang; and since Mai Ling generally walks to work, I borrowed the Beemer."

"So you guys trade off cars?"

Alex nodded as he pulled away from the curb. "Technically they're all company cars, so we don't really own them. But as a practical matter the Mustang is mine, the Vette is Nguyen's and the Beemer is Mai Ling's."

A little confused, I asked him if he had meant that they were CSS vehicles. That didn't make sense to me, because I knew that neither of them were employed by the Center. Nguyen handled their investments, and was in the office a lot – which was why he had a reserved parking place – but I was pretty sure Mai Ling wasn't involved with the CSS at all.

With his eyes fixed on the traffic, Alex shook his head to signify 'no'. But it wasn't until we had pulled to a stop at the first traffic light that he explained he and Nguyen owned another company in common.

They had been buying old cars and fixing them up since they were 16, and when Nguyen had returned to Washington after the war they'd started doing it again as a hobby. Things had eventually gotten to the point where they'd bought a used car lot in order to make sure they could always find the cars – and especially, the parts – they were looking for. The Mustang, the Vette and the Beemer all belonged to their hobby business, which they had whimsically named Fly By Night Motors, Inc.

That was pretty funny, but I was a lot more interested in what he had said about Nguyen than I was about old cars. It seemed as though he had come here alone after the war, and I was curious about how he had met Mai Ling. So as we turned right onto Constitution Avenue, I asked Alex to tell me about them.

Alex sighed and looked away, and for a moment I thought that he wasn't going to answer me. But then he looked back at the road in front of us and explained that their presence in America was the result of a rather long and tragic series of events. From the look on his face I could tell that I had touched on some painful memories, and I realized I had overstepped my bounds again. But before I could apologize, he explained that they had met at a diplomatic function in Saigon in 1971. Mai Ling's father had been a wealthy merchant and a strong supporter of the Thieu regime, and of course Nguyen's father was a member of the South Vietnamese foreign service. At the time, Nguyen had just returned to Vietnam to join the South Vietnamese Marines and Mai Ling had just finished her freshman year of medical school. Alex looked over at me again and laughed. She must have cast a spell on Nguyen, he said, because he'd left the party a blithering idiot. He had fallen head over heels in love with her.

Alex had been in Vietnam at the time with the U.S. Marines, and he and Nguyen had been stationed in fairly close proximity to one another just south of the so-called Demilitarized Zone. In violation of their treaty obligations, the North Vietnamese launched regular attacks across the frontier and those had kept them both busy. But they talked on the radio every couple of days, and every now and then they had been able to get together for a two or three day pass.

Alex had been wounded and sent home the following year, but they had managed to keep in fairly regular contact. Through letters and occasional international phone calls, Nguyen had kept him abreast of his courtship of Mai Ling – it hadn't been easy, he said, because both the Vietnamese and the Chinese had serious hang-ups about intermarriage. Each of their families had been violently opposed to the match, but Nguyen was not a man to be cowed by social opprobrium and Mai Ling turned out to be every bit as obstinate as he was. Over the next two years, his family had gradually come around, although Mai Ling's father had remained adamantly opposed.

At that point Alex broke up laughing. When one married in Vietnam, he said, the bride usually came with a substantial dowry. But on those relatively rare occasions when the girl's father refused his consent, an unmarked envelope stuffed with cash was considered a perfectly acceptable gesture. It was called "bride money," he said, and in this case it came to $50,000 American. It was an astronomical sum for that time and place, and not surprisingly it prompted a sudden change of heart. With cash in hand, Mai Ling's father gave the happy couple his blessing, and a year later they were married in a magnificent ceremony at Saigon's main cathedral. Which Nguyen had paid for, as part of the deal.

Mai Ling was attending school in Hue at the time, which was fairly close to where Nguyen was posted. They bought a house near the university, and began their life together. The interminable nature of the Vietnam conflict had persuaded the South Vietnamese military to adopt a relatively liberal leave policy, so they had actually been able to spend quite a bit of time together for the first couple of years. But their married life had been ripped apart when the North Vietnamese launched an all-out invasion in the spring of '75. By that time Mai Ling had graduated from med school and was doing her internship at a hospital in Saigon, and Nguyen had been promoted to executive officer of an elite battalion stationed at the southeast corner of the DMZ.

Nguyen's battalion had borne the brunt of the first day's fighting. They had been attacked at dawn by an armored regiment, but even though they lacked anti-tank weapons they'd managed to hold their own until nightfall. Fighting back with improvised satchel-charges and Molotov cocktails, they destroyed scores of enemy tanks. But there was a price to be paid for that sort of heroism, and by the time the sun rose the next morning, only a quarter of the Marines were still standing. The North Vietnamese had brought up reinforcements in the night, and their second attack broke the South Vietnamese lines.

With the battalion commander dead, Nguyen assumed command. Although he had been seriously wounded, he had rallied what was left of his men and deployed them along the top of a ridge overlooking the coastal highway. Unable to raise either his regimental or division command on the radio, he reported his position to I-Corps headquarters as "The Little Bighorn" and scratched out a last, loving letter to Mai Ling.

But the expected attack never came. Instead Nguyen and his men spent the day watching in horror as an endless stream of North Vietnamese tanks and motorized infantry rolled past them, driving south towards Hue.

With less than a hundred Marines left – half of them wounded – Nguyen faced the choice of staying behind and harassing the enemy's supply lines, or attempting an exfiltration. He chose the latter, and when night finally fell he led what was left of his command to the nearby seacoast. There they commandeered a couple of fishing boats, and put to sea – which in Alex's opinion was a damned courageous thing to do, because none of them knew how to navigate on open water, or even operate the sails.

Nguyen reasoned that the South Vietnamese Marines would throw up a second line of defense north of Hue, and he reckoned they could make it there in two days or less. But within a matter of hours, a raging storm had come up. The smaller of the two boats had capsized almost immediately, and over the course of the next three days the howling winds had blown the larger craft far out to sea. Two weeks later a Japanese freighter en route to Australia chanced upon the drifting hulk and pulled 42 half-dead survivors from the sea. Miraculously, Nguyen had been among them.

Alex looked away from me again, struggling to maintain his composure. When he looked back, he told me that Mai Ling hadn't been so lucky. When the Communists had captured Saigon, special paramilitary troops had gone from door to door, searching for people who appeared on their lists. When they found her father and her two brothers, they had shot them on the spot. Her mother and her little sister had been arrested and sent to a re-education camp, where they later died. But the North Vietnamese had needed doctors, so they kept Mai Ling at the hospital until their wounded had been cared for, before sending her to a camp as well. The South Vietnamese casualties weren't so lucky. They had been shot where they lay, or simply left to die.

We had crossed over into Virginia by then, and were heading west on Washington Boulevard. That wasn't far from where I had been earlier that morning, but I was too upset to notice. Alex, Nguyen and Mai Ling had all suffered horribly from the war, and I felt terrible about it. On the verge of tears, I asked Alex how they had ever managed to get to America.

Alex shrugged, and told me that it had been easy for Nguyen. The Japanese freighter had dropped him and his men off at Sydney, and as an allied power the Australians had taken them in without question. They had sent them to a naval hospital for evaluation and treatment, but by the time the doctors certified them as fit for service Saigon had fallen and the South Vietnamese government had been dissolved. So the Australians found them a barracks and some uniforms, and assigned them to one of their naval squadrons as allied naval infantry until their foreign ministry could sort things out.

There had been some talk of sending them back into South Vietnam as guerillas, or perhaps as intelligence agents. To keep his troops busy while Australians made up their minds, Nguyen had instituted an intensive training regimen. But in the end, the Australian government decided that he and his men were an American problem, so just before Thanksgiving they boarded a U.S. Air Force transport. When it touched down at Andrews Air Force Base, Alex had been there to greet them.

But Mai Ling had been a different story. Alex had pulled every string he could lay his hands on in an effort to find out what had happened to her, but she seemed to have vanished without a trace. A year and a half had passed without a word, and he and Nguyen had almost given up hope when a U.S. destroyer plucked a South Vietnamese army nurse from the South China Sea. She had escaped from a re-education camp in the Central Highlands, and like an estimated two million other South Vietnamese, she'd risked her life on the ocean rather than submit to tyranny.

In the course of a perfunctory debriefing, the nurse mentioned in passing a woman doctor she had encountered in a transit camp just north of Saigon. Although she was clearly an ethnic Chinese, the nurse remembered her because she had a Vietnamese surname. It was Trang, she said, or maybe Tranh. The information had been forwarded to Washington and eventually passed along to Alex and Nguyen.

Buoyed by the news, Alex began beating the bureaucratic bushes for more specific details, and Dr. MacLaughlin quietly agreed to help. Six months later, a friend-of-a-friend of his in the CIA's South East Asian Division pinpointed Mai Ling's location. After that, it was just a matter of opening a communications channel and negotiating a bribe.

Tears were welling in my eyes when Alex suddenly looked over again and laughed. "Nguyen is still teasing her about that...

"Whenever she gets on his case about smoking or throwing his dirty socks in the corner, he tells her to cut him some slack...

"Because you just can't expect much from a guy dumb enough to pay for the same bride twice."

Now that was one of those typically stupid jokes guys like to tell about their wives or girlfriends, and it had an unmistakably chauvinistic overtone about it. Under almost any other circumstances I wouldn't have thought it was funny, but by that time I had become so depressed that I decided to look at the bright side of the story – which was the rather obvious fact that Nguyen was still very much in love with Mai Ling. So as Alex slowed the car before turning onto a miniscule parking lot, I laughed a little and asked him what she had to say about that.

As we pulled to a stop in front of a brightly painted trolley car, Alex grinned. "She says he got off cheap."

Laughing, Alex pulled up the parking brake. "Which is true, and Nguyen knows it. So he usually ends up picking up his socks or whatever."

Alex climbed out of the BMW and walked around to open my door. After extending his hand and helping me out, he asked me to hold on a second. Then he opened the trunk and started rummaging around.

After a minute or so, he stood back and closed the trunk. Looking puzzled, he told me that he knew Nguyen had stashed some Marlboros someplace. Then a flash of recognition spread across his face, and he dropped down on one knee and began feeling around underneath the car. A moment later, his hand reemerged holding a pack of cigarettes wrapped in a plastic baggie. "There they are."

I was incredulous. "Nguyen hides his cigarettes underneath the car?"

Alex laughed. "Pretty extreme, huh?" Then he grinned, and told me that's what happens when you marry a doctor.

After that he placed his hand in the small of my back and guided me in the direction of the trolley.

I had never seen a trolley car before – let alone one that sold burgers and fries – so this was a whole new experience for me. Taking the lead, I climbed up the metal steps. And then after Alex opened the door for me, I went inside. A little bell attached to the door alerted the attendant to our presence, and after a moment he looked up from the magazine he had been reading and asked for our order. Alex nodded at me, so I asked for an Ollieburger with the special secret sauce, an order of fries and a Diet Pepsi.

It turned out that they didn't have Diet Pepsi, so I settled for a cup of ice water instead. Alex ordered the same thing, except for the ice water. He ordered a large Coke, with extra ice.

While we waited for our order, Alex told me that he had become an Ollie's junkie in ninth grade and he still stopped in a couple of times a month for one of their burgers. Ollie's had three or four trolley car stands in the DC area, and had become as much a part of the local culture as Bob and Edith's. Responding to the puzzled look that passed across my face, Alex explained that Bob and Edith's was a greasy spoon on Columbia Pike, open 24 hours a day, seven days a week. They had good food, reasonable prices and a great location, and they had been there so long that even the high and the mighty dropped in now and then.

That seemed really weird to me, but before I could ask him to tell me more about the place the attendant pushed two paper bags through the partition's window, and took the twenty dollar bill that Alex had laid on the counter. After stuffing his change in his pocket, Alex picked up both bags in one hand and pushed open the exit door with the other.

Alex led me to a wooden picnic table set in the shelter of a huge oak tree growing on the neighboring property. After I sat down, he took a seat across from me and opened the bags. By now thoroughly starved, I unwrapped my burger. But it turned out my curiosity was even stronger than my appetite, because I asked him if he was finished traveling before I took the first bite.

"More or less," he said. "I'm going to Louisville for the weekend, but after that I'm back until Christmas at least." Then he started eating.

Remembering my manners, I thanked him for lunch. The Ollieburger really was fabulous, I said, and the fries were even better. Alex smiled and told me that he was glad I liked it, then asked me how I was getting along at the CSS.

I probably should have seen that coming. He was the boss, after all, and I was his employee, so it was only natural for him to ask. But I had been far too busy enjoying his company to even think about work. So I had to pause for a moment to gather my wits, before telling him how much I liked my job. Dr. MacLaughlin was not only a brilliant economist, I said, but a joy to work for as well. In all honesty, I told Alex that I had learned more from him during our weekly project meetings than I had learned in all four years of college. And the fact that I had made a lot of good friends at the CSS was icing on the cake.

Alex nodded, and told me he was glad it was working out. He had heard nothing but good things about my performance to date, especially from Dr. MacLaughlin. "Scotty was quite impressed by your study."

Sitting straight upright, I grinned. "Really?"

Alex nodded emphatically. "Yes, he was. He called me in Tokyo last Friday, to let me know how well it had turned out."

"Wow! So I done good, huh?"

Smiling at my colloquialism, Alex assured me that I had. And then very seriously, he told me that he was confident that I would do as well on the next project.

It was my turn to be serious, so I asked him if we could talk about it. Alex paused for just a moment, before saying no. Although we were probably safe from eavesdroppers, he said, very strict protocols were in force and I would have to get used to following them precisely. Any questions or discussions would have to wait until we were back in the Executive Offices.

But I had already gotten used to that idea, so I nodded and took another bite from my burger. But since I felt like I had the upper hand, I pretended to pout. "Then you have to tell me about yourself instead."

Alex had just finished off the last of his fries, and was wiping his hands with a napkin. Raising one eyebrow, he looked at me sternly for a long moment before the corners of his mouth began turning up. "And why is that?" he asked.

Flustered, I searched for a sensible answer. "Well, if you can buy me an Ollieburger you can at least tell me where you're from."

Alex had shaken a Marlboro from Nguyen's pack of cigarettes, and was twirling it between his fingers at the time. After finally putting it in his mouth and lighting it, he said "Savannah."

"Savannah, Georgia?" I asked.

Alex laughed and shook his head. "Oh, no! Georgia is some place you Yankee folk are always talking about...

"But I'm from *Jaw-juh*," he said in an exaggerated southern accent. Then he grinned and asked me if I had ever been there.

I shook my head and said no, and began telling him how much I would like to. I hadn't traveled much, and I was just dying to see the world. I couldn't wait to visit Paris and London and Rome, not to mention Athens and Istanbul and Rio and just about everywhere else.

Seemingly fascinated, Alex followed my every word with rapt attention as I rattled on and on about all the places I wanted to visit and the sights I wanted to see when I finally got there. Then very suddenly, I caught myself short.

"Oh, no, you don't," I said.

Taken aback, Alex asked me what I meant.

"This is exactly what you did the night we met. You kept the conversation focused on me the whole time...

"You didn't tell me a darned thing about yourself, and you're not going to get away with that again!"

Gripped by a sudden insight, I looked at him suspiciously. "Did they teach you that in spy school?"

Alex pulled on his cigarette, and exhaled slowly as the faintest hint of amusement danced across his face. "Spy school?"

He was toying with me – or at least I thought he was – so there was no way in the world I was going to let it slide. I slammed my hand down on the wooden table and gave him my *Mildly Irritated Look*. "Oh come on, Alex. You used to work for the CIA!"

The angelic look he had worn faded from his face, replaced by one of practiced confusion. "I did?"

Exasperated, I leaned forward and looked at him over the top of my sunglasses. "Yes, Alex, you did. Dr. MacLaughlin told me you were a spy, so don't deny it!"

Alex looked away as he pulled on his cigarette. Then he looked back at me as he exhaled, and shook his head in mock sadness. "I should have known he'd rat me out." Alex stubbed his cigarette out in the little foil ashtray on the picnic table before looking up again, this time with feigned resentment. "He flunked me in Econ 101, you know."

I had just taken a sip of my ice water when he said that, and I almost choked on it. Of course that wasn't true – Dr. MacLaughlin had already told me that he'd passed him, with a "Gentleman's C" – but it was still riotously funny. So with my sides splitting from suppressed laughter, I had to turn away and spit most of it into a napkin. Hiding my face with my left hand, I sat there on the bench and laughed until the pain became unbearable. Then with tears still rolling down my cheeks, I looked back at him.

By then the angelic look had returned, and he apologized. He hadn't meant to be secretive, and he was truly sorry if he had offended me. "It's just that I find you fascinating."

I knew he was trying to divert my attention, but since that's the sort of compliment every girl wants to hear, it worked anyway. Forgetting all about the CIA, I just sat there and stared at him with my mouth half open.

Alex shook another cigarette from Nguyen's pack and lit it before looking up at the sky. Remarking on the weather, he said it was perfect for sailing. "I hope I can get my boat in the water before it turns cold," he said rather wistfully.

Still almost in shock, it took me a moment to respond. "You have a boat?"

Alex smiled and said yes. It was one of his favorite diversions. Whenever he could find the time, he liked to sail it along the coast.

That's so cool, I thought. "Does it have a name?"

Alex nodded. "The Jolly Roger," he said. "Named in honor of a great, great ancestor. The first de Vris to settle in America."

"The Jolly Roger," I asked. "Was he a pirate or something?"

Alex grinned, and said that was a matter of opinion. "You see, the French had originally attempted to colonize Georgia, but they were driven out by the Spanish. Jean Philippe – that was my ancestor's name – claimed the King of France had granted his family a large stretch of land along the coast, and when the Spanish refused to recognize his claim, he took to the sea and began attacking their ships."

"Really?"

Alex grinned, and nodded. "We have no idea where he came from, or even if his name was really de Vris. But we know that was the rationale he offered in court, because a transcript of his trial still exists."

"He got caught?"

Alex nodded and laughed. "A couple of Spanish galleons took him by surprise once, and trapped him between their guns and the shore…

"The Spanish cannons were larger and longer ranged, so he really took a pasting. They shot off his main mast and riddled his sails, but even though his ship was on fire he was able to make it into the shallows, and take refuge behind a small island where the larger Spanish ships couldn't follow…

"So Jean Philippe foxed 'em. He put in on the far side of the island, and built a huge fire upon it. And to make it convincing, he rolled a couple of kegs of gunpowder into the flames…

"From their position at sea, the Spanish could see the smoke billowing up from behind the island, and when the gunpowder went off, they were convinced that they had seen the last of the Pirate de Vris."

Alex laughed again. "Big mistake. Jean Philippe was able to make temporary repairs and limp up the coast to Albemarle Point, which was then the main British settlement in South Carolina…

"The Brits knew of him by reputation, of course, so they threw him and his crew in jail. And they would have hanged the lot of them, if someone hadn't pointed out that he had never once attacked a British ship...

"Since the Brits were in the middle of a war with Spain at the time, that stood him in good stead. So they dismissed the charges for lack of jurisdiction, and a few weeks later he put to sea again, after his ship had been repaired and provisioned by an anonymous benefactor."

"So what happened to him?"

"Business as usual." Alex took another long drag from his cigarette, and exhaled slowly. "But his luck improved – or perhaps he became a bit more cautious – because he lived to a ripe old age...

"After the British gained control of Georgia in Queen Anne's War, he bought a plantation just north of what's now Savannah and retired as a rich and well-respected subject of the Crown."

"And your family has been there ever since?"

Alex nodded. Although they had moved to Washington in 1961, his father had maintained the familial home in Savannah out of respect for tradition. Alex had eventually inherited it and, in fact, "Jaw-juh" remained his legal state of residence.

It was such a great story that I just couldn't pass up the opportunity to do a little teasing. "It sounds like old Jean Philippe was quite a character...

"So are there any other 'blackguards' in the family?"

Alex laughed and said, "Just me."

Grinning, I asked him if he was a pirate, too. Alex laughed again, and said no. "I'm more of a privateer."

Curious, I asked him what that was.

"A privateer? Well, back in the old days, governments sometimes licensed civilian sea captains to wage war on their enemies...

"It was a sort of officially sanctioned piracy." Then he looked down at his watch, and told me that we would have to get going. He had a ton of work piled up on his desk, and somehow or another he had to find time for a haircut as well.

Disappointed, I helped him pick up our trash and carry it over to the nearby refuse can. I had just shoved my crumpled up water cup through the swinging door when the thought suddenly struck me. "Alex, is what you do dangerous?"

Alex stopped and looked at me. Standing in the middle of the tiny parking lot, he cocked his head thoughtfully before shaking it ever so slightly. "No," he said softly. "It's what I've already done."

CHAPTER SIXTEEN

Confused and suddenly frightened, I stared at him as he turned back towards the car. "Alex, wait!"

He stopped and turned as I scurried after him across the crumbling asphalt – which wasn't easy in a tight skirt and three inch heels. "What's that supposed to mean?" I demanded to know.

A puzzled look crept across his face and then abruptly vanished. Looking down, he studied my face for a long moment before shrugging it off as "nothing." Then very suddenly, he said he had to buy Nguyen a new pack of cigarettes at the 7-11 on the adjacent lot.

Frustrated, I seized his arm just as he began to turn and demanded an answer. "Alex, are you in trouble?"

Grabbing him like that probably wasn't the best of ideas – which I realized, as I felt his muscles tense beneath my grip. Turning about, he looked down at my hand before gazing silently into my eyes. Mortified, I released him and stammered out an apology.

Too embarrassed to look at him, I stared at the ground. "I just want to know if someone is trying to hurt you."

When I finally looked up again, I was amazed to find him more amused than angry. He smiled, and shrugged. "Probably," he said. "I've stepped on some pretty important toes."

His matter-of-fact acknowledgement sent chills up my spine. I inhaled sharply, and my eyes opened wide. "Alex, you have to do something!"

Breathlessly, I told him he should hire some bodyguards or ask President Reagan for Secret Service agents.

Then suddenly curious, I stopped abruptly and cupped my hands above my eyes to shield them from the sun. "He'd give them to you, right?"

Laughing softly, Alex said the President would probably provide him with a Secret Service detail if he asked. Then he grimaced and said, "But that would take all the fun out of it."

What???

Transfixed by disbelief, I stood there stared at him.

Fun???

What's fun about having people chasing after you? And more to the point - what kind of knucklehead makes jokes about something like that???

I didn't know, and I didn't even care – because by that time, my temper had flared all over again. With my fists balled together, I slammed my foot down on the pavement.

"Alex, are you stupid?"

Glaring at him with my fists still clenched tightly by my sides, I didn't wait for a reply. "That wasn't funny, Alex, and now I'm scared!"

Suddenly aware of the fact that I had been shouting, I cut myself short. With tears welling in my eyes, I looked down at the asphalt and shook my head back and forth. Very softly, I told him I was afraid for him…

"I just don't want you to get hurt."

Feeling completely awful, I wanted to throw my arms around him and hold him like a great big teddy bear. But by then my mind had finally caught up with my mouth, and I knew I was in trouble enough already. An outburst like that would have gotten me fired anyplace in town, and as that sinking realization grew in the pit of my stomach, I figured my next stop was probably going to be the unemployment office.

But lucky for me, Alex was in a really good mood that day. After he stopped laughing, he admitted that he could be a bit dense at times. But then he turned suddenly serious, and looked deep into my eyes. Life is an inherently hazardous undertaking, he said, and politics was even more so. Then he paused for a moment, before telling me how important it was for me to understand that.

And rather pointedly, he reminded me that President Reagan had been shot and almost killed by a deranged twenty-something not so long ago, despite the host of Secret Service agents that accompanied his every move. Reasonable precautions were all well and fine, he said. But at the end of the day, character is one's first and often only defense in life…

And that was especially true in Washington.

Yeah, right, I thought sullenly. *That, and learning how to keep your big mouth shut…*

Taking the latter lesson to heart, I backed way off. Releasing my fear and anger to the four winds, I looked down at the pavement again and nodded my head. "Yes, Sir."

Apparently satisfied that he had made his point, Alex looked down at his watch. We really had to get going, he said. So without another word, I followed him across the parking lot and into the

7-11, and stood behind him while the clerk found two packs of Marlboros and rung up the sale.

After stuffing one pack into his T-shirt pocket, he poured the change into the right pocket of his jeans before gesturing for the door. Following him back across the parking lot, I waited while he wrapped up the other pack of cigarettes and slipped it into Nguyen's hiding place in the frame of the car. Then after he got up and opened the passenger side door for me I got in, still silent and very much on edge. Although I couldn't put my finger on it, my instincts told me that something dark and dangerous was going on behind the scenes here in Washington, and with a strange admixture of fascination and foreboding, I wondered what it was.

For the briefest of moments, I was tempted to ask Alex but I quickly dismissed the thought. I had pushed my luck far enough for one day, and in any event, I didn't think he would tell me even if he knew. I had been at CSS long enough to know that he was one of the most important men in the world – and that I was just a lowly research assistant.

When I'm not yelling at him, anyway…

Suddenly reminded of my outburst, I turned away in embarrassment and looked out the passenger side window. *Way to go*, I thought. *Bet he never buys you lunch again!*

Depressed by the thought, I barely noticed when he started the engine and put the car in gear.

Mai Ling had the radio set to a classical music station, and it had played almost imperceptibly on the way to Ollie's. But as we pulled back onto Washington Boulevard, Alex began fiddling with the dials. A moment later, *The Lion Sleeps Tonight* began filtering through the speakers. Grateful for the diversion, I asked Alex to turn up the volume.

"Like Oldies?"

I was surprised and disappointed that he asked, because we had already had that conversation before. He had been playing the Oldies station when he had driven me to James' apartment at the beginning of the summer, and I had told him all about My-Mom-the-Oldies-Fan. I had grown up on 50s and 60s music, and for some reason or another I had expected him to remember that. But since he didn't, I explained it all over again.

By the time I finished, my mood had brightened, and it improved even more when he smiled and asked what my favorite Oldies song was. It was a tough question, so I had to think about it before answering. "That song about Dooley. You know, the guy that wore all the goofy clothes?"

"Tan Shoes and Pink Shoe Laces. Dodie Stevens sang that in '57 or '58, I think."

Suddenly buoyant, I grinned and told him that was it. "So what's your favorite?"

Alex cocked his head over and pursed his lips. "I'm not sure I have any single favorite," he said. "But Bruce Channel's *Hey Baby* is one of my favorites. And then there's Chuck Berry's *Johnny B. Goode*, and Clyde McPhatter's *Lover Please*, and his version of *Does She Love Me?*

"And then of course there's *Blue Moon*, by the Marcels, and *If You Want to be Happy* by Jimmy Soul."

I smiled because I liked all of those songs, too. But the last one — the full title of which was *If You Want to be Happy for the Rest of Your Life, Never Make a Pretty Woman Your Wife* — was way over the top by contemporary feminist standards, so I decided to give him a hard time about it.

"Pretty good choices, except for that last one," I said. Grinning, I asked him if he was going to marry an ugly woman.

I had thought that was a pretty good trap, but Alex danced through it with ease. Without the slightest hint of a smile, he nodded gravely and said "Oh, yeah. I love ugly women."

Laughing, I was tempted to give him a good-natured whack. But since that was an obviously bad idea, I decided to tease him some more. "So how ugly does a girl have to be to qualify for your attentions?"

Alex had been fumbling in his T-shirt pocket for another cigarette, and after shaking one free from the package and lighting it, he looked over and told me she would have to be "way ugly."

I was laughing at the funny expression that had crept upon his face when it suddenly occurred to me that he should spend the night with me some time. *If he likes ugly women,* I thought, *he'd love seeing me in the morning!*

I was still snickering at the imagery when I suddenly realized that I had just touched on a rather important question — that being, specifically, the sort of women he actually liked. Alex was rich, powerful, brilliant, and devastatingly handsome — but he wasn't married, didn't have a girlfriend, and as far as I knew he wasn't even dating anyone.

And to me, at least, that was the biggest mystery of all.

Of course, that's not the sort of thing a girl wants to ask a guy about, because it always leads back to his old girlfriends — and that just doesn't work out. So to keep the conversation going, I turned in my seat instead and told him how much I had enjoyed his book.

Alex smiled, and asked which one I was referring to.

"Oh, the one about geopolitics," I said. "It was really good."

With his eyes still focused on the traffic, he nodded and told me that he was surprised that I had enjoyed it. "It's a textbook, you know."

Suddenly serious, I explained that Dr. MacLaughlin had told me to read it before moving up to the Eighth Floor. "He said it was the best book ever written on the subject, and he thought I should know something about it before I started the new project."

Turning a bit more in my seat, I tugged on my skirt before continuing. "I was really amazed, Alex. I had no idea that geography played such an important role in shaping international conflict."

As we eased to a stop at the light just before Columbia Pike, Alex nodded. "It's enormous, and largely unappreciated in America...

"Geopolitics is taught at the undergraduate level in Europe, but in the U.S., it's only taught in graduate school and usually then at the doctoral level." Which was unfortunate, he said, for it left even well-educated Americans ignorant of the underlying dynamic of the Cold War.

Hoping to score a few points, I smiled brightly and told him I had read it twice. "I even outlined it."

Alex chuckled and said, "Well, then you know the Cold War isn't something that just happened. It follows in part from the physical structure of the world."

Flashing back to a moment of recognition at the hotel pool, I told him that was the really scary part. "So there's just no way to compromise, is there?"

Alex shook his head. "Not really. There's a place for negotiations, in terms of common interests. Neither side wants to start a nuclear war by accident or miscalculation, and both have a vested interest in making sure regional conflicts don't spread beyond certain geographic bounds...

"But other than that, there's really very little to talk about.

"Unfortunately," he continued, "Most of the Congress seems intent upon ignoring that fact."

The light turned green, and Alex fell silent as we accelerated through the intersection.

Curious, I asked him why that was. "They're not all idiots, are they?"

Alex chuckled, and told me that was a matter of opinion. But in any event, the real problem lay elsewhere. Congress was a reflection of the policy-making elite, he said, which was badly fractured. Their post-war foreign-policy consensus had shattered in the crucible of Vietnam, and the elite had split into warring camps. The bottom line was that not everyone wanted to see the United States emerge from the struggle victorious – and given the nature of government in America, that sentiment had found expression on Capitol Hill.

Huh?

Shocked and confused, I asked him what he meant.

Alex paused for a moment, as if to measure his words more carefully. "That's really complicated," he said.

Frustrated, I told him I understood the complicated part. "But isn't Congress supposed to reflect the will of the people?"

Alex shrugged. "Well, that's the theory. But in practice, it doesn't always work that way…

"Most of American politics is epiphenomenal, as is government policy."

Since I didn't know what that meant, I sat there and stared at the dashboard as I puzzled it out. "You mean it's not real?"

"Oh, it's real enough," he said. "It's just not what it appears to be."

Well, everyone knows that, I thought.

But since I had never really considered the implications before, Alex's assurance made me feel suddenly foolish. *So if politics isn't what it seems to be…*

Then what the heck is it?

After thinking about it for a minute, I realized that I didn't have a clue, and as we passed over the Fourteenth Street Bridge into the District, that really began to bother me. As far as I was concerned, a democracy should be just exactly what it pretends to be. The fact that ours wasn't entirely on the up-and-up just didn't seem right.

I wanted to ask Alex about that, but he appeared lost in thought. In fact, he didn't say another word until I finally broke the silence by telling him how much I liked living in DC. He seemed genuinely happy to know that I had adapted to Washington life. Much to my surprise, he turned out to be the only person at CSS that didn't know Julia was getting married. After thinking about it for a moment, he said he was concerned that she would be moving out of the apartment and leaving me on my own.

After making a U-turn on North Capitol Street, Alex brought the Beemer to a stop in front of the lobby of our building. I was about to thank him for the Ollieburger and a wonderful afternoon when he turned in his seat and suggested I keep the dogs – and the Vette – until I found another roommate.

Since I still hadn't caught up with Julia, I didn't know if she would be staying in the apartment or not, so his offer to let me keep the dogs was a real relief. And of course, the idea of hanging onto Nguyen's Vette was completely cool. "Really?"

Alex nodded, very seriously. "I'd feel a lot better if you did."

Suddenly concerned, I asked him about Nguyen. "Won't he need his car?"

Alex shook his head. "Oh, no. We've got a bunch of cars, and Nguyen has already started rebuilding a MGB, so it's no big deal." Then he laughed and said, "Unless you wreck it, of course." Grinning, I promised to be really careful.

Alex smiled, and told me that would be a good idea. Then he got out and walked around the car to open the door for me. As he helped me out of the Beemer, he explained that he had to go get a haircut so he probably wouldn't be back that afternoon. But since there was plenty of dog food under the counter in his galley, and some extra bowls, he told me to buzz Jennifer Two when I got back to my office and ask her to box some of it up for me. And if I needed any help getting it down to the Vette, he said I should call Security and have one of the guards carry it for me.

Still holding his hand, I smiled and promised that I would. Then I thanked him for a wonderful afternoon, and darted towards the Lobby.

I had just pushed the big glass entryway door open when I heard him call after me. When I turned back, he was standing in the driver's side door. Smiling, he told me to whack Big Minh upside the head if he gave me any more trouble.

Smiling back, I gave him a little wave and slipped inside.

Two minutes later the elevator doors opened and I stepped into the Seventh Floor hallway. Having forgotten all about my outburst, I was basking in the afterglow of an almost perfect afternoon as I headed down the hall for the Econ shop. Although my most important priority was tracking down Julia, I figured I'd better check in with Jennifer first. I'd been gone almost two and a half hours by then, so it was a safe bet that someone or another had been trying to find me.

And since it was an even safer bet that Jennifer was going to give me the Third Degree the moment I walked in, I was trying to figure out what I was going to tell her when I heard Tom Andrews start swearing down the hall. A moment later there was a tremendous crash inside his office, and then a loud thud as something really heavy hit his interior wall. Mystified, I stopped to watch as he backed into the corridor, pulling a moving dolly with his desk loaded on top.

Sweating heavily and still cursing under his breath, he finally managed to get the dolly lined up properly. Then he jerked on it really hard, and dragged it halfway into the hallway. But he had lost his grip on the handle, and after stumbling backwards several steps he lost his balance and fell over against the far wall.

It was such a great performance that I was tempted to applaud. But since I could tell he wasn't in the mood for my sarcasm, I asked him what he was doing instead.

Tom had been too busy tugging and hauling to notice me until he hit the floor, and I could tell he was acutely embarrassed. After wiping his brow, he shook his head and told me that Christine had booted him out of his office.

"So what happened," I asked sweetly. "Bounce the rent check again?"

Getting to his feet, Tom gave me an irritated look and told me that she was moving him down the hall so a contractor could reinforce the floor above. They were going to install a vault directly over his office, but the building's architect wouldn't let them proceed without putting in an elaborate series of re-shores on the Seventh Floor. And since contractors were scheduled to start work bright and early the next morning, he had to get all his stuff moved by close of business.

Grinning, I told him to look at the bright side: One of these days he'd be a real economist like me, and then he could have someone else to do all the heavy lifting for him.

"Real funny," he snorted. "A Bachelor of Arts from Bumpkin University, and you call yourself an 'economist.'"

Under almost any other circumstances, I would have taken offense to that. But since I knew I had him over a barrel, I decided to tease him instead. Putting my hands on my hips, I gave him my *Seriously Irritated Look*. "That's a BA with a Magna Cum Laude attached to it…

"And it's from a perfectly fine school, Mister, so let's have a little respect!"

Glaring at me as he turned back to the dolly, Tom desperately tried to get the upper hand. "Big deal," he said. "I've got a Magna Cum Laude with both my degrees already, and as soon as I finish my doctoral dissertation, I'll have a third…

"From Johns Hopkins, by the way."

Although that really was impressive, I wasn't about to cut him any slack. Because Tom was a complete geek – and as every normal person knows, you have to smack geeks around now and then just to keep them in line. Otherwise, they'd take over the world and we'd all have to wear pocket protectors and big thick glasses held together with scotch tape. So I rolled my eyes and said *"Ouuuuuu"* as I sauntered off down the hall – shaking my rear end a bit extra, just to make sure he got the point.

Halfway down the hall, I was still reveling in my victory when the awful thought came upon me. I froze in mid-step, and then turned ever so slowly. Looking back at Tom, I asked him just exactly where Christine had put him.

He was about twenty feet behind me, still struggling with the dolly. Suddenly delighted, he looked up and smiled expectantly. "Right next to you – room 718," he said. "We'll be like office mates."

He stopped very suddenly, and knitted his brow together. "Well, not exactly office mates, but almost."

"Oh." Forcing a thin smile, I said "How nice." Then I turned and ran for the department office.

The door was open when I got there, so I slammed it shut behind me and slumped against it. Glaring at Jennifer, I asked her if she knew that Tom Andrews was being moved down to our end of the hall.

As she looked up from her keyboard, consternation passed across her face. Then she scrunched up her nose and said, *"Ewwwwwww...*

"He's gonna spend all his spare time in here, looking at my boobs."

Then she shook her head and sighed. "He's a complete geek, you know."

Still leaning against the door, I scrunched up my nose in sympathy. "Tell me about it," I said.

Jennifer shrugged and went back to her typing. "I suppose we'll just have to start dressing like 'bag ladies'...

"Ya think he'll take the hint?"

Pushing myself off the door, I headed for the coffee pot. "Not a chance, girlfriend...

"That's his idea of high fashion."

Jennifer was still banging away on the keyboard when I started pouring the coffee into a cup. Looking up, she asked me if I wanted to spike it with some of Dr. MacLaughlin's triple malt scotch. "He keeps the bottle in the top drawer of his filing cabinet."

Putting the coffee pot back on the warmer, I looked at her incredulously. "Really?"

Jennifer nodded. "Really." But just for special occasions, she said. "Like the time you drove him crazy arguing about inflation."

Looking up again, she told me that he had made a wild dash for the file cabinet the moment I had walked out the door, and taken a giant slug straight out of the bottle. "Normally, he just puts a drop or two in his coffee after lunch."

Grinning from ear to ear, I demanded that she tell me all about it. "So did he finally break down and admit I'm right?"

Jennifer looked up with a truly fiendish smile. "Not telling," she said. "At least not until you've told me everything about your lunch with Mr. Chairman of the Board...

"And I do mean everything."

Still stirring creamer into my coffee, I turned and looked at her sharply. "Hey, that's blackmail!"

Jennifer smiled sweetly. "So it is...."

"And since Dr. MacLaughlin is still out at Langley, you can sit your butt down in that chair over there and tell me every last detail."

Then her eyes popped open, and she sat bolt upright. "Oh my God, I almost forgot!"

Turning in her seat, she picked up a gigantic binder that had been lying next to her computer monitor. "Here's the manuscript for Dr. MacLaughlin's latest book. Since you won't be going up to the Eighth Floor until they get your new office put together, he wants you to read through it and look for obvious errors, typos, and stuff like that."

Flattered that he would want me to proof his manuscript, I put my cup of coffee down on the side of her desk and took it from her outstretched hands.

I had just started thumbing through it when I heard Jennifer command me. "Now sit down, girl, and start talking."

CHAPTER SEVENTEEN

For some reason it sounded more like a fog horn than an alarm clock, and for a long confused moment I just lay there under the covers wondering what it was doing up in my loft. But then the pounding of eight furry paws on the spiral staircase penetrated my consciousness. Suddenly wide-eyed and awake, I pulled the comforter over my head and rolled over the side of the bed. An instant later I heard a thud as Big Minh slammed down on the mattress, and then another as Lady Godiva landed on it.

Feeling very pleased with myself for having outfoxed them, I pulled myself into an upright position on the floor, and stuck my head out through the tangled comforter. Peering over the bed, I couldn't resist a little taunt. *"Nah-nah, ya missed me!"*

Then I made a funny face at them, and struggled to my feet with the comforter still wrapped around me.

Remembering my manners, I asked them how they had slept. But after a moment went by without reply, I decided that they were too polite to complain. Realizing that it must be awfully uncomfortable sleeping on the floor, I reached down and scratched each behind the ears in turn. Obviously pleased by my attention, Lady Godiva sat down on the bed and wagged her tail. But Big Minh apparently wanted to return the favor, because he reared up on his hind legs. Planting his gigantic front paws squarely upon my shoulders, he proceeded to lick my face.

Letting the comforter drop to the floor so that I could lower his feet back down on the bed, I tried to explain to Big Minh that most girls really aren't thrilled with big sloppy kisses first thing in the morning. But since he had been so clearly well-intended, I smiled and patted him on the head anyway. "But I do appreciate the thought!"

Then I pulled on the pair of sweatpants I'd left lying on the chair, and crawled across the bed to turn off the alarm. Halfway across, I got another big sloppy lick from Big Minh, and a slightly more delicate kiss from Lady Godiva as well. But given the circumstances, I figured that was something I could get used to.

To tell you the truth, I was really happy to have them there.

Julia had finally turned up about 7:00 pm the night before. The Accounting Department had replaced their old IBM 360 computer the week before with the newer desktop models that had just hit the market, and they had made a total mess out of the payroll. To make sure that Christine wouldn't find out about it, her boss had loaded one of them up on a dolly and pushed it into an unused storage room in the print shop.

Then after barricading the door, he and Julia had spent the rest of the day straightening it out in secret – which accounted for the fact that I couldn't find her all afternoon, even though I'd searched the CSS from top to bottom.

Julia had only stayed a minute. She had just dropped in to pick up some fresh clothes, and Mike was waiting for her outside. But she showed me her ring, and gave me the super abbreviated account of his proposal. Sure enough, he'd gotten down on one knee in front of the embers of their campfire, and as the light from the fading flames danced across his face, he had asked her to marry him.

It was really romantic, she said, and with a wolf howling far off in the darkness, just spooky enough to make for a wonderful story. Needless to say, between the campfire and the proposal and the cries of the wolf, things had become a bit passionate, and she couldn't wait to tell her children and her grandchildren all about it someday.

Then she stopped very suddenly, and corrected herself. "Well, not all of it," she said with a mischievous grin. "Just the romantic parts."

The whole thing was so cool that I hated to even bring up the subject of the apartment, but she assured me that it was OK. Although she was going to be moving in with Mike, his apartment wasn't that big and it didn't have enough closets for the two of them.

Since she was going to leave her furniture and some of her clothes until they found a new place after the wedding, she said she'd cover her share of the rent through mid-summer. Then after making me promise to help with all the planning, she scooped up her clothes and rushed out.

Grinning from ear to ear, I closed the door behind her. *Way to go, girl!*

Even though I hadn't known Julia very long, we'd become really close over the past couple of months, and like everyone else who knew the two of them, I thought they made a perfect match. An up-and-coming corporate lawyer, Mike was tall and modestly handsome. But he was smart, riotously funny, and completely devoted to Julia – and that's what I liked about him, most of all.

After she left, I'd curled up on the couch with a big bowl of microwave popcorn and mused about the two of them as an old episode of Gilligan's Island played across the screen. Safe in the knowledge that they had a great future ahead of them, I began wondering about my own. And since one thing always seems to lead to another, it wasn't very long before I started thinking about Alex.

Except for the part where I blew up at him, I thought the afternoon had gone really well. Although it really hadn't been a date, I was pretty sure it had been more than just lunch. Because after all, Alex could have just called the hotel and told them to bring me another cheeseburger.

But, since he'd spent most of the afternoon with me at his all-time favorite burger joint instead, I figured it had to count for something. So after thinking about it for a moment, I decided to call it a half-date. Because as far as I was concerned, that's exactly what it was.

Sitting cross-legged on the couch with my mouth stuffed with popcorn, I slipped into a gentle reverie to relive the afternoon, moment by moment. Still basking in the afterglow, I realized just how special it had been.

But as I pushed my shoulders back against the couch to stretch, I was gripped by a sudden sense of unease. For despite all that I had learned about him, Alex remained a total mystery. He had an elusive quality about him that was mysterious and exciting and – to be honest – dark, dangerous, and deeply erotic.

Just being around him stirred an ancient and indefinable longing within the depths of my being, and for one terrifying moment, it threatened to overwhelm me.

Trembling and breathing heavily, I forced my eyes closed and grasped the bowl nestled between my knees. *I could lose myself inside of him...*

Fighting hard to reassert control, I leaned my head back on the couch and slowly opened my eyes.

But as I stared at the high ceiling, I felt a sinking sensation in the pit of my stomach. Had it been only my fear and fascination, I could have handled it. But I was convinced that Alex was involved in some sort of behind-the-scenes power struggle with forces unknown, and I sensed that it could turn deadly.

But for some altogether maddening reason, Alex didn't seem concerned.

Now that's brilliant, I thought. *He's playing Gotcha! with the Grim Reaper, and you're falling in love with him!*

Getting up from the couch to put the empty popcorn bowl into the sink, I couldn't help but shake my head in disbelief. *You really put your foot in it this time...*

But since I wasn't in the mood for the truth, I rationalized instead. Conveniently ignoring the fact that he had almost been ripped in two, I tried to reassure myself. *He got through Vietnam, OK....*

The whole thing was so distressing that I pushed it from consciousness, and climbed into bed.

I slept well – at least until Big Minh and Lady Godiva so rudely awakened me – and I'd forgotten all about the conundrum that had vexed me the night before. But as I opened the apartment door and led the dogs out onto the street and into the early morning mist, it all came rushing back.

Good God, I thought. *What am I going to do???*

Confused, frightened, and suddenly angry, I realized that I hadn't the slightest idea. But in any case, I knew I couldn't do it in an old T-shirt and sweats. So after calling for the dogs, I went back inside and began getting ready for work.

Halfway through my shower, I realized what bothered me the most. Something really dark and sinister was going on in the shadows of government, but I didn't have the slightest clue as to what it might be. Rendered impotent by ignorance, all I could do was hold my breath and hope for the best...

Figuratively speaking, that is. Because nothing important ever happens fast in Washington...

Most people attributed the excruciating slowness of government to the deliberate design of the Founders. But after four months in the capital city, I had come to suspect that it had more to do with physics. *In this town,* I thought, *even Evil moves at the speed of molasses...*

Snickering at the imagery, I turned off the water and reached for one of Julia's oversized bath towels. But as I wrapped it around me and stepped out of the shower, I suddenly realized I could turn that fact to my advantage. Since I was the New Kid in Town, I was looking at a pretty steep learning curve. But in a slow moving environment, a fast learner has an edge, right?

So if I can just figure out what's going on, I can cut the Bad Guys off at the pass...

Lost in the thought, I padded over to the mirror above the vanity and wiped the condensed moisture from it with my hand. Dripping water onto the tiled floor, I stood there for a long moment studying the determined face that stared back at me. *One way or another,* I promised myself, *I'm gonna get to the bottom of this...*

And when I do, those Bad Guys are gonna be in a world of trouble!

Suddenly buoyant, it occurred to me that I might even get another statue out of the deal!

But after thinking about it for a moment, I had to discard the idea. *Nobody gets two statues in Washington…*

Which was true. So I decided they'd just have to make the first one a bit bigger. And put it in a really nice park, of course…

I was still basking in the imagery when the towel I had wrapped around my head came undone and fell onto my face. Rudely reminded that I had to get a move on, I reached for the blow-dryer hanging from the hook on the wall. Which was important, because I knew that there was a rule somewhere or another that said girls aren't allowed to save the world with wet, stringy hair…

Because you have to look pretty for that!

I was still chuckling about The Wet Hair Rule when I pulled Nguyen's Vette up to the gate of the parking garage, an hour later. Male egos being what they are, I was pretty sure that Wilbur would come up with one pretext or another to stop me – because there was just no way in the world you could chew a guy out like that without inviting some sort of petty revenge. So I was surprised and more than a little bit puzzled when he waved me through. But when I saw the look in his eyes as I drove past, I realized why. Wilbur wasn't just intimidated – he was terrified!

Feeling kind of bad about that, I made a mental note to spank my Inner Tomboy at the first available opportunity. Because she's not supposed to pick on people unless they're at least twice our size…

Grinning, I made the turn at the bottom of the ramp and wheeled the Vette into Nguyen's parking place. After leaning across the cabin to open the passenger side door for the dogs, I climbed out and began putting the top up. That turned into something of an ego trip, because Admiral Taylor and General Thomas were walking my way at the time, and I couldn't help notice they were checking out my legs – which, by the way, were looking really good after the long weekend at the pool.

Pretending hard not to notice, I had to struggle to keep a straight face as I locked the car and herded the dogs into the building.

There were all kinds of stories floating around CSS about how smart the dogs were, but it wasn't until we walked into an open elevator that I actually started to believe them. Once inside the cab, Big Minh stood up on his haunches and hammered at the button for the Eighth Floor. His paws were so big that he had a hard time depressing it, but after three or four whacks the light came on and the elevators doors slid shut. Barely believing my eyes, I just stood there and stared at him.

Pretty neat trick, I thought.

Forgetting the fact that I had to stop at my office to change into heels and fix my hair, I had stepped out into the Eighth Floor hallway before suddenly remembering. Wondering where my mind had been, I was in the process of turning back around when I heard Christine calling me. Making a half-turn in the direction of her voice, I was surprised to see her scurrying in my direction. Since I had never seen her do that before, I figured something must be up.

"I'm glad I caught you," she said. "There was a communications foul-up, and the attorneys from the Agency arrived early. They're waiting for us in the Executive Conference Room." Then she stopped very suddenly and looked at me. "But do something about that hair first!"

Realizing that I must have looked pretty frightful after zooming across town with the top down, I gulped and said "Yes, Ma'am." I had just begun to turn back towards the elevator when she reached out and put her hands on either side of my head. Tilting it to get a better look in the light, she studied me intensely. After looking down at my suit, and then back up at my face, she said my makeup was fine but the eyeliner needed work. "Darken it up just a bit."

Stepping back, she told me I had five minutes. She was going on to the conference room, but she wanted me to run by her office and tell Linda to bring down two carafes of fresh coffee and a plate full of doughnuts – just as soon as I finished making the necessary repairs. Understanding the need to make haste, I dashed down the hall to the ladies' room. After changing into my heels, I began frantically brushing out my hair. And after searching through my purse for the necessary supplies, I piled it up on top of my head and pinned it into place. Leaning close to the mirror, I ran my eyeliner pencil along the top of each eye once more. Then after finishing, I fumbled through my purse for my glasses.

I had worn big thick glasses all the way through grade school and junior high, but for some strange reason my eyes had improved as I grew older. Although I didn't really need glasses anymore, I'd put them on every now and then when my eyes got tired from reading or when I wanted to look really smart. So after putting them in place, I stepped back from the mirror.

Because I knew the meeting was important, I'd given a lot of thought to what I was going to wear. I had finally settled on a very conventional dark blue pinstripe suit and a white blouse, and as I stepped back to survey my handiwork, I commended myself for having made just the right choice. Although I hadn't worn a tie, I had wrapped a red silk scarf around my neck and tucked it into my blouse.

Perfect! I thought. With my hair on top of my head and my glasses perched upon my nose, I simply reeked of professionalism.

Gathering up my gear, I made a mad dash for the Executive Offices. After telling Linda about the coffee and doughnuts, I stashed my shoe bag under her desk and ran for the conference room. When I finally pushed the polished oaken doors open and walked inside, I had exactly nine seconds to spare.

Christine stood as I walked in, as did the two men who had been seated across from her at the conference table. After escorting me around the other side, she introduced me. The first identified himself as Tom Smith and the other as Bob Jones, and I shook hands with each in turn. But I disliked them both immediately, because I knew they were blowing smoke.

I may have just fallen off the turnip truck, I thought, *but I'm not entirely stupid...*

Suppressing a rather sarcastic desire to tell them I was actually Tinkerbell in disguise, I smiled politely instead. Then I followed Christine back around the table and seated myself in the chair beside her.

The so-called Mr. Smith started to make small talk, as the alleged Mr. Jones hoisted an oversized briefcase up onto the table and opened it. "I understand you've just co-authored a study with Dr. MacLaughlin," he said.

Nodding politely, I said, "Yes, Sir, I did."

To which Mr. Smith, so-called, responded with a practiced smile. "I'm looking forward to reading it...

"Dr. MacLaughlin expressed a great deal of admiration for your work and for your ability, and on the basis of his unqualified recommendation, Director Casey has approved your participation in this project."

Feeling only slightly more receptive, I folded my hands together on the conference table, smiled politely, and thanked him.

By that time, the alleged Mr. Jones had produced four thick, bound documents from his briefcase and a like number of black ballpoint pens. Separating them on the table, he placed a pen on each and slid one to his colleague before matter-of-factly pushing two more across the table towards Christine and me. He kept the last one for himself.

The so-called Mr. Smith thanked him before continuing. "As you know, we are about to undertake a review of the CIA's 'Black Budget.'

"Under almost all circumstances, such exercises are conducted 'in house' – that is, within the Agency itself.

"But in this instance, Director Casey has determined that the interests of the United States Government shall be best served by an independent review conducted by the Center for Strategic Studies."

"At the recommendation of Dr. MacLaughlin, he has decided to exercise the authority vested in him by law to clear you for this project...

"As the lead analyst, you shall be cleared for what is known as 'Sensitive Compartmentalized Information.'"

Having spoken the works with exceptional gravitas, the so-called Mr. Smith adjusted his glasses and looked at me sternly. "Which, for your information, is the highest security clearance in the land...

"No more than a few dozen people in the entire government have been cleared for this particular subset of information, and that number includes the President and the Director of Central Intelligence."

Suitably impressed, I nodded gravely.

Satisfied that he had made his point, the so-called Mr. Smith continued. "Although the law specifically provides for such waivers, they have been made so infrequently in the past that the General Counsel's office has been unable to find a clear precedent in its files...

"Indeed, according to our records this is the first instance in which the Director of Central Intelligence has exercised this authority, although past presidents have invoked it on at least two other, prior occasions....

"And so for that reason, the General Counsel has decided to cast this waiver in the form of a legally binding contract."

After looking down to open the document in front of him, the so-called Mr. Smith continued. "The terms and conditions of this waiver are in the folder before you, and in accordance with my instructions I am to read this document to you paragraph by paragraph...

"You will read along with me, silently, and on the completion of each paragraph I will pause and ask you if you understand what I have read to you. In the event that you do not understand, I have been directed to explain it to your satisfaction.

"Once you are satisfied that you understand what I have read to you, and what you have read for yourself, I will ask you to initial the paragraph with the black pen provided. After that, we will move on to the next paragraph...

"Mr. Jones shall serve as a witness for the Government, and Mrs. O'Connell shall serve as a witness for the CSS. Upon completion, they shall sign an affidavit attesting to the fact that I read each paragraph to you sequentially, and fully answered all of your questions, and they shall also attest to the fact that the initials you have placed beside each paragraph have been made by your hand."

"Now, Miss McAllister, do you have any questions?"

After I shook my head to signify that I didn't, the so-called Mr. Smith nodded and asked us all to open our binders to Page One, Paragraph One.

I had just opened the folder in front of me when Linda knocked on the door. Surprised, the alleged Mr. Jones leapt to his feet and dashed forward. After physically blocking Linda's passage, he took hold of the cart she had been pushing and pulled it into the room. Then he pushed the door shut and locked it, before returning to his seat.

As Christine rose to her feet, she suggested that the proceedings be temporarily suspended while she served the coffee. Smiling at the so-called Mr. Smith – who was unmistakably irritated at the interruption – she insisted that the coffee, at least, was essential to the contract. Although the doughnuts were problematical, she said, the courts would surely find that the absence of caffeine provided just grounds for abrogation.

I thought that was pretty clever, and so did the alleged Mr. Jones. But the so-called Mr. Smith was far from amused. Although he tactfully conceded the point, I could tell he was fuming as Christine carefully poured each cup.

Five minutes and a doughnut and-a-half later – Christine caught me eyeing hers, and had wisely decided to share before I succumbed to temptation and stole it – the meeting resumed.

Linda had brought two carafes of coffee, as per her instructions, and that turned out to be a really good thing. Because after about 15 seconds of the so-called Mr. Smith's droning voice, I was half way to La La Land. And the fact that the conference room was a little warmer than usual didn't help matters. The so-called Mr. Smith was as boring as the subject matter, and despite my best efforts to keep focused upon the task at hand, I found my mind wandering. Convinced the CIA had found a sure-fire cure for insomnia, I was trying to figure out how I could pirate their technique when the so-called Mr. Smith rudely interrupted. *Given the number of insomniacs in America, it's worth a fortune...*

"Miss McAllister? I asked if you had any questions."

Jerked back to reality — well, the legal version of it anyway — I shook my head and muttered, "No."

Reaching across the table, the so-called Mr. Smith turned the page in front of me and instructed me to initial Paragraph 67. Which I did, after taking another huge gulp from my coffee cup.

Time began to dilate, and as seconds turned into minutes and minutes into hours, I began to suspect that I had somehow journeyed into the Twilight Zone. If I'd heard Rod Serling's voice in the background, I would have actually believed it.

Contract my foot, I thought as I dutifully initialed Paragraph 118. *This is some kind of really sick, twisted experiment to find out how much I can take before I crack!*

But even really bad things come to an end eventually, and just before the clock on the wall registered 11:30, I heard the so-called Mr. Smith ask if I had any final questions.

Shuddering, I said no. Whereupon the so-called Mr. Smith said, "Very well. Please sign your full name at the bottom of page 47, and return the contract to Mr. Jones." Relieved, I scribbled my signature on the line above my typewritten name and pushed the folder back across the table. As soon as the alleged Mr. Jones had picked it up and placed it back in his briefcase, Christine closed hers and handed it to him as well.

Having collected all of the binders, the alleged Mr. Jones smiled and pulled another document from the accordion file in his briefcase. Handing it to Christine across the table, he informed her that this was the affidavit of witness, and asked her to sign it. After reading it closely, Christine placed her signature at the bottom of the second page and returned it.

Seeming very pleased with himself, the so-called Mr. Smith smiled and congratulated me. I was now a member of the inner sanctum, one of the privileged few permitted access to the nation's most closely guarded secrets. Then he rather forcefully reminded me of the provisions spelled out in Paragraph 146. If I disclosed any aspect of this project without prior written authorization — even the mere fact of its existence — I would be charged with espionage, and prosecuted to the full extent of the law.

So unless I wanted to spend the rest of my life in a federal penitentiary, I should begin observing the operational security requirements outlined in paragraphs 128 through 136, effective immediately. And just to make sure I got the point, he glared at me for a full minute.

By now convinced that he was a complete creep, I assured him that I would. And when he finally took his beady eyes off of me, I looked at Christine. She smiled, and nodded. "Very well, gentlemen. As soon as Ms. McAllister's new office is complete and all of the security features have been installed, you can start delivering the raw data for the project."

The so-called Mr. Smith and the alleged Mr. Jones smiled and gave Christine the adult version of "yup yup yup." Then we all shook hands, and Christine unlocked the door for them.

After the door swung shut behind them, she commended me for my fortitude. Shaking my head in disbelief, I asked her where creeps like that came from. Dodging the question, she reminded me that I had been properly warned. So after conceding the point, I asked her if we were finished. After guzzling coffee for more than two and a half hours, I really needed to be excused.

Christine looked down at her watch. Pursing her lips, she paused for a moment and then told me that her schedule had been trashed. If I didn't have anything more pressing to do, she suggested that we take a ten-minute break and then meet back in her office. There was no way she was going to be able to keep our three o'clock appointment, so we might as well pick out the furniture, drapes and artwork for my new office now.

Excited, I nodded in agreement. Satisfied, Christine turned and flipped a red switch on the wall before heading out the door. The instant the switch fell home, the air was suddenly filled with the sound of a pneumatic hammer banging on concrete.

What the ...

Racing after her into the hall, I asked her what had just happened. The conference room had been dead silent a moment ago, but the instant she threw the switch, it had been filled with noise. As she turned to lock the door behind us, Christine smiled and said that she couldn't go into any detail. Suffice it to say that the Executive Conference Room and several other rooms on the Eighth Floor were equipped with electronic baffling devices to protect them against unauthorized snooping. "You could set off a bomb in there, and no one would ever hear it..."

"And vice versa, of course."

"You're kidding!" I said

Christine smiled and shook her head. "Not at all. It's one of the Agency's brighter ideas, and because the CSS sometimes works on classified projects, they were kind enough to share it with us." Then she grinned mischievously, and added: "Along with a few other interesting gadgets."

"Wow!" I wanted to ask her more about it, but I had run out of time. After promising to meet her back in her office, I hurriedly excused myself and made a mad dash for the ladies' room.

By the time I arrived at the Executive Offices, the sound of the pneumatic hammer had been replaced by the hand-held variety. Pausing at the threshold, I was stunned by the sudden changes that had been wrought. A footpath of plywood ran between the secretarial desks before suddenly changing course into Christine's office, and a barrier of heavy plastic sheets had been hung from the ceiling just beyond the couch and chairs that had stood along the far wall of the reception area. And of course, all of the furniture had been either covered in drop cloths or wrapped in protective padded blankets.

But the most amazing thing of all was the big paper hat Jennifer Two was wearing – which looked very much like the sort of paper hats that little boys make when they play pirates. Stopping in front of her desk, I complimented her on the new look.

Two looked up from her typing and scowled. "Very funny."

Puzzled, I asked her what was up. Turning in her chair to face me, she pointed up at the ceiling. Tilting my head, I could see half a dozen ceiling tiles were missing. "The workmen were running some wires up there, and they screwed up...

"Half the ceiling landed on my desk, and I've still got dust raining down all over me...

Still grimacing, she shook her head. "So lighten up with the hat thing. I don't want that stuff in my hair."

Looking around me, I could see that the air was filled with particles. And while the paper hat made a certain amount of sense, I couldn't resist teasing her some more. Grinning, I told her she'd look even better with an eye patch and a mustache.

But Two really wasn't in the mood. "Don't you have an elsewhere to be?"

Suitably chastised, I conceded the point. "I'm supposed to meet with Christine."

Two lifted the sheet of folded paper off the top of her coffee cup, and after taking a sip, she pointed at Christine's open door. "So go."

Then she turned around again, and went back to her typing.

With all the banging going on in the background, knocking would have been a waste of time. So I stopped in Christine's doorway instead, and waited till she noticed me.

From that vantage point, I could see that she was talking to one of the workers. Since he was dressed a bit nicer than most of the others and was holding a set of plans, I assumed he was the foreman. And while I couldn't hear what they were saying over the racket that was coming from my new office, I could tell from the expression on Christine's face that she wasn't pleased. But after a minute or two, they seemed to reach some sort of agreement, and after nodding rather emphatically, the foreman returned to the construction area.

Shaking her head, Christine turned in my direction. "There you are!"

Waving me forward, she turned to her desk – which was the only piece of furniture that hadn't been entirely covered with the protective blankets – and picked up a set of heavy binders. Clutching them to her chest, she told me that we would have to use Alex's office. He was at the White House briefing the Chief of Staff on his talks with the Japanese – negotiations, really – and he wouldn't be back for another couple of hours.

Intrigued, I peppered Christine with questions as we crossed the reception area. "What was he doing in Japan?"

Stopping just short of the double doors that lead into Alex's office, Christine informed me that President Reagan had sent Alex to Japan as his personal emissary. The Japanese automakers had been giving Detroit a real pasting for the past couple of years, and there was strong sentiment on Capitol Hill to impose harsh new tariffs on Japanese cars. But since the President was opposed to restrictive tariffs as a matter of principle, he had asked Alex to try to persuade them to accept voluntary quotas.

Almost breathless, I asked her if it had worked. Since trade negotiations are right up my alley, I was intrigued.

As Christine handed me the binders so that she could unlock the doors, a conspiratorial grin crept across her face. "That man could talk a snake out of its skin."

Shaking her head, she gave me a wry smile. "I don't know how he did it, but the Japanese agreed to cut their exports to the U.S. by 30 per cent for the next two years...

"And that pretty much clinches the election for President Reagan. Since the autoworkers in Detroit are already leaning in his direction, this agreement pretty much guarantees their support. And with Michigan in his pocket, Senator Mondale doesn't stand a chance...

"No possible combination of electoral votes will give him a majority in the electoral college."

Wow! I thought. "So Alex just wrapped up the election?"

Pushing the door open, Christine grinned again. "That's the ole de Vris charm for ya."

Then almost absent mindedly, she said he had inherited it from his father.

"You knew his dad?"

After turning on the lights and closing the doors, Christine said she'd met him during her freshman year at Georgetown.

"Really? What was he like?"

Christine rolled her eyes and looked skyward. "Let's just say it was a really good thing his wife was there…

"Because otherwise, I might have thrown myself at him."

Then after making a sexy growl, she thrust her arms down to her sides and marched over to the couch with her face and eyes fixed on the heavens.

Snickering, I scurried after her. "So he was really handsome, huh?"

Christine didn't answer until she had sat down on the leather-bound couch that ran along the southern flank of Alex's coffee table. *"Ohhhhhh, yeah!"* she said.

And after instructing me to lay the binders out on the table, she gave me a knowing look. "Alex looks just like his father, so just wait till he turns fifty…

"Hearts are going to be breaking all over town."

Fascinated – and by now grinning from ear to ear – I was about to demand details when the air hammer started up again. To my complete dismay, the pounding noise pulled Christine back into the present. Exasperated, she shook her head. "God, what a mess!"

With the moment broken, I was forced to bow to the inevitable. Knowing that I wasn't going to be able to pry any more of the really good stuff out of her, I leaned back on the couch. Having forgotten all about what Tom Andrews had told me, I asked Christine what was going on. "I thought they just had to move out all the boxes, and do a little finish work…

"Replace the carpet and paint the walls and stuff."

Still leaning back in the couch, Christine wished that had been the case. "But after looking over the logistics, the Agency decided that it would be better to store the new project data here on premises than to cart it back and forth. So they insisted that we install a vault to keep it in…

"And since the vault has to have all sorts of electronic stuff attached to it, that meant new wiring, some new fiber optic cables and – for some reason – some new duct work as well."

Leaning forward to open the top binder, she said that she was nonetheless determined to look on the bright side. She and Alex were getting cable TV out of the deal, so they'd be able to monitor the news as it happened.

"Yeah? Are you gonna get Home Box Office too?"

Christine chuckled, and raised a finger to her lips. "Alex doesn't know about that yet."

After making me promise I wouldn't rat on her, Christine got down to business. "OK, the good news is you are going to get new carpeting. The bad news is that Alex wants it to be the same color as all the rest…

"So I thought you might want to emulate my practice, and put some Oriental rugs down over it."

Suddenly cheerful, I said, "Oh yeah!"

Christine nodded, and began flipping through the glossy pages. "These rugs are all in stock and available, so let's pick some out for you…

"You'll need an 8x10 to center the room, and a couple of 5x8s on either side to provide some balance…

"Now since the walls will be painted off-white, you'll want rugs that contrast. But bear in mind that you are getting new furniture, drapes and artwork, so it will all have to work together."

Nodding, I began studying the photos of the Oriental rugs as Christine laid the other four binders on the table. The first held paint color samples, and after thumbing through it for a minute, she opened it to the right page. "OK, here's your off-white wall color." After propping it open so I could compare the paint to the rugs, she opened the third. "This one has drapes and liners, and the others have furniture and art work, respectively."

As I sat there looking through the binders, it began to seem a lot like Christmas. Because even though I knew all the stuff we were going to order wasn't really for me, I was going to get to use it for a good long time. And everything was really, really expensive. The cheapest 8x10 rug listed at $5000, and even the prints – which were reproductions, rather than original paintings – started at $450 apiece. And that didn't even include the frames, or the recommended non-glare glass!

But the really fun part was watching Christine. She knew decorating as well as she did fashion, and she had an amazing ability to put things together. The final result was a gorgeous mix-and-match that blended reproductions of French Empire furniture and drapes with impressionist paintings and Dynastic rugs. By the time we had it all worked out on the table, I was dying to move in. But that, unfortunately, was going to take another week.

Closing the last binder, Christine smiled and asked me if I was happy with our choices. That was a big mistake, because I could have spent the next six months telling her how much I loved them. And if Linda hadn't stuck her head in the door to tell Christine that Senator Helms was on line three, I probably would have. Excusing herself, Christine walked over to Alex's desk and hoisted herself up upon it. After crossing her left leg over her right and turning towards the window, she picked up the handset and greeted the senator.

By that time the air hammer had stopped as suddenly as it had begun, and in the comparative silence I could overhear her talking to the senator about the B-1 bomber program. Since they were speaking 'Washingtonese' – which I still hadn't completely mastered – I couldn't follow the conversation exactly, but it had something to do with a defense appropriations bill bottled up in committee. Senator Helms apparently wanted the CSS to help him shake it loose.

As interesting as that was, I was beginning to feel a bit uncomfortable about eavesdropping on such an important conversation. So I was wondering if I shouldn't excuse myself, when Christine suddenly turned around and gestured for a pen.

After a hurried search I found a BIC ballpoint at the bottom of my purse, and I got up to hand it to her. But as she leaned backwards to take it from my outstretched hand, she accidentally knocked over a framed picture that had been sitting near the edge of the desk.

I caught it just before it hit the floor. And after standing back up to hand Christine the pen, I looked down to inspect it. Nestled beneath the glass was a photograph of a young girl dressed in a cheerleading outfit. She was fifteen or perhaps sixteen, with a beautiful smile, huge milk-chocolaty eyes, and light brown hair cascading to her waist. She was breathtaking.

Captivated, I looked on her in amazement. *She's so beautiful...*

A dim sense of recognition took hold as I studied the photograph before me. And so as Christine hung up the phone and turned back to me, a huge, excited smile spread across my face. "I didn't know Alex had a daughter!"

Clearly uncomfortable, Christine looked down at the picture and then back up at me. "He doesn't," she said.

CHAPTER EIGHTEEN

After jotting something or another down on Alex's calendar, Christine took the photograph from my hands and carefully replaced it on Alex's desk before explaining it had been taken five or six years before. The girl was 20 or 21 by now, but Alex kept the photo on his desk for sentimental reasons.

Anguished, I asked if she was Alex's girlfriend. After staring at me for a long moment, Christine looked away. In a very soft voice, she told me that the girl was "a close family friend."

That hadn't been much of an answer, and a part of me wanted to ask her more. But since another part of me didn't want to know the answer, I dropped my eyes and looked at the floor instead. My stomach had become queasy and my knees weak, and for a brief moment I thought they might give way.

The touch of Christine's hand beneath my chin caused me to stiffen, and as she lifted my face to her eyes, she seemed both stern and sympathetic. "Alicia, you have to understand that Alex and I have been friends for many years...

"Our friendship is based upon mutual respect, and that includes a respect for one another's private lives...

"Although you probably haven't been around him enough to realize this, the real Alex is somewhat different from his public persona. He can be a bit shy at times, and he's intensely private. He rarely shares his feelings with others, or even with his close friends, and as frustrating as that may be, I've learned not to pry."

Lowering her hand from my face, she softly – but emphatically – suggested that I do the same.

Not knowing what to say, I looked back down at the carpet. "Yes, Ma'am."

After finally being excused, I left Alex's office in a daze. Oblivious to the dust and the debris and the bone-rattling sound of the jackhammer, I wandered down the hallway to the Library. Pushing open the doors, I walked inside and made my way deep into the stacks until I came upon a study carrel and sat down.

I think that I cried a lot, but I really can't remember. Looking back on it, it almost seems as though I had stumbled into a Salvador Dali painting because everything seemed so jumbled and out of place. All I really remember is sitting slumped in the chair, staring mindlessly at the polished writing surface before me.

An hour or so after the construction noise subsided, I noticed the evening shadows creeping through the windows, and I realized that I should collect the dogs and go home. I didn't know what time it was and I didn't care, so I didn't bother to check my watch. But close of business had come and gone, and it was time for me to go as well. So I gathered up my purse, and walked numbly into the darkened hall.

The double doors to the Executive Offices were still open, and from where I stood, I could see the lights were still on. But everyone had long since departed, and if it weren't for the sound of a vacuum cleaner far off in the distance, I would have thought that the building was entirely deserted.

During the course of the summer I had been alone in the CSS on many an occasion, and often late at night. Since there was always a security guard or two patrolling the halls, I had never felt uneasy about staying late or coming in on weekends. But as I pushed open the door and started down the stairs to the Seventh Floor, it began to feel really creepy. Even though I knew there were other people there, it didn't feel like it – and that made me really uncomfortable. So when I finally emerged onto the Seventh Floor, I was relieved to find Big Minh and Lady Godiva curled up outside my office door.

It was almost 8:30 by the time we got home. Having forgotten to feed the dogs at lunchtime, I apologized and gave them an extra can of Alpo each. Then I threw a bag of popcorn in the microwave for myself. After it finished popping, I pulled a can of Diet Pepsi out of the fridge and sat down on the couch. I ate the popcorn mechanically, as I stared at the darkened TV.

Thinking that I was a complete idiot, I began to berate myself. *He's just a really nice guy, and you blew it all out of proportion...*

Not a word, not even the slightest gesture...

What the heck were you thinking???

Bitterly angry, another part of me insisted that wasn't true. *There's something there, I can feel it...*

Why else would he have bailed me out at the bus station? Put me up in the suite? Got me the interview with Dr. MacLaughlin? Or given me all ten million of his phone numbers when he went to Europe?

And why did he want me to keep the dogs and the Vette?

And what about Nguyen? Didn't he say Alex was fond of me?

And how come he didn't fire me for blowing up at him? *I suppose he's just using me for sex, right?*

My sarcasm may have stilled the voice within, but it left me feeling even worse than before. Angry, hurt, and humiliated I wadded up the popcorn bag and hurled it savagely towards the kitchen sink. I missed it by a country mile, but by that point I didn't care. Sinking back on the couch, I began to cry.

Lost in my own pain, I didn't notice that Lady Godiva had crawled up on the couch. In an unmistakable effort to comfort me, she pressed her head against my shoulder and softly rubbed it up and down. Smiling through my tears, I wrapped my arms around her and gave her a big hug. Still holding her close, I told her what had happened that day, and how foolish I felt.

She seemed to understand, because when I finally finished she nuzzled my face before pulling back just enough to look deep into my eyes. Then she lay down, and placed her head in my lap.

It was such a nice gesture that I began crying again. "Guess you've been there, huh?"

After stroking her head for a few minutes, I finally decided we should do something. "Let me get your brush, and I'll make you all pretty." Lifting up her head ever so gently, I slipped out from underneath her and made my way over to the box Two had prepared for me. I found her brush lying next to a couple of chew toys, beneath a box of extra-large milk bones. Walking back to the couch, I sat down beside her and began brushing her coat.

I had never had a dog, so I wasn't quite sure how to go about it. But after a few minutes I'd pretty much figured it out. It wasn't all that different from brushing my own hair, except there was a lot more of it and I had to be really careful with her tail.

After about ten minutes of gentle stroking, her coat looked all shiny and bright. Satisfied, I led her over to the full-length mirror Julia had hung on the wall. Kneeling down beside her, I asked her what she thought.

Lady Godiva seemed very pleased, but for some reason I wasn't. After a long puzzling moment, I finally realized that something was missing. Standing up, I told her to come with me. "I'll show you how to accessorize."

Washington has a leash law, and you're not supposed to take dogs out on the street without one. But Big Minh and Lady Godiva were so well trained that I never bothered. Grabbing my keys off the coffee table, I picked up my purse and herded them both out the door.

The District of Columbia isn't the safest place at night, especially for a young woman. But with a gigantic dog padding along on either side, I wasn't concerned. There weren't many people on the sidewalk at that late hour, and the few we encountered gave us an extra wide berth. Still chuckling after an especially scruffy-looking character crossed the street to avoid us, I patted them both on the head and told them to wait when we reached the People's Drug on Dupont Circle. Then I ducked in the door and headed for the aisle that had the gift cards and wrapping paper.

Five minutes later, I re-emerged with three rolls of two-inch ribbon and a pint of triple thick chocolate fudge ice cream. The ribbon was for Lady Godiva; the ice cream for myself. Considering what I'd been through that day, I figured I deserved some high-calorie comfort.

Back at the apartment, I put the ice cream on the counter to thaw out and began searching for a pair of scissors. After finally finding one in the bottom of Julia's dresser, I cut off a 3-foot piece of pink satin and led Lady Godiva back to the mirror. After telling her to sit, I wrapped it around her neck and tied it into a neat bow. Then I stood up and stepped out of the way, so she could take a look.

It seemed that Lady Godiva had never had a bow before, because she seemed puzzled when she looked in the mirror. After padding a few steps closer for a better look, she turned right and then left so she could see herself in profile. Suddenly very pleased, she trotted across the room to show it to Big Minh. After walking back and forth for him a couple of times she trotted back to me, wagging her tail all the way.

Reaching down, I patted her on the head. "It's amazing what a touch of color can do for a girl," I said. *Or a pint of ice cream, as the case may be...*

But no matter how many calories it may have, ice cream is only a temporary fix – so when I woke up the next morning, I felt almost as bad as I had the day before. Just the idea of walking back into the CSS filled me with dread.

But there wasn't much I could do about it. There was no way I could find a better paying job without a lot more experience, and I wasn't sure I'd want to even if I could. The CSS was a fascinating place to work, even if I factored Alex out of the equation – and of course, I had made an awful lot of friends there and I didn't want to lose them. All things considered, quitting wasn't much of an option.

Guess I'll just have to grin and bear it...

Deeply depressed by the thought, I wasted an extra half-hour getting dressed and putting on my makeup. By the time I finally got going, traffic was backed up from one end of town to the other so I was fifteen minutes late when I finally made it to the

Econ shop. Lucky for me, Jennifer and Dr. MacLaughlin were both out at Langley, and according to the note she had posted on the department door they probably wouldn't be back until well after close of business.

Dr. MacLaughlin didn't usually take Jennifer with him when he went to the Agency's headquarters. But as a former CIA officer, he was required by law to submit all his books and articles to the Agency for advance clearance – and since Jennifer was more or less in charge of all CSS publications, she served as the Center's unofficial liaison for published materials.

Although Jennifer was technically just a secretary, during the year and a half she'd been working for Dr. MacLaughlin she had developed a really good working relationship with the peer-review committees at all five of the major universities in DC, and the local printers, binders, and proofreaders as well. Perhaps more importantly, the heads of the major publishing houses all thought she walked on water; whenever something came up regarding a CSS-sponsored book, they always insisted on talking to her.

Given her uncanny ability to turn drafts into finished publications, Christine had wanted to put Jennifer in charge of publications production. But when she had broached the idea, Jennifer had flatly refused. Dr. MacLaughlin might be a complete flake at times, but she really loved working for him. And in any event, someone had to look after him. Genius or not, the man was so absent-minded that he had to wear loafers because he couldn't remember to tie his shoelaces.

Conceding the point, Christine had been forced to accept a reasoned compromise: Jennifer would remain as Dr. MacLaughlin's secretary, provided that she took care of the publications process as well. That had made her the *de facto* chief-of-publications, which is why she made a whole lot more than I did.

When I had first found out what the CSS was paying Jennifer, I couldn't believe it. But after seeing the first draft of Dr. MacLaughlin's latest book, I decided she deserved every penny. After finishing the hand-written draft, Dr. MacLaughlin had dumped 1800 indecipherable pages on her desk, most of which he had written on legal pads in his notoriously illegible scrawl. The rest of it had been put on whatever scraps of paper that had been handy at the time, including the backs of discarded envelopes and napkins from McDonald's. Making matters worse, Dr. MacLaughlin had apparently drawn the bulk of the charts and graphs on the back of old Christmas wrapping paper. But by the time Jennifer had handed it to me, it was 345 neatly typed and formatted pages. And so far at least, I hadn't found a single typographical error.

But as impressive as all of that may have been, it didn't help my caffeine cravings. And since I didn't have a key to the department office, that meant I was going to have to bum my morning coffee from another department. Normally I would have gone upstairs to the Eighth Floor, but since I wanted to avoid Alex, I went down to Reception on the Sixth. I knew I would have to face him eventually but I hoped and prayed it wouldn't be anytime soon. I had a lot of things to sort out, and I knew it was going to take some time.

After climbing back up the stairs to the Econ shop, I unlocked my office and turned on the lights. Putting my coffee down on the edge of my desk, I set my briefcase down along its side and began digging through my purse for my red felt-tipped pen. After pulling off the top and sticking it on the other end, I sat down and flipped open the binder that held Dr. MacLaughlin's draft. I had completed a mere 20 pages so far, and since he wanted it done by close of business Friday, I was really going to have to focus.

But unfortunately, that was a lot easier said than done.

Dr. MacLaughlin was a brilliant economist, and a skilled writer as well. But even though I was fascinated by the topic – which was a radical reconsideration of national security economics – I had a hard time concentrating. Despite my best efforts, my mind kept wandering. When I wasn't berating myself for being a fool, I was cursing the girl in the photo or damning Alex for leading me on. Three hours and a mere 25 pages later, I banged my head on the desk in disgust.

Outraged by the inequity, I cursed the Fates for what they had done. *It's not fair,* I protested. *No one should be that beautiful...*

It ought to be against the law, I thought. *And as for Mr. Chairman of the Board Alexander M. de Vris...*

Well, he's just a complete jerk, and he doesn't deserve me anyway!

Unable to concentrate for more than a few minutes at a time, I spent the rest of the afternoon alternating between Dr. MacLaughlin's manuscript and raging silently against the Heavens. I was bitterly angry, but I didn't know who to take it out on. Sometimes I blamed the whole thing on myself. But for the most part I blamed it on Alex or "that girl," as I had come to call her. Needless to say, I didn't get much done.

Thinking that things couldn't possibly get any worse, I was in a slightly better mood when I arrived at work the next day. But the sight of Jennifer dragging a huge box into my office made me stop, and wonder. "What the heck is that?"

Since the box was almost as tall as she was, Jennifer had tilted it over at an angle so she could drag it across the carpet. After pushing it back into an upright position and rotating it around, she peered around the side and informed me that it was my new computer. "Central Processing Unit, Monitor, and a brand-new laser printer all in one box."

"Really?" I was surprised, because Christine hadn't said anything about a computer.

Pushing herself through the tiny crevice left between the box and the edge of my desk, Jennifer said "Really."

"Christine's ordered 'desktops' for everyone, but they won't be delivered for another week or two and this one is different anyway." Having scrunched through the opening, she leaned back against my desk and explained that the CIA had sent it over. "It has all kinds of special software, so you can crunch numbers and draw charts and graphs and stuff."

That was pretty cool, and under almost any other circumstances I would have been excited. Because let's face it – shiny new toys are fun, right?

But at that particular moment, I just wasn't in the mood. All I could think about was how much I had to get done before I moved up to the Eighth Floor. And how to handle it when I did...

Seeing the dispirited look on my face, Jennifer asked me what was wrong. "Somebody swipe your Cheerios?"

After giving her a nasty look I told her "nothing," but Jennifer wouldn't let it go. After pushing past me to see if anyone was in the hall, she turned back. With a look of genuine concern, she told me to stop blowing smoke. Something was really bothering me, she said, and she wanted to know what it was.

Having tried and failed to brush it off, there wasn't much I could do. Jennifer could be relentless about that sort of thing, and aside from Julia, she was the best friend I had in Washington. So after telling her to close the door, I told her about how Christine had accidentally knocked the photograph off Alex's desk, and how I'd caught it, and how stupid I was for having thought it was his daughter, and what Christine had said about how she was a "close family friend." Shaking my head in disbelief, I told her that I felt like a complete fool.

Jennifer scrunched up her nose, and looked at me as if I were. "You mean that picture of Bunni?"

Embarrassed, I shrugged and told her that I didn't know. "The girl in the cheerleading outfit."

Jennifer rolled her eyes and shook her head. "Not to worry, girlfriend. That girl is dumb as a post...

"Definitely not the sort that Alex would ever be interested in."

After glancing at the door, I asked her how she knew that. Jennifer raised a finger to her lips. Then after poking her head out into the hallway and looking left and right, she pushed the door shut again and spoke in a hushed whisper. "Listen," she said, "this is serious business, so you have to promise you won't ever tell anyone I told you this."

Perplexed, I whispered back. "What?"

Jennifer gave me an irritated look, and explained Christine went ballistic when anyone talked about Alex's personal life. "He's really important, and a lot of people resent that," she whispered. "They say he's a spoiled rich kid and all that stuff, but Dr. MacLaughlin told me the real issue is his influence on strategic policy...

"There's something really big going on behind the scenes at the White House, and they think Alex is pulling the strings."

By that time, my mouth had dropped open and I could feel my eyes bulging. "Like what?" I demanded.

Jennifer glared at me, and whispered for me to be quiet. "It's got something to do with the Soviets, but Dr. MacLaughlin won't tell me what it is...

"But he said a lot of really powerful people are opposed to it, and they think they'll be able to derail the whole thing if they can get rid of Alex...

"Anyway, Dr. MacLaughlin said it's only a matter of time before they move against him. He thinks they'll try to ensnare Alex in some sort of scandal, and Christine is probably thinking the same thing...

"And trust me on this," she said. "When it comes to Alex, she's like a mother hen...

"She's like super-protective – and if she finds out I'm telling you any of this, I'm gonna be in deep trouble. Understand?"

Knitting my eyebrows together, I nodded quickly. "I promise. I'll never tell anyone, ever."

Jennifer looked at me sternly, and nodded. "OK, here's the thing. Bunni is a flight attendant for an airline, and she turns up every couple of months or so looking for 'Uncle Alex'...

"He puts her up in the suite at the hotel, and he takes her out to lunch or dinner but that's all there is to it."

The suite? He puts her up in MY suite???

Suddenly livid, I asked her how she knew that.

"Because Two takes his calls and has his appointment book, and she told me."

"Yeah, right." I said. "You mean to tell me that 'Uncle Alex' puts her up in the most expensive hotel in Washington and takes her out for lunch and dinner and nothing is going on???"

Angry and disgusted, I told Jennifer to give me a break.

Jennifer glared at me. "No," she said in a definitive whisper. "Nothing, nada."

"Trust me, that girl's a moron and Alex likes his women smart."

Deeply suspicious, I asked her how she knew that.

Jennifer rolled her eyes and shook her head. "I already told you. Two takes his calls and makes his appointments. She knows where he is and who he's with every minute of the day...

"And she knows who he's seeing and who he's not."

That part seemed to make sense, so I leaned back against the wall to mull it over. "So is Alex dating Two?"

Jennifer snickered. "Only in her dreams, girlfriend."

Puzzled, I asked Jennifer what she meant.

Jennifer looked at me like I was a complete moron again. "What do you think it means? Two sits outside his office every day routing his calls, taking his messages, typing his letters and handling his appointments...

"You think that's just a job for her?"

Knitting my eyes together, I grimaced and looked down at the floor. "I guess not."

Jennifer nodded emphatically. "Don't be stupid, girl. You're all worried about Bunni when you should be worried about Two."

Suddenly incredulous, Jennifer demanded to know if I was blind. "Haven't you noticed the way that girl acts when Alex is around?"

Feeling incredibly foolish, I laid my head back against the wall and stared at the ceiling. Finally, I looked back at Jennifer and confessed to terminal stupidity. "So Two's after Alex?"

Jennifer tilted her head over, and stared at me. *"Well, duh,"* she whispered. "Just check out what she's wearing when he's in the office."

Then she gave me a knowing look. "If it wasn't for Christine, she'd come to work naked."

Outraged by her unfair advantage, I shook my head in disgust. "OK, so Two's a big slut...

"But I still don't understand why Alex is hanging out with some mentally deficient flight attendant."

Jennifer knitted her eyebrows together and confessed she didn't know. "But I'll find out when she gets back."

"When who gets back?"

Jennifer nodded as she reached for the doorknob. "When Two gets back. She sprained her ankle roller-blading last night…

"It swelled up so bad that her roommate had to take her to the emergency room at Georgetown Hospital, and the doctors thought it was broken."

Opening the door, Jennifer told me that it wasn't, but they'd kept her overnight anyway. "The hospital let her go this morning, but she has to stay home until the swelling goes down."

Turning back to me, Jennifer explained that Two would probably be back in the office by Friday and promised to get the whole story for me then. But in the meantime, I'd better get my computer out of the box and up on my desk. It was only a matter of time, she said, before Christine stopped in to check up on me. Then she leaned back into my office and gave me a really stern look. "And don't tell anybody what I told you – understand?"

Nodding, I thanked her and promised not to breathe a word. Then I turned back to the box, and started prying at the half-inch thick cardboard packing.

It took two hours and Dr. MacLaughlin's help to get the darned thing out of the box. But I had it set up and running before Jennifer came back to ask me if I wanted to order lunch from the hotel. Glancing up from the complex software documentation, I told her to order me my usual cheeseburger and fries. Then I turned back to the part that explained how to set up a heuristic exercise that would permit me to make long-range projections with incomplete data.

I was familiar with computers and computer programming because that had been a requirement for graduation. But desktop computers were brand new at the time, and the idea of entering data directly into the machine was an entirely novel concept – back at Township College, we'd entered our input data onto punch cards and then fed them into the machine. The new keyboard entry system was a lot simpler, but I was worried about accuracy. When you made a mistake with punch cards, the IBM 360 would have a hissy fit. But as far as I could tell, this new one didn't care what you entered. Which concerned me, because I didn't want to be the first person at the CSS to blow up a computer…

As it turned out, Christine didn't show up until the next morning. I'd worked late and made a lot of progress on Dr. MacLaughlin's manuscript, and come in early so I could get back to the computer. By the time she walked in, I had just completed a practice run with the accounting program. After gesturing for her to come look at the monitor, I showed her how I had calculated the projected national debt for the next thirty years – rounded upward, to the nearest tenth of a cent. Of course, given the number of variables involved, I'd been forced to make a bunch of assumptions regarding fiscal and monetary policy across time. But just as I was explaining how I had arrived at them, Christine suddenly remembered an urgent appointment. Which was really unfortunate, because that kind of number crunching is the most fun you can have with your clothes on.

OK, so not everyone likes a good time...

Or maybe I'm a little bit weird. But at least it gave me something else to think about, because I was still obsessing about Alex and the girl in the picture.

It's not that I didn't believe Jennifer. But somehow, the whole thing about Two just didn't make sense to me. Two was gorgeous, and next to Christine she had the world's greatest figure. She was bright, too – but even so, I just couldn't see her with Alex. Bunni, however, was a very different story. I knew there was something there, because I could feel it.

Angry and disgusted, I slammed my hand down on my desk. *Bunni??? What kind of name is that?*

Shaking my head in anger and disbelief, I wondered why her parents didn't just name her "Fluffy"? Or maybe "Cottontail?"

Now that's a good one, I thought. And it was – until a rather unfortunate anatomical comparison popped out of the darkened recesses of my mind.

Oh good God, I thought. *I have got to go on a diet!*

Horrified by the intruding imagery, I made a promise to start losing weight. Then I made a mental note to scratch Bunni's eyes out, the very first chance I got.

Of course, I didn't really mean that. Because when I finally did meet her, a gruesome death seemed much more appropriate.

I was working on the last chapter of Dr. MacLaughlin's manuscript after lunch on Friday, when Linda buzzed me and told me that Christine wanted to see me in her office. So after locking my door, I bounded up the steps to the Eighth Floor. But by the time I got there, she was on the phone with Senator Somebody-Or-Another, so I had to wait. After a quick calculation, I decided the Senator's phone call provided me a perfect opportunity to grab a Diet Pepsi. So I told Linda I was going to run down the hall to the lounge.

Had I been paying attention, I would have seen her as soon as I walked out of the Executive Offices. But at the time I was too busy rooting through the bottom of my purse to notice the girl in a flight attendant's uniform, pulling a little cart behind her with a suitcase strapped upon it. It was only after I had found the requisite quarters and snapped my purse shut that I looked back up and saw her.

She had stopped, directly in front of me. Smiling cheerfully, she tilted her head over and introduced herself. "Hi!" she said. "I'm Bunni." Then almost breathlessly, she asked if I had seen her "Uncle Alex."

I hated her the moment I laid eyes upon her. She was even more beautiful than the image in the picture, and she had the sort of figure that drove sensible men crazy. Which she deliberately accented, with her carefully tailored uniform.

She simply reeked of sensuality, and as she stood there waiting expectantly for my reply the thought of wrapping her brightly colored scarf around her neck passed briefly through my mind. But in the end, my better instincts prevailed. In a voice so cold that it dropped the hallway temperature a good 20 degrees, I told her that I hadn't. Then I brushed past her, and marched on down the hall.

My disdain didn't seem to bother her, because she called after me in an all-too cheerful voice. "Well, thank you anyway, Ma'am. I'm sure he's here somewhere."

Ma'am?

Convinced that was a deliberate insult, I was snarling when I entered the lounge. I shoved the two quarters in the soda machine's slot, and slammed the flat of my hand against the Diet Pepsi button. "Don't even *think* about messing with me today!"

Obviously intimidated, the machine released a can with unusual dispatch.

When I got back to the Executive Offices, Christine's door was closed and so was Alex's, and Bunni was nowhere to be seen. But Two had returned from somewhere or another, and after hobbling across the carpet she leaned her crutches against the edge of her desk and sat down. Apparently on the same wavelength, she looked over at me as I seated myself in the waiting area, and shook her head in disbelief. "A couple more brain cells," she said, "and that chick could outsmart an amoeba."

The words were still hanging in the air when Alex's door suddenly opened. Ashen-faced, Two turned back to her typewriter while I grabbed a magazine off the end table to cover my face. Trying desperately not to laugh at Two's *faux pas*, I eavesdropped on their conversation.

After asking Two for his plane tickets, Alex apologized to Bunni. The President wanted to see him right away, so he wouldn't be able to drive her to the airport. But his meeting at the White House wouldn't last more than fifteen or twenty minutes, so he'd still have plenty of time to catch his 2:15 flight. Then very seriously, he promised her that he would be there in time for the party.

I was peeking around the side of the magazine when Alex reached into his pocket and pulled out a wad of bills. After handing it to her, he told her to take a cab to the airport so she wouldn't be late for her flight back to Louisville – and to use the rest of the money for the dress she had put on layaway.

From that distance I couldn't see how much he'd given her, but it must have been a lot. Bunni's eyes bulged, and she squealed with delight. Then she threw her arms around his neck and kissed him on the cheek. "Oh, thank you, Uncle Alex! Thank you! Thank you! Thank you!"

With her face still fifteen shades of red, Two was hunched over her typewriter and I was pretty sure she was praying that Alex hadn't heard what she'd said about Bunni. Thinking that Two was a goner if he had, I didn't even notice Christine. When I finally glimpsed her out of the corner of my eye, my heart almost leapt through my throat.

Oh, my God, I thought. *I am soooo busted...*

After forcing me to suffer through a good 30 seconds of her most severe Adult Authority Figure Stare, Christine curtly apologized. My new office would be ready by Monday morning, and she had wanted to talk to me about it, but something had come up. After another wilting stare, she told me to report to her first thing Monday, and then turned on her heel. Mortified, I tossed the magazine down on the end table and scurried out of the office while Alex's back was still turned to me.

Idiot!

Hoping to find refuge in my office, I made a mad dash for the stairs. But Fortune had deserted me, because Dr. MacLaughlin was striding up the hallway when I emerged from the stairwell onto the Seventh Floor. "There you are, Lass! Have you finished with my manuscript?"

Taken aback, I began to stammer. "Well, uh, no, Sir," I said. "But I promise I'll have it done by close of business."

Dr. MacLaughlin smiled amiably as he walked past me. "Very well. I'll be down the hall in Dr. Findley's office if anyone needs me."

After replying with a crisp "Yes, Sir" I ducked into the department office. In my haste to escape from the Executive Office, I'd forgotten my Diet Pepsi, and I was hoping that Jennifer would have an extra in the little bar refrigerator underneath the table that supported the coffee pot. But finding out if she'd had a chance to talk to Two at lunch was even more pressing. After my encounter with Little Miss Perfect, I was more desperate than ever for details.

Unfortunately for me, neither Jennifer nor the Diet Pepsi were there. Frustrated, I taped a note to her computer monitor saying I wanted to see her the moment she got back.

Back in my office, I tried to finish up Dr. MacLaughlin's manuscript. But even though I had only a few more pages to go, I just couldn't focus – because no matter how hard I tried to concentrate, my mind kept whipsawing back and forth between Bunni and Alex.

So it's 'Uncle Alex,' huh? And I suppose that makes her his 'niece'...

Uh-huh, sure. I thought. *I guess that's what he tells them at the hotel when she checks into my suite!*

Furious, I slammed my fist down on the desk. Conveniently ignoring the fact that I couldn't possibly be more than a year older than Bunni, I damned him for robbing the cradle. *He should be ashamed of himself,* I thought bitterly. *She's just a baby!*

Flushed with rage, I seized my red felt-tipped pen and hurled it through the doorway. It had ricocheted off the far wall and was cartwheeling across the floor when Jennifer stuck her head in the door. Looking puzzled and confused, she asked me what that was all about.

Growling, I demanded to know where she'd been.

Taken aback by my tone, Jennifer gave me a nasty look before explaining that she had gone up to the Eighth Floor to see Linda, after straightening out a problem with Adm. Taylor's latest monograph in the print shop. Glancing over her shoulder, she gave me an intense look and told me that I wouldn't believe what had happened up there.

Uh-oh, I thought. "Did it have anything to do with Bunni?"

After giving a furtive look over her shoulder again, Jennifer put her finger to her lips to quiet me. "Let's go up on the roof."

Suddenly worried, I grabbed my purse and followed her out into the hallway. As I was locking my office door, I very quietly asked her what had happened. Jennifer shook her head and raised her finger to her lips again. "Come on," she said.

By the time we reached the rooftop patio, I was really worried. "So what happened," I asked again. But Jennifer didn't say anything. She grabbed my wrist instead, and pulled me through the chairs and tables to the railing at the far edge.

The rooftop was a popular place to eat lunch when the weather was nice, but during the summer it was unbearably hot. Since I had started at the CSS at the beginning of a heat wave, I hadn't been up there before and the view surprised me. Although it wasn't all that much different from the pool at the hotel next door, from our perspective on the far west edge you could see the planes taking off from National Airport.

But since I had far more urgent things on my mind, I turned back to Jennifer. "So what happened?"

After glancing over her shoulder again to make sure we were alone, she told me. "Christine heard Two make some crack about Bunni being an amoeba or something, and she went postal...

"She had a telephone conference call, but as soon as she finished she called Two into her office and chewed her butt up one side and down the other."

Oh my God, I thought. "Did she get fired?"

Jennifer looked over her shoulder again, then shook her head. "No, but Christine said if she ever heard anyone say anything like that again she'd can them on the spot...

"Then she told Two she didn't want to see her face until Monday, and told her to get the hell out of the office!"

Harsh, I thought. *Two's gonna spend the next century living that down...*

Suddenly worried, I asked Jennifer if Christine had said anything about me. Puzzled, she said no. "But you're in luck because I had lunch with Two before all this happened, so I got the story on Bunni."

Relieved, I asked Jennifer what she had said.

Shrugging dismissively, she told me there was nothing to it. "Bunni's dad was Alex's platoon sergeant during his first tour in Vietnam..."

Puzzled, I interrupted. "Platoon sergeant? What's that?"

Looking slightly confused, Jennifer knitted her eyebrows together. "I'm not sure, but I think he was like Alex's main man...

"His second in command or something. Anyway, they became really good friends and they stayed in touch afterwards....

"To make a long story short – after a couple of weeks back in the States, the Marine Corps sent Bunni's dad to San Diego and Alex went back Vietnam. Then Bunni's dad was diagnosed with leukemia, and they gave him only a few months to live. So before he died, he wrote Alex and asked him to look after Bunni and her mom..."

A quick calculation told me that she must have been about the same age as I was when my father died. *Oh God*, I thought. *That poor girl!*

"Well, you know Alex. He wrote back and promised he'd take care of them, and he did. After the poor guy died, Bunni and her mom moved back home to Louisville, and Alex helped them buy a house...."

"And he was going to put Bunni through college, but she wanted to be a stewardess. So Alex pulled a few strings instead, and got her on with the airline...

"Anyway, she was dating this guy at West Point, and after he graduated last May, he proposed to her. But she won't accept until Alex meets him, and give her his blessing...

"So that's why Alex is on his way to Louisville."

More ashamed and embarrassed than I had ever been in my entire life, I had to look away. I knew what it was like to lose a father, and knowing that Bunni had endured the same agony wrenched my heart.

That poor girl, I thought. *How could I have been so cruel?*

Staring out across the river, I could only shake my head and wonder as tears began to well in my eyes.

I stood there for a minute or so, until Jennifer finally broke the silence by asking me what time it was. Glancing down at my watch, I told her. "Two-fifteen."

Jennifer pointed across the river. "Well, hey! That must be Alex's plane."

Lost in my own thoughts, I hadn't noticed the passenger jet as it took off from the airport. It was only a hundred feet or so off the ground when I saw it, and as I watched the plane struggle for altitude, something deep within warned me that it wouldn't make it. As my eyes fixed upon the aircraft, it shuddered and for a moment it seemed to hang motionless in the air.

Horrified, I watched as it faltered and then fell, just beyond the Fourteenth Street Bridge.

CHAPTER NINETEEN

Transfixed by shock and horror, I seized the railing in a death grip as the sound of the impact rolled across the Potomac. It wasn't until the cloud of black, oily soot began to rise above the tree line moments later that I was able to push myself away from the rail, and bolt for the stairs.

Mindless of my three-inch heels I tore down the stairwell and crashed through the fire door onto the Eighth Floor, barely avoiding a collision with Admiral Thomas and General McGreggor – who were pounding down the hallway, with Big Minh and Lady Godiva in hot pursuit.

Since most of the CSS staff had radios in their offices, they heard about the crash almost immediately. Moments after it occurred, the local radio stations interrupted their scheduled programming to announce the disaster, and within a matter of seconds CSS personnel were pouring out of their offices and racing towards Christine's. Apparently, I wasn't the only one who had heard about her cable TV.

Hard on the heels of Admiral Thomas and General McGreggor, I burst through the double doors of her office to find her standing in front of the screen. The normally vibrant color had drained from her cheeks, and her skin had turned ashen.

Ignoring the clamor behind me, I brushed past the dogs and squeezed between the General and the Admiral to stand next to her. That was fortunate, because when the news anchor cut to the site of the crash, my knees went weak. Without thinking, I seized hold of her arm.

A local Washington station had a film crew on the Virginia side of the river that day, reporting on the ongoing efforts to clean up the Potomac's polluted waters. By chance, the cameraman had seen Alex's aircraft falter and he'd turned his camera on it as it fell upon the river's bank. Within a matter of seconds, they were broadcasting live from the scene of the crash. But mindful of the carnage that lay within the aircraft's broken fuselage, the TV station had inserted a three-minute delay to ensure that the images were carefully screened before going out on the open airwaves.

Christine had reflexively wrapped her arm around my shoulder, and pulled me tight against her – which was the only reason I was still standing when Alex appeared on the screen 15 or 20 seconds later. Stumbling through the billowing smoke and flames, he was leading a group of six or seven dazed and bewildered survivors to safety.

By then, almost the entire CSS staff had packed into Christine's office, and the moment Alex emerged on camera a thunderous cheer went up. Overwhelmed by relief and exhaustion, I turned to her. Pressing my face into her chest, I began to sob.

With my face buried in the polished wool of Christine's suit, I didn't see Alex turn back into the flames when the little group emerged into open air. But I felt Christine's body go suddenly rigid, and I heard the explosion of profanity.

From just behind me, Gen. McGreggor bellowed: *"Goddamnit, Alex – get the HELL outta there!"*

A dead silence fell on the room, and as the minutes passed the fear and anxiety became unbearable. Trembling and by now deathly afraid, I lifted my head from Christine's breast just in time to see Alex stumble through the smoke and flames once again. He had a young girl of perhaps six or seven slung across his left shoulder, and a much younger boy clutching a smoldering teddy bear cradled in his right arm. Blood was pouring from a gash somewhere above his hairline and running down his forehead into his eyes.

Blinded by the blood and choking on the smoke and fumes, Alex staggered another 15 or 20 steps before slumping to his knees. Still holding the children as before, he arched his back in a desperate effort to breathe before falling face forward into the grass.

His momentary loss of consciousness probably saved their lives. For the instant his face struck the ground, what remained of the aircraft exploded with incredible violence, hurling thousands of shards of twisted aluminum in all directions. But by the grace of God they passed over him, and the children.

The explosion must have wrenched him back to consciousness, for he lifted his head slightly and shook it. Then grasping the girl by her hand and the little boy by his collar, he began dragging them toward the GW Parkway. As he did so, the first rescue team arrived on site.

There was another deafening cheer behind me, followed by yet another as the firemen reached Alex. But when he forced himself up on his knees to grasp an oxygen mask from the hand of a paramedic, the room exploded in frenzy. People began jumping up and down, laughing and screaming in relief.

At that point, Christine finally broke down. Wrapping both arms around me, she pulled me tight against her and wept. As the tears streamed down her cheeks and into my hair, I heard her whispering "Thank God" over and over. Which was my sentiment, exactly.

After a long minute or two, Christine finally released me. Walking stiffly back to her desk, she slumped into her chair and dismissed the staff for the weekend. Then she placed her face in her hands, and sobbed.

Emotionally exhausted, the jubilant staff filed out of her office. Most of them packed it in for the day and headed for home. But I was still too badly shaken to drive, so I wandered down to the Econ shop. Jennifer and Dr. MacLaughlin had beaten me back there, and by the time I found them they were silently working their way through his bottle of Scotch. After noticing me standing in Dr. MacLaughlin's door, Jennifer poured three fingers into a Styrofoam cup and handed it to me without speaking.

I'm not much of a drinker – let's face it, Demon Rum and I just don't get along. But given the circumstances, an alcoholic stupor was the least of my concerns. I took the cup from Jennifer's hand and gratefully downed it all. Then after setting the empty cup back on Dr. MacLaughlin's desk, I thanked her softly and wandered back to my office. Except for my expression of appreciation, not a word had been spoken.

I'm still not sure if it was the Scotch or emotional strain of the day, but after that it all became a big blur. I don't really remember what I did for the next two or three hours, or even driving home. In fact, the first thing I can clearly recall is herding the dogs through the apartment door and locking it behind me, a little after 6 o'clock that evening.

I must have stopped at the grocery story on the way home, because I was carrying a six-pack of Diet Pepsi and a half-gallon of chocolate mint ice cream. So after feeding the dogs and giving them a bowl of fresh water, I retreated to the couch and mindlessly attacked the ice cream. It was still frozen almost solid, so I had to work the spoon up and down along the edges in order to pry little chunks out of the carton.

Five minutes later, it had thawed enough for me to scrape little wavy lines of chocolate off the top by dragging my spoon across the surface. Half way across the container, I glimpsed the dogs out of the corner of eye. Playing with a tug-toy near the entranceway, they seemed unnaturally relaxed and cheerful.

That struck me as odd, because Big Minh and Lady Godiva had some sort of sixth sense about Alex. If you couldn't locate him in the office, all you had to do was tell them to "Find Alex" and they'd take you straight to him. They charged for their services, of course – the going rate was an Oreo cookie apiece – but it was a lot easier than searching all over the building. So after puzzling over their strange behavior, I suddenly realized they'd picked up on something that had escaped me. Seizing the remote control, I pointed it at the TV and pushed the on-button.

The TV was an older model that Julia had inherited from her big brother, so it took a couple of moments to warm up. But as the picture began to emerge from the cloud of white snow on the screen, I realized that it had something to do with Alex. Bounding to the refrigerator, I grabbed a can of Diet Pepsi and raced back to the couch.

By the time I got back, the image of a newscaster had formed on the screen. Turning up the volume, I listened intently as he summarized the afternoon's disaster. "It was," he said, "a terrible tragedy tempered only by the extraordinary courage of President Reagan's friend and foreign policy advisor, Alexander M. de Vris, who risked his own life to save the lives of his fellow passengers...

"As we extend our prayers and heartfelt sympathy to the friends, families and loved ones of the 67 passengers and crew who perished this afternoon, we are also thankful for those that were spared...

"And we would like to extend our deepest thanks and appreciation to Mr. de Vris, who after leading seven survivors to safety, returned to the flaming wreckage to save a little girl, a little boy, and a teddy bear, from certain destruction."

After staring intently at something off to his left, the newscaster looked directly into the camera and informed the audience that they would be joining the station's on-the-scene reporter at Arlington Hospital. The screen flickered for an instant, and was replaced by the image of a slightly plump middle-aged woman standing in front of the hospital's main entrance. After a momentary pause she introduced herself as Saundra McMaster of WJXA Television, and announced that after being treated for smoke inhalation and minor cuts and abrasions, the emergency medical staff at Arlington Hospital had released presidential advisor Alexander M. de Vris from their care just minutes before. "Having been pronounced fit for travel, he left the hospital at approximately 6:10 pm, with his close friend and business associate, Nguyen Kao Tranh."

The screen flickered again, and the image of Ms. McMaster was replaced by footage of Alex settling himself into the passenger seat of a partially restored MGB. The left side of his face seemed swollen, and he was moving a bit stiffly. But despite all the partially dried blood caked in his hair and smeared on his shirt, he seemed to be in pretty good shape.

Unfortunately, the same could not be said about Nguyen's latest restoration project – which looked a lot more like a junkyard on wheels than an automobile. As I watched it disappear down the street belching smoke, I could only shake my head in disbelief.

Good God, I thought, *He's just traded one wreck for another!*

Feeling suddenly guilty about the perfectly restored 1963 Corvette I had parked out back, I flipped the channel.

As a somber image of President Reagan filled the screen, the hushed voice of a newscaster announced that he would be making a short statement regarding the loss of Flight 197. Snatching up my now thawed half-gallon of ice cream, I watched intently as the President expressed his deep sympathy and sorrow for the tragic loss of life. Addressing the friends and families of those that had perished, he made a veiled reference to the death of his first child, and assured them that he understood the depths of their grief. And then in a moment of stunning sincerity, he expressed his almost child-like faith in the ultimate beneficence of the Creator. The departed had surely gone on to a better place, he said, and those of us who remained behind could take comfort from the fact that they now basked in the eternal presence of a loving God.

After bowing his head for a moment of silent prayer, the President looked up again and expressed his thanks for those that had been spared and, especially, for his friend and confidant, Alexander de Vris, who had saved so many lives. President Reagan glanced away for a moment and shook his head before looking back into the cameras. "I just can't help but think the Good Lord put Alex on that plane today for a purpose." Then after another pause, he asked the American people to pray for both the living and the dead, and said goodnight.

Despite the fact that I was still shoveling ice cream into my mouth, I was stunned as he walked away from the podium. I had never seen a man of President Reagan's stature so deliberately exposed and emotionally vulnerable before, and for the very first time I began to understand the depth of his appeal. For however controversial some of his policies may have been, Reagan was a sincere and deeply compassionate man.

As the President receded from view, I clicked the remote again and flipped to another station. With pictures of the flaming wreckage on a giant screen behind him, a newscaster had just finished reviewing the terrible event.

After glancing down at the papers on the desk before him, he announced: "In honor of Mr. de Vris' gallantry, we are presenting a special report dedicated to this courageous and controversial figure." With the camera following his lead across the newsroom floor, he looked to the left where a half-dozen distinguished looking people were seated around the far side of a polished conference table.

When the camera focused on the man in the center, he looked in the direction of the newscaster and said, "Thank you, Jim." Then he shuffled the papers in front of him and looked into the camera. "I'm Robert Marsten, director of Network News research department, and I am here in Washington this evening with a panel of distinguished biographers, historians and political scientists to discuss the life and times of Alexander Michael de Vris, one of the most important and, indeed, heroic figures of our times...

"Currently the Chairman of the Board of Directors of the Center for Strategic Studies, Mr. de Vris is widely recognized as President Reagan's most influential advisor on foreign policy and defense issues, and is reputed to be the architect of a still secret policy initiative designed to force the Cold War to a close. Although Mr. de Vris declined an appointment to high government office after President Reagan was elected in 1980, he is regarded by many as the *éminence grise* of the Reagan Presidency. Indeed, his influence upon the President is such that his critics have compared him to Cardinal Richelieu of 17th-century France."

Still looking into the camera, he continued. "In fairness, Mr. de Vris' many admirers maintain that a comparison to Merlin of the Arthurian legend is far more apt."

Suppressing a slight smile, he noted that either comparison made an implicit reference to black magic or white, and that it was perhaps appropriate given the many remarkable and often inexplicable occurrences that had characterized Alex's life. After a calculated pause, the moderator noted that this was an interesting point to which he and the panel might later return. "But since we are unanimous in our belief that that one cannot fully come to grips with the complex and compelling character of Alexander de Vris without first taking into account his family's distinguished history, we shall first present an historical overview of the de Vris' experience in America."

Fascinated, I scraped some more of the now-pliant ice cream from the carton as he nodded into the camera. After kicking off my shoes and pulling my legs underneath my skirt, I positioned the container on my lap and leaned towards the television screen.

The moderator – the Marsten guy who had been doing all the talking – faded from the screen and was replaced by an aerial view of an incredibly graceful antebellum mansion, set in the midst of billowing cotton fields just north of present day Savannah. According to the announcer, the sprawling three-story white stone structure had been first built by Captain Jean Philippe de Vris, the first de Vris known to have settled in the New World – who was, as the voice duly noted, either a pirate or an early patriot, depending upon one's point of view.

Although the house had been destroyed a half dozen times by hurricanes, naval bombardment or invading armies, the de Vris family had always rebuilt it from the original plans, and even though the present structure incorporated modern materials and conveniences such as running water, electricity, and air conditioning, it was considered an historic landmark. According to the Georgia State Historical Society, it symbolized the enduring Spirit of the South.

But for me, it held a much more personal meaning. It was the house where Alex had grown up, and it took only the slightest bit of imagination to see him racing barefoot through the fields as a young boy, or wading through the creek that meandered through the distant woods. And despite the obvious differences – such as the sheer size of the house, or the Olympic-sized swimming pool and the tennis courts in back – something about it reminded me of my own home in Glen Meadows.

The de Vris house in the city, however, was much more quaint. A rather small brick building set on a quiet side street in "Old Savannah," it reminded me of the sort of home one might find in Georgetown. Jean Philippe had built that too, because the young wife he had taken in retirement preferred the riverside settlement to his plantation manor. Although Captain de Vris spent most of his time in the fields with his hired hands – it seems that he had been an early and vociferous opponent of slavery – he nonetheless spent enough time in town to father three children in quick succession. The first two were girls, while the third and final child was a boy.

According to local historians, very little is known about the next two generations of de Vris. Church records recounted the dates of their births, marriages and deaths, and fragmentary property tax records suggested that they prospered both at planting and maritime trade. They seem to have lived quiet and unassuming lives, passing their accumulated fortune from one generation to the next.

But it wasn't until the American Revolution that the de Vris family's fate and fortune became inextricably entwined with that of the nation.

Now of course, all that was very interesting. But since I really wasn't in the mood for a slow-moving historical documentary I picked up the remote, and flipped the channel again.

I was in the process of shoveling yet another huge spoonful of ice cream into my mouth when I suddenly stopped and stared at the screen. With the pile of ice cream balanced precariously in midair, I scrunched up my nose in disbelief. *This has got to be some kind of mistake...*

I was staring at a picture of a shirtless Alex standing on a dock in front of a PT boat, with his arm draped around the shoulder of President Kennedy. Which was really strange, because Alex didn't have his mustache, and they both looked like they were in their early 20s. Then the picture switched to a group of young men playing poker on top of a fuel drum outside some sort of makeshift grass hut, and there they were again – Alex and Kennedy were sitting across from one another, intently studying their cards. I was in the process of thinking that Alex couldn't possibly be that old when I suddenly realized that it wasn't Alex at all. *Holy Cow*, I thought. *Christine wasn't kidding!*

They were pictures of Alex's father – Lt. Michael de Vris, as I later learned – taken in the South Pacific during World War Two. As it turned out, Alex's father and President Kennedy had served in the same PT boat squadron – and despite their very different politics, the two had become close friends.

By then, the documentary had changed from still pics to colorized motion picture footage, and as I finished off the last of the ice cream they were showing PT boats racing across the ocean seas. The boat commanded by Alex's father was in the lead, with Kennedy's boat following just behind it.

Then the still pics reappeared, and an announcer began describing the sort of odd-couple friendship that had developed between the elder de Vris and President Kennedy. According to other PT boat commanders that had served with them, they were temperamental opposites: where Kennedy was brash to the point of recklessness, Alex's father was cool and calculating. But both were exceptionally bright young men, and they shared an irreverent sense of humor. Perhaps most importantly, they were both fanatical poker players as well. Although none of the other officers in their squadron knew exactly how many millions of dollars' worth of IOUs went back and forth between them, Kennedy and the elder de Vris were so evenly matched in terms of their poker skills that they were rarely more that $15 or $20 apart.

A sort of friendly rivalry arose from their endless card games, and that permeated their relationship. Although the Boston political machine was later quick to present Kennedy as a war hero when he went into politics, the documentary pointedly noted that Alex's father was as heavily decorated as his friend. In fact, he had been awarded the Navy Cross of Gallantry for saving an American hospital ship packed with wounded Marines.

Alex's father had been escorting the ship to a convoy rendezvous point when three Japanese destroyers appeared out of the darkness of night and opened fire. Although the wooden hulled PT boat was only armed with machine guns and a 20-millimeter cannon, it was small and fast and it carried two torpedoes in launch pods along either side. Even though the torpedoes weren't very accurate when fired from a boat speeding along the ocean's surface, a lucky hit could sink a large warship. So after signaling the hospital ship to make a run for it, Alex's father had turned his boat into the enemy in an effort to draw their fire.

Mindful of the havoc a torpedo could wreak on their ships, the Japanese broke formation and took evasive maneuvers. But the elder de Vris didn't make the launch – he raced through them instead, before turning back for another run. And so it went on for hour after hour as he harassed and harried the enemy with machine gun fire and faux attacks.

When dawn finally broke and American fighter aircraft arrived on the scene, they were amazed to find the battle still raging. Lt. de Vris was wounded, his boat was on fire, and half of his crew were dead. But he was still attacking, and as a result more than 800 American lives had been saved.

Somehow or another, the TV station had found some old footage taken just after the battle, showing Alex's dad bringing his boat back into the island lagoon that had served as their base. It had been riddled with holes and was listing badly, most of the paint had been scorched from it, and black smoke was belching from where I supposed the engines must have been. According to the official report, Alex's father had collapsed from loss of blood and gone into shock just before the vessel slowly careened into the dock – but the guns were manned by the surviving crewmen, and a shredded Stars and Stripes still flew from the mast.

Having finished off the last of the ice cream, I watched intently as they displayed some other wartime footage. It took a while, but they finally showed a close up of Alex's dad being decorated in a hospital bed. Half-dead or not, he was an incredibly handsome man – so I wasn't the least bit surprised that the red-headed nurse hovering in the background had fallen madly in love with him. He must have fallen for her too, because they were married six months later.

But the fact that Alex's dad had been a PT boat commander in the South Pacific was important for another reason as well. Fifteen years after the war ended, his old friend and poker partner was elected President, and one of his first acts was put the elder de Vris in charge of a super-secret organization he had hidden in the Department of Commerce. A CIA report prepared in the waning months of the Eisenhower Administration warned that the Soviets were in the process of stripping the United States of its high technology, and not just through espionage. KGB-controlled front companies in Western Europe were acquiring most of it from American corporations, and President Kennedy needed someone he could trust to quietly and discreetly shut down the illicit trade. Since Alex's father was by then the CEO and principal stockholder of the Southern Export Bank – which financed most of the large export deals on the East Coast and the Gulf – he was perfectly suited for the task. So in 1961 he put the de Vris family fortune in a blind trust, accepted a million dollar a year pay cut, and moved his family to Washington.

Now that's cool, I thought. *Kinda like what I was doing with my report!*

Except for the fact that I didn't have to take a million dollar a year pay cut. But then, I wasn't making a million bucks a year to start with…

Figuring that was kind of a wash, I turned my attention back to the TV. Since most of the documentary had focused on Alex's father and his service to America, it naturally blended into Alex's service in Vietnam. But I have to tell you – I was totally unprepared for what followed

At first it was a collage of still photographs and amateur movies taken or made at various firebases along the Demilitarized Zone, or some more or less indistinct combat footage taken by television crews in the field. But when they switched to a film taken from a helicopter, my blood ran suddenly cold. Sensing the presence of an indefinable evil, I instinctively glanced over my shoulder to reassure myself that I was alone.

Shifting uneasily on the couch, I watched the battle raging beneath me from the vantage point of the camera high above. The sun hadn't quite cleared the horizon, so what I saw was mostly jungle, illuminated by gunfire and the ghastly light of flares. In the background, I could hear the chatter of the crew as they searched for a place to land.

Artillery shells were shredding the dawn's light with hellish explosions when one of the crewmen suddenly yelled, "Smoke to starboard, 1500 meters." The helicopter banked sharply and moved in for a landing. As it came to a rest, Marines jumped up from the tall grass that had concealed them and began racing toward the aircraft in groups of four. Each group was carrying a wounded man between them, using ponchos as makeshift stretchers.

Holding the ponchos with one hand and their helmets in place with the other, they ran crouched-over into the wash of the rotors. But it wasn't until they lifted the first wounded man onto the waiting deck that the camera passed across Alex's limp and almost lifeless body.

My blood went cold as I looked at his ashen-gray face. His eyes were vacant and staring as though he were looking into some dark abyss, and if his bloody lips hadn't been trembling I would have thought that he was dead.

Crying out in anguish, I fled from the ghastly image. Twisting away violently, I hurled myself into the back of the couch, and with my hands pressed hard against my eyes, I pushed my face deep into the overstuffed leather. Shaking uncontrollably, I didn't notice the wind and the rain lashing against the walls.

The sky had turned strangely dark after the plane crash that afternoon, and in the half-hour or so since I had returned home, the black clouds that had rolled over Washington had built into a raging storm. The air inside the apartment had suddenly become thick with static electricity, and as bolts of lightning exploded outside, an eerie glow danced upon the opaque glass bricks that ran the upper length of the exterior wall.

And as the lights began to flicker, I became vaguely aware of the emergency storm warning issuing forth from the TV. Gale force winds were moving up the Chesapeake Bay from the Atlantic, and residents of the DC Metropolitan Area were advised to seek immediate shelter.

Now most people would have dismissed the storm as mere coincidence. But we Irish are a superstitious lot, and in the very depths of my soul I knew better. It wasn't the storm that was raging outside my walls, but the Banshee that had come for Alex's soul. Cheated of its prize in Vietnam and denied it again this day, it had hurled its wrath against Washington instead.

Suddenly overwhelmed by a hatred as dark as the night itself, I sprang to my feet and seized the still unopened can of Diet Pepsi from the end table. As I hurled it at the oddly illuminated glass bricks along the wall, I screamed at the evil beyond.

"You can't have him, you son-of-a bitch!"

CHAPTER TWENTY

Historians have argued about the crash for decades, and most of them have attributed Alex's survival to pure chance. But due to the carefully crafted cover-up, they've never had access to any of the true facts. Except for a handful of routine forms, all of the information they've obtained over the years – including the CIA and FBI reports that were eventually declassified – were carefully calculated fabrications. One thing leads to another and if they'd ever found out the aircraft had been sabotaged, they would have eventually figured out the rest.

And trust me on this – given what followed, no one in Washington wanted *that* public.

One of the many things hidden behind the government's wall of secrecy was the fact that Alex had given his first-class ticket to an elderly nun just before boarding. So crippled by arthritis that she could barely walk, the aged sister had thanked Alex for his kindness and bestowed her blessings upon him. And as a result of this simple act of decency, his life had been spared. Scrunched into the very last row of the cheap seats, Alex survived the crash with only minor cuts and bruises. But I had no way of knowing that when I arrived at the office the following Monday, and neither did any of the other CSS staff.

To an outsider, the CSS must have seemed remarkably calm that day. The staff went about their business as per usual – phones were answered, copies were made, vending machines were cursed, and meetings were held – but beneath the placid exterior ran a deep current of unease.

No one spoke about it openly, of course. But in the hallways and the restrooms, staffers huddled together in small groups and talked in hushed whispers. The crash hadn't been Alex's only close call since Vietnam – there had been at least two and perhaps three others when he was in the CIA. Although no one knew any of the details, one of them had supposedly been in Moscow, another in East Germany and – reportedly – yet another in the Middle East.

The unspoken question that hung in the air was how long his luck would hold – and judging by the almost palpable sense of fear and anxiety that haunted the hallways, most of the staff figured that it couldn't last much longer. I had initially come to the same conclusion, but by the time I parked the Vette in the underground garage my fear had given way to a sense of guarded optimism.

I had spent the entire weekend at home, thinking about all the weird stuff that had happened since the morning I'd arrived in Washington — meeting Alex at the bus station, James' sudden disappearance, the insistent sense that someone had followed me the night I explored Capitol Hill, the break-in at the apartment, and now the plane crash. And even though I didn't have a shred of evidence at the time, I was convinced that someone had tried to kill Alex and make it look like an accident.

Somehow or another, it all tied together - and in the very depths of my soul, I knew the attempt against Alex had something to do with me.

But what?

That just didn't make sense — because let's face it, I was just a flunky research assistant. And in Washington, research assistants were a dime a dozen. There were plenty of other junior economists around, and some of them already had security clearances. So in the grand scheme of things, I was no big deal.

But it didn't take a rocket scientist to make the connection between the plane crash and my own weird experiences. Obviously, the same people who had tried to kill Alex were trying to intimidate me…

But why bother?

Because even if I packed up my bags and ran home to Glen Meadows, it wouldn't make any difference. The CSS could replace me in 15 minutes flat…

I had spent the entire day Sunday turning that over and over in my mind. But no matter how I looked at it, I kept coming up with a complete blank. The only thing I could think of was that somebody had made some sort of dumb mistake. *Maybe they think I'm some sort of super spy?*

Snickering to myself, I thought: *Yeah, that's me all right — Mata Hari in a mini skirt!*

But as I drifted off to sleep that night, it occurred to me that wasn't their only miscalculation. *Because if they think they're gonna get rid of Alex, they're way mistaken…*

Because I'd already made up my mind, and that just wasn't going to happen.

And as for that stupid Banshee — well, I didn't take four years of Tae Kwon Do for nothing. If he ever showed his face around Alex again, I was gonna kick his worthless butt all the way back to Hades…

Satisfied that I had put the world aright, I pulled the covers up over my head and went to sleep.

Much to my surprise, Christine was waiting for me when I marched into the Executive Office Monday morning. So after greeting Linda and Two with a curt nod, I followed her into her office and waited silently as she withdrew a new set of keys and a half-inch thick binder from a locked drawer in her desk. Seemingly more relaxed than the rest of the staff, she smiled as she tucked the binder under her arm and handed me the keys. "Guard these with your life."

I knew Christine was as upset as everyone else. But as the Center's Executive Vice President the task of shoring up morale fell to her, and she did a really good job of it. Her cheerful disposition seemed genuine enough, and it was definitely contagious. So as a big smile crept across my face, I took the keys from her outstretched hand. "Yes, Ma'am!"

Looking down at me in mock seriousness, she asked if I was ready. After nodding, I followed her back into the reception area to the locked doors of my new office. Giddy with excitement, I was practically walking on air when we reached them. Which was a welcome change, because there was a limit to how long I could fixate on all the weird, spooky stuff that was going on.

After several moments of fumbling with the keys, Christine told me to try the gold one. After slipping it into the keyway and turning it, I closed my eyes and slowly pushed the doors open. Grinning from ear to ear, I asked Christine if I could look.

Laughing softly, she told me to go ahead.

I couldn't believe my eyes when I looked inside, because everything worked – the Oriental rugs, the polished cherry desk, the impressionist paintings upon the walls, and the curtains all blended together in a perfect harmony.

And lo and behold! I even had bookcases!

Breathlessly, I told Christine that it was beautiful. "Absolutely beautiful!"

Standing in the doorway, I had this really cool sense that I had "arrived." Feeling very much like the Jeffersons when they moved uptown, I turned to Christine and told her that I just had to show it to my Mom.

"Can I take some pictures?"

Chuckling, Christine said yes, but not today. Handing me the binder, she informed me that it contained the security protocols that were now in effect, and rather sternly explained that we had a great deal of work to do. She was going to walk me through the procedures one by one, and after that she expected me to memorize them word-by-word. "It's not enough to know what you are supposed to do," she said. "It has to become instinctive."

Then she gave me another one of her Adult-Authority Stares. "*Comprende?*"

After I nodded again, she informed me that from that moment forward my doors would remain open at all times unless I had some compelling reason to close them during the business day. "If you find that the activities in the reception area are distracting, you may close them while you are in the office working. But other than that, they are to remain open."

Extending her arms with her index fingers pointing more or less toward either end of the ceiling, Christine did a half-turn and informed me that dozens of hidden cameras had been installed along the ceiling line in my office and the reception area as well. "Anyone entering or leaving this office from either the reception area or from the adjacent offices" – meaning her's or Alex's – "will be videotaped by at least three different cameras, and their movements within it will be continuously monitored."

"There are also cameras mounted on the building across the street, covering the windows."

Seeing me gulp involuntarily, Christine smiled and paused for a moment before continuing. "The only space in this office that isn't subject to direct video surveillance is your desk and the area immediately surrounding it..."

"So if you're having a really bad hair day, just make a mad dash for your chair."

Yeah, right, I thought. But since I wasn't about to say that to Christine, I scrunched up my nose and made a yucky face instead.

"Oh, come on. It's not that bad...

"You'll look great on camera."

Horrified by the imagery that had popped into my head, I turned and gave her a distrustful look. "We're talking color, right?

"Cause this whole strawberry blonde thing just doesn't work with black and white."

Christine knitted her eyebrows together and cocked her head to the right. After thinking about it for a moment, she agreed that could be a problem. "But I'm almost positive they're using color." So after promising to find out for sure, she led me over to the vault.

It was hidden behind a set of polished oak double doors, secured by a deadbolt and a key-in-knob lock. Taking the keys from my hand, she explained that the two locks were office-standard, and had been installed largely for cosmetic purposes. After unlocking them in turn with the brass colored key, she pulled the doors open to reveal the vault. "But the locks on the vault are an entirely different story."

Pointing to the keyways located on either side of the steel frame, she instructed me to take note. "Although these appear to be locks, they are actually designed to enable the electronic keypad that actually controls access to the vault...

"Alex, Dr. MacLaughlin, and I have copies of the first enabling key, and you will have the second...

"So one of us will have to assist you in enabling the keypad each morning, in accordance to the security protocols listed in the binder."

Then she reached inside her blouse and pulled out a key attached to a 20-inch chain. After lifting the chain over her head, she studied the key for a moment before handing it to me. "I think this one is yours." Then she fished inside her blouse again and pulled out another. After pulling that one over her head as well, she slipped it into the keyway on the right side of the vault.

After instructing me to insert my key, she continued. "The security system has been deliberately designed so that both keys have to be turned simultaneously to activate the electronic keypad...

"That doesn't make it impossible for a single individual with both keys to activate the keypad, but it does complicate the procedure, and the gymnastics involved will provide the cameras with obvious evidence of a security violation."

Turning back to me, Christine asked me if I was ready. After I nodded she said, "On three" and began counting. When she reached the magic number, we turned our keys together and the keypad came to life. Then she punched six of the illuminated numbers, before turning the handle on the vault door and pulling it open.

The door opened noiselessly, with little apparent effort. That surprised me, because it was at least eight inches thick. *Holy cow!* I thought. *These guys are serious!*

There were two wheeled carts inside, with curved handles at either end. One was for my special computer, and the other was for transporting the raw data the CIA was going to deliver the next morning. According to Christine, the CIA's security experts had decided to make them semi-mobile, so I could wheel them out each morning at start of business, and push them back when I finished up or left the office for any reason.

Which made sense, except for the two-key enabling system. Anytime I left the office I would have to secure the loaded carts in the vault, and that meant I'd be constantly interrupting Alex or

Christine or Dr. MacLaughlin to open it again. But Christine said that wasn't the case – once the vault was opened in the morning, I'd be able to close it and then reopen it myself using just the keypad until I pressed the red SECURE button beneath the numbers at close of business. Once I did that, the security system would reset and I'd need the second enabling key again. "That way," Christine said, "You'll be more or less free to come and go during normal business hours."

Picking up on the look of relief that passed across my face, Christine teased me. "Or if that's too complicated, we can just chain you to the carts."

Yeah, right. I thought. *Like those carts are gonna fit through the door of the ladies' room...*

Chuckling, Christine assured me that she was just kidding. But given all the security precautions they were taking, I had my doubts.

Changing the subject, Christine told me that we had a couple of other things to go over before we started on the protocols in the binder. First and foremost, I had to reset the combination on the vault. And since I was the only one authorized to know that, I had to come up with a secure six-digit combination. "So don't use anything obvious like your high school locker combination or your birthday."

After walking me through the procedures for resetting the electronic lock, Christine walked out into the reception area and closed the doors behind her. *Piece of cake,* I thought. *This is what prime numbers and square roots are for!*

So I picked the first six sequential primes, crunched the square roots in my head, rounded them up, and laid them out in a sequence. Then after reversing their order, I punched the first six digits of the resulting string into the keypad and pushed "SECURE." After the keypad blinked at me, I called for Christine.

Since she had gone to great lengths to impress upon me how important it was for me to remember the combination, I assured her that it was locked into memory. Satisfied by my confidence, she nodded and told me there were two other things we had to go over before taking a break. First on the agenda were the new security guards.

"You may have noticed that the retired policemen that guard the building have been augmented by a group of much younger men...

"Although they are wearing the uniforms of the private security company, that's just a cover. They're from the Agency's

Office of Security, and they'll be here for the duration of the project...

"They're highly trained professionals, and they are deadly serious."

"So don't mess with them. Be polite, respectful, and cooperative at all times – but otherwise keep out of their way, and let them do their jobs."

Puzzled, I nodded.

Christine smiled, and warned me that it might not be that easy. "Some of them are really cute, and I want to make sure the girls all understand this is a case of 'look but don't touch'"

Ahhhh, I thought. Grinning, I asked her just exactly how cute they were.

Christine looked down and to her left, shook her head and sighed. "One of them is just adorable!"

Unable to resist the temptation, I asked her if 'window shopping' was OK.

After giving me a frustrated look, Christine nodded and said it was. "Just make sure you stay on your side of the glass."

After glancing at the open door, Christine told me there was one other thing I should be aware of. "Alex often comes back to the office after dinner...

"Sometimes he catches up on his reading or his correspondence, and sometimes he just relaxes...

"I know that you are in the habit of working nights and coming in on weekends, so you need to understand that the office is his 'quiet place' after hours. Most of the time he just listens to music, but now and then he likes to play his guitar."

Cool! I thought. "Alex plays the guitar?"

Christine raised her eyebrows and nodded. "Anything with strings...

"Guitar, cello, mandolin, violin, you name it."

"Really?"

Christine nodded again, with much more emphasis. "Oh yeah," she said. "He's an incredibly talented musician."

Then she smiled, and told me that he used to play in Georgetown's bars on weekends when they were in school. Not for the money, of course, but to meet girls.

Then she smiled, more to herself than to me. "And every once in a while, he'd take me along to sing backup."

For some reason that really surprised me. "You sing?"

Christine smiled again, and nodded. "A little bit...

"I majored in finance because I needed a marketable degree. But I minored in voice, because I liked it."

"You're kidding!"

Christine pursed her lips together. "Not at all…

"It was a pretty strange course of study," she said. "But I enjoyed it."

"So you sang with Alex in bars?"

Christine nodded again. "It was a lot of fun, and we made a ton of money off the tips."

"That is so cool!" I said.

Christine smiled almost wistfully before she agreed. "It really was."

Grinning, I asked her if she had met any cute guys that way. Christine chuckled, and started to blush. "Well, maybe one or two," she said.

Raising my eyebrows, I said: "Oh yeah?"

Still smiling, Christine tried to look stern. "Maybe one or two" she said, with just a bit too much emphasis.

Thinking that Dr. MacLaughlin might not have been entirely correct when he'd described her as a "perfect angel" while at Georgetown, I quickly changed the subject. "Yeah, well I bet Alex was a big hit with the girls, huh?"

Christine huffed, and shook her head. *"Oh dear God,"* she said. "Don't get me started on that!"

Then she stopped very suddenly and shook her head in wonder. "It was just amazing…

"We'd set up in Clyde's or Nathan's at 10 o'clock on a Friday night, and by 10:30 the place would be packed to the rafters with girls…

"And every single one of them wanted a date with him…

"So we'd perform until closing time, and then he'd walk out the door with a girl on each arm and about a hundred phone numbers stuffed in his pocket!"

Then she rolled her eyes together and scrunched up her face in a look of genuine puzzlement. "It's a wonder he managed to survive college!"

It wasn't so much what Christine had said, but rather how she had said it — because her tone of voice conveyed a whole lot more information than I really wanted to know. But before I could say anything, she sighed and shook her head again. "But he plays so beautifully…"

After a long moment of wistful silence, Christine snapped out of her reverie. Suddenly all business again, she rather sternly reminded me again that the office was Alex's "quiet place" at night, and asked me to respect that.

Grinning from ear to ear, I figured I'd teased enough information out of her for one day. So I pulled myself up straight and made the Girl Scout sign. "Promise!"

Christine chuckled, and asked me if I had any further questions. I started to shake my head, but caught myself in mid-act. Raising both hands in an involuntary gesture, I quickly apologized and asked her if Alex was back from Louisville. "Cause I was going to work on some stuff tonight, and I want to make sure I don't bother him."

"Like if he's going to be in the office..."

"Or, uh, well..."

"Around?"

Oh God, I thought, *that was lame!*

After wincing involuntarily, I started praying that Christine hadn't seen it. Or more importantly, seen through my design.

Lucky for me, she hadn't. Because she said no, without hesitating, and explained that he was lying low in Kentucky for a few days. "He generated a great deal of favorable publicity when he rescued all those people from the crash, and of course that benefited the President...

"But it also had the unfortunate effect of diverting the public's attention at a rather critical time. President Reagan is headed for a landslide victory, and since Alex doesn't want to distract them from the campaign, he's decided to stay out of sight until things calm down...

"But he'll be back later this week."

Knowing that I was really pushing the limits, I asked Christine how he was.

For the first time, a worried look passed across her face. "Well, he's bit beat up, you know. He has a black eye, some cracked ribs, and a bunch of torn muscles...

"But he's doing OK."

Looking down at the floor, I nodded and softly thanked her for telling me.

Christine cleared her throat, and looked down at her watch. We were running a bit behind, but she was going to walk me through the security protocols in the binder one by one. After that, she wanted me to wheel one of the carts down to the Seventh Floor and load up my computer, monitor, and printer, and anything else I want to bring up to the new office. Although I wouldn't have any actual work to do until the CIA delivered the financial data in the morning, she wanted to make sure I was ready. After that, we went back to her office, and after sitting down on the couch, she began walking me through the security protocols.

The binder wasn't very thick, and all of the procedures were printed in big print. But Christine was both careful and methodical in her presentation, and she frequently digressed to explain the jargon – which she called "spook speak" – and to relate them to both the protocol and the larger issue of securing classified documents. Although she carefully avoided any hint or implication to the effect, it didn't take long to convince me that she had a great deal of experience in handling classified information.

In fact, her mastery of the procedures and the terminology was so complete that I found myself wondering if she'd been to spy school, too.

CHAPTER TWENTY-ONE

The question remained unanswered three hours and fifteen minutes later, when I pulled my cart to a stop outside the Econ shop. Hoping I could talk Jennifer into helping me load up my stuff, I walked into the department with my very best smile on my face.

Which was – unfortunately – wasted on the piles of boxes that filled the room, stacked halfway to the ceiling.

Squeezing through the narrow passageway that led between them, I called out her name. "Jennifer?"

I heard a big thud toward the back of the room, followed by a couple of clunks and a muted grunt. A moment later, Jennifer stuck her head up over the top of the boxes. "Hey, what's up?"

Looking up at her incredulously, I asked what she was doing.

"Oh, well, the pre-publication copies of *The Washington Journal of Political Economy* just arrived, and Dr. MacLaughlin wants to send copies to all 500 of his closest friends...

"So I'm putting address labels on the mailing envelopes and stuffing them because the mail shop is backed up."

Holy Cow! I thought. "The one with my study?"

Jennifer laid both elbows on top of the box she was leaning on and said, "Yup."

Kewl! I thought. "Can I have one?"

This time it was Jennifer's turn to look incredulous. "Are you kidding? We ordered 500 *copies* and they sent us 500 *cases*..."

"So take all you want."

Then she paused a minute and looked around. "But could you help me get out of here first?"

Puzzled, I peered down the raggedy path that led toward the back of the room. "Are you blocked in?"

After rolling her eyes, Jennifer gave me a disgusted look. "Oh, no. I just like kneeling on the top of my desk."

Grinning, I warned her to be nice. Otherwise, I might leave and lock the door behind me. Then I began working my way through the narrow crevice towards the back of the office.

It took me a while, but I finally managed to squeeze through the cartons and make my way back to Jennifer's desk. Peering through a four-inch gap between the piles, I couldn't resist a little jibe.

"Well, this is cozy," I said.

From the other side of the boxes, Jennifer gave me a sarcastic look. "Oh yeah. Just like home…

"Now help me get out of here."

Pursing my lips together, I rolled my head over to one side and shook it. "Nuh-uh." Then I looked at her bit more sharply. "At least not until you tell me how you managed to get bricked up like that."

Jennifer gave me another disgusted look. "Dr. MacLaughlin was out, and I was on the phone when the delivery guys came…

"And since I didn't know what he wanted to do about all the extras, I told them to stack the boxes along the walls…

"And the next thing I knew, I was stuck."

Thinking they weren't exactly stacked along the walls, I scrunched up my nose and looked at her incredulously. "And you didn't notice?"

Obviously irritated, Jennifer pursed her lips together. "I told you I was on the phone."

By now suspicious, I asked her with whom.

Jennifer rolled her eyes. "With David, if it's any of your business…

"Now will you help me get out of here? I have to go to the bathroom!"

Grinning, I ignored her distress and asked her who David was. "Boyfriend of the week?"

Which was a pretty good guess, because Jennifer went through boyfriends the way I go through ice cream.

Jennifer scowled at me with righteous indignation. "Boyfriend of the past two weeks, I'll have you know!" Then she made a half turn, and after rooting around on her desk she thrust a framed photograph through the gap.

"Wow!" I said. "Where did you find him?"

"At The Boyfriend Store," she quipped. "That's where I get all my guys."

Snickering, I was about to ask her for directions when I heard Dr. MacLaughlin's voice booming from the hallway. *"BLOODY HELL!!!*

"WHAT'S GOING ON HERE, LASS?"

Snatching the photograph back through the gap between the boxes, Jennifer asked Dr. MacLaughlin for just a moment. After setting the framed picture back on her desk, she climbed back up on the surface and stuck her head up over the boxes. Smiling cheerfully, Jennifer told him that there had been some kind of mistake. "I ordered the 500 advance copies of *The Washington*

Journal of Political Economy, but I think they goofed and sent us 500 cases instead."

I couldn't see him from where I stood, but I could hear the perplexity in his voice. "500 cases, you say?"

"Yes, Sir." she replied. Then she put on her "Poor Little Girl" face, and told him that she and I were about to move all the cases out in the hall. "But they're just *too* heavy!"

My mouth fell open, and my eyes rolled involuntarily. *There's no way he's gonna fall for that,* I thought.

But he did. "Of course they are, Lass." Then I heard him bellow across the hall for Tom Andrews.

Jennifer climbed down off her desk, and pressed her smiling face against the gap. "He's such a sweetheart," she whispered.

"Yeah," I whispered back. "He's a sweetheart and you're a con artist!"

Jennifer looked offended. "Am not!"

I started to say, "Are too" but I was interrupted by Tom Andrews' voice. "Yes, Sir?"

Dr. MacLaughlin explained that there had been some sort of mix up with the journals, and instructed him to carry them out in the hallway and stack them against the walls. From the tone of his reply, I could tell Tom wasn't particularly happy about the assignment. But he was an intern, and interns always get the short end of the stick. So rather than feel sorry for him, I leaned against the boxes and chatted with Jennifer until he'd moved most of the stuff out into the hall. Then I gathered up a whole stack of journals from the open case Jennifer had been working on and sauntered down to the mailroom.

I wrote a quick note to my mom, and taped it onto the cover of a journal. Then I banded it together with five other copies, and stuffed them into an oversized mailing envelope. After addressing it, I borrowed the mailroom's typewriter and wrote a slightly longer note to Dr. Watkins, my academic advisor at Township College. Thinking that he'd be pleased to know his star pupil had made the big time, I signed it before carefully folding it in half and banding it to two copies of the journal.

Since I didn't remember the address, I just addressed it to Professor Watkins, in care of the Department of Economics and Finance at Township College. Because let's face it – there's no way the post office could mess up a delivery in a town the size of Glen Meadows.

Then I dropped the two packages in the outgoing mail bin, and headed back up the stairs.

By the time I reached the Eighth Floor, I was in a really good mood. Hardly anyone gets a job like the one I had straight out of college, and I'd put my heart and soul into it. I knew I'd done a really good job with the study, and even though I knew both my mom and Professor Watkins would be proud of me, I just couldn't wait for their reaction!

But as it turned out, my eagerly awaited response came from an entirely unexpected source.

President Reagan had gotten an advance copy of the study, too – and despite his hectic schedule on the campaign trail, he'd found time to read it. Holding up a copy in front of a huge crowd at an outdoor mall in Des Moines late that afternoon, he presented it as proof of his policy towards the Soviet Union and urged every concerned American to read it.

Glancing down at the cover to check the names, he said: "Two of America's most distinguished economists – Charles Lawrence MacLaughlin and Alicia Elizabeth McAllister – have provided us with irrefutable proof that the Soviets are engaged in a global criminal conspiracy, trafficking in guns and narcotics throughout the Third World!"

Pressing his case, he argued neither the international community nor the United States should tolerate that sort of wanton illegality by a nation that professed to be a great power. Nations that claim title to greatness must conduct themselves in a manner that befits their aspirations, and he called upon the Soviets to abandon their destructive policies and to instead join with the United States to create a better world.

America's opposition to the Soviet Union was based upon solid principles, and his opponent – Senator Mondale, in case anyone had forgotten – was just plain wrong in calling for an end to the East-West confrontation. For until the Soviets abandoned their aggressive policies – which now included global criminality – an accommodation between the United States and the USSR would have to be built upon a foundation of cynicism.

But the last part of the President's speech slipped right past me when I turned on the evening news that night, because I got wrapped up in the whole "distinguished economists" thing. Nobody had ever referred to me as distinguished before, and I really liked it. Pulling one of the big throw pillows to my chest as I leaned back on the couch in front of the TV, I grinned from ear to ear. *Now, that was cool!*

Looking back on it, I suppose I should have seen what was coming. But at the time I was still something of a hayseed when it came to Washington politics – which explains how my picture ended up on the front page of almost every newspaper in America.

You see, almost every girl has a fashion outlaw buried somewhere deep down inside of her, and I'm no exception. Now most of the time, we keep that part of ourselves under heavy lock and key, to avoid mischance. But as luck would have it, mine broke jail the next morning.

When I emerged into the sunlight, I was wearing a pale lavender top with spaghetti straps. Made out of a silk satin-weave and adorned with tiny sequins, it fell just below the top of my hips, to contrast a slightly darker lavender mini skirt. Made out of a smooth satin, it was slit on the side to mid-thigh – a bit daring for the office, of course, but with the silvery-strapped shoes with the clunky heels, the outfit was just adorable!

Now, that's not the sort of outfit I normally wore to the office. But with the eggshell silk jacket – the one I had gotten on sale in Georgetown, with the Chinese collar – covering the sexy top, I was pretty sure Christine would let me slide. So after stuffing my briefcase behind the driver's seat and shooing the dogs inside, I put the Vette's top down and climbed in.

Normally, it took me about 20 minutes to make it to work in the mornings, and most of the time I enjoyed the drive. There was a new radio station in DC that had an entirely different kind of format, and I liked listening to it on the way to work. About 70% of the songs they played were on the current charts, but the remaining 30% were pulled from the top twenty of each year dating all the way back to 1940 – so you got a really eclectic range of popular music, including all the really great artists like Glen Miller, Elvis Presley, the Beatles, and of course, all the current hits. Even better, they played them in sets of three.

The theme song from *Ghostbusters* was filtering through the speakers when I turned onto Mass Ave, so I reached past Big Minh – who was sitting in the passenger seat, as per usual – and cranked up the volume. The movie had been the smash hit of the summer, and the song cracked me up. Laughing, I started singing along.

Tooling along Mass Avenue with the top down and the volume up was a lot of fun, even if I did get some strange looks now and then, and I was having a lot more fun than usual that day because they were playing all my favorite songs. Three or four blocks short of First Street, *Karma Chameleon* really got me going.

Boy George – the guy who sang it – was not only a flamboyantly gay cross-dresser, but a druggie to boot. But since I really liked his style of high-energy music, I was inclined to overlook his weirdness.

The Vette seemed to like it too, because it always accelerated when Boy George was playing. But unfortunately, some knucklehead had blocked off the intersection of Mass Ave and North Capitol and created a huge traffic jam that morning. So rather than zigzag through the light and zoom up the side street that led to the alleyway and the parking garage, I had to make a right turn on New Jersey and then a left on E. I had planned on entering the alley from there, but no such luck – a police van had it blocked off, so I was going to have to find another way in. But it wasn't a total loss, because just then the radio station started playing *Let's Hear It For The Boy,* by Denise Williams. Which, of course, reminded me of Alex, so it was one of my all-time favorite songs.

Totally oblivious to all the people around me, I was singing along and doing a little dance in my seat when the light turned green. But halfway through the turn, I had to slam on the brakes.

What the ...

There was a huge mob out in front of the CSS building, held at bay by a solid line of DC police officers, and dozens of TV trucks were parked all along the right side of the road. Cameras mounted on tripods were all over the place, and as I sat there tying up traffic in disbelief, I could plainly see a guy perched in one of the trees across the street, balancing a big TV camera on his shoulder.

With horns blaring behind me, I put the Vette into first gear and began edging forward through the crowd. Fifteen minutes later – and with the help of a half-dozen traffic cops – I made an otherwise illegal left turn onto the side street running parallel to Mass Ave, and headed for the alley.

Four police officers were blocking the back street entranceway, so I had to bring the Vette to a halt. Holding my CSS ID badge above the windshield so they could see it, I explained that I had to use the alley to get to the parking garage. One of the officers nodded and waved me through, but as the other three stepped back to let me pass, someone on the corner yelled: "Hey, that's her!"

An instant later, a mob charged in my direction.

My jaw dropped, and my eyes widened. *Holy cow!*

I had no idea what was going on, but with the charging horde bearing down on me, I decided it wasn't a good time to find out. So I stomped on the gas pedal and roared down the alleyway. Fortunately, Wilbur had seen me coming and had already raised the gate.

Accelerating through the turn, I slammed on the brakes and downshifted when the front tires hit the ramp. Hitting the gas again at the bottom, I fishtailed around the corner before screeching to a stop in Nguyen's parking place. Shooing the dogs out of the car, I snatched my briefcase out from behind my seat and jerked the top into position. After locking the door and slamming it shut, I made a mad dash for the Executive Offices.

Christine was in the reception area talking to Linda when I rushed in. Coming to a halt just before her, I breathlessly demanded to know what was happening.

In the midst of a half-turn, Christine suddenly froze. After eyeing me up and down, she looked over at Two – who was wearing this incredibly flimsy see-through blouse – and then back at me. After looking over at Two again, a knowing grin crept upon her face as she turned back to me. "Don't even think about it!"

Then she gestured for me to follow her into her office.

After closing the doors behind us, Christine looked me up and down again and smiled. "Cute outfit," she said. "But really bad timing."

Confused, I demanded again to know what was going on. "There's a mob down there, Christine, and a bunch of them tried to chase me down the alleyway!"

Suddenly serious, Christine nodded. "As you may know, President Reagan received an advance copy of your study yesterday and he made a major issue out of it at a campaign rally...

"We had asked him to give us a couple of more days to get copies in the hands of the press, but the request apparently fell through the cracks at his campaign headquarters...

"And as a result, Washington is in an uproar. The Democrats are trying to represent the President's statements as irresponsible and unsubstantiated allegations, and the press seems inclined to agree – because they're acting like a bunch of sharks that smell blood in the water."

Allegations? "Those weren't allegations," I said quickly. "Those were facts!"

Christine nodded. "So they were. But in the absence of the advance copies – which would enable them to check your facts and assess your methodology – they aren't buying...

"Which is why we're putting on a dog and pony show at the hotel for the press, and congressional staff members." Glancing down at her watch, she said, "In precisely 46 minutes."

Huh???

Since I didn't know that a "dog and pony show" was Washington-speak for a "media event," I was confused. "Why don't we just hand out some of the advance copies that are down in the Econ shop?"

Startled, Christine asked me what I was talking about. "The 5,000 copies that were delivered yesterday," I said. "Dr. MacLaughlin ordered 500, but somebody messed up the order and they sent 5,000 instead."

As a big smile spread across her face, Christine asked me if I was kidding. Shaking my head, I said "Nuh-uh...

"There's hundreds of cases of them, stacked up along the walls on the Seventh Floor."

Clenching her fists together, Christine raised them above her head and thrust them toward the ceiling. *"YES!!"*

After doing a little "Happy Dance" on the Oriental carpet, she clasped my shoulders with both hands. Staring directly into my eyes, she told me to run down to the Econ shop, and round up a couple of interns.

"Tell them to load up half the boxes on push carts and take them over to Conference Room Three at the hotel, and stack them just inside the doors as neatly as possible...

"And then wait until the press and staffers arrive. When they do, I want them to give each one a copy as they enter the room."

Still looking at me intently, Christine asked me if I understood. After I repeated her instructions back to her she nodded and told me to come back as quickly as possible, so she could do something about my hair and makeup. Because next to gravity, she said, TV cameras are a girl's worst enemy.

Perplexed, I scrunched up my nose and leaned my head over on its side. "Christine, what are you talking about?"

"The dog and pony show," she said. "You and Dr. MacLaughlin are going to be our 'talking dogs'."

Now most people probably would have caught on by then, but I was still totally confused. So I scrunched up my nose again, and looked at her incredulously. "You want us to go over to the hotel and *bark*???"

Christine cocked her head and stared at me for a long moment. And then as a sudden flash of recognition spread across her face, she cracked up. "A dog and pony show," she said, "is a press conference."

"A press conference?" I repeated in a high squeaky voice.

Christine nodded, this time with emphasis. "A press conference," she said. "And you and Dr. MacLaughlin are going to speak."

Huh???

My mouth was moving, but none of the words were coming out. But rather than wait for me to recover my wits, Christine opened her eyes wide instead, and nodded emphatically.

Aghast, I looked down at myself. "Christine!" I protested. "I can't go out there looking like this!"

Folding her arms across her chest, Christine pursed her lips together and gave me her "Nazi-look" before doing a slow walk around me.

Stopping just short of a full circle, she paused for a long moment before nodding. "You're right," she said. "The jacket has to go."

After studying me for another moment, she pursed her lips again and said I was going to need some diamonds.

Then she told me to get a move on, because we were running out of time.

CHAPTER TWENTY-TWO

Exactly 37 minutes later, Dr. MacLaughlin and I followed Christine up the steps of the raised dais in Conference Room Three, with Admiral Taylor, General Thomas, and General McGreggor bringing up the rear. Convinced that the whole press conference thing was a really bad idea, I glumly settled into the seat that had been assigned to me next to Dr. MacLaughlin.

Chatting amiably among themselves, the men were obviously at ease in front of all the lights and cameras. But I wasn't.

After I returned to Christine's office, she had sent me down to the ladies' room to wash off my face. After that, I spent the next fifteen minutes staring into her ceiling light while she redid my face and hair. Acutely conscious of the fact that I now had on more make-up than I had ever worn in my entire life, I was fidgeting in my chair and hoping no one would notice.

Because as far as I was concerned, the only good thing that had come out of Christine's makeover was the matching diamond necklace and earring set she'd had sent over from the hotel's boutique. They were truly exquisite, and as I sat there in front of the lights playing with the necklace, I realized that I'd never even seen anything that beautiful before.

But the thought was unfortunately short-lived, because a couple of guys from the hotel staff diverted my attention by carrying a huge blackboard up the steps onto the dais. So while everyone else was waiting for the show to get on the road, I started checking out the exits – just in case I did something stupid, and had to make a run for it.

I had pretty much settled on the one behind and to my right when a high-pitched squeal interrupted my planning process. Apologizing to the audience, Christine spent a moment adjusting the volume before asking the assembled press if they were ready. After a murmur of agreement from the audience, she asked someone in the back to dim the lights. Getting the thumbs-up signal from one of the cameramen, Christine lifted the microphone from the stand on the podium and walked to the edge of the dais. Smiling, she welcomed one and all.

Although I couldn't see her face from where 1 was sitting, I could hear her as she walked the press through the events that had led to my study. Captivated by her melodic speaking voice, I watched as the camera lights followed her up and down the edge of the dais. Speaking without notes, she paused only occasionally to smile into a lens.

Man, I thought. *She's good!*

But it wasn't until the lights followed her swaying hips back to the podium that I realized just how good she really was. Suppressing the surprised look that had attempted to steal upon my face, I was betting dollars to doughnuts that she had mesmerized the mostly male audience.

Christine! I thought. *You are soooo naughty!!!*

I was snickering to myself when she turned toward the table and introduced each of us in turn. Following Dr. MacLaughlin's example, I smiled and nodded into the lights when she called my name.

After everyone was properly introduced, Christine informed the audience that Dr. MacLaughlin would make a presentation outlining the study and its economic implications. After Dr. MacLaughlin finished, Admiral Taylor and Gen. Thomas and Gen. McGreggor would discuss the strategic ramifications of Soviet black marketeering within the larger context of the Cold War, and then open the floor to questions. Nodding to Dr. MacLaughlin, she replaced her microphone on the podium and stepped back into the shadows.

Feeling enormously relieved that Christine hadn't mentioned me, I looked over at Dr. MacLaughlin as he reached for the mike in front of him. Although I wasn't quite sure what I was supposed to be doing, I thought it would be a good idea to follow his remarks carefully. So I sat up straight in my chair, and with my most serious look, focused my eyes on him.

But it turned out that Dr. MacLaughlin was as good at working a crowd as Christine. After issuing a cheerful good morning to all present, he remarked that he hadn't had the opportunity to bore a group this size since he'd retired from active teaching.

There was a little laughter and a great deal of snickering from the audience in front, and then a loud boo from the back. Grinning, Dr. MacLaughlin quipped into the microphone that one of his former students must be in attendance.

Leaning back in his chair and thrusting his arm out for dramatic effect, he pointed into the haze and demanded the heckler identify himself. After a moment of complete silence, an uncertain voice called back: "Thomas Alfonso, Professor. Class of '76."

After that, the whole place broke up laughing.

Once the laughter died down, Dr. MacLaughlin looked to the far back again, and addressed the culprit in his most severe professorial voice, "I did fail you, didn't I?" When the Alfonso guy replied no, and reminded him that he had received a "B" in Introductory Economics, Dr. MacLaughlin looked over at me and deadpanned "Remind me to call Georgetown when we get back to the office, so I can change his grade to an F."

The audience cracked up again, and by the time the laughter finally subsided Dr. MacLaughlin had them eating out of the palm of his hand. Getting up from his seat, he walked over to the podium and picked up the microphone Christine had been using, and began speaking. Pacing back and forth across the dais, he presented a brief historical overview of the Cold War and then described the role that economics played in the conflict. Pivoting on his heel at the far end of the dais, he marched back to the center and began explaining the difficulties involved in analyzing Soviet economic performance and potential before explaining the significance of price in developed economies. These economies were so large, he said, that it was physically impossible to take accurate inventories of raw materials, plants and equipment, or finished products. The only way to estimate their numbers or to allocate their use was to measure their relative scarcity by allowing prices to float in an open market, and in his opinion the Soviets' failure to do so had ultimately doomed their effort. By artificially fixing prices in response to what were fundamentally political considerations rather than actual scarcities, the Soviets had created an entirely new and often subtle form of inefficiency that ran throughout the warp and woof of their centrally planned economy.

After a brief discussion of the failed Lieberman Reforms of the 1960s – which were designed in part to remedy that error – he addressed the cascading problems generated by the Soviet economic system. Reeling off one statistic after another as he paced back and forth, he explained how one set related to another, and then to all the rest, until he had at last built a mental image for the audience of the Soviet economy. It was, he said, very much as if one had built a towering, ramshackle structure on a cliff overlooking an ocean, where each angry wave eroded its foundation. Aghast at the imagery that had taken root in my mind, I realized that it wouldn't take much to bring the whole thing crashing down…

As Dr. MacLaughlin brought his lecture to a close with all the storm and fury of a Wagnerian opera, I suddenly realized that was precisely his point. The Soviet economy had frayed badly along the edges, and in a desperate effort to keep the whole thing from unraveling, the Soviets had resorted to black marketeering. Thus the world was now faced, he said, with an unprecedented and potentially catastrophic challenge: a failing, nuclear-armed superpower engaged in global criminality.

Good God! I thought. *He did that without notes???*

Thinking I couldn't do that if I lived to be a hundred, I sat in stunned silence as he replaced the microphone at the podium. The audience must have been thinking the same thing, because there was a long moment of utter silence. Then a smattering of applause spread through the crowd, until it had built into a thunderous roar.

I was still shaking my head in awe when Christine returned to the podium. After waiting for the applause to die down, she thanked Dr. MacLaughlin for his remarkable presentation, and then turned to Admiral Taylor. As the ranking military officer – he had four stars, as I later learned – she suggested that he lead the discussion of the military implications of the Soviet Union's involvement in the global black market.

Adm. Taylor was tall and thin, and in civilian clothes he looked more like a high school English teacher than a career naval officer. But he had flown more than 120 combat missions over North Vietnam before being promoted to flag rank, and as he began speaking I realized that there was a lot more to him than met the eye as he crisply described the Soviet naval threat.

After providing a brief overview of the enormous Soviet naval build-up that had started in the mid-1960s, the admiral turned his attention to their Merchant Marine. In order to earn hard currency, he said, the Soviets had built a huge fleet of relatively small oceangoing merchant ships – most of them around 10,000 tons – and deployed them in the Third World.

For the most part, these Soviet merchant ships plied the coastlines of the undeveloped world, where they did a brisk business hauling smaller cargos that Western and Japanese ships disdained. But according to intelligence reports, they were also dropping off loads of illegal weapons and – almost certainly – picking up large quantities of drugs as well. According to the Admiral, the problem had been overlooked for far too long. For in addition to the fact that the ships were hauling contraband, they would automatically transfer to military control in the event of war. The fact that these were civilian ships didn't mean they were unarmed, and intelligence reports indicated that many of them carried a small arsenal of naval mines and surface-to-surface and surface-to-air missiles below decks. Although none of these ships were likely to last long in combat, they were a serious complicating factor in naval war planning.

They were also a perfect platform for launching *Spetsnaz* naval commandos against vulnerable targets inland, and their ports-of-call provided a perfect opportunity for the Soviets to insert Spetsnaz scouts into selected countries to reconnoiter possible wartime targets such as docks, warehouses, electric grids, and oil terminals and oil tanks – and not just in the Third World.

Soviet merchantmen routinely plied the Caribbean Basin – through which almost half of our total oil imports flowed – and at any given time, dozens of Soviet merchantmen were docked in our southern ports. To make his point, the admiral ticked off a list of high-value targets that lay within easy reach of sea-borne raiders along the Gulf Coast, and cited FBI reports that Soviet "merchant seamen" on shore leave were routinely observed on apparent scouting missions in their vicinities. In the event of war, the admiral believed Soviet merchant marine assets could wreak havoc on our coastal infrastructure. In all likelihood, they would inflict enough damage on our ports to effectively close them for 10 to 15 days.

The admiral then nodded to his right, and informed the audience that Gen. Thomas could elaborate upon that point.

After clearing his throat, Gen. Thomas began describing the U.S. military's mobilization plans, and the role the Gulf Ports were expected to play in them. In the event of a Soviet attack upon Western Europe, current plans called for airlifting the bulk of America's regular ground forces to Europe, where they would pick up pre-positioned supplies before heading for the front line in Germany. However, current NATO ammunition stockpiles were sufficient for only 30 days of high-intensity fighting, so it was critical that additional arms and ammunition begin flowing on the very first day of hostilities. Given their bulk weight, these could only be transported by sea, and if Adm. Taylor's estimates for port closures were anywhere close to correct, the war effort would be crippled. In all probability, Allied conventional forces would collapse on $D + 45$ – that is, on the 45_{th} day of hostilities – leaving civilian policymakers with the stark choice of surrender or nuclear war. Nodding to Gen. McGreggor, Gen. Thomas asked him to place the problem in context.

After thanking Gen. Thomas for the floor, Gen. McGreggor provided the audience with what he called a *tour de horizon* of Soviet grand strategy. Although he did not believe that the Soviets had any interest in actually fighting a war, they were clearly attempting to achieve a global strategic advantage so unmistakably pronounced as to make armed resistance futile. Should they achieve it, the Soviet leadership believed – accurately, in his opinion – the political leadership of the NATO countries would have no choice but to accommodate their demands. The NATO alliance would be dissolved of necessity, leaving the United States to stand alone. Then over a period of years, the socialist democracies of Western Europe would inevitably slip into a form of Soviet-style Communism.

Within this grand strategic framework, gunrunning and narcotics trafficking played multiple and important roles, he said. They provided the Soviets with a source of illicit hard currency, access to a wide range of ports throughout the world by way of their merchant marine, and an almost perfect platform for launching naval commandos against littoral targets.

In addition, they provided the Soviets with a global web of criminal connections and – by virtue of their money laundering activities – unprecedented access to and influence upon major Western banks and financial institutions. The nature and extent of the contacts they inevitably developed in criminal and banking circles had undoubtedly provided their intelligence services with a bonanza, and as the former head of the Defense Intelligence Agency, he had no doubt that they had employed it to blackmail and suborn corrupt politicians throughout the West. It was his best judgment then, that the Soviet's involvement in gun running and narcotics trafficking was motivated by much more than financial interest. Taken together, the two provided the Soviets with a range of strategic opportunities, and for that reason they should be viewed in a broad strategic context. In bringing his presentation to a close, he thanked the audience for their attention and opened the floor to questions.

Lost in thought, I barely noticed when Christine returned to the podium. During the course of the study it had become obvious that the Soviets were up to their ears in money laundering, but the possibility that they were using their financial contacts – supposedly respectable, or otherwise – to dig up dirt on politicians hadn't even crossed my mind. Thinking that was a really foolish oversight, I made a mental note to kick myself as soon as the press conference was over. Because let's face it – a financial statement tells you just about everything there is to know about a person.

By that time, Christine had completed a few brief remarks, and called on a rather slender middle-aged man in the front row. After rising to his feet, he identified himself as Franklin Pierson of *The Wall Street Journal*, and asked Dr. MacLaughlin about his level of confidence in the data the study was based upon.

Dr. MacLaughlin was busy stuffing his pipe with tobacco as the question was asked, so he didn't look up until he had finished. Nodding gravely, he stuck the pipe in his mouth and lit it. Then after pulling on it a few times, he commended Mr. Pierson for asking. Explaining that the data had originally been obtained by the CIA's Clandestine Service, Dr. MacLaughlin said it had been checked and cross-checked against a multitude of different sources before it had been accepted as genuine. Pulling the pipe from his mouth, he pointed it at Pierson for emphasis, and told him that he had "every confidence" in the factual accuracy of the information.

After the Pierson guy thanked Dr. MacLaughlin and sat down, Christine called on a more portly man in the front row. Standing and introducing himself as Guy Randolph of *The Washington Post*, he asked Adm. Taylor if he could cite the intelligence reports that suggested the Soviets had armed their merchant ships, provide an estimate as to how many merchant ships had been armed, and a description of their armaments. After listening carefully, Adm. Taylor apologized and said the intelligence reports were still classified so he couldn't discuss them further without authorization.

However, he had read them during his tenure as Chief of Naval Operations, and had found them so alarming that he had personally checked their "sources and methods." Moving on to the remainder of the question, Adm. Taylor stated that approximately 300 Soviet merchant ships had been armed with an assortment of surface-to-surface, surface-to-shore, and surface-to-air missiles, as well as several different types of naval mines.

The next question was posed by a reporter from *Business Week*, who asked Dr. MacLaughlin about the prospects for expanding trade with the USSR. After drawing on his pipe, Dr. MacLaughlin said he really wasn't qualified to say one way or another. Given the centralized nature of the Soviet economy, trade with the Soviets depended more upon treaties than economics and that made it very much a diplomatic issue. But if he were forced to hazard a guess, he would say that Soviet exports of oil and natural gas were likely to increase substantially. Whether or not they would increase their imports of Western goods, however, remained very much an open question.

After that, the questions began moving more or less up and down the line. Economic questions were directed to Dr. MacLaughlin, naval questions to Adm. Taylor, and military questions to either Gen. Thomas or Gen. McGreggor. Which made me a happy camper, because I was really hoping everyone would ignore me.

But no such luck. Because about a half-hour later, someone in the back noted that I had been listed as co-author of the study and asked Dr. MacLaughlin to explain my role in the project.

Oh, rats! I thought. Then I stole a quick glance over my shoulder, to make sure my escape route was still clear.

Dr. MacLaughlin must have read my mind because he looked over and whispered, "Just be yourself" before turning back into the cameras. Smiling broadly, he thanked the questioner for the chance to introduce his young colleague.

Turning slightly in his seat, he reiterated my name – just in case anyone had somehow missed it – and described me as a "truly remarkable product" of Township College who he had been fortunate enough to hire as a research assistant. Then he went on to describe the study's design, and the role that I had played in the project's completion.

That part was all true, but when he started in on all my supposed qualities I began to blanch. Praising my "perceptive insight" was one thing, but the whole "brilliant analytical mind" bit was like, way over the top. Blushing badly, I clenched my teeth together and whispered out of the corner of my mouth. "Stop that! You're embarrassing me!"

But he didn't. Instead, he suggested that the remaining questions regarding either the study or economics in general be directed to me. Smiling amiably, he asked for the next question as I growled under my breath.

"I'll get you for this!"

I knew he heard me, because he snickered. But by then Christine had called on some guy seated in the mid-section. After standing and introducing himself, he asked what had led me to specialize in Soviet economics.

The question kinda threw me, because I hadn't thought of myself as a Soviet specialist before. Moving quickly to correct his misapprehension, I explained that I had double-majored in international finance and economics, and that any specialized knowledge of Soviet economics I had acquired had been learned in the course of the project, through individual study and Dr. MacLaughlin's tutelage. Seemingly satisfied, the guy thanked me for my explanation and sat down.

The next question came from a journalist who identified himself as a reporter from London's *Financial Times*, and it seemed innocuous enough as stated – basically, he just wanted a cursory assessment of the Soviet civilian economy. But as I began to formulate my reply, I realized that he had thrown me a curveball. Trying hard to steady my voice, I told him quite honestly that I wasn't sure the Soviets actually had a civilian economy. Because in my view, civilian economics are ultimately reducible to supply and demand, with price determining the point where the one intersected the other. But the hyper-centralized Soviet economy was based upon planned production and presumed consumption, with little regard to price and none at all to demand. For that reason, the so-called civilian economy of the USSR more nearly resembled a governmental purchase and distribution plan.

The reporter paused for a moment, before asking me for additional clarification. It was a most interesting observation, he said, but he wasn't sure his readers would immediately grasp my point. Smiling, Dr. MacLaughlin leaned forward and seconded the request, and suggested that it would perhaps be better taken visually. "Why don't you graph that on the chalkboard," he said.

Although ashen-faced and trembling, I hadn't entirely lost my wits. So I made a special point of stepping on Dr. MacLaughlin's foot as I rose from my seat.

Proceeding to the blackboard, I picked up a piece of chalk and sketched an X–Y axis. Then in a slightly squeaky voice, asked the audience to take widgets for example. Since widgets are very valuable things to have – for economists anyway, because we always use them as an example when we're trying to illustrate supply and demand – everyone wants at least one. But since widgets cost money, the number of people that actually buy them depends upon their price in the market place. Turning halfway around to look over my shoulder, I asked the audience if everyone was with me so far. Seeing the audience nod, I turned back to the board and continued. Drawing a big dot on the vertical Y Axis, I labeled it Point A. "Let's assume that this represents the number of widgets produced in our hypothetical society." Then I drew another dot on the horizontal X Axis, and labeled it Point B. "And let's assume that this represents the number of people who are able and willing to buy widgets at $100 a piece." After extending a horizontal line from Point A on the vertical axis about two feet across the board, I dropped another line down to where Point B lay on the horizontal axis, and then connected the two dots with a curve.

Stepping back for a moment to survey my handiwork, I continued. "This is your supply and demand curve at $100 a widget....

"But let's suppose that selling widgets at $100 a pop is really profitable," I said. "In that case, investors are going to put their money into new widget factories and the supply will increase...

Marking Point C in the vertical axis above my original Point A, I said, "So all of a sudden we now have a lot more widgets offered for sale, but more or less the same number of people willing to buy them at $100 each. So the only way widget makers can sell their product is to increase demand by cutting their price." Drawing another big dot to the right of Point B, I labeled it Point D and scrawled $90 underneath it. Then I drew another curve connecting Point C and Point D. "Excess supply prompts price cuts which increase consumer demand, and new sales bring the market back into balance."

Stepping back so the audience could see my revised graph, I explained that this was one simplified example of how supply and demand operated in a free market economy. "But in the USSR, comparable market forces are entirely lacking. Production targets are set by government ministries that may or may not take into account the number of potential consumers, and prices are artificially established on the basis of multiple criteria that have little or nothing to do with actual costs of capital investment, production, distribution and sale."

Stepping back up to the blackboard, I drew another X-Y axis. "Let's say X represents supply in the form of planned production, and Y represents projected consumption – in effect, a bureaucratic estimate of demand...

"So the Ministry of Light Industry orders its factories to produce a zillion widgets which it plans to sell for 100 rubles each. But since the Soviet economy is geared to production rather than sales, they have very poor quality control in their civilian factories. As a result, Soviet widgets are so poorly made that Soviet consumers aren't willing to buy them at any price – they'd rather make their own at home, or simply do without."

Turning back to the board, I drew a big dot near the top of the vertical axis and labeled it Point A, and another big dot at the bottom of the vertical axis where it intersected the horizontal axis X, and labeled it Point B, and then I drew a heavy line up and down to connect them. "Thus the phenomenon of a high level of government-mandated consumer production coupled to low or non-existent levels of consumption and inflexible prices...

"Which makes accurate assessments of national wealth impossible, because all the consumer goods no one will buy are stuffed into warehouses and carried on the books as list-value inventory."

Turning back to the audience, I explained that when it came to the Soviet civilian economy there just wasn't a bottom line. "It's pure fantasy," I said.

Putting down the chalk, I started back to my seat. But unfortunately, the interrogation wasn't over. Someone from *The New York Times* jumped up and shouted a question. Because I hadn't fully heard it, I halted in mid-stride and asked him to repeat it.

After thanking me for what he called "a most illuminating presentation," he said he remained puzzled. Since I was unwilling to call the Soviet civilian economy an economy, he wondered what term I might use to describe it.

Now that's a good question, I thought as I stood in the middle of the dais. Pondering it for a moment, I settled into my "thinking pose" – that funny little thing I do when I'm grappling with a problem on my feet. Placing my left hand on my hip, I raised my left foot and balanced it on its toes. As I did so, my skirt slipped up and revealed a whole lot more of my thigh than it should have.

But unfortunately, I wasn't paying attention as my hem ascended into the Forbidden Zone. Oblivious to the sudden pop of flashbulbs, I raised my right index finger to my lips and laid my head over on my shoulder. Looking up to my right, I thought about it for a long moment before I reverted to a more ordinary stance to reply. "I would have to call it a negative-value system, because the value of the finished consumer goods are often less than the value of the raw materials they were produced from."

Suddenly uncertain, I glanced over at Dr. MacLaughlin. Clapping his hands together, he bellowed "Bravo!" Then he leaned forward into the microphone on the table, and assured the audience that it was "a truly inspired description."

Since the audience had suddenly started chattering amongst themselves, I wasn't quite sure what to do. Hoping for some guidance from Christine, I looked over at the podium. But unfortunately, she was studying her watch. Then after looking back up at the audience a moment later, she apologized and informed them that we were nearly out of time. Pointing to a rather plump but elegantly dressed lady in the third row, she said, "The last question is yours."

After taking to her feet and juggling the small notebook that had been resting on her lap, she identified herself as Lydia Sykes from the *Style* section of *The Washington Post*. Smiling sweetly, she looked at me. "I just have one question, dear…

"Do you have a boyfriend?"

Taken by complete surprise, I stammered for a moment. Then I frowned and shook my head. "No, Ma'am," I said sadly. "I had a guy, but he dumped me."

There was a sympathetic *"Awwwww"* from the audience, followed by complete silence. Ashamed and bitterly angry, I shook my head again as I looked down at my feet.

Completely oblivious to the fact that you could have heard a pin drop in the stillness, I muttered a bewildered curse. *"The schmuck!"*

CHAPTER TWENTY-THREE

Now from any logical standpoint, a completely silent room can't possibly become any more silent. But for just an instant, it did. Then the whole audience cracked up.

Suddenly aware of what I had just said on live TV, my jaw dropped and my eyes bulged, and without even thinking I threw my hand over my mouth.

But by then it was far too late. They were howling!

Oh dear God! I thought. *What have I done???*

Horrified, I stood transfixed on the stage as a sense of despair crept upon me. Desperate, I turned toward Christine, but to no avail. Almost doubled over the podium laughing, she had clasped the sides of the wooden stand in a death grip in an effort to remain standing. So after a quick glance to my right, I made a run for it.

But for a man who stood 6'2" and weighed well over 280 pounds, Dr. MacLaughlin was amazingly agile. The moment I bolted for the exit, he leapt to his feet to block my escape, and before I could take another step he'd wrapped a huge arm around my waist and pulled me to his side. Holding me there with crushing force, he whispered out of the side of his mouth. "Just smile and wave, Lassie, and they'll think it's all part of the show." Then he thrust his other arm into the air, and bellowed out his thanks to one and all.

By the time I managed to force a thin smile on my face, Christine appeared in my peripheral vision. Still chuckling as she wrapped an arm around my waist from the other direction, she announced that a press release would be available from her office later that afternoon. Then after a final wave to the audience, she and Dr. MacLaughlin guided me across the platform and down the far steps to the exit doors.

Christine and Dr. MacLaughlin were both a lot taller than I was, and Dr. MacLaughlin at least was a whole lot stronger. So when they had wrapped their arms around my waist, they sort of lifted me up in the air a bit. But there wasn't a whole lot I could do about it except kinda float along between them and hope that no one noticed my feet weren't exactly touching the ground.

After more or less carrying me through the exit doors, they set me down in the service hallway that ran parallel to the conference room. Which was a really good thing, because that meant I could breathe again.

But as soon as my shoes were planted on the carpet, they looked at one another and broke up laughing again. Burying my face in my hands I tried to apologize to them, but Christine cut me off with a chuckle. Draping her arm around my shoulder, she explained that everyone has problems with their first press conference. Looking up at her, I scrunched my nose in disbelief. "Really?"

Christine chortled, and repeated herself emphatically. "Really!"

For some reason that surprised me, so I took a moment to think about it. But as we pushed through the exit doors that led from the hotel to the alleyway, I looked up at her hopefully. "So you blew your first one too?"

Christine rolled her eyes as she pulled her arm off my shoulder, and then shook her head back and forth in disbelief. As she began swinging her arms forward and back, I could hear Dr. MacLaughlin chuckling off to my left. Then as we approached the rear entrance of the CSS building, Christine explained that it hadn't been a press conference. "It was my first big modeling job in New York," she said. "I tripped on the runway, and fell flat on my face."

My jaw dropped and my eyes bulged. "Oh my God!" I exclaimed. "On live TV?"

By that time Dr. MacLaughlin's chuckling had turned into sly snicker, so I figured he must have seen it. Looking back up at Christine, I watched as she sighed and pursed her lips together. By this time we had finally reached the door that led to the First Floor Lobby, and as she reached for the door handle to open it, Christine shook her head back and forth and sighed again before finally nodding. "Uh-huh."

Harsh, I thought. "That must have been really embarrassing."

Christine nodded again. "Oh yeah," she said. Then she gave Dr. MacLaughlin a nasty look and said, "And believe it or not, some people still tease me about it."

Dr. MacLaughlin 'harrumphed,' and hotly denied it. But after a withering look from Christine, he backed down a bit. "Well, not very often at least."

After giving him another withering look, Christine turned back to me. "Anyway, I was pretty sure that was the end of my modeling career..."

Then after pausing for a moment, she smiled and explained the public was remarkably forgiving. "They want to be able to relate to those in the spotlight, and television encourages them to do so because in one sense you're right there with them, in their living room....

"But in fact you're physically distant, and that creates something of a paradox...

"And that forces the audience to make a choice as to how they want to see you, and that choice occurs at a very deep psychological level...

"Tripping on the runway revealed my humanity to the audience. They looked at me and thought, 'Hey, she's a klutz, too!'"

Smiling and looking down at me, she explained that her blunder had given fashion aficionados something they could not only laugh at, but relate to as well. The same thing applied to the press conference, she said. "As embarrassing as it may have been, your little *faux pas* was endearing." Then very emphatically, she pointed out that everyone gets dumped at one time or another, so she was pretty sure the audience would relate to that.

Then she pursed her lips together, and nodded to no one in particular. "And if they don't...

"Well, to hell with them anyway!"

Surprised and suddenly buoyant, I asked her if that meant I still had a job. As a grin spread across her face, Christine winked and said "Maybe."

Then she chuckled, and assured me that I was still on the payroll. "Everyone stumbles the first time out of the box," she said. But all things considered, she thought I had done very well.

As a smile of relief spread across my face, I looked over at Dr. MacLaughlin. We had reached the elevators by then, and he was in the process of pressing the up button when he noticed. Standing back and folding his hands in front of him while we waited, he smiled. "I quite agree, Lass. All in all, it was a superb performance."

Suddenly suspicious – and more than a bit curious – I looked up at him as we entered the elevator cab. "So what about you?"

Looking suddenly uncomfortable, Dr. MacLaughlin made a vague clucking sound before replying. "What about me, Ms. McAllister?"

Grinning, I told him to fess up. "Tell me about your first press conference. Did ya mess it up?"

Chuckling, Dr. MacLaughlin strenuously denied it. But as a crimson look of embarrassment crept across his face, he claimed it was only because they didn't have the media back then.

"Gutenberg was still working out the bugs in his printing press, as I recall."

Uh-huh, I thought as Christine rolled her eyes and gave him another sarcastic look. "Charles," she said, "You are such a liar!"

Dr. MacLaughlin chuckled. "So I am." But before I could say anything, the elevator came to a halt on the Seventh Floor. With a triumphant grin on his face, Dr. MacLaughlin excused himself and took off down the hallway.

As the door closed, I looked up at Christine. "So he's blowing smoke, huh?" Christine chortled and said, "Big time."

Grinning, I asked her for the 411. But as the door opened onto the Eighth Floor, she shook her head and grinned. "You'll have to get that out of him yourself."

Thinking there wasn't much chance of that as we turned the corner and headed up the hall to the Executive Offices, I apologized to Christine again. "I'm really sorry about that whole schmuck thing."

Halting in mid-stride just in front of the open doors, Christine cracked up again. Seizing the edge of the drinking fountain with one hand, and placing the other across her side, she laughed again until tears started rolling down her cheeks. "I still can't believe you said that!"

Since I didn't know what to do I just stood there, shifting uncomfortably on my feet until she stopped laughing. "So am I ever going to live this down?"

After straightening herself up, Christine grinned and shook her head. "Not in this lifetime!"

Then she rather pointedly told me it was time to get back to work, and strode down the hall.

Suddenly aware of the fact that Two had been peering over the side of her desk to eavesdrop, I tossed my hair back and leaned over the fountain for a drink. *Oh Lord,* I thought. *She's just gonna love this!*

But since there wasn't anything I could do about it, I figured I might as well be the one to tell her. So in response to her whispered question as I passed by her desk, I stopped and explained that I had messed up at the press conference.

With a less than convincing look of concern, she asked me if I was serious. "Oh no," I said. "I just made a fool out of myself in front of a national audience, that's all."

Two's eyes widened. "Oh, God!" she said in a hushed whisper. "Does Alex know about it?"

After I shrugged, she flipped her hair back before returning to her keyboard. "Oh, well," she said snidely. "Better you than me."

I gave her a disgusted look, but I didn't say anything because I had enough problems without getting into it with the boss's secretary. So after making a mental note to even-up with Two later, I turned toward my office. I had a ton of work to do – which I suddenly realized was a problem, because we hadn't opened up the vault yet.

Pausing in my doorway, I was trying to decide whether I should knock on Christine's door or go down to the Econ shop to get Dr. MacLaughlin when the intercom on my phone buzzed. When I picked up the receiver, Christine asked me to join her in her office – she had to call Alex, and she wanted me to sit in on the conversation. But first and foremost, she wanted me to bring her a fresh cup of coffee.

Three minutes later, I pushed one of the double doors to her office open with my shoulder. With two 16-ounce styrofoam cups of steaming coffee precariously balanced on a tray, alongside a creamer, a half-dozen packs of sweetener, some stir sticks, and napkins, I carefully made my way across the Oriental rug before setting the whole thing down on the side of her desk. Relieved I hadn't spilled anything, I handed her one of the cups and then arranged all of the rest of the stuff between us before sitting down in the chair across from her.

After thanking me, Christine looked over the legal pad she had been scribbling on. Apparently satisfied, she picked up the phone and started punching the keypad. After a ten or fifteen-second silence, she straightened in her chair and asked for Mr. Alexander de Vris. "Room 310, please."

After another pause, Christine suddenly smiled. "Hey stranger, how ya doing?"

Nestling the mouthpiece between her cheek and her shoulder, Christine reached across for the creamer. As she poured some into her cup, she chuckled. Placing the vessel back on the desk, she reached for two packets of sweetener, and a stir. "So what did you think?" she asked.

Holding the mouthpiece with one hand and stirring the sweetener into her coffee with the other, she nodded as she glanced down at the pad before her. Then after carefully depositing the stir into the trash can beside her desk, she picked up a pen and scribbled a quick note before grinning as she leaned back into her chair. "We got lucky, to tell you the truth...

"Dr. MacLaughlin had ordered 500 advance copies for the Econ shop, but they messed up and sent us 500 cases instead."

After listening intently for a moment, Christine nodded. "Right," she said. "Enough for everyone there, and another 3,500 or so to distribute on the Hill…

"We should get quite a bit of play on the evening news."

There was another pause as Christine listened, before nodding again. "I'll put a press release together as soon as we're finished. I told them they could pick it up here this afternoon, but I think we should fax a copy to all the major national and international news outlets. Want me to send you the draft before we release it?" Leaning back in her chair as she took a sip of coffee, she nodded again. "Oh yeah, I think we hit it out of the ballpark!"

Although I couldn't hear what Alex was saying, it had been easy enough to follow the conversation. So when she looked at me and grinned, I knew that Alex had asked her about me.

Leaning back in her chair again, Christine smiled mischievously. After another moment of silence, she nodded rather emphatically. "Very well indeed!"

Nodding again, she told him that Dr. MacLaughlin concurred. "He was particularly impressed by her characterization of the Soviet economy as a 'negative value system.' He thought that was a great description."

Glancing at her watch, Christine said "Uh-huh" a couple of times. "I think we should play it for all it's worth."

Shifting in her chair, Christine listened intently for a moment. Then she smiled and told him it could have been worse. Slipping into a really bad imitation of my New England accent, she grinned and muttered "the schmuck." Then she broke up laughing.

As the crimson spread across my cheeks, I buried my face in my hands in a futile effort to hide. *Oh good God*, I thought. *I'm never going to hear the end of this!*

But just as I was about to take the exit marked "Self Pity," I heard Christine growl. "Not even funny, Alex!

"I've told you a hundred thousand times….

"The seamstress who tacked the hem on my gown did a lousy job, and when it fell I went with it!"

Pulling the handset away for a moment, she gave it a disgusted look before returning it to her ear. "And besides, Dr. MacLaughlin already made fun of me today so don't even think about it!"

A look of mock surprise and outrage passed across her face. "Yeah, well you've done some dumb stuff too," she said. "Need I remind you about Mary Lou Steinhoff?"

Caught completely off guard, I scrunched up my face and sat back in my chair. *Who the heck is that?*

Laughing as a triumphant look spread across her face, Christine sarcastically said "Uh-huh" before falling quiet. Pretty sure she'd just won a game of *Gotcha!*, I leaned forward and grinned.

Suddenly serious, Christine fell silent and listened intently. After a long moment, she nodded and said she agreed. "Have a number in mind?" she asked. Then she nodded again, and after a long pause, told him not to worry about it. She'd think of something.

Leaning back in her chair, Christine asked him when he was coming back. Then after a brief pause, she asked how it had gone with Bunni and her beau. After reversing direction and leaning forward to take another sip of coffee, she grinned happily. "So you liked him, huh?"

After listening for another couple of moments, she asked him if Bunni had picked out her dress. After a short pause, she smiled again. "Oh Alex, that was so sweet of you!"

"Are you going to give her away?"

After another short pause, Christine smiled wistfully and leaned back in her chair again. "She'll make such a beautiful bride, Alex..."

With the smile still lingering on her face, Christine listened again intently. "OK," she finally said. "We have a lot of stuff to go over, so why don't I pick you up at the airport?"

Nodding, she reached across her desk for her Day-Timer. After flipping the page, she scribbled something across the bottom. "No," she said, "I think it's a good idea..."

Scribbling in the Day-Timer again, she nodded. "Right. Working dinner, 7-10 pm. I'll reserve a private dining room at the hotel." Then she nodded again, and looked over at me. "Yes, she's right here..."

"Want to talk to her?"

Uh-oh, I thought.

But lucky for me, Alex apparently had something more pressing on his agenda. Nodding again, Christine smiled and looked over at me. "I'll be sure to tell her," she said. Then she hung up the receiver, and picked up her coffee.

Grasping the cup with both hands, Christine leaned back in her chair and smiled. "Alex wants you to know that he thinks you did a terrific job with the press conference."

Incredulous, I scrunched my brow together. "Even with the schmuck thing?"

Christine laughed again, and nodded. "Even with the schmuck thing." Then she reached into her lower side drawer, and pulled out the case for the diamond earrings and necklace set. After pushing it across her desk, she said, "There you go."

Thinking that nothing really good lasts forever, I sighed and turned the necklace around. Looking down sadly, I was in the process of opening the clasp when Christine asked me what I was doing.

Puzzled, I looked up and told her I was returning the diamonds.

Leaning forward across her desk, she smiled and said I'd misunderstood. "Alex told me to give you a bonus," she said. "They're yours."

Dumbstruck, I sat frozen in my chair until Christine repeated herself. Then my eyes bulged, and my jaw dropped. Inhaling sharply as I looked down at the incredibly beautiful stones, I asked her if she were kidding.

Christine shook her head back and forth and smiled. "No, they're yours," she said. "Given in appreciation for a stellar performance."

Oh my God! I thought. Stammering, I tried to protest. "But Christine!" I gasped. "These must be worth a fortune!

Chuckling, Christine assured me that they didn't cost quite that much. And in any event, it was a mere trifling when compared to what the CSS dropped at the hotel every year. With a twinkle in her eye, she assured me that Alex wouldn't even notice it in the expense report.

Well, kewl! I thought.

Snatching up the case, I asked her if there was anything else. Shaking her head, Christine said no. But she had a ton of work to do – specifically, the press release – so she'd appreciate it if I would gather up the serving tray and the assorted debris, and close her door on the way out. Grinning from ear to ear, I assured her that wouldn't be a problem.

Because after the diamonds, I would have scrubbed the floors and washed the windows!

But as I was picking up the tray, it suddenly dawned on me that I still needed someone to help me unlock the vault so I could get started. But after pausing for just a moment, Christine smiled mischievously and suggested that I go get Dr. MacLaughlin. Giving me a sly wink, she said it would give me a chance to show off a bit...

With a smile reaching from one ear to another, I said "Yes, Ma'am!" And with the tray in one hand and the velvet jewelry case in the other, I darted out the door.

Wondering how long it would take before someone noticed the treasure I was wearing, I slipped the case into my top drawer and took the short cut into the galley. After dumping the trash into the trashcan and washing off the tray, I retraced my steps to the lobby of the Executive offices and headed for the elevators.

But this time Two wasn't at her desk – which was really irritating, because flaunting the diamonds would have been the most perfect revenge. She must have known they were on loan from the hotel's boutique, because she had studiously ignored them when I'd come back to the office – so I just couldn't wait to see her face when I told her they were a bonus.

Oh, well, I thought. *This will give me time to figure out a way to insinuate Alex gave them to me!*

Thinking I'd have to be sly about that, I chuckled wickedly as I sauntered down the hall.

As the elevator doors closed behind me, I suddenly realized that my jacket was still draped across Christine's couch where I had left it hours before. Which had suddenly become relevant, because some knucklehead had set the office thermostat too low again and goose bumps were rising on my arms. Not to mention certain other things in more intimate places, but we really don't have to go into that...

But even more importantly, with all the excitement over the diamonds, the whole thing about Mary Lou What's-Her-Face had slipped right past me.

So who the heck is she? I wondered as I stepped off the elevator onto the Seventh Floor. Thinking that Jennifer would probably know, I made a mental note to ask her as I rounded the corner.

But Jennifer was on the phone when I walked into the department office. Scribbling furiously on one of those pink message pads, with the telephone handset wedged between her ear and her shoulder, she didn't look up.

"Uh-huh, uh-huh. Yes, Sir, I'll be sure she gets the message." Then she jabbed another blinking button on the console, as she ripped the top sheet off the pad and tossed it on top of a huge pile already stacked on her desk. "Center for Strategic Studies, Department of International Economics."

Glancing up as I poured a cup of coffee, she gave me an evil look before informing the caller that yes, Ms. McAllister was a staff research assistant. Which kinda gave me the willies, because that was the first time anyone had ever called the office asking about me.

Looking down at the sheet of paper in front of her, Jennifer nodded and said that was correct. "Department of Economics and Finance, Township College," she said. "Class of 84." Then after perfunctorily thanking the person on the other end, she jabbed another blinking button. "Center for Strategic Studies, Department of International Economics."

Thinking the whole thing was really weird as I stirred some sweetener into my coffee, I leaned forward a bit to look at the pile of messages. After slapping my hand as I tried to turn them around, Jennifer looked up and bared her teeth.

Then she smiled sweetly into the handset, and replied to the caller. "Yes, Sir," she said. "Dr. Charles MacLaughlin is the senior author; Ms. McAllister is the junior author."

After nodding a couple of times, Jennifer said "Yes, Sir" again. "She's an economist."

After a moment's pause, Jennifer nodded again. "We'll be happy to send you a copy, Sir. May I take your address, please?" After scribbling it on another pink sheet, she thanked the caller and slammed the phone down on the cradle.

Ignoring all the other blinking lights, she looked up and glared at me. "This is all your fault!"

Then she punched a series of numbers into the console's keypad and switched the phone over to the answering machine. Shaking her head back and forth as it picked up the next message, Jennifer sighed and leaned back in her chair. Folding her hands together in her lap, she looked up at me and glared. "What the hell did you do over there?"

Uh-oh, I thought. Scrunching my eyebrows together, I asked her what she meant. Giving me an exasperated look, she leaned forward again and crossed her arms on the edge of her desk. "The phone's been ringing off the hook for the past hour, and every single call has been about you."

"Really?"

Glaring at me again, Jennifer nodded before picking up the mass of pink sheets. "Oh, yeah," she said as she began sorting through them. "In addition to the hundred or so guys who wanted your phone number, we have *Esquire* magazine, *The New Yorker*, and just about every foreign embassy in town."

Tossing a bunch of the pink slips in my direction, Jennifer looked down and began sorting through the rest. "And let's see...

"Fifty or sixty foreign newspapers, some guy who says he's a junior staffer at the NSC, Ambassador Reynolds at the State Department, and *Glamour* magazine – they want to know what your favorite color is, and your favorite fashion accessory, and what you cook for 'that Special Someone'...

"And *Soldier of Fortune* magazine, *World Economics Today*, *Time*, *Newsweek*, *U.S. News and World Report*...

"Not to mention the two or three perverts who wanted to know if you were wearing underwear."

Incredulous, I asked Jennifer if she was jerking my chain. "Oh no," she said. "It's been like 'Freaks-R-Us' on the phone today."

Had I been thinking, I might have made the connection between the weird phone calls and the break-in – but I was so wrapped up in the moment that it slipped right past me. So rather than getting worried, I cracked up instead – because it had never occurred to me that perverts watched C-SPAN.

All that serious stuff we were talking about, and they're obsessing about my underwear???

So rather than be offended, I decided to ask Jennifer what she had told them. Scrunching up her nose, Jennifer gave me a disgusted look. "Nuthin'," she said. "I hung up on them."

Still chuckling, I told Jennifer she was ruining my social life. Then after taking a sip of my coffee and shaking my head in mock sadness, I sighed. "Well, maybe they'll call back."

Jennifer scrunched up her nose again. *"Ouuuuuu,"* she said. Then she sat up suddenly, and started thumbing through the pink slips again.

Pulling one from the stack and handing it to me, she said, "Speaking of perverts, I almost forgot...

"*Playboy* called and they want to know if you'll pose for them. They're doing a pre-election special called 'The Girls of Washington,' and they want you to be the centerfold."

Huh?

Setting my coffee down on the edge of Jennifer's desk, I took the slip from her and looked at it suspiciously. She was obviously playing a joke on me, so after giving her a sarcastic look, I wadded up the slip and tossed it back on her desk. "Oh, sure," I said. "I guess Congresswoman Baxter must have turned 'em down, huh?"

Which I thought was pretty funny, because let's face it – she wasn't the sort of woman you'd want to take a picture of, even with all her clothes on.

But Jennifer was too busy straightening out the crumpled piece of paper to get the joke. Looking back up at me, she said she was serious. "They want you to pose."

After staring at her for a long moment, I finally realized she wasn't kidding. Mystified, I hooked the neck of my top with my right index finger and pulled it outward. After peering downward for a long moment, I scrunched up my face and released it. Thoroughly confused, I asked Jennifer, "Why?"

Momentarily puzzled, Jennifer stared at me for a couple of seconds before cracking up. "Those aren't real," she said.

Huh?

Shocked and offended, I hotly denied it. *"Are too!"* I said.

Still laughing, Jennifer managed to say "Not you, silly…

"The girls in those magazines!"

Startled, I cocked my head and looked at her suspiciously. "They're not?"

Still chuckling, an exasperated look crept upon Jennifer's face as she looked back at me. "You know, you really are a hayseed."

Shifting uncomfortably back and forth on my feet, I took a couple of moments to mull it over.

Yeah, well OK, that's fair…

After a couple more moments of silence, Jennifer leaned forward across her desk. "They airbrush all those pictures."

Suddenly aware of the fact that I had spent the better part of a decade comparing myself to some artist's fantasies, I just stood there dumfounded. "Oh," I finally said.

Grinning from ear to ear, Jennifer kept teasing. "So you really didn't know that, huh?"

Flustered, I shook my head before finally shrugging my shoulders. Then after summoning my wits, I asked her how she knew about that stuff.

After sighing and shaking her head again, Jennifer reminded me that she had three brothers.

Then she gave me a mischievous grin, and asked me if I was going to do it. "They pay really well, you know."

"They wouldn't get their money's worth," I said after glancing back down at my chest. "And besides," I said. "My Mom would kill me!"

At that, Jennifer's eyes widened and she sat up straight in her chair. Hurriedly sorting through the rest of the slips, she told me not to worry. "She was the first one to call, girlfriend…

"And by the tone of her voice, I'd say you're good as dead already."

CHAPTER TWENTY-FOUR

Jennifer was right.

I managed to dodge my Mom for the rest of the afternoon, but when she finally caught up with me at home later that night, I really got an earful.

She didn't say a word about the schmuck thing – because I'm pretty sure she thought James had it coming – but she went completely postal over my outfit. My skirt was too short, she said, and it was slit way too high. And oh, by the way, what the heck was I doing wearing a skimpy little top like that on TV? When the spotlight hit it, people could see right through it!

I tried to explain to her that I'd been blind-sided by the press conference – and that I'd worn a perfectly proper jacket over the top to work, thank you very much – but she just didn't want to hear it. It turned out that President Reagan's campaign-trail reference to my study had made me an overnight celebrity back in Glen Meadows, and just about everybody with a TV set had tuned in for the press conference. So when my skirt slipped up into the stratosphere, the tongues back home had started wagging…

Well, that figures, I thought…

Probably the most excitement Glen Meadows has seen since Old Man Higgins drove his 18-wheeler through City Hall…

But since there was no way to reason with her, I just sat there on the couch and let her vent for a good fifteen minutes or so. But when she finally began to calm down, I managed to steer the conversation toward the really important stuff. Such as my silvery shoes with the little straps, which she had to admit were just totally adorable…

And of course my presentation, which she thought had been really good.

Wrapping my legs underneath me, I grinned triumphantly as I shifted the handset from one ear to the other. "So you think all those years of college paid off, huh?"

Having successfully switched the subject, I was tempted to ask her for some pointers for the audit – because after 17-odd years as a CPA, she knew a thing or two about financial analysis – but my sense of caution warned me not to. Christine had been dead serious when she warned against discussing the project with anyone, and ever since I met those guys from the CIA I'd had this really creepy feeling that they might be tapping my phone. Convinced that caution was the better part of valor, I decided I'd just have to dig out my old *Introduction to Accounting* text, and figure it out on my own.

Which I did the next morning, before leaving for work.

I'd been around the CSS long enough to know that Alex's travel plans were subject to change, so I was hoping that he'd come back early. But when I arrived at the Executive Offices, his doors were still closed, and since Two was nowhere in sight, I figured he was probably still in Louisville. So after feeding the dogs, I got Christine to help me open up the vault instead.

Once it was opened, I got down to work. After loading a big cardboard box onto one of the carts, I dragged it over to my desk before returning to the vault for the other cart that held my computer. After pausing for a moment to think the whole thing through, I decided I'd keep the monitor and the keyboard on my desk, and just move the CPU back and forth on the cart.

But that meant I'd have to find a really long extension cord and a power strip, so after a half-second's hesitation, I pushed everything back in the vault and closed it, before heading down to the supply room on the Fifth Floor.

Now something like that wouldn't normally have taken me more than 10 minutes, but when I got down to the supply room, the door was locked, so I had to go up to Reception on the Sixth Floor and have the receptionist page Herman Rowlings – that was the guy who was in charge of maintenance. But as it turned out, Herman was down on the Fourth Floor arguing with a plumbing contractor about something or another – which made no sense because the CSS didn't occupy that floor and, as far as I knew, didn't have anything to do with it at all.

So my ten-minute excursion turned into a forty-five minute wait, compounded by a frustrating five-minute exchange over the extension cord and power strip.

Herman had been happy to give me the requested items, but when he pulled them out of a storage locker in the supply room they were all covered in some nasty stuff that might have once been oil, but had since morphed into some sort of semi-hardened gunk – so I had to convince him that icky electrical stuff just wouldn't work in my brand-new office, with all the expensive Oriental rugs. But since the logic of the situation didn't seem to compute with Herman, I had to play on his emotions.

Now normally I don't approve of manipulating guys like that – because let's face it, it really is a bit underhanded – but every now and then they're so thick that a girl just has to. So I took a leaf out of Jennifer's book and conned him.

Since Herman had been around the block once or twice already – he was at least 50 at the time – I wasn't quite sure if he was going to fall for it. But after putting on my very best "Little Girl Sad" face, he reluctantly put the old extension cord and power strip back in the locker and gave me new ones, still wrapped in their plastic packaging. The extension cord was about 25 feet longer than I needed, but under the circumstances I wasn't about to argue. So after thanking him profusely, I snatched them out of his hands and scurried out the door.

By 10:15, I had everything hooked up and ready to go, so after opening the box of financial records I hopped into my big leather chair and pushed the computer's ON button. But as the monitor warmed up, I suddenly realized there was a slight problem: my big leather chair had been sized for my oversized executive desk, which had been sized for an average man or a really tall woman. Since I was neither, that meant my feet were dangling in empty space, a good eight inches off the floor. But after swiveling back and forth a couple of times, I suddenly realized what telephone books are for. So after loading everything back up on the carts and securing them in the vault, I headed back down to the supply room for a couple of sets of Yellow Pages and some strapping tape.

Twenty minutes later, I sat down at my desk again and put my feet on the bundled books.

Perfect! I thought.

Reveling in my sense of victory, I was about to turn the computer back on when Julia stuck her head through the door and looked around. "Wow!"

"Julia!"

Since I'd barely seen Julia since the night after the break-in, I jumped up and rushed to the doorway. After glancing around to make sure no one was watching, I gave her a big hug before apologizing. My office had been declared off-limits to everyone but Alex, Christine, and Dr. MacLaughlin, so I couldn't give her the nickel tour.

Julia scrunched her eyebrows together, and gave me a conspiratorial look. "Yeah, I heard," she whispered. "Some kind of top-secret project, huh?"

After glancing around quickly to make sure no one had overheard, I nodded and whispered back. "Yeah, but I can't tell you about it or I'll end up in the slammer."

With a very serious look on her face, Julia nodded before breaking into a big grin. "Then tell me about your new digs," she said. So I happily pointed out all my new furniture, and the rugs, and the drapes, and the artwork on the wall, and explained how Christine had helped me put it all together.

After listening with rapt attention, Julia turned back to me with a wicked grin. "Better not let anyone else see this," she said. "They'll think you've been sleeping with the boss!"

Snickering, I said, "Yeah, right."

Then I struck a sexy pose and grinned. *"Behold!"* I said in my most sultry voice. *"Alicia McAllister, Seductress-Extraordinaire!"*

Which probably wasn't the best of ideas, because wouldn't you know it – Christine had picked that precise moment to stride into the reception area.

Oops…

After seeing the frosty look on her face, Julia whispered out of the corner of her mouth. "Wasn't here, didn't see it." Nodding curtly, I whispered "Right." Then I turned on my heel and marched back to my desk.

After making a quick mental note to kick myself, I pulled the box of financial records open again and sat down. Hoping really hard that Christine wasn't going to suddenly appear in my doorway, I pulled the top sheaf of copies out and started thumbing through them. Completely bewildered, I set them aside and pulled out another.

Fifteen minutes later, I pushed my chair back and stared at the mass of paper piled in the center of my desk. *What is this stuff?*

After puzzling over it for another ten minutes or so, I scooted my chair back up to my desk – which was no easy feat, with my legs dangling in midair – and started turning it back over, in reverse order. When I finally got to the first sheaf of papers, I picked it up and studied it again.

A title had apparently been printed across the top of the original, but someone had blacked it out with a magic marker before copying it again, and they'd scribbled a series of numbers beside the blacked out portion in a red felt tipped pen. *Now that's weird*, I thought. Finally concluding that the number was some sort of substitute project designation, I turned my attention to the columns of numbers and dates below.

At the top left there was a typed figure – $42,000,000 to be precise – and then in the next column, a half-inch or so below it, a six digit number prefaced by the letters QN. In the next column was a date, and in the next column over a figure of $18,326.29.

At first glance there seemed to be certain logic to the layout, except for the two additional columns to the right that were blank. Not at all sure what I was looking at, I flipped through it again page by page. I had expected to find some sort of balance on the final page, but there wasn't a darn thing on it when I got there. Tossing it aside, I picked up the next sheaf of copies.

The title had been blacked out on that one too, but after studying it for a few minutes it seemed a lot more logical. A series of the QN number sequences ran down the left hand column; and in the next column over, a capitalized letter "T." A long series of numbers appeared in the column immediately to the right of the "T," followed by a list of dollar figures in the next column over, and a final column that was altogether blank. Although I was just guessing at that point, I was pretty sure the blank one was a dummy. *Probably generated by the accounting program,* I thought.

Setting the two side by side, I flipped through them one page at a time. Eventually persuaded that the first sheaf represented either purchase orders or payment authorizations, I deduced that the "T" thing probably stood for Treasury, and the number next to it the actual amount paid out by the government. But on the other hand, the first sheaf might represent progress payment requests, and the second might be progress payment authorizations. Thinking that there was no way to be sure at this point, I put the first two sheaves aside and started thumbing through the rest.

Three hours later, I tossed the last batch of papers back on my desk and pushed my chair back. Using my taped together telephone books for leverage, I arched backward and stared at the ceiling. Although I hadn't even come close to figuring out all the stuff in the box, I had reached four critically important conclusions.

First, there was no way that they had sent me all the data for Project OO/29862. Second, the accounting program they had installed on my computer was totally inadequate – which meant I was going to have to go deep into the program code and rewrite a big chunk of it. Third, if the first box was any indication of the rest, I was pretty much guaranteed lifetime employment. Fourth – and most importantly – I was really hungry.

So after glancing at my watch, I stuffed the documentation back in the box and loaded up my cart. Because as far as my stomach was concerned, lunch was way more important than the national security.

After rolling the carts back into the vault and securing it, I started across the carpet for the door. Halfway there, my phone buzzed.

After a half-seconds pause, I turned back to my desk and picked up the hand piece. It was Herb Randolph from the Press Office, down on the Sixth Floor, and he wanted to see me right away.

Puzzled, I scrunched up my nose and looked at the hand piece suspiciously. "Really?"

"Really," he said. Following my presentation, the Econ shop had received so many calls from reporters that Jennifer had demanded some help. The only solution, he said, was to put together a press packet containing a biographical sketch of all the speakers to accompany the videotapes they were sending out. That wasn't a problem with Dr. MacLaughlin, Admiral Taylor, or the Generals – he already had plenty of stuff on file for them – but he was going to need some additional information from me.

Thinking I didn't have much of a choice, I reluctantly agreed. But since I'd skipped lunch, I had to stop by the canteen first.

Two Twinkies, a Ho Ho, a bag of Doritos, and half a Diet Pepsi later, I pushed open the door of the Press Office. Since no one was at the reception desk, I glanced around for a minute before walking towards the open doorway at the far end of the room. "Mr. Randolph?"

I heard a loud whirring sound, followed by some muted cursing. Then after a moment of silence, a rather exasperated masculine voice called out. "Yeah, I'm back here."

Not quite certain what to do, I peered around the doorframe and announced my presence. "You wanted to see me, Sir?"

Although I had seen Mr. Randolph up on the Eighth Floor a couple of times, somehow or another I hadn't actually met him. But since he was a member of the senior staff, I figured I should be on my best behavior.

He was seated on a stool in front of a workbench, wrestling with what appeared to be a VCR. Without turning around, he told me to take a seat. Then he slammed his fist down on the top of the machine.

Still watching as I settled into a chair by the door, the machine bounced up and down before suddenly spitting out the tape that had been jammed inside it. After examining it carefully, Randolph tossed it in the general direction of the industrial-sized trashcan on the other side of the bench before peering inside the apparatus.

Apparently satisfied, he pushed it away to greet me. After carefully wiping his hand on a shop towel, he stood up and extended it to me. "I'm Herb Randolph," he said. "Thanks for coming down."

After motioning for me to follow, he led me back into the Press Office's reception area and pushed open the door to his private office. Waving me towards a chair, he made his way around his desk and picked up a file. After glancing through it for a moment, he sat down and told me that he needed to ask me a couple of questions for the press packet he was putting together. "You're the new kid on the block, so everyone wants to know about you."

Well, isn't that just peachy, I thought.

"I have your resume, but Washington is a small town – political Washington, anyway – and the press likes details. So we're going to put together a little bio to make them happy...

"Ok, your resume says you're from Glen Meadows, Connecticut, and that you graduated from Township College with a double major in economics and international finance." Glancing up from the folder, he asked me where Township was located.

"Oh, it's in Glen Meadows, too." I said.

After scribbling a note on a legal pad, he continued. "So you were a day student?" Nodding, I told him that I had lived at home with my mom.

"OK, so what's she do?"

"She's an accountant," I said.

After scribbling another note, he asked me about my dad. Shifting uncomfortably in my seat, I looked down at the floor before answering. "He was an engineer for the state highway department," I said. "But he was killed in an accident when I was four."

Randolph stiffened in his seat for a moment, then sighed and shook his head. "Oh, damn," he said softly. With a look of genuine compassion, he told me how sorry he was. Then after a moment of silence, he asked me if it had been a traffic accident.

Still looking down at the floor I told him no. "There was an explosion and a fire at one of their warehouses, and after they put the fire out he went into the building to assess the structural damage…

"And it collapsed."

After a long moment of silence, Randolph shook his head again and swore softly. "I can't begin to tell you how sorry I am…

"I know that must have been very hard for you."

Then seeing the tears welling in my eyes, he asked me if I'd like to take a break. Shaking my head, I told him I was OK.

"Alright," he said kindly. "Any pets?"

Surprised, I shook my head again. "Just Mr. Fenwick, my mom's cat."

Grinning at the name, Randolph said OK. "But you're dog-sitting for Alex?"

Not quite certain how to respond, I shifted uncomfortably in my seat. After pursing my lips together and looking down at the floor, I told him there was a whole long story there.

Leaning back in his chair, Randolph looked at me knowingly. "Want me to talk to Christine about that?"

Nodding, I told him that would be a good idea.

"OK," he said. "Favorite colors?"

Perplexed, I thought about it a moment. "Well, forest green goes with my hair really well."

Scribbling again on his legal pad, he asked me if I had any hobbies or outside interests.

Nodding, I told him that I had been on the Girl's Track Team at Glen Meadows High School, and that I'd taken four years of Tae Kwon Do in college.

Grinning, Randolph looked up. "Yeah? Can you smash bricks and stuff like that?"

"Oh yeah," I said. "But I'm a lot better with two-by-fours."

Startled, he looked up incredulously. "Seriously?"

Nodding emphatically, I said "Oh yeah! Master Lee – my martial arts instructor back home – clamped three together and made me punch through them for my brown belt."

Chuckling, he told me he'd make a note to stay on my good side. "Anything else?"

"Well," I said, "I've been too busy to enroll in a Tae Kwon Do class here in Washington, but I want to get my black belt eventually…

"But I still run, and I work out at the gym a lot."

Grinning again, Randolph said, "Ok, so you're a gym rat. What else?"

Perplexed, I sat there for a moment. "Well," I said finally, "I like music…

"Classical, contemporary, rock, and a little country-western now and then." Reminded of Alex for some really weird reason, I blurted out, "Oh yeah! And Oldies, too!"

Suddenly switching the subject, Randolph asked me if I had made straight A's in high school. After I nodded, he asked me about college.

"Almost," I said. "I got an A-minus in geology."

Chuckling, he said you have to be careful with rocks. "They'll get ya every time."

Snickering, I agreed. "Tricky little buggers."

"Ok," he said. "You were born in Glen Meadows, right?"

After I nodded again, he continued. "Where you lived with your parents until you lost your father in a professionally related accident at age four...

"You attended elementary school in Glen Meadows, and you were a straight-A student and an athlete in high school; and later, an outstanding scholar and martial arts expert at the local college...

"Phi Beta Kappa, right?"

After I nodded, he continued. "You took a double major in economics and international finance, and graduated Phi Beta Kappa with a near-perfect grade point average...

"Your favorite color is forest green, you like a wide variety of music, and you like cats and dogs."

"So what led you to move to DC?"

After scrunching up my nose and making a funny face, I told him that was kind of a long story.

"Boyfriend, huh?"

Scrunching up my nose again before grimacing, I nodded.

After scribbling a brief note, Randolph looked up and grinned. "And that would be the schmuck who dumped you?"

Exasperated, I shook my head and sighed. "Do we really have to go into that?"

Chuckling again, Randolph shook his head. "Nah, we'll finesse it...

"If anyone one else asks, I'll tell them it's a private matter."

"Anyone else?" My eyes crossed involuntarily as I jerked upright in my chair.

Randolph shrugged. "Andy Warhol once said that in the future, everyone will be famous for 15 minutes...

"So just think of this as your turn."

I didn't say anything, but I rolled my eyes. Chuckling, Randolph told me that was the bad news. The good news was the media had the attention span of a two-year-old, so they'd forget all about me in a couple of days...

Or at least until the next time they needed to write a story about me – which was the whole point in putting together a biographical sketch.

Shrugging, I asked Mr. Randolph if there was anything else. "Just a couple more things," he replied. "You drive a Corvette?"

Uh-oh, I thought. Realizing that the Vette could open up the same can of worms as the dogs, I shifted uncomfortably in my seat.

After pausing for a long moment to gather my thoughts, I explained that the car wasn't actually mine. "I was in kind of a tight spot a couple of weeks ago, and Mr. Tranh lent it to me...

"But it's really kind of a long story, so I think maybe you'd better talk to Christine about that too."

"OK," he said. Then after glancing over his notes, he informed me that he had the month and year of my birth, but not the actual date.

"Oh," I said. "April 24th, 1962."

After writing it down, Randolph told me he had one last question. Then after looking at me very sternly, he asked me if I had any skeletons in my closet that he should know about.

Not quite tracking, I asked him what he meant.

"Well," he said carefully. "Is there anyone in your past that might tell the press really bad things about you?"

Shifting uncomfortably in my seat, I tugged at my skirt as I mulled it over.

Thinking I was as good as busted, I decided I'd better fess up. "Well, yeah," I said...

"Sister Mary Allison – that was my sixth grade teacher at Catholic school – said I was the most rotten kid she'd ever met, and I'd probably burn in Hell."

Randolph stared at me for what seemed like an endless moment, before the corners of his lips began creeping up the sides of his face. Then he broke up laughing.

"I think we had the same teacher," he said finally.

Still chuckling, he tossed his pen on his desk and told me that he'd buzz me if he needed anything else. Then he grinned and told me to feel free to call him anytime. Washington reporters made sharks seem all cute and cuddly by comparison, so Rule Number One was never to talk to them without a member of the senior staff present. Rule Number Two was he was always available for that, because Rule Number Three prohibited the junior staff from talking to them unless he was there to cover their backs.

Which was in the *CSS Policy and Procedure Manual*, by the way...

Feeling incredibly foolish about that whole Sister Mary Allison thing, I thanked him for his time and headed for the door. But before I made it through the reception area, he came chasing after me with a huge wad of papers folded inside part of a newspaper. "I almost forgot," he said. "Jennifer brought these down for you."

Puzzled, I asked him what they were.

"The *Style* section of today's *Washington Post*," he said with a big grin. "The rest is Fan-Mail-by-Fax."

"Jennifer said there's a job offer or two in there, and a couple of marriage proposals. But for the most part they're from guys who just want a date."

You have got to be kidding, I thought.

CHAPTER TWENTY-FIVE

He wasn't.

Since Christine was prowling about, I stuffed the four-inch wad of papers in the lower right hand drawer of my desk. But after I heard Linda buzz her to let her know that Senator Hecht was on Line Two, I succumbed to temptation. With the carts in place and my computer hooked back up, I opened the drawer and teased the *Style* section from its hiding place. After a quick guilty glance around, I spread it out on the top of my desk.

Yikes!

My eyes bulged and my jaw dropped as my left hand suddenly landed on my chest – because right there on the first page was a huge picture of Yours Truly at the press conference, standing in front of the blackboard with a piece of chalk in my hand. They must have taken it just after I'd completed the first supply and demand curve, and turned around to face the audience.

Relieved that the *Style* section hadn't splashed my skirt-in-the-stratosphere pic across their front page, I studied the photograph for a couple of minutes before deciding that it was pretty good. Suddenly very pleased with myself, I started reading the story below. As I did, a big grin spread across my face.

That Lydia Sykes woman must have really liked me, because she had titled the article *Brilliance, Beauty, and Charm: The New Face of Feminism in the Reagan Era* – of which I was, supposedly, an exemplar.

After an exceedingly brief biographical sketch that must have been gleaned from my resume, she did a quick *tour d'horizon* of my presentation – which she clearly hadn't understood – before launching into her story about how the "next generation" of smart, saucy, and oh-so-chic young women were transforming the face of Washington. But that was OK with me, because she just adored my outfit. Calling it "trendy, but ever so sophisticated," she described it down to the last tiny detail before attributing it to my supposedly "perfect sense of style, poise, and elegance" – mentioning in passing the "brilliant balance" I'd achieved with the diamonds and my silvery shoes with the little straps.

Which I really appreciated, because those were my all-time favorite shoes.

Still grinning as I turned the page to find the rest of the story inside, I chuckled happily when she noted that President Reagan had described me as a "distinguished economist" and cracked up altogether when she started recounting all of Dr. MacLaughlin's superlatives. Leaning over in my chair laughing, I wondered where he'd come up with that stuff.

I mean, let's face it – I may be a bit sharper than the average tack in the box, but I'd already figured out that the world is full of people who are a lot smarter than I am. Like Alex, and Dr. MacLaughlin, and Christine just for starters...

But it was a fun read, and I really liked the way she tied it into the much larger changes that were happening in Washington as more and more bright young women began their careers in fields that had been more or less closed to them just a few years before.

To tell you the truth, I'd never really given the feminist movement much thought because my mom had had her own business for as long as I could remember, and as far as I knew, her gender had never been an issue. But I have to admit that I kinda liked the idea of being a part of the changes that were supposedly sweeping through the corridors of power. And since there was no way us girls were going to mess up the world any worse than the guys already had, I thought it was a pretty good idea on balance.

Which is not to say that I didn't have any reservations about the whole feminist thing. I wanted to get married and have a family someday, and when that happened, hearth and home were going to come first. But in the meantime, I figured could save the world once or twice.

Grinning, I slipped the *Style* pages back in the drawer. But before I turned back to the task at hand, I made a quick note to pick up a copy of *The Washington Post* on the way home, so I could send it to my mom. Because after the press conference, I knew she'd want to show the Lydia Sykes article to all her friends.

So after scribbling a reminder on a Post-It-Note and sticking it at the top of my computer monitor, I pulled the documents back out of the big cardboard box and started sorting through them again. This time they seemed to make a lot more sense, because after about 10 minutes I had become so immersed in the columns of numbers that I lost track of time.

Six hours later, I was suddenly startled by a loud noise off to my right. Having almost jumped out of my skin, it took me a minute to realize it was Big Minh banging his dog bowl against the door jamb of the Galley. Which, of course, was his way of reminding me that it was long past his dinnertime.

Oh my God, I thought as I looked up at the clock. *Where have I been?*

Getting up from my desk, I suddenly realized that everyone else had left hours ago. Except for the security guards – who were nowhere in sight – I was probably the only one left in the whole building.

Now that had never bothered me when I was down on the Seventh Floor, because my office was small and cozy, and I could hear almost everything going on out in the hall from my desk. But the Executive Offices were a lot larger, and a lot more quiet, and as I stood there in the ghostly silence it started to seem really creepy. So after feeding Big Minh and Lady Godiva, I loaded my stuff up on the carts again and pushed them into the vault. After pushing the door closed and punching the SECURE button at the bottom of the keypad, I hurriedly locked the outer oaken doors. Then after changing into my sneakers and gathering up my briefcase, I shooed the dogs out the door and down the hall, and headed for home.

By the time I pulled the Vette into Nguyen's parking space the next morning, my late night moment of trepidation had begun to seem rather foolish – because let's face it, with the three or four retired police officers that normally prowled the halls after hours, the half dozen or so CIA security guards, the closed circuit cameras, and two really big guard dogs, the office was probably the safest place in Washington. So I pushed it out of mind, and focused upon the more pressing issues at hand – such as the expected return of a certain Mr. Alexander M. de Vris, and the incredibly well tailored suit I had worn just for the occasion.

I had found it on a sale rack at Macy's at the beginning of July, which was pretty strange since it was made of really high quality summer wool that had been dyed a deep maroon. Since that's not one of my favorite colors I probably would have passed it by, except that it had been marked down to a mere $69. Tempted, I pulled it off the rack and tried it on.

The first thing I noticed was the fit – the jacket was just perfect, and the skirt was nearly so. But as I studied myself in the store's three-panel mirror, I suddenly realized that the color accentuated the natural contrasts in my hair. The more I thought about that, the more I liked it. Because with an off-white silk blouse and delicate gold necklace, it would look fantastic!

Which in fact, it did. Especially after the seamstress took in the skirt just a bit, and raised the slit ever-so-slightly.

Smiling happily at my reflection as I approached the big double glass doors that opened into the basement lobby, I paused for just a moment to ask Lady Godiva what she thought. Momentarily puzzled, she cocked her head over and looked up at me. But after I did a half turn to the right, and then another to the left, she wagged her tail and barked approvingly.

After reaching down to scratch behind her ears, I nodded at her and winked. "This ought to turn a head or two!" Then I pulled open the door, and sauntered over to the elevators.

As per usual, Big Minh reared up on his hind legs and whacked the "UP" button for me. Then after the door opened and we stepped into the cab, he whacked the button for the Eighth Floor as well. But before I ventured into the Executive Offices, I wanted to stop by the Econ shop to pick up my messages – and calm my nerves. It had been almost a week since I'd seen Alex, and after all the stuff that had happened I was both excited and really nervous.

So after Big Minh sat back down on his haunches, I pushed the button for the Seventh Floor.

When I walked into Dr. MacLaughlin's outer office two minutes later, Jennifer was hunched over her keyboard and typing furiously. And since she was wearing a set of headphones, I didn't think she'd noticed me when I strolled over to the coffee pot and poured a cup. But just as I was sliding the pot back onto the burner, she sat up suddenly and stabbed the keyboard with her right index finger before pulling off the headset. Still holding it in her hand, she gestured with her head. "Over there."

Huh?

Puzzled, I asked her what she meant as I finished stirring the creamer into my coffee.

Pointing at the big plastic mail tub wedged into one of the upholstered armchairs on the opposite wall, Jennifer grinned and told me it was my fan mail. "And I've got a really rough day ahead of me, so don't even think about asking me to sort through it!"

After tossing the plastic stir into the trashcan underneath the table, I scrunched up my nose and eyed it suspiciously. "Fan mail?" I asked incredulously.

Jennifer tossed the headset in the center of her desk and grinned. "You're famous, girlfriend."

Still skeptical, I walked over and peered at the hundreds of cards and letters stuffed in the tub. "They're all for me?"

Jennifer snickered. "Well, let's see," she said. "Most of them have your name on the envelope, but the mail shop figured the ones addressed to 'The Really Hot Economist Chick' and 'The Fox in the Mini-Skirt,' are for you too."

Then she giggled. "But they sent all the ones addressed to 'Super Chick' to Christine."

Which was really unfortunate – because I had just started to swallow a swig of coffee, and I almost choked on it. After throwing my free hand over my mouth, and somehow managing to force it down, I gave Jennifer an incredulous look. "You have *got* to be kidding!"

By now almost doubled up laughing, Jennifer shook her head over and over. After finally calming down enough to speak, she said no. "Every time Christine goes on TV she gets tons of fan mail."

"Well, that figures," I said with a shrug. "She's gorgeous."

Then suddenly mischievous, I asked her about Alex.

Jennifer snickered, and for a moment I thought she was going to break up laughing again. "Well that's one reason he tries to avoid TV appearances," she said. "Every time he's on *Meet the Press* or *Agronsky and Company*, he gets about a zillion love letters from all over the world."

Thinking I probably would have been better off if I hadn't asked, I frowned. "Well I guess there just aren't enough young, handsome, and brilliant gazillionaires to go around."

Jennifer chuckled. "The guys in the mail shop think it's a riot," she said. "You wouldn't believe the stuff they send him."

Scrunching my eyebrows together, I looked at her over the edge of my cup. "Like what?" I demanded to know.

Jennifer shrugged. "The usual...

"Sexy pictures, lingerie, promises of undying devotion."

Suddenly irritated, I closed my eyes and shook my head. "Please tell me you're kidding."

Wide-eyed, Jennifer shook her head. "Nuh-uh," she said. "All the important stuff goes straight to Alex, but the mail shop opens and sorts everything else that's addressed to him before sending it up to Two."

After taking another sip of my coffee, I snickered. "I bet she loves that."

Jennifer grinned. "Drives her crazy, girlfriend."

Then very suddenly, Jennifer shifted in her chair and looked over at the mail tub. Grinning wickedly, she asked me if I was going to open any of the letters.

Knitting my eyebrows together as an embarrassed grin spread on my face, I hesitated for just a moment before picking up a letter perched on the top of the pile. It was addressed to "The Fox in the Mini-Skirt."

After balancing my coffee cup on the edge of Jennifer's desk, my face began to flush as I peeled back the flap. Teasing the neatly folded two-page letter out of the envelope, I opened it up and scanned the first page.

Jennifer must have seen my eyes bulge, because she grinned from ear to ear. "So what's it say?" she demanded to know.

Flustered, I was about to tell her it was none of her darned business when the phone rang. "Center for Strategic Studies, Department of International Economics," Jennifer said sweetly.

"Oh, hi Christine...

"Yes, Ma'am, she just walked in. Would you like to speak with her?"

There was a moment's pause, before Jennifer nodded into the handset and said, "Yes, Ma'am. I'll let her know."

Hanging up the phone, Jennifer told me to beat feet. "Alex is back, and he wants to meet with you and Dr. MacLaughlin in the Executive Conference Room in five minutes"

Yikes! Glancing down at my watch, I realized that I barely had time to change my shoes and fix my hair.

Grabbing up all my stuff – which included my purse, my briefcase, and my overpriced designer shoe bag – I asked Jennifer to do me a favor and find a place to stash the mail tub, before darting out the door. But after about two steps, I suddenly stopped short. Pivoting on the ball of my foot, I retraced my steps before sticking my head back through the doorway. Grinning, I pointed my index finger at Jennifer. "And don't even think about reading that stuff!"

Looking up with an angelic face, Jennifer placed her left hand upon her chest. "Why, I wouldn't dream of it," she said, with feigned innocence.

After staring at her for a long moment, I rolled my eyes and shook my head. "You're such a liar!" Then I bolted for the stairs.

Precisely five and a half minutes later – which was how long it took me to put my hair up and change my shoes, give or take 15 or 20 seconds – I breathlessly pushed open the doors of the Executive Conference Room and stepped inside. Christine was agonizing over the selection of pastries the hotel had sent over on a refreshment cart, while Alex and Dr. MacLaughlin were standing by the windows, engaged in an intense and very quiet conversation.

Glancing over her shoulder, Christine smiled and invited me to help myself before finally settling on a chocolate éclair. "The pastry chef has outdone himself."

Which, unfortunately, he had. Because there were at least a million calories of pure, unadulterated joy on that cart, and not a Diet Pepsi in sight…

So according to my *House Rules on Calorie Counting*, that meant I was going to have to add at least 10,000 points to my Guilt List.

But after hesitating for a moment, I suddenly realized I could blame it on Christine. "This is all your fault," I whispered, as I picked up an oversized pastry stuffed with whipped cream and fresh strawberries.

Laughing softly, Christine told me to hush up and take a seat. Which I did, just as soon as I set my briefcase on the table and poured a fresh cup of coffee.

Happily immersed in my pastry, I failed to notice that Alex and Dr. MacLaughlin had finished their conversation and taken their seats, or that the room had fallen strangely silent. In fact, it wasn't until I licked the last tiny bit of whipped cream off my left index finger that I noticed all eyes were on me.

Oops…

Momentarily frozen, with my finger still at the edge of my half-opened mouth, my eyes flitted first to the left and then to the right. Realizing that I had been caught in the act, I forced a thin smile as the crimson spread across my face. "Great pastries, huh?" Then I grabbed my purse and began hunting through the bottom for my glasses – not because I needed them, but rather to create a distraction.

After perching them on the end of my nose, I folded my hands in my lap and sat back in my chair. "Ready," I said.

By this time, Christine and Dr. MacLaughlin were chuckling, but Alex just smiled. Opening up the manila folder in front of him on the table, he asked everyone to give him a moment to look over his notes. Which was a really good thing, because Alex had this dazzling smile and I was about to melt in my chair. Desperately trying to concentrate, I pinched myself just above the knee. *Focus, dummy!*

Which was really hard, because Alex was wearing this dark and incredibly elegant three-piece suit with a red silk tie. He simply reeked of refined masculinity and power, and as I stared at him the conference room suddenly seemed a whole lot warmer. Shifting uncomfortably in my seat, I averted my eyes and hoped no one had noticed.

Alex jotted something in the margin of whatever he was reading, and then closed the file and pushed it across the table to Christine. After apologizing for his prolonged absence from the office, he smiled and congratulated us for our performance at the press conference.

It had been superbly well done, and he wanted to commend Christine, in particular, for having pulled it all together on such short notice.

As Christine smiled, Dr. MacLaughlin began banging his pipe in the ashtray in front of him. Apparently unsatisfied with the result, he pulled a pipe tool out of his pocket and began scraping the inside of the bowl. "It did go rather well," he said absentmindedly.

Strenuously resisting the sudden urge to bolt for the door, I was hoping and praying that Alex wouldn't mention my little *faux pas*. But my luck held, and instead of bringing up the schmuck thing, he commended me for my presentation instead. My characterization of the Soviet economy as a "negative value system" was brilliant, and it had already gained a great deal of currency within the Administration.

By this time Dr. MacLaughlin had finished cleaning his pipe, and was busily stuffing it with tobacco. "Indeed," he said.

Smiling again, Alex glanced in his direction and suggested that he had found himself yet another outstanding protégée.

Dr. MacLaughlin lit his pipe, and after puffing on it several times he gave Alex his most severe professorial look. "After putting up with your antics for four interminable years at Georgetown, I'm bloody well entitled to it!"

Christine cracked up, as Alex's face flushed. Lacking a witty rejoinder, he fished in his coat pocket for a pack of cigarettes and a lighter. After shaking a Marlboro free, Alex lit it as the slightest hint of an embarrassed smile crept across his face. "So you are…

"And now if you are through reminding me of my less than distinguished collegiate career, perhaps we can address the business at hand."

Grinning like a Cheshire cat, Dr. MacLaughlin chuckled and agreed. "Christine?"

Suddenly serious, Christine brought Alex up to date. "The vault and the associated security systems are complete and operational, and the first batch of source material has been delivered…

"Alicia moved into her new offices on Monday, and after allowing for the press conference that's given her, what? One full day to work with it?"

Realizing that all eyes had shifted to me, I sat up in my chair and nodded. "About that," I said. "I had to spend an hour or so down in the Press Office."

Nodding casually, Alex asked me if I had anything to report so far.

After shifting in my seat again, I explained that the accounting program the CIA had sent over with my computer was inadequate for the task, and that the source material was pretty chaotic. "I'll have to rewrite a big part of the program, and I'll need Dr. MacLaughlin to explain the spreadsheets because they didn't identify the numeric value categories."

Ill at ease with the silence that followed, I was about to elaborate on the latter point when Alex cut me off. "You know how to write computer programs?" he asked incredulously.

Thinking it was no big deal, I nodded. "Oh yeah," I said. "Piece of cake."

Then suddenly remembering I was speaking to the Chairman of the Board, I added a hasty "Sir."

After staring at me with a look of disbelief, Alex looked over at Dr. MacLaughlin. "Scotty?"

Dr. MacLaughlin pulled on his pipe a couple of times, before taking it out of his mouth and leaning forward on the table. "Well, it's no surprise that the program isn't up to the task, but the Agency claims it's state of the art." After pausing for a long moment, he finally shrugged. "Oh, what the hell. If the girl says she can do it, why not?"

After nodding, Alex turned back to me. "How long will it take?"

After thinking about it for a moment, I told him that I wasn't sure. "Two weeks, maybe three."

Alex shrugged as he put his cigarette out in the ashtray. "That's fine."

Then he looked back over at Dr. MacLaughlin. "Since the conceptual problem ties into the lack of adequate value identification, why don't you take a moment to explain it for Alicia?"

Dr. MacLaughlin pulled on his pipe again before saying "Right."

After tapping it in the ashtray again, he pulled a pipe cleaner out of his suit pocket and wriggled it into the pipe stem. "Knowledge rather easily translates into power, and that is especially true with regard to knowledge of government activities. And while most government activities are innocuous, a substantial number are not. And so to prevent enemies or potential enemies from gaining knowledge of them, they are carefully hidden...

"For the most part, such activities are conducted by intelligence services behind a veil of secrecy, and protected by physical, bureaucratic, and legal barriers – secure installations defended by armed guards, strict information-handling protocols, and severe administrative and legal sanctions for the misuse or unauthorized disclosure of classified information."

"Nonetheless, the fact remains that intelligence services are vulnerable to penetration by enemy agents, and in recent years – since the effective dissolution of the Agency's Counterintelligence shop, to be precise – ours have been at particular risk."

"One way of dealing with the problem is to tighten procedures and protocols, and to increase the level of physical and personnel security...

"But another and perhaps more fruitful approach is to diminish the number and the size of the 'footprints' that intelligence activities invariably leave behind...

"In other words, to reduce the paper trail to an absolute minimum by consciously and deliberately maintaining only the barest of records...

"Hence the extraordinary growth in the size and significance of the 'Black Budget' in recent years."

Pausing for a moment to stuff his pipe with tobacco, Dr. MacLaughlin fumbled with his lighter before igniting it once again. Apparently satisfied after puffing on it two or three times, he finally resumed.

"The problem with that, of course, is that the deliberate abandonment of proper record-keeping renders oversight problematical at best...

"So, when taken to the logical extreme, one ends up in the uncomfortable position of exchanging accountability for a very high and – perhaps – excessive level of secrecy."

After tapping his pipe into the ashtray again, Dr. MacLaughlin leaned forward on the table and fastened his penetrating blue eyes on mine. "At the end of the day, Lass, 'Black Budget' accountability depends almost entirely upon the integrity of the program managers."

Dr. MacLaughlin had never stared at me like that before, and the fact that he had locked his eyes on mine made me feel decidedly ill at ease. Shifting uncomfortably in my seat as I sorted through what he had just said, it suddenly occurred to me that my new project seemed more like some kind of super-secret counterintelligence operation than an exercise in number crunching.

After mulling that over for a long moment, I folded my hands together on the table. Scrunching up my nose, I leaned forward and took a wild guess. "So you think the Bad Guys are messing with the Black Budget?"

CHAPTER TWENTY-SIX

I was still leaning on the conference table when the room became deathly quiet.

For some weird reason, Christine had become suddenly fascinated with her coffee cup. As she studied the liquid sloshing around within it, Dr. MacLaughlin looked down and began stuffing his pipe with tobacco again. Surprised and suddenly suspicious, I looked across the table to my left.

While Dr. MacLaughlin was explaining the Black Budget to me, Alex had propped his elbows up on the surface and folded his hands together, and he was still holding that pose when I fastened my eyes upon him. Difficult to read under the best of circumstances, Alex met my gaze impassively. But as I searched his face for the slightest hint of emotion, I thought I saw his eyes narrow ever so slightly.

Gotcha!

As a triumphant grin spread across my face, I leaned forward even farther and exclaimed excitedly. "That's it, isn't it?

"The Bad Guys are manipulating the Black Budget, and we're gonna bust 'em!"

Since Alex was holding his impassive gaze, I turned first to Christine and then to Dr. MacLaughlin. Wide-eyed, I demanded an answer. "Right?"

But Christine was still studying the bottom of her coffee cup, and Dr. MacLaughlin seemed completely immersed in his pipe bowl. Looking back and forth in search of an answer, I repeated my question a bit more anxiously. "I'm right, aren't I???"

But it wasn't until I turned back to Alex and saw the corners of his mouth turn up ever so slightly that I knew. In fact – as I suddenly realized – they had been leading me toward that conclusion all along.

Now that was clever! I thought. *They weren't authorized to tell me the truth, so they laid out a trail of breadcrumbs instead...*

Leaning back in my chair, I stared at Alex as I began working my way through the logical implications. But before I could finish, Dr. MacLaughlin disrupted my chain of thought. After lighting his pipe again and taking a few puffs, he cradled it in his hand for a few moments before shifting in his seat and shrugging his shoulders. "We're not at all sure what we will find in the course of this project, Ms. McAllister...

"Nothing like this has ever been undertaken before, so we're venturing into rather uncertain waters."

Then after stuffing his pipe back in his mouth and puffing on it again, he leaned back in his chair. Then through a dense cloud of tobacco smoke, he mused that exploratory efforts tend to turn up the unexpected. "So who knows?"

Nice dodge, I thought as another big grin spread across my face. But before I could press the point, Alex pushed back his shirt cuff and looked at his watch. "It looks like we're out of time," he said. "But barring unavoidable schedule conflicts, we'll meet here each Friday from 11:00 am to 1:00 pm for project planning and review."

Glancing around the table, Alex asked if there were any objections. After thumbing through her Day-Timer, Christine informed Alex she had a schedule conflict on the coming Friday, but other than that, she could block out the time. Alex nodded, and turned to Dr. MacLaughlin.

After pursing his lips together, Dr. MacLaughlin shrugged and said he had no objection. Then he grinned, and asked Alex if the company was buying.

Chuckling, Alex nodded and assured him that a mid-day meal had been included in the project's budget. "But since the hotel tends to be busy on Fridays, make sure you drop off your order with Two before we get started."

Well, kewl! I thought. *Not only do I get a free lunch – Two's gonna have to call it in for me!!!*

Thinking that would really get her goat, I grinned wickedly as I began calculating what the free Friday lunch was going to do for the projected rate of return on my brand new investment account. Figuring an additional six bucks a week at an assumed 4.5% over thirty years, I had just started crunching the numbers in my head when Alex pushed his chair back from the conference table and dismissed us. Realizing it amounted to a pretty good chunk of change, I put the exercise on hold at Year Eight and gave Alex a happy "Yes, Sir!" before gathering up my gear.

Since Christine had asked Alex for a minute to discuss something or another in private, I followed Dr. MacLaughlin out into the hall. Pausing by the water fountain, he told me that he needed to take a look at the spreadsheets I was working from before he could explain the numeric value categories. But since he had to check in at Econ shop first, he said he'd meet me in my office in 15 or 20 minutes. Thinking that was almost exactly how much time I need to get set up – assuming, of course, that I could catch Christine before she got tied up on the phone – I nodded my agreement before scurrying down the hall.

As luck would have it, Christine wasn't far behind me. So after she helped me open the vault, I pulled my carts out and started plugging in the computer. By the time Dr. MacLaughlin turned up – carrying an oversized Styrofoam cup of coffee and an ashtray – I had everything ready.

After glancing over the top spreadsheet, Dr. MacLaughlin spent about five minutes walking me through the various categories. Those were simple enough – and pretty much what I had already guessed – but redesigning the computer program was a whole different story. Because first of all, Dr. MacLaughlin didn't know anything about computers. And second, he didn't really want to.

But to his credit, he patiently sat through my explanation of how the machine worked, and then my slightly more complicated critique of the CIA software program. After setting up a dummy account and demonstrating what the program could and could not do, he agreed with my assessment. As far as he was concerned it was totally inadequate for our purposes, so after Maintenance brought up a folding table we sat down and started working on the software redesign. Dr. MacLaughlin didn't know anything about writing code, but he knew exactly what he wanted in terms of the final output. So we spent the rest of the day writing up the list of features and functions I needed to add to the program, and puzzling out the logical relationships between the existing code and all the stuff I was going to add on to it.

After that, my life went into high gear again.

Ever since I had started at the CSS, I had kept a fairly fixed schedule. Barring unforeseen mishaps – such as a really bad hair day, or running out of eyeliner – I generally arrived at the office 10 or 15 minutes before start of business, and worked through the day. For the most part I ate lunch at my desk so I could read *The Wall Street Journal* or *The Economist*. But every now and then I'd take the dogs out for a noonday stroll or – more rarely – join Julia and some of the other girls for lunch over at the hotel.

Close of business was formally defined as 5:30 pm, and since I almost always worked way late, I usually left on the dot. After working out at the gym, I'd make a quick stop at the hotel's coffee shop for a burger or a chef's salad before taking the dogs on their evening walk. For the most part, I was back at my desk by 7:15, and I'd usually work until 9:30 or 10.

But of course, that was my schedule while I was down on the Seventh Floor. Now that I had moved up to the Eighth Floor – and Alex was finally back in the office – I realized that a few changes might be in order. But of course, I had to figure out his schedule first.

Which just happened to fit right in with my assigned tasks.

Since the first order of business was to figure out the existing software code, I called my Mom and had her overnight my old textbooks on programming. Then after deciding to blow off the gym for one night, I ran up to the bookstore on Capitol Hill to pick up a couple of manuals. Because even though programming isn't particularly hard, it requires meticulous attention to detail, and I wanted to make sure I knew what I was doing before I started messing with the CIA's accounting software. So after obtaining all the reference materials, I spent the rest of the week going through the program code line by line, with occasional time-outs to consult my textbooks and manuals.

Which was incredibly boring, even for a number cruncher like me.

But by the time the first Friday meeting rolled around, I had a pretty good handle on things. So after dazzling Alex and Dr. MacLaughlin with my presentation on rewriting the Agency's software, I didn't feel the least bit guilty about gulping down the really expensive seafood salad the hotel had sent over.

Well okay, maybe just a little...

But aside from the sheer monotony of writing computer code, I really liked my new life up on the Eighth Floor. For one thing, the big double doors of my office allowed me to see and hear almost everything that happened in the reception area, and it was fascinating to watch all the important people come and go. The other thing was that Alex was usually there during the day, and even though he was really busy he almost always managed to find a couple of minutes for me. He smiled and waved good morning when he arrived at the office, and every now and then he'd even stop in to see how things were going. And as difficult as he was to read, I kinda got the feeling he liked having me around.

At least I hoped he did...

Despite the creepy feeling I had experienced the first time I was alone there, I had come to like the Executive Offices even better at night. Since I usually left at 5:30 pm sharp, I wasn't sure when Alex took off, but for the most part he was back at his desk when I returned from the hotel. And even though he usually kept his doors pulled to in the evenings – it turns out he had just started work on his seventh book – I still got to talk to him for a few minutes every night. Because by that time I'd worked my way up the Executive Office food chain to become the DCM – which was CSS shorthand for the Designated Coffee Maker. It turns out that I made *way* better coffee than either Two or Linda, so whenever Alex or Christine wanted a fresh pot they always buzzed me.

Now some girls might have resented that – because let's face it, I was professional staff while Linda and Two were not. But since people at the CSS took their coffee seriously, the DCM carried a lot of weight. And in the Executive Offices, it was *definitely* a high-status slot.

The only downside was that I still hadn't heard Alex play his guitar. But he had an incredible stereo system hidden in his office somewhere, and almost every evening around 9:00 he'd put on some classical music. Since I didn't know much about classical music at the time, I usually didn't recognize the pieces he played. But as the light, airy operas or the more intense orchestrals wafted through the open galley door, I enjoyed them nonetheless.

Life was good, I thought. And then two unexpected developments made it even better.

The first was I'd finally found someone to snuggle with. The second was Christine's memo.

I had gone to Macy's on a weekend shopping expedition to find a pair of shoes to match my new navy blue blazer, but as I passed through the children's section, I stumbled across the most *adorable* teddy bear I'd ever seen. He was sitting on a white display box in the middle of the aisle when I first glimpsed him, welcoming kids to the store. Five feet tall in his padded feet and covered in brown fuzzy fur, he practically begged me to take him home. So even though I blanched when the sales clerk told me how much he cost – which was $250, on sale – his big brown eyes and his cute little nose were just irresistible.

Forgetting all about the shoes I'd come for, I forked over the cash and carried him out the door – which was no small feat, given the fact that I was only three inches taller than he was. But I managed to get him to the Vette, and after convincing Big Minh and Lady Godiva that my newfound friend wasn't a threat – they'd initially been very skeptical, of course – I put the top down and strapped him in with the seatbelt. Big Minh wasn't very happy about having some stranger ride in his seat, but after a rather long and complicated explanation and the solemn promise of a doggy treat when we got home, I finally persuaded him to crawl into the passenger well with Lady Godiva.

But Christine's one-page memo surprised me even more than Teddy, because for some weird reason, no one had bothered to tell me that the CSS sponsored social events. But they did, and it turned out that the first item on the social schedule was the annual CSS Halloween party. As per corporate custom, employees were encouraged to wear costumes to work on Halloween Day, and business would close at noon. In prescribed order, personnel from each department would then make the rounds of every other Department, trick-or-treating for candy, popcorn balls, candied apples, and other treats. Then at 4:00, busses would pick up the entire staff for a cookout and a bonfire in North Arlington, followed by a hayride back to the office that would wend across the Key Bridge into Georgetown, then past the White House and back to the front of the CSS building where a $200 prize would be awarded for the best costume.

That really sounded like fun, because I hadn't been trick-or-treating since I was in Eighth Grade. But the annual Homecoming Dance was even better. It turned out the CSS held a formal Homecoming at the hotel every year for all past and present personnel, and a rather lengthy list of VIPs. Dress was Black Tie – which meant formal evening gowns for the girls – and for me at least, that was really exciting.

I had desperately wanted to go to Homecoming when I was in high school, but no one had ever asked me. I'm still not sure if it was the braces, or the big thick glasses I wore back then, or my intimidating grade point average – but whatever the reason, I always ended up spending Homecoming night with all the other female outcasts. And despite my Mom's constant reassurances that I would become a beautiful swan one day, it really hurt. So the idea of being invited to the CSS Homecoming – of actually being *wanted* there – made my spirits soar.

And of course, the thought of wearing a beautiful evening gown made it even better. Because as far as I'm concerned, every girl deserves to be a princess at least once in her lifetime – and the CSS Homecoming was going to be my very first chance.

Normally the CSS held its Homecoming later in November, but because this was a presidential election year Christine had decided to combine it with an election-night party. So this year they were going to have a truly memorable gala on November 7th. Then the memo concluded with a brief statement that the annual CSS Christmas Formal had been scheduled for Thursday, December 20, and that more information would be forthcoming.

Well, kewl! I thought. *Two formals for Yours Truly!*

Still holding the memo in front of me, I sat back in my chair and chuckled. *Hey! A Handsome Prince and a Pumpkin Carriage, and I'm all set!*

Then my eyes suddenly crossed and my face scrunched up involuntarily. *That and a boatload of money,* I thought – because I hadn't the slightest idea how I was going to pay for *two* formals.

Oh well…

There goes my six bucks a week, and about 50 years of compound interest…

Then I turned back to the business at hand.

As I look back on it now, the six and a half weeks that followed were a lot of fun. But at the time, I was so busy that it seemed almost crazy. It took two and a half mind-numbing weeks to rewrite the CIA software program, and another couple of days to get all the bugs out. But I finally wrapped it up just before September turned into October, and after that, I started entering the source data. Which wasn't exactly exciting work, but at least I had the weekly project meetings to look forward to.

As per the established schedule, we met every Friday in the Executive Conference Room at 11:00 am sharp. Then after Alex opened the meeting, I'd brief everyone on my progress. That was a lot of fun, because for the first three or four meetings they hadn't the slightest idea what I was talking about. And more to the point, it provided me with the perfect opportunity to exact my revenge for the Press Conference.

Since I knew Dr. MacLaughlin was the project liaison with Langley – and responsible for providing Director Casey with periodic updates – I made a point of using my very best computer gobbledegook in my presentations. Which meant he had to borrow my *Dictionary of Data Processing*, and spend endless hours puzzling out terms like bits and bytes, floppy disks, hard disks, random access memory, and relational databases. Although Christine wasn't at our first meeting, she attended all the others, and about halfway through my second meeting presentation she figured out what I was up to. While Dr. MacLaughlin was furiously scribbling notes on a yellow pad, she gave me a sly wink.

I'm pretty sure Alex caught on as well, because whenever I laid it on too thick the corners of his lips would turn up ever so slightly, and he'd interject a comment or a question. But I think he was enjoying my little prank as much as Christine, because he never actually said anything. And in fact, he made a point of including me in the subsequent luncheon discussions.

Since there really wasn't that much to go over for the first three or four weeks, we usually broke early and then came back when the hotel delivered our food. After that, Alex, Christine and Dr. MacLaughlin would discuss various CSS projects and – more often than not – related areas of interest like the election campaign, the economy, and what was happening overseas.

The economic stuff was easy enough to follow, but I got lost in their nuts-and-bolts analysis of the election, and the international stuff was way over my head. But they were really nice about it, so whenever my eyes crossed or a puzzled look crept upon my face, they'd always pause for a moment to walk me through whatever it was they were talking about. I liked that, because it made me feel like I was part of the gang – a very junior part of the gang, to be sure, but a part nonetheless.

Which was like, *way* cool.

By that time, my work-a-day life alternated between entering data and prepping for the weekly meetings. But since the data entry was mindless and the progress reports still relatively simple, the forthcoming festivities consumed most of my attention. Finding the right dress for the Homecoming Dance was going to be difficult, but doable – but figuring out what I was going to wear to the Halloween party was really tough. I'm mean, let's face it – that particular holiday doesn't present all that many options for girls, and I wanted to do something really original. So that pretty much ruled out the traditional witch, ballerina, or fairy princess thing.

Three weeks into October, I was still stumped. But late one night, it finally hit me.

Big Minh and Lady Godiva had joined Teddy and me on the couch for the Sunday Late Nite Movie, and as we watched Jimmy Cagney shoot it out with a rival gang in an old black-and-white film, I became suddenly intrigued. As I leaned forward to study his on-screen character, I realized that Cagney wasn't much taller than I was – and that the suit he was wearing could cover a whole lot of curves.

That's it! I thought. *I'll go as a gangster!*

With a fake mustache and my hair up under a hat, I was pretty sure I could pass for a guy.

Of course, I'd have to lower my voice a few notches and walk funny. *But hey! How hard can that be?*

Guys do it all the time…

Suddenly excited, I jumped up grabbed my briefcase. Then after retrieving a legal pad and a mechanical pencil, I started making a list of all the stuff I'd need:

A dark pinstripe suit - with pleated pants, of course, to hide my hips…

A dark shirt and white tie, with a fake diamond pin – 'cause gangsters always tack their ties with a big gaudy diamond...
A hat, shoes, and a fake mustache.
And maybe a big Ace Bandage to kinda flatten my chest a bit.
And, oh yeah! A toy machine gun and a violin case to carry it in! Because that's how gangsters always carry their machine guns around, right?

Looking over the list, I figured I could get most of the stuff at a second-hand store, and I was pretty sure I could pick up the rest at a costume shop.

Well, kewl! I thought. *Now all I have to do is figure out how to walk like a guy!*

Turning back to the screen, I began studying the men in the film. It turned out they had just tossed a bomb through some poor guy's window, and were running like mad to escape the blast. Getting up from the couch, I waited for the next scene before trying to mimic their movements.

Harder than I thought...

Because as I quickly discovered, men walk way different from women. We girls hold our shoulders straight, and more or less keep our arms at our sides, and we kinda roll our hips forward as we move. But as I studied the guys on the TV screen, it seemed to me they did almost the exact opposite. Trying hard to mimic Cagney's swagger, I strutted back and forth in front of Julia's full-length mirror a couple of times before deciding I looked ridiculous.

Gonna have to work on that, I thought.

But all the rest of the stuff was pretty easy. I found a dark pinstripe "Gangster Suit" that more or less fit me at a Goodwill store for $20, and a of pair fake alligator-leather shoes for $5. Getting the suit tailored cost me twice that, but I managed to find a cheap black polyester shirt in the Boy's Section of a really cheesy discount store, along with a white polyester tie. And after searching all over the District and Northern Virginia, I finally found a decent replica of a one of those 1930's era machine guns, and a really cheap, third or fourth hand violin case at a music shop in Arlington.

The hat and the mustache turned out to be a bit tougher, but I finally tracked them down at the magic store on Vermont Avenue. In addition to their standard fare of books, materials, and stage props, they also had a huge selection of costumes, capes, and disguises for would-be magicians. So by the time Halloween rolled around I had everything I needed, and after trying on the whole kit and caboodle, I was pretty sure I could pass for a guy.

Not bad, I thought, as I walked back and forth in front of the mirror.

Well, as long as I don't have to say anything. Because that baritone thing just wasn't working out...

Even though the CSS staff was encouraged to wear their costumes to work, I decided to wear my regular clothes for the morning and change into my costume at lunch. That way I wouldn't feel embarrassed if anyone really important showed up before the party started. So I stuffed everything into a hanger bag, and decided that I'd stash it in my old office on the Seventh Floor. So after saying goodbye to Teddy and shooing the dogs into the Vette, I took off for work.

After I arrived, everything seemed pretty normal until I walked into the Econ shop. Coming to an abrupt halt just inside the door, my eyes bulged when I saw Jennifer standing by her desk licking an oversized lollypop – dressed in a Catholic schoolgirl's outfit, with her hair up in pigtails. Just shy of scandalous in her short pleated skirt and knee socks, she did a little curtsy and asked me what I thought.

Scrunching up my nose as I slowly walked around her, I told her she could get arrested for wearing something like that. After huffing dismissively, she turned up her nose and informed me that everyone else thought it was cute. "And in any case," she said, "You should see what Two's wearing."

Then still pretending to be cross, she demanded to know where my costume was.

Holding out the hanger bag, I told her I was going to change at lunchtime. Then I set it down on one of the chairs against the wall and poured a cup of coffee, and asked her about Two.

By this time Jennifer had sat down behind her desk, and after licking her lollipop again, a wicked grin spread across her face. "You *aren't* going to believe it girlfriend...

"So go see for yourself."

Knitting my eyebrows together to suppress a triumphant smile, I picked up my Styrofoam cup and told her I would. But first I had to stash my costume across the hall.

Having laid the hanger bag out on my old desk, I was backing out in the hallway when Dr. MacLaughlin rounded the corner. "Ah, there you are, Lass...

"No costume today?"

I explained that I had put it in my old office for safekeeping, until lunch. And after eyeing his smartly tailored suit, I asked him where his was.

"Oh," he said nonchalantly. "I'm wearing it!"

Huh?

That threw me, because Dr. MacLaughlin almost always wore Scottish wools to work.

Eyeing him up and down suspiciously, I asked him what he was.

Grinning, he said he was a *spy*. Then chuckling as he breezed past me, he strode down the hall.

It took me a couple of minutes to get the joke.

After emerging from the stairs on the Eighth Floor, I encountered Alex and Christine just outside the doors of the Executive Offices. Alex was wearing a three-piece wool business suit, as per usual, but Christine was dressed up like Glenda the Good Witch from the Wizard of Oz. Resplendent in her beautiful satin dress and silver crown, she was granting wishes to everyone that passed by with her magic wand. Thinking that she looked absolutely gorgeous – she'd even colored her hair red for the occasion – I pretended to be a Munchkin.

Since my skirt was a bit too tight to actually curtsy, I did a little dip and bowed my head instead. "Good Morning, Your Majesty."

Having already been taken by Dr. MacLaughlin, I looked over at Alex and gave him my *Mildly Irritated Look*. "Let me guess," I said. "You're a *spy*."

But Alex shook his head to the contrary. "Oh no," he deadpanned. "I'm a *counterspy*."

Since there was no way he was going to get a laugh out of me for *that*, I gave him another irritated look – only this time, it topped out at "Moderately Severe" on the Alicia Scale. Tilting my head again, I stared at him for a long moment before sighing.

"You spooks are *weird!*" I said as I brushed past him.

As I marched into the office, I could hear Christine laughing behind me. Grinning, I looked around the Executive Office for my next victim.

But unfortunately, Two was nowhere in sight. So after signaling Christine from just inside my doorway, we opened up the vault. Complimenting her on her gorgeous costume, I explained that I had left mine down at the Econ shop. "Since people can see me from the hallway, I thought I should wear business clothes until the party starts."

As she pulled the door of the vault open, Christine smiled and said that would be fine. Then she told me to close my eyes and make a wish. After I'd closed my eyes tight, she tapped me on the head with her magic wand. "Granted" she said, after I opened my eyes. Then she gave me a sly wink and added, "But in the fullness of time." Then she lifted the hem of her dress, and breezed out the door.

Since it didn't take a rocket scientist to figure out her implication, I flushed rather badly. But after a moment or two of embarrassed reflection, I decided to be an optimist. *At least she's on my side...*

Cheered by the thought, I began rummaging through the box of source material I was working on. Then after the computer finished booting up and bleeped at me, I sat down and started banging on the keyboard.

Thinking I could probably train a monkey to do the data entry for me, I spent the better part of an hour pondering the issue as row upon row of numbers appeared on the screen. Still debating whether or not I should ask Dr. MacLaughlin to order me a chimp, I glanced up just in time to see Two pad into the reception area.

When I did, my eyes bulged and my jaw dropped – because I just couldn't believe it.

Oh my God!!!!

Two was dressed in an all-black cat costume with a little set of pointy ears poking out of her hair. And with the long tail and the whiskers she'd glued to her face, it would have been really cute if it hadn't have been so tight. As she sauntered up to her desk twirling her tail in an oh-so-provocative manner, it didn't leave much to the imagination.

Definitely not the Cowardly Lion, I thought.

After shaking my head a couple of times to make sure I wasn't dreaming, I turned back to the keyboard. Alternately focused upon the task at hand and fuming at Two, I lost all track of time – in fact, it wasn't until I heard Christine announce the close of business that I realized it was time to break for lunch. Hoping that my costume would be a big hit, I loaded up my carts and pushed them into the vault. Then I made a mad dash for the Econ shop, because I needed Jennifer to help me bind my chest.

After about forty-five minutes of tugging and hauling – and couple of Ho Hos from the Seventh Floor Lounge – I stood before the mirror in the ladies' room, completely transformed. Cocking my hat at a rakish angle and setting my face into a tough guy look, I stepped back a couple of feet to take stock. *Not bad*, I thought, as I adjusted my tie.

Because I actually looked like a gangster...

OK, so maybe a really short one...

Pleased with myself, I thanked Jennifer for all her help and grabbed my beat up violin case. After shaking it to make sure my machine gun was still inside, I stepped out into the hall.

Not quite sure what to do with myself until 1:00 o'clock, I paused for a moment before heading up the stairs.

As I emerged from the stairwell onto the Eighth Floor, I overheard Alex and Christine. After creeping up the hallway quiet as a mouse, I peeked around the corner and realized they were standing in front of the big double doors of the Executive Offices again, chatting amiably with a much taller man who stood with his back to me. Four or five other men were standing around them, deferential and apparently idle.

After looking down at his watch, Alex excused himself and disappeared through the doors. When he emerged a few moments later, he was carrying a huge plastic bowl packed with expensively wrapped candies.

Oh, boy, I thought. *Chocolate!*

Chuckling, I placed my violin case down on the carpet and quietly opened it. After withdrawing my toy machine gun, I peeked around the corner again just in time to see Alex hand the gigantic bowl of goodies to the big tall guy that had his back to me.

Figuring this was my chance, I stepped around the corner and took a half-dozen quiet steps before dropping my voice three or four notches and leveling my gun.

"ALL RIGHT, YOUSE GUYS!" I bellowed in my best Cagney imitation. *"GIMME DA CHOCOLATE, AND NOBODY GETS HURT!"*

Which I thought was like, *really* funny.

But unfortunately, no one else seemed to get the joke. Alex's eyes bulged, and his mouth dropped, and Christine fainted dead away.

I was still wondering what was up with that when the first Secret Service agent tackled me. But it wasn't until the second one slammed into me that I realized what I had done.

Holy Cow! I thought. *I just jacked the President!!!*

CHAPTER TWENTY-SEVEN

When I came to a couple of hours later, I found myself lying in a hospital bed with a starched white sheet pulled up to my neck. After blinking a couple of times to make sure I wasn't dreaming, I suddenly realized I wasn't alone. Three very large young men were standing off to the side, and from the stony looks upon their faces, I was pretty sure they weren't delivering flowers.

Startled, I was trying to push myself upright when I felt something cold tug against my right wrist. *Uh-oh*, I thought, as I looked down at the stainless steel handcuff that bound me to the bed.

This can't be good!

Forcing a thin smile, I looked over at the three men along the wall. Then I threw myself back on the bed and stared at the ceiling. *Now you've done it!*

Not quite sure whether I was going to get life or just 99 years for robbing the president, I crossed my fingers and hoped for the latter. Because if it was just 99 years, I figured I'd be out on good behavior before I turned 70...

But hey, I might get lucky...

If they give me a basement cell, I can tunnel my way out!

Thinking that would take an awfully long time, I had just started mulling over another escape plan when a really cute young guy walked in the room. Dressed in one of those white doctor coats with a stethoscope around his neck, he was wearing a nametag that identified him as "Dr. W. R. Francis" of Capitol General Hospital.

Now acutely conscious of the fact that someone had undressed me when I'd arrived at the hospital, I started praying that it wasn't him. Because there was no way I wanted a gorgeous guy like that to see me without makeup, wrapped in an ace bandage and wearing a pair of men's boxer shorts! Flushing badly, I looked up at him when he reached my bedside.

But lucky for me, he seemed even more ill at ease than I was. *Must be an intern*, I thought. *Because real doctors know how to deal with us hard-core felons.*

After fumbling with a clipboard for a moment, he laid it down on the bed beside me and asked me how I felt. Thinking it was a really dumb question, I raised my right hand off the bed and showed him my handcuff. "Been better," I said.

Trying hard to suppress a nervous smile, he told me that he needed to take a look at me. So after taking my blood pressure, he pulled out one of those little doctor flashlights with the pointy ends out of his coat pocket and leaned over the bed.

After looking into each eye, he put the flashlight away and grasped my wrist to take my pulse. Having stared at his watch for what seemed like an interminable time, he finally released me.

Then he pulled a thermometer out of a glass jar on the table beside the bed, and after jamming it in my mouth he started doing this massage thing on my shoulder. "Is this painful?"

Thinking his exam was coming perilously close to groping, I shook my head and balled up my left fist.

But you better watch it, buddy – or I'll teach you what pain's all about!

Apparently satisfied nothing was amiss, he walked around to the other side of the bed and did the same thing to my other shoulder. Which was pretty amazing, because by then I'd realized that my shoulders were about the only things that *didn't* hurt. But before I could say anything, he pulled the thermometer out of my mouth, and after glancing at it, he scribbled something on his clipboard and hurried out the door.

So what's up with that? I wondered. *I've got insurance!*

But before I could make an issue out of it, a nurse came in and gave me a shot. And the next thing I knew, I was half way to La La Land.

I must have fallen asleep again, because when I came to, the sun was settling behind the horizon. The shift must have changed, too, because the three guys who had been standing guard had been replaced by two slightly older men, and a woman who looked like she might be in her mid-thirties.

Definitely an improvement, I thought. Because they didn't look *half* as tough as the other guys.

Realizing that I was awake, the older of the two men strode over to the side of the bed and held up a black, wallet sized ID. "Ms. McAllister, I'm Special Agent Jordan of the U.S. Secret Service...

Then he gestured with his head at the others. "And these are special agents Rawlings and Jacobs. We're here to ask you a few questions."

Under almost any other circumstances, I would have been impressed. But I *really* had to go to the bathroom, so after forcing a thin smile back upon my face, I explained my predicament.

Much to my surprise, they seemed sympathetic. The woman stepped around the bed, and after unlocking the handcuffs she offered to help me to the restroom. Which turned out to be a really good thing, because I could barely move. Every bone in my body ached, and I was pretty sure I'd torn a bunch of muscles.

Must be the "good cop," I thought as I hobbled to the toilet. Which in fact she was – because after promising I wouldn't try to escape through the 6 x 8 inch ventilation duct, she even let me shut the door.

Five minutes later, I painfully crawled back onto the bed. Then after a nurse came in and elevated it, Special Agent Jordan pulled out a little notebook and asked me if I was ready. After I nodded, he explained that the Secret Service was responsible for the President's security. As such, they were obliged by law to investigate all actual or potential threats to his safety. Given the apparent threat to the President that had transpired at the CSS office, the Secret Service had taken me into custody as a material witness. Although I had not been charged with any crime, he emphasized that anything I said could and would be held against me in the event that charges were filed.

Whew, I thought. "So I'm not going up the river?"

Suppressing a thin smile, Agent Jordan reiterated that no charges had been filed against me so far. Then very seriously, he informed me that a willingness to cooperate with their investigation would weigh heavily in my favor.

Having picked up on the implied threat, I assured them that I would be happy to cooperate. Then suddenly contrite, I apologized profusely. "I'm really sorry," I said. "There's no way I would have 'jacked' that chocolate if I'd known it was President Reagan's…"

Looking hopefully into each of their faces, I continued. "Really," I said. "Because I'm a big fan…

"But you already know that, right? You guys keep files on everybody, don't you?

"So just look in my file."

Then nodding emphatically, I said, "Really! I'm the President's *biggest* fan."

Suddenly aware that I had exaggerated just a bit, I scrunched up my nose and crossed my eyes. "Well, maybe not as big a fan as Mrs. Reagan," I admitted, "but almost."

Nodding again hopefully, I said, "That's me. A big, *BIG* fan."

By that time a grin had crept across Agent Jordan's face. "So we are told, Ms. McAllister. But we do have a number of other questions, so I'd like you to address them."

"Sure," I said, before settling back against the pillows. Because I could tell it was going to be a long night.

So I spent the next two and a half hours answering all kinds of questions – and much to my surprise, not a single one of them involved either the President or the chocolates. Instead they wanted to know all kinds of weird stuff like whether or not I wet my bed when I was a kid, and if I liked animals, and which of my grade school teachers I liked, how I got along with my parents, if I'd ever owned a firearm, or if I'd ever traveled abroad, and stuff like that. And then finally – after a short break so I could eat my hospital food – they wanted to know why I had moved to Washington after graduating from college, and how I'd gotten my job at the CSS.

Which was a rather delicate subject, because after getting busted by the Secret Service I was pretty sure that my next career opportunity was going to involve parking cars or busing tables.

But despite the weirdity of it all, I answered their questions as honestly and as accurately as I could. After a while, though, it started getting old because they kept asking me the same things in different ways. At first I thought they were just trying to trip me up, but after a while it slowly dawned on me that they weren't really questioning me – they were giving me some sort of psychological exam, to find out if I was some kind of chocolate-crazed psycho case.

Me? I thought incredulously. *OK, so I get a little weird when it comes to free candy...*

But hey! Who doesn't???

But then I realized they probably had to file a mountain of paperwork, and they needed something to put in it. So I played along until about 9:30, when the phone on the nightstand suddenly rang. Not quite sure what to do, I asked them if I should answer it. So when they said they had no objection, I picked it up. Rather cautiously, I said hello.

There was a moment of dead silence, and then a very official-sounding woman came on the line to inform me that Air Force One was calling. "Ms. Alicia McAllister?"

Dumbfounded, I nodded into the handset before replying. "Yes, Ma'am," I said. "This is she."

Then the voice instructed me to hold for President Reagan.

Holy Cow! I thought. *President Reagan???*

A moment later, the President's familiar voice filled the line. "Well, hello there, feller..."

"Are they treating you OK?"

Barely able to believe I was talking to the President, my eyes crossed involuntarily as I searched for something to say. After taking a big gulp, I asked him if he meant the Secret Service. "Oh yes, Sir, they've been very nice."

There was a moment of static on the line – because as I later learned, the Air Force One radiophone didn't interface all that well with ordinary civilian telephones – so I wasn't quite sure what he said next. But I caught the part about "quite a caper."

Scrunching up my nose in embarrassment, I hastily apologized. "I'm really sorry, Mr. President. I had no idea that was you..."

"I was just playing a little joke on Alex and Christine." Suddenly remembering I was talking to The President of the United States, I added a hasty "Sir."

There was another little bit of static, but I could hear him chuckling. "Well feller, have you learned your lesson? Crime just doesn't pay, you know."

"Oh yes, Sir!" I said earnestly. "No more chocolate-rustling for me!"

President Reagan chuckled again before responding. "Well OK, then. If I let you off the hook, will you promise to go straight?"

Forgetting all about the Secret Service agents, I held up my hand and made the Girl Scout sign. "Yes, Sir!" I exclaimed. "Straight as an arrow...

"Promise!"

"Well OK, then, I'm going trust you." Then after inviting me to come by the White House sometime to discuss my study, the President said he was going to have to sign off. He had a hard day of campaigning ahead of him, and he had to get some shuteye. So after I thanked him for his call, the line went dead.

Still holding the handset, I turned to the Secret Service agents. *"That was President Reagan!"* I exclaimed. *"Can you believe it???"*

An indulgent smile passed across Agent Jordan's face, but the other two seemed strangely disinterested. I was thinking their reactions were pretty weird when it suddenly occurred to me that they probably worked at the White House. Flushing a bit as I scrunched up my nose I said, "Oh, right...

"You guys probably talk to him all the time, don't you?"

Another smile passed across Agent Jordan's face – this time, apparently genuine – and he nodded slightly. "On occasion."

Then he snapped his notebook shut and informed me that they were going to release me from custody. If the Secret Service had any other questions, they would contact me.

Well, kewl! I thought. "Does that mean I can go home?"

Agent Jordan shook his head and said no. The doctors were concerned that I might have a slight concussion, so the hospital was going to hold me for observation. But barring an unforeseen turn for the worse, I could probably leave in the morning. Then almost apologetically, he told me that I'd hit the floor pretty hard. "Your head took quite a knock."

Disappointed, I lay back in the bed as they retrieved their handcuffs. *Oh well*, I thought. *Maybe they'll give me another one of those shots...*

Which in fact they did, just as soon as the Secret Service agents cleared out.

The next morning I was awakened by the sound of a woman whistling *The Nick Nack* song at the end of my bed. Not quite sure what to make of that, I pushed myself up on an elbow and peered at the diminutive figure through sleepy eyes.

Mai Ling?

Thinking that I might still be dreaming, I watched as she pulled a footstool over and climbed up upon it. Looking down at me, she smiled and said: "Goo morning, sweepy head. How patien today?"

"Mai Ling? What are you doing here?"

Still smiling, she told me that Alex had asked her to check up on me. "Have privileges at Capitol General...

"So I take case now."

Impressed – and more than just a little bit flattered – I told her she really didn't have to do that. The hospital had already assigned me a doctor, and in any event I knew she had more important things to do.

Mai Ling rolled her eyes before grinning. "Dat boy maybe goo doctor someday, if supervisor yell at him 'nuff...

"But right now, he jus cause trouble." Then she hopped off the footstool, to get my chart off the end of the bed.

"Anysway no botherer," she said as she glanced over it. "Mostly write an do research, but treat special patien now an den...

"Have old friend of father here now."

Then after a moment of silence, Mai Ling looked up incredulously. "He prescribe you dis?"

Then she shook her head in disbelief and held up the chart. "In Vietnam hospital, senior doctor beat intern for dat!"

Uh-oh, I thought. "Did he give me something bad?"

Mai Ling paused for a moment, before shrugging her shoulders. "Not really bad," she said. "Jus not advise for concussion."

Then she shrugged again, and hung the chart back on the bed. "I chew on him later."

After climbing back on the footstool, she told me that she was going to examine me. "Maybe go home today."

As she turned to pull a thermometer out of the glass jar on the table, I asked her if I really had a concussion. Because that just *didn't* sound good.

After gently sliding the thermometer under my tongue, Mai Ling pursed her lips. "You lose conscious for while, so maybe little one…

"Head hurt?"

After I shook my head, she nodded. "Chart say no vomiting, dat goo…

"Any nausea?"

As I shook my head again, she asked me about my vision.

Rolling the thermometer to the side with my tongue, I told her that I thought it was OK.

After pulling the thermometer out and looking at it, Mai Ling leaned over the bed and asked me to sit up. After I managed to get in an upright position, she put her index fingers together in front of my eyes, and told me to follow them as she pulled them apart. Apparently satisfied, she placed her right index finger in front of my nose, and slowly pulled it back. "Now up," she said.

"OK, now down…

"Goo, now lef…

"OK, now righ."

Seemingly pleased, she pulled out her doctor flashlight and peered into each eye. Then apparently satisfied, she put the flashlight away and asked me if I remembered what happened.

Scrunching my face up into an embarrassed smile, I tried to dodge the question. "Well, I was making a little joke at the office and things sorta got out of control."

Which wasn't meant to be humorous, but Mai Ling cracked up anyway. Placing her left hand on her abdomen, she pointed at me with her right index finger. "You steal candy from Prezdent…

"Ha ha ha, *dat* funny!"

Oh, well, I thought. *The best laid plans of mice and men…*

After Mai Ling stopped laughing, she slipped back into the doctor mode. Rattling off a rather long sequence of words, she asked me to repeat them in order. Nodding after I finished, she did the same thing with a group of numbers.

"Dat goo," she said. "Long term, short term memory OK. No headache, nausea, vomiting. No eye problems, no perseverating...."

"I tink you jus little banged up, not serious...."

"You sore three four days, maybe. But if everything else OK, I sign release." So after listening to my chest and taking my pulse, she wrapped the blood pressure cuff around my arm and pumped it up. Nodding as it slowly released, she said, "Dat very goo."

"Christine send bag from office wit clothes, so you take shower an dress. I come back in few minutes after I see Mr. Huang." Then after helping me out of the bed, she scribbled something on my chart and signed it before walking out the door.

Lucky for me, Jennifer had stuck a note and a little travel kit in the hanger bag that held my purse and clothes, so I had all the basics – toothbrush, toothpaste, shampoo, a comb, hairbrush, a really cute little fold-up blow dryer, and make-up necessities. So by the time Mai Ling returned 35 minutes later, I looked halfway presentable.

She had already disposed of the white coat and the nametag that identified her as a physician, and with her huge almond-shaped eyes and long black hair cascading to her waist, she looked absolutely gorgeous in a dark blue wool skirt and an off-white silk blouse. "Ready?"

Since I had already stuffed my Halloween costume in the hanger bag along with the travel kit, I nodded.

"OK," she said as she handed me a small bottle of medication with a prescription wrapped around it. "Dis for pain an muscles, but don try drive or operate equipmen...."

"We check you out an den I drive you home. Three day rest, doctor order."

I started to protest, but she silenced me with a wink. "But I tell Christine maybe shopping OK for exercise an fresh air."

Grinning, I said "Yes, Ma'am!" before following her out the door.

It turns out I had been on the third floor, and the patient discharge area was on the first. So after stopping off at the Nurses' Station to let them know I was being discharged, I followed Mai Ling down the hall toward the elevators. She was telling me how much fun the hayride had been when she abruptly halted before a little alcove that contained a stainless steel sink and a bunch of cabinets. As I followed Mai Ling's line of sight, I was surprised to see Dr. Francis wrestling with a defibrillator unit.

But I was even more surprised when Mai Ling marched over and grabbed the defibrillator out of his hands. "You stupid boy," she yelled. "You want grill cheese, you go buy in cafeteria!"

As she turned the paddles up to inspect them, two pieces of bread fell out from between them, and she started hollering again. "Defibbelator make electric, not heat...

"Ruin samich, mess up 'spensive equipmen!!!"

Then after rubbing some gooey, half-melted cheese off the paddles onto his starched white coat, she stuffed them back into his hands. "You clean up mess!" she demanded.

Seething, she turned on her heel and marched out of the alcove. But just before she reached me out in the hallway, she turned around and jabbed her finger at the now-stricken intern. "When I come back," she growled, "I beat you like redhead step chile!"

Resuming her march down the hallway, Mai Ling shook her head and sighed in disbelief. "Worle full of knucklehead."

CHAPTER TWENTY-EIGHT

As I finished signing out, Mai Ling explained that she had to stop by her office to pick up her purse and her jacket, and collect the dogs. She had called the hospital to check on me the night before, and since she was reasonably sure I'd be released in the morning, she'd brought them with her. "Alex concern," she said. "Not good for young girl be alone in city."

Since I wasn't *that* young, I started to protest. But before I could say anything, she suddenly remembered that she hadn't finished telling me about the hayride. As a huge smile spread across her face, she placed her overlapping hands out in front of her chest and did a little back and forth dance. "I go as China Doll." But Nguyen had gone as a cowboy, and it turned out there was a story there.

Mai Ling had grown up in a deeply traditional Chinese family, and except for her brothers and the students and professors who she had met in the course of her studies, she had very little experience with men. Naturally shy, she had been ill at ease at the diplomatic function where she had first met Nguyen, and her innate reticence had been compounded by the uneasy relationship that prevailed between the Vietnamese political elite and the rich, ethnically Chinese merchants who dominated the South Vietnamese economy. So even though her father had given President Thieu permission to formally introduce the two, she had found it difficult to say more than a few words to the dashing young officer.

Sensing her discomfort, Nguyen had assured her that she wouldn't be violating any taboos by speaking to him – because he wasn't really Vietnamese. It turned out that he was actually a Texan, and it was only due to a tragic accident that he had ended up in Vietnam. His mother had tripped one day, and accidentally dropped him into a hole out in the Back Forty. After falling all the way through the earth, he'd ended up in Asia. But as luck would have it, a kindly Vietnamese family had seen him pop out of the ground, and they had taken him home and adopted him.

As we exited the hospital onto 8th Street, a shy smile crept across Mai Ling's face as she turned to me. "But I tink maybe he make dat up so I talk wit him."

Since guys are always making up lines like that, I couldn't help but laugh – which turned out to be a really bad idea, because it made my ribs hurt. So I ended up holding my sides as I followed her across the street to the four-story brick building that housed her medical office and laboratory. Still trying to suppress my laughter as we approached the door, I was impressed by the big brass plaque that identified the occupants. The top portion read:

M. L. TRANH, MD
Practice Limited to Gerontology

And then a few inches below it:

RED DRAGON LABORATORY, LTD.

Making the connection, I pointed to the lower inscription and asked Mai Ling if that was her company, and after she nodded I complimented her on the name. Still smiling shyly, she nodded again. "Dragon very important to China people. Symbolize great wisdom an power."

Then she pulled the big glass door open, and waved me inside.

After stopping at the receptionist to pick up her messages, Mai Ling led me down the hall to the elevator; and after I hobbled in, she pushed the button for the fourth floor. "Have medical office on first floor, but business office upstairs."

After a few moments, the elevator shuddered to a halt and we emerged into a broad hallway. Gesturing for me to follow her, Mai Ling strode across the floor and unlocked a set of double doors. Behind them was a large laboratory that looked like something out of a movie set. After adjusting the shoulder strap of my hanger bag, I followed her past the maze of beakers, test tubes and odd-looking machines toward a door at the far end. Just before we got there, I asked her what all the equipment was for.

Mai Ling explained that the healing arts were as old as humanity, and some of the more sophisticated medical traditions – such as the Egyptian, Indian, and Chinese – appeared to have achieved remarkable success in treating illness and disease with herbal remedies. But unfortunately, Western physicians had subjected very few of these traditional treatments to rigorous, empirical tests.

Since many of the most successful modern drugs were derived from compounds isolated from herbs and other plants, that had puzzled her and piqued her interest. So after completing her internship and residency at the George Washington University Hospital, she had incorporated Red Dragon Laboratory for the express purpose of systematically evaluating traditional remedies. And so far, at least, she and her associates had achieved impressive results. Although they had chalked up fewer hits than misses, quite a number of the traditional treatments had proved to be effective.

As we reached the door to her private office, Mai Ling explained that these empirically validated results had made it possible for her to license the Red Dragon name commercially, and that dozens of herbal supplements marketed under that name were now available in the health food stores that were springing up all over America.

Wow! I thought, as I did a quick mental calculation. "I bet you're going to make a ton of money off that!"

Mai Ling smiled as she unlocked the door and pushed it open. "Make goo profit now," she said. Then she chuckled wickedly, and winked. "But hit jackpot when love potion prove."

"Love potion?" I asked quizzically.

As a huge grin spread across her face, Mai Ling nodded and picked her purse up off her desk. "Old China wive potion," she said. "Put in husban drink, make him *very* loving."

Suddenly remembering my position as Designated Coffee Maker, I grinned wickedly as I wondered if it would work on single guys too. But since I didn't dare pose a question like that to the wife of Alex's best friend, I asked if she was kidding instead.

Suddenly very serious, Mai Ling tapped the side of her forehead with her right index finger. "China wive very smart," she said. "Put potion in tea, husban stay home wit her!"

"Really?"

Mai Ling paused for a moment before shrugging her shoulders. "Not prove 'sperimentally yet," she said. "But Mother swear by it."

Then she giggled as she pulled her coat on, and shut the door. "Maybe dat why so many China people."

Trying hard not to laugh again – because by then my ribs *really* hurt – I followed her back out into the hallway. After locking the outer door again, Mai Ling looked around quizzically. "Dogs must be down on three floor," she said. "Prolly begging food again."

After walking down the hall and pushing the fire escape door open, she put two fingers in her mouth and whistled loudly. A moment later, muted barking floated up the stairs.

"I go get dem," she said. "You take elevator an meet me at street door." Then she disappeared into the stair well.

Three minutes later, she emerged on the ground floor with Lady Godiva and Big Minh in tow. Apparently happy to see me, they rushed over wagging their tails.

The dogs always seemed to have some sort of sixth sense about people, and today wasn't any different. Apparently realizing that I'd been hurt, they didn't jump up on me like they usually did. They sat down in front of me instead, and waited for me to bend over to greet them. Thankful for their courtesy, I pressed my right hand against my ribs and bent over to scratch them behind their ears. "Did ya miss me?"

After I finished, Mai Ling pulled her car keys out of her purse. Suddenly pensive, she looked at her watch before asking me if I had time for a quick stop in Chinatown. "Have to pick up dress for dance."

Oh, my God! I thought. *That's just six days away!*

Exhaling sharply, I nodded before asking if she was going to a store. "Because I have to find one quick!"

As I followed Mai Ling out of the door and around the building to her car, she suddenly smiled. "We go to *Madame Henri*, maybe you get dress dere."

Not sure whether Madame Henri was a store or a person, I asked Mai Ling what she meant as I set my hanger bag on the back seat and shooed the dogs inside. After starting the car and backing out on the parking lot, Mai Ling explained that Madame Henri had been an exclusive dressmaker in Saigon. "She marry French soldier in colonial day, an go to Paris wit him after France leave Vietnam...

"Husband away a lot in military, so while he gone, she go to famous fashion school...

"Den poor guy killed in Algeria war, an she come back an open dress shop in Saigon."

As she pulled the Beemer out onto the street, she explained that Madame Henri was equally adept at traditional Oriental and French fashions, and for that reason she had quickly become the dressmaker of choice for stylish South Vietnamese women. Then she smiled softly, and told me that Madame Henri had made her wedding dress. "It so beautiful," she sighed. "Feel like princess when Father walk me to altar."

Caught up in the romantic imagery, it took a minute or two for the awful realization to sink in. *There's no way I can afford a custom-made dress...*

Shifting uneasily in my seat as Mai Ling navigated through the Washington traffic, I explained that since I had just graduated from college, I didn't have a lot of money to spend on a dress. "I'm going to have to find one in a store," I said sadly.

As she scooted through the intersection at Louisiana and Mass Ave, Mai Ling shook her head thoughtfully. "Madame Henri not so 'spensive in America...

"Mostly Vietnam customers, and dey can't pay Paris price now." After turning left on 6th Street NW and then making a dogleg onto 5th Street, Mai Ling pulled to a stop. Grinning, she pointed at an empty parking space in front of a small storefront. "See? Dat prove God still love us goo people!" she said as she put the car into reverse, and deftly backed into the slot.

After clambering out, Mai Ling told the dogs to stay put as she pumped three or four quarters into the parking meter. Grinning, she turned to me.

"In Vietnam, you pay policeman not to take car. In America, you pay machine." Laughing, she placed her hands together and did a little bow to the parking meter before turning back to me. "I guess dat progress."

Then she led me inside Madame Henri's shop.

The door had brushed against an oriental wind chime, and its sounds filled the room as I looked around. The building was old and in rather bad condition, and faded paint was peeling off the plastered walls. But the shop itself was spotless, and it had been tastefully decorated in a subtle blend of French and Vietnamese cultures. As I glanced around the customer reception area, a welcoming voice greeted us in French.

Mai Ling stepped forward as an elderly Vietnamese woman emerged through the curtain that hung in the doorway of the partition wall that separated the front of the shop from the back. Stopping a few paces before us, she smiled and bowed. After placing her hands together and returning the courtesy to the much older woman, Mai Ling replied in French. I couldn't really follow what she said, but from the respectful tone of her voice, I surmised that the woman must be Madame Henri.

Which, in fact, she was.

After brief moment of conversation, Mai Ling turned slightly and introduced me. Madame Henri smiled again, and in heavily accented English said "I greet you." Then she placed her hands together and bowed again.

Since my French was even worse than her English, I smiled politely, and attempted to imitate the custom by bowing in turn.

Apparently pleased, Madame Henri said something to Mai Ling before gesturing for us to follow her through the curtain. After pulling it back to allow us to pass, she followed us into the much larger space that served as her work area. Row upon row of expensive rolls of cloth hung from the walls, and the two large tables that stood in the center of the room were cluttered with half-assembled finery. Far away in the back, two young oriental girls labored over sewing machines, while another was cleaning one of the half-dozen or so adjustable plastic fitting forms that stood in odd places past the sewing machines. My first impression was one of a small dressmaking factory, but after eying the huge stacks of books and magazines piled on the floor by what looked like drafting tables, I realized it was more of a school than a factory. Thinking that was a wonderful way to learn fashion and design, I felt a twinge of envy for the girls in back.

Because to tell you the truth, I hadn't *always* wanted to be an economist.

After sorting through the rack of finished dresses standing along the left wall, Madame Henri withdrew one covered in heavy dark plastic and carried it to Mai Ling. After hanging it on the post of a steamer, she pulled up the plastic to reveal a beautifully patterned red, orange and yellow silk dress, cut and crafted in traditional Vietnamese style. Beaming, Mai Ling reached out to examine the garment. After whispering something under her breath in French, Mai Ling apparently asked Madame Henri if she could try it on. Smiling, Madame Henri gestured toward a fitting room nestled against the partition wall.

A minute or two later, Mai Ling emerged wearing one of the most stunning gowns I had ever seen. As was customary in Asia, the form-fitting top had a Chinese collar, while the lower portion of the dress hugged her hips before falling straight. But unlike other oriental dresses that I had seen, the bottom had a slight curvature to it, and the side slit ran slightly above mid-thigh. It was bold, brilliant, and breathtaking.

But what really astonished me was the pattern. Although you couldn't see it close up, from the seven or eight feet I stood from Mai Ling I could discern the subtle outline of a dragon that began at her right shoulder and wrapped down and around to the corresponding rear hem. Realizing that the dragon must have been printed upon the red silk cloth with wooden blocks, my jaw dropped – and not just because of the price. Having always bought machine-made clothing from shops and department stores, I'd never seen such artistry before. In fact, I hadn't even known it existed.

As I looked on in near disbelief, Mai Ling turned happily in the three-way mirror. Then letting out something that almost sounded like a squeak, she scurried over to Madame Henri and bowed again and again. *"Merci, Madame! Merci!"*

With a huge smile upon her face, she reached down and grasped Madame Henri's hand, and after folding it into her own, she raised it to her lips and kissed it. After exclaiming something in French – which I think loosely translated as "the most beautiful dress in the world," Mai Ling ran back into the dressing room.

Still smiling when she emerged a couple of minutes later, she placed the bag back on the post of the steamer and addressed Madame Henri again. After a moment or two of back and forth discussion, Mai Ling asked me if I could speak French. After I shook my head to the contrary, Mai Ling shrugged. "Maybe dat make harder, but I try translate."

Then after she addressed Madame Henri again, the older woman gestured for me to follow her to one of the drafting tables. After pulling a huge sheet of thin white paper from a box angled against the wall, she taped it to the white plastic surface with masking tape and picked up a pencil. Holding it in her fist, she drew a large X on the paper before turning back to me and speaking. Standing by her side, Mai Ling listened attentively and translated.

"Fashion philosophy express in cloth…

"Woman Goddess, she know *mystery* of creation. Dat knowledge give power over man, make him humble…

"So woman dress – how you say – exude dat power. But young girl spring flower, pretty an delicate…

"She know *beauty* of creation…

"Young man not understand what he see, become intrigue. So we show beauty of girl, mystery an power of woman…

"Dey both aspects of female essence…

"We make fashion to show dem."

Turning back to her drafting table, Madame Henri began making quick broad strokes. "You pretty girl, we use dress like frame…

Then she turned around again and held up her hands in front of her eyes, with her thumbs touching and her fingers raised at right angles. "Dress focus attention on beauty."

After she turned back to the table, I watched in fascination as a dress took form before my eyes. But even as I did so, my heart began to sink – because I knew there was just no way I could afford one of Madame Henri's creations. "Mai Ling," I finally whispered. "You have to tell her that I can't afford this!"

But Mai Ling smiled. "I already tell her you poor college kid, she say dat OK...

"You friend, so she charge same price as store dress...

"You tell American friends about Madame Henri, maybe pay little more when you get 'stablished."

Forcing a thin smile, I wondered if Mai Ling knew what stores were charging for formal dresses these days. Because I was pretty sure I could get a nice one for a couple hundred bucks at Macy's...

Madame Henri suddenly laid her pencil down on the table and walked over to a floor lamp. Pulling it closer to the table, she bent the adjustable neck toward her just a bit before motioning for me to walk around and stand before her. After staring at me for a long moment, she picked up an oversized art gum eraser and made a few short strokes across the paper. Then she picked up the pencil again and resumed sketching.

Still translating Madame Henri's words from the French in which they were spoken, Mai Ling explained. "She say make dress from different silks, French, Italian, China...

"Dye them same dark blue color, contrast weave.

"Only expert tell, but dey reflect differen' an make dancing rainbow under light...

"Den she say make high slit off center in front, but overlap fabric...

"Dat sort of tease – overlap make very modest, but young man tink maybe he see pretty thigh...

"Den she round hem little like my dress, but make angle and overlap...

"Dat make man little confused, so he watch."

Then after another exchange between Madame Henri and Mai Ling, she continued. "Angle neckline with hem, so it off lef shoulder...

"But we take very fine French silk an it sweep up from right waist over bare shoulder, like Sari kinda...

"Den hang down back just below hem."

At that point Madame Henri turned around again, and said something to Mai Ling. Grinning, Mai Ling turned back to me and translated again. "She say man hunter, attract to motion...

"Over shoulder cloth maybe move wit body, maybe move wit wind...

"Either case dey can't help look. Dat man nature."

Thinking that Madame Henri had just explained one of the great mysteries of the universe, I nodded thoughtfully. "That's right," I said softly. "They hunt, we gather."

I was still pondering that when Madame Henri laid her pencil down again, and pulled the light closer. After angling the neck again, she gestured for me to come around the table and look.

Almost hesitant, I walked around it slowly. Which turned out to be a good thing – because when I finally looked upon what she had drawn, it took my breath away.

Madame Henri hadn't merely sketched the dress – she had sketched me *in* the dress. And as I looked down upon her creation, it seemed as though the world had suddenly melted away. For just an instant, it seemed as though I was actually wearing it, and as I began to dance and twirl across the stage of my imagination, I knew that I wanted it more than I had ever wanted anything else in my life. Exhaling softly, I whispered. "*It's me...*"

As I fumbled through my purse for my Visa card, it occurred to me that Madame Henri was a genius. For as if by magic, she had summoned forth and captivated a part of me that I had but dimly known.

And for the very first time, I recognized the feminine archetype of creation, and I knew that in the fullness of time it would manifest through me in mystery and power.

The Goddess within, I thought. *The Goddess to be...*

CHAPTER TWENTY-NINE

To this day, I still don't know how the Secret Service managed to keep *The Great Halloween Chocolate Heist* out of the newspapers. But it was a really good thing they did – because if my Mom had found out I'd been busted for jacking the President, it would have been curtains for Our Hero.

And to tell you the truth, I had enough problems hobbling around Washington, trying to find shoes, gloves, and a handbag for my Homecoming dress. Madame Henri had given me swatches of the silks she was going to use, all dyed to the same dark blue. Since she used custom dyes it's really hard to describe the color precisely, but under the store lights, it looked a lot like midnight blue.

Which I really liked, because it brought out my eyes.

Now you would think it wouldn't be all that hard to find shoes and an evening bag to match a color like that, but I ended up spending the whole weekend trekking through one store after another to find what I wanted. Now normally I would have enjoyed a two-day shopping expedition, but since Julia and Jennifer were nowhere to be found that weekend, I had to make the rounds all by myself. And of course, just about every bone in my body still hurt.

But I finally found the last item on my list just before closing time Sunday evening, so I managed to get back to the apartment just before seven – happy, relieved, and a whole lot poorer. But unfortunately, I'd forgotten all about the steak bones I'd promised Big Minh and Lady Godiva. Since they were already miffed at me for leaving them home two days in a row, I realized an apology just wasn't enough. So I bought them off with a big bowl of strawberry ice cream.

Apparently mollified by the treat, they took up their positions by the door as I hauled my aching body up the spiral staircase and crawled into bed.

Much to my surprise, I felt a lot better when I woke up the next morning – which was a really good thing, because the Vette was still parked in the underground parking lot at work. Since I'd already discovered that Washington cabs won't stop if you're accompanied by two oversized dogs, I had to get up early and take the metro to the office to retrieve the car and then go back to apartment to pick up Big Minh and Lady Godiva. Lucky for me, the traffic wasn't that bad so I managed to make it to work just in time.

Since there's just no way you can steal chocolate from the President without getting razzed, I figured I was in for a pretty tough day. So as I pulled the Vette into Nguyen's parking place, I was still debating whether I should put a bag over my head and pretend to be invisible, or just try to laugh it off.

Alone with the dogs on the elevator, I was leaning toward Plan A on my way up to the Econ shop. But since I'd been lost in thought, the fact that Big Minh had whacked the floor button slipped right past me. So when the doors opened I found myself on the Eighth Floor, face to face with Gen. McGreggor – who promptly threw his hands up in the air.

"Don't shoot," he cried in mock terror. "I surrender!"

After staring up at him for a long moment, I forced a thin smile upon my face and jabbed the Seventh Floor button.

Looks like I'm gonna have to go with Plan B...

Lucky for me, Dr. MacLaughlin wasn't in the Econ Office when I rolled in to pick up my messages. But Jennifer was, and the instant she saw me she cracked up laughing. "Get out on good behavior?"

After giving her a deeply sarcastic look, I shook my head. "Nah, I blew the joint."

Pulling a stack of pink slips out of my box on the wall by the coffee pot, I explained as I sorted through them. "Staged a fight in the mess hall, and while the screws were busy breaking it up I hid in the dumpster..."

"Rode out in the garbage truck."

Jennifer grinned wickedly. "So that explains the hair, huh?"

Ouuuuu, I thought.

Since I'd been pressed for time that morning, I was wearing my hair half-up/half down, with a plastic barrette holding the top in place. Maybe not the best look for a young professional woman – but with the blue pinstripe suit and the white cotton blouse with the round collar I was wearing, I thought it looked cute.

Kinda like a high school cheerleader, right?

Even though I spent the better part of the next minute searching for a witty comeback, I was at a complete loss for words. But since there was no way I was going to let Jennifer know she'd got me, I stuck out my tongue before marching out the door.

But after about five steps down the hall, I realized that I'd been a bit too harsh. So I pivoted on the front of my foot, and retraced my steps. Sticking my head though the door, I thanked Jennifer for sending the little travel kit over to the hospital. "That was really nice," I said. "I'll bring it back tomorrow."

Looking up from her keyboard, Jennifer grinned and winked. "Next time I'll include a file."

I was feeling a bit more at ease by the time I emerged from the stairway onto the Eighth Floor – but unfortunately, things didn't get any better. Adm. Taylor snickered when I passed him in the hallway, and Two broke up when I walked into the Executive Offices. But on the slightly brighter side, Linda was a bit more restrained. Somehow managing to maintain a semblance of a straight face, she informed me that Christine wanted to see me. "And man, is she gonna chew your butt!"

Which in fact she did – in grand style.

But after being chewed up one side and down the other for a good five minutes, it began to dawn on me that Christine was more upset than angry. She'd been around Washington long enough to know that the Secret Service didn't mess around, and my little prank had scared her half to death. As far as she was concerned, it was a minor miracle they hadn't shot me full of holes.

Which it probably was, when you take into consideration all the rotten stuff that was going on behind the scenes.

But since I didn't really understand all that at the time, I shifted uneasily on my feet in front of her desk. Then after taking a deep breath, I looked up from the floor and apologized. "I'm really sorry," I said earnestly. "I didn't mean to scare you like that."

Taken off guard by my sudden confession, Christine closed her eyes for a moment and shook her head softly. After opening her eyes again, she placed her elbows on the top of her desk and clasped her hands together. Then after a long moment of silence, she told me that I had to understand that we were in enough danger without brandishing guns in the presence of the Chief Executive.

"You could have been killed," she said softly. Then after pausing for a dramatic moment, she locked her eyes upon mine. "Not only that, you may have exposed yourself to other threats downstream."

There was another long silence, as I shifted uneasily in front of her desk. Then Christine exhaled sharply, and shook her head again. "God help us if the Secret Service has gone bad."

Huh?

Since I'd already figured out how close I'd come to departing Planet Earth, the part about getting shot was no surprise. But her statement about being "in enough danger" was a real News Flash, and the bit about the Secret Service was positively creepy. So as I watched her lay her forehead against her clasped hands, I glanced around nervously as I wondered what she'd meant.

But before I could ask, Christine looked up again and locked her eyes upon mine. "Never, **EVER** do a dumb stunt like that again…

"Understand?"

Looking back down at the floor again, I nodded. "Yes, Ma'am." Then after a long silence, Christine abruptly changed the subject. Since the election and Homecoming were both the following day, it was going to be a short workweek. Anyone who needed to take the morning off to vote had been excused to do so, and she was going to close business at four pm so everyone would have a chance to dress for the dance. Nonetheless, she expected me to be prepared to present a full briefing at our Friday meeting – and after staring at me for another long moment, she emphatically suggested that I "make it good."

Wincing at the implication, I fidgeted a moment before asking. "So is Alex upset with me?" I asked in a high squeaky voice.

Exasperated, Christine clasped her hands together again and sighed. "*No*," she said emphatically, "that's *my* job!"

Then suddenly returning to normal, she told me to get my duff into the galley and make some coffee. "Then get to work!"

Deeply relieved, I was thinking that the day simply had to get better as I scurried out the door. And as Fate would have it, it did – because I got three lucky breaks in a row.

First of all, Mai Ling had called while I was in Christine's office to let me know my dress was ready for the first fitting. Madame Henri was going to be working late that night, so I could go by her shop after work. She would make the alterations on the spot, and she thought I would probably be able to take the dress with me when I left.

Which was like, *way* cool…

But the gossip mill was even better. As soon as I finished making the morning's coffee, I ran down the hall to the Eighth Floor lounge to grab a pack of Ho Hos for breakfast. Debbie Stevens was already there, and after she finished pounding on a machine for stealing her quarters, she told me that Christine had gone through the roof over Two's cat costume. So after chewing her out the next business day, Christine called all the girls into the auditorium for an hour-long lecture on appropriate office dress, among other things.

After going over all the basics – hair, nails, makeup, jewelry, etc. – she delivered a rather pointed talk on style. Although Debbie couldn't remember exactly what she'd said – at least not word for word, anyway – the bottom line was pretty emphatic: form fitting was good, tight was bad; and see-through tops only worked when you couldn't actually see through them.

And as far as flirting in the office went, certain people – who unfortunately went unnamed – were skating on thin ice. And when she said thin ice, she meant *really* thin ice.

Oh, man! I thought. *I have got to work on my timing!*

Because if I hadn't gotten busted, Two would still be catching flack...

But best of all was the big bag of goodies I found on my chair after coming back from the lounge – a whole big grocery bag stuffed with just about every Halloween treat imaginable: popcorn balls, candied apples, gum balls, lollypops, tootsie rolls, miniature candy bars of all descriptions, and tons and tons of chocolates. And when I say chocolates, I mean chocolates! The really good imported stuff from Holland, Belgium, Switzerland, and England, all individually wrapped in colored foil.

Wow! I thought, as I pawed through it. *I haven't seen this kinda loot since third grade!*

And since anything eaten on Halloween, Thanksgiving, Christmas, Easter, my birthday or the Fourth of July doesn't count according to *Alicia's House Rules on Calorie Counting*, I didn't hesitate for a moment. I unwrapped three of the little chocolates, and popped them all into my mouth. Then I buzzed Christine to help me open up the vault.

So after opening it up and dragging my carts out, I set up my computer and got down to work. Or at least I tried to. Because to tell you the truth, I just couldn't get into it. All I could think about was my dress, and the dance.

So I spent the rest of the day watching the clock, wondering where Alex was – because for once, even Two didn't seem to know – and crunching some occasional numbers in between. When 5:30 finally rolled around, I was out of there like a shot.

Unlike the morning, the traffic that evening was unusually heavy, so it took me almost half an hour to cover the ten blocks or so to Chinatown. But I lucked out and found a parking space right in front of Madame Henri's shop, and I got even luckier with the fitting. Madame Henri had taken dozens of different measurements when I'd ordered the dress, and the fit was almost perfect. After taking in the waist ever so slightly and raising the hem a fraction of an inch, she added a little tiny clasp on the back to anchor the Sari-like wisp that came up over my left shoulder and fell down my back. Then Madame Henri led me over to the three-way mirror. "You Belle of Ball," she said with a big smile. "Handsome Prince come carry you away."

Captivated by the wonder of her creation, I twirled in front of the mirror and hoped she was right. "It's beautiful, *Madame Henri!*" So even though I couldn't really afford it, I gave her an extra $20 before carrying it out the door.

Since I'd left the dogs at the office, I carefully laid the dress in the Vette's trunk and headed back to work. Since Alex wasn't there, I decided to feed Big Minh and Lady Godiva and take them for their nightly walk before heading home. Exhausted for some inexplicable reason, I fell into bed just after 9 o'clock.

Which was really ironic, because the next day was a total write-off at work. Half the staff was out voting, Alex was still AWOL, and I had an appointment with the hairdresser at 3 pm. But on the brighter side, Julia's fiancée was away on business, so she and two of the other girls in accounting had rented a suite at the hotel for the night, and they had room for one more. Thinking that a place to change was well worth the additional expense, I anted up for a share. So after some serious pleading with Christine – well, actually, it was a lot more like begging – I zoomed back to the apartment, where I took a quick shower and crammed my overnight bag full of necessities. Arriving back at the office just before 3:00, I dropped my dress off at the dry cleaners to be steamed and made a run for the hairdresser.

Raphael – that was the name of the stylist who owned the little shop – was pacing up and down waiting for me when I arrived. Flamboyantly effeminate and almost certainly gay, Raphael was high-spirited, high-strung, and notoriously intemperate with his clients. But as hair stylists go, he was a true genius, so his clients happily suffered his tirades.

Since I was at least five seconds late, I figured he was probably going to blow his stack. But as it turned out, he was in an unusually good mood that day. So he merely huffed, and motioned me toward one of his chairs.

Explaining that I wanted to wear my hair up to the dance that night, I told him that I'd like it washed, trimmed on the ends, and styled just a bit. After huffing again, Raphael questioned me intently about the dress I would be wearing, my makeup, jewelry, and a host of other seemingly insignificant details. Finally satisfied, he called for the girl who served as his assistant. Then in his most charming Italian accent, he told her to wash my hair.

An hour and a half later, I hefted my overnight bag up on my shoulder and stepped out into the hotel lobby. Raphael had put the slightest hint of a red tint into my hair to bring out the highlights before sweeping it up and piling it on my head, so I felt almost regal as I slowly walked across the lobby to pick up my room key and my dress before heading upstairs.

The suite was on the fifth floor, and although it wasn't quite as nice as the one Alex kept in the penthouse, it had two bedrooms and four way oversized beds. Julia and the other two girls were already there, so after making sure I knew their names, Julia suggested we go down to the restaurant and get something to eat. Homecoming didn't kick off until 7:30, so we would have plenty of time to get ready. Since I was already starving, I was all in favor – but I took my overnight with me, because I had my diamonds in it.

Precisely two hours and fifty-five minutes later – which included a leisurely dinner, a good half-hour in front of the mirror applying my makeup, changing, and then another half-hour showing off my dress and explaining where I'd found it – the four of us arrived at the ballroom, five fashionable minutes late.

Resplendent in his dress uniform, Adm. Thomas was escorting his wife through the formal receiving line. Between us stood a couple of CSS staffers with their dates and a half-dozen or so distinguished looking men dressed in tuxedos, with their wives – presumably – on their arms. I recognized two of them as Senators, but the others looked foreign. Judging by the medals they were wearing on their chests, I figured they were probably ambassadors from someplace or another. Glancing around, I found there were a dozen or more congressional staffers standing behind me, followed by another admiral and his lady. Farther back, I was surprised to see Wilbur from the parking garage approaching with a rather shy-looking girl on his arm. Thinking it was really nice of Alex to invite the non-professional staff, I turned back towards the door.

The line had started moving faster, and when I stood up on my tiptoes I could see Alex and Christine standing just inside, greeting each guest in turn. With her hair piled high on top her head, she was dressed in this incredible full length black gown that fell moderately low in the front and daringly so in the back. Dripping with diamonds and standing at least six feet tall in her heels, she looked like an otherworldly vision of beauty.

Alex was wearing a tux, of course, and since I'd never seen him in formal dress before, I was stunned. I mean let's face it – sexy enough to drive a sane woman crazy in a three-piece suit, he was totally irresistible in black tie. So without even realizing it, I growled under my breath.

Come 'ere Loverboy...

CHAPTER THIRTY

After two or three minutes, I finally made it through the doorway. Standing behind my former roommate, Christine didn't see me until she had finished welcoming Julia – but when she did, she did a double-take, and broke into broad smile. Taking my hand in hers, she locked her eyes upon mine. "*Where* did you get that dress?" she whispered. Grinning, I told her Madame Henri had made it for me as I moved up to Alex.

Alex smiled warmly as he took my gloved hand. "Ms. McAllister, thank you so much for coming."

Since he had addressed me so formally, I decided to reply in kind. "Thank you for inviting me, Dr. de Vris." Momentarily taken aback by my use of his academic title, Alex recovered quickly. After glancing around furtively, he focused his eyes upon mine and raised a finger to his lips.

"Don't blow my cover," he warned in a hushed whisper. "They think I'm stupid!"

Laughing, I promised Alex that his secret was safe with me.

So after Alex smiled again and told me to enjoy the evening, I set out after Julia.

After getting a glass of white wine from the bar, I asked Julia to fill me in. This was my first time at a CSS Homecoming, but she'd been to the one the year before. "Well, this one will be a little different," she said as she pointed at all the big screen TVs mounted on the walls. "The Eastern states are going to start reporting election returns any minute now, so that will keep people focused for a while. But as soon as Reagan gets 270 Electoral College votes, the orchestra will start playing so all the VIPs can dance. And then after they get finished – like about 11:00 or so – they'll bring in a band, so the rest of us can have some fun too."

Suddenly curious, I asked her if Alex danced. After taking a sip of her wine, she nodded. "Oh yeah, he'll lead Christine out on the dance floor for the first dance, and after that, they'll dance with the VIPs…

"And then at least one dance with everyone on the staff."

Then she stopped suddenly, and screwed up her face. "That didn't come out right," she said. "But you know what I mean. Alex will dance with all the girls, and Christine with all the guys."

"*Really?*" I asked incredulously.

After taking another sip of her wine, Julia nodded again. "Oh yeah," she said dismissively. "It's a morale thing."

"Well, I think it's *really* nice." Then I took a little tiny sip of wine, and looked away so Julia wouldn't see me beaming – because if she'd caught me, she would have teased me without mercy.

The ballroom was beginning to get crowded, so we began edging away from the bar. But we hadn't made it more than a few feet before a sudden cheer went up, and people started clapping. Glancing up at a TV screen, I saw that President Reagan had carried the first state.

Well, kewl! I thought. *Forty-nine to go!*

We hadn't made it more than a few feet when another cheer went up – President Reagan had carried another state, and according to the TV reports five more of the early-reporting states were leaning in his direction.

Wow, I thought. *This won't take long!*

Taking another little sip of my wine to celebrate, I glimpsed Nguyen and Mai Ling working their way through the crowd. Excusing myself, I began heading in their direction. Trying hard not to step on anyone's toes, I lifted the hem of my dress and slipped through a knot of diplomats. Fortunately, she heard me call her name, and as she turned, her face lit up in a smile. "Dress sooo pretty!" she said. "You look like Princess tonight!" Then she stood up on her toes and gave me a hug.

After thanking her over and over for introducing me to Madame Henri, I complimented her on her dress – because to tell the truth, it was just amazing. Standing just behind her, Nguyen grinned and made this funny little clicking sound twice. "Chinese dresses," he said with a wink. "Ya gotta love 'em."

Which of course, all the guys did.

Laughing, I took his outstretched hand and agreed. I was in the process of telling him how much I appreciated everything that he and Mai Ling had done for me when another deafening cheer went up. Three more states had reported in, all of them for Reagan.

When I turned back, Nguyen apologized for them both. "Alex asked us to help out a little tonight, so we're going to have to go shake some hands," he said. Saying I understood, I thanked them both again and started to turn away. But Nguyen called after me, and asked me to save him a dance.

Taken aback, I glanced over at Mai Ling, but after she smiled again and nodded, I promised him I would. Hoping that meant another small step toward becoming a part of the gang, I began working my way through a bunch of tables to where I'd left Julia.

I hadn't taken more than a few steps when I almost dropped my glass – because there was Dr. MacLaughlin, dressed in a formal Scottish kilt.

Since I'd never actually seen a man wearing a kilt before, it took me a minute to adjust. But as I surveyed his finery – a formal jacket, black tie, a ruffled shirt, and this purse-like thing hanging on a gold chain from his waist – I had to admit I liked the look.

But I was going to tease him about it anyway – or at least I was, until I noticed the hilt of a dagger protruding from the top of his knee sock.

Hmmmm, I thought. *Better wait till he's unarmed.*

But since I wanted to say hello anyway, I worked my way through the crowd.

He was shaking hands with a distinguished-looking man dressed in an unfamiliar uniform when I arrived. "Charles MacLaughlin," he was saying. "Of the Clan MacLachlan."

The other man – who spoke with a British accent – seemed to grasp the significance of that immediately, and the two of them began chatting amiably. It turned out that they probably shared a common ancestor from around 1300 AD or so, but since the Scots were forever changing the spellings of their last names, they weren't entirely sure. Back in the old days, whenever a Scotsman got in trouble with the law he'd change the spelling of his surname just enough so it wouldn't turn up in the warrant file, and hide out with distant kin. And if the King's Men ever showed up to arrest him, the miscreant would swear on his mother's grave they had the wrong man, and the whole clan would back him up. Thinking that sounded a lot like the old "Wasn't there, didn't do it" ploy, I stood patiently off to the side until Dr. MacLaughlin noticed me. When he did, he broke into a big smile. "There you are, Lass!"

After draping an arm over my shoulder and pulling me to his side, Dr. MacLaughlin introduced me to Air Commodore Walter MacKinstry of the Royal Air Force, and then to his wife Cynthia, who had mysteriously reappeared from someplace or another. After shaking hands with the Air Commodore, I shook hands with Mrs. MacLaughlin, and told her what an honor it was to work for her husband. "He's a brilliant economist, you know." A just ever-so-slightly plump woman with a beautiful face and a lovely smile, Mrs. MacLaughlin thanked me for the compliment as the Air Commodore quipped. "It's a damned pity we lost him, then...

"We might still have the Empire if he'd stayed home."

After toasting to that, Dr. MacLaughlin informed the Air Commodore that I had been the co-author of his recent paper on the Soviet economy. Obviously taken aback, the Air Commodore studied my face intently before turning to Dr. MacLaughlin to express his surprise. "That paper made quite an impression at our Embassy," he said. "And I must say it was superbly well done."

Then after a moment's pause, he continued. "You're fortunate to have such a capable young lady to assist you."

After tossing back his drink, Dr. MacLaughlin chuckled. "Well, I do need someone to blame my mistakes upon."

The Air Commodore laughed politely, but Mrs. MacLaughlin interjected. "Don't believe a word of it, Commodore. Charles tells me she's *brilliant*!"

As my cheeks flushed, I was trying to think of something gracious to say when another huge cheer went up. Another six states had been posted in the Reagan column, bringing his total to 11. After glancing at the digital clock that had been inserted in the lower right-hand of the TV screen, I was amazed to see it was only 8:30.

Holy Cow! I thought. *This is going to be a wipeout!*

When I turned back, Dr. MacLaughlin was explaining the Electoral College to the seemingly fascinated Air Commodore, so I waited for a lull in the conversation before excusing myself. After shaking hands again with the Air Commodore and Mrs. MacLaughlin, I set out in search of Julia again.

Less than ten steps later, I ran into Jennifer, but before I could compliment her on her dress another deafening cheer went up. "Good God!" I said. "The election is going to be over in another 20 minutes!"

Clinking her glass against mine, Jennifer said "The sooner the better," and explained that that the VIPs would only dance for an hour or so before leaving. "Once they're gone, Alex will crank up the music, and we'll have some fun!"

Then she dropped a shoulder and gave me a sultry look. "Ready to break some hearts?"

Now Jennifer had a figure to die for, and believe me – she was dressed to kill. So I figured the odds were way better than even that at least one of the guys was going to get carried out on a stretcher that night.

But as for myself...

Well, let's just say I didn't think any of the guys were going to end up crying over me.

So I kinda smiled, and told her that I didn't know about breaking hearts – but I really would like a dance or two. Holding out the skirt of my dress, I smiled hopefully. "I got all pretty."

Jennifer grinned, and told me to have fun. "But avoid Alex until close to the end, because that's when they'll play the really romantic songs." Then she winked, and told me she was off to find her first victim.

As I started making my way through the crowd again, there was another tremendous roar as people started jumping up and down cheering. It was only five minutes to 9:00, but the major networks had already projected President Reagan the winner. As champagne bottles began popping all over the ballroom, the volume suddenly increased and I heard the newscaster declare: "No possible combination of the remaining states can give Senator Mondale the 270 Electoral College votes needed to win the presidency."

After the cheering subsided, the high-pitched sound of a microphone coming to life filled the ballroom, and after standing on my tiptoes, I could see Alex standing behind an elevated podium along the north wall next to the orchestra's platform. "Ladies and gentlemen, may I have your attention please."

Dodging an errant champagne cork, he welcomed one and all to the CSS's Seventh Annual Homecoming, and started to congratulate President Reagan on his landslide victory. But before he could even finish the sentence, his words were drowned out by a deafening cheer. Smiling from the podium, he waited for the din to die down before informing the assembled crowd that he'd decided to dispense with his prepared remarks. "So, let's just enjoy the evening."

Then as the lights dimmed, his eyes followed a spotlight into the audience. "Mrs. O'Connell, may I have this dance?"

I couldn't see Christine from where I stood – because let's face it, I'm barely 5'7" in 3 inch heels – but Julia told me all about it later that night. As the crowd parted, Christine placed her hand upon her neckline and curtsied, and then the two of them met in the center of the dance floor. As the orchestra began playing, they danced in the spotlight.

Which was like, *really* cool.

After they finished, a dozen other couples made their way onto the dance floor, and Alex escorted Christine to her husband, who was waiting at the edge. Since I didn't get to see that either, Julia told me that after Alex thanked Christine for the dance and Dan for the privilege – which was her husband's name, as I learned – he began dancing with the female VIPs.

By that time I had worked my way up to the front of the spectators and I began watching with awed fascination. *So this is how the other half lives*, I thought to myself in half-jest.

I was about to turn away, when I noticed Mai Ling dancing with Nguyen, and for just a moment I fixated upon them. Nguyen returned the smile that danced upon Mai Ling's face with a look of utter contentment, and for a moment it seemed as though I could read his mind.

He had chosen his love wisely and well, and he knew it...

Suddenly wondering if anyone would ever love me the way Nguyen loved Mai Ling, I turned back into the crowd and made my way through another group of tables to the bar. Although I had barely touched my wine, I traded it in for a new glass and moved off to the side. Heeding Jennifer's advice, I hid in the shadows.

I stood there for a long time thinking about a lot of things, but my mind kept drifting back to my Mom and my Dad. I knew she had worshiped the ground he walked on, but what about him? Did he feel the same way about her? I didn't know, and rather sadly, I knew there was no way I ever could know.

But for her sake, I really hoped so...

My reverie was finally broken when I heard Nguyen calling me by name. "Still with us?" he asked.

Blushing, I nodded. "I was just thinking."

"Well, if you've finished solving the world's problems, you owe me a dance." Smiling, he took my hand and led me across the ballroom to the dance floor, and we danced a long, slow waltz.

It turned out that Nguyen was not only a really good dancer, but was riotously funny as well – and in a less-than-subtle effort to cheer me up, he kept dropping these hilarious one-liners. By the time the music faded, I was laughing so hard my barely-healed ribs had started hurting again.

"Stop that, Nguyen!"

Chuckling as he led me from the floor, he said he was just teasing. "And by the way, everyone but my wife calls me Nu." Smiling as I retrieved my glass of wine from Mai Ling, I said "OK, Nu."

Then I thanked Mai Ling for letting me borrow her husband.

"Borrow?" she said with a big grin. "Dat rent! I send bill in morning."

Figuring fair was fair – because after all, she hadn't charged a dime for seeing me in the hospital – I laughed and said OK. "Just remember I'm still paying off my college loans."

Mai Ling grinned again. "He step on toe? I give discount den."

Joining in the jest, Nguyen apologized. "I usually don't do that, you know."

I was working on a comeback when someone tapped on the microphone. Turning around, I could see it was Alex. After asking the audience for a round of applause for the orchestra, he explained that it was traditional to bring in a contemporary band to conclude CSS Homecomings. But this year they had prepared a special treat instead. So without further ado, he asked for a big round of applause for their guest DJ.

And then with a big grin on his face, he introduced Nguyen Tranh. *"The Prince of Pop, The Regent of Rock, The Sultan of Soul!"*

Who by the way came cheap, because he wasn't union...

Taken by complete surprise, I looked over at Mai Ling – who was looking down at the floor, with one arm across her midsection, and the other had hand placed over her face. "Oh no, big trouble now...

"Nguyen play disk jockey again."

By that time he already bounded up to the platform, and seated himself behind a console. Then after a series of riotous one-liners, he finally bellowed: *"GooooooodEveningWashington!!!*

Then he demanded to know what time it was. But before anyone could answer, Bill Haley's *Rock Around the Clock* filled the ballroom.

Still puzzled, I turned to Mai Ling. *"Nguyen is a disk jockey?"*

Looking up, Mai Ling sighed and shook her head. "Only in fantasy life...

"He play cowboys and Viet Cong when little boy. Now he preten DJ."

Cracking up at her joke – at least, I *thought* it was a joke – I commiserated. "Guys never really grow up, do they?"

By that time the dance floor was crowded again, and I saw Jennifer doing the Jitterbug with some guy I didn't recognize – which I thought was a pretty amazing accomplishment in a floor length dress.

Mai Ling must have thought so too, because she pointed at Jennifer. "She gooo!"

I was about to respond when Alex suddenly appeared off to the right. After smiling at me, he pulled Mai Ling out on the dance floor, where they danced to Carl Perkins' version of *Blue Suede Shoes*. It turned out that she could jitterbug too, and as I watched her dance, it suddenly dawned on me why Madame Henri had cut her slit so high.

Gotta remember that, I thought.

But just as I was finishing making my mental note, I spied Tom Andrews approaching out of the corner of my eye. Making a quick about-face, I had almost escaped into the crowd when he caught up with me. "Will you dance with me?" he asked plaintively.

I was about to tell him I couldn't because they'd mistakenly amputated my foot in the hospital, but I just wasn't a big enough liar to carry it off. So I forced a thin smile and reluctantly followed him out on the dance floor – after making another note to kick myself in the duff. But Tom wasn't a bad dancer, and as soon as the music stopped a really cute intern from the Press Department asked me for the next dance. After convincing myself that a one-year age difference didn't quite qualify as cradle-robbing, I agreed.

And in fact, five or six other guys asked me to dance. Which, to be honest, was something of a record.

But it got even better, because Christine and her husband were in the middle of the dance floor when *The Devil with a Blue Dress On* began pouring out of the speakers. Laughing, she kicked off her shoes and let her hair down as they picked up the beat.

Now I don't know if you have ever heard that song, but it has this incredible high-energy beat, and back in the day – which was like a couple of years before I was born – girls used to Shimmy to it. And while The Shimmy is pretty tame by contemporary standards, it was considered rather risqué at the time.

Which I happen to know, because my Mom turned bright red and changed the subject when I asked her about it...

So to make a long story short, Nguyen was playing an extended version of the song that had a long drum solo in the middle. And you guessed it – Christine started to Shimmy.

On my God! I thought. Because I just *couldn't* believe my eyes!

Snickering, I slipped up alongside of Gen. McGreggor and Adm. Taylor to get a better view. Entirely oblivious to the fact that I was standing there, Adm. Taylor shook his head and sighed. "General, I do confess – I just *love* watching the little girls shake their booties."

With his eyes still locked upon Christine, Gen. McGreggor nodded approvingly. "Truly one of life's great pleasures, Admiral."

Which of course, cracked me up completely.

Suddenly aware of the fact that I had been standing right there, Gen. McGreggor turned bright red, and a stricken look spread across Adm. Taylor's face. Realizing this was the perfect chance to get the general for razzing me at the elevator, I turned into him and stood up on my tiptoes.

Taking his face in my hands, I looked him straight in the eyes. *"Pervert!"*

Then grinning from ear to ear, I laid a big kiss on his cheek, and scurried off laughing.

I was still chuckling about that when the music faded out. Christine and her husband were holding hands in the middle of the dance floor laughing, as the guys in the crowd whistled and cheered. *"Encore, Encore!"*

But Christine – who was both beaming and blushing by then – shook her head, and after picking up her shoes, she started to lead her husband off the dance floor.

Nguyen had other plans, though. Speaking low in the microphone, he told her to hold it right there – because he had another song for her. Then getting halfway up out of his seat, he looked around the crowd and bellowed for Alex. "Come on bro, it's time to do your penance."

Puzzled, I spotted Alex in the crowd just as his face began to flush. Holding up his hands in protest, he shook his head back and forth. Then someone started yelling *"Alex! Alex!"* and the CSS staff picked up the chant. But it wasn't until Christine marched over and grabbed him by the wrist that he finally conceded.

Glancing around the crowd, Nguyen informed them that there was a whole long story here. But since he was a dead man if he told it, he was just going to dedicate the next song to Alex and Christine...

Who, by the way, had spent four long years driving each other nuts at Georgetown...

Then he depressed the lever on the turntable, and lowered the needle onto the vinyl.

More than just a little bit confused, I tried to figure out what was playing as Christine turned her back on Alex and began rhythmically walking away from him, clapping her hands to the beat – which wasn't easy, because it kept shifting from a 2:3 to a 3:3:2 and back to the 2:3. Or at least I thought it did, because I just couldn't keep up.

Man! I thought. *You have gotta be coordinated to do that!*

As I watched Alex follow her around in a circle, clapping his hands to the beat, I suddenly realized it was a variation of Clyde McPhatter's *Lover Please (Please Come back).*

Oh, my God! I thought. *They were an item!*

More intrigued than angry, I watched Alex close the gap with Christine as the refrain began.

Lover please, please come back
Don't take that train coming down the track
Don't, please don't, don't leave me,
Don't leave me in misery

After the instrumental transition to the first verse of the lyrics, Alex placed his hands on Christine's hips as she lifted her arms above her head. Still dancing the circular dance, she began moving her hips to the beat.

You would never hold me so near
You would never call me dear
Don't 'cha know I'd die for you
Now you're gone that's what I'll do

As the lyrics faded into the instrumental before the refrain, Christine turned into Alex, and as she danced backward to the beat she wagged a remonstrative finger under his nose. Laughing, Alex grabbed her hand and spun her out.

Lover please, please come back
Don't take that train coming down the track
Don't, please don't, don't leave me,
Don't leave me in misery

After dancing away from Alex, Christine turned back and put her hands on her hips. Still moving to the beat of the music, she watched dismissively as Alex circled her, clapping to the beat. And then as the song moved into a long instrumental, she ignored him altogether and danced alone.

After what must have been at least two or three minutes – because this was the long dance version, you know – Alex pulled her back to him as the second verse began.

All those stories, not too long
About a love that went all wrong
The girl left the boy, just as bad
Now she's gone, he's so sad

Christine had spun away, but when the lyrics faded into the refrain, she locked her eyes upon Alex and began moving back toward him in this incredibly sexy, sultry dance.

Lover please, please come back
Don't take that train coming down the track
Don't, please don't, don't leave me,
Don't leave me in misery

Taking the sultry thing to a whole new level, she stopped just before him. Reaching out with her index finger, she put it under his chin and pulled him towards her. Pursing her lips just millimeters from his, I thought for sure she was going to kiss him — but at the last instant, she spun away just as lyrics began to repeat.

You would never hold me so near
You would never call me dear
Don't 'cha know I'd die for you
Now you're gone that's what I'll do

Throwing her hair back over her shoulders, she stuck her nose way up in the air and fell back into the beat. And then with a triumphant smile upon her face, she danced away, clapping her hands to the music before finally stopping to dance in front of her husband.

Then as the music faded away, she laid this *monster* kiss on him.

Alone and abandoned in the center of the dance floor, Alex threw up his hands and shrugged his shoulders. Then as the refrain came back around, he walked over to Dan and shook his hand.

Now that was kewl! I thought. *A class act from start to finish…*

But class act or not, Nguyen hadn't been kidding. There was *obviously* a whole long story there, and it didn't take a Rocket Scientist to figure out that Alex and Christine had just told a part of it in their dance. Grinning from ear to ear, I joined in the deafening applause.

After making a note to squeeze *every* last lurid detail out of Christine just as soon as we got back to the office, I decided to make a strategic withdrawal as the applause died down. Nguyen was still playing fast music, and I really wanted to have a slow dance with Alex.

Hoping that Nguyen would hurry up and change the tempo, I headed for the bar. Although I'd barely tasted my second glass of wine – and to be truthful, the first one as well – it had become warm during the hour or two that I'd been holding it. So I handed it to a passing steward, and picked up a glass of champagne from his tray.

As luck would have it, Nguyen slowed it down after the next song. But since I didn't like the next three or four tunes that much, I held back. Glancing around, I realized that the lights had dimmed again and the spotlight had returned. I was still trying to decide whether or not I should reposition myself forward, when Alex appeared in my peripheral vision. As I turned to greet him, he smiled. "The last dance is coming up, Ms. McAllister, and I wondered if you would share it with me."

Well, duh, I thought. Wondering how he could possibly be *that* dense, I was tempted to ask him why he thought I'd been hanging around.

Because after all, I could be doing something really exciting, like painting my toenails or memorizing statistical tables…

But since that really wasn't the time to mouth off, I smiled instead and told him it would be my pleasure.

Then I extended my hand.

As the spotlight followed us out onto the dance floor, I wondered what song we would dance to. Still holding his hand when we reached the center of the dance floor, I turned into him and placed my other hand upon his shoulder as The Righteous Brother's *Unchained Melody* filled the room – which just happens to be *the* most romantic song *ever* written.

Smiling, I turned away so he wouldn't see the mist in my eyes.

There's no denying it, I thought. *This night is mine.*

Hoping Alex was thinking along the same lines, I laid my head against his shoulder as we swayed to the music.

But Fate had conspired against me. Because the very moment I closed my eyes, an authoritative voice intruded from behind.

"I beg your pardon, Sir. The President is calling on a secure line."

CHAPTER THIRTY-ONE

A week later, I was still fuming about the dance. *It's all President Reagan's fault*, I thought as I pounded away on my keyboard. *Saving the world is all very well and fine, but my dance was way more important...*

He couldn't wait three minutes???

I still had no idea what the President had wanted. But it must have been important — because after Alex left with the Marine general who had so rudely interrupted us, he seemed to have dropped off the face of the earth. Two swore up and down that she didn't know where he was, and the fact that even Christine seemed to be in the dark only added to my ire. But since there was a finite limit to how long I could stay mad, I let go of my anger and began plotting my revenge.

Growling under my breath, I sent President Reagan a mental warning. *You better watch it, buddy...*

Because next year I'm gonna steal ALL your chocolate!!!

Figuring that would fix his wagon, I glanced at my watch. Thinking now was as good a time as any, I pressed the intercom button on my phone and buzzed Christine. After she picked up the handset, I told her I was going to make a fresh pot of coffee and asked her if she'd like a cup — which was more of a pretext than a courtesy, because I really wanted to talk to her. So after she thanked me and said yes, I loaded up my carts and secured them in the vault.

Five minutes later, I was standing in the galley watching the coffee drip into the pot below it. As I waited for it to fill, my mind wandered back to Homecoming and I realized there had been a bright side to the dance after all. *Actually several*, I thought, as a grin spread across my face.

Because first of all, Two was furious that Alex had chosen me for the last dance.

But as I chuckled to myself, I decided the flap over Christine's sexy dancing was almost as good — because there was a whole long story there, too. Back at Georgetown the other students had nicknamed her "Wild Thang" for the way she danced, and someone on the staff had found out about it. Christine had been mortified, of course — which probably accounted for the fact that she'd suddenly started dressing like the

Church Lady — but everyone else at the CSS thought it was hysterically funny.

Which, of course, included me. But since this was the first chance I'd had to talk to her in private since the dance, I suppressed my snicker and poured her a cup of *Alicia's Finest* instead. Then, after loading up the tray with cream, sweetener, and stirs, I poured one for myself as well.

After making my way across the reception area of the Executive office, I balanced my tray in one hand and knocked on Christine's open door with the other. When she looked up from whatever it was she was reading, she smiled and told me to come in.

As I set the tray down on the edge of her desk, Christine raised an eyebrow. "Two cups?"

After straightening up, I paused for a moment to gather my courage. "Well," I said. "I was hoping maybe we could talk."

Suddenly realizing she'd been ambushed, Christine gave me an irritated look as she took the proffered cup of coffee from my hand. Then after reaching across her desk for the little pitcher of cream, she sighed and told me to close her office doors.

Grinning, I said "Thanks!"

Once I'd pushed the double doors shut, I turned back. Then after Christine waved me into one of the upholstered leather chairs seats in front of her desk, she poured some sweetener into her coffee and stirred it. Then she leaned back in her chair, and gazed at me. "I suppose you want to know about Alex and me."

Nodding as I fixed my own coffee, I paused for a moment in order to choose my words more carefully. "Well, yeah," I said. After scrunching up my face, I told her I was confused. "You had told me that you and Alex hadn't dated, but then Nguyen played that song for you and said there was this whole long story there…"

"And then there was that dance."

Suddenly aware of the fact that I was probably skating on thin ice — what with that whole "Wild Thang" and all — I hastened to compliment her. "Which was like, really cool," I said quickly. Then knitting my eyebrows together, I told her she was a great dancer.

Forcing a fast smile upon my face, I nodded emphatically. *"Really!"*

Flushing, Christine sighed before leaning back in her chair and looking up at the ceiling. "It's not what you're thinking."

Then she leaned forward, and after taking a sip of her coffee she reached into her top drawer and pulled out a pack of cigarettes, a lighter, and a small glass ashtray. After shaking a cigarette free and lighting it, she put the pack and the lighter back into her drawer and closed it. "I don't do this very often," she said in a voice tinged with guilt. Almost shocked, I nodded with widened eyes.

After a moment of silence, Christine told me that she had met Alex the first day at Georgetown. "He and Nguyen were standing in line behind me at registration, and it took forever to sign up for our classes…

"So we started talking while we stood in line, and it turned out that we were going to take most of the same classes…

"I can't remember exactly, but I think the three of us had four classes together the first semester; and after that, we had at least two and usually three classes together all the way through to graduation…

"And there were a couple of other students who shared them."

After taking another puff from her cigarette, Christine continued. "Max Allen, Steve Germain, Lois Peabody, Susi Thomas." Then she chuckled. "And, of course, Mary Lou Steinhoff."

Suddenly remembering that I'd made a mental note to get the 411 on Mary Lou, I briefly considered asking her for details. But since I didn't want to get Christine sidetracked, I nodded instead and hoped she would continue.

"Anyway, by the end of the first semester we were hanging out together – except for Mary Lou, because she just didn't like us very much – and when we weren't studying, we did a lot of stuff together as a group…

"Movies, concerts, parties, picnics, trail rides, things like that."

As Christine paused to take a final draw upon her cigarette, I sensed an opening. "So you *weren't* dating?"

After stubbing her cigarette out in the ashtray, Christine rolled her eyes in exasperation. Then finally she shrugged. "Sort of…"

"But most of the time it was with the group, or after tutorials."

"Tutorials?" I asked quizzically.

Much to my surprise, Christine laughed. "Well, Alex wasn't the best of students, so he used to pay me to tutor him for exams."

Grinning from ear to ear, I asked her if it did any good. Chuckling, Christine shrugged as a smile spread across her face. "Not much…

"But I pulled him through Econ 101 and 102, and a couple of finance classes."

By now fascinated, I asked her what tutoring Alex was like.

Christine grimaced. *"Torture!"* she said. "But the money was good, and he always threw in an 'End of Finals' dinner at a really nice restaurant."

"Well, that was nice," I said. Christine nodded and smiled. "It was…

"And he always took me someplace really special on my birthday."

As I puzzled my way through what she had told me, I took another sip of my coffee. "So you *were* dating?"

Suddenly exasperated, Christine sighed again before shaking her head. "Alicia, it's *complicated!*"

Then after taking another sip from her cup, she explained. "You have to understand the circumstances," she said. "I was a scholarship student from a small town in West Virginia, and I was the first person in my family to ever go to college – let alone a prestigious school like Georgetown…

"And I took my studies very seriously."

"But Alex was just having a good time, and that irritated me to no end."

Then as a look bordering upon disbelief crept upon her face, she explained. "And besides, he always had a dozen other girls in his stable."

Suddenly exasperated again, she looked at me across her desk before shaking her head again. "It's not like I wasn't attracted to him – because I was. But we were polar opposites back then…

"He was rich, I was poor. He thought college was a big four-year party, and I thought it was the chance of a lifetime."

Then she pursed her lips and shrugged. "And then, he was younger than I was."

Huh?

That caught my attention – and it caught Christine's too, because her eyes suddenly crossed as she realized what she had said. Leaning across her desk, she pointed a finger at me. "Don't you *dare* tell anyone that!"

Grinning, I promised I wouldn't. "But I thought you were in the same class?"

Frowning, Christine nodded. "We were. But Alex's mother hired a tutor for him when he was four, so he was a year ahead of his age group. And since my birthday fell in the spring, I was a year behind most of mine."

Grinning, I teased her. "So you robbed the cradle, huh?" Irritated, Christine shot back. *"I did NOT!"*

Suppressing the big grin that had spread across my face, I apologized. "I was just teasing."

Huffing, Christine told me I'd better have been.

Nodding quickly, I assured her it was just a jest. "So what happened then?"

Christine paused for a long moment, before sighing. "Alicia, it was hard…

"The chemistry was there," she admitted. "And we did a lot of things together, and sometimes we even went out on dates…

"And because we spent so much time together, everyone just assumed it was a serious relationship."

Quizzically, I peered over the rim of my cup. "But it wasn't?"

Christine sighed again. "I told you it was *complicated*…

"It's not like we didn't try, because we did. But every time we started getting close – I mean really close, emotionally – things just got crazy, and we always ended up having a big fight."

"Because of all his other girls?" I asked softly.

Christine frowned and shook her head. "That didn't help matters, but it wasn't really the issue."

By now mystified, I asked what was.

After a long moment of silence, Christine sighed again and leaned back in her chair. "My stubbornness," she said softly.

Suddenly sitting upright, I almost spilled my coffee. "Really?"

Christine nodded, almost sadly. "Alex had already decided on a military career before he arrived at Georgetown, and there was just no way I was going to traipse all over the world as a Marine Corps wife…

"I had dreams of my own," she said. "I wanted a career. I wanted to do something important with my life."

Shifting uneasily in my seat, I tugged at my skirt. "So, you couldn't talk him out of it?"

Christine shook her head as a guilty look stole across her face. Looking down at her desk, she shook her head. "Nope."

After a moment, she looked up again. "My father only made it through the eighth grade, and he was a truck driver all his life…

"He worked hard, and he saved and invested. And by the time he retired five years ago, he owned his own freight company and a whole fleet of trucks…

"But success came late in life for him, and things were tough when I was growing up. We didn't have much money, and there were just so many things I wanted out of life...

"And there was just no way I was going to stay in the hollows of West Virginia, and end up married to a trucker or a coal miner."

Thinking I could really relate to that, I nodded, and asked her how it had finally ended.

Shaking her head, Christine said not very well. "I didn't understand myself very well back then, so I wasn't able to put it into words...

"So we really weren't able to talk it through.

"We hung out together, studied together, did things together with the group and – every once in a while – we went out together."

"Then we graduated. And Alex left for the Marine Corps, and I went on to grad school."

Thinking it must have been awful leaving things up in the air like that, I told her that it must have been hard.

Christine nodded. "It was, and the fact that we kept in touch probably made it worse...

"He called me every once in a while before he left for Vietnam, and we wrote back and forth while he was away...

"Then after he returned from his first tour of duty, he came to Boston to see me and we spent a week together...

"Sightseeing, taking in the local plays, quiet dinners."

Lowering my eyes, I asked her what that was like.

Christine shrugged. "It was nice," she said. "Or at least it was until I asked him about his plans."

Uh-oh, I thought.

"Things got tense after he told me he was staying in the Marine Corps, and we got into a huge fight the night before he left."

Oh, gawd, I thought.

After looking down and studying my shoes for a minute or more, I asked her what happened.

Christine raised her eyebrows and inhaled sharply. "I kicked him out."

Startled, I sat bolt upright in my chair. *"You kicked him out???"*

After raising her eyebrows and exhaling slowly, she nodded her head and confessed. "Yeah, I threw him out on his ear."

Oh, Jesus! I thought. *BAD, BAD move!*

I don't know if Christine read my mind, or if I had actually said it aloud. But Christine nodded in agreement. "It really was...

"And then a couple of weeks later, Max called to see how I was doing, and in the course of the conversation he mentioned Alex had gone back to Vietnam."

Christine sighed again, before taking another sip of her coffee. "I didn't know that he had already volunteered for a second tour before he'd come to Boston, and I was sure he had gone back there because I'd dumped him."

Then she shuddered involuntarily. "I just had this awful feeling," she said. "By that time the fighting had become furious, and the Marines were bearing the brunt of it."

After wiping a tear from the corner of her eye, she told me that she had gotten down on her knees and prayed for him every night. "And then one morning I got up and turned on the news, and they said the whole family was gone...

"His Mom and his Dad had been killed in a car wreck, and he had been killed in Vietnam."

Oh my God, I thought, as I watched her face contort in anguish. *That poor girl...*

Struggling to hold back the tears, she continued. "I just came unglued...

"I curled up in a ball on the couch and cried for hours and hours...

"Then finally about six o'clock that night – at least I think it was about six, because the shadows had begun to fall across my living room – the Pentagon issued a correction...

"Alex was still alive, but in grave condition. They didn't expect him to live through the night."

Then Christine looked up at me in agony. "I know you've lost someone you love. But imagine what was like to be told Alex was dead – and then hours later told no, he's still alive, but he's going to die anyway...

"I just couldn't deal with it."

By that time, tears had begun welling at the corners of my eyes, too. Because I just couldn't imagine anything so terrible.

There was a long silence, and for the next couple of minutes you could have heard a pin drop on Christine's Oriental carpet.

"I went numb. I couldn't walk, I couldn't talk, I couldn't think, I couldn't feel...

"All I could do was sit in front of the TV and wait for Alex to die...

"So I sat there in front of the screen crying, all through the night and into the morning...

"Then about 10:00 am the next day, the Pentagon announced that Alex had improved during the night. They said he was in 'grave but stable condition' and the doctors were cautiously optimistic. If he lived through the next 24 hours, they said they'd be able to move him from the field hospital to the navy base at Da Nang."

"Thank God," I muttered.

After another long silence, Christine wiped another tear from the corner of her eye and nodded. "I did...

"I went to church every day for a month."

Thinking that was a no-brainer, I nodded in silent agreement. Because if that had happened to me, I probably would have joined a convent...

Christine finished off the last of her coffee, and dropped the Styrofoam cup in her trashcan. "There wasn't a whole lot of news after Alex was moved to Da Nang...

"But after about six weeks or so, I got a letter from the Tokyo Naval Hospital in Japan...

"Alex was still in such bad shape that he couldn't write it himself, so he had dictated it to a Navy corpsman. But he wanted me to know he was going to be OK, and he didn't want me to feel bad about throwing him out because it had been all his fault."

Christine paused for a long moment, and shifted in her chair. "Always the gentleman," she said, smiling through her tears.

"So then it wasn't his fault?"

Leaning back in her chair, Christine sighed and looked up at the ceiling before shaking her head. "No," she said softly. "It was mine."

I broke the long silence that followed by telling her how sorry I was.

Christine nodded, and told me that she was too. "If there was one thing in my life I could take back and do over, that would be it...

Then she shrugged again, and continued. "Anyway, Alex said he knew that things just couldn't work between us, but he hoped we could still be friends."

Then she looked up at me, and after brushing a tear from her eye, she continued. "The moment I read those words, I realized that I wanted to be his friend more than anything else I'd ever wanted in my whole life."

Then after wiping another tear from the corner of her eye, she told me how much she loved him. "But it's a different kind of love, Alicia...

"It's just not the kind you can build a marriage upon."

Wow, I thought. *That's gotta be a tough row to hoe.*

"So does Alex feel the same way?" I asked.

Christine smiled and nodded. "After he was transferred back to Bethesda Naval Hospital here in Washington, I took a semester off to look after him."

Suddenly sentimental, Christine smiled. "I pushed him around Washington in a wheelchair for months, so we had plenty of time to talk it through."

Wow! I thought. "Alex was in a wheelchair?"

Much to my surprise, Christine chuckled. "You know the way the handles stick out from the back?"

Puzzled, I nodded.

"Well they reminded Alex of the *Enterprise* from *Star Trek*...

"So he got one of those *Star Trek* shirts, and had *"Starship Enterprise"* painted on each side of the chair!"

By this time Christine was grinning from ear to ear. "You'd think that after getting almost blown in two, losing his family, and then getting stuck in a wheelchair, he would have been depressed...

"But he never let it get to him, not once."

Then as a look of admiration mixed with disbelief stole across her face, she shook her head again. "The one time we talked about it, Alex said that he was one of the lucky ones. He'd had his parents for 24 years, and he was grateful for that...

"And as far as his injuries went, well....

"He said it had been an honor to serve his country."

Deeply impressed by his fortitude and grace – well, actually, awed would be a better word – I just sat there in silence. Because to tell you the truth, I just didn't know what to say.

Seeing the look on my face, Christine shifted in her seat and smiled. "So anyway, we spent that spring playing *Star Trek*, zooming around Washington and 'going where no man had ever gone before'...

"And it was a lot of fun."

Then Christine suddenly stopped, and crossed her eyes. "At least when he wasn't yelling, *'Scottie! I need more power!'*"

Still laughing, she looked down at her desk and shook her head in amazement. "He can be such a *nut!*"

With a huge grin, I told Christine I wish I'd been there to see it. Then I asked her what happened next.

Smiling wistfully, Christine explained that spring turned into summer, and she had to go back to Harvard to catch up on her classes. "Alex was up on crutches by then, so I thought it would be OK to leave him. But before I left, we made a vow to be friends for life."

Then she smiled happily. "As we are, and ever shall be."

CHAPTER THIRTY-TWO

Happy for Christine, I smiled back. But after a moment's pause, I just *had* to ask. "So what's your husband think about all that?"

Laughing, Christine threw back her hair. "Well, he can't complain too much...

"Because after all, it was Alex who introduced us."

Laughing at the delicious irony, I asked her if she was kidding. After shaking her head and crossing her finger across her heart, she said nope. "He went to George Washington, so I didn't know him in college. But he's a guitar player, too, and he and Alex used to get together and jam every now and then...

"Anyway, Dan was in law school while Alex and I were playing *Star Trek*, and just before I left, Alex set us up on a date.

Well, kewl! I thought.

Then Christine smiled wistfully. "We started seeing each other, and since Boston's not that far from Washington, we were able to get together every month or so...

"And we kept that up even after I finished my MBA and moved to New York. So after a couple years of modeling, I moved back here...

"And we married the next year."

Smiling, Christine leaned back in her chair. "So that's the story." Then suddenly intent, she leaned forward again and asked me if there was anything else I wanted to know. "Because it really is very personal.

"*Comprende?*"

Miffed by her tone of voice, I thought *OK, Wild Thang, whatever you say...*

Since I valued my life, I didn't actually say that. So I nodded instead, and promised to keep my mouth shut. But since her relationship with Alex wasn't the only thing I had wanted to talk to her about, I knit my eyebrows together and told her there was something else. "But it's not really about you and Alex."

Obviously relieved, Christine nodded attentively.

"Well, it's about the way Alex and Dr. MacLaughlin think," I said finally.

Nodding again, Christine told me to go on.

"Well, it seems to me that their thought process is like, way different from most people," I said. "Dr. MacLaughlin isn't into details, but he can just glance at a column of statistics and tell you what they mean...

"Kinda like the way Alex skims the headlines of the newspaper, and knows everything that's going on in the world."

After Christine nodded attentively, I continued. "So I'm kinda thinking they're looking for some kind of pattern in all the numbers I've been crunching...

"It's almost like they expect something to just jump out of the data – something that would be immediately obvious to them, but would zip right past everyone else."

Uncertain if I had made any sense, I scrunched up my nose and asked Christine if she understood what I'd meant.

But Christine had stiffened in her seat, and her eyes had narrowed. Clearly ill at ease, she took a very long time to answer. Then after an unbearable silence, she nodded slowly and deliberately. Suddenly sounding very much like Dr. MacLaughlin, she said that was a penetrating insight – and then very firmly, she told me that I would do well to keep it to myself.

Not quite sure if that was a warning or a threat, I looked down at the floor. *Oh, way to go, girl...*

After intently studying the pattern in Christine's Oriental rug for a brutally long moment, I finally concluded that it had been a warning. "So the plane crash wasn't an accident, was it?"

Christine shrugged her shoulders, and averted her gaze. "The FAA attributed it to mechanical failure."

After another long silence, I looked up again. "But you don't really believe that?"

Christine sighed and shrugged her shoulders again. "Not really."

After staring at the floor for a long moment, I looked up again and fastened my eyes upon hers. "So is this like, really dangerous?"

Christine averted her gaze; and weighed the question for a long time. "For Alex, because he's the key player," she said finally. "But I don't think the opposition has any real interest in the rest of us."

Acutely conscious of the fact that Christine had slipped into "spook speak" – because intelligence professionals always refer to the Bad Guys as "The Opposition" – I turned the whole thing over in my mind a couple of times before somewhat hesitantly asking her about the break-in at my apartment.

Leaning back in her chair again, Christine crossed her legs as she pondered the question. "Maybe it was just some freak," she said finally. Then she shrugged again, and shifted in her seat. "But on the other hand, they may have been trying to intimidate you."

After pursing my lips together and looking down at the floor, I nodded. Then after looking back up, I asked Christine who they were.

"The KGB?"

Christine looked away, and for a moment I thought she was going to reach for another cigarette. But after hesitating for a long moment, she shrugged. "I'm not sure...

"All I know is they're inside the government, and they're very powerful and very ruthless."

Thinking that fit the known facts, I nodded. "So do you think they'll try to kill Alex again?"

As a worried look passed across her face, Christine exhaled sharply. Then after opening her eyes wide and pursing her lips together, she shrugged. "Probably."

"Over my damn dead body!"

Suddenly aware that I'd spoken out loud, I looked up in consternation as an indulgent smile flickered across Christine's face. Flushing badly, I squirmed in my seat. "Well, I'm pretty tough, you know!"

Then more to convince myself than anything else, I defiantly reminded Christine that I had a brown belt in Tae Kwon Do. Irritated by the implausible look that crept upon her face, I fired back.

"Really!" I insisted. "I can smash bricks with my bare hands!"

Now that wasn't meant to be funny, but Christine cracked up anyway. And after moment's reflection, I did too.

Yeah, like a couple of busted bricks are gonna scare 'em...

When we eventually stopped laughing, Christine smiled and said she could appreciate that. But it was very important for me to understand that being cautious was a lot more important than being tough – and she admonished me to think about that, long and hard.

So after promising her that I would, she again cautioned me not to discuss anything that we had talked about. "And that includes my relationship with Alex." she said sternly.

"Because it's really *very* personal."

Nodding, I promised her that I would.

Apparently satisfied, she glanced at her watch and informed me that she had work to do. Then after getting up from her desk, she walked me to her door. But before shooing me out of her office, she smiled and told me how much Alex had liked my

Homecoming dress. Then she winked, and told me I'd been a big hit.

Thinking that was like, way cool, my face lit up as I scurried out the door.

After taking the carrying tray back to the galley, I made a quick trip to the ladies' room before picking up a can of Diet Pepsi from the Canteen. Thinking that would be enough to keep me wired for the next three or four hours, I pushed the outer doors of my offices partway closed and settled into my oversized chair to mull over Christine's warning. But I just couldn't keep focused – because for some reason or another, I kept thinking about Alex and the Bad Guys instead.

So they think they're going to get him, huh?

Fat chance, I thought.

So after pursing my lips together, I picked up my Diet Pepsi and began studying the fine print along the bottom of the can while I analyzed the problem. Since it would be a whole lot easier to stop the Bad Guys if I knew what they were up to, figuring that out was obviously the first order of business.

Can't be that hard, I thought. *Because it's all in that data somewhere...*

So after pondering the issue for a few minutes, I finally concluded that the best way to proceed was by analogy.

It's kinda like an impressionist painting, I thought. *Stand up close and it looks like someone accidentally splattered paint all over the canvas. But if you take a couple of steps back, all of a sudden the picture emerges.*

Thinking that seemed about right, I nodded to no one in particular as I turned the Diet Pepsi can sideways to read the list of ingredients. *So at the end of the day, it all comes down to one simple question...*

Specifically: Just exactly where do I have to stand to see the picture?

After puzzling over that for five minutes or so, I finally had to admit that I didn't know. *But it's just a matter of trial and error,* I thought. *Just keep sorting the data in different ways, and you'll find it.*

Satisfied with my approach, I leaned back in my chair and stared at the ceiling. Snug and secure between the leather-upholstered arms, the room became suddenly warmer and as the tense muscles in my back began to relax, my eyes fluttered shut.

Drifting gently back through time and space, I gradually became aware of the deck that rolled beneath my feet and the saltwater breeze that played across my face. As I ran my hand along the polished wooden rail before me, I gazed upon *The Good Ship Alicia* once more, and wondered how many years had passed since we had so bravely sailed the Seven Seas.

Too many. I thought sadly, as the First Officer strode into my field of vision.

Seemingly oblivious to the curves that now pressed against my heavy frock coat and the tangle of hair that spilled from beneath my bicorn hat, he came to attention and saluted smartly. "It's good to have you back, Captain...

"Shall I set a new course?"

Still basking in the sun and the salt-laden wind, I rested my hand upon the hilt of the cutlass that hung from my hip, and nodded gravely. "Captain Hook is up to his old tricks again, and Peter and the Lost Boys need our help...

"So set the sails for Neverland, First Officer!"

Still at attention, he saluted again. *"Aye, aye, Sir!"*

Then he turned to the crewman manning the wheel behind me, and bellowed. *"NEW COURSE, HELMSMAN...*

"SECOND STAR TO THE RIGHT, AND STRAIGHT ON TILL MORN!"

After the helmsman acknowledged his instructions, the First Officer paused for just a moment as a smile spread across his face. *"AND BE SHARP ABOUT IT, LAD...*

"THE CAPTAIN'S BACK!"

Then after turning back to me, the First Officer asked for my orders.

Rather than answer him immediately, I pulled the telescopic spyglass from the pocket inside my coat, and extended it to full length. Then after spotting the tall sails of the pirate ship as they rose upon the horizon, I snapped it shut and nodded curtly. "Bring the ship to action stations, First Officer....

"Man the guns and make them ready!"

After acknowledging my orders with another crisp salute, the First Officer bellowed to the deckhands below. As the alarm bell clanged and the crew raced to their stations, I heard the gun ports bang open along the sides of the ship, and from deep within the hull the rumble of cannons being dragged into position.

Standing tall at my post on *The Good Ship Alicia*, I smiled to myself.

It's time to teach ole Hook a lesson...

CHAPTER THIRTY-THREE

One of the things I liked best about the CSS was the Guest Lecture Series. During the fall and winter months, they invited all kinds of really important people to come to the CSS and present a lecture to the staff in the auditorium. As a general rule, the lectures kicked off at ten in the morning, and usually consisted of an hour or so talk by the guest lecturer followed by another hour of discussion that blended into a catered, stand up lunch of deviled eggs, open-faced sandwiches, and other delicacies from the hotel.

Held every two weeks, the guest lectures broke up the day-to-day grind, so they were really popular with the staff. But the really cool part about it was the chance to meet some of the important people who came to give talks. Vice President Bush had given a lecture about his tenure as CIA Director the year before, followed by Paul Volcker, the Chairman of the Federal Reserve Board – who had given an incredible talk about monetary policy – and a whole bunch of other VIPs, including the Secretary of State, the Chief Justice of the Supreme Court, and the Chairman of the Joint Chiefs of Staff.

This year's guest lecture series was going to be opened by James Angleton, the CIA's former Chief of Counterintelligence – and since I figured it probably had something to do with my project, I was really looking forward to it.

Although the public had hardly heard of him, Angleton was a legendary figure inside Official Washington. Tall, gaunt, quiet and retiring, Angleton had headed the CIA's Counterintelligence staff for more than twenty years, and in the process, he had gained a reputation as an eccentric genius. Having already established himself as a poet of stature as an undergraduate at Yale – it turns out he had been a close friend of T.S. Eliot and an associate of Ezra Pound and E. E. Cummings as well – he had gone on to attend law school at Harvard. But by then, World War Two had intruded, and in 1943 he left graduate school for the Army.

After being selected for the Office of Strategic Services – that was the forerunner to the CIA – Angleton had trained as a Counterintelligence officer in London before being posted to Italy. And while his career was still officially classified, it was an open secret in Washington that he had performed brilliantly during the closing months of the war. After an extended post-war tour of duty overseas, Angleton returned to the United States where he had developed the first modern theory of Counterintelligence. And by all accounts, he became one of history's great practitioners of that "Dark Art."

But since being good at your job doesn't mean much in government, Angleton had been unceremoniously fired in December of 1974. According to the official story, the CIA had terminated him because of a supposedly disastrous "mole hunt" he had led. But according to Dr. MacLaughlin – who had been head of the Agency's International Econ Division at the time – Angleton had been dismissed for challenging the CIA's analytical methodology. It turned out that former National Security Advisor and later Secretary of State Henry Kissinger had negotiated a whole slew of treaties with the Soviets during the Nixon years, but Angleton had told Congress that the CIA's analytical approach was so fundamentally flawed that the Agency couldn't verify that the Soviets were actually carrying out their end of the bargain. In a situation like that, somebody had to go – and since Kissinger was way more powerful than he was, Angleton had walked the plank.

If the stakes hadn't been so high, the whole thing might have been just another tempest in the Washington teapot. But since the physical survival of the United States depended upon being able to accurately verify Kissinger's arms control treaties, the issue just wouldn't go away. It flared up again during the latter part of the 1970s, and again after President Reagan was elected in 1980. And most recently, with the publication of a book entitled *New Lies for Old*.

Written by former KGB Major Anatoliy Golitsyn, *New Lies for Old* described in chilling detail the Soviet strategy of deception that Golitsyn had personally helped develop while serving as a KGB staff officer in Moscow. According to Golitsyn – who had worked closely with Angleton after the Soviet's 1961 defection – the CIA's analytical methodology was hopelessly outclassed by the Soviet deception operation directed against it. The bottom line was that the KGB had taken the CIA's methodology for evaluating intelligence data and turned it back against them, and as a result we didn't know – and indeed, we couldn't know – a darned thing about what the Soviets were up to.

Unfortunately, Golitsyn had written his book for professional spooks rather than the average man in the street, and as a result it was almost impossible for ordinary Americans to wade through it. So to help rectify that problem, Angleton had agreed to make a special presentation at the CSS. And in order to get the word out beyond the Beltway, the CSS was going to videotape his talk and distribute it to civic groups and organizations on VHS tapes.

But of course, none of that was going to do me any good if I didn't get in gear, so as I pushed my carts into the vault, I glanced nervously at my watch. *Yikes!* I thought. *Five minutes to secure the carts, feed the dogs, and get down to the Sixth Floor!*

So after silently yelling at my First Officer to pour on the speed, I pushed the door of the vault shut before slamming the outer oaken doors into the closed position. Then I grabbed my purse and made a run for the galley. Since the dogs were nowhere to be seen, I dumped some dry dog food into their bowls before hurling the bag back into the bottom cupboard and making a run for the stairwell.

Screeching to a halt just outside the conference room some four minutes and thirty seconds later – after an unscheduled and entirely undignified stop at the ladies' room – I breathlessly pushed through the Auditorium doors. Pausing just inside the threshold, I could see Alex seated next to a much older man at a long table that had been draped in green baize on the elevated dais, and Dr. MacLaughlin waving to me from his seat in the center of the audience, close to the front.

Thank God for small favors, I thought. *He's saved me a seat!*

Hoping no one had seen me tear through the doors, I summoned forth all the poise I could muster and made my way down the center aisle to where Dr. MacLaughlin was seated. As I settled into the seat he'd held for me, I whispered my thanks. Smiling amiably in acknowledgement, Dr. MacLaughlin finished stuffing his pipe with tobacco before leaning over to explain that Angleton's lecture would provide me with important background information. "So pay close attention, Lass...

"But withhold any questions or comments you may have for either Alex or myself at a later date. I don't want you calling attention to yourself in this setting."

Somewhat puzzled, I nodded and whispered "Yes, Sir."

By that time, Christine had left her perch along the far left wall and approached the dais. Then after a short and inaudible exchange with Alex, she looked to the far back and asked the video crew if they were ready. After getting a thumbs-up from the crew leader, Alex pulled the microphone placed in front of him closer. Once Christine had retaken her seat, he smiled into the cameras and began to speak.

After welcoming the staff to the first lecture of the CSS's 1984/85 Guest Lecture Series, he introduced the CIA's former Chief of Counterintelligence. "Please welcome our guest speaker, Mr. James Angleton."

Dressed in an impeccably tailored English suit and hidden behind thick glasses, Angleton lit one of his trademark Virginia Slim cigarettes, and inhaled deeply. Then after releasing a thick cloud of smoke, he waited for the applause to die down before nodding shyly and saying that he had been honored by the invitation to speak at the CSS, and then thanked Alex for the opportunity. After smiling and stating that the honor was his, Alex began his prepared remarks.

"As most of you are aware, the publication of *New Lies for Old* by former KGB Major Anatoliy Golitsyn has sparked an enormous controversy here in Washington. In the past month alone, it has been cited more than a dozen times on the floor of the Senate, and at least twice that on the floor of the House of Representatives. *The Washington Post* and *The Washington Times* have both published extensive articles on or about the book, and senior members of the national security community have commented upon it...

"But thus far at least, the debate provoked by *New Lies for Old* has been more inflammatory than instructive."

After resting his elbows on the table and knitting his hands together, Alex continued. "Part of the difficulty lies in the fact that the subject matter is so abstract that it requires both a disciplined mind and a serious commitment of effort to merely comprehend the issues that *New Lies for Old* has raised. For contrary to public opinion – which has been shaped and conditioned by decades of Hollywood thrillers – counterintelligence is not an exercise in back-alley brutality. Although unfortunate incidents do occasionally occur in the field, Counterintelligence is fundamentally an exercise in applied epistemology."

As a grin crept across his face, Alex paused for an aside. "Which for those of you who cut class the day your professor explained it, epistemology is that branch of philosophy which asks: how can you know what you believe to be true is actually so?"

Feeling suddenly exposed, I slid down in my seat as my face began to flush.

Uh-oh, I thought. *How did he find out about that???*

Sinking even lower in my chair, I began fuming. Because I swear to God, I only cut class once the whole time I was at Township...

OK, so maybe twice. Let's not make a federal case out of it...

Seemingly oblivious to my flushed face, Alex continued. "But another part of the problem lies in the general lack of historical knowledge about the USSR, and especially that of the first decade of the Soviet state..."

"Which is why we have invited Mr. Angleton here today."

After another brief pause, Alex continued. "But before Mr. Angleton begins his presentation, I would first like to provide you with a brief overview of Maj. Golitsyn's career."

After another short pause, Alex explained that Golitsyn had first come to the attention of the United States in 1954, when Peter Deriabin defected to the West. Also a KGB major, Deriabin had served with Golitsyn as a counterintelligence officer in Vienna, and in the course of his debriefing he had identified Golitsyn as a potential defector. But Golitsyn had been recalled to Moscow before the CIA could approach him, so until December 22, 1961, he remained no more than a name on a file card at CIA headquarters.

"But on that date he arrived at the US Embassy in Helsinki in the midst of a heavy snowfall. Identifying himself to the Marine guards as a Soviet diplomat, he asked to see the CIA's chief of station. In accordance to the established protocol governing walk-ins — that is, potential defectors who appear unexpectedly — he was admitted to the embassy. To prove his bona fides, he presented the chief of station with a sheath of classified documents from the KGB's files, and promised more in return for asylum. A deal was quickly cut, and on Christmas Day, a U.S. Air Force transport lifted off from the Helsinki airport. In addition to the diplomatic pouch that served as its pretext, it carried Maj. Golitsyn, his wife, and their daughter, to freedom...

"It was a spectacular Cold War victory for the CIA, later celebrated in Alfred Hitchcock's thriller *Topaz*. But there was far more to the story than Hitchcock ever knew."

Forgetting all about my little problem with philosophy class, I sat back up in my seat. By now thoroughly engrossed, I leaned forward and focused on every word.

"Golitsyn's tour of duty in Vienna had been both unremarkable and unrewarding. As far as the CIA was able to determine, he had been a minimally competent field agent. To the best of their knowledge, he had failed to recruit even a single penetration agent in any of the Western intelligence services. But as later events made clear, this was due to temperament rather than ability. Reassigned to the KGB's headquarters in Moscow, Golitsyn quickly proved himself an exceptionally capable staff officer...

"After serving as a NATO analyst at Moscow Centre, Golitsyn was re-assigned to the KGB Institute. The Soviets formally represented the Institute as a "think tank" comparable to the U.S. Government's Rand Corporation, and that was perhaps partially true. But the larger truth was far more sinister, for it held within its walls the KGB's strategic planning group. Formed at the express direction of then-Soviet dictator Nikita Khrushchev, it was charged with developing a long-range policy for destroying the West. Golitsyn had been assigned to this group, and it was there that he began planning his defection. Convinced that the Soviet state was implacably aggressive, he took upon himself the task of warning the West. Lest he arouse suspicion, he carried out his duties with fervor and dispatch. Working late nights and weekends, he committed hundreds of classified documents to memory while planning his escape...

"After arriving in the West, Golytsin was subjected to an exhaustive debriefing. During the course of his interrogation, CIA officers were stunned by his detailed knowledge of the NATO intelligence services. Unwilling or unable to believe that he had actually handled the classified documents he claimed to have analyzed in Moscow, they subjected him to rigorous tests. Hundreds of authentic documents were intermixed with thousands of fabrications, and as he systematically identified the genuine with unfailing accuracy, their doubt turned to horror. The fact that Golitsyn not only knew the names and identification numbers of hundreds of top-secret NATO documents but could also identify them on sight proved beyond doubt that NATO's security had been breached on a massive scale. Worse yet, Golitsyn proved by deduction that Soviet moles had penetrated most and perhaps all of the Western intelligence services, and he provided specific and often detailed clues as to their identities. Beyond doubt, the British, French, West German and American intelligence services had all been compromised, and there was no way to assess the extent of the damage. The only thing that could be known with certainty was that KGB agents were operating with impunity throughout the highest levels of the NATO Alliance...

"The harm done to NATO and the NATO intelligence services was presumed catastrophic – but according to Golitsyn, that was merely the tip of the iceberg. For the KGB was no longer operating as a traditional intelligence service. Following the Shelepin reforms of 1958-1960, the KGB had emerged as the primary offensive instrument of the Soviet State, and its mission had been recast from traditional espionage to strategic deception.

"Convinced that the USSR could not hope to defeat the West in open battle, Khrushchev had devised a strategy of indirect aggression that would, in time, lead to a complete Communist victory. His plan included support for what the Soviets euphemistically called "wars of national liberation," international terrorism, so-called Active Measures operations against the Western political systems, and diplomatic initiatives designed to separate the United States from its European allies. To cover the inherently aggressive nature of their actual deeds, the Soviets would publicly pursue a policy proclaimed as Peaceful Co-Existence. Their ultimate objective was to persuade Western policy-makers to accept a convergence of Communism and capitalism on Soviet terms, through an admixture of force, fraud and enticement. To ensure that Western policy-makers would not recognize their peril, the KGB was recast and reconstituted to systematically mislead the Western intelligence agencies and the governments they served with a steady stream of carefully crafted disinformation."

After pausing for a moment of thoughtful silence, Alex softly cleared his throat before continuing. "And this is the essential message contained within *New Lies for Old*...

"But unfortunately, it is a message that is very difficult for the Western mind generally – and the American mind particularly – to grasp...

"We instinctively recoil from the possibility that our perceptions may be the instrument of our destruction, and we reflexively object to it – most often on pragmatic grounds. For surely, a deception of the size and scale presented in *New Lies for Old* would collapse under its own weight...

"And yet, history nonetheless records another Soviet operation of similar size and scope – *Operatsia Trist* or, in English, Operation Trust – which some of us believe is the historical template for the present Soviet disinformation campaign against us. Or as Maj. Golitsyn has termed it, the Soviet's Long Range Policy."

Then turning to Angleton, Alex nodded. "Jim?"

Shifting in his seat, Angleton didn't respond immediately. Instead, he dug another pack of cigarettes out of his coat pocket and shook one free. Then after carefully lighting it and inhaling deeply, he peered through his heavy black-framed glasses and studied the audience with a dispassionate gaze.

"Golitsyn is difficult," he said, "and for those without a working knowledge of the *Trust*, almost impossible to understand…

"One must understand that the *Trust* was far more than a mere counterintelligence operation. The *Trust* saved the Soviet Union from early destruction and, in a very basic sense, it is the source of our problems today."

Thinking it was weird that I'd never even heard of something that important, I leaned back in my chair and tugged on my skirt.

Angleton took another long draw upon his cigarette, before continuing. "Unfortunately, very few in the West are familiar with either the early years of the Soviet Union or the history of the KGB, and for that reason the *Trust* has almost been lost to history. It is for that reason that I have come here today, to present the same lecture that I gave to the new recruits down at the Farm."

By which he meant the CIA's training facility at Camp Peary, in southern Virginia.

After taking another long drag on his cigarette, Angleton stubbed it out in the ashtray before leaning back in his chair. Then after adjusting his glasses, he began speaking from memory.

"Despite the passage of more than six decades, the precise origins of the *Trust* remain obscure. But in retrospect, it seems as though Lenin's address to the Ninth Congress of Soviets on December 23, 1921 marked its advent."

Then after leaning forward to clasp his hands together, he rested his elbows on the table in front of him and continued. "It was there that Lenin ratified the New Economic Policy that temporarily restored private enterprise to Russia, and it was there that scholars assume that he approved, among other things, the strategic deception so closely associated with it.

"Communist rule was then far from assured. The Bolsheviks had little popular support, and the victorious Allied Powers of the First World War were arrayed against it. The danger was not immediate, for the Russian people were prostrate and the British, French and Americans were war-weary and distracted. But the Bolsheviks recognized that internal opposition would become acute as their economy recovered, and the external threat would steadily increase as the million or more Russians who had fled abroad coalesced. Some of the émigré organizations they formed in exile had the tacit support of Western governments and the actual support of their intelligence services, and the Bolsheviks understood it was only a matter of time before they would face internal and external opposition combined. It was therefore essential to neutralize both.

"A few weeks before Lenin's address to the Ninth Party Congress, a senior employee of the Soviet Ministry of Waterways had been arrested after returning from an official trip to Western Europe. En route back to the USSR, A. A. Yakushev had stopped in Tallin, Estonia, where he had met with a Yuriy A. Artomonov. According to some accounts, Yakushev was in love with Artomonov's wife, and hoped to persuade him to grant her a divorce. According to others, he was having an affair with Artomonov's cousin, and stopped only to deliver a letter. Whatever the actual case, Yakushev was a member of the anti-Communist underground and Artomonov a member of the external resistance.

"At this meeting, Yakushev informed Artomonov that the underground had so thoroughly penetrated the Soviet government apparatus that they were subtly transforming the regime. Anti-Communists had gained such power that it was only a matter of time before they achieved secret control. A silent *coup d'etat* was in progress, and it held every promise of success. For that reason, Yakushev advised Artomonov that armed action against the regime should be abjured, lest it awaken the Communists to their danger. An enthusiastic Artomonov promptly forwarded a detailed report of their conversation to his superiors at the Monarchist Council, then located in Berlin. Somehow the letter was intercepted by the Soviet intelligence service, which was then known as the Cheka.

"With Yakushev in captivity and with Artomonov's letter in hand, it was a simple matter for Soviet intelligence to deduce the biases, beliefs and expectations of the external resistance and to craft a strategic deception carefully tailored to fit them. A plausible cover story was concocted to account for Yakushev's disappearance, and a disinformation agent posing as his friend was dispatched to provide Artomonov with an even more detailed report on the underground's activities. Under threat of death, Yakushev was then "turned" to the Soviet cause and released from prison. Yakushev returned to the resistance as a Soviet penetration agent and, with his active assistance, the Cheka suborned its operations. Perhaps within a year, the Communists achieved effective operational control over extensive portions of the underground by maneuvering ever-increasing numbers of penetration agents into positions of influence, power and authority."

He paused for a moment and reached for the glass of water in front of him. After swishing it around, he took a deep drink before lighting another cigarette. Gazing off into space almost absentmindedly, he resumed the lecture.

"Having tamed the underground, the Cheka next moved against the external resistance and the Western intelligence services supporting it. Building upon the line of communication first established through Artomonov, the Chekists completed their feedback loop by establishing formal liaison missions in the major cities of Europe. Although some members of the external resistance harbored strong misgivings as to the underground's authenticity, the leadership nonetheless accepted it as genuine. Because the external resistance freely shared information with the underground's liaison, it was not strictly necessary for the Cheka to penetrate its inner sanctum.

"A flood of disinformation soon appeared in the West, most of it channeled through the liaison offices. Always, the message was the same: 'Don't attack the Soviet Union, for great changes are taking place and these are sure to result in the peaceful overthrow of Bolshevism.' This was convincing because it was carefully modulated to conform to the beliefs and expectations of the external resistance's leadership, and because the underground – by now almost entirely under Cheka control – provided further proof. Having established clandestine crossings along the Soviet frontier, the underground guided members of the external resistance in and out of the country on an almost routine basis. Unaware that their reconnaissance missions were in fact carefully staged deceptions, members of the external resistance were convinced by their own observations. They were thus easily persuaded to refrain from offensive operations against the USSR, as were the foreign intelligence services supporting them.

"Having achieved this most pressing objective by the summer of 1923, the Cheka proceeded to use the cross-border operations to selectively eliminate members of the external resistance. To maintain the fiction that the underground was engaged in a dangerous game of cat and mouse with the regime, border crossings were often made hazardous. Reconnaissance teams were sometimes fired upon, and agents killed or captured. The occasional disappearance, death or apprehension of external resistance leaders during border crossings was therefore attributed to misfortune. Only much later did it become apparent that they had been targeted for assassination. Foreign intelligence services supporting the external resistance were drawn in as well, and many of their intelligence officers and agents suffered a similar fate. It was by this means that the Cheka captured and killed the legendary British master-spy Sidney Reilly.

"A deception of this magnitude could not be sustained forever, and after seven years the days of *Operatsia Trist* were clearly numbered. Like the New Economic Policy, *Trist* had been conceived as a temporary expedient to assist the Soviet regime as it consolidated power. By 1927, this initial objective had been long achieved, as had other objectives later added.

"In April of that year, a senior underground-leader-turned-Chekist by the name of Eduard Opperput forced it to a close when he sought sanctuary in Finland. Whether he defected as claimed, or was a dispatched agent as most scholars argue, remains unknown. In either case, he caused chaos in the external resistance and the foreign intelligence services that had supported them by serializing his account of the *Trist* in a Russian language newspaper. Having invested all of its hopes and expectations in *Trist* – and most of its resources as well – the external resistance received a blow from which it never recovered. The closely associated Finnish, Estonian and Polish foreign intelligence services were also severely damaged. The British and French foreign intelligence services were similarly affected, though to a lesser extent.

"It was a brilliant exercise in perception management. The Soviet regime, which had been so precarious in 1921, was now safely established in power, where it has remained ever since.

"The same, I might add, applies to the KGB."

Crossing my arms across my chest, I leaned back in my chair in stunned silence as the audience began to applaud. *Incredible scam*, I thought...

So how come I've never heard about it before? It was a pretty good question, because I'd knocked down straight A's in history.

But apparently, I wasn't the only one who was puzzled because after Alex thanked Mr. Angleton for his presentation, he opened the floor to questions. An instant later, Bill Withers – the really cute intern from the Press Department I danced with at Homecoming – shot to his feet, and asked the same thing.

Smiling as he lit another cigarette, Angleton shook the match he had used to light it before tossing it in the ashtray in front of him. "As I said at the opening of my presentation, the *Trust* has almost been lost to history. Save for the handful of senior foreign officials who were actively involved in the effort to overthrow the Bolsheviks, its significance went largely unnoticed at the time.

Which was fortunate for them, for they had been swindled on a grand scale...

"Had the Western publics noticed, it would have ended a great many careers."

After Bill thanked him and sat down, Alex called on someone in the second row who I didn't recognize. Thinking he must one of the Congressional staffers who had been invited, I scooted up in my seat to get a better look. "So in your opinion, Sir, are the Soviets running a replay of the *Trust* against us?" he asked.

Looking almost cross, Angleton shook his head to the contrary. "I'm afraid you miss the point...

"I said you cannot understand Golitsyn – or the new methodological approach he has developed to cope with Soviet deception operations – without first understanding the *Trust*."

After taking another drink from his glass, Angleton continued. "It's impossible to run a major deception for any length of time using a conventional organizational structure. Penetration is a fact of life, and in the intelligence business it is a way of life."

"For that reason, a deception of the scale posited by Golitsyn has to be accompanied by an entirely different command and control system. It cannot be located within the intelligence service, because no matter how well defended it may be, that service is vulnerable to penetration and compromise.

"The command and control structure must therefore be located outside of the intelligence service. It must be entirely separate from that service, and physically distinct. And indeed, the service in question must not even know of its existence. At most, the head of the service and perhaps one or two of its most senior officers will know the source of their orders and directives.

"The service therefore ceases to be an intelligence service in any conventional sense of the term, and becomes instead the operational arm of a strategic planning group that is nameless, faceless, and indeterminately located. It becomes in effect a mere front for hidden powers that be, and for that reason its activities tell us nothing at all with regard to the strategic objectives they are pursuing.

"You have to understand: states have intelligence services for a reason. Intelligence services conduct operations in support of actual rather than declared policies. Historically, an accurate analysis of the activities conducted by a state's intelligence service has been sufficient to reveal its true intentions...

"It has been the gold standard by which states have been measured.

"In the past, we had assumed that a careful analysis of the KGB's global activities would reveal a more or less accurate image of the Soviet's true intentions. But given the methodological problems that plague American intelligence analysis, that presumption may no longer be valid. It is possible they have constructed an impenetrable Inner Line."

At that point, Alex leaned forward and asked Angleton to elaborate. "Except for the intelligence officers in attendance, I don't think our audience is acquainted with the term."

After nodding thoughtfully, Angleton agreed.

"The term 'Inner Line' is of Russian origin. It refers to the command and control structure I have just described. The external resistance actually tried to construct one in the early 1920s, but their senior leadership had already been penetrated. It seems that one of the members of their Inner Line was a Bolshevik agent."

After shifting in his seat and lighting another cigarette, Angleton pointed it at the audience. "The point is this: if an Inner Line is successfully constructed, it vanishes into the mist. The intelligence service it controls becomes a mindless automaton, doing the Inner Line's bidding without even knowing of its existence. At that point it becomes impossible to accurately infer anything from its operations. It is no longer possible to distinguish bona fide operations from cover or diversionary operations, even in theory. By the same token, it blinds us to the adversary state's true purpose. No matter how accurate our own intelligence, it is impossible to know whether their declared policy of peaceful relations is their actual policy, or an elaborate charade designed to mask aggressive intentions.

"In other words, the successful construction of an Inner Line by an opposition service places us in a position of total ignorance."

As Angleton paused to let his point sink in, I shifted uncomfortably in my seat as I re-crossed my legs. Thinking that Angleton had just overturned my intellectual applecart, I was working my way through the various implications when he resumed.

"What you need to grasp is one single, simple fact: If the Soviets have succeeded in constructing an Inner Line, everything – and I mean everything – we thought we knew about the KGB, the Soviet Union, and the entire Communist movement has been cast into doubt. Our intelligence has been reduced to rubble, and yet our policymakers must still make decisions of consequence based upon it.

"There is a realistic possibility that the Soviet Union is engaged in a deception of enormous magnitude, one that is designed to ensure our destruction. And yet we have no way to either prove or disprove the suspicion.

"At this point, we must assume that whatever evidence we may successfully gather is misleading and probably deliberately so. Logic and reason collapse in the face of such uncertainty."

I was still mulling that over when Adm. Thomas raised his hand. After Alex recognized him, the admiral stood up and formally introduced himself for the benefit of the cameras. Then rather casually, he posed his question. "Jim, I was just wondering if there is any means or mechanism for detecting an Inner Line once it has become operational?"

Thinking that was a really good question, I leaned forward as Angleton smiled. "Good to see you, George…I hadn't realized you were in the audience today."

Then he leaned forward, and folded his hands on the table. After a long moment's pause, Angleton explained that the Counterintelligence Staff had spent more than a decade working through that problem before finally deciding that a solution was logically impossible. "Even if a member of the Inner Line were to defect after the point of operationalization, we would have no way to establish his *bona fides*.

"And even if he were able to bring across massive documentation, we would have no way to verify or cross-check it against established data."

Adm. Thomas nodded, and said that was what he had thought. "So, if they've managed to establish an Inner Line, we're pretty much up the creek without a paddle?"

After the chuckling died down, Angleton smiled. "One might say so, George. But to say we're adrift upon the ocean without even a compass to guide us would be a better analogy. Until we recognize the flaws in our present analytical approach and adopt a new methodology which can account for strategic deceptions of the sort posited in *New Lies for Old*, we're going to be floating around rather aimlessly."

After a couple of really technical questions from some of the old spooks in the audience – or at least people I thought were old spooks, because of their really vague manner of introduction – Gen. McGreggor's new intern from Catholic University asked about the relationship of the hypothesized Inner Line to the Soviet political system.

Now I'm not sure if it was the question itself or Angleton's concise but somewhat speculative answer, but there was something about the exchange that touched the dark suspicion that had been lurking in distant recesses of my mind. Forgetting all about Dr. MacLaughlin's admonition to keep my mouth shut, I raised my hand.

Seeing it in the air, Alex pointed in my direction. "Ms. McAllister?"

Oblivious to the fact that Dr. MacLaughlin had stiffened in his seat, I stood up and identified myself as a research assistant from the Department of International Economics. Then after pausing for just a moment to organize my thoughts, I explained that since I was new to Washington, I really didn't understand politics very well.

"But after the last question, Sir, I was wondering if the United States has an 'Inner Line.'"

Unnerved by the fact that almost everyone in the auditorium had suddenly turned to stare at me, I shifted uneasily on my feet as my voice began climbing the octave scale.

"Because, like – wouldn't that explain all the really weird stuff that goes on around here?"

CHAPTER THIRTY-FOUR

As the silence grew louder, I broke away from Angleton's impassive gaze and glanced first at Alex and then at Christine. Alex was doing his inscrutable thing again, but Christine – who had returned to her perch along the wall – looked suddenly apoplectic.

Uh-oh, I thought. *Hope she doesn't faint again...*

I was still worrying about that when Dr. MacLaughlin rose to his feet, and draped his arm around my shoulder. "Jim, I think my young colleague lacks the experience and background to appreciate the operational requirements of an Inner Line...

"So perhaps you could take just a moment to expound upon them."

Then after stuffing his pipe back in his mouth with his free hand, Dr. MacLaughlin pushed me back down into my seat.

Angleton nodded, and flicked the ash from his cigarette. "Of course, Scotty." Then after pushing his glasses back into place, he explained that the Counterintelligence Staff had studied the basic operational requirements that would be imposed by such a venture. "We concluded that their minimal staff requirements would be in the range of three hundred or so...

"Fifty to seventy-five intelligence officers, and several hundred support personnel – security guards, communications specialists, secretaries, file clerks, housekeeping staff, etc....

"And while that's not a terribly large number, when you take into consideration the fact that they would have to operate from a separate, secret, and secure location, the operational requirements seem rather severe. In order to attract and maintain the caliber of personnel that would be required for such a venture, their salaries and benefits would have to be far above that commensurate with their normal grade, and since they would presumably be based in a remote location, the amenities that would be required to maintain their morale would have to be extraordinary...

"At the very least, they would have to have a modern, fully equipped hospital and an extensive network of sports, entertainment, and recreational facilities. And since married personnel would be preferable from a security standpoint, you would also need schools for their children and comparable athletic, entertainment and recreational facilities specifically geared to families."

After stubbing out his cigarette and lighting another, Angleton continued. "In short, an Inner Line of the sort hypothesized here would entail a small village numbering at least 2,000 people and quite possibly 2,500…

"And while that still isn't a great number, when all costs are considered – especially that of support and security – the total sum required would be many hundreds of millions of rubles per annum, and perhaps more. One of our estimates placed the total as high as one point five billion a year – and all of that would have to be carefully hidden from the scrutiny of any outside agency or organization."

After doing a quick ruble-to-dollar conversion in my head at the official exchange rate, I nodded intently. *That's a pretty good chunk of change…*

After pausing for a moment to tap his ash into the ashtray again, Angleton continued. "In order to maintain operational security, even the ruling Politburo would have to be kept ignorant of the Inner Line's existence – and as a practical matter, that would require the Inner Line to have an independent and entirely secret means of finance."

Well, duh, I thought. *But all they have to do is skim a billion or two off the top of the KGB's drugs and guns operation, right?*

After taking another deep drag off his cigarette, Angleton locked his eyes upon mine again and continued. "Simply put, even with the advantages conferred by the larger Soviet society – specifically, the secrecy and security of a totalitarian state – the operational requirements of an Inner Line would be imposing…"

Unconvinced, I shook my head in disagreement. *Nah,* I thought. *All you'd need is a good accountant with a sharp pencil and a really big eraser…*

"And in the far more open societies of the West – especially that of our own, here in the United States – the requirements would prove impossible. Setting aside all the other difficulties imposed upon intelligence services by democratic societies, the cost would prove insurmountable. After adjusting for price differentials, the amount required to first create and then sustain such an operation would run into the billions of dollars…

"And the money trail alone would virtually guarantee a fatal leak."

Well, yeah, I thought.

But before I could start working my way through that possibility, Dr. MacLaughlin had risen to his feet again. After thanking Angleton for his exposition, he excused us on the basis of urgent business in the Econ shop. Then after reaching down and seizing a hold of my hand, he pulled me to my feet and whispered harshly. "The Executive Conference Room, Lass…

"*Right NOW!*"

Confused and shocked by his uncharacteristic action, I forced a thin smile toward Mr. Angleton and Alex before following him out the door and down the hall to the elevators.

Although Dr. MacLaughlin was trying hard to maintain his composure, I could tell he was seething with anger. His face was taut and red, and as we waited for the elevator doors to open, I thought for a moment he would bite all the way through the pipe stem he'd jammed between his teeth. Too frightened to say anything, I followed him into the elevator wordlessly, and then after we arrived on the Eighth Floor, into the Executive Conference Room as well.

Acutely conscious of the fact that I'd really messed up, I stood off to the side while Dr. MacLaughlin locked the conference room door behind us, and threw the switch for the sound isolation thingy. But while I was still trying to figure out how I was going to convince him that it was an honest error, he suddenly wheeled around and thrust his pipe stem in my face. "You are *WAY* out of line, Lassie."

I started to apologize, but he cut me off before I could get a word out. "I specifically instructed you to withhold your comments and questions for a later date," he growled. "But you defied my orders!"

"Dr. MacLaughlin," I said plaintively. "I was just so wrapped up in it all that I forgot."

Still furious, Dr. MacLaughlin fired back. "I don't give a tinker's damn!" he bellowed. "The Inner Line is *WAY* beyond your pay grade, Lass…

"And you are never, *EVER* to ask a question like that again!"

Then after sticking his pipe stem back in my face again, he glared at me. "*Especially* in public!"

Frightened, confused and suddenly dejected, I protested as tears welled in my eyes. "But Dr. MacLaughlin," I said plaintively, "I don't understand…

"I know you told me not to ask any questions, and I'm sorry. But all I did was ask if we had an Inner Line."

Dr. MacLaughlin's glare was so fierce that for a moment I was afraid he might have a stroke. But instead, he shoved his pipe stem back in my face. "The question of the Inner Line is not merely controversial. It has implications that extend far beyond your current ability to comprehend, and for that reason you are NOT to speak of it again in public…

"And you will address any questions that you may have regarding it to either Alex or myself, and then ONLY in a secure area!"

Still glaring at me, he demanded. "Is THAT clear?"

By that time tears were rolling down my cheeks. Unable to answer at first, I meekly nodded. Then after sniffling, I said "Yes, Sir."

Dr. MacLaughlin was still livid, but I could tell the tears were getting to him. After handing me his handkerchief, he exhaled sharply and demanded that I stop crying. "You're making me feel like a bloody Nazi."

Still dabbing away my tears, I apologized softly. "But I just don't get it, Dr. MacLaughlin. Gen. McGreggor's intern asked a question about the Inner Line, so why shouldn't I?"

Clearly exasperated, Dr. MacLaughlin poked his pipe stem in my face again. "Because he's *bloody* well not working on our project!"

Then after glaring at me again, he stuffed his pipe stem back in my face. "That's why!"

Confused and suddenly angry, I looked up at Dr. MacLaughlin incredulously. "So what's the project have to do with the Inner Line?"

For a moment, I though Dr. MacLaughlin was going to completely lose it. But he didn't – he threw his hands up in the air instead, before turning on his heel. Pacing furiously up and down the conference room as he struggled to fill his pipe bowl, he finally stopped before me. Then after packing the fresh-cut tobacco into the bowl with the thumb of the hand that was holding it, he stuffed it back in his mouth and lit it.

After taking three or four deep puffs, Dr. MacLaughlin thrust it back in my face again. "You asked if the United States had an Inner Line, and speculated that such an entity might account for what you termed 'all the weird stuff' that happens in here in Washington…

"Now I can assure you, Lass, that the United States does NOT have an Inner Line, and for precisely the reasons Jim – Mr. Angleton – recounted…

"But we cannot discount the possibility that something very much like that might exist – and if it does Lass, I'm quite sure that those involved will do whatever they deem necessary to assure their secrecy."

Then a great deal more softly, he demanded to know if I understood. Looking down at the floor, I nodded my head. "Like sabotage Alex's airplane."

I had expected him to contradict me, but he didn't. So after a long silence, I looked back up to see him shake his head again. "You're far too clever to lie to, Lass."

Not exactly an open admission, of course. But under the circumstances, it spoke volumes.

Dr. MacLaughlin didn't say anything for a long moment. Instead, he puffed on his pipe as he gazed up at the far corner of the room. Then finally, he nodded to himself before looking down at me again. "This is my fault," he said finally. "I should have briefed you before the conference, but until this day I hadn't realized the depth of your insight...

"Clever, of course, even brilliant...

"But I never suspected you were that perceptive."

Thinking things were finally looking up, I smiled. "Yup, that's me," I said as I handed back his handkerchief. "Your basic brainiac, with a GPA to prove it."

Suppressing an indulgent smile, Dr. MacLaughlin nodded. "That's all very well and fine, Lass, but within the present circumstances, discretion is far more important than an agile mind." Then he pointed his pipe stem at me again, and remonstrated. "Before an audience that included at least a dozen serving and retired intelligence officers, you asked a question that will doubtless subject you to a great deal of unwanted attention, Lass...

"Now for the sake of all involved here, you MUST understand that the Inner Line is NOT your concern...

"Therefore I shall reiterate: you are not speak of it again publicly – indeed, you will not speak of it at all except to Alex or myself – and then only under the conditions specified." Then very seriously, he again asked if I understood.

Nodding intently, I assured him that I did.

Dr. MacLaughlin nodded in return, and instructed me to make myself scarce for the rest of the day. "Aside from the CSS staff and a number of my former colleagues, there were more than a few reporters in the audience today, and I want to make sure that you avoid them all...

"So I want you to go back to your office and lay low until we can be certain they've all left the building."

Oh rats! I thought glumly. *There goes my free lunch...*

But before I could get really irritated about being banished from the buffet, a sudden question popped into my head.

Interrupting Dr. MacLaughlin as he reached for the kill switch for the sound isolation thingy, I asked him if he had served with Mr. Angleton in the OSS.

Seemingly surprised by the question, he turned back to me and cocked his head. "Oh, no," he said. "Jim was assigned to X-2 – which was what we called counterintelligence in those days – and I was initially assigned to Research and Analysis...

"I'd just finished my undergraduate degree at Yale when the war started," he said. "So they decided to make use of my academic skills. I inventoried and prioritized German-controlled war production facilities in Occupied Europe."

"So you had a desk job?" I asked.

Reaching again for the kill switch, Dr. MacLaughlin nodded. "For about 18 months or so."

By now intensely interested, I asked him what he did after that. Chuckling, Dr. MacLaughlin turned back to me as he pushed the switch into the off position. "I was transferred to an Operations Group in the UK, and after sending me back home to Scotland for additional training they dropped me into France."

"Really?" I asked quizzically. "What did you do there?"

After hesitating for the slightest moment, he smiled softly. "I blew up my list of targets."

Holy cow! I thought. "That must have been really dangerous!"

Suddenly serious, Dr. MacLaughlin nodded sadly. "Yes, it was...

"But we were young men then, and death seemed a distant dream."

Then he suddenly chuckled. "And while I found it painful to watch so much capital blown to bits, I must say the delinquents the Army had placed under my command thought it was great fun."

Still chuckling, he shrugged and opened the door. "Now if you will excuse me, there is a delightful buffet waiting for me in the auditorium."

Forcing a thin smile upon my face, I waited until he sauntered out before sticking out my tongue.

Ya better bring me some, you jerk!

Which in fact, he did, about an hour later. I'm still not sure whether the oversized paper plate loaded with deviled eggs, thinly sliced cuts of Danish ham, roast beef, and turkey, and piled high with cole slaw and potato salad, was a peace offering or merely an act of consideration – but to tell you the truth, by then I was so hungry I just didn't care. So after thanking Dr. MacLaughlin profusely, I happily ate the lot.

By the time I finished off the last deviled egg, it was almost 2:00 pm. Since Mr. Angleton's morning presentation – and the little *contretemps* with Dr. MacLaughlin that had followed it – had made a mess out of my schedule, I decided to skip my usual hour at the gym and work straight through. That way I figured I could get back on track, before leaving for the night.

And I probably would have, if I'd been able to focus. But my mind kept wandering back to the Inner Line thing, and the more I thought about it, the weirder it seemed. From a strictly logical standpoint, of course, it all made sense – because if you're playing the "Great Game" of geopolitics and you want to make sure the enemy never discovers your true intentions, the Inner Line is definitely the way to go. And of course, it fit neatly with all the conspiracy theories that were floating around.

Mr. Pechello, for example – the old guy who lived down the street back in Glen Meadows – swore up and down there was some kind of "Secret Government" hidden away somewhere, and he'd tell anyone who'd listen that it was calling all the shots. According to his account, the "Secret Government" was responsible for just about everything that had gone wrong in America – sex education, forced busing, feminism, bra-burning, the breakdown of public morals, and the high price of beer. But then Mr. Pechello also believed in flying saucers and little green men, and every now and then, he'd go out in his backyard buck-naked and howl at the full moon.

Not exactly a credible authority, I thought.

But aside from old Mr. Pechello's nuttiness, there were other more serious factors that one had to account for. For while the Inner Line concept might work with a totalitarian society, as Mr. Angleton had implied, neither he nor Dr. MacLaughlin thought there was any likelihood at all that it could work in America, and the more I thought about it the more I had to agree. Aside from the fact that there's just no way you can hide that much money on an indefinite basis, I didn't think the political types would go along with it in the first place.

There's just no way they're going to give up that much control, I thought. *Because then they'd just be puppets on a string.*

Reasonably convinced, I had just turned back to my keyboard when a little voice spoke from the darkened recess of my mind.

Assuming, of course, they'd agreed to it in the first place. But suppose they didn't? Maybe it just sort of happened, as a result of something they did authorize?

That would be epiphenomenal, right — you know, a secondary thingy that kinda occurs in parallel with a primary thingy?

And wouldn't that be kinda like what Dr. MacLaughlin's worried about? Not an Inner Line — at least not in the strict sense, anyway — but something "very much like it"???

Lost in thought, it wasn't until the caffeine cravings caught up with me that I finally glanced up at the clock. *Holy cow!* I thought. *It's 6:30!*

Where the heck have I been?

Thinking it was more than just a little bit freaky that I'd been banging away on the keyboard for almost five hours without really being aware of it, I kicked off my shoes and pushed myself away from my desk. After deciding that the half-day old coffee in my porcelain mug was a bit more than I could bear, I decided to make a fresh pot. So after stretching my legs and yawning, I got on my feet and headed for the galley.

But halfway across the carpet, I came to a sudden halt. Alex had left his door to the galley halfway open, and from where I stood, I could hear him arguing with Christine. Grinning, I crept forward in my stocking feet.

Around Washington, most people thought Alex and Christine had a perfect working relationship, and as far as I could tell that was almost always true. But every now and then, they'd really get into it, and when that happened the staff — which included me, of course — thought it was really funny. Dr. MacLaughlin told me that they'd been battling it out for as long as he'd known them — which was like 15 years or so — and then after grinning rather wickedly, he'd admitted how much he enjoyed it. It was like watching an old married couple fight, he said.

Thinking the entertainment value outweighed the risk, I crept the last couple of feet to the doorway that opened from my office into the galley. Steadying myself against the door jamb, I could hear Alex swearing.

"Oh *Goddamnit*, Chrissy! We scheduled this *months* ago!"

I wasn't quite sure what Christine said in reply but it was pretty heated. Something about, "I told you my folks were coming for Christmas."

"Oh for God's sakes, Chrissy, they'll be here for two weeks, and this is just one night…"

"It's the White House Christmas Dinner, and I've already told the President and Mrs. Reagan we'll be there!"

Leaning forward a bit more, I heard Christine tell Alex he'd have to find someone else. "My parents are getting up there in years, Alex…

"They won't be around that much longer, so I want to spend as much time with them as I can…

"Surely, Alex, you can understand *that!*"

Although I couldn't really make out his reply, Alex's tone of voice told me that he had conceded the point. Then after a muffled exchange, I heard Christine tell him that he could find another date in 15 seconds or less. "Half the women in Washington would kill for the chance, and you know it!"

"Date?" Alex bellowed. "This isn't a social affair, Chrissy, and you damn well know it! This is strictly business, and I need to take someone to help represent the CSS…

"And besides – President Mitterrand is going to be there, and he wants to meet you!"

I couldn't hear exactly what Christine said to that, but I'm pretty sure it was something to the effect that the President of France was out of luck. "If he wants to meet me, he can come by the office like everyone else," she said dismissively. Snickering under my breath, I perked up my ears for Alex's reply.

The silence hung in the air for a minute, or maybe even more. Then in a weary voice, Alex finally conceded. "Alright, I'll take Two."

What???

You're gonna take Two to the White House??? For Christmas dinner???

But before I could come completely unglued, Christine fired back. "You most certainly will *NOT!*"

That apparently didn't go over very well, because something slammed down really hard on Alex's desk. And after the picture frames stopped banging against the wall, he demanded to know why not.

"Alexander!" Christine exclaimed. "In case you have forgotten, Two is a 24-year-old *secretary!*"

Although I couldn't see him, I could almost hear Alex shrug. "So?"

After a long pause, I heard Christine sigh. "She's a lovely girl, Alex – well, in terms of her appearance at least – but you need to take someone better suited to the occasion…

"Someone who can properly represent the Center – and given the fact that we've just opened up the new office in Paris, I think it's important to make a good impression upon President Mitterrand."

From the tone of her voice, I could tell she was laying it on pretty thick.

Oooooh, I thought. *You're good, girl!*

Betting dollars to doughnuts Christine had crossed her legs when she'd dropped that last one on him, I grinned wickedly. Then finally after a long silence, he asked her who he should take.

"Well," Christine said in a cheerful voice. "What about Alicia?"

"Ms. McAllister?" For some reason, he sounded puzzled.

Stiffening in the darkened passage, my eyes crossed involuntarily as my face scrunched up.

Hey! I thought. *Standing right here!*

I was still seething when Christine replied. "Sure, why not? She's a darling girl, Alex – she's charming and vivacious, and more to the point she's sharp as a tack…"

"She can more than hold her own in a White House setting."

Grinning from ear to ear, I made a mental note to get Christine something really nice for Christmas. Then after an interminably long moment, Alex agreed. "All true," he said. "But what makes you think she'd want to go?"

What??? I thought. *Are you stupid???*

Christine must have been thinking the same thing, because she laughed out loud. "Stop being such a blockhead," she said in a voice that reeked of exasperation. Then catching herself, she moved to reassure him.

"Trust me, Alex – she'd *love* to go."

Well, duh, I thought.

After another long pause, Alex finally said OK. "I'll mention it to her tomorrow."

"Oh *no* you won't, Alex. You'll forget, and then we'll end up having this argument all over again."

I couldn't make out what Alex said in reply, but Christine said I was working late. "She's still in her office, Alex, so you go ask her *right* now!"

Uh-oh! I thought.

So after a quick look over my shoulder to judge the distance, I made a mad dash for my desk. Trying hard to ignore the fact that my heart was pounding in my throat, I bent over the spreadsheet lying in front of me and pretended to be busy.

From that far away, I couldn't hear anything else. But after a minute or two of silence, I heard a knock on my open door. As I looked up, Alex asked if he could come in.

Well, yeah, I thought. *It's your office…*

But since there was no way I was going to actually say that, I pretended to be surprised. "Oh hi, Alex! Come on in…"

As he carried one of the leather-upholstered chairs over to my desk, I pushed the spreadsheet away and sat up straight.

After settling into the chair, Alex explained that he was expected to attend certain events here in Washington. Many of them were not strictly political, but since they provided an opportunity to promote the CSS, he normally took Christine.

Then looking suddenly uncomfortable, he explained that they had been scheduled to attend the annual White House Christmas Dinner. But unfortunately, something had come up and Christine wouldn't be able to make it.

Trying hard to suppress the smile that was attempting to steal across my face, I watched as the faintest hint of a flush crept across his face. "So if it's not too big an imposition, I was wondering if you'd be willing to fill in for her?"

Then rather hurriedly. "Not as a date, *per se* – but rather to help represent the CSS."

For a moment, I thought the desire to jump up and do my little "Happy Dance" would overwhelm me. But after fighting back the impulse, I smiled sweetly instead. "Well sure, Alex, I'd love to help out."

Being a team player is important, right?

CHAPTER THIRTY-FIVE

Needless to say, I didn't get a whole lot of sleep that night. My first impulse had been to call everyone I'd ever met to tell them I'd been invited to the White House Christmas Dinner, but by the time I finally got home, it was way too late to start making long distance calls. So after thinking about it as I got ready for bed, I realized it would probably be better just to let them find out about it on their own.

Which, of course, would come sooner rather than later in the office, because it was only a matter of time before Alex or Christine told Two to pencil it into his appointment book. Still chuckling about that, I turned off the light on the nightstand next to my bed and pulled up the covers.

Not that it did any good, because I was *really* excited. Or at least I was, until I crunched the calendar numbers in my head. *Oh, dear God!* I thought...

So if this is Thursday the fifteenth – Oops, it's after midnight so that makes it Friday the sixteenth...

And if the White House Dinner is on December nineteenth, and the CSS Christmas Ball is on the twenty-first, that gives me precisely 32 days to get ready for the White House and 33 days to get ready for the Ball...

But since only ten of those days are weekends – and two of those are over Thanksgiving – that leaves me with only about eight full shopping days to come up with two formals, shoes, gloves, evening bags, etc...

After flopping over, I pulled the covers up over my head and buried my face in the pillow. *Tough, but doable,* I thought...

But how the heck am I going to pay for all that stuff?

Because after buying a whole new winter wardrobe – not to mention my Homecoming dress – I was flat broke. I could sell some stocks of course, but that would pretty much clean out the tiny little account I'd established, and in any event, the market usually tanks in October and stays down until mid-January or so.

You do that girl, and you're really gonna take it on the chin...

Thinking there had to be a better way, I was trying to decide whether or not to ask Christine if the CSS would spot me the bucks against my Christmas bonus, when it suddenly occurred to me that girls really get the short end of the stick when it comes to formals and such.

See, if I was a guy, all I'd have to do is get a haircut and rent a tux, and I'd be set...

Thoroughly irritated, I was in the process of turning over again when a little voice from the back of my head corrected my logic. *But then if you were a guy, Alex wouldn't have asked you in the first place...*

True enough, I fired back. *But that's not the point...*

It's the principle of the thing!

So after making a mental note to have a serious talk with my Mom the next time I saw her, I finally drifted off into a really cool dream.

I'm not quite sure what I was dreaming about, because it vanished the moment the alarm went off a few hours later. Irritated beyond belief, I poked my head out from under the covers to find an apartment that had suddenly turned cold and dank.

Oh, rats! I thought. *Old Man Winter's finally arrived...*

Now people had been warning me about Washington's weather since the moment I'd arrived, but you really have to live here a couple of years to understand just how weird it can be. It can turn from one season to another in the blink of an eye – and somewhere in the depths of the night, the clear blue skies of Indian Summer had fled.

Pretty dreary, I thought, as I followed the dogs out to their favorite fire hydrant under the leaden skies of winter.

But there's a bright side to everything, including cold weather – and on this particular morning it was my downstairs closet, which was stuffed to the rafters with brand-new boots, hats, and winter weaves. Thinking Mother Nature had just handed me the perfect opportunity to show off the incredibly gorgeous suede suit that had been hanging there since late August, I pulled it out of the hanger bag and laid it across the back of Julia's couch. Sort of milk-chocolate-y in color, it would be absolutely gorgeous with an off-white silk blouse, matching boots and a contrasting scarf for color.

Thinking I was going to look incredibly chic and sophisticated at the office, I climbed into the shower.

And in fact, I got all kinds of compliments when I sauntered through the doors of the Executive Offices an hour and fifteen minutes later. After informing me that Christine wanted to see me in her office right away, Linda told me the outfit was absolutely stunning – and much to my surprise, even Two liked it.

Must not have gotten the word on the White House, I thought, as I made my way into Christine's office.

Christine was poring over a report when I walked in, but my suit caught her eye. She did a quick double-take before ordering me to turn around in front of her desk. "Nice suit," she said as she raised her coffee cup to her lips. Smiling happily, I thanked her for the compliment before asking her what was up.

"You wanted to see me?"

Nodding as she placed her coffee cup down on the coaster, she said she just had a minute. "I have to get a handle on last quarter's expense report before Alex gets back from his meeting at the White House," she said. "But I wanted to make sure that you understand that the Christmas dinner is a business function, and therefore a business expense...

"So the CSS will be picking up the tab for your dress, and for other associated expenses such as your shoes, your accessories, and your hair."

My eyes bulged as a huge smile spread across my face. "Really?"

Picking up her coffee cup again, Christine nodded. Then after smiling, she told me we'd get together later, and work on some ideas for a dress. "But right now, I'm really under the gun. Let's get your vault open so I can get back to work on these numbers."

So after she put her cup down and got up from her desk, we walked over to my office and opened it up for business. After that, my life went into hyper-drive again.

Somewhere or another during the course of the night, I'd finally decided to spend Thanksgiving with my Mom in Glen Meadows. I had really wanted to stay in town, because Dr. MacLaughlin and his wife had invited Jennifer and me over for Thanksgiving dinner. But since Mom had been hinting about how much she wanted to see me for weeks and weeks, I figured I'd better go home for the holiday.

She's lonely, and Thanksgiving can be pretty tough when you're on your own...

That – and the fact that I knew that I'd never hear the end of it if I didn't spend the holiday with her – had pretty much clinched it. So I picked up the phone and buzzed Christine to make sure it would be OK to take a personal day on the twenty-first. After giving me a breezy "sure," she warned me to remind her again when she wasn't buried. So after promising I would, I buzzed Two to get Nguyen's work number.

Much to my surprise, his secretary put the call through right away. So after asking about Mai Ling, I explained my predicament – with special emphasis upon the guilt trip my Mom was going to lay on me if I didn't show — before asking him if it would be alright to take the Vette to Connecticut. Somewhat fearful that I might have overstepped my bounds, I waited anxiously through an almost imperceptible moment of silence before he laughed.

"Tell ya what," he said. "I'll trade you favors...

"We're planning on spending Thanksgiving at Alex's place in Savannah, and getting Big Minh in one of those airline cages is almost impossible...

"So if you'll take the dogs with you, I'll let you take the Vette to Glen Meadows."

Then, after explaining that he'd already added me to the insurance policy, he told me to make sure I had the car serviced before I went. "Take it to the Exxon station just up Maryland Avenue, and have Jimmy change the oil, and check the tires and brake pads...

"*Fly-by-Night Motors* has an account there, so just tell him to put it on our tab."

Wow, I thought. *That's really generous.*

So after thanking him profusely and promising to make sure it was in tip-top shape before I left, I wished him a Happy Thanksgiving before putting down the phone. Then after taking a deep breath, I picked it up again, and punched in my Mom's business number.

She picked it up on the second ring. "McAllister Accountancy, Elizabeth McAllister speaking."

Forcing a cheery smile, I said "hi" and told her that I'd talked the warden into letting me out a day early for good behavior. "So I should be there about 7 or 8 Wednesday evening, depending on traffic." Grinning, I half-listened to the spiel that followed.

Moms are like that, I thought.

Suddenly jerked back to attentiveness by her unexpected question, I explained that I'd be driving. "Trying to get a plane out of Washington at Thanksgiving is pretty much impossible, Mom."

Then after another barrage of questions, I bent the truth just a little bit. "Well, it's kind of a company car, and Mr. Tranh — that's the guy who drives it most of the time — said it would be OK if I used it over the holiday."

OK, so that was a stretch...

But since there was just no way to explain the Vette without telling her about the break-in, I really didn't have much of a choice in the matter. So after making a mental note to come up with a really good cover story before I pulled into her driveway, I changed the subject. "Oh, by the way…

"I've been taking care of Mr. de Vris' dogs when he's out of town, and I promised to take them over the holiday so he could go home to Savannah…

"But they're super-well trained, so they won't be any trouble. Promise!"

Then before she could respond, I told her that the boss had just buzzed me. "Gotta go, Mom. Love ya!" I said hurriedly, before slamming down the phone. Thankful that I'd gotten *that* out of the way, I sank back in my seat and looked up.

Uh-oh…

Christine was leaning against my door jamb with her arms folded across her chest and her lips pursed together in a sly grin. "Warden, huh?"

Then as she pushed herself away from the door jamb and straightened up, she chuckled. "You are *soooooo* busted!"

The she turned on her heel, and walked away laughing.

Oh, gawd, I thought as I banged my head on my desk.

But believe it or not, things actually improved after that. Aside from Christine — who came back later to razz me about the warden thing — everyone else left me alone for the rest of the morning. So by the time our regular Friday progress meeting rolled around two hours later, I was totally prepared.

Which was a really good thing, because Alex and Dr. MacLaughlin asked me a whole bunch of really detailed questions. Puzzled by their sudden interest in what I had thought was little more than statistical minutia, I silently wondered what had piqued their curiosity. Thinking there was nothing particularly new or interesting in that week's report, I made a mental note to run a regression analysis the first chance I got.

Something's got them interested…

But since I figured I'd better do that on the sly, I decided I'd work on it after hours. So I spent the rest of the day alternately entering data, and wondering when Two was going to find out about the White House.

I had originally planned on taking some time off that weekend, but since I was going to take an extra day for Thanksgiving I decided to work straight through. That turned out to be good thing, because unfinished work weighs in at about Factor Eight on *Alicia's Guilt Scale*.

Which is substantially worse than cheating on my diet, but nowhere near as bad as stiffing Mom for Thanksgiving.

Having not only caught up on my work, but pulled way ahead, I was looking forward to a long, high-calorie holiday as I loaded up the following Wednesday afternoon. Because like I think I mentioned, I give myself a free pass on Christmas, Easter, Thanksgiving, and all recognized federal holidays. According to my *House Rules on Calorie Counting*, they're completely excepted.

So after stuffing my overnight bag into the car's tiny trunk, I slammed down the lid. Then after shooing the dogs into the Vette, I carefully laid my hat in the little space behind my seat and pulled the directions from my jacket pocket.

OK, I thought…

New York Avenue to U.S. 50 East, then I-295 North to I-895 until it becomes just I-95…

Till it becomes the New Jersey Turnpike. Then pick up I-95 again to U.S. 1 N/U.S. 9, and get off on I-87 N at Exit 3 toward Albany…

Then take Exit 4 to the Cross County Parkway – which will become Central Park Avenue for a while – then take the Cross County Parkway East Ramp to the Bronx River Parkway, and then get off on the Hutchinson Parkway…

Merge into Cross County Parkway E – which will become the Hutchinson River Parkway N – and exit onto I-684 N toward Brewster, and merge into I-84 East via Exit 9E toward Danbury and then merge into CT-8 via Exit 20 on the left toward Torrington…

And take US-6 east to Exit 39 toward Thomastown and Bristol on CT-202 before turning right on East Main Street – which might be marked U.S. 6 – then turn right on to Main Street before angling off to the right again on South Riverside Avenue, and follow it until it turns into CT-72…

And follow CT-72 until I hit the turnoff to Glen Meadows.

Since the total distance was just over 350 miles, I figured seven and a half hours driving time, after allowing for lunch and three stops for gas, snacks, and Mother Nature. *Piece of cake,* I thought, as I backed out of my parking space and nosed onto the street.

Driving to Glen Meadows alone would have been a bit scary. But with the dogs, it was more of an adventure, so I dressed for the occasion. To round out the jeans and cowboy boots I was wearing, I'd draped a white silk aviator scarf over my pink turtleneck before pulling on my genuine pre-scuffed Indiana Jones jacket. With my hair up to accommodate my genuine Indiana Jones hat and with the not-so-genuine aviator sunglasses perched on my nose, I figured I looked scruffy enough to saunter in to even the toughest truck stop.

And in fact, that turned out to be the case – because I got all kinds of looks when I roared into a massively oversized, but rather dubious-looking filling station an hour and a half later. Having pulled to a stop in front of the broad storefront windows of the attached restaurant, I climbed out the car and put on my hat. After pulling it down low the way Harrison Ford did in *Raiders of the Lost Ark*, I walked the dogs over to the access road so they could make a quick pit stop. Then I put them back in the Vette, and swaggered into the eatery.

I spent a leisurely half-hour putting away lunch, and trying not to laugh at all the truckers who kept turning around to stare at me. Then after perusing what passed for the local newspaper, I got up and casually tossed a ten-spot on the table before sauntering out the door – accompanied by a smattering of applause and one particularly loud wolf whistle. Thinking I probably should have forked over the extra hundred bucks for the genuine Indiana Jones bullwhip Nordstrom's offered as an accessory, I laughed as I climbed into the car.

Eat your hearts out, guys...

The rest of the trip was pretty uneventful. I made a couple of other quick stops for coffee, gas, and munchies, but I spent most of the next five and a half hours tooling along listening to the tapes I'd stuffed in the glove compartment. Having spent the past couple of months absorbing the sounds that wafted into my office at night, I'd become a real classical music junkie. And while I wasn't all that big on the operas Alex liked, but I'd had gotten deep into Vivaldi, Mozart, Bach and – especially – Pachelbel. I didn't know what it was about that guy, but his *Canon in D Major* brought tears to my eyes every time I heard it.

But since tears just didn't work with my outfit, I popped a Steppenwolf tape into the player when I hit Glen Meadows, and cranked it up. Naturally, *Born to be Wild* was blaring from the speakers when I roared into my Mom's driveway.

She must have been waiting by the door, because it opened the moment I clambered out of the car. After giving her a little wave, I reached behind the seat and pulled out my hat. Then after making sure that I'd put it on just right, I walked around and let the dogs out. But unfortunately, that turned out to be a bad move because Mr. Fenwick – that's my Mom's cat, you know – took off like a rocket.

Oops...

Thinking she was going to get all bent out of shape over the cat, I was about to tell her I'd go find him when she cut me off. After crossing her arms across her chest, she explained that she had been expecting her daughter. But it seemed that a short little man with two enormous dogs had turned up instead...

In a *perfectly* restored 1963 Corvette Classic.

"Where did you get *that* car?" she demanded to know.

Forcing a smile upon my face, I dodged the question by sticking out my hand. "Indiana Jones, here. World Famous Adventurer."

And then very quickly, I apologized about Mr. Fenwick and promised to go find him. "He's probably on top of the garage again."

After pulling down my sunglasses to make sure it was me, she chuckled and told me not to worry about the cat. "Come on inside, Dr. Jones...

"And bring your friends with you. I have a batch of brownies fresh from the oven, and a gallon of vanilla fudge swirl in the freezer." Then she gave me a big hug, and welcomed me home.

Well, kewl! I thought happily. "The kind with the little chunks of peanut brittle frozen inside?"

Mom smiled and nodded. "Yup!"

So after racing back to the Vette to get my overnight bag, I casually plopped down at the kitchen table as she banged two over-sized scoops into a bowl right next to a steaming hot brownie. Then after placing it in front of me, she put a little tiny scoop on top of half a brownie in another bowl, and sat down across the table from me.

So after prying a little bit of frozen heaven off the rest, I teased her. "Still watching your weight, huh?"

"Oh, yeah," she said matter-of-factly. "After you hit 40, it's a constant struggle.

Forty? I thought incredulously. *I'm only 22, and I've been fighting that battle for the better part of three years!*

Thinking the famous O'Malley "thin genes" must have skipped a generation, I decided to change the subject. "Hey, I should introduce you to my friends!"

Flanked by Big Minh on my left and Lady Godiva on my right, I looked first to one side and then to the other. Then after pushing my bowl into the center of the table – well out of Big Minh's reach – I patted the sides of the table and told them to stand up and be recognized. After they had reared up and planted their paws on the tabletop, I put my arms around their necks. Nodding to my left, I introduced Big Minh. Then as the color drained from my Mom's face, I introduced Lady Godiva.

Mom forced a thin smile and said hello, before turning back to me. "Do you let them put their paws on your table at home?"

Thinking she just wasn't a dog person, I grinned as I released them. "Oh sure, they're really clean…

"I give them a bath every week, and I brush them out every other night."

Then pulling my bowl back in front of me, I broke off two little pieces of my brownie and gave one to each of the dogs in turn. Then I picked up my spoon, and launched an all-out attack on the ice cream.

Incredulous – and by now more than just a bit suspicious – Mom asked if they lived with me.

"Well, not really," I said. "But Alex – uh, Mr. de Vris – travels a lot, so they stay with me whenever he's out of town."

Then suddenly reminded of my cover story, I explained that was why I was driving the Vette. "Because you can't take dogs on the Metro."

Realizing that wasn't entirely true, I hurriedly corrected myself. "Well, not unless you're blind and it's a Seeing Eye dog anyway." Hoping that would satisfy her, I spooned some melted ice cream on top of my brownie.

The subterfuge apparently worked, because after nibbling on her own brownie, she asked me what "Mr. de Vris" was like.

Grinning as I swallowed a huge spoonful of ice cream mixed with brownie bits, I told her that he was *really* cool. "Handsome, brilliant, rich, and powerful you know…"

Then almost as an afterthought, I laid my head over on my shoulder and gave her a puzzled look. "And a *really* nice guy…

"He knows everyone who works at the CSS by their first names – even the attendant in the parking garage, and the maintenance guys – and he always takes time to ask about everyone's families and stuff."

Mom gave me a knowing smile, and said she had thought so. She'd seen him on a news show a couple of weeks ago, she said. "He reminded me of your father."

Surprised and deeply perplexed, I looked up suddenly. "Really?

"I know Dad was really handsome and all that, but I just don't see the resemblance."

Mom smiled again, and said they weren't anything alike in terms of their appearance. "It was the way he related to the commentator and the other guests on the show…

"He was so very gracious…

"And of course, there's that hint of a Southern accent," she said.

"Dad had a Southern accent?" I asked incredulously. Because that was news to me.

Mom brought a paper napkin to her lips, and shook her head. "Just a touch," she said. "You know he was born in Alabama."

Nodding, I dug another scoop of ice cream out of my bowl. "But he didn't sound anything like Gramma McAllister."

Mom laughed. "Well, his father moved the family up here when he was 14 or 15, so he lost most of it."

Then very suddenly, she told me to make sure I called Gramma McAllister on Thanksgiving Day. "She's really proud of you, you know...

"And it's important to stay in touch, because we're all the family she has now."

Not a problem, I thought. Because to tell you the truth, she was my all-time favorite Gramma, and I called her all the time anyway.

Then after stuffing yet another huge spoonful into my mouth and swallowing, I grinned a wicked grin. "And you know what else?

"Alex is just *sooooooo* sexy!"

Suddenly aware of the fact that I'd just opened up a whole can of worms, I tried to put the lid back on fast. "Mr. de Vris, that is."

Still backtracking, I began frantically searching for words. "In a sort of really dignified, older adult kinda way."

"Ya know?" I asked in a tentative voice.

Realizing I had just gotten myself in deeper, my eyes crossed as my cheeks began to flush.

Bad move! I thought.

Which in fact it was – because from the look on her face, she obviously *did* know. So after giving me a withering look of disapproval, she pointed her spoon at me and warned me to mind my P's and Q's.

"Men like that are *dangerous*," she said. "And if you don't watch it, you're going to end up in *serious* trouble."

Thinking she just didn't know the half of it, I scrunched up my face and looked back down into my bowl. But since there was no way I was going tell her how right she was, I nodded dutifully and agreed. "No kidding."

Then after pondering the whole yin/yang thing for almost an entire minute, I looked up and grinned from ear to ear. "So guess who he's taking to the White House Christmas Dinner?"

Taken aback, Mom paused for a moment with her spoon frozen in midair. "Probably a famous movie star," she said thoughtfully.

"Now, let me guess – Demi Moore?"

Still grinning, I shook my head back and forth. "Noooo."

After swallowing her ice cream, she looked up and gazed off into space for a moment. "What's her name?"

"That girl who starred in *Splash*, with Tom Hanks – Daryl Hannah!"

Laughing outrageously, I leaned back in my chair and said "Nope!"

Then after pausing for a long moment, her eyes bulged. *"Oh, my God!"* she exclaimed. "Is he back together with Ashley Redmond?"

Huh?

As my eyes crossed, I asked her who the heck Ashley Redmond was.

Exasperated, Mom dropped her spoon into her bowl and leaned forward. "Ashley Redmond, *the supermodel!*"

Then she looked at me like I was from Mars or something. "Don't you ever read the tabloids?"

Scrunching up my nose, I recoiled. "Of *course* not..."

"I'm a highly trained professional!"

OK, so that was a big lie. Well, the part about the tabloids, anyway.

But honest to God – unless there's a really good story about Elvis turning up alive and well at a Buddhist monastery, or some famous actress having a love child with the Pope, I hardly even glance at the headlines.

Really!

Satisfied by the look on my Mom's face, I congratulated myself for having bluffed my way through that particular embarrassment. Then suddenly curious as to why I'd never heard of this Ashley Redmond chick, I looked up. "So when were they an item?"

After thinking about it for a moment, Mom said it had been a couple of years ago. "The tabloids had a real field day when they split up."

Thinking Christine probably had something to do with that, I played with my ice-cream-and-brownie-soup until Mom jerked me back to reality.

"OK, I give up," she said. "Who's Mr. de Vris taking to the White House Christmas Dinner?"

Still irritated about the whole supermodel thing, I kept playing with the bowl in front of me. But since there was an absolute limit as to how long I could contain my excitement, I looked up as a huge smile spread across my face.

"*Yours Truly*," I said triumphantly.

Still smiling from ear to ear, I watched as a look of shock spread across her face. Then suddenly aware of the fact that she was going to wig on me in three seconds or less, I quickly reassured her.

"It's not like he's taking me out on a date or anything, Mom. In Washington, these sorts of things are *strictly* business."

Which of course, was the truth.

Or at least it has been, I thought deviously.

CHAPTER THIRTY-SIX

But scheming is one thing and coming up with a good plan is another. After three weeks of wracking my brains, I was still drawing a complete blank. So as Alex opened the door of the limousine in the circular drive of the hotel, I decided to pack it in.

I'll just enjoy the evening, I thought excitedly.

Which wasn't going to be hard, because for the first time in my life I looked truly beautiful.

But let me tell you – turning a one-time ugly duckling into a beautiful swan is a job of work. And if it hadn't been for the combined efforts of Madame Henri, Raphael, and Christine, I probably would have arrived at the White House looking like a wannabe prom queen.

After knocking around ideas for the better part of a week after I returned from Thanksgiving, I finally persuaded Christine that we should get the dress from Madame Henri. So after close of business, she loaded me, the dogs, and a dozen or so sketches into her Mercedes sports coupe and drove us to Madame Henri's shop. After somehow managing to get lost in Chinatown – which was a pretty impressive feat, given the fact that it was only about six blocks square at the time – she finally found the place, and we arrived more or less on time for an after-hours appointment.

After finding a place to park, we left the dogs in the car and walked the half block to Madame Henri's door. Taken somewhat aback by the rather seedy exterior, Christine rang the buzzer next to the paint-flaked door.

Now Christine had never bought a dress from Madame Henri before, and despite my Homecoming dress and Mai Ling's unqualified recommendation, she had been deeply skeptical about entrusting this particular occasion to her. But after a cursory look around the shop, she was persuaded. Speaking confidently in French, she explained that I needed a dress for a formal White House dinner.

Upon hearing the words *"Maison Blanche,"* Madame Henri's eyes lit up, and a huge smile spread across her face. Placing her hands together, she bowed toward me three or four times. "Palace Ball," she said in a hushed and excited voice. "We make you Princess!"

With her eyes still twinkling, she gestured for me to climb up on the little wooden platform in front of her drawing table. Then as Christine peered over her shoulder, she began to sketch.

Ten interminable minutes later, Christine looked up and smiled. "It's perfect!" she said.

And in fact, it was. Because what Madame Henri had come up with was an incredible combination of what Christine called "age, season, and setting." Taking the princess concept as her motif, she had drawn a dress that harked back to Mediaeval royalty. Made from two different weaves of velvet dyed to the same forest green color, she fashioned a form-fitting bodice with a modest neckline that attached to a subtly flared floor-length skirt that flattered my hips. As was the custom in Mediaeval times, she had tapered the top into a "V" where it met the skirt, and attached a golden silk sash that angled down from my waist before looping over and falling almost to the floor. But to make sure I wouldn't trip and make a fool out of myself, she angled the front hemline up ever so slightly, and placed what Christine called an inverted pleat in the front.

Then in classic Madame Henri style, she had somehow managed to trim the edges almost imperceptibly with golden thread. The result was astonishing – because even though you couldn't really see the threads, they changed the way the light reflected from the velvet in a subtle way. So on the night of the dance, the overall effect was just stunning. With my Red-Hair-By-Raphael piled upon my head and my Pearls-Borrowed-From-Christine – not to mention the professionally perfect makeup she had applied just before Alex arrived – I actually looked like the princess Madame Henri had sketched.

So when Alex knocked on the door of the suite, Christine had given me a sly wink and told me to "Knock 'em dead, girl!"

And to tell you the truth, that seemed almost plausible. Because after walking around the limo and taking his seat beside me, Alex kept glancing over out of the corner of his eyes.

Smiling, I looked over my shoulder and joked. "I clean up pretty good, huh?"

Realizing that he'd been caught in the act, Alex flushed ever so slightly and smiled softly. "Very well, indeed," he said.

As the six or seven minute trip to the White House passed in comfortable silence, I turned in the plush leather seat to look at Alex. Resplendent in an elegantly cut tux and white tie, I watched as the shadows and lights of Pennsylvania Avenue played across his chiseled face. Thinking it was a good thing for him that it was such a short ride, I snickered to myself as we pulled up to the White House gate.

Because trust me on this – if it had been any longer, that boy would have been in *big* trouble!

As the limo pulled to a halt, I watched through the smoked glass partition as the driver lowered his window and displayed his credentials before announcing our arrival. "Mr. Alexander de Vris and his guest, Ms. Alicia McAllister" he said matter-of-factly to the uniformed Secret Service agent. Then after a moment's pause, the rear window next to Alex slid down as the guard walked back towards us. Leaning over for a better look, he nodded and smiled toward Alex. "Good evening, Mr. de Vris."

But after shining a flashlight in my face, the corners of the agent's mouth turned up and his shoulders began to shake. Although he managed to keep his composure while he greeted me, he cracked up as he asked if I'd brought my machine gun. "Because I have strict orders to arrest anyone that's armed."

Still laughing, he stepped back before I could answer and waved us through.

Chuckling as his window slid back into place, Alex turned to me and smiled. "Your reputation precedes you."

Oh, Gawd! I thought, as I twisted in my seat and scrunched up my face.

"Alex, am I ever gonna live that down?"

After pondering the question for the barest of milliseconds, Alex pursed his lips together and shook his head. "Nah."

But at least he winked when he said it.

By that time, the limo had pulled to a stop in front of the main entrance of the White House, and Marine guards in dress uniforms stepped forward to open the doors. Taking the proffered hand of a Marine sergeant or something, I gracefully exited the vehicle and looked up at the brilliant lights that illuminated the portico. Having forgotten all about the Secret Service guard who teased me at the gate, I took Alex's arm and accompanied him up the steps and into the foyer.

With eyes the size of saucers, I glanced around the elegant Entry Hall. Pausing for just a moment so I could take in my surroundings, Alex smiled softly as another Marine stepped forward to take my wrap. After handing it to a waiting valet and informing him that it belonged to Ms. Alicia McAllister, yet another Marine approached. "Good evening, Sir. Would you please accompany me to the East Room?"

Then after Alex nodded, we followed the Marine as he turned left into Cross Hall and then down the gold trimmed red carpet past the half-dozen or so military officers spaced at ten-foot intervals until we reached the far end. Stopping at the entrance of the East Room, the Marine gestured for us to proceed. "President and Mrs. Reagan and President and Mrs. Mitterrand will arrive shortly, Sir."

Christine had already explained that this particular state dinner would be quite a bit different from the more normal variety. Unlike most European heads-of-state, President Mitterrand was an open and outspoken admirer of the United States, and one of the things he liked best was the easy informality of Americans. Hoping to gain some insight into the typical American Christmas celebration, he had submitted a formal request through the French ambassador to President and Mrs. Reagan. Rather than suffer through yet another boring and minutely scripted state dinner, he hoped they would indulge him with a more common and typically American holiday feast. Never big on protocol themselves, the Reagans had been happy to oblige. So after informing the White House Office of Protocol that this would be more of a Reagan family dinner than an affair of state, Mrs. Reagan had planned it herself.

But as we walked into the stunningly ornate room, I had to wonder. Because my idea of informality is cut-offs and sandals – but as I looked at the other guests it became quickly apparent that the White House version was a whole lot different. All the men were in white tie, like Alex, and the women were bedecked in diamonds and fabulously expensive designer gowns. But as I studied their finery, I had to smile – because even though my dress had only cost a pittance in comparison, Madame Henri's masterful blend of fabric and lines had made mine *way* more elegant than the rest.

Feeling very pleased with myself, I followed Alex around the room as he introduced me to the various dignitaries and their ladies. After being introduced to the ambassadors from France, Morocco, and Mexico, and a half-dozen or so Senators and Cabinet Secretaries – and their wives, of course – I followed Alex's example and asked a passing steward for a Perrier water with a twist of lime. Before lifting the exquisitely cut crystal glass to my lips, I looked up at Alex. "So you know all these people?" I asked inquisitively.

Smiling softly, Alex nodded. "Political Washington is a lot like a small town," he said. "Hang around long enough, and you get to know just about everyone."

Well, yeah, I thought. *If you're handsome, rich, brilliant and powerful...*

But I don't think that works for us research assistants.

But since I wasn't going to actually say that, I took the outstretched hand of The Honorable Casper Weinberger – who was otherwise known around town as the Secretary of Defense. "I'm very pleased to meet you, Sir." Then after a brief exchange of pleasantries, I stepped back a bit and off to the side as the two men chatted.

It turned out that the now-immensely powerful Sec Def had once been an assistant junior gofer to Alex's dad way back when, so they'd known one another since Alex had been a high school kid. As I pretended to pay attention to their discussion of the new MX missile system and its likely effect upon the strategic balance, I noticed a familiar figure sidle up to me. *Uh-oh*, I thought. *Special Agent Jordan...*

Dressed in white tie, Agent Jordan would have been indistinguishable from all the other men except for the bulge under his left shoulder. Thinking his presence just *wasn't* a good sign, I stiffened as he whispered out of the corner of his mouth. "I'm watching you, McAllister."

Now under any other circumstances, I would have totally wigged. But the corners of his lips had turned up ever so slightly when he spoke, and the twinkle in his eye told me that he was just teasing. So after a quick glance to make sure that Alex was still engrossed with the Secretary of Defense, I looked back over my shoulder at the Secret Service Agent and stuck the tip of my tongue out real quick.

"Bite me," I whispered back.

I was still snickering at the sight of Agent Jordan choking on his Perrier, when all of a sudden, a band started playing *Hail to the Chief* from somewhere down the hall. Turning with the rest of the room, I watched as President and Mrs. Reagan entered, followed by President and Mrs. Mitterrand. Handing the still-suffering Secret Service agent my glass, I began clapping with the other invitees.

President Reagan gave the room a jaunty wave as he led Mrs. Reagan and their guests to a podium at the far end. After a brief speech introducing President Mitterrand and his lovely wife, and thanking them for being so kind as to visit him and Mrs. Reagan in Washington, the President made another brief remark about the two centuries of unbroken Franco-American friendship. After noting that France had been America's very first ally, he asked the assembled guests to welcome "His Excellency, *Monsieur le Président* Francois Mitterand."

Smiling graciously, the tall Frenchman stepped forward. But even though he was partially bald and at least as old as President Reagan, he had an amazing presence. Although he was charming – even elegant – he exuded a certain strength of character that suggested both courage and cunning. Later that night, I learned that he had been captured in World War Two, and had paid dearly for his first five escapes from a German Prisoner of War camp. Then after his sixth and finally successful escape, he had infiltrated the Vichy regime as a spy for the Free French Forces still fighting from abroad.

After thanking President and Mrs. Reagan for their wonderful hospitality, President Mitterrand made a few brief and gracious remarks before turning the microphone over to Mrs. Reagan, who spoke only briefly before turning the microphone over to Mrs. Mitterrand. Less eloquent than her husband – who spoke in charmingly accented but otherwise perfect English – she thanked President and Mrs. Reagan for inviting Mr. Mitterrand and herself to the White House, and the guests for honoring them with their presence. After that, a White House Social Aide stepped forward and announced the receiving line.

Queuing up behind Alex and the other guests, my excitement grew as we proceeded up the line. It turns out that diplomatic protocol is a lot different from other social graces, because in a diplomatic receiving line the ranking political figure comes first, followed by their spouse, who is followed by the next ranking political figure and their spouse. President Reagan and President Mitterrand were diplomatic equals of course, but since President Reagan was serving as the host, he took precedent.

Thrilled by the prospect of shaking hands with President Reagan, I waited for the Social Aide to announce my name after Alex had moved on to Mrs. Reagan. After what seemed like forever, the Social Aide finally intoned. "Ms. Alicia McAllister."

Much to my surprise, the President smiled in recognition and took my gloved hand in both of his. "Well, hello there, feller." Then he cocked his head and looked at me in mock seriousness. "Now you've gone straight like you promised, haven't you?"

As my cheeks turned crimson, I swore up and down that I'd left my life of crime behind.

"Promise!" I said, earnestly.

President Reagan smiled and laughed, but before letting go of my hand, he turned to Mrs. Reagan and winked. "Now you keep an eye on her, Nancy, and make sure she doesn't steal the silver!"

Although the Secret Service had somehow managed to keep *The Great Halloween Chocolate Heist* out of the newspapers, it apparently wasn't much of a secret in official Washington – because the whole receiving line cracked up at the President's quip. But even though it was really embarrassing, I had to laugh too.

But even so, I was thankful when Mrs. Reagan rescued me. Waving her hand dismissively at her husband, she told me to ignore him. Then smiling as she took my hand in hers, she winked and said that she'd swiped her share of chocolate, too. So after thanking her for the bailout, I moved up to President Mitterrand.

Smiling graciously, he said, "*Enchanté, Mademoiselle.* Your beauty and brilliance are known to us even in France."

Staggered by the compliment, I blushed as I shook his hand. "Well, thank you, *Monsieur le Président!*" Then I moved up to his wife, Danielle. After complimenting her on her beautiful dress, I met Alex in the hallway where a waiting Social Aide escorted us down Cross Hall to the State Dining Room. When we arrived, another Social Aide escorted us to our seats.

As a gesture of respect for our hosts, we were still standing behind our chairs when Alex looked over at me and grinned. "I think the President likes you," he whispered.

Although tempted to whack him with my evening bag, I decided to go for points instead. "Some people have good taste," I retorted. But before Alex could respond, the two Presidents and their First Ladies strode into the room.

Now, there is this whole protocol thing about seating arrangements at State Dinners, and under almost any other circumstances Alex and I would have been seated at separate tables. But since Nancy Reagan had planned the dinner rather than the Chief of Protocol, I found myself seated near the end of the long table with Alex to my left and President Mitterrand – who had been seated opposite of President Reagan at the far end of the table – to my immediate right, with Danielle Mitterrand directly across from me.

Which was like, *way* cool.

After President Reagan invited us to take our seats – and Alex helped me into mine – wine stewards miraculously appeared to fill our wine glasses with red and white respectively. But for better or for worse Christine had placed me on a strict regime of one glass of champagne, *after* the dance.

And there was a good reason for that, she explained. It seems that a prominent guest-who-shall-forever-remain-unnamed had arrived at a White House dinner three sheets to the wind some years before, and gotten positively plastered as the night went on. But since the gentleman in question was a congenial drunk, President Carter and his guests had actually enjoyed his exuberance. And aside from the fact that his stricken wife had supposedly made him sleep on the couch for a month, no real harm had been done.

But since I didn't want to end up dancing on the table, I'd taken Christine's admonition to heart. So I asked the steward for a glass of Perrier instead. "With a twist of lime, please."

Then like the other women present, I took off my long gloves one at a time, and laid them on the table to my right. After a toast by President Reagan – who was drinking the non-alcoholic version of sparkling cider – President Mitterrand replied in kind. Immediately thereafter, the serving staff suddenly appeared.

By the time they delivered our salads, Alex and President Mitterrand were chatting amiably in French. But after seeing the look of incomprehension that had spread across my face, President Mitterrand switched to English and apologized. "Forgive me, *Mademoiselle*. I presumed you spoke French."

Setting my fork back down on my salad plate, I shook my head apologetically. "I took a couple of courses in college to satisfy my language requirement for graduation, Mr. President…

"And even though I read it fairly well, I just can't follow it conversationally."

"A pity," said the President before smiling at Alex. "It is the language of love, you know."

Which was like *way* cool – because that was like the only time in my entire life that I actually saw Alex's cheeks turn crimson.

Must be doing something right, I snickered to myself.

But Alex recovered quickly, by observing that French was the language of diplomacy and war as well. Chuckling, President Mitterrand returned to his salad. After two or three refined bites, he turned his attentions to me.

"I am told that you are an economist of rare merit," he said.

Trying hard to suppress the flush that began spreading across my face, I explained that I had been fortunate enough to have had a whole series of outstanding teachers at Township College. Then suddenly remembering that I was there to help represent the CSS, I quickly added that I had been even luckier to find a position with Dr. MacLaughlin. "He's a genius, you know."

President Mitterrand nodded knowingly as he took a sip of his wine. "Ah yes, *Professeur* MacLaughlin…

"A great mind indeed. I have read several of his books."

Then suddenly serious, President Mitterrand asked for my opinion as to the persistent inflation that was bedeviling the economies of the developed world.

Thrusting myself back in my chair, I clapped my hands together in delight.

"Well, you know, Mr. President, Dr. MacLaughlin and I fight about this all the time," I said. "As a general rule, he believes that inflation is the result of misguided monetary policy, and in that sense he is very much in agreement with the so-called 'Chicago School' of economics...

"But in this particular case, he believes it's actually more of a 'Witches Brew' of monetary exuberance and what we call 'cost-push' inflationary pressures." Glancing over at Alex as the stewards removed our salad plates, I could tell that I'd lost him already. But President Mitterrand was following closely, and from the look on his face I could tell that he understood exactly what I'd said.

Nodding intently, he asked me to please go on.

"Well, sir," I said as the waiters delivered our dinners. "Although mainstream economists have offered at least six other plausible theories as to what is causing the so-called 'stagflation' we've been experiencing...

"I think Dr. MacLaughlin is right in attributing it to the 'Witches Brew' – at least, in so far as it goes. But I think there are other hidden factors at work that he doesn't sufficiently appreciate."

Slipping into French again, President Mitterrand said "*Vraiment?*" before returning to English. As he began cutting the layered slices of turkey and ham on his plate, he asked me what they might be.

After taking a quick sip of water, I explained the hidden costs imposed by regulation. "Every time government passes a law regulating business, they impose additional hidden costs.

"But because these costs don't lend themselves to precise measurement, and because they vary from business to business anyway, they're almost impossible to accurately calculate...

"Nonetheless, they are there – and they increase with every additional layer of rules and regulation ...

"So even if the production of goods and services remains constant, prices will continue to rise."

After placing his knife and fork back down on his plate, President Mitterrand leaned back in his chair and placed his hands together. "Yes, of course," he said thoughtfully. "But *Professeur* MacLaughlin does not agree?"

Placing my own fork down, I shook my head lightly. "It's not so much that he doesn't agree, Mr. President. But since we can't accurately calculate the costs of regulation, he thinks we should focus on the things we can calculate – like the effects of excess money within the economic system, and impact of 'cost-push' price increases."

Nodding thoughtfully as he resumed eating, President Mitterrand remained silent for a moment. "But you do not agree, *Mademoiselle?*"

Shaking my head much more firmly for emphasis, I said, "Oh, *not* at all…

"In my view, we have to make a major effort to develop new analytical tools so that we can at least approximate regulatory costs." Then I went on to explain that some of the world's best mathematicians were working on a whole new mathematical system that could be applied to problems like that…

"They call it 'Fuzzy Math' and they think they can build what they call 'Fuzzy Logic Systems' to cope with these sorts of problems in another ten or fifteen years."

"But until then," I said before digging into my mashed potatoes, "I think we oughta SWAG it."

Then suddenly realizing what I had just said, I froze in my seat as my eyes crossed involuntarily.

Oops…

Hoping that would fly right past President Mitterrand, I held my breath.

But unfortunately for me, the man was sharp as a tack. After taking another drink of his wine and commenting upon the excellent meal, he reiterated. "SWAG" he asked curiously. "I'm afraid I do not know the term."

Forcing a thin smile upon my face, I explained that was engineering slang for an approximation.

Puzzled, President Mitterrand cocked his head and looked at me. "An acronym of some sort, *mais oui?*"

Nodding, I silently uttered a quick prayer. *Oh, come on God, gimme a break!*

But the Almighty must have been busy just then, because President Mitterrand persisted. "Of course," he said. "But of what words is it constructed?"

After looking around furtively, I realized I was trapped. "Well you see," I said hesitantly. "Everyone thinks engineering is like a really precise exercise…

"But my dad was an engineer, and he told my Mom that there are an awful lot of things they can't accurately calculate either – like the sorts of forces that operate on bridges and dams and stuff, under variable conditions…

"So when they have to guess about things like that, they call it a SWAG."

Since it was obvious that the French President wasn't going to accept that kind of muddled answer, I took another quick look around before rising halfway to my feet. Then after gesturing for him to lean towards me, I cupped my hands and whispered in his ear.

"It means 'Scientific Wild-Assed Guess' " I said. "But *please* don't tell anyone I told you that, because my Mom would *kill* me if she ever found out!"

President Mitterrand had stiffened in his chair as I whispered, with his eyes locked straight ahead. But as I pulled away from him to sit back down in my seat, he broke up laughing. After howling for the better part of a minute, he looked toward Alex and unleashed a torrent of French.

Thinking my goose was cooked better than the turkey on my plate, I winced before stealing a look at Alex. He'd stiffened in his chair too, and his eyes had widened. But after the briefest of moments, he cracked up too.

I was sighing in relief when President Reagan suddenly addressed me by name from the head of the long table. "You must have told a pretty good joke down there, Ms. McAllister."

Squirming in my seat, I forced a thin smile. "I was just comparing some of the more technical problems we encounter in economics with the problems engineers face in construction, Mr. President."

Then after scrunching up my nose and forcing another thin smile, I fibbed. "But it just didn't come out right in translation."

Desperate to change the subject, I leaned over the table to divert his attention. "So how's that whole Cold War thing working out, Mr. President? I heard that new guy in the Kremlin is giving you a hard time."

OK, so that was lame…

But it worked. Because after President Reagan explained that the new Soviet leader – that Konstantin Chernenko guy – seemed like a pretty tough cookie, the conversation turned to his likely successor. It turned out that Chernenko was older than the guy he'd replaced, and was thought to be in even worse health.

Which I thought was kinda hard to figure, since the other guy was already dead…

But since glaring contradictions like that seem to fly right past most people in official Washington, no one else seemed to notice. Although the State Department gave Chernenko two years at most, the smart money around town thought that was a stretch. So there was a lot of speculation about who would take over when he kicked the bucket.

Would it be yet another of the Old Guard's octogenarians? Or would it be someone younger and presumably more flexible?

That question kept the conversation going all the way through dessert and coffee. But when President Reagan finally announced it was time to move back to the East Room for dancing, President Mitterrand placed his hand upon mine before rising from the table. After thanking me for my exposition, he told me to come to France if I ever felt the need for a more challenging position.

Then with a broad smile, he said he'd fire the fool running his Ministry of Economics and give me the job instead.

Laughing, I promised I'd keep it in mind.

After we moved back to the East Room, I was surprised to find the Marine Band set up and already playing. So after a quick trip to the ladies' room – well, actually, a rather long trip because I wanted to fix my hair and refresh my makeup – I returned to find Alex standing alone, drinking yet another cup of coffee. Taking a glass of champagne from a passing steward, I looked up at him as I took the first sip. "So tell me, Mr. de Vris…

"Will I finally get to dance with you this evening?"

Alex smiled, and shrugged. "If you can work me in," he said wryly. "But I think your dance card is pretty well filled."

Puzzled, I looked up and asked him what he meant.

"Well, aside from President Reagan, President Mitterrand, the Secretary of Defense, and the Secretary of State, there are about a half dozen other men with very important-sounding titles who would like to dance with you."

Incredulous, I was about to tell him to stop putting me on when President Reagan loomed into view. "Ms. McAllister," he said as he bowed slightly. "Would you honor me with this dance?"

Stuck somewhere between shocked and thrilled, I hesitated for a moment before handing Alex my glass. Then I returned the President's gesture with the modified curtsy that Christine had taught me. Placing my right hand upon my neckline, I extended my skirt with my left as I bowed and dipped in return. "Well of course, Mr. President," I said. "I would be delighted."

So as the band began playing an old-fashioned Southern waltz – I danced with *the President of the United States!*

Which was like *way* cool!

But believe it or not, it got even better — because just as soon as our dance ended, President Mitterrand approached and asked for the next. And after that, the Secretary of Defense, the Secretary of State, and then two or three ambassadors from countries that I'd never even heard of, followed by a couple of presumably important government officials with long and very impressive sounding titles.

Which by the way, did a lot for my ego — because aside from the CSS Homecoming Dance on Election Night, hardly anyone had ever asked me to dance before.

But as much fun as all that was, I had something else on my mind — specifically, the ambush I was plotting for a certain other big wheel by the name of Alexander M. de Vris. So after thanking the Under-Secretary-of-Something-or-Other as the music faded, I set out in search of President Reagan.

Finding him chatting with President Mitterrand and the Swedish ambassador, I waited off to the side until he noticed me.

Smiling when at last he did, President Reagan asked what he could do for me.

"Well, Sir." I said hesitantly. "I was supposed to have had the last dance with Alex at the CSS Homecoming on Election Night, but just as the music started, this Marine general or something interrupted and said you were calling on a secure line, so I didn't get my dance."

Then after putting on my very best Little Girl Sad face, I continued. "And to make matters even worse," I said plaintively, "they were playing *the* most romantic song *ever* written."

So having laid the guilt on as thick as I dared, I looked up at the President hopefully. "So, I was just wondering if maybe you could ask the band to play the *Unchained Melody* for us…

"You know, the really long dance version by the Righteous Brothers?"

Laughing softly, President Mitterrand remonstrated President Reagan. "*Monsieur le Président,*" he said with a teasing smile. "You have done *Mademoiselle* a grave disservice…

"And on behalf of the Republic of France, I must *insist* that you rectify it immediately!"

Playing into the jest brilliantly, President Reagan lowered his head. Then after shaking it back and forth several times, and muttering "The shame, the shame!" he looked up as a playful smile spread across his face. "Now don't you worry, Missy. I'll take care of it right away."

Suddenly delighted, I bounced up on my toes and grinned from ear to ear. "Well *thanks*, Mr. President!"

CHAPTER THIRTY-SEVEN

So that's how I finally got my dance with Alex – which actually turned out to be two, because President Reagan insisted. But by then it was getting late, and President Reagan and President Mitterrand brought the evening to a close by thanking all the guests for coming. After lining up and going through the reverse version of the receiving line, I accepted Alex's arm as we followed a Social Aide down Cross Hall to the Entry Hall, and then after another Aide placed my wrap across my shoulders, we walked down the steps into a gentle snow.

Now, that was cool! I thought.

I'm still not sure whether Alex read my mind, or just picked up on the huge smile that had spread across my face. But as the limo pulled to a halt in front of us, he looked down and smiled. "I'm glad you enjoyed it."

Which was like, the understatement of the century.

After yet another Marine had opened the door for me, I climbed in as Alex walked around to the other side. Then after stopping to say something or another to the driver, he got in as well. As we pulled up to the gate to exit the White House grounds, he asked me if I was in a hurry to get back to the hotel.

Taken completely off guard, my eyes widened as I shook my head.

Surprised as the limo turned left onto Pennsylvania Avenue rather than right, I turned in my seat to watch as the White House receded in the rear window. Apparently amused by the look on my face, Alex chuckled. "You did that the last time we were here."

Flustered, it took me a moment to make the connection. *He's right*, I thought, before wondering how long it had been since he'd driven me past the Executive Mansion that second day in Washington. *Seven months?*

It seems like a lifetime...

The limo turned left again on 17th Avenue before turning right onto Constitution Avenue two blocks later. Curious as to where we were going, but unwilling to break the comfortable silence I listened to the Christmas music that softly wafted through the limousine's speakers and watched as the snow transformed the capital city into a winter wonderland. Always beautiful at night, the flurry of snowflakes combined with the myriad holiday lights and decorations in a way that made Washington seem almost ethereal.

Crossing over the Potomac on Memorial Bridge into Virginia, the limo turned right onto the George Washington Parkway. Enthralled as we passed the brilliantly lit Kennedy Center on the other side of the river, I turned in my seat again as we proceeded up the Parkway past the spires of Georgetown University. Then a few minutes later, we made a sharp turn to the left and up a steep hill into what seemed like a dense patch of woods before looping back down onto the Parkway in the other direction. Looking over at Alex as we passed the Iwo Jima Memorial before coming up on Arlington National Cemetery, I thanked him for the diversion. "It's really beautiful at night."

Alex didn't say anything. He smiled and nodded instead, and then slipped into a private place somewhere deep within.

For those who didn't know him well – which was just about everyone, to tell you the truth – Alex always seemed calm and collected. But believe me when I tell you that still waters run deep – and from the moment we first met, I'd sensed the passion that lay beneath his cool exterior.

On that night, however, he was more relaxed than I had ever seen him. And for that moment at least, I could tell he was truly happy. Hoping that maybe I had something to do with that, I resisted the temptation to intrude on his silence. So instead, I smiled in return.

After making the loop up onto 14th Street and crossing over the bridge back into Washington, the limo driver took us past the Reflecting Pool to the Lincoln Memorial and the Vietnam Memorial, and then on to the Tidal Basin and the Jefferson Memorial. Amazed and delighted by how different everything looked at night, I stood up on my knees for a better view – perhaps not the most lady-like thing to do under the circumstances, but it did give me a chance to rest both hands on his shoulders for balance.

As I leaned forward to look out on the swirling snow, I felt a strand of fallen hair brush across his cheek. By now so close that I could smell the faint hint of his aftershave, and feel his shoulder rise and fall with rhythmic breath, it suddenly seemed as though the limo had somehow become much warmer. Closing my eyes as I leaned my head back, I imagined the touch of his lips upon mine.

As my face began to flush, an unfamiliar tension spread across my body. Lost in my own imagination, I held the pose for what seemed an eternity. But when we turned left onto Constitution again, I had to struggle to calm my heavy breathing. Now aware of the depths of my desire, I smoothed my skirt as I settled back into my place beside him and began plotting another ambush.

After we finally arrived back at the hotel, Alex escorted me to the door of the suite. Taking my hands in his, he smiled and thanked me for a wonderful evening. Then after a quick kiss on the top of my head, he turned to go.

But since there was just no way I was going to let him off that easy, I slammed my foot down on the carpet as the words tumbled from my mouth. *"Alexander de Vris!"* I exclaimed. "You come back here right now!"

Puzzled, he turned around. "Ms. McAllister?"

Exasperated beyond measure, I pointed my index finger at the floor before me. "Right here, right now," I said, before demanding a good night kiss.

"And I'm not talking about some little peck on the cheek, Alex – I want a *real* kiss!"

OK, so the stories are true. I threw myself at him...

But gimme a break – he'd been dodging me for months!

So to make a long story short, he finally kissed me – and believe me when I tell you that it wasn't just *any* kiss. It was one of those long, slow, delicious kisses that mothers warn their daughters about.

But nothing that good lasts forever, and as my knees grew weak and my consciousness began to dissolve, I summoned up the last of my strength and pulled myself away from him. By now flushed and trembling so hard that I could barely speak, I pulled him close to me again before saying goodnight in a husky voice.

I was fumbling for the key in my evening bag when he placed a finger under my chin and lifted it upwards to look at him. Smiling softly, he apologized. "If I've seemed indifferent, Alicia, I'm sorry...

"It's just that things are very complicated right now."

Stunned and grateful for the gesture, I nodded as tears began welling up in my eyes. "I know," I said sadly. "Saving the world must be a pretty tough job."

Smiling softly, Alex nodded. "Long hours, low pay, lousy benefits..."

"I've *got* to join a union."

Then he suddenly leaned forward, and after grasping the door handle he gave it a violent jerk. As the door popped open, he winked. "That's an old spy trick, you know."

Somewhere between shocked and amazed, I glanced over at the door before turning back to him. But since I'd already figured out that diverting my attention was another one of his spy tricks, I reached out and grasped his lapels. Unwilling to let him break the mood like that, I looked up into his eyes.

"But things won't always be so complicated, will they?"

Which translated from the feminine, means something *way* different...

Suddenly serious, Alex shrugged as a wistful look crept across his face. Leaning forward and kissing me on the top of my head again, he said goodnight. Then he turned on his heel and disappeared down the half-lit hall.

Oh, my God, I thought, as I leaned back against the door jamb and stared at the ceiling. Confident that Alex had not only caught my drift but answered my question with one of those mute moronicisms only guys are capable of, I placed my hand on my neckline and took a deep breath before tip-toeing around the half-opened door and pushing it shut behind me.

Suddenly exultant, I threw my clenched fists up in the air triumphantly.

YES!

Convinced that I'd *finally* made a dent in The Mystery Man's armor, I did my little Happy Dance thing right there in the foyer.

Then as a triumphant smile spread across my face, I began singing that old Sixties song *Then He Kissed Me*. Picking up the beat as memory supplied the "Wall of Sound" that had made the song so famous, I danced back to the bedroom. Then suddenly remembering I wanted a Diet Pepsi, I did my version of the Moonwalk – which was *way* better than Michael Jackson's, thank you very much – all the way back to the galley.

Cracking up as the song came to its stunning crescendo in my head, I strolled back down the hall to the oversized bed. Putting the unopened soft drink on the nightstand beside it, I flopped down and smiled at the ceiling.

Could this night have been any better? I wondered.

Not a chance, girlfriend, came the reply. *It made that whole Cinderella thing look lame!*

I was thinking that was God's honest truth when I suddenly remembered I'd promised to call home. Mom had made a huge issue out of the White House dinner, and she'd absolutely insisted that I call her the moment I got back to the hotel.

Knowing she was sitting by the phone back in Glen Meadows, I sat up suddenly and began frantically running through the list of things I was going to tell her – the gigantic limo that had taken us to the White House; meeting President and Mrs. Reagan and President and Mrs. Mitterrand; the delicious dinner and all the things we'd talked about at the long dinner table; dancing with the Presidents and all the other really important Washington VIPs; and the long ride home through the snow past all the important buildings and monuments.

Satisfied that pretty well covered it, I popped the top of the Diet Pepsi and took a quick drink before picking up the phone and punching in the number.

She picked up on the second ring, and from the sound of her voice I could tell she was wide-awake even though it was a bit past midnight – which was like the wee hours of the morning, by Glen Meadows standards. So rather than waste time with preliminary chitchat, I cut right to the chase and told her the whole story from start to finish – except for *The Great Hotel Hallway Kiss*, of course.

Because aside from the fact that she would have gone ballistic, I just didn't think it was any of her business anyway.

After almost an entire hour of incredibly detailed reportage, I finally said goodnight, and then after carefully hanging up my dress, I crawled into bed to get some much-needed sleep. There had been an awful lot of talk in the office when word got out that Alex was taking me to the White House, and if I didn't show up for work on time – looking halfway presentable, of course – the gossip was going to get *way* serious.

Or in the interests of accuracy, way *more* serious – because rumors were already flying all over the place, and some of them weren't very nice.

But for the most part, they were just plain silly, so as I sauntered into the building the next morning I had to really work hard to suppress the grin that kept trying to sneak across my face. Julia practically shrieked when I ran into her by the elevator, and Jennifer – naturally – gave me a ration of light-hearted grief when I stopped by the Econ shop to pick up my messages.

But to tell you the truth, I had more on my mind than gossip or my newfound celebrity status when I stepped out of the elevator onto the Eighth Floor. Knowing that Christine was going to want to see me first thing, I was thinking it was going to be positively weird talking about my evening with her college beau. I was still trying to wrap my head around that one when I walked into the Executive Offices.

Two was conveniently sick that day – which came as absolutely no surprise – but Linda was at her desk. Smiling as she looked up, she told me that Christine wanted to see me just as soon as I made the morning's coffee. So after dumping my gear in my office, I made my way into the galley. Then after feeding the dogs – who'd spent the night guarding my office, by the way – I fired up the coffee pot.

Precisely seven and a half minutes later, I tapped on Christine's doors with my foot before pushing through the double doors with a coffee tray. After looking up and smiling, she thanked whoever she was talking to for calling, and hung up the phone. As I set the tray down on the edge of her desk, she picked up her Styrofoam cup – which I'd already prepped with her standard two shots of cream and a packet of Sweet 'N Low – before leaning back in her chair and taking a sip.

After I sat down in the proffered chair, Christine smiled over the rim of her cup, and told me that she'd heard I'd been a big hit at the White House. But then she grinned, and said she just had *one* little question. "Did you get a kiss?"

Gulp!

Feeling my cheeks turn crimson, my eyes flitted back and forth involuntarily. Shifting in my seat, I tugged at the hem of my skirt before crossing my legs and folding my hands across my knees.

"Well, uh, kinda."

Chucking, Christine repeated my reply. *"Kinda?"*

Still trying to figure how I was going to weasel out of that one, I stalled for time. "Well, you see, Christine, it was like this…"

But since I knew that even a really good lie wasn't going to fly with Christine, I stopped short.

Oh bloody hell, I thought in silent imitation of Dr. MacLaughlin. So I threw my arms up in the air and 'fessed up.

"OK, so I threw myself at him…

"I'm a bad person, so can we move on?"

Chuckling, Christine assured me that I wasn't the first girl to succumb to the ole de Vris charm.

"Been there, done it myself."

Then she smiled, leaned forward, and told me she'd received a glowing report on my White House debut.

Thanking God for small favors – which in this case was Christine's willingness to let the whole kiss thing slide – I grinned and asked her where she'd heard that.

Smiling as she held her cup of coffee between both hands, she said "From none other than Nancy Reagan, herself."

"Really?"

Thinking that was just *incredibly* cool, I leaned forward in my chair. *"Mrs. Reagan said that?"*

Christine smiled and nodded before taking a sip of her coffee. "That was her on the phone...

"She said you were positively charming, and that she and the President hope you will come back."

Figuring Special Agent Jordan must have already counted the White House silver, I assured Christine that wouldn't be a problem. "I had a *great* time!"

After taking another sip on her coffee, Christine informed me that since she'd already got the 411 from Nancy Reagan, she was going to give me the boot. "Alex had to fly out to Oklahoma first thing this morning, and he stuck me with a ton of paperwork...

"So let's get your vault open, so I can get back to work."

Suddenly curious, I asked Christine what he was doing in Oklahoma – and when he'd be back, by the way, because the CSS Christmas Formal kicked off at 7:00 the next evening...

"Tribal Council meeting," she said as she pushed her chair back and stood up. "But he'll be back in time for the dance."

Huh? I thought.

Then wondering what that was all about, I repeated her words. "Tribal Council?"

Carrying her cup, Christine nodded as she rounded her desk. "One of Alex's ancestors married an Indian princess way back when, so he's an honorary member of the tribe."

Well, kewl! I thought. "So like, is Alex royalty or something?"

As a puzzled look spread across her face, Christine stopped dead in her tracks. Then after tilting her head to one side and weighing the question for a long moment, she confessed she wasn't sure. "But I think the Cherokee Nation abolished their aristocracy when they adopted a republican form of government."

Turning suddenly about, she walked back to the low bookcase that ran behind her desk and pulled a volume from one of the shelves. Handing it to me, she said I could probably find something on that inside. Then after admonishing me to return the book when I finished with it, she told me we had to get a move on because she was really under the gun.

So after she helped me open up, I dragged my carts over to my desk and got down to work. But my heart just wasn't in it – even though Madame Henri called to let me know my dress for the Christmas dance was ready, I really wanted to read the book Christine had given me.

Pirates, Indian princesses, presidential advisors – now how cool is that???

So at precisely one minute after 5:30 that evening, I took off like a shot. The first stop was the hotel, where I gathered up all the stuff I'd left there — and confirmed my appointment with Raphael for the next afternoon, of course — and then it was on to Madame Henri's. But after that, it was straight home for an evening of quality time with *In the Service of Honor: A History of the de Vris Family in America*.

And of course, a big bowl of triple-thick chocolate fudge ice cream...

But the Fates were against me that night — because the moment I slid my key into the lock on my door, I started cramping.

Thinking that was really weird — because it wasn't even close to *that* time of the month — I hung my Christmas dress from the top of the downstairs closet door and made my way up to the loft. Having changed into my sweats and my fuzzy slippers, I was padding down the spiral staircase when I noticed the floor below suddenly seemed awfully far away. Then, as beads of perspiration formed on my forehead, I seized the handrail to steady myself.

Realizing that whatever was going on just couldn't be good, I carefully made my way down the last five or six steps before hobbling behind the freestanding partition to Julia's sleeping area. Pulling the down comforter off her bed, I staggered to the couch. Realizing that I'd never make it all the way around to the front, I climbed over the top and tumbled onto the cushions below. Trembling from a sudden chill, I pulled the comforter over me and curled up underneath it.

Alternating between hellishly hot sweats and bitterly cold chills — interspersed by urgent and exhausting trips to the bathroom — I spent the night drifting in and out of consciousness. Awakening briefly just after 9:00 the next morning, I crawled to the end of the couch and used the phone on the end table to call the Econ shop. After telling Jennifer in a hoarse whisper I wouldn't be coming in, I dropped the handset back on the cradle and passed out again.

Although it seemed like no more than an indeterminate moment, three or four hours must have passed before I heard the apartment door first open and then softly close. Hoping an Angel had come to deliver me from my misery, I peered out from under the comforter to see Mai Ling kneeling by the couch.

Not quite an angel, I thought distantly. But under the circumstances, I figured a doctor was the next best thing.

Forcing a weak smile, I tried to greet her with a barely audible whisper.

Mai Ling smiled sympathetically as she laid Julia's set of keys on the coffee table. Then after struggling out of a heavy winter parka, she opened up her black leather physician's satchel and pulled out a disposable thermometer, a stethoscope, and a blood pressure instrument. After stripping the wrapper off the thermometer and sticking it in my mouth, she hunted through her pockets until she found her little flashlight. "I examine now," she said. "But I tink dat flu."

After peering in my eyes, taking my blood pressure, and listening to my chest, she poked and prodded me for a minute before removing the thermometer from my mouth. After glancing at it before tossing into the trashcan next to the TV, she asked me how long I'd had symptoms. Still so hoarse I could barely whisper, I explained what had happened the night before.

Then after telling her I'd never been so sick in my life, I asked her if she could give me something.

Mai Ling grinned, and shook her head. "Dat waste good medicine...

"Two, three hour, you die anyway."

What???

Mai Ling had been kidding, of course, but by that point I wasn't quite up to the finer points of bedside humor. Horrified, I hurled myself up into an upright position, and gasped. *"Die???"*

As Mai Ling erupted into laughter, I had to grab the back of the couch to keep the room from slipping out from under me. "Ha, ha, ha!" she bellowed. "Dat priceless!"

Almost doubled over with laughter, she pointed her finger at me. "You funny girl!"

Muttering under my breath, I held onto the couch until the twirling room slowed down enough to glare at her. "I'm gonna get you for that, " I croaked.

Mai Ling grinned, but ignored the threat. "Not much can do wit flu," she said. "Jus ease symptom till virus burn out, two day, maybe three."

Then with a look of professional concern, she explained how serious the flu could be. "Spanish flu kill tens of millions in 1918, maybe hundreds millions...

"So many die, most countries didn't even try count."

So after helping me ease back down onto the couch, she said that if I got any worse, she was going to put me in the hospital. "Flu dis year not so bad, but lots of complication...

"Make immune system vulnerable to opportunist infecting, 'specially respiratory. Den maybe bronchitis, pneumonia come."

Oh great, I thought. *Just what I need...*

Then Mai Ling bounced up on her feet. "I make special China tea now...

"Not kill virus, but alleviate symptom some."

Nodding glumly, I pulled the covers over my head again as Mai Ling busied herself in the kitchen.

Five minutes later, she returned with a steaming cup. After handing it to me and telling me to sip it slowly, she pulled a large smoked-glass bottle out of her satchel and explained it was Vitamin C.

"Best research say high level speed recovery...

"Start 1000 milligrams, increase by 'nother 1000 milligrams every four hour till you run to toilet...

"Dat mean you excess upper limit, so you reduce dose jus little bit den."

Then after setting the Vitamin C down and pulling a smaller bottle out of her satchel, she explained that it contained a blend that had been clinically proven to boost the immune system. "Olive leaf extract, astragalus, beta glucan, an other stuff...

"Take one capsule every twelve hour, an sip lot of tea. Better hot, but cold OK."

Then after informing me that she had left a half-pound of tea leaves on the kitchen counter next to the fresh-made pot, Mai Ling pulled a business card out of her satchel. After searching through her pockets for a pen, she turned it over and wrote her pager number on the back. "Dis beeper," she said. "You get even little worse, you call me right away...

"Already check, bed available at Capitol General...

"Understan?"

After I nodded, Mai Ling fed the dogs for me. Then after taking them out to the bushes, she urged me to try to eat something as she struggled back into her coat. Thinking she looked very much like an Eskimo in her parka, jeans, and knee-high padded boots, I teased her as she pulled on a red plaid hat with fold-down flaps.

"Cold out der!" she exclaimed. "Make Vietnam person icicle!"

Thinking she looked more like a Popsicle in a funny wrapper when she froze in place and mimed to make her point, I giggled as she gathered up her doctor gear and stuffed it back in her satchel. Then after reminding me to beep her if I felt even the slightest bit worse, she picked up Julia's keys and told me she'd stop by in the morning after she finished her rounds at the hospital.

Suddenly serious, she wagged her finger at me. "Never lose patien to flu," she said. "Mess up record, you in *big* trouble!"

So after making me promise I wouldn't die on her, she gave me a thumbs-up sign and scurried out the door.

CHAPTER THIRTY-EIGHT

When I awoke the next day, I found Mai Ling sitting next to the couch, engrossed in a paperback book. Noticing as I shifted under the comforter, she glanced over and smiled before holding up a finger while she finished the page. Then after slapping the book shut, she held it up excitedly. "Goo book!" she exclaimed.

Glancing over at the cover, I realized it was *Murder in the White House* – the book I'd bought at the little grocery store on Capitol Hill, my third night in Washington. Which was really weird, because I'd been looking for it for months.

So after pushing myself into an upright position, I asked her where she'd found it. Mai Ling pointed toward bookshelf. "You asleep when I come, so I find book to read."

So that's where the darn thing went, I thought.

Then as Mai Ling's eyes widened, she held it up again. "Someone make murder in White House," she said in a hushed whisper. "Big mystery!"

Then as her eyes grew even wider, she clasped the book against her chest. "Lend me, please?" she asked hopefully.

Thinking that was a complete no-brainer – because after all she'd done for me, I owed her a lot more than that – so I forced a weak grin and said "Sure." But then in a hoarse whisper, I made her promise not to tell me anything about it, because I wanted to read it too.

Smiling excitedly, she promised she wouldn't breathe a word as she stuffed the book into her physician's bag. Then suddenly serious, she asked me how I was.

So after lying back down and rolling over on my side so I could see her, I answered. "I feel like I got run over by a truck...

"Everything hurts, and I'm really dizzy."

Mai Ling nodded sympathetically as she pulled a disposable thermometer out of her satchel. "Dat par for course," she said. Then after telling me to open my mouth, she slipped the instrument under my tongue. "I tink one more bad day...

"Den maybe you feel little better."

As she waited for the thermometer to warm up, I weighed my options. *Let's see...*

I can spend another night of alternately freezing my butt off and burning up – not to mention dealing with aches and pains, and being so dizzy I can barely crawl to the bathroom — or I can just kick the bucket and get it over with...

Thinking that was a pretty tough call, I was wondering if they had chocolate in Heaven when Mai Ling suddenly reached over and pulled the thermometer out of my mouth. After studying it for a moment, she tossed it in the trashcan and told me my temperature was still elevated. Then she pulled me into an upright position and gave me another exam.

After taking my pulse and blood pressure, she peered into my eyes with her little flashlight before pulling a stethoscope out of her bag and listening to my chest. Frowning, she put the instrument away and started poking and prodding. "Dat hurt?"

Nodding, I told her just a little.

Sitting back in her chair, Mai Ling looked concerned. "Tink flu go away soon, but lymph nodes little swollen and some congestion in chest...

"Mostly worry you get chest cold, den maybe bronchitis...

"So take pills, drink tea, stay inside three four days more an keep warm...

"An try eat something. Sgt. Trung restaurant three block away an dey deliver...

"You probably not like Vietnam food very much but dey have big China menu, too." Then as a huge smile crept across her face, she winked and told me that Madame Trung was the world's greatest cook. "Make you little fat, maybe — but *very* happy."

Explaining that she and Nguyen were leaving for Savannah in just a few hours, she told me her answering service would forward her calls, and she'd already arranged for a Dr. Radcliff to cover for her in the event of an emergency. "Get sicker, you call answer service right away...

"I call pharmacy wit prescription, or maybe call Dr. Radcliff...

"He very goo doctor."

Then after fixing another kettle of tea while I staggered to the bathroom, she began telling me about the Christmas dance as she packed up her gear. "Sad you miss dance...

"Pretty decoration, goo food." Then she laughed and told me that they'd had a live band, too. "So Nguyen not play disc jockey an embarrass again."

Then after taking the time to tell me every last detail, she snapped her satchel shut. But just before walking out the door, she stopped and turned back. "Hope better by Chrismiz...

"Do all doctor can, so maybe I say little prayer in church."

JUST BEFORE MIDNIGHT

Thinking that was really sweet, I thanked her before rolling over and falling back into a deep sleep.

When I finally woke up almost twenty hours later, I was sore and stiff but feeling much better. My fever must have broken while I slept, and even though I was a bit wobbly when I got up, the dizziness had abated. So after making my way to the bathroom to pay homage to Mother Nature, I decided to take a shower and wash my hair.

Which was a really good idea, because by then I had acquired quite a scent.

Hoping I hadn't stunk up the apartment, I wrapped one towel around my head and another around my torso before making my way up to the loft to find some fresh clothes. So after pulling on a clean pair of sweats and toweling my hair, I padded back down the stairs and combed it out.

Mai Ling had taken the dogs out and fed them when she arrived, but since I felt guilty for keeping the poor creatures locked up for almost 20 hours, I took them out again just as soon as my hair was dry.

Suddenly hungry after we returned to the apartment, I pulled out the Yellow Pages and looked up the number for Sgt. Trung's restaurant. Since I didn't know the name of the place, it took me a couple of minutes to figure it out. Given the fact that *The Perfume River Inn* was the only Oriental restaurant anywhere close to the apartment, I punched in the number – but just to be sure, I asked the girl who answered the phone if Sgt. Trung was the proprietor.

After being assured that he was, I ordered half the menu. Or at least half the Chinese menu, anyway. Kung Pao Chicken – extra spicy, thank you very much – Chinese Dumplings, Hot and Sour Soup, and a side order of Pork Fried Rice.

Thinking that would probably last me through New Year's, I happily gave them my address and credit card number.

My order arrived a half-hour later – so after tipping the little Vietnamese kid who brought it over on his bicycle, I sat down and started eating. Forty-five minutes later, I found myself staring at the empty cartons that littered the coffee table in front of me. *No way!* I thought. *I couldn't possibly have eaten all that...*

But after looking down at my bulging stomach, I had to face the facts. *Either that, or you managed to get four months pregnant in fifty minutes...*

So rather than fess up to gluttony, I rationalized the whole thing instead. *It's that darned flu,* I told myself. *It makes people crazy...*

After finally convincing my conscience that it really wasn't *my* fault, I picked up the remote and turned the TV on before crawling back under the comforter. But as soon as I got all comfy and warm, the phone rang. It was Jennifer.

"Hey, girlfriend! How ya feeling?"

Thinking being home sick wasn't half as bad as being handcuffed to a hospital bed, I told her that I'd been worse. "But I'm still feeling a bit woozy."

After a sympathetic *"Awwww,"* Jennifer apologized for not having called before. "But Mai Ling left strict orders at the office not to bother you for a couple of days."

After I assured her that it wasn't a problem, Jennifer suddenly asked me if I'd heard about the dance. Nodding, I said that Mai Ling had told me all about it.

There was a long silence, until Jennifer rather hesitantly asked me if she'd told me about Two.

"Noooooo" I said, now suddenly suspicious by the manner of her question and the tone of her voice.

"Oh, my God!" Jennifer exclaimed. "You're just *not* going to believe it!"

Realizing that whatever happened must have involved Alex somehow, my stomach tightened – and since I wasn't even sure I wanted to know, I hesitated for a moment. Finally, I asked her what had come down.

"Well, it was close to the end of the evening," Jennifer said. "And Alex and Christine had finished dancing with all the VIPs and staff. So they were just sort of hanging out on the edge of the dance floor, talking to Christine's husband…

"And the band started playing *Fire* – you know that really sultry song by the Pointer Sisters?"

Since I could already tell where Jennifer was headed, I hesitated again before answering. "Yeah, I've heard it."

"OK, so the band's lead singer was this girl and she started singing this really slow, sexy version…

"So Two struts right up to Alex and grabs him – and I mean, *literally* grabs him – and drags him out on the dance floor."

Uh-oh, I thought.

"So anyway," Jennifer continued. "You know Alex…he takes that sort of stuff in stride. But then Two raised her arms above her head and started dancing really provocatively…

"And then she moved in really close and started crawling all over him…

"So after she ran her fingers through his hair and down his chest, she turned her back into him and pulled his arms low around her waist...

"And then she started doing this really sexy grind thing with her hips!"

That witch! I thought – using a slightly different word.

As soon as I figure out where to bury the body, I'm gonna kill her!

"Well anyway, girlfriend, you should have seen the look on Alex's face – he was like, totally stunned."

"So what happened?" I asked hesitantly.

"Well, as soon as Alex recovered his cool, he sort of spun her out, and they finished the dance...

"But I was standing right there, and let me tell you – Christine was *totally* livid!

"She was so mad I thought she was going to march right out on the dance floor and slap that girl silly!"

Thinking that would have served her right, I nodded into the mouthpiece.

"So anyway," Jennifer continued. "As the song ended, Two slipped around behind Alex and whispered something in his ear...

"I couldn't hear what she said, but as soon as the music stopped she left...

"Then Christine dragged Alex out into the hallway and they really got into it...

"I didn't hear any of that either, but Wilbur – you know, the parking attendant – he was coming back from the men's room, and he overheard the whole thing....

"Christine wanted Two fired right then and there, but Alex was insisting that it wasn't that big of a deal and said he'd take care of it when the office re-opens on the second."

"Oh, gawd." I said. "So how many people saw it?"

"Well, see that's the thing." Jennifer said.

"Since the CSS Christmas formal is such a big social event here in Washington, a couple of newspaper photographers had been invited to cover it – and some guy from the tabloids slipped past the ushers at the door with a fake invitation...

"So guess what's plastered all over the scandal sheets this morning?"

Feeling suddenly queasy again, I closed my eyes and shook my head. "Pictures of Two climbing all over Alex?"

There was a long silence before Jennifer said, "Uh, yeah...

"And, uh...

"Some really big headlines about you and Two fighting over 'The World's Most Eligible Bachelor.' "

Oh dear God! I thought. *Can this get any worse?*

Totally oblivious to the fact that it was by now Christmas Eve, I asked Jennifer what day it was. "December 24th," she said.

Uh, oh, I thought. *Mom's gonna call any minute now...*

So after a long pause, I asked Jennifer if there was anything else I should know about.

"Well, not really," she said. "Except *People Magazine* ran a really big story about the White House dinner, and said a lot of nice things about you...."

"And they published some really great pictures of you dancing with Alex, and President Reagan and that other guy, Mitterrand...

"Have you seen it?"

Shaking my head, I told her no.

So after promising to pick up a half-dozen copies from the convenience store, Jennifer told me not to worry about Christmas dinner. "Mrs. MacLaughlin said she and Dr. MacLaughlin were going to bring you a big plate of Christmas turkey tomorrow afternoon."

Thinking that was really nice, I asked Jennifer to thank them for me. After promising she would, Jennifer told me to make sure to turn on the local station at 8 pm, because Christine's choral group was going to sing Christmas carols at the White House. So after glancing at the clock, I thanked her for the heads-up call and wished her a Merry Christmas before hanging up the phone.

Putting the whole Two thing momentarily on hold, I hurriedly worked out a plan for dealing with my Mom.

Thinking that my best option was to play for time, I grabbed the answering machine next to the phone and faked a cheery message saying that I had gone to a Christmas party and wouldn't be home until late. "But please leave a message, and have a *very* Merry Christmas!"

Satisfied that would hold her off until the next day, I pulled the comforter around myself and started plotting Two's demise. Standing her up in front of a firing squad was out, because I'd need a crew for that. And of course, the same went with hanging. But pushing her down the elevator shaft at work seemed like a definite possibility, until I realized it was *way* too good for her...

Because if she doesn't land on her face, she might still be pretty at her funeral...

So, after considering a dozen or so other options, I was leaning towards boiling her alive in used vegetable oil when I suddenly started sneezing.

Thinking this just *couldn't* be happening, I turned my eyes to the heavens.

Oh, come on, God — gimme a break!

But He didn't.

By the time I changed the channel a few hours later to watch Christine's choral group at the White House, I was not only sneezing, but coughing as well. And to top it off, my nose had suddenly become all stuffed up.

So after pulling the comforter over my head and wrapping it around me, I pulled my legs underneath me as the cameras introduced the Georgetown Choral Society to the audience. After panning across their ranks as they assembled on the White House lawn, another camera zoomed in on Christine. Stunningly beautiful against the snow-swept background, Christine smiled into the camera as the newscaster introduced her and then thanked the audience for joining them. Then after giving a brief overview of the planned event she stepped back as a flame-bearer made his way up and down the ranks of the carolers, lighting each of their candles in turn. Once the last of the candles was lit, the TV lights dimmed and the cameras moved back as the conductor stepped forward and raised his baton.

After a moment of complete silence, he swung his arms apart and opened a thunderous rendition of *Hark the Herald Angels Sing* — and an instant later, the doors of the White House swept open to reveal President and Mrs. Reagan standing just inside the entry hall. Elegantly dressed in formal wear, they almost looked like figures in an old-fashioned painting through the flurries of snow. Thinking that was incredibly cool, between sniffles and sneezes, I took a slug of cough medicine right out of the bottle.

Totally awed by the unfolding spectacle, I huddled on the couch in stunned silence for the next forty-five minutes as they sang all of my favorite Christmas songs — *Joy to the World, What Child is This, The Little Drummer Boy, Jingle Bells, A Winter Wonderland, O Come All Ye Faithful* — and a whole bunch of others.

Then as the candles began burning low, they sang the most beautiful version of *Silent Night* I had ever heard.

Thinking the pageant was over, I watched as stewards suddenly appeared from off-camera and started handing out steaming cups of hot chocolate to the carolers. But just as I was about to turn off the TV, the newscaster cut in to inform the audience that Mrs. Christine O'Connell would close the evening with a solo performance of *Christmas Eve in Washington.*

Still peering through the little aperture formed by the comforter, I watched as Christine stepped forward and accepted a microphone. Then, as the choral society formed a half-circle behind her with what remained of their candles, she began to sing in an incredibly rich, melodic voice:

It's snowing tonight in the Blue Ridge
There's a hush on the Chesapeake Bay
The chimneys are smoking in Georgetown,
And tomorrow is Christmas Day.

The Tidal Basin lies quiet
The tourists have found their way home
Mr. Jefferson's standing the mid-watch
And there's a star on the Capitol Dome.

It's Christmas Eve in Washington,
America's hometown
It's here that freedom lives,
And peace can stand her ground

It's Christmas Eve in Washington
Our joyous wish to you
Is for peace, love and laughter,
To last the whole year through.

Snowmen peeking through the windows
It's warm with love inside
'Round the tree the children gather
Awaiting Santa's midnight ride.

Mom and Dad are counting their blessings,
Reflecting on all they've done
So thankful for another
Christmas Eve in Washington.

It's Christmas Eve in Washington,
America's hometown
For it's here that freedom lives,
And peace can stand her ground.

It's Christmas Eve in Washington
Our joyous wish to you
Is for peace love & laughter,
To last the whole year through.

As she dropped her voice to repeat the final verse, thunderous applause came from somewhere off camera. Then as Nancy Reagan wiped a tear from her eye, the misty-eyed President put his arm around her shoulder and pulled her close. As the camera zoomed in on him, I could see him saying "Thank You" over and over.

Then as a huge smile stole across his face, President Reagan raised his hand over his head and waved enthusiastically. "A Merry Christmas to all," he shouted. "And to all a Good Night!"

Still sniffling, I pushed my hand out from under the comforter and replied with a weak little wave.

"Merry Christmas, Mr. and Mrs. President."

CHAPTER THIRTY-NINE

So, I spent most of the next week on the couch, sniffling, sneezing and coughing. For the most part, I huddled under Julia's comforter and pretended to watch TV. Fortunately, I had quite a bit of company. Jennifer stopped by Christmas morning to drop off the magazines and the scandal sheets – which turned out to be a good thing, because my Mom finally caught up with me just before noon – and then Dr. and Mrs. MacLaughlin came by later in the day to drop off a really great holiday dinner.

Which I really appreciated – because believe it or not, there's an absolute limit to the number of Chinese dumplings I can eat.

And of course Mai Ling stopped by to check up on me just as soon as she got back from Savannah, three or four days later. Concerned by the cold, she spent an unusually long time poking and prodding me before delivering a very stern warning to stay inside and keep warm – and of course, to keep taking the supplements she'd left with me, and drink the herbal tea as well. It turned out that there was a particularly nasty form of viral pneumonia going around, and she wanted to make sure I didn't get it. After pursing her lips and shaking her head, she warned how serious it could be. "Antibiotic not work wit virus," she said. "Get sick wit dat, you in hospital for month."

But once she was sure she'd made her point, she shifted gears. After taking off her doctor's hat – figuratively speaking, of course, because she had turned up wearing the same goofy looking plaid hunting cap – she sat down on the couch and told me all about Christmas in Savannah.

The de Vris family mansion was incredibly beautiful, she said, and it was just a stone's throw from the ocean. So after exchanging gifts and eating a magnificent Christmas feast – which Alex had ordered from a caterer, so Mai Ling wouldn't have to cook – they took a boom box out on the beach and built a huge bonfire. Warming themselves by the flames, they spent the evening listening to Christmas carols and watching the waves as they crashed upon the sand. Then as the embers burned low, they went back inside, and after opening a bottle of expensive wine, Alex brought out his guitar and played for them.

After tucking her legs underneath her and pulling up a part of the comforter, Mai Ling smiled shyly. "Boys make Mai Ling wonerful Chrismiz."

But then it got even better, because after Alex finished playing they'd cracked open another bottle and sat around the kitchen table whispering secrets until almost dawn – which of course gave me the perfect opportunity to pry a few of them loose. It turned out that Alex had been as surprised as everyone else by Two's antics at the Christmas formal, and Mai Ling rather pointedly informed me that he hadn't been amused.

Then after another shy smile, Mai Ling looked down at the comforter before looking back up at me. "Maybe other girl steal heart away."

Which I thought was like, *way* cool.

But before I could squeeze any of the details out of her, Mai Ling jumped up and started stuffing her gear back into her satchel. Frustrated beyond belief, I told her she couldn't possibly leave me hanging like that – but she just grinned.

"Story of life," she said. "Little feet, big mouth – can't find shoes, say things make me trouble."

Then after smiling again, she slipped back into the doctor mode. Suddenly serious, she issued yet another stern warning to stay inside and keep warm, before hoisting her satchel and scurrying out the door.

Which, by the way, was a warning I actually tried to heed.

But by the time New Year's Eve rolled around, I just couldn't stand looking at the walls anymore. Thinking that all the excitement in Times Square provided perfect cover, I decided to break jail before they started the countdown to New Year's.

So after bundling up in a down ski jacket and pulling on a hat and mittens, I gathered up the dogs and shuffled down to the all-night drugstore. After cleaning out their ice cream freezer, I raided the packaged pastries and cupcakes before piling it all on the sales counter. After enduring the unspoken scorn of the petite teen-aged girl behind the cash register, I lugged the loot back to the apartment and plopped down on the couch to greet the New Year with a half-gallon of Strawberry Swirl and a package of those little Angel Food cakes...

OK, so I had a package of cupcakes too – but I gave half to the dogs, so let's not make a federal case out of it...

Now of course, that didn't do much for my diet. But it made me feel a lot better – so even though I wasn't sure whether it was the cakes or the ice cream or just the natural course of events that cured me, my cold was ancient history when I arrived at the office on the morning of January second.

Excited to be back, I gave Linda a cheery wave as I strolled into the Executive Offices – because after what Mai Ling had let slip, I was pretty much on top of the world.

And of course, I just couldn't wait to see what would happen with Two...

But before I even passed her desk, Linda called me back. Leaning across it to hand me a memo as I turned around, she warned me to look sharp and stay on my toes. "Lord Wythcliff is going to be here any minute."

Huh?

Scrunching up my nose, I gave her a puzzled look. "Lord Who?"

Sitting back down in her chair, Linda said "The new head of the London office...

"It's all in the memo."

After a disinterested shrug, I made a mental note to look it over when I got settled – and promptly forgot all about it the minute I saw the big pile of boxes stacked on my desk.

Realizing it was Christmas stuff from my Mom and Gramma and Grampa O'Malley, and of course Gramma McAllister, I transferred my briefcase to my left hand and thrust my right fist up in the air. "Yea, Santa!"

Thinking I'd really hit the jackpot, I was in the process of shaking the first one when Christine walked in. "Back from the dead, I see."

Still holding the box, I whirled around and grinned. "Yes, Ma'am!" I said. "Alive and kicking!"

Then after setting the box down, I started rummaging through my purse. After finding the exquisitely wrapped little box with the mashed-up bow near the bottom, I handed it to her. "Merry Christmas," I said.

It really wasn't much – just a little diamond bracelet – but it was elegantly crafted, and really expensive. Since I figured I owed her for the White House dinner, I'd gulped hard when I saw the price tag, and forked over the cash.

Seemingly surprised, Christine blushed a little as she took it from me. "You really didn't have to do that," she said.

Smiling, I told her she didn't have to hook me up with Alex, either. So after giving her a wink, I told her fair was fair.

Still blushing, Christine thanked me and told me she'd open it later. "Because right now," she said, we have to get organized...

"Did you read the memo?"

Oops...

After crossing my eyes and pursing my lips, I 'fessed up. "Not yet," I said. "I sort of got sidetracked with all the Christmas stuff."

After nodding, Christine walked me through it as we opened up the vault. "Lord Wythcliff is the eldest son of a wealthy and politically influential English family," she said. "After graduating from Oxford, he enrolled at the Royal Naval College and had intended to make a career out of the service...

"But he was badly wounded in the Falklands War, so he was forced to retire."

Bummer, I thought. "Sounds a lot like Alex."

After we turned our keys in the enabling mechanism, Christine nodded as she tucked hers back in her blouse. "He's only been with us a few months, so I haven't met him in person. But I've spoken with him on the phone once or twice, and that was my impression as well...

"And since he's still not fully recovered, I want to make sure that the staff extends him every courtesy."

Glancing up from the keypad as I punched in the vault's entry code, I asked Christine what had happened. Because even though I didn't actually know when the Falklands War had happened, it seemed like it had been a long time ago.

As I pulled the vault door open, Christine shrugged. "He was on the HMS Sheffield when it was hit by a missile," she said. "And as the senior surviving officer below decks, he assumed command of damage control operations...

"So he was fighting the fires when a secondary explosion almost ripped his leg off."

Grimacing as I jerked the first cart backwards, I shook my head sadly. "So what happened?"

Christine said that he'd ordered a sailor to tie off the bleeding, and stayed at his post until the Captain ordered the crew to abandon ship. "He was awarded the Victoria Cross for that," she said softly.

Huh?

Puzzled, I gave Christine a funny look as she helped me push the first cart over to my desk. "The what?"

"The Victoria Cross," she said. "That's the British version of the Medal of Honor."

"So did he lose his leg?" I asked as we walked back to the vault to get the second cart with my computer on it.

"No, he was lucky...

"But he underwent a half-dozen surgeries, and I understand he still has difficulty walking."

After giving the second cart an especially hard jerk, I looked up at Christine. "You know the more I learn about this war stuff, the less I like it."

After pursing her lips, Christine nodded gravely. "That's why we're here," she said.

With my cart halfway to my desk, I stopped suddenly. "It is?"

Nodding again as she grasped the back of the cart, Christine told me that's why Alex had set up the CSS in the first place. "Everything we do here is directed at avoiding another war," she said. "And in the event war should come anyway, to make sure that we win it as quickly and as painlessly as possible."

Still frozen in my tracks, I laid my head over on my shoulder and looked at her incredulously. Because to tell you the truth, the people at the CSS – which included myself, of course – had never really struck me as peaceniks.

Christine smiled indulgently, as though she had read my mind. The name of the game, she said, was "peace through strength." Then as she shoved the cart forward with her hip, she chuckled and dropped her voice a couple of octaves. "Nobody mess wit da big dog."

Laughing at her colloquialism, I pulled the cart into place and grabbed the extension cord from the shelf underneath the one holding the computer and monitor. Thinking there was a certain logic to that "Big Dog" thing, I nodded thoughtfully as I hooked up the cords.

Seeing that I'd finished, Christine told me to look sharp and stay on my best behavior, before informing me that she had to get back to work. But before she could turn and head for the door, I called her back. After summoning my most earnest look, I asked her about Two.

"I heard what she did at the dance."

Taken by surprise, Christine's eyes widened as she raised a finger to her lips. Pointing toward the galley's open door, she whispered that Two was in Alex's office pulling together some files for Lord Wythcliff. Then after leaning forward, she told me that she'd talked about it with Alex again over the weekend, and that he'd assured her he'd deal with it.

After taking a furtive glance at the open galley door, I asked in a hushed whisper if Alex was going to fire her.

Looking suddenly concerned, Christine shook her head. "He's going to chew her out, and he's asked me to find a place to reassign her..."

"Unless she mouths off – in which case, she's gone."

I was in the process of whispering my thanks when I glanced through my open door and saw Alex and another man enter the Executive Offices from the hall. "Hey," I said softly. "That must be Lord What's-his-face."

After glancing over her shoulder, Christine smiled and told me to come on. "Let's go shake hands."

Noticing our approach, Alex and the other guy stopped alongside Two's soon-to-be-former desk. As the stranger rested on his cane, I could see that he was a lot younger and a whole lot more handsome than I had imagined. Tall and blonde with soft blue eyes and a short, neatly trimmed beard with reddish highlights, he looked a lot more like a dashing sea captain than an aristocrat.

Which was really weird, because I always thought there was some sort of rule that said British Lords had to be old and fat, and really stuffy.

Stopping just before the two men, Christine smiled and extended her hand. "You must be Lord Wythcliff..."

"Please allow me to introduce myself," she said. "I'm Christine O'Connell, Executive Vice President of the Center for Strategic Studies."

Shifting on his cane, Lord Wythcliff smiled shyly as he extended his hand. "Christine, it's so good to meet you at last..."

"And please, call me Tim." Then he grinned, and reminded her that this was America.

Chuckling, Christine promised she would. Then after turning to me, she introduced me as Dr. MacLaughlin's research assistant. "Ms. Alicia McAllister."

Which of course was entirely proper, but way off in terms of timing – because while they'd been chatting, I'd been busy imagining Lord Wythcliff in an Old Spice commercial. And as luck would have it, I had just started humming the Old Spice jingle in my head when he extended his hand.

"So pleased to meet you, Alicia..."

"A smashing piece of work, that study. The Prime Minister raved about it!"

Huh?

Thinking I must have missed something, I grasped his hand as my eyes crossed involuntarily.

"Well, uh...

"Thank you, Sir!"

Realizing how lame that must have sounded, I was in the process of making a mental note to kick myself when Two suddenly emerged from Alex's office carrying a huge box of papers Apparently engrossed in reading whatever was on top, she didn't even notice us until she reached the far side of her desk.

What followed can only be described as a "Hollywood Moment."

Suddenly aware of our presence, Two looked up at Lord Wythcliff and Lord Wythcliff looked down at Two – and as their eyes met, the heavens opened and far off in the distance a choir of angels sang. Transfixed by the moment, they stood speechless as they stared into one another's eyes.

Holy cow! I thought. *Anybody got a camera?*

Because it was just amazing – especially when Two dropped the box she was carrying on her foot, and didn't even notice.

Thud!

So I was thinking that was really funny when Alex suddenly cleared his throat, and introduced them. "Lord Wythcliff, I'd like you to meet my secretary, Jennifer Rogers."

Still speechless, Lord Wythcliff limped around her desk and extended his hand.

Looking up with eyes the size of saucers, she took his hand in both of hers. "I'm Two," she said in a husky whisper.

Oh, Gawd, I thought. *I'm gonna yak...*

But before that could happen, Christine excused us on the basis of urgent business – which Lord Wythcliff either didn't hear or chose to ignore. With his attention fixed upon Two, Christine placed her hand in the small of my back and guided me into her office.

As she silently pushed the doors shut, I looked up at her incredulously.

"Did you see that?" I whispered.

Deferring my question as a huge smile spread across her face, Christine did a little Happy Dance on the carpet. "Oh, yeah!" she finally said.

Then after looking reverently to the heavens – which in this case was actually an acoustic tile in the ceiling grid – she gave thanks to God.

Thinking she must have gone suddenly mad, I looked up at her in consternation.

"Christine!" I demanded, as I pointed toward the door. "Didn't you see that?"

Looking down at me as a huge grin stole across her face, she nodded. "*Uh-huh.*"

Then she grinned even wider. "The *perfect* solution!"

Staring at her incredulously, I shook my head. "Christine, what are you raving about?"

Looking down at me again, Christine chuckled wickedly. "Alex told me to reassign Two…

"So I'm going to ship that little trollop off to London!"

Not quite sure I if should believe my lying ears, I just stood there and stared at her while it slowly sank in. Then I cracked up completely. "Oh my God, Christine…

"You wouldn't!"

CHAPTER FORTY

But she would, and she did.

By the time Lord Wythcliff left in the early afternoon, the fix was in. Two was now Lord Wythcliff's Executive Secretary – which meant that exactly one week from the day, she was going to be his problem as well.

As things began returning to normal later that afternoon in the Executive Offices, Christine and I shared a big sigh of relief before getting back to our regularly scheduled tasks. But since everyone but Linda mysteriously vanished well before close of business, I decided to sneak out a bit early for once.

Normally, I would have felt guilty about that, but since Two was getting booted I figured a little celebration was in order. So after taking the dogs out for their evening walk, I met Jennifer at the hotel for dinner and a glass of wine. I had arrived thinking that Jennifer might be a bit disappointed by Two's imminent departure, because the two of them had occasionally hung out together. But as dinner progressed, it became clear that she was almost as happy about it as I was.

"The girl's a trip," she said as she drained her glass.

So, after figuring out my share of the bill and paying the waiter, I went back to the office to collect the dogs. After hunting all over the building, I finally found them down on the Fifth Floor where they'd cornered a mouse behind one of the oversized trashcans in the Print Shop. So after leaning over the far edge to let the terrified creature know this was his lucky day, I shooed the dogs down the hall and into one of the elevators. Having forgotten all about my Christmas stuff still locked in the vault, I headed home for a little quality time with the book Christine had lent me.

I arrived at the apartment a little after 7:30, and after making a pot of Mai Ling's tea – to which I'd become completely addicted – I plopped down on the couch and wrapped Julia's comforter around me as I opened the book. Fascinated, I finished all but the last ten pages or so before finally conking out around midnight.

Written by Alistair Manning – one of the pre-eminent biographers of the post-war era – the book was not only well-crafted but incredibly interesting as well. Starting with the legends that swirled around Captain Jean Philippe – which Manning stressed were legends, because no one really knew anything about him before he began raiding the Spanish Main – it traced Alex's family in America through the eleven generations that preceded him. Although I was disappointed that it stopped in 1961, when Alex's family had moved to Washington, I felt the vivid portrayal of the lives and times of his ancestors gave me a certain degree of insight. For the very first time, I was beginning to understand what made the Mystery Man tick.

I was still thinking about what I'd read the next morning after Christine helped me open up. So after setting up my computer – and opening my Christmas gifts, of course – I started on the data. But since I could do that in my sleep, it wasn't long before my mind began drifting back to what I'd read the night before.

The persistent familial traits that characterized the de Vris family throughout their long history in America were one of the things that intrigued me the most – because it was these traits, rather than their wealth or power, that set them apart from other distinguished American families like the Rockefellers, the Du Ponts, and the Kennedys.

The first of these familial traits was their paradoxical attitudes toward war and peace. Without exception, the de Vris' had opposed to every war America had ever fought – but once the bullets started flying, the de Vris men were always the first in line to enlist.

That didn't make much difference during the French and Indian War, because the frontier was already in flames by the time word of the conflict reached Georgia. But during the run up to the Revolutionary War, their outspoken opposition to the insurrection had led the good people of Savannah to brand them as Tory sympathizers, and there had been some rather serious talk about throwing the lot in jail.

Given the animosity that had been directed at them by their more militant neighbors, you can imagine their surprise when Arnaud Montagne de Vris – Jean Philippe's grandson – placed his sword and his ships at the disposal of the Continental Navy when word arrived that Congress had declared independence. But according to the author of the book, they were even more surprised by his two underage sons – because the moment Captain de Vris' sails disappeared over the horizon, 16-year-old Henri and his 14-year-old brother Anton ran off to join the Continental Army.

Fortunately, they all survived the war more or less unscathed. Captain de Vris lost an arm exchanging broadsides with a British Ship-of-the-Line off Newfoundland, and Henri had been grazed on the shoulder by a musket ball at Yorktown. The younger brother Anton – whom the elder de Vris had promised a whipping for following his damned fool brother – got off with a tongue lashing when he finally returned home from the war. The Manning guy who wrote the book attributed the Captain's leniency to the youth's distinguished performance at the Battle of Cowpens, and that might have been true.

But I was thinking it probably had more to do with the Captain's loss than anything else. Because let's face it – spanking the kid with one arm seemed like a practical impossibility.

Be that as it may have been, the same pattern repeated itself again with the War of 1812, the Civil War, the Spanish-American War, World War I, World War II, Korea, and Vietnam – although with occasionally more humorous results.

Here "Admiral Jack," as he was universally known, was a case in point. Because he was not only willing to stand up for what he thought was right – which according to that Manning guy, was the second of the de Vris family's recurrent traits – but riotously funny as well.

The only member of the family to ever hold public office, Jacques Binot de Vris studied law at William and Mary College in Virginia before returning to Savannah to join the local bar. The son of naval Captain Olivier Marcel de Vris of the War of 1812 fame, and the grandson of Anton the Delinquent of Revolutionary War renown, Jacques had established a thriving law practice before becoming the youngest judge ever appointed to the Circuit Court. And in fact, many of his contemporaries were convinced it was only a matter of time before he was elevated to the state Supreme Court.

But since appointments to the bench are fundamentally political in nature, his prospects were dashed by the growing tensions between North and South. In the run-up to war, his pro-Union and abolitionist sympathies aroused such ire that the Georgia state legislature had all but decided to impeach him when General Beauregard fired upon Fort Sumter – and if he hadn't resigned to join the Confederate Navy, they probably would have.

After spending eight weeks and tens of thousands of dollars of his own money retrofitting a family-owned ship for war, the newly commissioned naval commander set sail in July of 1861. Ordered south into the Caribbean, he proceeded to wreak havoc on Union commercial shipping before eventually turning north into the Atlantic, where he established his reputation as a tactical genius. Unlike other naval commanders of the day, Jacques preferred to fight at night and in the worst possible weather. Running without lights, he would suddenly emerge from fog or storm to unleash a broadside against his unsuspecting foes. Fired at point-blank range, his cannonades spread fear and panic throughout the Union Navy. For within less than a year, Jacques had captured five Union warships and sent another dozen to the bottom.

After slipping through the Union blockade with his new flotilla – now manned by Southerners recruited abroad, and a handful of foreign volunteers – Jacques sailed into his officially designated homeport of Charleston in October of 1862. Following a tumultuous welcome by the local townspeople, he was promoted to the rank of Captain and ordered back to sea. After two months of repair and re-supply, he led his flotilla out of the harbor in the dead of night and made another run for the Caribbean where he spent the remainder of the war shredding the warships sent against him and seizing Union merchantmen at sea. Auctioning off the cargos of the civilian ships in Nassau and other friendly ports, Jacques deposited untold millions into Confederate accounts abroad. Used to purchase war materiel in Britain and France, by 1863 his proceeds had become the single largest source of gold for the Confederacy.

In the meantime, Jacques' flotilla had grown to become the largest in the Confederate Navy, so in December of 1864, he was promoted to the rank of Commodore – which is what they called admirals back in those days.

But neither Admiral Jack's ships nor the treasure they captured could turn the tide of war on the ground, and in April of 1865, Lee was forced to surrender. Immediately thereafter, the Union ordered all Confederate ships still at sea to strike their colors and return to their homeports under a white flag of surrender.

After being personally served with the order by the senior Union diplomat in Jamaica, Admiral Jack reportedly unleashed a torrent of expletives "most marvelous in their creativity and invention" before personally throwing the hapless counsel overboard into the waters below. Then, after locking himself in his cabin for three days – during which time it is said he consumed the better part of a case of whisky – he finally staggered out, and ordered his crew to comply with the Union demands.

Since Admiral Jack had been a lawyer in civilian life, he had been quick to note the Union démarche hadn't specified the size of the white flag to be flown – and had said nothing at all about his sails. So when his flotilla returned to Charleston a month later, a six by eight inch flag of surrender flew from the top of their main masts. But much to the merriment of the local populace, each and every one of their sails had been painted with the Confederate Stars and Bars.

Needless to say, the Union occupation authorities were not amused. So rather than accept Admiral Jack's surrender, they marched him off to the brig instead.

Now, under almost any other circumstances, a prank like that would have got him six months of hard labor. But after Admiral Jack questioned the paternity of the presiding judge at his court-martial, the authorities threw the book at him: eight years of confinement.

But if the sentence was harsh, the circumstances of his incarceration were not. The sympathetic commandant of the improvised Union prison gave him a third story cell with a fine view of Charleston Harbor, which Admiral Jack greatly admired. And while he took breakfast and lunch with the other incorrigibles confined there, he made a point of losing a few dollars every night in the card games he played with his captors. So, when a local restaurateur turned up at the back door with a six-course gourmet meal each evening, the guards were inclined to look the other way – although they did make a habit of seizing one of the two bottles of wine and half the accompanying cigars as contraband.

Admiral Jack looked upon the guards' larceny as money well spent, and I was inclined to agree. Because in addition to the fare delivered to his cell each night, they studiously ignored the pens and ink and writing paper that he mysteriously obtained – and of course, his after-dinner brandy – and pretended not to notice as he composed his memoirs.

Smuggled out of prison and published in June of 1869, Admiral Jack's book was an overnight sensation in the North and South alike. Entitled *My War at Sea*, the detailed accounts of his naval exploits were interspersed with reflections on the nature of warfare so profound that military scholars still quote them today.

The book not only earned him a place in American folklore as "The Grey Ghost of the Seas," but a Presidential pardon as well. Released from prison in August of 1869, Admiral Jack traveled north to Washington to personally thank President Grant for his freedom before returning to Savannah to put the family's affairs in order. Then, just before the first winter snow, he embarked on a nation-wide speaking tour to promote his memoir and, incidentally, to assist in the process of post-war reconciliation. Astonished to learn the Confederacy's greatest naval hero had not only been a Unionist but an abolitionist as well, many Northerners were persuaded to look upon the South in an entirely new light.

Although there was no question that he could have easily won a Senate seat or even the governorship of Georgia, Admiral Jack resisted the siren call of politics. Instead, he devoted the rest of his life to public speaking, and promoting the cause of national unity. And somewhere along the way, he found the time to write another two books on strategy and tactics that are still studied at the Naval War College today.

But it turned out that Admiral Jack wasn't the only jailbird in the de Vris family – because Cousin Willy, as he has come to be known, did him one better.

The only son of Admiral Jack's youngest half-sister, Marie Anne de Vris, and her husband, James Bedford Allen, Cousin Willy had attended prep school in Virginia before implausibly enrolling at Harvard to study Divinity. But his academic career was cut short after he locked a diarrheic cow in the Dean's office over a holiday weekend. Expelled from the institution after one of his classmates ratted on him, Cousin Willy decided to seek his fortune out West rather than return home in shame. To no one's surprise, he took up cards to make ends meet.

Now, much has been made of the de Vris' willingness to take risks, and in fact the guy who wrote the book identified that willingness as the third of their distinctive familial traits. That may be true when it comes to other endeavors, but believe me when I tell you it just doesn't apply to cards, dice, or any other so-called game of chance. Because when a de Vris sits down and puts his money on the table, you can bet your boots he's got the game rigged sixteen ways to Sunday.

And since cheating at cards seems to be as deeply imprinted in the de Vris family genes as their other more laudable traits, Cousin Willy had amassed a small fortune by the time the Spanish-American War broke out. So upon hearing that his old classmate Teddy Roosevelt was raising a volunteer cavalry unit, Cousin Willy headed south into what was then called the Indian Territory to enlist.

Having achieved the exalted rank of corporal, Cousin Willy received a meritorious citation for bravery during the charge up San Juan Hill before eventually mustering out as a buck sergeant.

And since he had more or less redeemed himself through his courageous deeds, most of the de Vris family was prepared to welcome him home after the war.

But it seems that Cousin Willy had other plans, because he dropped out of sight for almost a decade before finally turning up at a saloon just outside Santa Fe.

That proved to be an unfortunate choice of venue, because there was an exchange of gunfire after one of the locals accused him of cheating in a poker game. So when the smoke cleared, Cousin Willy found himself in jail facing capital charges. And even though he swore up and down that he'd only fired in self-defense, neither the judge nor the jury was inclined to believe him. But in fairness, the reporters who covered the trial thought that probably had something to do with the fact that the magistrate and eight of the jurors were kin to the deceased.

Since that hardly seemed right, the de Vris' sent a whole team of Philadelphia lawyers out west to draft an appeal to a higher court. Unfortunately, neither their appeal nor their subsequent plea for the Governor's clemency was favorably received, so Cousin Willy's last hope was a Presidential pardon. But since President Taft had never forgiven Cousin Willy for a swindle some twenty or so years before, just about everyone figured his goose was cooked.

But the night before the hanging, someone started a ruckus in the saloon, and while the sheriff and his deputies were busy breaking it up, somebody blew up the jail. After the bits and pieces of bricks and mortar finished falling from the sky, the sheriff and his men started the long task of sorting through the wreckage for Cousin Willy. But after finding what was left of his watch a day or two later, and then one of his boots all covered in blood and gore the day after, they chalked it up as a jail break gone bad. Figuring justice had been done, the Sheriff declared Cousin Willy legally dead.

And that probably would have been the end of it, had it not been for the fact that an occasional correspondent for *The New York Times* managed to get lost in a blinding snowstorm at the far end of Patagonia some years later. Pulled from a snowdrift by an expatriate rancher who claimed to be of French origin, the sometimes-journalist spent more than a month at his benefactor's sprawling hacienda recovering from the effects of frostbite and exposure. Although deeply grateful to the man who saved his life, he couldn't help but notice the subtle discrepancies that cast doubt upon the rancher's story. For one thing, the supposed former Parisian spoke French with a decidedly North American accent, and for another, he kept a faded photograph of a much younger man on his fireplace mantle. Dressed in an American uniform and standing next to Colonel Theodore Roosevelt, the journalist couldn't help but notice the soldier bore a striking resemblance to his host.

But by then the world had moved on, and after returning to the United States the writer felt justified in maintaining his silence. By the time he finally published the story a month or so before his death in 1940, it was no more than a curiosity. As far as the law was concerned, Cousin Willy was a one-paragraph entry in a dusty register. In any event, Monsieur LaChance, as the rancher had called himself, had long since departed this earth. And so aside from the journalist, there was no one left alive who cared about Cousin Willy one way or another.

That had seemed somehow poignant to me when I'd first read it, but I'd put that particular story aside in order to follow the rest of the de Vris line. The chapters on Alex's grandfather and father especially intrigued me, because according to the author, they exemplified the last two of the de Vris family's enduring traits, which were, respectively, loyalty and integrity. For over the centuries, they'd established a well-deserved reputation for standing by their friends through thick and thin. And, by all accounts, they were unfailingly honest...

Well, as long as you don't try to play cards with them, anyways...

But I have to tell you – the vignettes about the de Vris women woven into each chapter were, like, *totally* cool.

It seems that Eleanor Elizabeth Montford de Vris – who was Jean Philippe's wife, and the first of the de Vris women in America – had not only been smart, tough, and headstrong, but an amazingly independent woman as well. And since almost all the girls in the family who followed were just like her, it appeared that she had left an indelible genetic impression on the female side. But what I found even more amazing was that she had, in some mysterious way, cast a continuing influence over her male descendants as well. For the next eleven generations, they'd all married women very much like her.

Which I thought was incredibly fascinating, as I banged away on my keyboard. But before I could explore that particular twist any further, a sudden insight sent me bolt upright in my chair. In addition to the fact that the de Vris men liked their women smart, tough, headstrong and independent, they had a thing for redheads as well. So after hurriedly running my hands through my hair, I jabbed the SAVE button on the keyboard before snatching up the phone and dialing Raphael's number.

Since I'd missed my last appointment while I was sick, I figured it was a safe bet he was going to throw another one of his hissy fits. So as the phone began ringing on the other end of the line, I was trying to guesstimate how much groveling I was going to have to do to get back in his good graces.

At least a week of utterly shameless flattery, I concluded. *Not to mention a bottle of really good wine...*

But to my utter amazement, his receptionist – the one with the orange and pink and purple punk hairstyle – was actually nice to me when she finally answered the phone. So after going on and on about how worried Raphael had been when he'd found out I was ill, she penciled me in for the next week before making this really weird kissing noise into the mouthpiece and hanging up.

Thinking that girl just *had* to be the strangest person I'd ever met, I stared at the mouthpiece for a long moment before finally hanging it up. Then after shaking my head back and forth a couple of times, I started banging on the keyboard again.

After about fifteen minutes of that, my mind had started slipping away again when an unexpected knock jerked me back to reality. Startled, I looked up to find Mai Ling standing in the doorway holding the book she had borrowed.

Delighted to see her, I jumped up from my desk and rushed over to greet her.

"Mai Ling!" I said excitedly. "What are you *doing* here?"

Smiling shyly, she held out *Murder in the White House*. "Finish last night," she said as her eyes opened wide. "So I bring back story."

After taking the paperback from her outstretched hand and telling her how glad I was she'd enjoyed it, I apologized for not asking her into my office. "Security protocol," I explained in a soft whisper.

After smiling a conspiratorial smile, Mai Ling nodded. "Linda already tell, *verrry* secret work..."

Then as her eyes opened wide, she grinned and said it must be exciting.

Pressing the book to my chest, I leaned back against the door jamb and pursed my lips. Mindful of the fact that I'd been promised about twenty years' worth of free lodgings in a federal penitentiary if I so much as breathed a word about the project – and frankly unwilling to admit just how mundane it actually was – I suppressed the smile that was trying to creep across my face.

"No comment," I finally said.

Mai Ling chuckled and told me that was all right. "Use to dat," she said. "Know Alex years now, he never say about work."

Then after pursing her lips together, she nodded to no one in particular. "Like dat big stone cat in Egypt...

"Always look, never say."

Then suddenly changing the subject, she told me she had to get back to her office right away. "Left tricky 'speriment running wit lab assistant. Have to supervise las stage."

"But you read story," she said as her eyes opened wide again. "*Verrry exciting!*"

So after I promised to start on it that night, she placed her hands together and gave me a little bow. "I thank you," she said, before making a run for the elevators.

Feeling very pleased that Mai Ling had come by the office, I was thinking I should ask her to lunch sometime as I sat back down at my desk. Placing the book off to the side, I hit the SAVE button again. After first checking my watch, and then standing halfway up in my seat to make sure no one was watching from the reception area, I began reviewing the data.

I'd been aggregating and disaggregating the data ever since Alex and Dr. MacLaughlin had suddenly perked up during one of my Friday presentations. But for the life of me, I couldn't figure out what had caught their attention. After analyzing that particular data set at least a hundred different ways, I hadn't come up with a thing. So after finally concluding that whatever it was they'd picked up on couldn't possibly have been contained within that particular batch, I'd hypothesized that it wasn't that particular data set *per se*, but rather some sort of pattern it had brought into focus. But whatever it was, it had slipped right past me – which was like, *really* irritating.

So whenever I was more or less caught up – and I was sure no one was looking – I'd been working on a relational data base program, so I could sort the data fields from the various projects to search for overlaps and commonalities.

President Reagan liked to tell this story about a man who encountered a young boy digging through a big pile of horse manure with a pitchfork. Puzzled by the kid's behavior, the man asked him what he was doing. "Well, Sir," the boy replied. "This here pile's so big, I figure there just has to be a pony in there somewhere."

For the past five weeks or so, I'd felt a lot like the kid in the President's story. *Keep banging away*, I told myself, *and you're bound to find something*. But by the time I finished the data base program and worked all the bugs out of it, I was beginning to wonder.

So after loading it in the machine and pushing the RUN button, I leaned back in my chair and began wondering again about what Alex and Dr. MacLaughlin had picked up on. But as the little bar that tracked the machine's progress popped up on the screen and started blinking, I suddenly made an intuitive leap.

With the hair on the back of my neck suddenly standing upright, my eyes frantically searched for the ghostly presence that had somehow crept into my office. There was nothing there – or at least nothing I could see…

But I could *feel* something dark and ghastly, lurking just beyond my awareness.

Scared out of my wits, I gripped the edge of my desk with both hands. Desperately wanting to flee from the unseen evil, I was on the verge of panic when some sort of supernatural force seized control of my body, and forced me to turn ever so slowly toward the paperback I'd so casually laid aside.

Then as the blood ran cold in my veins, I gasped. *Oh dear God*, I thought…

They wouldn't…

CHAPTER FORTY-ONE

As I sat there transfixed, my body temperature plummeted and beads of cold sweat began forming on my forehead. Without thinking, I reflexively wrapped my arms across my chest as fear washed across my body.

Then I began to quake.

Because if the Bad Guys found out I knew – or if they even suspected I knew – I was dead as a doornail.

Now death is not something that the average twenty-something contemplates very often, and I had hardly thought about it at all. Having barely crossed the threshold into adulthood, it seemed a distant, and at times, implausible possibility. But as I sat behind my desk trembling, it suddenly became all too real…

And I wondered how it would come.

An auto "accident," so-called? Or perhaps a bullet through the head, in an apparent robbery gone wrong?

Then as a tear ran down my cheek, I wondered if it would hurt or if I'd even know…

It's not fair, I thought in bitter despair. *I'm only twenty-two!*

I don't know how long I sat there shaking, but I think it was a long time. But it wasn't until a little voice from the back of my mind assailed my cowardice that my composure began to return.

Pull yourself together, it demanded. *And stop being such a wimp…*

Do you think Alex cries and trembles every time the Bad Guys go after him?

No, I thought bitterly, as I wiped another tear from my eye. *But Alex is a de Vris – he was born to greatness…*

And I'm just a girl from a two-stoplight town in the backwoods of Connecticut.

Having stilled the little voice with my rebuttal, I shook my head and sighed before placing it between my folded hands. *Dear God*, I thought. *How did I get in this mess?*

Still deathly afraid, I got up stiffly and lurched to the double doors on wooden legs. Pushing them halfway shut, I made my way back to my desk and sat down to weigh my options.

I desperately wanted to go home to Glen Meadows and just pretend that none of this had ever happened – that I'd never come to Washington, that I'd never met Alex, and that I'd never taken the job at the CSS.

But for once, my rational consciousness and my survival instinct were in complete agreement: running just wasn't an option.

Kinda like sending them a telegram, I thought...

Dear Bad Guys...I know what you're up to, come get me...

By now disgusted, angry, and still gripped by fear, I spent the next hour just sitting there trying to think my way out of the box.

By any reasonable standard, I should go to Alex and lay it all out the first chance I got.

But if I'm right, he already knows – he's known from the very beginning, and so has Dr. MacLaughlin...

You were thinking that the idea was to uncover the Bad Guys, and catch 'em in the act...

But it's really a trap...

A trick designed to flush them out of the bushes and force their hand, and Alex is the bait...

So why go and stick your neck out? Doesn't it make more sense to just play stupid?

Well, yeah, I thought as I looked up at the clock. The day had somehow slipped away, and it was already well past 5 pm. So I punched the SAVE button and typed in the SHUT-DOWN command. Then moving stiffly, I got up and began unhooking all the cords before loading up my carts.

But how do you do that?

Because let's face it – there was no way I could pass myself off for Wilbur, the parking garage attendant.

And what makes you think they don't know that you know?

Desperately praying the computer hadn't been bugged – because if it was, it wouldn't take a rocket scientist to figure out what I was up to – I popped the deliberately mislabeled data base program out of the CPU, and hid it in a stack of papers. Then I loaded the unit onto the cart and pushed it into the vault. After shoving the data cart in behind it, I pushed the heavy door shut, and jammed the SECURE button with my index finger.

Still lost somewhere deep within my own thoughts, I shuffled over to the coat stand and pulled on my heavy woolen overcoat, my mittens, and the really cute 1920s-style flapper hat I'd worn to work that day, before stuffing the paperback in my briefcase and setting off in search of the dogs.

By the time I got home an hour and a half later, I was exhausted and my nerves were completely shot. I'd taken Big Minh and Lady Godiva for their usual walk up to the Capitol and back, which took 20 minutes or so – and given the number of Capitol Police that patrolled the grounds, I'd felt reasonably safe. But on the way home, some jerk smashed his Cadillac Coupe De Ville into a UPS truck at Dupont Circle, so I spent the better part of an hour nervously looking around as I sat stalled in a massive traffic jam.

Someone could walk up and blow my brains out in this mess, and no one would even notice...

So by the time I walked through the apartment door, I was on the verge of coming unglued again. Completely exhausted by the stress of it all, I changed into a clean pair of sweats and curled up on the couch under Julia's comforter. With the dogs and the locks and the stainless steel stopper Nguyen's locksmith had installed, I didn't think they were going to come crashing through my door while I slept. But just to make sure, I got up and rooted through the trash for empty Diet Pepsi cans. After retrieving almost 20 of them from the bin, I stacked them up in a little pyramid against the door before crawling back onto the couch.

Convinced that the cans would make a God-awful racket if the door was forced, I slipped into a fitful and uneasy sleep.

At least I'll be awake when they get me...

I awoke early the next morning, still exhausted and with dark circles under my eyes. But my mind was clear, and far more focused. After examining Julia's knives in the kitchen drawer, I picked one of medium size. Then after breaking two pencils in half and securing them just below the blade with a couple of feet of looped and twisted twine, I wrapped the newly fashioned guard with strapping tape. After checking the balance by resting it on my finger, I nodded in self-satisfaction.

Not exactly the best weapon for hand-to-hand combat, I thought as I slipped it into the pouch of my sweatshirt. *But it will do for now...*

Then I disassembled my little pyramid of Diet Pepsi cans at the door, and stacked them off to the side before taking the dogs out to the bushes in the pre-dawn light.

After a nervous and deeply unsettling two or three minutes just outside the apartment building, I shooed the dogs back inside. Then after carefully locking the apartment door behind me, and reinserting the stopper, I fired up the coffee pot and popped a couple of slices of cinnamon toast into the toaster oven. Since I'd moved in with Julia, I'd fallen into the habit of skipping breakfast – but given the circumstances, I figured I might need the extra energy.

Hit the low-lifes hard, and run like hell...

Then after gorging on the cinnamon toast and slamming down two overlarge mugs of coffee, I headed for the shower.

Since I'd gotten up way early, I washed my hair and wrapped myself in oversized towels before spending a leisurely half-hour perched on the edge of the tub shaving my legs. Then after carefully washing them off, I traipsed over to my downstairs closet to pick out my outfit and shoes.

During the winter months I usually wore mini-skirts and hose to show off my legs, but as often as not Christine turned up wearing boots underneath a gorgeous full-length skirt. Normally belted at the waist, they looked spectacular on her and I just loved the look. So even though I didn't have her figure, I'd hunted all over town until I'd found an ankle-length, chocolate brown A-line I could wear.

Might slow me down a bit if I have to run, I thought. *But it's perfect for a side-kick to the knee, or a round-kick to the head...*

Satisfied with the trade-off, I marched upstairs to the loft to lay out my skirt and shoes and retrieve an off-white cashmere turtleneck from my dresser, before heading back downstairs and investing an inordinate amount of time on my hair and makeup.

Because if I'm going to die – I'm gonna look really good!

Finally content with the look, I went back upstairs and finished dressing before gathering up my stuff for work. Then, after wrapping the point of my knife in tissue paper so I wouldn't poke a hole in my overcoat pocket, I pulled on my winter gear and hustled the dogs out the doors, around the corner and into the car.

But I have to tell you – driving to work that morning was just plain *weird*.

For the first mile or so, I kept glancing in the rear view mirror to see if anyone was following me. But the closer I got to the office the stranger it became – because as I gradually came to realize, the mass of humanity that clogged the road with rush-hour traffic were just ordinary people going about their daily lives.

There must be a million people on their way to work right now, I thought. *And not one of them has a clue...*

A couple of days, a couple of weeks, maybe a couple of months – their whole world is going to be turned upside down and they haven't the slightest inkling...

Then after biting my lip as I turned into the alleyway that led to the parking garage, I wondered if they'd even realize what had happened. Lost in thought, I didn't even notice when Wilbur waved me a cheery good morning.

Aside from the fact that Wilbur sat at the gate all day long and monitored who came and went from the garage, there were at least a half-dozen security cameras down there and Christine had assured me that the security guys monitored them carefully. So once I pulled into the garage, I breathed a deep sigh of relief.

I felt even better after I entered the building because I ran into one of the CIA security officers at the elevator and then another one – the really cute one who Christine thought was adorable – in the hallway just outside the Executive Offices. But since we weren't supposed to even talk to them, I smiled and gave him a little wave as he passed by.

Once inside the big double doors, I stopped and did a double take. Aside from the fact that Two wasn't there – she had the week off to pack up her gear before moving to London – the doors to Alex's and Christine's offices were both closed. Puzzled, I asked Linda what was up.

Glancing up from her keyboard, Linda informed me that Alex was at the White House going over a speech that President Reagan was going to deliver in St. Paul the next day and Christine was attending a meeting on Capitol Hill. And for what it was worth, she added, Dr. MacLaughlin was over at the Federal Reserve Bank for something or another.

So after looking around at the deserted office again, I scrunched up my nose and asked her who was in charge.

Smiling sweetly, she informed me that she was. "At least until Christine gets back, anyway."

Well, kewl, I thought.

So after glancing around to make sure no one was in the hall listening, I leaned over her desk and whispered. "Linda, I need a big favor…

"I have to go out for a couple of hours, and I need you to cover for me."

Taken aback, Linda stared at me for just a moment before promising she would. "But what's going on?"

After glancing around again, I shook my head. "It's kind of an emergency situation, and I can't tell anyone…

"But trust me – it's *really* important."

So after shrugging, Linda said OK. "Just be here by 11:30, because Christine's supposed to be back by then."

After promising I would, I hung up my hat and coat and stowed my gear in my office. Then after slipping my knife into a sheath of papers, I palmed a roll of duct tape and headed to the ladies' room. After slipping into a stall and locking the door behind me, I fashioned a makeshift sheath for the knife from the papers that had hidden it before pulling up my skirt and taping it to my inner thigh. Satisfied after practicing the movement I'd have to make to draw the blade, I left the tape on the toilet and headed for accounting.

Finding Julia at her desk, I very quietly told her that I had to speak with her in private. Concerned, Julia got up and followed me out into the hallway.

"You have access to the petty cash, right?"

Nodding as she knitted her eyebrows together, Julia asked me what was up. "I can't tell you," I said. "But I need to borrow $200 from the cash box for a couple of hours – until after lunch."

After studying my face for a long moment, Julia shrugged and said "Sure." But since her boss wouldn't even count it until just before close of business, she told me to take my time. "As long as you have it back here before 5:30, no problem."

Then I told her I needed one more favor. "I need to borrow your coat and your hat, if you wore one."

At that point, Julia looked at me like I was crazy. "Is this part of that weird project you're working on?"

After glancing around to make sure no one else was in the hallway, I nodded. "But don't you dare tell anyone, OK? It's *really* important."

So after promising me that her lips were sealed, she pulled the two hundred bucks out of the cash box, and pointed at her coat and hat hanging against the wall. "Take care of the coat," she whispered. "It cost me $300!"

After thanking her, I struggled into her winter coat and pulled her knit hat down low over my eyes. Then I stuffed the wad of bills in the left coat pocket, and headed for the stairs.

Emerging on the ground floor three minutes later, I pushed through the double doors and hailed a cab. "The corner of Eighth and H streets, please."

At the time, Eighth and H was Washington's most notorious outdoor drug market, so it was no surprise when the cabbie did a double take and asked me if I was sure I wanted to go there. After insisting that I knew what I was doing, he shrugged and told me to get in.

Less than five minutes later, he pulled to a stop in front of a boarded-up shop. "That'll be six bucks, lady."

Thinking it was an outrage that he was charging me that much for a trip that was barely two miles, I gave him a disgusted look and flipped him a ten. As I clambered out the door, I told him to keep the change.

So far — so good, I thought as I looked around at the street toughs lounging on the corner. *If the Bad Guys were following me this morning, they're probably still watching the alleyway...*

Waiting for a redhead — well, sort of — in a dark gray coat and a black beret to come barreling out the garage in the Vette...

Instead of me coming out the front door wearing a red coat and contrasting pink knit hat.

Feeling very pleased with myself, I marched up to the big tall guy with a cigarette dangling from the corner of his mouth. "So who's in charge here?" I demanded to know.

Not quite sure he had heard me correctly, he paused before responding. "What the hell do you care, bitch?"

Standing my ground, I tilted my head up and looked Ghetto Dude square in the eye. "I want to know because I came down here to do a little business...."

"So are you gonna tell me or not?"

Chuckling, he tossed his cigarette on the sidewalk. "That depends, girl..."

"If you want to sell that scrawny white butt of yours, you talk to my man LeRoy. But for anything else, you talk to me."

Now normally I would have taken offense at that kind of language. But the way I figure it, anyone who thinks my butt's scrawny can't be all bad. So I nodded instead, and said OK. "But this is private — the rest of your friends don't need to hang around."

After jerking his head at the others, he waited until they moved on down toward the bus stop.

"So what are you looking for, girl? Weed, maybe a little cocaine?"

After glancing around to make sure no one was in earshot, I told him no. "I want a four inch stiletto, a smallish set of brass knuckles that will fit my hand, and one of those flat wide-blade throwing knives with a modified metal guard...

"Four inches from tip to hilt, no more, no less."

Ghetto Dude looked at me like I was crazy. "What's a white bitch like you want with all that hardware?"

Giving him a steely look, I told him it was none of his business. But if the stuff miraculously appeared in the next ten minutes, he was going to walk away a hundred bucks richer.

"A hundred bucks? Forget it, *bitch*...

"That'll cost you two hundred."

After giving him a disgusted look, I told him I could get the stuff on any street corner for a buck and a quarter. "Get real, Jack, or I'm outta here."

So after giving me a threatening stare, Ghetto Dude demanded $150 – half up front, half on delivery.

"Not a chance, mister. Twenty now, the rest when you get back."

After mulling it over, he asked how he could be sure I wasn't a cop. Chuckling, I told him the DC cops carried nine-millimeter semi-automatics. After sliding my hand in my pocket, I told him I was packing a thirty-two snub nose instead. "But it's loaded with hollow points, so I can mess you up good if you jack me around."

I was bluffing of course, but there was no way for him to know that. So after giving me a wary look, he told me to give him the twenty. "You wait over there, across the street."

Nodding, I palmed a twenty in my other pocket and slipped it into the hand hanging at his side. "You've got ten minutes."

After glancing around, he vanished into the alley, and after making sure he was gone, I turned around and walked across the street. Leaning up against the building, I suddenly realized that I must have looked a lot like one of the working girls H Street had become famous for. Chuckling at the stares I was getting from the passing cars, I lifted my right foot up and placed it against the bricks behind me. I was still laughing at the imagery when a scruffy-looking white guy walked up and propositioned me.

Now under almost any other circumstances, that would have cracked me up. But since I could tell he was dead serious, I gave him a dangerous look instead. "More than you're gonna make in a lifetime, fool…

"So get the hell out of here before my pimp comes back and kicks your sorry ass."

Shocked and obviously frightened, he mumbled an apology and shuffled off.

I was trying to decide if lounging against the wall like that was really a good idea when my business associate suddenly reappeared in the alleyway across the street – so I pushed myself off the bricks and crossed the street against the light. "Got the stuff?"

"Yeah, I got it – so gimme the money."

"Oh, no," I said. "Toss it on the ground in front of you so I can take a look at it."

After glancing around, he protested. "You're crazy, bitch! The cops are all over this corner."

"So back into the alley, and do it there."

Disgusted, he took a couple of steps backwards – cursing me all the way. But once he was in the shadows, he laid the stuff out on the ground where I could see it.

"Now back up a couple more steps," I said as I pulled six twenties and a ten out of my pocket. After folding them over twice and creasing them a couple of times, I tossed them beyond my newly acquired arsenal. "Now you're gonna stand there while I pick this stuff up and inspect it, and then you're gonna keep standing there until I disappear...

"Got it?" Just to make sure, I slipped my hand back into my right pocket again and gestured with it.

Looking disgusted, Ghetto Dude turned away. So after going down on one knee, I tested the stiletto before slipping the brass knuckles on my hand. "Nice," I said. "I like the feel."

Then I stuffed the two knives and the knuckles into my left coat pocket, and told him it had been a pleasure doing business as I backed out of the alley.

"You got a name, girl?"

Nodding, I grinned and dropped my voice a couple of octaves. *"Bond,"* I said. *"James Bond."*

Snickering, he nodded. "Yeah, well it looks like your white ass is in a world of trouble, 007...

"So if you ever want to trade up on that popgun you got in your pocket, you jus' come back and see Bobby, ya hear?"

After promising I'd keep him in mind, I stepped backward out of the alley way and onto the sidewalk before suddenly turning on my heel and marching away. Relieved to find myself alive and still in one piece, I flagged down a cab and told him to take me to Union Station.

Because if they saw me leave the building in the cab, I thought, *returning on foot oughta fry their minds...*

Or at least I hoped it would.

After stopping at the hotel to bum one of the plastic bags Raphael gave customers when they bought hair gel or shampoo from his salon – so I could sneak my new hardware into the office without anyone seeing the contraband – I took the elevator up to the Eighth Floor and slipped into the ladies' room. Finding the tape in the stall where I had left it, I stripped the improvised dagger from my thigh and replaced it with the new four-inch throwing knife. Then after taking the stairs back down to accounting, I returned Julia's coat and hat before bounding back up the stairs to the Eighth Floor. Rolling into the Executive Offices at precisely 10:33, I had almost an entire hour to spare.

Linda was talking to someone on the phone, but as I approached her desk she stuck up her index finger and signaled for me to wait. After she finally informed the caller that she would make sure Mrs. O'Connell got the message, she returned the handset to the cradle. "I forgot to tell you about Friday," she said. "Christine's organizing a going away party for Two at the hotel, and she wants all the girls to kick in $10 for a going away present."

Thinking ten bucks was a small price to pay for getting rid of her, I laughed and promised to kick in twenty. "But I have to run to the bank first, and cash a check."

So after strolling into my office and discretely transferring the stiletto, the brass knuckles, and my improvised dagger into my shoulder bag, I pulled on my beret and my coat and headed down the stairs again. Fortunately, my bank had a branch just around the corner, so it only took me fifteen minutes to cash the check, return the $200 to Julia, and fork over the promised twenty to Linda. "Glad to contribute to such a worthy cause," I said. "But as far Two's party goes – one glass of wine, and I'm gone."

Chuckling, Linda nodded. "You and everyone else," she said. "She's not exactly Ms. Popularity, you know."

Then after reminding me I was the Designated Coffee Maker, she ordered me to get my rear into the galley and make a pot before she went into withdrawal. Throwing her a snappy salute, I said, "Yes, Ma'am!" before retreating from her view.

Fifteen minutes and a half-cup of *Alicia's Finest* later, Christine finally turned up and helped me open the vault. So after pulling my carts into place and hooking everything up, I sat down at my desk and started banging on the keyboard. Since the project had by then taken on an almost surrealistic quality, I had to keep reminding myself over and over again that my safety and survival depended on playing stupid.

As my mood darkened, my mind whipsawed back and forth with growing anger. Blaming Alex for my predicament one minute and myself the next, I completely lost track of time. In fact, it wasn't until the dogs trotted in with their empty bowls clenched between their teeth that I realized it was almost 6 pm.

"*All right*," I said as I got up to feed them. "I *got* the message."

As I was filling up their bowls, I suddenly realized that I was hungry, too. So after retrieving my shoulder bag from the back of my chair, I headed down the hall to the canteen. After stocking up on Ho Hos, corn curls, and cheese and peanut butter crackers, I beat the soda machine until it finally surrendered my Diet Pepsi.

Thinking the stupid machine had it coming for trying to steal my quarters again, I was really hoping Christine wouldn't figure out who put the fist-sized dent into it when I settled back into my chair. So after opening and closing my hand a half dozen time to work the pain out of it, I popped the top of my drink and ripped open the Ho Hos.

Then having surrendered to one temptation, I promptly fell victim to another. Knowing full well I that I was taking my life in my hands, I reloaded the data base program I'd designed to sort what I called "overlaps" – numeric designations that identified stuff like which bank the checks were drawn on, and the vendors that must have cashed them. Then I hit the RUN button again.

Back in those days, computers were a lot slower than they are today and it wasn't uncommon to wait three or four or even five minutes for the machine to load a complicated program. So after the little box containing the progress bar appeared on the screen, I leaned back in my chair and polished off my junk food. Then after *that* box was replaced by another announcing the data base program had been successfully loaded, I bent over the keyboard and started typing.

Satisfied with my logic, I pulled a pad of graph paper out of my desk and began my first data-sort. Drawing an X-Y axis on the paper, I began systematically sorting and re-sorting the data every way I could think of to create a scatter plot, two data fields at a time – carefully recording which project I had sorted and what data fields I'd used, and how the data had fallen out, before penciling in the results. Totally absorbed by the process, I lost all sense of time and place.

In fact, it wasn't until I heard Alex making a fresh pot of coffee in the galley that I became aware of my surroundings again.

Suddenly angry that he hadn't even bothered to say hello, I turned my attention to the charts I'd constructed. Since the Black Budget projects were supposed to be completely separate in order to complicate any effort to trace them back to their true origins, I should have ended up with a series of dots running along a 45-degree slope from the left vertical axis to the right horizontal – and that turned out to be more or less the case.

Thinking that couldn't possibly explain why Alex and Dr. MacLaughlin had reacted to that one data set way back when, I decided to fudge by adding a third variable and re-plotting the whole thing in three dimensions, rather than two. That took a while, and since three dimensions are a lot harder to plot on two-dimensional paper, I had to graph the whole thing in my head. After the first four or five tries produced gibberish, I froze as a pattern emerged from the seemingly random relationships.

"*Uh-oh,*" I whispered.

Because I'd just found something that *definitely* wasn't supposed to be there.

Now even after all these years, I can't tell you exactly what I'd uncovered – because Black Budget projects are the Intelligence Community's version of the Crown Jewels, and I'd end up busting rocks in the Big House if I did. So let's just say *someone* had taken a great big project and hidden it in the Black Budget, by breaking it up into little itty-bitty pieces.

And after the freaky experience I'd had the day before, I was pretty sure I knew why they'd done it.

So after leaning back in my chair and taking a really deep breath, I typed in the print command and sent the whole file to the laser printer. As it formatted the pages, I tore another sheet of graph paper from the pad, and made a rough reconstruction of the three dimensional chart I'd traced in my mind.

When the last page fell from the machine, I placed my graph on top and clamped it together with a binder clip. Knowing that I'd really put my foot in it this time, I got up from my desk, took another deep breath, and marched through the galley to Alex's office.

Oscillating between mind-numbing fear and righteous anger, I stopped just inside his door as he looked up to greet me. Holding out the sheath of papers, I demanded to know who was behind the plot I'd uncovered.

Now most people wouldn't have noticed as Alex shifted into his detached and coolly professional spy mode – but by then I was one of the few people in the world who knew him well enough catch the transition. So as his eyebrows rose to mask his surprise, I watched him tilt his head ever so slightly.

"I'm not sure what you're talking about, Alicia."

Outraged by his denial, I screamed at him. "That's horse poop, Alex!

"They're going to kill the President and take over the government," I snarled. "And I want to know who the hell they are!"

By now hidden behind an impassive gaze, Alex leaned back in his chair. "We're not sure," he said softly.

Livid, I slammed my foot down on the floor and hurled the bundled papers at him.

"DON'T LIE TO ME, ALEX!"

And then as the papers arced toward their intended target, my eyes were for some inexplicable reason drawn to the clock on the far wall. It said 10 o'clock.

"But that can't be right," I whispered. *"It's just before midnight."*

CHAPTER FORTY-TWO

Still fixated on the clock, I didn't notice as Alex batted the thick bundle aside. Momentarily entranced, I didn't even realize what I'd done until the clamped papers cartwheeled across the floor. Then suddenly aware of the affront I'd given, I threw up my hands in horror.

"*Oh my God, Alex, I'm so sorry...*"

"*I didn't mean it – I swear, I didn't mean it!*"

Thinking I had just made what Washingtonians call a "Career-Ending Move," I stood there shocked and humiliated, and waited for the axe to fall. But rather than fire me, Alex shrugged dismissively.

"You need to work on that pitch," he said. "You throw like a girl."

What???????

As my jaw dropped, another wave of anger washed over me – because back home in Glen Meadows, I'd been the star pitcher of our neighborhood sandlot team, and I had a record that would have made Nolan Ryan green with envy.

Six winning seasons, I growled to myself. *That's S-I-X, Mister – you count 'em!*

And since I'd pounded Johnny Winters about three feet into the schoolyard for saying that to me in eighth grade – and almost gotten expelled for it – I was on the verge of storming over Alex's desk and punching his lights out, when I suddenly realized what he was up to.

Seething, I balled up my fists and slammed my foot down on the floor.

"*You jerk!*" I sputtered. "*You're just trying to divert my attention again!*"

Chuckling as he rose from his chair, Alex said he'd been wondering when I'd finally get wise to that particular trick. Then he grasped his coffee mug and told me he needed a refill. "May I bring you a cup?"

I was about to tell him that I could get my own darn coffee, when it occurred to me that was the very least he could do after insulting me like that. So I nodded instead, and told him how I liked it. "A touch of cream," I said in my most haughty voice. "And two Sweet-N-Lows."

I was still standing when he returned a minute or two later. So after handing me a cup, he gestured toward one of the leather-bound chairs in front of his desk. As I seated myself, he walked around his desk and settled into his own chair. Pulling a crumpled pack of Marlboros out of his of his vest pocket, he shook one free before putting the filtered end into his mouth, and lit it with an elegant silver lighter.

After inhaling deeply, Alex placed the hand holding the cigarette on his desk. Then after gazing at me for a long, disconcerting moment, he commended me. "That was a brilliant exercise in deduction," he said.

With an acute sense of discomfort now added to my anxiety and fear, I looked down at the floor before crossing my legs and tugging on my skirt. "So I'm right," I said softly before looking up.

Alex took another deep draw from his cigarette, before exhaling slowly. "As far as we have been able to ascertain."

Looking down again, I studied the floor for a long moment. Then as the tears began welling in my eyes, I looked up and asked again. "So who *are* they?"

Alex raised his eyebrows as he shrugged his shoulders. "Their critics usually refer to them as 'The Financial Elite," and that's a more or less accurate description...

"But the financial media – *The Wall Street Journal, Forbes*, and other specialized financial publications – usually refer to them collectively as 'the bond market,' which is a great deal more informative in terms of their core interests and motives...

"And the organizations and institutions they've created or control as "the Establishment"...

"Over the past century, they've established a dozen or so front organizations and for the most part they work their will through them...

"The Ford and Rockefeller foundations, for domestic policy and especially education...

"The Carnegie Endowment for International Peace and the Council on Foreign Relations for foreign policy generally, with the CFR focused on European policy particularly...

"The Trilateral Commission for Asian Policy, and the Bilderberger Group for global financial issues...

"And of course, the newspapers and media outlets they own, and the politicians they've bought."

Intensely focused on the Financial Elite thing, the bit about the Establishment slipped past me altogether. *"The bond market?"* I said incredulously.

After taking another sip of his coffee, Alex nodded before stubbing his cigarette in the ashtray.

"Yeah…

"The people that buy and broker large-scale debt."

As I tilted my head over, I leaned forward and stared at him in disbelief. "But why would they want to kill the President?"

Shaking my head, I told him I just didn't get it.

Alex nodded. "Few people do…

"It's probably the world's best kept secret." Then after lighting another cigarette, Alex asked me what I knew about "political economy."

Huh?

Seeing the bewildered look on my face, Alex changed tack. "You studied American history in college?"

By now totally confused, I nodded. "The basics…

"From Jamestown through the Civil War in American History 101, and from Reconstruction to present in AH 102."

Nodding, Alex leaned back in his chair. "And what were the two great national controversies from the founding of the Republic through the Civil War?"

Taken aback, I made a funny face as I shifted in my chair. "Well, slavery," I said slowly. "And then there was that whole bank thing I just didn't get."

Trying hard to suppress the smile that was creeping across his face, Alex took another drag on his cigarette. "That bank thing?"

"Well, yeah," I said defensively. "There was that whole big controversy over the Bank of the United States – and then the entire argument started up again after the first one expired and the second one was chartered."

After stubbing his cigarette out in the ashtray, Alex nodded. "So if the Bank of the United States was so controversial, why was it chartered in the first place? And why was a second one chartered after the first one expired?"

Hmmmmmmm…

Leaning back in my chair, I looked up at the ceiling as I searched my memory. After finally making the connection, I pursed my lips together.

"OK," I said. "Alexander Hamilton promised the states the new federal government would assume their debts from the Revolutionary War if they ratified the Constitution, and he needed a national bank to come up with some serious cash."

Leaning forward, Alex nodded. "So the first Bank of the United States was chartered to manage the debts the federal government assumed from the states?"

"Well, yeah," I said.

Alex nodded again. "So why was it controversial?"

After knitting my eyebrows together and scrunching up my nose, I re-crossed my legs and smoothed out my skirt. Realizing that I was completely stumped, I decided to fess up. "Alex, I haven't a clue."

Leaning back in his chair, Alex said OK. "So what about the Second Bank of the United States?"

Looking up dumbly, I shrugged my shoulders. "I dunno."

Alex nodded again, and reached for another cigarette. "Simply put, the first Bank was chartered to retire the Revolutionary War debts. But it was not a government institution, as the name deliberately implied, but rather a privately-owned bank in which the government owned a minority share...

"Nonetheless, because the notes issued by the bank – that is, the currency – were specifically recognized by law as valid for the payment of taxes and other debts owed to the United States Government, Bank of the United States notes became the *de facto* national currency."

"After its charter expired in 1811, the national currency vanished with the bank and we were forced to rely upon banknotes issued by various state-chartered institutions...

"But since these banks were both local and perhaps less ably run, their notes were heavily discounted. The result was rampant inflation – which led to the creation of the Second Bank of the United States five years later."

Thinking that sounded familiar, I nodded as Alex continued.

"But even though the Second Bank managed to stabilize the economy, it was as feared and distrusted as the first, and for all the same reasons...

"It was so widely hated that President Jackson vetoed an extension of its charter in 1832, and effectively killed it."

After pausing for a moment to light his cigarette, Alex leaned forward and looked directly in my eyes. "So why do you think so many exceptionally able people – including almost all of the Founders – feared and distrusted the First and Second banks?"

Suddenly intrigued, I leaned forward. "Well see, that's the part I just don't get. For all intents and purposes, the First and Second banks operated like modern-day central banks, maintaining the value of the dollar and expanding the economy...

"So where's the downside?"

Alex smiled softly as he toyed with his cigarette. Then after flicking an ash into the ashtray, he nodded. "Precisely the answer one would expect from an economist," he said. "But the issue isn't about economics *per se*, but rather about political economy – which is an altogether different beast."

Scrunching up my nose again, I leaned back in my chair. After asking him what 'political economy' meant, I demanded to know why I'd never even heard of it before.

After drawing upon his cigarette again, Alex shrugged. "The meaning of the term has changed a half-dozen times or more over the last three hundred years...

"These days it is generally used to refer to the interaction of politics, law, and economics in a given society. Public works programs, for example, are politically motivated efforts to influence the economy...

"As are particular tax provisions and, more broadly, deficit spending – all of which are, inevitably, enshrined in public law."

Frowning as I gazed at the long bank of windows lining the exterior wall, I mulled over Alex's examples. Finally persuaded that I understood the term, I turned my attention back to Alex.

"So 'political economy' refers to pretty much any government action designed to move the economy in a politically desirable direction?"

Leaning forward again, Alex nodded. "That's as good a definition as any."

Then after uncrossing my legs and shifting in my seat again, I asked him what all that had to do with the banks.

Alex stubbed his cigarette out in the ashtray, and waited while the siren of a passing police car faded into the distance. "As I stated before, the first and second banks were privately owned, as is their present successor, the Federal Reserve Bank...

"As a practical matter, the federal government has subcontracted monetary policy to a succession of privately held monopolies...

"Put differently, it has delegated the power to determine how much currency shall circulate at any given moment – in effect, the power to expand or contract the economy at will – to a narrow group of self-interested and entirely unaccountable private citizens...

"Specifically, those engaged in the business of banking and finance."

Lurching bolt upright in my chair, my eyes bulged.

Holy cow! I thought – except I kinda used a different word, which I probably shouldn't repeat.

Why didn't I see that?

"And that has profound implications that run throughout the warp and woof of American society."

Well, no kidding, Sherlock...

Because as every economist knows, government only has two mechanisms for influencing the economy: fiscal policy – which basically refers to levels of government taxation and expenditure – and monetary policy, which refers to the amount of money in circulation, and its availability and costs, i.e., interest rates.

So if the government subcontracts monetary policy to a private monopoly...

Seeing the look on my face, Alex smiled softly. "I can see the wheels turning."

"Well, yeah," I said.

"We're talking about a privately-owned monopoly that has been delegated the legal right to fix interest rates, expand or contract the money supply, and effectively control the nation's debt...

"Financially speaking, that gives them the power to determine who shall live and who shall die."

"That," Alex said softly, "And a great deal more..."

Nodding, I sat there for a long moment taking it in.

So that's what he meant when he said American politics is epiphenomenal...

After toying with another cigarette, Alex continued. "The existence of a privately owned central bank – which for all practical purposes, is what the First and Second banks were, and what the Federal Reserve Bank is today – has broad political and economic effects...

"From the standpoint of economics, it means an economy based upon public debt, because it requires the federal government to sell debt instruments to the Federal Reserve Bank in exchange for the Federal Reserve Notes we use as currency...

"Which means that the number of dollars in circulation is theoretically equal to the size of the federal government's debt, plus the money banks have 'multiplied,' – that is, the total amount of loans and credit they've extended, based on a multiple of their cash reserves...

"So as a practical matter, the only way to increase the amount of currency and credit for economic growth is to increase the size of the federal debt."

Nodding as Alex finally lit the cigarette he'd been playing with, I congratulated myself. *Well, yeah, I knew that!*

After inhaling deeply, Alex continued. "The bottom line is that the debt-based currency system we employ has introduced a systemic requirement for perpetual government growth...

Oops.

I hadn't thought of that...

"Which is precisely what the Founders had wished to avoid when they drafted the Constitution."

Uh-oh, I thought. *That can't be good...*

"Perhaps more to the point, the privately controlled, debt-based currency system has the effect of subverting the democratic process by making the federal government dependent upon the relatively small number of stockholders who control the banks that own the Federal Reserve System...

"And it is that dependency that has made it possible for the wealthy few to exert an inordinate influence over government policy – and in certain select areas, to control it altogether...

"The bottom line is our present system of debt-based currency has given rise to a self-interested oligarchy whose wealth depends upon the perpetual expansion of the size and cost of the federal government."

"No surprise then, that they are prepared to protect their interests by any means available – personal persuasion, political contributions, bribery, corruption, or even murder, if necessary."

There was a long silence as I struggled to assimilate what Alex had said. The more I thought about it, the more it seemed to me the debt-based currency system Alex described was little more than a mechanism for sneaking socialism through the back door. So after turning it over in my mind a couple of times, I said so.

After taking another sip of his coffee, Alex nodded. "Precisely – capitalism and socialism intersect at the point of public debt."

I should have known that, but it had apparently zipped right past me in school.

Neeeeowwwwwwwww...

Thinking I was a complete idiot for having missed what should have been obvious to any freshman, I just sat there and shook my head.

Finally, I looked back up at Alex. "So what's that have to do with the bond market?"

Leaning forward again, Alex clasped his hands together on his desk. "The bottom line is that the federal government routinely spends more money than it takes in...

"To make ends meet, it sells interest-bearing debt securities, primarily to the Federal Reserve Bank. The Fed holds some of them as a reserve, and sells the rest if it wants to decrease the amount of liquidity in the economy and raise interest rates – or buys others from private investors, if it wants to increase the amount of available cash and lower interest rates.

"But as a practical matter, it's nothing more than a gigantic scam to fleece the American people...

"Because the same small group of people who own the banks that own the Fed are precisely the same small group of people who profit from government debt...

"As far as they're concerned – the bigger the debt, the better the government."

Muttering another bad word under my breath, I re-crossed my legs and leaned forward. "So why do they want to kill President Reagan?"

Alex chuckled, and for a minute I thought he would laugh out loud. "Because President Reagan wants to reduce the rate of government growth from a gallop to a crawl – which will have the effect of shrinking their market and cutting their margins."

Confused, I laid my head over on my shoulder. "But if economic growth is tied to government expansion by way of the money supply – won't that crash the economy?"

Alex nodded thoughtfully. "It would – except for the fact that the Constitution permits the federal government to issue its own currency on the basis of perceived need...

"So a reduced number of Federal Reserve Notes can be offset by issuing U.S. Treasury Notes in their stead – Greenbacks, if you will – and save the taxpayers a great deal of money, because there's no interest to be paid upon them."

Suddenly curious, I leaned forward again. "Well, if the federal government can issue its own currency notes – what's it need the Fed for?"

Alex gave me a penetrating look before shaking his head. "Nothing," he said. "*Nothing at all.*"

Oh, my God! I thought. "President Reagan is going to pull the plug on the Fed, isn't he?"

Alex shrugged. "He's going to try – if he lives long enough."

By now terrified, I started crunching the numbers in my head to ward off the fear that threatened to overwhelm me.

There's gotta be billions at stake, I thought. *No – it's more like trillions, when you factor in the interest on almost a century of outstanding debts.*

Knowing there were an awful lot of people who wouldn't think twice about killing the President for a fraction of that amount, I was wondering how many people understood the currency scam Alex had just described, when an even more appalling thought hit me.

"Alex," I said softly. "How much are you really worth?"

Surprised, Alex leaned back in his chair. Then after a long silence, he said he wasn't sure.

"*Forbes Magazine* said you're one of the richest men in the world."

Suppressing his irritation, Alex frowned before shrugging again. "Probably."

"Well, there's a point to all this, Alex…

"You're the principal stockholder in Southern Exports, which is the single largest commercial bank on the East Coast."

"Yes," he said.

"So you're not only one of the richest men in the world – well, probably, anyway – but you also own a bank that owns a big chunk of the Fed."

"That's correct," he said softly.

"So why are you helping President Reagan put the Fed out of business???"

Alex shook another cigarette out of his pack and lit it. Then after inhaling deeply, he shrugged.

"It's the right thing to do."

Oh, Gawd, I thought. *A Boy Scout with a death wish…*

But after studying his face for a long moment, I realized there was more to it than that. "Alex, there's something you're not telling me."

Shifting back into his spy mode, Alex returned my gaze impassively. "And what might that be?"

Uncertain, I looked down at the floor for a long moment. And then it all fell into place.

"When your Mom and Dad died – that wasn't an accident, was it?"

Alex held my gaze for a long moment, before finally looking away. "I'm not sure."

"Was the driver who hit them killed as well?"

Alex shrugged. "A body was found near the wreckage, but the police were unable to identify it – or even connect it to the stolen vehicle."

Thinking *that* figured, I looked down at the floor while I formed my next question. "Was your father involved with the Fed?"

After taking another draw on his cigarette, Alex nodded. "He had been a member of the Board of Governors, but he resigned after a couple of years…

"And then after we moved to Washington, he helped President Kennedy draft Executive Order 11110 – which has been completely misconstrued...

"It wasn't the frontal assault on the Fed that some people have claimed – it was much more subtle than that...

"But it was the opening gambit of a much larger game that would have eventually cut the Fed out of the loop by returning the currency function to the Treasury Department, where it belongs...

"But since Uncle Jack was assassinated six months later, nothing ever came of it...

"Much like President Lincoln, and for essentially the same reason."

Now I should have picked up on that immediately, but at the particular moment I was hung up on the familial reference. "Uncle Jack?"

Alex smiled softly. "President Kennedy...

"He and my Dad served together in the Pacific during World War II, and they became close friends...

"And our families spent a lot of time together when I was a kid." Then all of a sudden, Alex chuckled. "Uncle Jack taught me how to deal off the bottom of the deck when I was maybe eight or nine."

Suddenly laughing, I told Alex he *had* to be kidding.

Shaking his head, he swore up and down it was a true story. "Those two were world-class card sharks."

Incredulous, I asked what his father had said about "Uncle Jack" teaching him how to cheat.

Clearly enjoying the memory, Alex leaned back and laughed. "He said dealing off the bottom only worked with fools, drunks, and greenhorns...

"So if I tried it with an experienced player, I'd probably end up like Cousin Willy."

Exasperated, I shook my head and sighed. *There's something definitely weird going on with that family...*

But since there was a finite limit to how long I could keep all this stuff separated in my mind, that thought was soon pushed aside as a disconcerting pattern forced its way into my consciousness...

The Establishment, so-called – the Carnegie Endowment, the Council on Foreign Relations, the Trilateral Commission, the Bilderbergers, the Federal Reserve Bank, the media, and the crooks on Capitol Hill – were merely pawns of the Financial Elite...

Which was intimately involved in a series of brutal killings that had claimed the lives of President Lincoln, President Kennedy, Alex's parents, and God knows who else.

So that's it, I thought...

The "Inner Line" Dr. MacLaughlin's so worried about — and now they've got their very own intelligence service, hidden inside the CIA...

Suddenly gripped by mind-numbing fear, I looked up and told Alex I was scared.

Nodding sympathetically, he assured me that he understood — and apologized for getting me into the mess. "It never occurred to us that you'd figure it out."

After looking down at the floor for what seemed like forever, I angrily informed him that an apology just wasn't good enough.

"I want you to *do* something!"

After gazing at me for a long moment, he nodded slightly. "And what would you like me to do?"

Still staring at the floor, I told him I wasn't sure, before suddenly changing my mind. "Make me feel safe again."

"I wish I could," he said in a voice tinged with sorrow.

"But you've stumbled into a very dangerous game, so any reassurance I might offer would be deceptive at best."

"Well, then *lie* to me, *Alex!*"

After stubbing his cigarette out in the overflowing ashtray, he laughed softly and agreed.

"Then there's nothing to worry about, kid...

"Because we're the Good Guys, and we wear the White Hats — and as you know from the movies, Good always triumphs over Evil...

"So we'll cut the Bad Guys off at the pass and get the drop on 'em — and then we'll tie them up and wait for the Sheriff to come haul them away."

"And *then* what?" I asked hopefully.

"Well, we'll saddle up our horses and ride off into the sunset like the Good Guys always do."

After mulling it over for a minute or two, I decided that was completely absurd. So I locked my eyes upon his, and gave him my *Seriously Irritated Look.*

"Alex — that's ridiculous!"

CHAPTER FORTY-THREE

Needless to say, I didn't get a lot of sleep that night. I was scared out of my wits, and the fact that Alex had called the security office and instructed them to have armed guards follow me home didn't help matters.

Making a complete fool out of myself in the parking garage made it even worse. Because after I pushed the carts into the vault and secured it, Alex walked me down to the Vette – and along the way, I had started worrying about his trip to St. Paul. So while we were waiting next to the car for the CIA guys, I grasped the lapels of his coat and made him promise he'd be careful.

After kissing me on the top of my head, Alex smiled softly and told me that "careful" was his middle name.

My mind must have been on the goodnight kiss I was plotting, because that particular figure of speech flew right past me. After my eyes crossed in confusion, I made a funny face and looked up quizzically. "I thought it was Michael?"

To his everlasting credit, Alex managed to maintain a straight face for, *oh...*

Two or three milliseconds, before cracking up – which was just slightly less than it took me to realize what I'd just said.

Oh, Gawd, I thought. *What kind of an idiot...*

But before I had time to find a rock to crawl under, the double doors of the basement level suddenly swung open and two of the security agents marched out onto the tarmac. Slipping into his command mode, Alex ordered them to follow me to my apartment and make sure I entered it safely.

After the men acknowledged their orders, Alex turned back to silently gaze into my eyes for what seemed like an eternity. Then after another soft smile crept across his face, he turned on his heel and strode back into the building without another word. Knowing that was his way of saying goodbye, my stomach knotted. Because as he walked away, I had this terrible feeling that I'd never see him again.

But I didn't have long to dwell on the premonition, because just then one of the CIA guys pulled up in a white Bronco. The other one, who had been silently standing by with a submachine gun resting on his hip, gestured for me to get in the Vette, and waited while I stowed my briefcase behind the driver's seat and shooed the dogs into the car. Once I was safely inside, he clambered into the passenger side of the Bronco and made a hand signal for me to proceed.

Needless to say, the drive home was like, *totally* weird. Because let's face it – it's not every day that a twenty-two-year-old research assistant gets escorted to their door by CIA agents armed with automatic weapons.

Especially when they already have two well-trained guard dogs…

I was still mulling that over when I slipped the key into my lock twenty minutes later. Not quite sure what I was supposed to do after pushing the door open, I turned to my two stone-faced companions and thanked them for seeing me home. The taller one – the one who seemed to be in charge – nodded curtly. "Our pleasure, Ma'am."

Then the two of them turned on their heels, and marched back down the hallway and out into the cold of the moonlit night.

Leaning with my back against the now-closed door, I pressed my eyes shut and exhaled deeply. Still cycling between being scared out of my wits, frightened for Alex, and feeling like a complete idiot for what I'd said in the parking garage, I finally summoned up the strength to turn around and slip the door stopper into position before reassembling my little pyramid of Diet Pepsi cans against it. Then after pulling the dogs close to me, and earnestly warning them to be especially vigilant that night, I washed off my face before trudging upstairs and pulling off my clothes. After climbing into a pair of sweats, I slipped my brass knuckles onto my hand before turning off the light and crawling under the covers.

Draping my arm over my big stuffed animal, I pulled Teddy close before whispering a little prayer and drifting off into a troubled sleep.

I can't really remember much about my dreams that night, except that something dark and evil with hideous red eyes was chasing after me. No matter how fast I ran or how hard I dodged and weaved, it got closer and closer until I could hear its heavy breathing just behind me – and then the smell of its rancid breath on my neck. As a clammy hand seized my shoulder, I suddenly awoke in a cold sweat.

I must have screamed in my sleep, because the dogs came charging up the spiral staircase barking and snarling. Too frightened to speak, I waited until I stopped hyperventilating, before patting the bed next to me. After they'd bounded up on the comforter, I gathered one on either side and draped my arms around their necks. Holding them close to my trembling body, I watched the full moon trace across the glass bricks at the top of the exterior wall until I finally fell back into an uneasy sleep.

Exhausted and still deeply ill at ease when I stepped out onto the sidewalk the next morning, I waited while the dogs made a quick pit stop at the bushes before walking them around the building to retrieve the Vette from the parking lot in back. As I turned the last corner, I was still trying to shake the memory of the *thing* that had haunted my dreams when I came to an abrupt and involuntary halt.

Incredulous, my jaw fell slack as I stared at the huge black bird perched on the top of the car.

What the...

Thinking that just *couldn't* be, I stood there and stared in disbelief as the dogs raced around the Vette barking at the winged apparition. Entirely unconcerned, the bird returned my stare with a cruelly indifferent gaze.

Refusing to be intimidated, I grasped my briefcase in both hands and marched to within a few feet of the bird before demanding to know what it was doing on the roof of my car.

"Don't you know it's January?

"You're supposed to be down south, where it's warm!"

After waiting an interminable moment for a reply, I decided the bird was asking for it. After giving him fair warning, I swung the case at him.

"Go!"

After leaping up in the air to dodge the satchel, the bird settled back down on the canvas top and glared at me. So after poking the briefcase at him three or four times, I yelled at him again.

"Go on now...

"Shoo! Shoo!

Finally taking the hint, the bird leapt into the air again and circled the parking lot before perching on the roof of the apartment building. Still staring at me as I searched for my car keys, I couldn't escape the disconcerting suspicion that the feathered freak was some sort of supernatural harbinger. Unsettled by the weirdness of it all, my hands were trembling so hard I could barely fit the key into the lock on the door.

By the time I arrived at the Executive Offices a half-hour later, I was firmly convinced the Forces of Darkness were in play. But the familiar surroundings had a calming influence, so when I noticed Christine's office doors were closed, I stopped at Linda's desk and asked where the boss was.

Glancing up from whatever it was she was typing, she explained that Alex was en route to Minnesota with President Reagan – which I already knew – and that Christine was testifying before the Armed Forces Committee on Capitol Hill. After quickly adding that she would probably be there all day, she informed me that Dr. MacLaughlin would be up in a few minutes to help open the vault.

But before I did anything else, he wanted me to review and comment on an article he'd just finished before he sent it off for publication.

"So you're in charge again?"

Looking back up, Linda rolled her eyes and shook her head. "You've *got* to be kidding, girl...

"The inmates have taken over the asylum."

Puzzled, I was about to ask her what she meant by that when I heard the dogs racing up the hallway, barking for all they were worth. A moment later, a whirring sound added to the cacophony as a miniature tank careened around the corner and raced through the doors with the dogs in hot pursuit.

Incredulous, I watched Big Minh and Lady Godiva chase the little vehicle around in circles before finally turning back to Linda. "What's up with that?"

Looking up again, Linda sighed. "Some electronics company in Japan sent Alex some remote-controlled toys – that tank thingy, and a big red fire truck – and Alex told the Brass they could try them out...

"So Gen. McGreggor and Adm. Taylor have been racing that stupid thing up and down the hallway, driving everyone crazy."

By that time, Big Minh and Lady Godiva had cornered the tank in the far end of the office, so I had pretty much written it off as an overpriced chew toy when it suddenly leveled its cannon and opened fire.

BANG! BANG! BANG!

Confused by the unexpected turn of events, the dogs backed off slowly. Still growling with bared fangs, they reluctantly gave ground as the tank advanced in my general direction.

Looking disgusted, Linda shook her head before muttering to no one in particular. "When the cat's away, the mice will play."

Chuckling, I asked her how they were driving that thing, because neither Gen. McGreggor nor Adm. Taylor were anywhere in sight.

Looking up again, Linda sighed. "Well see, that's the thing....

Pointing over her desk at the still-advancing tank, she asked me if I could make out the little rectangular gizmo mounted on the turret alongside the barrel. So after turning around to look at it, I nodded.

"That's a little TV camera, so you can operate it around corners and stuff."

Then as the tank approached me, Linda suddenly looked up and warned me. "Better watch that thing," she said as the tank came to a halt by my feet. "I caught those two perverts trying to look up my skirt a few minutes ago."

Shocked, I pressed thighs together and pulled my skirt tight around me. "*You jerks!*"

Then I turned slightly and lifted up my left foot. Pointing down at the spiked heel, I warned them if they tried that with me I'd ram the point straight through their little TV camera.

"You can hear me, right?"

Staring straight into the camera, I continued. *"You've got a microphone in there, don't you?"*

I wasn't really expecting an answer, but when the turret swung back and forth in denial I decided enough was enough.

Slamming my foot down on the carpet, I pointed at the door and hollered. *"Out!"*

Having apparently decided that discretion was the better part of valor, the tank backed up a few inches before suddenly shooting forward between the dogs. It was racing for the door with Big Minh and Lady Godiva in hot pursuit when Dr. MacLaughlin suddenly appeared in the aperture.

"Bloody hell!" he screamed as he leapt out of the way. *"What is this, Romper Room?"*

Thinking his reaction was really funny, I grinned and pointed at Linda and told him it was all her fault.

Obviously irritated by my whimsical attitude, Dr. MacLaughlin marched over and thrust his draft into my hands before reaching into his vest pocket and retrieving his key to the vault. Then in what later seemed like prophecy, he muttered to himself. *"Fetch the Devil..."*

After checking to make sure he had the right key, Dr. MacLaughlin resumed his march to my office. "Now come on, Lass, let's get your vault opened up."

As I slipped back into my work-a-day world, a semblance of normalcy returned. So after thanking Dr. MacLaughlin for his assistance – and apologizing for my insolence back in the reception area – I pulled my carts into place and hooked up my computer before starting on his article. Unlike most of his other work — which tended to be pretty theoretical — this particular paper was an historical overview of John Law, an early Scottish economist who first developed the concept of the managed inflationary economy. Fascinated by the opening paragraph, I pulled a red felt-tipped pen from my drawer and began working my way through it.

Lost in thought, the day almost slipped away from me — and if Jennifer hadn't buzzed me around 3:30, I probably wouldn't have even noticed. "One of the guys in the mail shop brought up a package for you, and told me it's been sitting around there since before Christmas."

"A package?"

"Yeah, and the guy that brought it up — the new guy, Rick — he said the mail shop manager was mad as hell because he'd left a dozen messages with Two, telling you to get your butt down there and pick it up."

Thinking *that* figured, I told Jennifer the package was news to me. "She never said a word."

After telling me that was par for the course with Two, Jennifer asked me if I was going to come down or if she should bring it up. "I'm way ahead of the curve, so Dr. MacLaughlin won't mind."

After glancing at my carts and the open vault, I asked Jennifer if she would mind bringing it up.

"Not a problem," she said. "But you have to open it, because it's from Tiffany's in New York."

Tiffany's???

Puzzled and more than a bit excited, I told Jennifer I'd meet her in the reception area before putting down the handset. Stuffing Dr. MacLaughlin's paper in my top drawer, I jumped up and scurried through the door.

A minute or two later, Jennifer strode in carrying a goodly sized box and handed it to me. Grinning, she told me to hurry up and open it.

After glancing up from her keyboard, Linda pulled a single-edged razor from her center drawer and gestured at the open space in front of her. Hesitant, I shook the box before setting it down on her desk and accepting the razor blade. But just as I was about to cut the packing tape, I suddenly froze.

"What if it's a bomb or something?"

After giving me an incredulous look, Linda rolled her eyes. *"From Tiffany's?"*

Thinking the point well taken, my face turned crimson. Then I shrugged, and cut the brown cardboard box open.

Inside lay one of Tiffany's trademark blue boxes, tied with a red satin ribbon and surrounded by those little Styrofoam peanut thingies. Thinking the bow looked really cool, I pulled the Tiffany's box out of the shipping carton without spilling too many of the Styrofoam bits on the floor. "No card," I announced before shaking the box again.

"What do you think it is?"

Jennifer gave me an impatient look. "Well, open the damn thing and find out!"

Not wanting to ruin it, I gently untied the bow before teasing open the box.

"*Oh, my God!*" I whispered. "*Look at this!*"

As Linda and Jennifer gathered around, I reached inside and carefully extracted the lead crystal Unicorn contained within. Gasping at its beauty, Linda whispered that it must have cost a fortune.

In a voice tinged with awe, Jennifer agreed. "*Two grand, at least…*"

Carefully setting it down next to the big box on Linda's desk, I reached back inside the gift box and pulled out the spare Unicorn horn encased in a little plastic sheath, and then the silver mounting stand and the certificate of authenticity that lay underneath. Puzzled, I turned the box upside down and shook it.

"There's no card," I said.

At that point Jennifer broke up laughing. "So, just exactly how many people do you know who can afford a gift like that?"

After crossing my eyes and thinking about it for a moment, I laid my head over on my shoulder.

"Well, uh…"

"*Alex?*"

After staring at me for a long moment, Linda looked at me like I was some kind of dunce.

"*Duh-uh!*"

Then after shaking her head in disbelief, she shrugged. "Next time you're in Oz, girl, you better ask the Wizard for a brain."

Thinking that was unfair, I protested. "*But there's NO card*," I said. "How do you know it's from him?"

Linda looked at Jennifer, and Jennifer looked at Linda, and then they both shook their heads.

"Dumb as a post," said Linda.

Chuckling, Jennifer told her she shouldn't insult fence posts like that. "Some of them are pretty smart, you know."

But before she left, she grinned and gave me a high-five. "Enjoy your gift," she whispered.

Thinking the mystery wouldn't make that easy, I gathered up the Unicorn, the stand, and all the other stuff and tiptoed back to my office. Scared to death that I would trip and drop the exquisite treasure, I let out a sigh of relief when I reached the shelf that stood across the room from my desk.

After making a mental note to lock it up in the vault every night before I went home, I carefully assembled the display. Then after taking a step back, I marveled as the ceiling lights played upon it.

It's so beautiful...

Realizing I probably wouldn't accomplish another thing for the rest of the day, I walked around my desk and sat down in my chair. Since it doesn't take a rocket scientist to know that the Unicorn is a symbolic representation of all that is best and beautiful about the masculine sex, I smiled to myself.

Guys really are magnificent, I thought as I gazed on the crystal figure.

Well...

At least when they're not acting like jerks, anyway...

Then, as a huge grin spread across my face, I forgot all about the weird stuff that had happened.

Card or no card, I thought. *That boy is mine!*

Suddenly excited, I pulled Dr. MacLaughlin's paper out of my drawer and got back to work.

Happy, content, and completely absorbed, I stayed focused until almost 8 pm. Suddenly aware of my growling stomach, I scribbled my final comments on the bottom of the last page and pushed it back across my desk. Then after stretching in my seat – and taking an inordinately long moment to admire my Unicorn – I stood up and lifted my purse off the back of my chair. Confident that there was at least ten bucks worth of quarters hiding on the bottom somewhere, I stuffed my feet back into my heels and headed into the galley. Then after banging the dogs' bowls against the doorjamb a couple of times to let them know that dinner was about to be served, I filled them with food before heading down the hall to the canteen.

Returning five minutes later with a microwave cheeseburger, a bag of Doritos and a can of Diet Pepsi, I turned on the boom box I kept on the windowsill behind me. Then as Beethoven filled the air, I cranked up the volume.

About halfway through the Ninth Symphony, Big Minh and Lady Godiva emerged from the galley. Apparently sated by their meal, they plopped down in front of my office doorway – but after less than a minute, Big Minh's countenance suddenly changed. After baring his fangs and uttering a low growl, he jumped up.

By now joined by Lady Godiva, he began prowling back and forth in front of the door as though he sensed the presence of an unseen enemy. Suddenly reminded of the big black bird that had perched on the Vette that morning, the hair on the back of my neck stood up and my skin began to crawl.

Slowly turning back to the pacing dogs, I could see from the froth forming on their lips that they were on the verge of frenzy.

Something's way wrong, I whispered to myself.

Then, very suddenly, Big Minh let out a blood-curdling howl as a massive convulsion hurled his body into the air. After being suspended in space for an unnaturally long moment, he slammed down on the carpet and began writhing on the floor.

Then as the blood in my veins turned to ice, I made the instinctive connection. *Oh, dear God…*

Something terrible just happened to Alex…

Horrified, I raced over to Big Minh and knelt beside him. As I placed my hand on the dog's chest to see if he was still breathing, he let out a low moan. Shouting at Lady Godiva to watch over him, I raced back to my desk and snatched the handset off the phone. After punching in the number for the CIA security team, I struggled to regain my composure as I waited for them to answer. But on the seventh or eighth ring, I finally realized the truth.

They set me up…

An instant later, the radio crackled and hissed as a pirate signal overwhelmed the broadcast. Transfixed by fear, I stood there and stared at the silvery box as Creedence Clearwater Revival's *Bad Moon Rising* poured from the speakers.

> *I see the bad moon arising*
> *I see trouble on the way*
> *I see earthquakes and lightning*
> *I see bad times today*

Lurching forward, I spun the dial to the next station.

> *Don't go 'round tonight*
> *It's bound to take your life*
> *There's a bad moon on the rise*

Frantic, I spun the dial again.

I hear hurricanes a-blowing
I know the end is coming soon
I fear the river's overflowing
I hear the voice of rage and ruin...

Don't go 'round tonight
It's bound to take your life
There's a bad moon on the rise

Convinced that something awful had just happened in St. Paul – and now certain that something even worse was about to happen right there in Washington – I snapped off the radio and hurriedly loaded up the carts. Then after pushing them into the vault, I swung the door shut and jabbed the secure button before racing back to Big Minh. Still whimpering, but now on all fours, I had just knelt down beside him when I heard the beating sound of helicopter blades above. Then there was a thud from somewhere up on the roof, followed a few moments later by the sound of a muffled explosion.

As my blood turned cold, the lights flickered off and plunged the office into total darkness. Then as the dim, emergency backup lights came to life, I saw it...

Or at least I *thought* I saw it – that *thing* that had chased me through my dreams, standing right there in the reception area...

Its hideous red eyes ablaze, staring right at me...

The Banshee...

Struck numb by horror as it raised a claw-like finger towards me, I barely heard the sound of heavy boots pounding down the stairs.

Then there was another explosion at the stairwell, and I heard Mai Ling calling for me.

"*ALIZA, ALIZA!*"

Unable to see through the smoke that billowed through the hallway and into the Executive Offices, I started to call out. But before the words could form, Mai Ling and four heavily armed Vietnamese men dressed in loose-fitting jeans and black hooded parkas stormed into my office. One of them I recognized as Sgt. Trung.

"*ALIZA, BAD MEN COME, WE RUN AWAY...*"

"*DEY KILL US!*"

Then with pleading eyes, Mai Ling urged me to my feet. "*VITE, VITE!*"

With my wits suddenly back about me, I needed no further convincing. Bounding up from the floor, I snatched my Unicorn off the shelf and ran after Mai Ling. With one of the Vietnamese close by either side, I raced through the reception area and the lingering smoke in the hallway to the stairwell they'd blown to gain access to the Eighth Floor. As I pounded up the stairs, I heard the rattle of automatic weapons fire from somewhere far below.

As we charged through the wreckage of the roof door, Sgt. Trung turned and shouted something, but his words were drowned out by the sound of the helicopter blades. Then after pointing in the direction of the aircraft, he slung his weapon over his shoulder before grabbing my arm and hustling me across the deck. As we raced into the rotor wash, he reached down and picked me up as I stumbled on an unseen obstacle. Then after bounding another two or three steps, he hurled me into the aircraft next to Mai Ling.

Backing out of the wash, he gave the pilot a hand signal before clenching his fist and defiantly holding it high over his head. Then after screaming something in Vietnamese, he signaled for his men and charged back into the stairwell.

The aircraft had just begun edging forward when I suddenly remembered the dogs. Thrusting my Unicorn into Mai Ling's shaking hands, I crawled to the open hatch. Uncertain as to whether they should turn to face the enemy or stay with me, Big Minh and Lady Godiva had taken up defensive positions alongside the helicopter. Seeing me wave for them, they leapt past the door gunner and slid across the floor.

The aircraft suddenly lurched skyward before sliding laterally through the air above the street. Grabbing the canvas cargo netting that lined the sides of the helicopter to keep from slipping as the aircraft banked, I watched through the still-open hatch as flashes of automatic weapons fire eerily illuminated the upper floors of the darkened structure.

As the aircraft slipped over the desolate buildings of a city now plunged into darkness, a tremendous explosion blew out the face of the building below. Transfixed by the orange-red fireball that blossomed from what had once been my office, I watched as bits of shattered glass and concrete rained down upon the street.

Then as we surged into the dark of night, I closed my eyes and prayed for Sgt. Trung and the other brave men below.

CHAPTER FORTY-FOUR

Driven back from the hatch by the frigid air that howled through the open port, I crawled across the floor of the helicopter to Mai Ling. Safe and warm with her parka and fur-lined boots – and that goofy plaid hunting hat of hers – she was tugging at one of the cargo blankets that had been stowed behind the canvas netting. Gesturing for me as she wrested it free, she held the blanket up as I crawled into it and wrapped the folds around me. I tried to thank her, but my chattering teeth choked off the sound.

As I huddled next to her, the dogs must have sensed my discomfort. After crawling across the floor, Lady Godiva climbed into my lap as Big Minh lay against my exposed side. Grateful for windbreaks and the shared warmth, I pulled the cargo blanket over my head in an effort to stop the bone-rattling shivers that convulsed me.

Gradually regaining control as my body's heat built up inside the blanket, I tried to make sense of the jumbled imagery cascading through my mind. Desperate to know what had happened, I pushed my face through the edges of the blanket and turned toward Mai Ling. Barely visible in the darkness, I could see that she was weeping.

Shouting over the noise of the engines and rotor blades, I called out to her. *"MAI LING...*

"WHAT'S HAPPENING??"

Still sobbing as she turned to me, she shook her head. *"DON' UNDERSTAN,"* she shouted.

"NGUYEN COME TO OFFICE LAST DAY...

"HE SAY WAR COME, HE TAKE MEN TO BATTLE ...

"DEN HE SAY WE LOSE ONE COUNTRY, NOT LOSE ANOTHER...

"TELL ME PACK LITTLE BAG, SGT. TRUNG COME FOR ME. HE SAY NOT ASK QUESTIONS, DO EXACTLY WHAT SERGEANT TELL ME."

Then she threw her arms around me and sobbed. *"ALIZA, I SO AFRAID..."*

Pulling her close to me, I had just started to comfort her when the door gunner put his hand to the side of his helmet and nodded. Locking his machine gun into position, he shouted toward the front of the aircraft and gave the co-pilot a thumbs-up sign before stepping over to us and kneeling before Mai Ling. After shouting to her in Vietnamese, she wiped the tears from her eyes and nodded before turning back to me.

"*WE LAN SOON, RUN TO AIRPLANE.*"

Not quite sure I had heard her correctly, I was about to shout and ask her to say it again when the helicopter banked sharply. A moment later, the nose of the aircraft reared up as the noise from the engines and rotors suddenly increased. Then there was a thud, as we settled onto the frozen ground next to a runway.

Pulling Mai Ling to her feet, the door gunner pointed through the hatch and shouted above the engine noise. Although I didn't understand a word of Vietnamese at the time, the tone of his voice told me to run for my life. So after pulling off my heels, I bounded out the door and raced after Mai Ling to the little two-engine jet idling on the darkened runway. Painted flat black, its dark silhouette seemed strangely ominous.

Although the helicopter hadn't landed more than a hundred feet from the jet, the distance seemed enormous as I tore across the frostbitten ground. Finally reaching the boarding ladder after what seemed like an eternity, I raced up the steps after Mai Ling. The padded footsteps that followed a few feet behind reassured me that the dogs were still with us.

A forty-something Vietnamese man, dressed in a military flight suit with a handgun protruding from his shoulder holster, grabbed my wrist and pulled me through the door. Then after pointing to the leather upholstered seats of what was normally a luxury corporate jet, he pulled the door shut and secured it. Shouting to the pilot as he turned back, he barked something in Vietnamese to Mai Ling.

"He say don' open window shade, fasten seat belt an hold dogs in lap…

"We make combat take-off."

Given the circumstances, it's hard to imagine that I could become more frightened. But as I secured my seatbelt and called for Big Minh, the 'combat take-off' thing managed to scare me even more. Closing my eyes as he climbed into my lap, I clutched him hard against my chest and said a little prayer.

In the chaos and the darkness, I hadn't gotten a good look at the runway. But I could tell it was short – as in *way* short – and as the engines began howling, I wondered how the pilot had managed to land the aircraft on that tiny little strip in the first place. Hoping against hope that jets needed more room to land than take off, I crossed my fingers as the aircraft lurched forward.

With the window shades drawn, I couldn't see what was going on as we hurtled down the runway, but the high-pitched scream of the engines told me we were running out of tarmac fast. As my heart crawled up my throat there was a loud bump, and then the nose of the aircraft tilted skyward. Pressed back into my seat by gravity and the weight of the dog, I froze as the bottom of the fuselage raked across the top of a tree.

By now certain that we were going to get splattered all over the Maryland countryside, I closed my eyes tight for a long, heart-pounding moment.

But miraculously, the fiery end I feared didn't come. The jet leveled off instead.

As the dim red emergency lights came on in the cabin, I let out a huge sigh of relief as I pulled Big Minh's head close to my own. Massacring the metaphor, I whispered in his ear. "Looks like we dodged the bullet!"

I had just turned to look at Mai Ling when the co-pilot reappeared. Kneeling in the tiny aisle that separated the single row of seats that ran along each side of the aircraft, he said something to Mai Ling in French before switching to fluent English. Then after turning to me and asking if I was OK, he told us to keep the window shades down and the seat lights off. "Intelligence reports the enemy may have jets up looking for us, so it's important to observe operational security...

"Any breach of protocol might give us away."

Then after backing up just a bit so he could look at us both in the dim red light, he asked if we understood. As the color drained from my face, I nodded.

Chuckling at my facial expression, the co-pilot told me there was nothing to worry about. Jerking his head toward the cockpit, he grinned. "Colonel Kao can out-fly the Devil."

Hearing the name, Mai Ling gasped. "Col. Kao pilot?"

Nodding, the co-pilot smiled. "Five hundred missions over the North, without even scratching the paint on his F-5."

Visibly relieved, Mai Ling reached around Lady Godiva and placed her hands together and did a little bow over and over again. *"Oh, tank God,"* she whispered. *"Colonel keep us safe."*

Then very suddenly she looked at the co-pilot again, and in a pleading voice asked for news of Nguyen.

Suddenly serious, he apologized. "I'm sorry, *Madame*...

"Our forces have been observing radio silence for more than an hour. We haven't received any news at all."

Then after glancing down at the carpeting he looked up again at Mai Ling and gently took her hand. *"Madame Docteur,"* he said before switching back to English

"Maj. Tranh is a brilliant soldier, there is nothing to worry about."

Bursting into tears, Mai Ling buried her face in Lady Godiva's fur and nodded her head. "Dat true," she whispered. "Nguyen always come back to me."

Standing, the co-pilot nodded and promised he would let her know if they received any word. Then he turned on his heel, and marched back into the cockpit.

After looking down at the floor for a long moment, Mai Ling shooed Lady Godiva from her lap and reached inside her parka. Pulling my Unicorn from the inside pocket, she held it out in front of her as a smile crept across her face. *"Soooooo beautiful,"* she whispered.

Smiling shyly, she turned in her seat and handed it across the aisle. "Magic horse remine me of Nguyen..."

Then as a blush spread across her face, she told me about the night they had met. "When little girl, I always wonder who I marry someday...

"Sit in garden, an wonder where he is, what he doing den...

"Sometime I imagine he tink about me too...

"Den Father take me to Palace for diplomat reception, and I see handsome young soldier stan next to President Thieu...

"So – what dat word? *Dashing???*

"Dat right – so dashing in dress uniform, wit sash around waist and sword at side...

"An I know right away – *dat him!*

"Dat man I marry someday!"

Giggling, Mai Ling put her hand across her mouth. "Den I tink 'Father catch me stare at Viet man, he send me to convent!' so I look away. But Nguyen see me, he ask President ask Father if maybe he speak to me...

"Put Father in dilemma. Relations not so good between China people and Vietnam people den, lot of – how you say – etnik tension...

"But Father can't say no to President, so he agree."

Laughing softly through teary eyes, Mai Ling smiled. "So Nguyen come to me, tell me silly story dat he really cowboy from Texas...

"Make me laugh and smile."

Even though Mai Ling had told me how they'd met once before, it was such a wonderful story, I laughed with her again.

Then after reaching across the aisle, I took her hand in mine and told her how lucky she was to have such a great guy.

Smiling shyly again, she nodded. "But I worry," she said. Then after squeezing my hand, she told me she was worried about Alex too.

"Alex wonerful friend…

"Save me from prison camp, bring me to America so I be wit Nguyen again."

Tightening my grip on her hand, I closed my eyes and inhaled deeply. "I'm scared, too, Mai Ling…

"The Bad Guys want him dead."

Mai Ling nodded. "Nguyen tell me," she said. "But he say me not worry – Alex like cat, always land on paws."

Thinking I probably shouldn't add to her worries by mentioning Big Minh's bizarre seizure in my office – or the intuitive connection I had made – I smiled at the mangled phrase instead. Closing my eyes again, I crossed my fingers on my other hand, and whispered a little prayer before responding.

"Dear God," I said in an anxious voice. "I hope so."

In the long, emotionally laden silence that followed, we shared the age-old dread of women whose men had gone off to war. Too far from the battle lines to help them, and uncertain of their fate, all we could do was comfort one another as we prayed for their safe return. Unable and perhaps unwilling to say anything more, I held tight to Mai Ling's hand.

The intimacy of our unspoken anguish might have lasted an hour or more if it hadn't been for the sudden buffeting of the plane. Shaking and shuddering, it lurched violently upward before edging back down. Urgently reminded that my choice of Doritos for dinner hadn't been one of my better ideas, I clenched my teeth together as I looked toward the back for the restroom.

I was about to get up when the aircraft shuddered and jerked again, throwing me against the side of the fuselage. As my shoulder slammed into the window, the lowered shade slipped up three or maybe four inches.

Seeing the color drain from my face, Mai Ling's eyes widened. "Aliza, what wrong?"

My mouth moved in reply but the words just wouldn't come. All I could do was point down and out with my index finger.

After staring at me for an interminable moment, Mai Ling's eyes bulged as a look of fearful recognition spread across her face. "How low?" she asked in a high-pitched, squeaky voice.

After slowly turning my head to look out at the treetops flying by just below the aircraft's wings, I tried to utter the words. After the third try, I finally succeeded.

"*Trees*," I squeaked. "*Fifteen, twenty feet.*"

Mai Ling's eyes bulged again. *"Uh-oh."*

Nodding, I echoed her. Then I reached over and slammed the shade back into position.

Pressing back in my seat, I seized the armrests in a death grip and stared straight ahead. "Mai Ling?"

"Aliza?"

"This Col. Kao. He's a really good pilot..."

"Right?"

After a moment, Mai Ling squeaked again. *"*Best pilot in Republic Vietnam Air Force."

Thinking her voice didn't sound altogether convincing, I nodded stiffly. "That's good," I said in a high squeaky voice.

"Really good..."

There was a long silence before the aircraft shuddered and jerked again. With my stomach lodged in my throat, I realized it was then or never – so I unbuckled my seat belt and made a dash for the lavatory. After jumping over the dogs and ripping open the door, I jammed myself between the interior wall and the exterior of the fuselage and leaned over the stainless steel toilet. But despite the violent pitching and rolling of the aircraft, the stupid Doritos just wouldn't come up. They just sat there in my stomach, making me nauseous.

Shoulda had the Twinkies, I thought dejectedly.

After hitting another air pocket some five minutes later, the spicy corn chips *finally* obliged me. Now weak and shaky, I summoned the strength to push myself back into an upright position. Then after flushing the toilet and washing out my mouth as best I could, I opened the door and stepped back into cabin. Realizing there was a little galley just to my left, I put one hand on each side of the narrow corridor and made my way back there. Spying the automatic coffee maker built into the space above the little sink – and desperate to wash the disgusting taste from my mouth – I rooted through the drawers until I found a little foil packet of Folgers, a stack of filters, and a big box of sugars. So after preparing the machine and pressing the start button, I opened up the little bar refrigerator below and pulled out a pint of artificial creamer.

After the little light changed from red to green, I unlocked the stainless steel coffee pot and poured the contents into two of the overlarge Styrofoam cups I'd found. Then after fixing them –

a little creamer and no sugar for Mai Ling, a bit of each for myself – I swayed back down the aisle to where we were sitting.

I had just handed Mai Ling her cup when the aircraft began a long, gradual climb upwards. Relieved, I sat back in my chair and placed my cup in the holder on the armrest. After buckling my seatbelt, I asked Mai Ling where they were taking us.

"Dunno," she said. "Nguyen say someplace safe, but not tell where."

By now convinced there was no such thing as a truly safe place, I had just started pondering our predicament when the door of the cockpit suddenly opened and the co-pilot re-emerged.

"I apologize for the rough flight, *Mesdames*, but we had to stay below radar until we left American air space."

Huh?

"We're not in the U.S. anymore?"

Shaking his head in reply to my question, the co-pilot said no. "We're over the Atlantic, just beyond American territorial jurisdiction."

"The *Atlantic!*" I exclaimed. "Where are we going?"

The co-pilot kneeled again between our seats, and shook his head. "I don't know," he said. "Our orders were to evacuate you from the Washington region and fly you to a specified set of co-ordinates to rendezvous with Canadian fighter aircraft...

"They will escort us to our destination."

Then the co-pilot continued. "We're in radio contact with the Canadians, and they should appear on either side in a matter of moments...

"If you look out the window, you may be able to see their approach."

Incredulous, I scrunched up my face. *"Fighter jets?"*

Nodding again, the co-pilot said yes. "A flight of Canadian F-18s will escort us to a landing field."

After taking a few moments to let that sink in, I reached over and gingerly raised the window shade. A few hundred feet or so off our wingtip, I could see an aircraft bristling with missiles pulling up alongside. A moment later, the cockpit lit up and the pilot looked over and gave me a "thumbs up" sign. After I returned his signal with a little wave, the pilot clicked his light off and disappeared into the darkness.

Confused by the Canadian involvement into what I thought was a domestic crisis, I settled back in my seat and began puzzling it through. *The pirate radio signal, the rooftop evacuation, the jet and now Canadian fighter planes...*

Obviously, someone had done serious planning...

But who?

The fact that almost everyone involved so far were former Vietnamese military personnel pointed toward Nguyen – and the more I thought about it, the more it seemed like he'd created some sort of secret army...

Consistent with all the known facts, I thought. *But why would a more or less ordinary stockbroker do that?*

To protect Mai Ling? Obviously...

To help Alex? No doubt...

But as far as I knew, she didn't know anything about the Black Budget project at all. So why would the Bad Guys go after her?

And why would Nguyen risk her life – and the lives of so many of his men – to save mine?

Because once I had uncovered the plot, I realized that I was of no further use to anyone. My life had become an expendable commodity...

So Nguyen could have just let me die back at the office...

But he didn't – he risked a dozen lives instead to save mine...

Thinking that it just didn't add up, I pushed myself back into my seat to mull it over.

Incomplete data, I thought.

But on the off chance that I might be able to deduce the missing pieces from the parts of the puzzle I already had, I went back to Square One and started rethinking everything that had happened since I climbed off the Greyhound Bus that first day in Washington.

But as I lifted my coffee cup to my lips I was entirely unaware of the attempt against President Reagan's life, or the savage retribution even then being visited upon the conspirators back in the States.

As I learned much later, the first to fall was Joshua Holloway, the CIA's chief-of-station in New York. The recently divorced intelligence officer had left work a bit early that night, to make sure he would be on time for a new off-Broadway play the critics were raving about. But unfortunately for Holloway, the stunningly attractive twenty-something who accompanied him had so consumed his attention that he didn't notice the motorbike carrying two leather-clad riders following a discreet distance behind. As he climbed out of the cab in front of the theater, the bike jumped the curb and roared through the panicked crowed, slowing only slightly as the passenger fired two rounds from a large caliber handgun. The first bullet ripped through Holloway's skull, the second pierced his heart.

The gunmen had roared off before his lifeless body had even hit the ground, so the horrified bystanders were unable to give the police more than a vague description. But one of the witnesses thought the driver had looked kind of Oriental. "Chinese guy, I think."

Halfway across the city in a luxurious penthouse apartment, Alan Fitzsimmons was sitting at his desk writing a draft memo he intended to circulate throughout the upper echelon of the Federal Reserve System later that week. In his judgment, the financial system lacked sufficient liquidity to sustain the current economic expansion, and so, as the Chairman of the Federal Reserve Bank of New York – the largest, and by far the most important, of the twelve regional banks that made up the Federal Reserve System – he felt obliged to advise his colleagues that a fresh infusion of cash was required. Startled by the pair of armed men who had somehow managed to gain entry to his suite, he leapt from his desk and demanded to know what they wanted. "Just a little drink, Mr. Fitzsimmons," one replied in heavily accented English.

An hour later, the NYPD found his broken body sixty stories below. According to the coroner's report, the subsequent autopsy revealed a blood alcohol level at near lethal proportions. In all likelihood, the official report concluded, he had fallen from his balcony in a drunken state.

Fifteen minutes later, and eleven hundred miles to the south, beachfront residents of Miami witnessed a spectacular fireball some ten miles out to sea when the luxury yacht of Julius Farberg suddenly exploded. Farberg, the crew, and the sixteen international bankers he had been entertaining perished in the blast, which the Coast Guard later attributed to the dozens of propane gas tanks that had been erroneously loaded and improperly stored in the hold. The sole survivor was Farberg's wine steward, a former South Vietnamese navy commando who had somehow managed to swim through the dark, shark-infested waters and reach shore alive.

And so it went from city to city, all across America. In Chicago, the Chairman of the area's largest bank hanged himself in his bathroom, leaving behind a rambling and at times incoherent suicide note that two of the three experts hired by the Chicago police deemed genuine; in L.A., the head of the entertainment industry's largest studio was found dead from a heroin overdose. His estranged wife professed to be shocked by the news, claiming that he had kicked the habit years ago. But his mistress shook her head sadly before the news cameras, confirming the fast-circulating rumors that he had suffered a relapse.

"It's tragic," she said. "Bernie was amazingly talented, a wonderful man." Then after placing her hands together, she bowed from the waist and whispered a Buddhist prayer in Vietnamese.

Scores of others died that night as well. But as we flew through the darkness high above the Atlantic, I had no way of knowing the bloody havoc Nguyen and his secret army were visiting upon the traitors.

Or that Alex had fallen, in a desperate attempt to shield the President from an assassin's bullet.

JUST BEFORE MIDNIGHT

CHAPTER FORTY-FIVE

About four hours later, we touched down in a blinding snowstorm. After what seemed like an interminably long time, the aircraft slowed to a crawl before pivoting to the left, and then creeping forward. Deeply relieved that the flight was finally over, I let out a long sigh as I peered out the window. Between the snow and the bright lights that played on us I couldn't see much, but as we passed through a shadow, I glimpsed hundreds of heavily armed soldiers standing at the ready. Beyond them, I could see batteries of anti-aircraft missiles mounted on armored vehicles and a mobile radar unit sweeping the skies just beyond.

As I turned back to Mai Ling, the plane suddenly jerked to a halt, and a moment later, the engines powered down. As the lights switched to battery power, the cabin door opened and Col. Kao and his co-pilot emerged. Stopping just short of us, the colonel knelt down and apologized for the turbulent flight. While the co-pilot wrestled with the door, he explained they had used the storm system to mask their movement. "There's no way the enemy could have tracked us through that mess."

Grateful to be alive and in one piece, I was about to join Mai Ling in thanking him when I heard heavy boots pounding up the gangway. A moment later an older, silver-haired man dressed in combat garb stepped into the cabin, followed by a taller and somewhat younger man dressed in civilian clothes. After returning salutes from Col. Kao and his co-pilot, he identified himself as General Pierre Fontaine of the Canadian Armed Forces, and welcomed us to Newfoundland. Then before we could reply, he brusquely informed us that his orders were to ensure our safe transfer to French control. Nodding to the tall man in civilian clothes, he introduced Colonel Gerard Fortescue of the French intelligence service.

Confused and alarmed, I glanced over at Mai Ling for reassurance. But the puzzled look that crept across her face told me she was as surprised as I was. As she sputtered something in French, Col. Fortescue stepped forward and explained in English that the Republic of France had placed us under its protection. Then very seriously, he instructed us to gather whatever belongings we might have and follow him with all due haste to the French Air Force transport idling on the runway.

"Time is of the essence, *Mesdames*. We must move quickly to ensure your safety."

On the verge of panic, I turned from the French colonel to the Canadian general, and then back to Mai Ling before scrunching up my nose. As Mai Ling unleashed a torrent of French, I demanded to know where they were taking us. Ignoring whatever Mai Ling had just said, the colonel turned to me. "To Paris, *Mademoiselle*, where you will be safe."

Then after turning back to Mai Ling to issue a brief reply, he glanced at his watch and commanded us to follow.

Normally I would have protested, but by then I was scared out of my wits again. Since it didn't take a rocket scientist to figure out the Canadians and the French wouldn't have gone to so much trouble to protect us if they didn't think the threat was real, I reluctantly stood up and handed my Unicorn to Mai Ling for safekeeping. "Let's go," I said softly.

After whispering my thanks to Gen. Fontaine, and then again to Col. Kao as I passed by him, I followed the French officer down the gangway and into the snowstorm. As I reached the ground, two tall and rather athletic young women dressed in parkas fell in beside me while another pair waited for Mai Ling. Not quite certain as to where they fit into the grand scheme of things, Big Minh and Lady Godiva hesitated for a moment before padding after us.

As Mai Ling and her escorts hurried to catch up, Col. Fortescue turned around and gestured as a group of soldiers armed with automatic rifles closed in around us. "Quickly" he said, before breaking into a trot.

Struggling against the howling blizzard, I glimpsed the outline of a much larger jet looming beyond the next phalanx of soldiers. By now nearly frozen stiff, I muttered a little prayer through my chattering teeth. Somehow the girl trotting next to me on my left heard it, because she moved in close and wrapped an arm around my waist. Half carrying me, she shouted over the wind to encourage me.

"Eez only leetle more," she cried in heavily accented English. "We weel make eet, even eef I must carry you!"

Unwilling to bear the shame of that, I lowered my head into the storm and drove myself forward. Another ten or fifteen seconds later, I found myself clambering up the icy gangway. By now shaking almost uncontrollably, I stumbled past the soldier at the top and into the warmth of the cabin. With her arm still wrapped around my waist, my escort guided me halfway down the aircraft before gently pushing me into an aisle seat and shooing

Big Minh in after me. "Fasten seatbelt," she said as she pulled a blanket out of the overhead compartment. Handing it to me as she moved out of the way for Mai Ling and her escorts, she paused for a moment before sitting down behind me. "When we take off, I bring you hot café."

Huddled under the blanket, I barely noticed as another group of soldiers filed by, their weapons at the ready. In fact, I probably wouldn't have noticed at all if it weren't for Mai Ling.

"*Mon Dieu,*" she exclaimed in a hushed voice. "*Légion étrangère!*"

Too miserable to really care, I peeked out from under my blanket and stared at her dully.

Apparently mistaking my indifference for interest, she pointed at the soldiers settling into the seats four or five rows ahead. "*Foreign Legion,*" she said. "Very fierce!"

"*Foreign Legion?*"

Nodding emphatically, Mai Ling pointed forward again and forced a wan smile. "Hope dey protect us…"

Still shivering under the blanket, I wondered how the Foreign Legion was going to defend us at 30,000 feet.

Guess they'll stick their guns out the windows, or something…

Just then the pitch of the engines suddenly changed, and after a shouted warning from somewhere toward the front, the jet lurched forward. As it accelerated down the runway, I turned in my seat to look through the window as the ground began slipping away from us. Then after a loud bump, we were in the air.

As the ground fell away from us, I heard a stirring behind me. Still too cold and miserable to care, I stared numbly out the window into the snowstorm, vaguely aware of the fighter escorts forming up alongside us. Still lost among the glittering snowflakes, I was startled by the voice of a woman behind me. "*Mademoiselle?*"

Wrenched from my reverie, I turned around to see the security agent extending a steaming cup of coffee. "Drink theez," she said. "Eet weel help warm you."

Thanking her, I shook my left arm free from the blanket and took the cup. Shaking my other hand free, I clutched it with both hands to extract the heat from the porcelain as I raised the steaming beverage to my lips. Too hot to gulp down, I held it there and took little sips instead. Then after wondering if my feet would ever feel warm again, I looked across the aisle at Mai Ling.

Still dressed in her parka, she was just finishing her cup when she sensed my presence and turned towards me. Dark circles had formed under her eyes and she looked exhausted, but she forced another smile as she raised her cup. "Maybe things little better now."

Nodding, I downed the last of my coffee as a steward in a white coat approached carrying a bottle of wine and two ornate glasses on a silver tray. After ceremoniously lowering the fold-down trays from the seats in front of us, and placing a glass on each, he silently filled each to the halfway mark. "Dinner will be served momentarily, *Mesdames*."

Suddenly aware that I was ravenously hungry, I thanked the steward and lifted the glass from the tray. After taking a small sip, I pushed the tray back into position and unbuckled my seatbelt, so I could turn around and take stock of my surroundings. Realizing for the first time that we were on a large, luxury jet that normally must have been reserved for military VIPs, I shrugged the blanket off my shoulder and pushed myself up higher in my seat. There were about twenty rows of large, leather-upholstered seats in front of me, with two abreast on each side of the center aisle. Soldiers occupied the first five rows, but the next five that separated us were empty. Behind us, the same pattern repeated itself, except for the security agents who had settled in behind us. Mistaking my curiosity for hunger, the girl who had half-carried me into the aircraft smiled and assured me that the promised food would be momentarily forthcoming. Then almost as an afterthought, she smiled again and introduced herself.

"You must be *Mademoiselle* McAllister," she said. "I am *Capitaine* Michelle Gaston, of zee *Direction General de la Securite Exterieure*...

"Col. Fortescue ees een command of zee operation, but I am een charge of zee detail assigned to ensure your personal security."

Since she hadn't extended her hand, I decided to acknowledge her with a smile instead. "It's nice to meet you, Captain." Then without even thinking, I blurted out the obvious question. "What's happening?"

Capt. Gaston – or Michelle, as she asked me to call her – shrugged and said she didn't know. "But eet must be very serious, because our orders came straight from zee President of zee Republic."

"So you're taking us to Paris?"

Nodding, Michelle assured me we would be safe there. In addition to the three agents who had accompanied her to Canada, another dozen would be waiting at a military airport outside of Paris – along with the battalion of Foreign Legionnaires that had been placed under Col. Fortescue's command.

"Zee enemy weel never reach you," she promised. "We weel fight to zee death."

Thinking that whole "fight to the death" thing wasn't *entirely* reassuring, I was struggling to come up with a reply when the steward returned carrying two silver trays. After excusing himself, he lowered my seat tray again before placing one of them on it. After he turned to Mai Ling and repeated the action, he lifted the silver covers from our plates and wished us "*Bon appétit.*"

A moment later, a second steward appeared with chopped and un-garnished steaks for the dogs.

Having excused myself from the conversation with Michelle, I thanked God for small favors. Because let's face it – given the choice between scary stuff, and sautéed steak and vegetables with little tiny potatoes covered in butter sauce on the side, the food's gonna win every time.

In a state of near starvation, I inhaled everything on my plate – including the exquisite salad, and the little tiny loaf of fresh baked bread – before draining my wine glass. Entirely unaware of the fact that the steward had been standing in the aisle behind us, I settled back into my chair as he refilled our glasses. But since Mai Ling had wolfed down her meal almost as quickly as I had, he had two gluttons to snicker at rather than just one.

Less embarrassed than I probably should have been, I was in the process of finishing off the second glass of wine when I suddenly realized Michelle was standing over me in the aisle. Having taken off her parka by then, I couldn't help but notice the grip of the semi-automatic handgun protruding from the modified shoulder holster she was wearing. Impressed by the clever way she had adapted it to her figure, I didn't even see the little travel case until she handed it to me. "I'm afraid theez has only the barest necessities, *Mademoiselle*, but eet weel have to do for now. When we get to Paris, I weel summon zee cosmetologeest."

Suddenly aware of what I must look like, I froze in my seat as my eyes involuntarily crossed. Then after taking a deep breath, I tentatively took the travel kit from her hand before asking where I could freshen up. After she pointed toward the rear and stepped aside, I pulled my still frozen feet out from underneath Big Minh – who had for some reason decided he liked the floor better than the leather upholstered seat – and edged into the aisle before self-consciously making my way past the soldiers.

They must be really brave, I thought.

Because even though they looked straight at me as I passed, not one of them cringed in terror.

Which happens to be a great deal more than I could say for myself. After I entered the rest room and locked the door behind me, I almost fainted when I looked in the mirror. Unable to believe the wretched image reflected in the glass could possibly be me, I stepped back against the wall and raised my fingers to my face. My hair was not only tangled, but matted, too – and my makeup was just too awful to describe. Most of it had been washed away in the snow, but my mascara had run all over the place and left dark streaks trailing down my cheeks and onto my collar. And to top it all off, I had big dark circles under my eyes, just like Mai Ling.

Thinking I looked like a raccoon who'd been caught in a rainstorm, I placed the little case on the marble vanity cover and opened it up. Peering inside, I found a comb and a brush and some hairpins, a compact with powder, moisturizer, a little bottle of foundation, some blush, an eyeliner pencil, a little case with various shades of eye shadow, a tube of mascara, a half dozen lipsticks of various shades and colors, and a toothbrush and a little tube of toothpaste that didn't actually belong there but which someone – presumably Michelle – had very thoughtfully enclosed anyway.

After reviewing the damage and prioritizing the repairs, I unwrapped the little bar of perfumed soap sitting next to the sink and got down to work.

Twenty minutes later, I emerged from the restroom and began making my way up the aisle to my seat. The emergency repairs I'd made on my face and hair had rendered me passable for polite company, but there wasn't a thing I could do about my clothes. Aside from the fact that I had no idea where my shoes were – I think I left them in the helicopter, back in Maryland – my jacket and skirt were torn, and the exposed part of the white blouse I was wearing was covered in grime. As for my hose – well, let's just say I gave them a decent burial.

So rather than force the Foreign Legionnaires to dwell upon my pasty white winter legs, I hurried back to my seat. After tucking the travel kit between the cushion and the armrest, I got up on my knees again and thanked Michelle for her kindness. Then, as an embarrassed look forced itself across my face, I asked her if there was any chance she could find me a pair of shoes and some hose to go with them.

After thinking about it for a moment, she shook her head. "I'm sure we have some travel slippers here somewhere, but I'm afraid zere are no shoes or stockings…

"But eef you weel give me your size, I weel call ahead and make sure zey will be waiting for you when we land."

Nodding, I thanked her. "Six and a half medium, or sometimes a seven, depending on the style." I said. Then I very hopefully informed her that a pair of travel slippers would do just fine for now.

Smiling, Michelle leaned across the aisle and said something in French to one of her subordinates. Nodding silently, the woman got up and headed toward the back of the plane. A few minutes later she returned with a pair of one-size-fits-all travel slippers wrapped in a plastic bag. The color didn't exactly go with my outfit, but since they were toasty warm I didn't care.

As my toes finally began to thaw, it occurred to me that I should probably ask Mai Ling about frostbite. But she had raised the armrest that separated the two seats on her side of the aisle, and curled up. Seemingly fast asleep under a blanket – with Lady Godiva alongside – I decided not to wake her. So instead, I reached across the aisle and retrieved my Unicorn from the interior pocket of her parka, which she had draped over the back of the seat in front of her.

Holding it with both hands as I settled back into my seat, I gazed at it for a long moment to admire its exquisite beauty. Then suddenly reminded of the terrible things that must have happened back in the U.S., I closed my eyes and clutched it to my chest. After praying for Alex and Nguyen, and for Sgt. Trung and his men, and for all the other Good Guys who had put their lives on the line to save ours, I prayed for President and Mrs. Reagan as well.

But most of all I prayed for Alex, and for us. After pleading with God to get him through this safe and unharmed, I begged Him to find a way for us to be together again.

And for the first time since I got kicked out of Catholic school, I even crossed myself when I finished.

Seriously hoping God would forget about that particular indiscretion – well, that and a couple of other little tiny things we don't need to go into – I opened my eyes before leaning back in my seat. I was still holding my Unicorn against my chest as my mind began drifting back through the series of deadly events that had driven me to this particular time and place.

Maybe I missed something…

I was still pondering that possibility when lightning struck. After jerking bolt upright in my seat, my jaw dropped and my eyes bulged. *Oh, my God…*

Vice President Bush used to be head of the CIA!

And at that moment, everything fell into place.

The CIA – well, the black operations types anyway – were going to kill the President, and put their guy in the White House!

Why didn't I see that before???

Thinking I was a complete idiot for missing the obvious, I pulled one hand away from my Unicorn just long enough to smack myself in the head. Although I didn't know a whole lot about the vice president, I did know that his father – Prescott Bush – had been a founding director of the Union Banking Corporation. I also knew that he had somehow managed to sell his single, publicly recorded share in UBC for a reported $1.5 million – and according to my history professor back at Township College, that was *after* UBC got busted laundering money for a Nazi bigwig during World War II!

Thinking there was no way in Hades anyone was going to pay a million and a half bucks for one share of tainted bank stock, I raised the armrest that divided my seat from the one next to it, and scooted over against the fuselage of the aircraft. Then after shifting around so I could lean against it, I pulled the blanket Michelle had given me up around my neck. I was still pondering the mysterious stock trade that had made the Bush family rich, when emotional exhaustion and physical fatigue combined with the warm glow of the wine. Without any awareness at all, I slipped into a deep and dreamless sleep.

I must have slept for five or six hours, because the sun was high in the sky when I looked out the window. Startled, I sat up in my seat and glanced around.

Mai Ling and Lady Godiva were still sound asleep, but there was a flurry of activity toward the front of the aircraft. Apparently awaiting orders, three of the Foreign Legion officers were arranged around Col. Fortescue while he talked to someone on a wall-mounted telephone. I was thinking that probably meant we were approaching our destination, when Michelle leaned over the backrest and wished me a good morning. "Did you sleep well, *Mademoiselle?*"

Shrugging off the blanket, I nodded and asked her where we were.

"Approaching zee French coastline," she said. "We weel land een less than an hour." Then she suggested I go brush out my hair while she summoned the steward. "He weel bring you orange juice and coffee and a baguette."

Thinking that was an excellent idea, I handed her my Unicorn and asked her to care for it while I was gone. Smiling, she took it from my hand and promised to guard it faithfully.

When I returned some ten minutes later, Mai Ling had mysteriously vanished but the promised breakfast tray had arrived. Deeply grateful for the coffee, I spent another ten minutes savoring the rich brew before turning to the juice and the roll. Halfway through the latter, Mai Ling suddenly reappeared before slipping into her seat and starting on her breakfast. "Goo morning," she said. "Soldier say we lan soon." Which turned out to true, because the moment she said it, the plane banked to the left and slowed. As we began descending, I could see the rich farmlands below and a scattering of little houses.

A minute or so later, the captain came on the intercom and announced we would be landing in just a few minutes. Then after repeating the message in English, the FASTEN SEAT BELTS signs came on. As we banked and slowed again, I caught sight of the perimeter fence of a military base and then a whole series of runways beyond it. Three minutes later, the wheels touched down.

After we came to a stop, Michelle leaned over my seat and explained that we would wait on the aircraft while the first group of soldiers filed out. Once they had taken up positions outside on the runway, we would follow with the rest of the troops behind us. But first, one of her subordinates would bring me shoes and a parka. Grateful that I would be spared the indignity of treading French soil in fuzzy slippers, I whispered my thanks.

A minute or so later, there was a loud bump from somewhere outside, and then a gust of cool air as someone opened the forward door. As the soldiers in front got up and began to file out, I wrapped my blanket around me and pondered the irony. I'd dreamed about traveling to France all my life, and here I was – a refugee in tattered clothes and borrowed slippers, with dirty hair, minimal makeup and the wrong shade of lipstick. Glancing toward the heavens – well, actually, the ceiling of the cabin – I gave the Almighty an irritated look.

Way to go, God…

But before I could bewail my predicament any further, a young woman appeared in the aisle. Tall and thin and obviously athletic, she said something to Michelle in French before handing me the parka she had slung across her arm and then a pair of flats that matched my tattered outfit. *Not exactly my style*, I thought as I slipped them on. But since they fit well – and looked *really* expensive – I decided I shouldn't complain.

Once I'd struggled into my parka, Mai Ling's minders took up positions in front and behind her and escorted her forward.

Repeating the drill, Michelle fell in behind them and gestured for me, "Welcome to France."

After we made our way down the stairs, the soldiers fell in alongside of us and we began marching towards a large hanger. By this time, Michelle had changed our formation, so that Mai Ling and I were walking abreast with the dogs between us, with one security agent in front, one in back, and one on either side.

After thrusting out her chest and imitating the soldiers' march as we trooped along, Mai Ling began whistling the theme song from *The Bridge Over the River Kwai*. After a moment or two of that particular weirdness, I finally looked over my right shoulder and demanded to know what she was doing.

Mai Ling looked back at me and grinned. "Been prisoner before...

"Vietnam camp very harsh. Little food, brutal guard...

"So I whistle merry tune an lift spirit. Den one day guard catch me, an beat me long time wit stick...

"Den he get political officer. Political officer come ask what I whistle...

"But I know him stupid man, so I tell him it 'Great Proletarian Anti-Fascist Resistance Song' an say I learn in other camp.

"Political officer very impressed, say I make progress in re-education."

Grinning from ear to ear, Mai Ling looked over at me again. "Fool tell me teach it everyone in camp, so we whistle song when guard around an laugh under breath."

Seeing the shocked look on my face – because I knew they would have shot her if they'd ever figured out the truth – Mai Ling chuckled triumphantly.

"Dey *neeeeeev-er* catch me!"

Then she started whistling again.

Amazed by her courage – not to mention her wacky sense of humor – I was still shaking my head when we filed into the hanger, and the huge doors began rolling shut. Then after the lights came on and my eyes adjusted, I could see a couple of armored limousines surrounded by at least a dozen police cars. But when I saw the two doubles standing next to the second limo, my jaw dropped. Dressed in identical ragged outfits with minimal makeup and bedraggled hair, they could have easily passed as our twins. Except the girl impersonating me – the one with the not-entirely-legal red hair – was prettier than I was.

Which was like, *really* irritating.

At that point Col. Fortescue began barking orders, and the two girls climbed into the back limo with their four female security agents. Then as the hanger doors began opening again and the limos and the police cars started their engines, Michelle grabbed Mai Ling and me by our arms and steered us to a rather battered delivery van off to the side. Still irritated and by now deeply confused, I turned to her and demanded to know what was going on.

"Motorcade ees diversion," she said matter-of-factly. "We weel ride in zee van."

Disappointed, I clambered into the clunker and waved for the dogs before sitting down on one of the customized benches someone had installed. After looking around, I had to admit the accommodations were passable – it was neat and clean inside, and the bench I was sitting on was well padded and comfortable. But all things considered, entering Paris for the first time in a limo would have been *way* cool.

After Mai Ling and the other three security agents climbed in, Michelle pushed the side door shut and locked it before telling us to be patient. The motorcade would leave first, and exit the main gate of the air force base. We would leave after them, and take the service gate.

After the wail of the police sirens faded into the distance, Michelle shouted something to the driver and the vehicle jerked forward. But since the van didn't have any windows in the cargo section, I couldn't see a darn thing. Except for an occasional stop or start, I was entirely clueless as to our progress.

About an hour later, the van finally slowed and tilted forward as we entered what I guessed was an underground parking lot. Then after the vehicle stopped, backed up, and then stopped again, Michelle got up and opened the side door. After we clambered out, she led us through a heavy steel door into what seemed like an ancient, stone-walled basement. Then after pressing a button set on the exterior of an ornate iron cage, a rickety old elevator began slowly descending. Unlike most of the old-fashioned elevators in France, this one was roomy enough to accommodate all six of us humans and still have a bit of room for our furry companions.

A couple of minutes later, it stopped on what I thought must be the third floor. After Michelle opened the door, we stepped out into what looked like an exceptionally elegant hotel with deep, plush carpeting and elegant off-white walls adorned with original seventeenth-century artwork. As she led us down the hall and past a series of statues to our suite, Michelle turned around and welcomed us to our new home. "Theez was once zee Paris residence of a great French lord, so I theenk you weel like eet here. Eet ees equipped weeth every amenity, including an open courtyard and a magnificent chef."

Then after opening a door that led into an opulent suite, she gestured to either side. "Theez parlor overlooks zee courtyard, and on each side zee bedroom for each weeth bath and sauna…

"And zere are telephones een every room, so all you need do ees lift zee receiver for immediate assistance."

Then after looking back and forth, she smiled. "You weel weesh to bathe, *mais oui?*"

"New clothes weel be delivered momentarily."

After looking around in astonishment, I concluded I had to be dreaming. But since I'd acquired something of a scent over the past 14 or 15 hours, I decided to suspend my disbelief on the off chance it might be real. So I was just about to tell Michelle how much I'd love to climb into a steamy, hot tub when Col. Fortescue suddenly appeared in the doorway.

After summoning her out into the hallway, the two conferred in a hushed whisper. Then after apparently reaching some sort of an agreement, the colonel strode back into the room and cleared his throat. "I am afraid, *Mesdames*, that I have what you Americans call a good news-bad news story."

Then as my stomach knotted, he continued. "*Madame Docteur*, Major Tranh's forces are everywhere victorious…

"He is alive and unharmed…

"But I regret to inform you that *Monsieur* de Vris has been wounded."

Then after turning to me, he continued gravely. "I can tell you only that he is alive, *Mademoiselle*. I have no other information."

CHAPTER FORTY-SIX

After a moment of shocked silence, all hell broke loose.

Stricken, I slumped back upon the couch, as Mai Ling surged past me and unleashed a torrent of rapid-fire French. Apparently unwilling to wait for Col. Fortescue's reply, she switched to English. With her balled-up fists pressed tight to her sides, she slammed her foot down on the floor and ordered him to summon an aircraft immediately. "Alex patien, you take me him now!"

"*Madame Docteur*," he began in a sympathetic voice. But before he could complete the sentence, Mai Ling stood up on her tiptoes and thrust her hands in his face.

"Surgeon hands!" she screamed. "Saigon battle, make thousands procedures…

"Terrible circumstance…

"No electricity, operate wit flashlight. Run out of drug, bandage, blood, glucoze…

"Sterilize instrument wit rice pot!"

Lowering her hands before her face, she stared at them as tears welled in her eyes. "Even all dat, save many, many soldier lives."

After struggling to regain her composure, Mai Ling looked up again and repeated her demand for an aircraft. "Take me America now, hands save Alex too."

Then as she burst into tears and began sobbing, Col. Fortescue stepped forward and gently placed his hands upon her heaving shoulders. "*Madame Docteur*," he said in a soft and deeply sympathetic voice, "I do not doubt your skill…

"But you must understand that *Monsieur* de Vris has already received the finest medical treatment the United States can offer…

"He was with *Monsieur* Reagan when he was struck down, so he received immediate care from the President's physician."

Still sobbing, Mai Ling wiped the tears from her eyes. Then after another struggle to regain her composure, she sniffled before nodding and looking up. Switching back into French, she began rattling off a series of words and phrases while touching one finger after another on her left hand with her right index. Gently releasing his hands from her shoulders, Col. Fortescue nodded earnestly. "Of course, *Madame*, I will see to it myself."

"You not forget?"

"No, *Madame*, you have my word. I will cable Washington for the information immediately."

After thanking him in an almost child-like voice, Mai Ling sank down on the couch beside me as the Colonel and Michelle retreated from the suite. After putting her arms around me, we both burst into tears.

Shaking and trembling as she wept, Mai Ling switched from one language to another as she cursed the Fates. Then finally in English, she said it wasn't fair. Alex had won her freedom from the concentration camp in Vietnam, and for that she owed him her life. But now that he needed her, she wasn't there to help.

And even though it wasn't true, she berated herself for having run away and left him to face the enemy alone.

Having retreated to somewhere deep inside, I barely heard her lament. Overcome by fear and overwhelmed by anguish, I leaned my head against hers and wept. Then after a long time, I finally summoned the wit to ask her what it all meant.

Puzzled, Mai Ling pulled back and stared at me through teary eyes. "What mean?"

So after sniffling and rubbing my nose, I refined my question and asked her what it meant when someone is shot. "From a medical standpoint."

Looking down, Mai Ling shook her head. "Many variable involve, Aliza...

"Size an velocity of bullet, where it impak...

"Whether hit bone or vital organ...

"How much blood loss, natural health an strength of victim...

"Many, many things."

Nodding desperately, I pressed her again. "But what are the odds of survival?"

Still looking down, Mai Ling shook her head. "Dat depen," she said. "If bullet not hit vital organ an he get immediate medical attention, dey pretty goo...

"Maybe two in three...

"But Alex strong man, so odds prolly little better."

Then she looked up at me. "Can't say witout more information, so I ask Colonel for medical file. He send request to Washington."

"So you'll know if you get the file?"

Mai Ling nodded. "Pretty sure," she said, before turning very serious. "But wit trauma case, God decide...

"Even best surgeon not save all, even when patien not seem hurt so bad."

Then after pulling a tissue from a box on the end table beside her, she rubbed her nose and shook her head. "It funny thing, Aliza…

"Sometime, I feel God presence an I know patien be OK. Den other time, I sense Angel presence an I know dey come take patien to Heaven."

Then after a long moment, she exhaled sharply. "Den times I feel something awful, and I know Evil Spirit come for patien soul."

Then after looking up at me with eyes the size of saucers, she crossed herself. "I call priest, tell him drive Demon away wit prayer."

Suddenly scared out of my wits, I pulled back and stared at her with bulging eyes. "Does that work?"

Mai Ling shrugged. "Dunno for patien. Make me feel better, tho."

Then she lowered her head again, and choked back more tears. "Dat what scare me, Aliza…

"Alex good man, he kind an generous an I know God love him for dat…

"But he cheat Death in war, an I tink maybe it chase after him now."

As a chill crept up my spine, I shivered involuntarily. "You're not the only one, girl."

Mai Ling sniffled again. "So I go Church every morning, pray God protect him."

Then very suddenly, Mai Ling stood up and ran her fingers through her long, disheveled hair. "Too much stress, I sleep now." Then without another word, she marched off to the bedroom Michelle had assigned her.

Too exhausted to make the trek to mine, I curled up on the couch instead.

When I awoke the next morning, I found myself lying on a bed underneath a comforter in the room Michelle had assigned me. I hadn't the slightest idea how I got there, but since I was still wearing everything but my shoes, I guessed one of the Legionnaires had carried me in. But with a pounding headache – and a mouth as dry as the desert – I was just too miserable to really care. So after crawling out from under the comforter, I stumbled to the bathroom in search of water.

Had my wits been about me, I probably would have noticed the pitcher of water and the ornate crystal glass on the silver tray sitting on top of the nightstand. But in my disoriented state, that slipped right past me, so I turned on the cold water in the bathroom. After pulling back my hair, I leaned my head under the faucet and drank.

Not exactly ladylike, but I was just too out of it to care.

Having sated my thirst, I hobbled back into the bedroom. Noticing for the first time the pile of clothes sitting on the dresser, I walked over and examined them. In addition to a really elegant robe and a pair of slippers, there were three sets of casual tops and jeans, a pair of sweats with a hooded pullover, and three pairs of casual shoes lying on the floor. Nothing special except for the robe, but everything – including the rather sexy undergarments – was my size.

So after stripping off my clothes, I stuffed my feet into the slippers and grabbed the robe before returning to the bathroom to finally shower – which was like, way overdue, because my scent had reached toxic levels by then. Had any children or small animals been within a three-block radius, they probably would have asphyxiated.

After a long, luxurious shower, I pulled the bedroom door open a half-hour later and walked into the main room of the suite, wearing a pair of jeans, the hooded pullover, and the cordovan penny loafers I'd found on the floor. Mai Ling was seated at the table near the balcony doors, gnawing on baguette and reading a newspaper. Off to the side, a French newscaster was reporting the news on the big screen TV she had somehow managed to drag across the room.

Sensing my presence, Mai Ling half-turned in her chair and gave me a wan smile. "Goo morning," she said, in a voice still edged with fear.

After crossing the room, I pulled out a chair and sat down across the table from her. As I reached down to scratch the dogs behind their ears, I asked her if there was any word on Alex.

Mai Ling frowned and shook her head as she reached to pour me a glass of orange juice. "Not yet..."

"Jus big lie from media."

Unsettled, I played with the glass of juice before reaching for a pastry. "What are they saying?"

After polishing off her baguette and reaching for another, she pointed at the stack of newspapers she'd tossed aside. "Dey say Arab terrorist attack office."

"Arab terrorists?"

Mai Ling nodded. "Uh-huh...

"An den dey say security guards fight very brave an shoot dem. Bad news terrorist all dead so no one know why dey attack...

"President make statement condemn violence, say guards big hero."

Yeah, right, I thought disgustedly. *Those low-lifes set me up!*

Then Mai Ling pulled a newspaper off the stack and showed me the huge front-page picture of what was left of the CSS building. Gasping as I surveyed the damage, I shook my head in disbelief. "Good God," I muttered. "My Mom must have had a heart attack!"

Mai Ling shook her head as she poured us cups of rich French coffee. "Not worry," she said. "Colonel come hour ago, say *Professeur* MacLaughlin call mother an tell her you safe, an say he put you on plane to Brussels for NATO study hour before attack."

Thank God, I thought. *Because if she ever finds out the truth, I'm toast...*

Finally summoning up the courage, I asked her if there was any word about Sgt. Trung and his men.

Mai Ling nodded. "Dat good news...

"Sergeant an three men wound little, not so serious. Already release from doctor care."

After breathing a deep sigh of relief, I began mindlessly nibbling on my baguette. Half-finished, I was reaching for my coffee when the hallway door suddenly opened and Col. Fortescue marched in with a large manila envelope tucked under his arm. Stopping just before the table, he handed the envelope to Mai Ling. "The information you requested, *Madame.*"

Snatching it from his hands, Mai Ling ripped it open and hurriedly thumbed through the contents. Then after seizing what looked like an X-Ray, she bounded over to the courtyard window and held it up to the light. As she studied the film, I could see the tension drain from her face.

"Oh tank God," she whispered. "Big thick skull save life!"

After crossing herself, she turned to me. "Swear to God," she said. "Never ever call Alex blockhead again, long as live!"

Then after tucking the X-Ray under her arm, she placed her hands together and looked up. "Dat promise, Lord!"

After closing my eyes and letting out a huge sigh of relief, I asked her how he was.

Looking back at me, Mai Ling chuckled. "Bullet make new part in hair," she said. "An he have big headache two day, maybe three."

Still grinning, she wagged her finger at me. "But he deserve dat, for make me worry!"

After sitting back down, she began skimming through the rest of the material. Suddenly irate, she slammed her tiny fist down on the table before holding up a sheet covered with incomprehensible scrawl. "See dis?" she demanded. "I tell Alex quit smoke, but he don' listen...

"So I yell at him till he promise jus five cigarette a day."

Then after scrunching up her face, she shook the paper in front of my face. "But dis make me tink he cheat."

Stuffing the X-Ray and the other pages back into the folder, Mai Ling shook her head. "Nguyen prolly cheat too...

"Jus wait till I get hold of boys," she muttered ominously. "I beat dem wit stick!"

Snickering as Mai Ling thanked the Colonel, I briefly considered ratting on Alex – because after all, Mai Ling was his doctor. But after a moment's thought, I decided some gentle chiding downstream might be better.

Maybe he'll listen to me...

As Col. Fortescue excused himself and made his exit, I suddenly realized I was starving. "So what's up with the French?" I whispered. "Don't they believe in breakfast?"

Mai Ling shook her head. "Juice, pastry, an coffee...

"But goo lunch, wonerful dinner."

"That's nice," I said. "But right now, I'd really like a big plate of bacon and eggs, and an English muffin covered in butter...

"And some of those little microwave sausages, too."

Mai Ling grinned and nodded enthusiastically. "Dey really goo!"

Then after looking down at her watch, she informed me lunch would be in an hour. "Den Colonel give us briefing."

Thinking that was a good thing, I asked her about Nguyen. After she told me Col. Fortescue had reassured her once again, the conversation turned back to the office and all the absurd news stories about the attack. But somehow or another we got sidetracked, because by the time the stewards arrived with our lunch, Mai Ling had told me all about the magical summer she'd spent in Paris after graduating from college, and of course, about all the shops and stores and museums we just had to visit while we were here.

I was thinking that was a fantastic idea when the first steward set my salad plate in front of me and totally derailed my train of thought. "Oh, my God," I whispered. "I've died and gone to Heaven!"

Which in fact, wasn't that far from the truth – because in addition to the salad, the main course consisted of sautéed steak, peas, raw carrots, a small serving of mashed potatoes artistically arranged, and of course, a loaf of bread fresh from the oven. More to the point, the very first bite revealed a master chef had prepared it all. So rather than dawdle, I followed Mai Ling's example and began shoveling food into my mouth.

Twenty minutes later – after finishing off the little cup of ice cream the steward brought after he removed my plate – I leaned back into my chair and lifted my wine glass to my lips. Noting that Mai Ling was on her third serving of the frozen treat, I was suddenly struck by the astonishing incongruity.

The girl eats like a horse, I thought. *And she still has a perfect figure???*

Envious, I had just made a mental note to ask her about that when Col. Fortescue marched into the room accompanied by Michelle. After apologizing for interrupting our meal, he strode to the far end of the table and informed us that circumstances beyond his control had compelled him to advance our schedule. Still standing, he waved Michelle to a chair on his right, and asked for our indulgence.

"As I presume you know, *Mesdames*, the attack upon the Center for Strategic Studies has received enormous publicity throughout the world. This is not an accident...

"The American authorities have attributed the attack to Arab terrorists, and done all that is possible to exploit the incident in order to divert attention from the attempted assassination of *Monsieur le Président* Reagan, the wounding of *Monsieur* de Vris and – of course – the many conspirators killed in reprisal."

Unable to restrain myself, I suddenly interrupted. "So how many Bad Guys did Nguyen take out?"

Suppressing the frown that had attempted to creep across his face, Col. Fortescue replied in a brusque, military tone. "I am not in possession of all the details, *Mademoiselle*, but I believe the total amounts to some hundreds so far...

"And since perhaps a dozen of these individuals were exceptionally prominent and well-known, your government has deemed it necessary to prevent the public from making the connection between their sudden demise and the attack upon your President...

"Unfortunately, however, it appears that the plot went deeper than your intelligence had imagined and a number of lesser figures are still at large. Because our own intelligence reports that they are well-organized, well-armed, well-funded, and undoubtedly desperate, we believe they remain a potent threat. Given the chance, we believe they will attempt to exact vengeance – and loyalist elements of your CIA agree...

"For that reason, *Monsieur le Directeur* Casey has asked that we provide for your security here in Paris until the threat is eliminated."

"You mean we can't leave?"

"No, *Mademoiselle*, you must remain with us for the time being. But we will do everything within our power to make your stay as pleasant as possible."

Clearly irritated, Mai Ling leaned forward and locked her eyes on the colonel. "When Nguyen come?"

After hesitating for a moment, Col. Fortescue apologized. "*Madame Docteur*, I am sorry to inform you that it may be several weeks or perhaps even months before the Major can come for you. He has been tasked with hunting down the remnants of the conspiracy, and that will undoubtedly take some time." Apologizing again for the change of schedule, he informed us that he had to attend to urgent business elsewhere. "*Capitaine* Gaston will complete your briefing."

Once the Colonel left, Michelle asked the steward to bring us fresh coffee. After he placed new cups before us and filled them, she hoisted a slender briefcase onto the table and opened it. Pulling two thick manila envelopes from within, she handed the first to Mai Ling and the second to me.

"Inside zeez folders you weel find zee complete documentation we weel use to establish your cover identities here in Paris...

"Passports, drivers' licenses, and what we call 'backstop' – for you, *Madame Docteur*, a French birth certificate, a French national identity card, a physician's license, and an employee ID from zee Paris military hospital, a letter from a purported lover, a check book, credit cards, and miscellaneous receipts. All zeese in your cover name of *Docteur* Lydia Chang...

"Please take note of zee address listed, and your telephone number. You must memorize zeese, and all other details of your cover identity."

Turning, she instructed me to open my folder. "You weel find a Canadian passport and driver's license inside, *Mademoiselle*, a student identification card listing you as a graduate student from zee University of Toronto, a checkbook from a Canadian bank, a bundle of travelers checks, assorted credit cards and receipts, a library card from zee Canadian town in which you are supposed to be from, and a small notebook listing zee telephone number of your landlord here in zee city, and various friends, faculty members, and acquaintances at zee American University of Paris where you are conducting research for your graduate thesis in zee economics."

Then after taking a moment to prepare her coffee – two sugars, believe it or not, and a ton of cream – she informed us that the *Palais* was not a prison. "You are guests of zee *République*, and we hope eet weel soon be possible for you to enjoy our city…

"But your security ees first and foremost, so eet is essential you completely memorize every detail of your cover identity. Do you understand?"

After nodding, I glanced down at my new driver's license.

They have got to be kidding, I thought. *Rebecca Ann Holland? From 'Lost Moose Creek,' Ontario???*

Then after wondering where they got the photo – which wasn't bad, by the way – I glanced down at the written description and did a quick conversion of kilos to pounds in my head.

What???

"A hundred and twenty-three pounds?" I sputtered.

Sitting bolt upright in my chair, I gave Michelle my *Completely Evil Look* before holding up the license and pointing at the metrics.

"Now, that's a *damned* lie!"

CHAPTER FORTY-SEVEN

After an extended argument that lasted the better part of ten minutes, Michelle rolled her eyes and sighed before finally conceding. "Very well, *Mademoiselle*, I weel order a new set of documents listing your weight as 118 pounds, as you say." Then after giving me another irritated look, she asked if there was anything else before she resumed.

Thinking I'd pushed my luck far enough for one day, I decided against arguing the Rebecca Ann thing. So I shook my head instead, and placed my hands together on the table.

"Very good," said Michelle.

Then after pulling another two thick envelopes from her briefcase, she handed them down the table. "As you have already discovered, we placed a few casual clothes in your rooms thees morning…

"But you will need additional items of clothing, so I have brought you zeese catalogues so you may choose your own colors and styles…

"Thees of course weel cost money, but I am informed that your CIA has placed you on a per diem allowance of $150 per day. Theese funds will be deposited in your cover accounts each Friday, so you weel have money to cover zee expense…

"So you may order what you weesh using zee credit cards we have supplied, and have zee clothes sent to your cover address. Once zey arrive, we weel have them delivered here to zees suite." Then after glancing from Mai Ling to myself, and then back again, Michelle asked if we understood.

Nodding as I flipped through the first catalogue, I had just started calculating what kind of a wardrobe I could put together with my per diem when it occurred to me the term implied we'd have to pay for room and board. Looking up from a gorgeous sundress, I asked Michelle how much the suite was going to cost us.

"Nothing, *Mademoiselle*. As I have said, you are zee guests of zee *République*."

Grinning, I told her I'd have my first order ready by morning.

"Good," she said. "Now we can move on to zee more important things." Then she reached into her briefcase again, and withdrew two sheets of paper. "Zees ees zee schedule that we weel follow here at zee *Palais*."

After handing one to Mai Ling and the other to me, she gave us a minute to look them over. "You shall awaken at 6:00 am, and have one half-hour to dress before breakfast. Breakfast weel last from 6:30 to 7:15, followed by fifteen minutes to change into your athletic clothes...

"From 7:30 to 9:00 we weel have zee physical training in zee gymnasium, followed by 20 minutes to shower and dress. After that, *Madame Docteur* will report to zee *Palais* clinic where she will be available to treat personnel until 11:45...

"During zees time, *Mademoiselle* weel report to her office on zee second floor where she weel conduct her analysis."

Huh?

Sticking my index finger up in the air, I asked Michelle just exactly what analysis she was referring to.

"I do not know, *Mademoiselle*. *Monsieur le Président* will brief you when he calls."

"President Mitterrand?"

Rolling her eyes, Michelle informed me that *Monsieur Mitterrand* was the only president France had. "Until zee election, anyway."

"President Mitterrand has a project for me?"

"Oui, *Mademoiselle*. I am told he is most impressed by your expertise."

Wow! I thought. *Economist-Girl strikes again!*

So after making a mental note to have Madame Henri make me a Super Hero suit – you know, with boots and a red cape and everything – I asked Michelle what the project was about.

Suppressing her irritation at my interruptions, she sighed. "I do not really know, *Mademoiselle*. Something about zee European Economic Community's planned expansion, I believe."

Then after pausing, she asked with thinly disguised sarcasm if she might resume.

Slumping back into my chair, I nodded.

"Very well, *Mademoiselle*....

"Zee mid-day meal shall be from noon until 1:30 pm. After that, you weel return to your assigned duties until 4 pm."

Then she grinned. "However, eef you weesh to sneak out a beet early so as to join us in zee lounge by 4 pm, no one weel be offended."

Puzzled, I asked her what was in the lounge.

"Zee large TV, *Mademoiselle*. Here at zee *Palais*, we have made eet a habit to gather there each afternoon to watch *Les Mensonges du Coeur*."

Smiling again, she translated. "In zee English, 'The Lies of the Heart.'"

After glancing over at Mai Ling – who was engrossed in a lingerie catalogue – I turned back to Michelle. "What's that?"

Laughing, Michelle explained it that it was a fantastically popular soap opera in France. "But for those of us in zee service, eet has become something of – how do you say – an addiction?"

Then she smiled again, and winked. "You weel see."

After pausing again for a moment, she explained that dinner would be served at 7 pm, and we could eat at our leisure. After that, our time was our own until lights out at 11 pm. "But I am not a baby seetter, so eef you weesh to stay up a bit later, I weel have no objection."

Then after glancing at Mai Ling – who was intently studying a rather scandalous black lace bustier – Michelle explained we would have weekends off, except for the obligatory workout at the gym on Saturday mornings.

"You are Catholic, no?"

Shaking my head, I pointed at Mai Ling. "She's a Catholic – I'm a sinner."

Snickering, Michelle informed me that they were trying to find a priest to hold Sunday services. "But unfortunately, zee military has zee shortage of chaplains right now so eet may be a few weeks."

Thinking I'd lucked out again, I told her not to worry about it. Then I asked her about the weekends. "Can we do any sightseeing?"

Michelle nodded, and said they were working on it. But our doubles had to establish their presence in Brussels first, and the French security service had to make a sweep of Paris. "We are working on thees, *Mademoiselle*..."

"We hope to take you sightseeing, and to some of zee cultural attractions soon."

In the meantime, the French had just set up a special landline routed through Belgium so I could call my mother. "Eef zee call ees intercepted, eet will appear to have originated in Brussels."

Then after explaining to a crestfallen Mai Ling that they were unable to contact Nguyen because he was still in the field with his men, she glanced down at her watch. "Zee line should be open by now, *Mademoiselle*, so you may place your call. But you must not deviate from zee cover story that you are in Belgium for zee month to attend a NATO Economic Conference...

"If she asks you any questions, you must tell her that all details are classified and you are not permitted to speak of them...

"You understand?"

Nodding, I asked her where I could make the call.

"Use zee telephone een your room," she said. "Merely lift zee receiver and tell zee operator zee number you weesh to call."

Thinking I might as well get it over with, I got up slowly and walked back to my bedroom. After closing the door for privacy, I leaned back against it for a moment to compose my thoughts.

She's gonna have a cow...

But since there was nothing I could do about it, I shrugged and walked over to the small telephone table and pulled out a chair. After calculating the time difference and taking a deep breath, I lifted the ivory and gold handset from the intricately carved base and gave the operator my mother's residential number.

"Hi, Mom."

Convinced that she was going to come unglued, I reflexively pulled the handset away from my ear and grimaced. But Dr. MacLaughlin must have laid it on really thick, because her voice was actually calm. After telling me how glad she was I'd called, she went on and on about how thoughtful my boss had been. "He called me before I even heard of the attack, to let me know you were en route to Europe...

"And then again this morning to let me know you'd safely arrived...

"Otherwise, I would have been scared to death!"

So after nodding and agreeing with her, I let her rattle on and on about how terrible it all had been. "Can you imagine?" she said. "Terrorists blowing up a building in our nation's capital???"

Having actually seen the explosion, I could do a lot more than imagine it. But since I didn't want to worry her, I just played along. "Yeah, Mom, it's awful...

"Those terrorists have a lot of nerve."

So after another five minutes or so of nodding into the phone and saying "Uh-huh" and "Right," she finally asked me about Brussels.

"Well, there's not a whole lot I can tell you, 'cause it's all very hush-hush. But the conference is really interesting, and they've put us up in a really nice hotel...

"And after we get our Study Group up and running, they're gonna let us do some sightseeing and stuff."

Confused by her response, I pulled the telephone away from my ear and looked at it. *Huh?*

Having finally figured out what she was asking, I nodded. "Oh yeah, Alex was with the President in St. Paul or someplace, so he wasn't there."

What?

"Well, Christine – you know, Mrs. O'Connell, our Executive Vice President? – she told me President Reagan was going to send him on some sort of secret mission somewhere, so you probably won't be seeing him on TV for a while."

"Bangladesh? What's he doing there?"

Nodding as she recounted the news report, I told her that made sense. "No, Mom, Christine can handle the rebuilding. She's got a Harvard MBA, you know."

"Yeah, well, that's the thing – my office was really gorgeous, so I'm kinda bummed out about it...

"I mean, you should have seen the Oriental rugs, and the artwork!

"Yeah, well, I guess that's life in Washington. But I'm gonna call her the first chance I get and ask her to put it back together just exactly as it was."

"Yeah, Mom, really, *REALLY* busy...

"No, I'm not supposed to give you the phone number because this whole thing is like super-secret and they don't want anyone to know we're even here...

"So don't say anything to the neighbors, OK?

"Especially Mrs. Albright, 'cause you know how she likes to talk...

"But I'll give you a call in a couple of days, OK?

"Yeah, I promise...

"Love you."

Thinking that had gone a lot better than I expected, I returned the handset to its cradle and let out a big sigh of relief before heading back into the main room. Finding it empty, I walked across to Mai Ling's room and looked inside the open doors. Puzzled to find it empty too, I went back out into the main room and shook my head.

Musta gone someplace, I thought.

After hesitating for just a moment, I walked over to the hallway entrance and tugged the doors open. Finding two gigantic Foreign Legionnaires dressed in civilian clothes standing guard on either side, I craned my neck back and asked the one on my right if he spoke English.

Smiling, he nodded and replied in a thick Irish accent. "That I do, Missy..."

"What can we do for you?"

Strangely surprised, I asked him if he'd seen my friends. "A not-so-tall Oriental woman, and two really big dogs."

"That I have...

"Your lady friend took them down to the courtyard...

"But we'll be happy to escort you there, if you care to join them."

Thinking I could use some fresh air, I nodded. "Please."

So after I'd dashed back into my room to grab my parka, he hoisted a walkie-talkie to his mouth and said something in a weird French dialect – which, as I later learned, is called "Legion French" – then jerked his head at his companion. "Come on Lad, we'll take the young Miss to her friend."

Following the first Legionnaire up the hallway toward the elevator, with the second one in tow, I had just started wondering how he had ended up in the Foreign Legion when he suddenly started swearing. Pointing at a handwritten sign taped over the control buttons, he informed me we would have to take the stairs. "Bloody thing is out of service again."

Gesturing to an unmarked door 15 or 20 feet beyond, he told me to follow him. "Now you'd think the damn government could come up with a few francs to keep the contraption running, wouldn't you?"

Not quite sure what to say, I followed him the rest of the distance and through the door he had opened for me. After thanking him, I fell in behind and started traipsing down the steps. Hoping my Irish ancestry would stand me in good stead, I asked him what his name was.

"Liam," he said, as he glanced back over his shoulder. "Corporal Liam O'Toole, at your service, Miss."

"It's nice to meet you, Liam. I'm Alicia – Alicia McAllister."

Then after a moment's hesitation, I asked him what a nice Irish lad like him was doing in the Legion.

Turning half around this time, he smiled. "Well I had me a bit of an accounting problem back in Dublin Town, so I thought I'd best seek my fortune elsewhere."

Puzzled, I echoed his statement. "An accounting problem?"

Nodding as he turned back to the steps, he explained that he'd made a rather large withdrawal from a bank one night and the management had taken exception.

By now thoroughly confused, I asked him how they could possibly object to that. "After all, it was your money."

Laughing, the Legionnaire turned around on the stoop, and explained that was the point of contention. "Well you see, I didn't actually have an account there."

Huh?

Then it finally sunk in. *"You robbed a bank???"*

Chuckling, he said preferred to think of it in terms of an unorthodox loan. "I meant to pay it back, of course."

Seeing the look on my face, he leaned toward me and pointed at the Legionnaire following behind. "But my fine German friend here, 'e killed ten men."

Then leaning in further, he lowered his voice to a whisper.

"Snuck into their rooms as they lay sleeping, an' slit their throats!"

Horrified, I shrank back against the wall and looked up at the killer standing on the steps just behind me. Leaning forward, the sandy-haired Legionnaire made a hideous face as he slid his right index finger across his throat.

Oh, dear God…

Thinking it was then or never, I was about to make a run for it when the two men broke up in gales of laughter.

Huh?

Then suddenly realizing they were jerking my chain, I just stood there for a moment before shaking my head.

Then I gave them my *Most Evil Glare.*

"Jerks!"

So after slamming my elbow into Liam's side, I stomped past him and headed down the steps alone.

Unfazed by the blow, the oversized Irishman raced past me to take up his position in front. Still laughing, he turned around and began walking backwards down the steps – which was actually pretty impressive, to tell you the truth – as he smiled apologetically. "To be honest, Missy, I had me a bit of woman trouble…

"So I decided I'd get away for a while."

Harumph!

"And me friend Gunther here, 'e was just looking for a little adventure."

Having tried and failed to ignore the jerk, I rolled my eyes and gave him my *Truly Disgusted Look.* Then I pointed down the stairway, and barked a command. "March!"

Two and a half flights of stairs later, we emerged into a large, well-manicured courtyard. Still chuckling, the Legionnaires joined two others who were standing on either side of the doorway as I stomped over to Mai Ling. Wresting a tennis ball from Lady Godiva's mouth, she took a couple of steps backward before hurling it toward the brickwork at the far end of the quadrangle. Barking like there was no tomorrow, the dogs raced after the ball before screeching to a halt and making a frantic U-turn when it bounced off the masonry.

Running for all she was worth, Mai Ling beat the dogs to it by a fraction of a second, spun around and hurled it back at the wall in a single graceful motion. Laughing, she raced forward again but this time she was too late. Big Minh got it first.

Noticing me out of the corner of her eye, Mai Ling waved me over. "Goo game," she said. "Mai Ling fifteen, dogs twelve...

"But tired now, so glad you come."

Then after persuading Big Minh to surrender the ball, she handed it to me. "We make team, Peoples verzes Dogs."

Looking down at the saliva-covered orb, I persuaded myself that I'd seen worse spitballs back in Glen Meadows. So after shaking out my arms, I winked at Mai Ling. "Watch this."

Then I reared back, and let loose my *World Famous Sandlot Slider*.

Apparently unfamiliar with a ball that slipped sideways rather than traveling in a straight line, Big Minh and Lady Godiva were taken by complete surprise. Snickering as they piled up against the wrong part of the wall, I raced forward to where I knew the ball would bounce back and caught it as it skipped across the ground.

"One for the Peeps!" I exclaimed as I tossed the ball to Mai Ling.

As I got into the game, my fears and worries dissolved. For the first time in weeks, I really had fun.

CHAPTER FORTY-EIGHT

I spent the first couple of days with Mai Ling at the clinic, helping her sort through the medical records of the people assigned there and inventorying supplies. So I was slowly losing my mind counting wooden tongue depressors in the storeroom when President Mitterrand finally called to discuss the project he wanted me to do. Which was a really good thing, because one more day of counting little wooden sticks would have put me in therapy for the rest of my life.

As it turned out, *Monsieur le Président* had a sticky wicket on his hands. The European Economic Community was planning on admitting Spain and Portugal to their already established free trade zone that summer, but there were still a ton of problems that had to be ironed out before the treaty of accession could be signed. Spain and Portugal were far less developed than the existing members of the EEC, and everyone involved was concerned about the possible economic dislocation that might result if the trade barriers were dropped without adequate preparation. At the very least, it was going to cost the current EEC members a ton of money to bring Spain and Portugal up to par in terms of basic infrastructure, and President Mitterrand was pretty sure his economists were blowing smoke up his butt with their estimate of $60 billion. So to make sure he wasn't committing France to a European version of the Money Pit, he wanted me to check their calculations. Thinking that sounded a lot more interesting than counting tongue depressors, I happily agreed.

The very next day, a nice young man turned up with a truckload of boxes packed with reports, studies, analyses, and raw source data. It turned out that Yves – that was his name – was working on an advanced degree in statistics at the Sorbonne. He was Mrs. Mitterrand's nephew, once or twice removed – which meant he could be trusted – and a wizard with numbers. Although he was only vaguely acquainted with French economic terminology, he spoke perfect English, and was an absolute genius when it came to picking up on statistical sleights-of-hand. So after the Legionnaires lugged all the boxes up to my grandly titled office – which was just a big room with a conference table and an old beat-up coffee maker – we got down to work.

True to her word, Michelle made sure we got out once or twice a week to see the sights in Paris. But she was an absolute stickler about security, and she insisted that we wear disguises whenever we left the building. Parisian street clothes and Parisian-styled makeup were mandatory, of course, as were sunglasses, wigs, and hats. Discreetly surrounded by layered teams of security agents, Michelle made sure our jaunts were tightly choreographed and controlled. But the security details were so good it was almost impossible to tell them apart from all the other Parisians we encountered strolling along the Seine, wandering through art museums, or sipping espressos at the hundreds of sidewalk cafes. But as much as I enjoyed the art and the architecture and the incredible history, what I really liked about Paris were the hats.

Now for some reason my biographers all seem to think I developed my hat fetish after meeting Queen Elizabeth – which makes a certain amount of sense, considering the Queen was a big fan of headwear, and that's what we always talked about whenever I visited Buckingham Palace. She'd send Alex and Prince Phillip off to look at an old suit of armor or something – just to get them out from under foot – so we could drink our tea and talk about our latest acquisitions. But in the interests of historical accuracy, though, I have to tell you it wasn't the Queen who got me hooked – it was this really cool velvet Cat-in-the-Hat number in the window of a little shop on the Left Bank. It wasn't quite as tall as the one in the Dr. Seuss book, but it had the exact same colored stripes. And as I stood on the cobblestone street and peered through the window, I fell totally in love with it.

Of course, Mai Ling cracked up when I emerged from the shop with it perched on my head, and the normally staid Michelle snickered. But I didn't care what they thought – I loved that hat!

And from then on, I was hooked...

But that wasn't the only thing I got addicted to in Paris, because I got sucked into Michelle's soap opera before the first commercial break.

Set in the fictional *Ville du Coeur* – supposedly a resort town at the base of the French Alps favored by the political, military, and bureaucratic elite – *The Lies of the Heart* revolved around Monsieur Paul Douay, the Communist mayor; Commissioner Tomas Rayneaud, the scheming chief of police who was constantly plotting against Douay; the jaded Madame Annette Bagot, the proprietor of the luxurious vacation lodge; Mademoiselle Sophie Entange, who was ostensibly the head of maid service at the lodge, but was in fact the key operative in the mayor's Soviet espionage ring; His Eminence Antoine Nefis, a retired Catholic bishop; Sister Anna-Marie, the bishop's housekeeper and beloved friend of 50 years; the rich, beautiful, and mysterious widow, Madame Chantal Blanc, who had settled in the village after spending many years traveling abroad; and a constantly changing cast of Very Important People who vacationed there. Last but not least, of course, was the nameless and deeply sinister *"Monsieur X,"* who could be glimpsed watching from the shadows at the end of almost every episode.

Naturally, everyone in *Ville du Coeur* was hiding at least one deep, dark secret – except for the mayor, of course, who was hiding at least a half-dozen.

Because it turns out Mayor Douay wasn't really a Communist at all, but rather a deep-cover agent of the *Direction de la Surveillance du Territoire* – which was what the French security service was called back then – who had infiltrated the KGB years and years ago, and was using his espionage ring to feed the Soviets disinformation.

Of course that wasn't his only secret – because aside from being a double agent, he was also madly in love with the mysterious Madame Blanc. But because he was convinced a woman of such wealth, beauty, and sophistication would scorn such an ordinary and – to be honest – not exactly handsome man like himself, the mayor hid his feelings. Totally oblivious to the fact that Madame Blanc was deeply in love with him too, he suffered the agony of unrequited love in silence.

Madame Blanc, of course, had a reason for hiding her love for the mayor – a reason never quite explained, but had something to do with the disquieting circumstances surrounding the death of her husband in Africa. Unwilling to believe that a man as good and decent as Monsieur Douay would have anything to do with her, she hid her feelings, too, and suffered as well, while Commissioner Rayneaud – who hated Mayor Douay, and either knew or suspected Madame Blanc's secret – did everything he could to keep them apart by playing on her guilt and his self-doubt (Rayneaud was a total jerk).

That suited Madame Bagot just fine, because like almost everyone else in the village, she had a hidden agenda, which for reasons that still weren't clear, involved playing the chief of police off against Madame Blanc. It also suited the curvaceous and lustful head maid, Sophie, who had been trying to bed the mayor for years, not out love of course, but just to chalk up another conquest.

Unfortunately, all this put Bishop Nefis in something of a bind, because as a young priest he'd ministered to Madame Douay

– the mayor's mother – and it turned out she'd had some deep dark secrets of her own. After her husband had run off when the young mayor-to-be was just ten, she'd sent her son away to boarding school in Switzerland. And in the course of a tempestuous affair that followed with a much younger attorney from Marseilles – who just happened to be the son of a Corsican mobster – she'd become pregnant.

Unwilling to take the chance the attorney's mobster family would find out about the unborn child and use their power and malignant influence to wrest the baby from her, she'd turned to her priest. Saddened and deeply concerned for Madame Douay and her unborn, then-Father Nefis had arranged for her to take refuge in a convent in Brittany. Seven months later, she gave birth to a daughter who would grow up to become...

You guessed it – the mysterious Madame Blanc of our story.

To keep her daughter safe, Madame Douay had entrusted the girl to the Church, before returning to the village with none but Father Nefis the wiser. Educated first in the convent school and later at the Sorbonne, Chantal eventually married the much older Edouard Blanc – a man who was as rich and handsome as she was beautiful, and every bit as mysterious. Aside from the fact that Edouard had been an officer in the French Foreign Legion and fought at Dien Bien Phu, very little was known about him. Although he claimed to be a diamond merchant with business interests throughout southern Africa, hardly anyone actually believed his story. Most people assumed his trafficking in precious stones was a front for illegal arms exports – a suspicion seemingly supported by his untimely death in the Congo.

Because Madame Blanc had been the only witness, the police had accepted her story of a deadly encounter with smugglers deep in the jungle. But while no one was prepared to entirely rule out that possibility, the suspicion that one or more of Edouard's many enemies had finally caught up with him lingered. And given the fact that Chantal had somehow survived the hail of gunfire that killed her husband, there were whispers that she'd set him up.

Whatever the actual case – Michelle, for one, thought she'd probably been tricked into luring him into an ambush – Madame Blanc had returned to her ancestral village a very different woman. Once outgoing and vivacious, she had become quiet, deferential and – according to some – deeply repentant. She kept to herself, attended mass at the little village church every morning, spent endless hours working in her garden, and loved the mayor from afar.

But of course, that wasn't the end of the story – because of all the villagers, Madame Blanc alone had glimpsed the sinister "Monsieur X" skulking in the shadows. Whether or not she knew him was still unclear when the last episode ended, but when she encountered him outside the Mayor's house on a late-night walk, the blood had drained from her face as he raised a silencer-equipped rifle to his shoulder. The episode – naturally – had ended in a cliffhanger as her scream mingled with the muzzle flash.

Having been left hanging the day before, almost the entire company of the *Palais* had crowded into the lounge by the time Mai Ling and I arrived just before 4 pm. After we'd settled down in the chairs Michelle held for us, she gave us a quick synopsis of the characters and the plot during the commercial break. She'd just finished her summary when someone switched off the lights and cranked up the sound.

The episode opened with a recapitulation of Madame Blanc's scream and the muzzle flash from the rifle, and then shifted to a hospital room where the savagely beaten Madame Blanc lay barely conscious, surrounded by doctors, nurses and of course, Commissioner Rayneaud, who was scribbling in a small pocket notebook. Unfortunately, I couldn't hear a word of the dialogue because Madame Blanc was the Legionnaires' favorite fantasy girl – they'd plastered pictures of her all over their quarters – and when they saw her lying there beaten black-and-blue they went berserk. In the midst of the explosive profanity that followed, the Legionnaire next to Mai Ling leaped to his feet and swore revenge. "I kill zee bastard who haas done zees!"

As the other Legionnaires hollered their approval and volunteered to help, Michelle jumped up and – I think – demanded their silence. Then as the room quieted down, we watched as Commissioner Rayneaud exited the hospital with a uniformed officer in tow. Leaning over so I could hear her, Michelle began translating in a whisper. "Zee stupid beetch had eet coming," said the Commissioner.

At that point the room erupted again, as the Legionnaires swore at the crooked cop in a welter of languages. Shaking her head, Michelle informed me that today was going to be a write-off. "I am afraid zee Legionnaires are all in love with *Madame*," she said. "Zey will not tolerate zees mistreatment of zere fantasy girl." But since I couldn't really follow the dialogue anyway, I nodded and shrugged and focused upon the actors.

Madame Blanc's scream must have thrown off the assassin's aim, because aside from her battered body, no physical evidence had been left behind at the crime scene. Not that it actually mattered, because the Commissioner hadn't the slightest interest in investigating the alleged attempt on the Mayor's life, or even the actual attack on Madame Blanc. Despite her painfully whispered testimony that she had been beaten by an assassin outside the Mayor's residence, Rayneaud dismissed her claim as the product of a disturbed mind. "Zees was a random attack," Michelle translated. "Zee beetch murdered her husband in Africa, and now she expresses her guilt through zees delusion."

Yeah, sure. I thought. *Blame the girl, you schmuck...*

With the Legionnaires interrupting the story every couple of minutes with outraged profanity, it was really hard to follow what happened after that. But as far as I could tell, the rest of the hour-long show revolved around the reaction of the main characters. The mayor was stricken, of course, and the Bishop was dismayed. Sister Anna-Marie – who had actually cared for the infant Madame Blanc, and sometimes thought of herself as Madame Blanc's mother – was horrified. Madame Bagot apparently believed the fast circulating rumor of an assassin, but seemed far more interested in working through the implications than worrying about Madame Blanc, while Sophie-the-Spying-Slut could barely disguise her glee at her rival's misfortune.

"Zee girl ees disgusting," said Michelle contemptuously.

Thinking that was an understatement, my eyes bulged as the scene shifted to the Paris headquarters of the *Direction de la Surveillance du Territoire.* Inside the building, a uniformed officer marched into a palatial office, stopped in front of a huge ornate desk and came to attention. After saluting the much older man dressed in civilian garb who sat behind it, the officer apologized for the interruption. "I'm sorry, *Mon General,* but there has been an incident in *Ville du Coeur...*

"It seems an assassin has attempted to murder Colonel Douay."

Then the scene suddenly shifted to the KGB's headquarters in Moscow, where a uniformed KGB agent silently handed a file across an equally ornate desk to another older man also in civilian garb. As he took the file from the officer's hand, the name "Douay" was clearly visible on the protruding tab. Then the picture faded to black, ending the episode.

Outraged at yet another cliffhanger, the Legionnaires began swearing again. And as empty soda cans arced across the room at the TV screen, even Michelle uttered a muffled curse at the writers.

"Damn zem!" she swore. "Zee bastards always do zees to us!"

But since I was even more outraged than she was, her protest barely registered. *Bloody hell*, I thought, as my mouth dropped open. *They can't leave me hanging like this!!!*

But they could, and they did. So like everyone else in the *Palais*, I spent the next twenty-three hours and fifty-nine minutes alternately agonizing over what the next episode would bring, and cursing the writers and the director for leaving me twisting in the wind.

Realizing that I'd been suckered by a stupid soap opera, I shook my head in disbelief. *They got me...*

After that, things at the *Palais* settled into a routine. I got up every day at 6 am sharp, ate breakfast with Mai Ling and Michelle, went to the gym, worked on my project with Yves, and worried about the Mayor and Madame Blanc. At precisely 3:45 every afternoon, I slammed the office door shut and locked it before taking off for the lounge at a dead run to make sure I'd get a good seat for the next episode. And then after playing ball with the dogs if the weather was good, or running them up and down the steps if it wasn't, I spent dinner and most of the evening discussing the latest twists and turns in the *Ville du Coeur* with Michelle and Mai Ling.

Other than that, the only things that broke the comfortable monotony of our gilded cage was my weekly phone call to my Mom, our occasional outings to shop for the latest fashions, visits to art museums or symphonies and, of course, the weekly dance Michelle had organized in the lounge. Somewhere or another, she'd come up with one of those rotating silver balls you always saw in discos and a reasonably good sound system, so every Saturday night Mai Ling and I would slip into our latest fashion acquisitions and go downstairs to dance with the Legionnaires and the handful of male security officers who turned up from time to time.

It was a lot of fun, especially when Legionnaire Pierre showed up. Even though Pierre had been in the service for the better part of two years, he barely looked sixteen – and according to the other Legionnaires, he probably wasn't even that. But he was cute as a button, and he had a huge crush on me that he tried to hide but just couldn't. So whenever he was off-duty, he'd come up with some excuse or another to drop by my office and flirt with me in that clumsy, self-conscious way of adolescent boys.

Now that probably would have irritated most girls my age, but Pierre was such a sweet kid that I just couldn't bring myself to kick him out. So I made a point instead of letting him know that my heart was already taken, and gently reminding him that at almost twenty-three, I was way too old for him. But since he was as homesick and lonely as I was, I liked to talk to him – as long as he behaved himself, anyway – and I always saved a dance for him at Michelle's makeshift disco.

But as the days turned into weeks and the weeks turned into months, I began to get irritated with my captivity. Mai Ling was a little bit better off than I was, because she received letters from Nguyen on a fairly regular basis – and in fact, they'd even been able to speak once for a couple of minutes. But we were still totally in the dark as to how long we were going to be locked up in Paris, and to make matters worse, I was doing a slow burn over Alex. So far at least, I hadn't heard a single word from him. Even though I knew saving the Free World was hard work – and that he'd almost been killed in the process – my patience began to wear thin.

The big jerk! I thought...

Since I've met him, I've been tailed, my apartment's been trashed, my office has been blown up, and I've got Bad Guys out there who want me dead...

And he thinks he's got problems??? Gimme a break...

He can at least pick up a phone and call me!

I was still fuming about that at breakfast one Sunday morning, when Mai Ling bounded in from somewhere and demanded that I follow her to the briefing room.

"Briefing room?" I asked as she grabbed hold of my hand and started pulling me out of my chair.

"What for?"

Blowing off my question, Mai Ling told me I'd see when we got there.

Hoping it might have something to do with the situation in the outside world – that's what briefing rooms are for, right? – I got up and followed her out into the hall and down the steps. Then after emerging on the second floor, I followed her into a large and unfamiliar room before screeching to a sudden halt.

Uh-oh...

At one end of the room, a conference table had been converted into a makeshift altar, and at the other end, there was one of those portable confessionals that itinerant priests lug around with them.

This can't be good...

So I was about to make a run for it, when a priest strolled in through a connecting door on the left. "*Bon matin,*" he said ominously, followed by a bunch of rapid fire French I just couldn't follow.

I had just started backing out of the room when Mai Ling pressed the palms of her hands against the small of my back and shoved me forward. "Father say you make confession now."

Confession???

A nervous glance over my shoulder and a quick calculation told me I was trapped. With Mai Ling behind me and the priest now standing just a few feet from my side, there was no way I'd make the stairs before they tackled me.

Rats!

Since there was no way out, I decided to bluff. I smiled at the priest as sweetly as I could, and thanked him. "But this really isn't necessary, Father…

"I've been really good."

I was still smiling at the priest when Mai Ling slugged me from behind. "Lie to Father big sin," she hissed over my shoulder. Then she pushed me forward again, and pointed at the confessional.

"Goo for soul."

Realizing I was busted, I shook my head in disgust before shuffling across the room. Feeling like a prisoner on her way to the gallows, I was hesitating before the confessional when it suddenly occurred to me that the priest hadn't spoken a word of English.

My lucky day! I thought. *Tell him you don't speak French, and you're outta here!*

No such luck…

Because the moment I explained to him I didn't speak French, he replied in perfectly comprehensible English. "Don't concern yourself with language, my child. Although I am of French parentage, I was educated in England."

Rats! I thought again, glumly. *Can't win for losing!*

So after shaking my head again, I warily stepped into the booth and pulled the door shut before sitting down. A moment later, the priest pulled back the little sliding partition, and softly enquired. "Tell me, my child, how long has it been since your last confession?"

Scrunching up my face as I shifted uneasily in my seat, I mulled it over. Although there was no way I'd actually lie to a priest — let's face it, Mai Ling was right about that — shading the truth just a bit was a whole different matter.

"Not so long, Father," I faked in a cheerful tone.

"And how long might that be, my child?"

After crossing my arms across my chest, I pressed back in my chair as I tried to figure out how to finesse it. "Well, let's see, Father...

"Ohhhh, about 11 years...

"That's not so long, right?" I asked hopefully.

There was a long, deafening silence.

He's not buying it...

The seconds stretched into a minute or more before he finally spoke again. "What sins do you wish to confess, my child?"

Shifting uneasily in my chair again, I thought it over.

"Well let's see...

"I've been cheating on my diet...

"So that's Gluttony, right?"

"It can be, my child. To eat more than one requires for life is unquestionably a sin – an abuse of the body God has given you and, potentially, deprivation of others in greater need of sustenance."

Yeah, right, I thought. *Gimme a stamp, and I'll mail 'em my leftovers...*

"And your other sins, child?"

Hmmmmm...

Suddenly aware that I was furious with Mai Ling, I 'fessed up to Anger. "Anger's a sin, right?"

"A grave sin, my child. Anger is corrosive to the soul, and leads to destructive actions."

Hoping he would let me slide on Gluttony and Anger, I cleared my throat. "Well, I think that about covers it, Father."

Silence...

Deafening silence...

All right, all right!

After shifting in my seat and clearing my throat, I searched my conscience. Realizing I hadn't given as much to charity as I should have, I 'fessed up to Greed.

"A sin as common as humanity, my child."

"Oh, yeah." I quickly agreed. "Everybody's got that problem!"

Silence...

Deafening silence...

All right, all right!

"And then I guess you can add Sloth, Wrath, Envy, and Pride to the list."

"Those are grave sins, my child."

Dejectedly, I nodded in silent agreement.

Silence...

Deafening silence...

Aw, come on, gimme a break!

After shifting again uneasily, and crossing my legs, I thought of Two for some weird reason.

"And Jealousy..."

After shifting again before leaning forward to rest my chin on my folded hands, I made an unhappy face.

"And then there's Lust..."

But suddenly defensive, I leaned forward and insisted. "But that's *NOT* my fault, Father."

"No?"

Shaking my head, I emphatically assured him it was not. "You see, there's this guy, and he's like way more handsome than the law allows...

"And he's really rich and smart and important, and every time I see him — even when I just think of him — I just lose all sense of...

"*Uhhhhhh*...

"Dignity...

"Yeah, let's call it 'dignity' — if you know what I mean."

"Yes, my child, I do."

"But, Father!" I demanded. "What girl wouldn't?"

"He's got this really handsome, chiseled face, and these huge broad shoulders and a little tiny waist, and when he moves it's like watching a tiger prowl through the jungle...

"I mean...

"You can actually see the muscles rippling under his three-piece suit!"

Completely oblivious to the fact that my voice had dropped to a husky whisper, or even to the fact that I'd become flushed and was inhaling long, deep breaths, I prattled on. "He's just like, irresistible, Father...

"So it's all *HIS* fault...

"Really!"

There was another silence, but this time it wasn't quite so deafening.

"And do you love this man selflessly and without reservation?"

Uhhhhhh...

Then as my voice climbed a couple of octaves, I heard myself squeak. "Father, did I mention Lust?"

CHAPTER FORTY-NINE

Needless to say, he threw the book at me – ten Our Fathers, forty Hail Marys, an act of contrition, and an act of selfless service to the poor. Not to mention a pilgrimage to the shrine of Our Lady of Devotion at Chalonvalle, wherever the heck that was.

But it would have been even worse if I'd caught up with Mai Ling. Because after my confession, the Father had said a mass, and being nobody's fool, Mai Ling had made a run for it the instant the service ended. But since she was not only amazingly fast, but agile to boot, she'd made it back to her bedroom and slammed the door in my face just before I caught up with her.

Which was probably a good thing, because I would have pounded her through the floor.

But since I realized that was going to have to wait – the big oaken doors to Mai Ling's bedroom were just too thick to kick in – I decided to pull out the final draft of my report to President Mitterrand instead. Although Yves and I had wrapped it up the Friday before, I still wanted to tweak the language a bit and make sure I'd caught all the typos before I sent it over to the President's office at the Elysée Palace. So after retrieving the text from my bedroom and digging a red felt-tipped pen out of my work purse, I plopped down at the parlor table and started working my way through it again, page by page.

Although most people find statistical tables and technical summaries pretty dull, it took me only a minute or two to get wrapped up in the minutiae. In fact, I was so engrossed I didn't even notice Mai Ling crawl past on the exterior ledge and make her escape. But it wasn't until Michelle interrupted me two or three hours later that I realized I'd become lost in the details. Startled by her presence, I looked up her and wondered where I'd been.

"*Mademoiselle*," she said gravely. "I must speak weeth you concerning a matter of great importance."

"Well, sure." I said. Then as I pushed my chair back from the table, I asked her what was up.

After sitting down catty-corner from me, Michelle folded her hands together on the table and leaned forward. "Seex days ago, a rather large group of zee traitors crossed over zee East German border and entered zee West…

"After spending zee night in Strasbourg, zey spleet into two teams – one headed to Brussels, zee other came here to Paris...

"Zen late last night, zee ones who had traveled to Belgium arrived here in Paris to join zere colleagues."

Startled, I pulled back in my chair. "So they've figured it out?"

Michelle nodded gravely. "*Oui.*"

After looking down, I sighed. "And the East Germans are helping them?"

Michelle nodded again. "And the Soviets, of course. Zee East Germans wouldn't have dared act upon zere own."

After thinking about it for a minute, I looked back up at Michelle. "So why don't you arrest them?

After glancing down again, Michelle explained that they had no legal basis for making an arrest. "Your government has chosen not to publicly acknowledge zee *coup*, and has filed no charges against zem...

"And so far at least, zey have broken no laws here in France."

Thinking that figured, I shifted in my seat and smoothed my sweater. "So what's the game plan?"

After an intense stare, Michelle cleared her throat. "Col. Fortescue intends to lure zem into a trap and wipe zem out, *Mademoiselle*...

"But zee plan requires your assistance."

After a long silence, I looked up again. Then very softly, I asked her what she wanted me to do.

With sympathetic eyes, Michelle explained. "Tomorrow we go to zee café at midmorning, and we wait."

Thinking that did not sound good – with extra emphasis on the "not" – I looked at her incredulously. "So he wants us to be the bait?"

As a deadly serious expression spread across her face, Michelle nodded. "Zee Colonel has already passed zee information to zee Soviets through a double agent, so zey weel be expecting us...

"But what zey do not know is zee Colonel weel have hundreds of security officers and Legionnaires in place before we arrive...

"Zere will be an incident, a pretext, and we weel kill zee traitors dead!"

Works in theory, I thought glumly.

But after mulling it over for a few moments, I realized I didn't have much of a choice...

If we don't take 'em down now, I'm gonna be stuck here for the rest of my life...

After shifting uneasily in my chair, I cleared my throat. "I have a question, Michelle...

"Actually, two..."

"Yes, *Mademoiselle?*"

After locking my eyes on hers, and staring intently, I told her I just didn't get it. "Why are they after me?"

A puzzled look passed across Michelle's face as she shrugged. "I do not know, *Mademoiselle*. Eet is far above my pay grade." Then she paused a moment before she resumed speaking.

"Perhaps it ees because you could demonstrate zere conspiracy to a court...

"Or perhaps eet is because you made public reference to zee Eenner Line."

Then after shaking her head, she gently admonished me. "Zees ees never a good idea, *Mademoiselle*."

"Right," I said softly. "Next question."

Opening her eyes expectantly, Michelle replied. "Yes, *Mademoiselle?*"

Not quite sure how to put it, I squirmed in my seat before tugging on my sweater again. "You're French, Michelle...

"But when you talk about the Bad Guys, your voice seethes with hatred and contempt...

"So I was just wondering, how come?"

Michelle paused for a moment, before smiling softly. "Perhaps zee American people have forgotten, but we French have not...

"Zee great banking houses that are behind all zees have no nation, no loyalties...

"Zey betrayed zee *République* to zee Nazis during zee last war, and now zey collaborate with zee Communists...

"They love nothing but zee money, and zee power."

After thinking about it for a moment, I nodded softly. "That's what Alex says."

Chuckling, Michelle straightened in her chair. "Ah, yes," she said with a smile. "Zee gallant and handsome *Monsieur* de Vris!"

Then as her eyes twinkled, she asked if he was my lover.

Taken aback by so blunt a question, I cracked up. "Only in my dreams, girlfriend."

Smiling softly, Michelle reached across the table and laid her hand on mine. "You must remember zat *Monsieur* has been busy zeese past few months." Then she smiled again and reminded me that French blood ran in his veins.

"Zee French are not always so obvious in matters of zee heart, *Mademoiselle.*"

"Really?"

Nodding emphatically, Michelle smiled even more broadly. "For zee French male, zee seduction ees high art…

"Zey employ zee utmost subtlety, *Mademoiselle*, and for zee beautiful woman zey show zee most astonishing patience."

As she rose from the table, I leaned back and looked at her quizzically. "Really?"

She nodded again, even more emphatically. *"Vraiment, Mademoiselle!"*

Then she winked, and told me to enjoy the game. "For zee woman, eet ees one of life's great adventures!"

Thinking the French had a whole different take on things, I shrugged. "Maybe so, but this being all alone stuff is getting old."

Michelle rolled her eyes and sighed. "Yes, *Mademoiselle*, I know…

"I have not slept with my lovair since zees all began!"

Shocked and more than a little bit embarrassed by her candor, my eyes crossed involuntarily. *"Uh, right…"*

Laughing at the look on my face, Michelle thanked me for my cooperation. "Now go to bed early, and get zee full night's sleep…

"I weel awaken you at 7:00 tomorrow, and brief you over zee breakfast."

The mention of which – naturally – reminded me of the fact that condemned men are supposed to get anything they want for their last meal. "Any chance we can have a real breakfast for once? Like bacon and eggs, and an English muffin?"

After pausing for a moment, Michelle shrugged. "I don't know about zee English muffin," she said. "But I weel ask zee cook for something more American."

Then as if she had just remembered, Michelle suddenly informed me that *Madame Docteur* had left the *Palais*, and would be gone for several days. "A Legionnaire has fallen ill, and she has accompanied him to zee hospital."

Bloody hell! I thought. *She escaped???*

After shooting a look over my shoulder at the still closed and locked doors of Mai Ling's bedroom, I decided there was something definitely wrong with that picture. So after giving Michelle a suspicious look, I demanded to know if the sudden medical emergency had anything do with that ambush of hers earlier that morning.

"You know…the one with the Priest, and the confessional?"

Seemingly puzzled, Michelle shrugged and told me she didn't know. Then she pointed her finger at me and commanded me to get a good night's sleep. "Tomorrow we engage zee enemy…

"So you must be alert and well-rested."

Then she turned, and strode out the door.

Propping my chin under my balled up fists, I sat there for a long time and just stared out the window. Thinking I'd really put my foot in it when I agreed to be Col. Fortescue's bait, I wondered where I'd be this time tomorrow.

Probably shot full of holes, I thought glumly.

But on the bright side, I reminded myself that the stylist Michelle had brought in had done a fantastic job with my hair. Cheered by the fact I'd be the best-looking stiff in the graveyard, I finished up the last page of my report for President Mitterrand before taking it down to my office and making the corrections on the clunky word processor they'd brought me.

Having blown off lunch, I wandered down to the canteen for some high-calorie comfort. Then after snarfing down two bags of chips and a diet drink, I made my way to the lounge and spent the rest of the afternoon watching a safari show with a couple of Legionnaires before finally heading back upstairs for dinner.

All alone for the first time since my arrival in January, I toyed with my food after the steward placed it on the table. After staring out the window for an interminable length of time, I realized that I was bored beyond comprehension. So I grabbed the bottle of wine that had accompanied my dinner, and strolled over to the couch. Pulling one of the fashion magazines out of the pile that had accumulated on the end table, I began flipping through the pages. Spring had come late to Paris that year – or at least that's what everyone said – and I still hadn't quite finished rounding out my wardrobe.

Hmmm…

So what goes good with blood and gore?

Thinking polka dots and stripes just wouldn't work with gunshot wounds, I decided I'd better stick with solids.

Maybe something in a dark red…

Suddenly amused by my ghoulish humor, I tossed the magazines aside and picked up the remote for the big screen TV. But since Mai Ling had dragged it over by the table again – which was pretty amazing, given how much it weighed with the console and the VCR – I had to rotate the couch 180 degrees just so I could see it.

After spending the better part of an hour channel surfing – the satellite TV delivered 683 stations, believe it or not – I finally settled on a really bad knock-off of *The Night of the Living Dead*. It was pretty much standard fare as Zombie movies go, but in this particular film, the football team had cleaned out the local gun shop after the Zombies ate all the adults, and holed up in their high school. Ably assisted by the cheerleading squad – and a science nerd who turned the chemistry lab into bomb-making factory – the jocks and the cheerleaders kicked Zombie butt in ferocious, room-to-room fighting before falling back into the gym to make their last stand.

Naturally, the head cheerleader got eaten along the way. But since she was blonde and disgustingly beautiful, I figured she had it coming.

Less competition for the rest of us, right?

Retreating into the middle of the basketball court, the jocks and the airheads – well, what was left of them anyway – formed up in a circle, and did General Custer proud. Blazing away with shotguns and semi-automatic hunting rifles, they mowed down wave after wave of the flesh eating freaks.

And those stupid liberals want to take away our guns!

By this time, of course, the National Guard had reached the outskirts of town and I was pretty sure a tank was going to burst through the wall any second now and save the day, when the last jock standing ran out of ammunition. Nonplussed, he bashed the head of the closest Zombie with his rifle butt before laying a lip-lock on the cheerleader beside him.

"This is it, baby…the score's all tied up, and we're on the one-yard line."

Then he threw himself on the makeshift plunger the science nerd had made, and blew the whole school to smithereens.

Well, kewl! I thought, as the scene shifted to an aerial shot of the gigantic mushroom cloud that billowed from the wreckage.

That'll teach those Zombies!

But since the high school had lost their entire first string – not to mention the whole cheerleading squad – I figured their prospects for the next football season were pretty bleak. So after taking another swig of wine, I began questioning the wisdom of that whole General Custer thing.

They shoulda got out of Dodge while they had a chance…

Suddenly realizing how late it was, I polished off what was left of the wine and set the empty bottle on the floor. Then after turning off the TV and pushing myself to my feet, I made my way into my bedroom and pulled off my clothes. Leaving them in a pile on the floor, I pulled on a Foreign Legion T-shirt I'd bummed off of Legionnaire Pierre and shooed Big Minh and Lady Godiva off the bed. Ignoring their unhappy looks, I crawled under the covers.

The light that spilled through the doors from the parlor created a rainbow effect as it passed through my Unicorn, still perched upon the nightstand where I'd placed it so many months ago. Pushing myself up on one arm, I lay there for a long time to watch the colors dance through the brilliantly cut crystal. Except for Mai Ling and the dogs, the Unicorn was all that was left of my life in Washington.

As I reached out to run my fingers along its side, tears welled in my eyes. Brushing them away, I wondered if I'd still be alive to appreciate it when the dust settled the next day. Frightened and dispirited, I had just rolled over and pressed my face deep into the pillow when I heard the music wafting from below. So faint that I could barely hear it, it took me a moment to realize it was *Que Sera, Sera* – the song my mother had sung to me as a child, whenever I was fearful or anxious.

Pulling the covers up tight around my neck, I sang along in a whisper until at last, I fell asleep.

CHAPTER FIFTY

Almost exactly nine hours later, I found myself scowling into the three-way mirror in my bedroom. After turning first to the left, and then to the right, I glared at Michelle. "I look like a boy!"

Michelle shook her head in disagreement, and gave me an irritated look. "You look like a perfectly lovely young woman," she insisted.

"Michelle! Perfectly lovely young women have curves!"

Then after tugging at the bulletproof vest she'd strapped on me, I pointed to where my breasts were supposed to be and scowled at her again. "This thing makes me look flat!"

Exasperated, Michelle handed me the bulky knit sweater she'd brought. "No one weel know zee difference weeth zees on."

"Exactly!" I said. "I'll look like Legionnaire Pierre!"

"*Mademoiselle*," she said sternly. "No one weel ever mistake you for a Legionnaire…

"You are far too lovely."

Yeah, right. I thought.

"So how come you have breasts?" I demanded to know.

Michelle sighed and shook her head before looking down at the floor. "*Mademoiselle*," she explained in an authoritative voice, "Because I wear zee body armor on zee routine basis, zees vest was specially fabricated to conform to my figure…

"Now eef zee vest we have geeven you does not flatter you, I am sorry – but we are en route to a potentially deadly encounter, and zee vest weel keep you safe." Then after glaring at me again, she thrust the sweater into my hands and demanded I put it on. "Now feex your makeup, and pull on zee matching knit hat. You have five minutes…

"I weel wait for you by zee chamber door."

Scowling at the mirror again, I pulled the sweater over my head before pinning up my hair. After examining the hat – which was actually kinda cute – I pulled it on and tucked some wayward strands of hair underneath.

Not bad, I thought as I turned in the mirror again. *Gimme a couple of boobs and I'm good to go…*

So after stuffing a couple of wads of tissue paper down the front, I finished my face and applied my lipstick. But since my effort at curve-enhancement hadn't made the slightest bit of difference – the vest was just too thick – I pulled the wadded up balls out from under the body armor, and tossed them in the general direction of the waste can. Completely oblivious to the fact that I'd missed the target by three or four feet, I wrapped my white silk aviator scarf around my neck before pulling on my bomber jacket with the Army Air Corps insignia. Then I turned on my heel, and marched into the parlor.

Stopping in front of Michelle, I came to attention and saluted like the Legionnaires. "Legionnaire Pierre Look-A-Like reporting for duty, Sir!"

Chuckling, Michelle waved me through the now-open door. "Zat ees *'Madame Capitaine'* to you, Legionnaire…

"And feex zat salute – eet ees terrible!"

Whatever you say, boss…

After walking down the hall, we paused in front of the elevator and waited as it lumbered up from the first floor. After surveying me, Michelle laughed. "Weeth zat jacket, you really do look like a boy," she said. "I must take a picture for my young seestair…

"She would love such a handsome young man!"

After pulling my aviator sunglasses out of the inner pocket and perching them on my nose, I dropped my voice a couple of octaves and told her not to break the poor girl's heart. "My squadron's bombing Berlin today, and intelligence anticipates heavy losses…

"I might not be coming back."

Then I whacked the call button again.

Five minutes later, we finally emerged from the front doors of the *Palais* and crossed the street. As we turned left onto the sidewalk, Michelle instructed me to take the interior position closest to the buildings. So after hesitating just long enough to judge the distance, I hopped over a puddle left by the early morning rain to make sure I didn't splash my brand-new $300 soft-leather boots with the two and a half-inch heels. Or my brand-new designer jeans – which had had set me back another hundred bucks American.

Pulling up alongside *Madame Capitaine*, I asked her where we were going. "To a café," she said. "Called *La Résistance.*"

"So how far is that?"

Madame Capitaine shrugged. "About two kilometers."

Uh-oh, I thought as I converted the kilometers into miles. Because I'd just taken my boots out of the box that morning, and they were already starting to hurt my feet.

"No chance of taking a cab?"

Madame Capitaine shook her head back and forth. "Zat ees not zee plan."

As we crossed the next street, I shrugged. *Gonna have to gut it out...*

We walked another three blocks in silence before turning down a short street that led to the River Seine. As we crossed over the street that ran alongside the river, I turned up my fleece collar to protect my ears from the cold wind coming off the water.

Michelle had been too busy scanning our surroundings to talk to me before, but as the layers of security details closed in around us, she began to relax. Pointing ahead, she asked me if I saw the bridge about a mile or so down.

Nodding, I asked her if that was where we were heading.

Michelle pointed again. "Can you see zee three-story building on zee opposite side?"

After I nodded again, she told me that the café was in the ground level. "During zee Battle for Paris, Colonel Fortescue's father and hees Résistance team fought zee Germans from zere...

"Zey held off zee German tanks for an entire day – until zee Free French Army arrived."

"So that's why they call the café *La Résistance?*"

Michelle nodded. "Eet's quite famous, you know. All of the chairs and tables – even zee bar – ees made from zee steel plate of the German tanks and armored vehicles zey destroyed on zee bridge."

Well, kewl, I thought. Then I asked about Col. Fortescue's father. "He survived the battle, right?"

Michelle shook her head softly. "No, *Mademoiselle*. He died for France."

Not knowing what to say, I plodded along for a few minutes in silence. Then for no particular reason, I started whistling a tune Mai Ling had taught me.

"What ees zat you wheesel?"

Grinning, I looked up at Michelle. "Something Mai Ling taught me. It's called *The March of Heroes...*

"Kinda appropriate, don't you think?"

Michelle chuckled, and then shrugged. "Perhaps, *Mademoiselle*, but I assure you – eet ees far better for you to be zee live coward zen zee dead hero...

"So you must promise me you weel take no foolish chances today."

Thinking that was a no-brainer, I hurriedly gave her my assurance. "That thing about bombing Berlin was just a joke, you know."

Then after what seemed like an impossibly short time, we turned right onto the bridge. After snickering at the young lovers making out against the marble rail, my face turned crimson as the guy slipped his hand up his girlfriend's sweater. Seeing me blush, Michelle laughed softly. "Eet ees not as you imagine, *Mademoiselle...*

"Hee's weapon ees hidden under her clothing."

"They're security agents?" I whispered incredulously.

Nodding softly, Michelle whispered back. "Zee love-making diverts zee attention, no?"

Well, yeah, I thought...

But aside from the fact that being groped in public just didn't appeal, the idea of having a loaded handgun stuffed in my bra was just too weird for words. So I shrugged it off, and asked her how come I couldn't see any of the others.

Whispering back, Michelle assured me they were there. "But zee stationary teams take special care to avoid detection."

Which was definitely an understatement, because after all the time I'd spent wandering around Paris, I'd gotten pretty good at picking up on the mobile security types. But as we neared the end of the bridge, I couldn't spot a single security agent anywhere.

There were plenty of people around – lots of them, in fact – but the guy selling tourist trinkets from the pushcart at the end of the bridge looked utterly harmless, as did everyone else I could see. In fact, the only person who looked even remotely menacing was the really heavy-set old woman manning the counter of the open-air shop across from the café. Shrugging again, I plodded across the street after Michelle, and entered the sidewalk café.

"Zees ees eet," she said as she pushed open the wooden-framed glass door.

Given the hour, I was surprised by the number of patrons. But after Michelle discreetly identified herself, the maître d' escorted us to a rather large, square table situated against the far wall. After gesturing for me to take a seat that backed up against the masonry, Michelle settled into the chair on my right. Pointing to a brass plaque riveted to the heavy steel plate table, she read the inscription for me. "Zees table was made from zee armor plate of a German Panzer tank destroyed by zee Résistance on zee twenty fourth of August, 1944."

Then after pointing to the bar – beyond the hallway on my left, and backset three or four feet to the rear – she explained again how all of the furnishings had been made from German steel salvaged from the battle. Then she pointed to the large framed photograph that hung above the door, depicting the carnage. After counting the number of tanks and armored vehicles the Résistance had destroyed, she directed my attention to the score of smaller photographs which adorned the walls. "Zey are zee fighters who died here, holding zee bridge for our General Leclerc."

Smiling, Michelle crossed her hands on the table. "Ees history, you know?"

Deeply impressed, I nodded. "So, what's next?"

Michelle narrowed her eyes. "Zee ladies' room for me. But I'll be right back."

And then without another word, she got up from her chair and strode around the corner and down the hall immediately to my left. But she must have crossed paths with a waiter somewhere along the line, because one mysteriously appeared with coffee and pastries a minute or so later.

Not quite sure what to do with myself, I poured a cup of coffee from the carafe he had placed on the table and, after failing to bridge the language gap with my request for sweetener and skim milk, I fixed my coffee with sweet cream and natural sugar. After deciding the extra calories shouldn't count due to my good-faith effort to obtain the less fattening alternatives, I began analyzing my surroundings.

The building itself was obviously way old – from what I had gleaned from Michelle, it had probably been built around 1600 or so. But German tank fire had pretty much leveled it during the Battle for Paris, so it had been rebuilt with more modern materials. The wall behind me, and the one to my far right, seemed to be exceptionally thick masonry and were probably left over from the original construction. But the wall to my left and the wall facing the main street were obviously newer, as they were mostly wood-framed glass. But whoever had been in charge of rebuilding it after the war had known what they were doing, because the barefaced brick, the white painted masonry, and the wood-framed glass worked well together, and the steel furnishings added to the effect. All in all, I thought it was pretty cool.

By now bored waiting for Michelle – and more than a bit curious as to what was taking her so long in the ladies' room – I began surveying the customers. Seated at an angle to me in the next row of tables was an elderly gray-haired man with a neatly trimmed beard and glasses, reading what looked like a book of poetry as he sipped his coffee. Although I couldn't see his face very well, he had a kindly look about him and, for the briefest of moments, I had this really odd feeling that we'd somehow met before.

Realizing that was impossible, my eyes flitted to the left as the patrons from another table stood up to leave. And then my jaw dropped!

Off to the left against the windows, I could see Legionnaire Pierre dressed in civilian clothes with some blonde girl in his lap, crawling all over him.

Why, that two-timing little twerp!

Forgetting all about the fact Pierre was supposed to be the best pistol shot in the entire Legion, I grinned from ear to ear. Snickering under my breath, I was wondering what *Madame Capitaine* was going to do when she found out her under-aged Legionnaire was getting it on with a strange chick in an adult establishment, when the girl finally came up for air. As she brushed her hair out of her face, my eyes bulged and my jaw dropped again.

Oh, my God...

Because that wasn't just any girl giving Legionnaire Pierre mouth-to-mouth resuscitation – it was Michelle's executive officer, Lieutenant Jollie!

Who, by the way, was at least ten years older than my poor little Pierre!

Why, that Jezebel!!!

Outraged that a grown woman would be having her way with a sixteen-year-old boy, I had just made up my mind to march over and slap the little trollop senseless when the front doors flew open, and in walked...

You guessed it...

None other than James – that schmuck of an ex-boyfriend who'd lured me to Washington and dumped me without so much as a fare-thee-well.

As my jaw sagged again, I froze halfway out of my seat, unable to believe my eyes.

His eyes locked upon mine, and as a huge smile spread across his face, he pulled a gun out from under his coat and raised it against me. Then everything went into slow motion.

Off to my left, I could see Lt. Jollie shove the heavy table away as Legionnaire Pierre rose to his feet and wheeled toward James, a semi-automatic pistol cupped in both hands, and ahead and off to my right I glimpsed the old man who had been reading poetry racing towards me with a gun in hand. Tables were being overturned all over the café as men and women pulled firearms from their coats, purses, bras, and waistbands.

Then the entire place exploded in gunfire.

Which was like, totally weird...

It was as though reality had almost frozen in time – or at least that's how it seemed, until the old man threw himself over the table and slammed into me. Still unable to comprehend what was happening, I watched numbly as he grabbed the outer edge of the table and pulled it over as we fell to the floor. As he slammed down on top of me, I observed the hail of bullets tearing into the wall above us from somewhere far away, and listened to the distant sound of lead slamming into the steel table he'd brought down as a shield.

Then, in the midst of the deafening clamor, my mind suddenly snapped back. Looking up at the man lying on top of me, I recognized a familiar face.

"Alex???"

Grinning, he tossed aside the fake glasses and peeled off the beard. "Hey, kid...

"How ya doing?"

Twisting my shoulders and pushing with my hips, I told him I was having a minor breathing problem. "But other than that, Alex, pretty good ...

"And you?"

After shifting his weight a little, he shrugged. "Well, I got shot," he said nonchalantly. "But other than that, not bad."

Nodding, I had started to tell him I'd heard about that shooting thing when a burst of automatic weapons fire hammered against the table. Barely able to hear myself over the gunfire, I yelled at him. *"I THINK IT'S TIME TO GO!"*

As another burst of fire raked the wall above, he nodded emphatically. Then after rolling off me – which was like, weirdly disappointing – he yelled in my ear. "Nu is out back with an armored personnel carrier and a couple of squads of anti-terrorist police."

Then pointing toward the hallway corner with his gun, he yelled again. "Two part movement – on the count of three, get up and run like hell for the space behind the bar...

"Keep low, and I'll cover you...

"Then after you get across, I'll follow...

"From behind the bar we have to make it down the hallway, past the restrooms and dog-leg through the kitchen to the courtyard behind the building. Nu will have us covered from there...

"Got it?"

Nodding emphatically as another burst of automatic weapons fire ripped into the wall above, I kicked away some of the debris and got ready to bolt. After positioning himself sideways against the table, Alex pushed himself up on one knee and held up one finger, then two, and then three. As he leapt to his feet and began firing, I raced across the seven or eight foot distance and threw myself onto the floor behind the steel bar.

Now some girls will say you just can't run in heels. But trust me on this – when you've got people shooting at you, it's *not* a problem.

But dodging bullets is a whole 'nother story – which I suddenly realized, as I threw myself toward the floor behind the bar. Because I'd heard the round zip past, and after sniffing a couple of times, I could tell something was wrong...

Thinking that just couldn't be good, I gingerly raised my hand to my head and groped around. Finding the smoldering hole in my hat, I pulled it off and swore under my breath.

That low-life son of a ...

Then I got mad.

Grabbing an unbroken bottle of brandy from the floor, I calculated the angle the bullet must have traversed before flexing my throwing arm. Then after taking a couple of deep breaths, I popped up and let fly.

BANG!

Fool hadn't seen it coming, so he dropped like a rock.

GOTCHA, SUCKER!!!

Excited – and really, really pleased with myself – I was doing this little victory dance when Alex slammed into me again. Which turned out to be good thing, because less than an instant later another burst of automatic weapons fire raked across the big mirror behind the bar

"*WHAT THE HELL ARE YOU DOING???*" he roared.

Ignoring the shards of glass that rained down on us, I looked up indignantly and told him I was getting a little payback. "That low-life shot my hair!"

Completely bewildered, Alex stared at me for a long moment before repeating my words. "He shot your hair?"

"Yeah, Alex" I sputtered. "The dirtball shot my hair – and I just had it cut and colored, and it was perfect!

"So I beaned the jerk!"

As a look of masculine incomprehension spread across his face, Alex tried to stammer out something, but the words just didn't come. So after shaking his head in disbelief, he popped the magazine out of his semi-automatic and reloaded it. After slamming the new magazine into place, he told me we had to make a run for it. "The French wiped out the main force before they got here, and they have the place surrounded...

"And they've got a half-dozen of their people inside with us...

"But three or four of the renegades who were already inside survived the first volley, and they're still firing from behind the steel tables."

After I nodded over the din, I followed him as he crawled toward the hallway. Looking up, I was astonished to see Michelle inching her way along the wall, with a gun in each hand. Sheltering behind a column protruding from the wall, she looked down at Alex and mouthed the words. "On zee count of three, *Monsieur...*

"I weel cover you."

Realizing she faced almost certain death, Alex started to object but Michelle cut him off with a wave of a gun. "*Pour la France, Monsieur.*"

Alex hesitated for a moment, then nodded grimly. "*Pour la France, Madame.*"

"*Un...deux...trois!*"

Then she wheeled into the hallway, and advanced upon the enemy with both guns blazing.

Before I had time to react, Alex grabbed my hand and pulled me up on my feet.

"*NOW!*"

Given the number of bullets flying in our direction, I didn't need any encouragement – because I was halfway down the hallway before the word even left his mouth. Careening around the corner of the kitchen door, I dodged to the right and raced around the butcher-block prep table standing in the middle of the room before slipping on what had once been a salad.

I hit the ground hard and slid, but an instant later Alex caught up with me. Grabbing the back of my fleece collar, he pulled me up on my knees just short of the open door. Offset and to the right, it was just outside the line of fire.

Since Alex had knelt in front of me, I had to peer around his shoulder to see what lay beyond. From my vantage point I could see a rather large courtyard where a stable had probably stood way back when, and beyond it an alleyway that looked like it led out onto a street. But since some sort of armored troop carrier had backed down the narrow passage and blocked my view, I couldn't be sure. Off to my left, I could see Nguyen holding an automatic rifle, pressed against the wall of the alley, and a dozen heavily armed anti-terrorist police behind him. A bit farther back on my right, another squad of anti-terrorist police knelt down alongside the vehicle.

But what really surprised me was the sight of Mai Ling. Clearly visible through the open double doors of the vehicle, she was kneeling inside and clutching a medical kit to her chest. Drowning in body armor that was at least three sizes too big, she was struggling with an equally ill-fitting helmet that kept slipping down over her eyes. When she finally managed to get it perched on the back of her head, a big smile spread across her face and she gave me an excited, palms up wave. Happy to see her – and more than a little bit relieved to know an experienced doctor was on hand – I waved back.

By that time, Alex was absorbed in some sort of remote conversation with Nguyen, who was making funny gestures with his hands. After Alex gestured back, he turned to me over his shoulder.

"Nu thinks there's a sniper on the roof of the building to the left, or maybe in one of the third floor windows, so here's the drill...

"I'm going to pop out and fire a few rounds at the roof, to see if I can draw fire...

"Got it?"

Thinking I didn't really like that idea, I frowned before telling him to be careful.

Grinning, Alex told me "Careful" was his middle name.

But since he'd already suckered me with that one before, I gave him an irritated look and started whacking him on the shoulder. *"NO – IT'S – NOT...*

"It's Michael!"

After grinning over his shoulder again, Alex made another hand signal to Nguyen, and then leapt to his feet. Wheeling halfway through the open door, he fired off three rounds before ducking back inside. But since the din from the firefight in the café hadn't abated, I couldn't tell if anyone fired back.

After another exchange of hand signals, Alex turned back over his shoulder and shouted. "Nu didn't see a muzzle flash, so we're probably OK."

Then after pointing off to the right, he asked if I could see the overloaded dumpster that stood two or three feet off the wall to my right, about 30 feet from where I knelt.

Peering over his other shoulder I shouted, *"YES"* in his ear.

"OK...I'm going to run half-way, wheel about, and give you covering fire...

"You count to three and run like hell for the dumpster...crawl in between it and the wall, and I'll meet you there...

"If we aren't fired on, we'll run from there to the APC – got it?"

Nodding emphatically, I told him I was already there. Then after another exchange of hand signals, Alex bolted through the door.

So after a hurried 1-2-3, I took off like a shot. I'd just passed Alex – standing out in the open, blazing away at something or another – when a burst of automatic weapons fire tore into the wall beside me.

Rats!

Thinking it was then or never, I dove for the safety of the dumpster. Fortunately, the cobblestones around it were littered with rotting lettuce so I slid when I hit the ground. In less than an instant I was lying face down in a pile of garbage, behind the safety of the overflowing metal box.

A half-second later, Alex landed on top of me as a hail of bullets hammered against the steel barrier. Pressed flat against the cobblestones as Alex crawled over me, I was thinking that whole jumping thing of his would work a lot better someplace else.

Having traversed my near-lifeless body, he knelt at the end of the dumpster and popped an empty magazine out of his gun before slamming a new one into place. Then after cycling the action, he leaned around the edge to establish visual contact with Nguyen. After another exchange of hand signals, he turned back to me.

By that time blood had begun flowing through my torso again, and I was pretty sure I was still breathing. So I pushed myself up on my knees – rather painfully – and waited expectantly.

Stating the obvious, Alex informed me that the sniper hadn't fallen for the trick.

So after brushing a bunch of three-day old lettuce off my jacket, I asked him what we were going to do.

"Nu caught the muzzle flash – the sniper's on the third floor, second window from the end...

"I'm going to peek around the edge to get a handle on the geometry, and then we're going to do the same drill again...

"Only this time Nu is going to pop out with me, and fire on full auto."

Now, that's a plan, I thought sarcastically…

You're both gonna get killed, and I'm going to be stuck behind this stupid dumpster for the rest of my life…

Alex suddenly grinned, as though he had read my mind. "Not to worry," he said in a veiled reference. "We've done this stuff before."

"Uh-huh," I said before pushing him forward. "Get a fix on that sniper."

Ignoring my sarcasm, Alex shifted on his knee and leaned out a bit farther – just in time for another hail of automatic weapons fire to rip into the wall and shower his face with little tiny bits of brick and mortar. Jerking back reflexively, he unleashed a torrent of profanity as he began rubbing his eyes to clear away the debris.

I beg your pardon???

My jaw dropped and my eyes bulged – because Alex had said a *really* bad word. But I recovered quickly, and whacked him over the head.

"Alexander Michael de Vris!" I exclaimed. "Shame on you!"

My remonstrance apparently had the intended effect, because his face turned crimson. Still blinking and rubbing his eyes, he turned half-around and sheepishly apologized.

Given the circumstances, I decided to accept his apology – but not until I'd pointed my finger at him, and warned him not to do it again. "It's not nice."

Nodding, Alex moved forward again. Then after exchanging hand signals with Nguyen, he turned back to me. "Change of plans…

"I'm going to pop up in place and draw him out, and Nu's going to nail him…

"So the instant I'm on my feet, make a run for the APC, but remember, stay as close to the ground as you can."

Nodding, I asked him when.

"Now's as good a time as any…

"Ready?"

After I bit my lip and nodded, Alex leapt to his feet and began firing – and I was out of there like a streak of greased lightning. An instant later, there was a burst of fire from Nguyen and then a scream from somewhere above.

As the anti-terrorist police surged forward – one column toward the café, the other toward the back door of the sniper's building – I counted the remaining steps…

Five – four – three…

Then after judging the distance, I hurled myself through the open hatch of the APC. After slamming down on the plate metal deck and sliding forward, I let out a deep sigh of relief...

Safe at last...

Until I realized Alex was right behind me.

OH, NO...

Tensing my muscles and balling my fists, I pressed my eyes shut and waited for 200 pounds of solid muscle to smash me flat again. But seconds passed, and the expected blow never came.

So after counting to ten, I slowly opened my eyes and glanced around. Alex and Nguyen were wrestling the doors shut in the back, and Mai Ling was pounding on the bulletproof glass window that connected us to the vehicle's driver.

"*Vite! Vite! Vite!*"

Thankful to be alive and in one piece – a little smooshed, maybe, but still in one piece – I pushed myself up into a sitting position and leaned back against the fold-up bench that ran along the side. Then as the vehicle jerked forward, I let out another deep sigh before glancing back across the cabin.

Looking over at Alex, Nguyen grinned. "Just like old times, bro."

Alex smiled softly and nodded, before pulling a battered pack of Marlboros out of his shirt pocket. Ignoring Mai Ling's withering glare, he shook three of the crumpled cigarettes free. After lighting one and handing it to Nguyen, he lit another and handed it across the way to me.

After I took it from his outstretched hand, he lit the last one for himself. Then after inhaling deeply, he leaned back and smiled.

"Ya done good, kid."

"Bloody hell," I retorted. "I done great!"

Still smiling, Alex nodded again. "So you did," he said.

Then after glancing at Nguyen and Mai Ling, Alex called the Membership Committee into session.

"All in favor of admitting Alicia to the Gang, say 'Aye.' "

After a chorus of 'Ayes,' Alex spoke again. "All opposed say 'Nay.' "

After a moment of silence, Alex said he held proxies for Christine and Dr. MacLaughlin. "So the vote's unanimous." Turning back to me, Alex grinned. "You're in, kid. Welcome to the club!"

Thinking it was about time I got some recognition, I grinned back before leaning over and snatching the helmet off Mai Ling's head. Then after putting it on my own, I stuffed the filtered end of the cigarette in my mouth and smoked the first and only cigarette of my entire life.

Then as the APC swayed through a pothole, I became suddenly curious.

"So, do we have a name?

"Because we just saved the world, so we're like, Super Heroes right?"

As the Membership Committee broke up laughing, my face began to flush.

OK, I'll be quiet now...

CHAPTER FIFTY-ONE

After they stopped chuckling, a silence settled in. Mai Ling crawled over to Nguyen, who wrapped his arm around her and pulled her close. Happy and content, she lay her head against his shoulder and put her arm around his waist before closing her eyes. More than a little bit envious, I looked over at Alex hopefully. But by then, he'd withdrawn to someplace deep within.

Since it took more than a half-hour to make it back to the *Palais*, I figured the driver had taken a meandering route to flush out anyone who might be tailing us. Since I was pretty sure we'd just wiped out the Bad Guys, the maneuver struck me as a bit anticlimactic. But I'd been around the French security types long enough to realize it was probably just standard procedure, so I shrugged it off and leaned back against the fold-up bench.

After swaying through another couple of potholes, the APC made a sharp left turn and began rolling down an incline. Suddenly alert, Alex rose to a half crouch and made his way back to the doors. After receiving a shouted 'all clear' from somewhere outside, he opened up the doors and jumped out. As I reached the exit, he placed his hands on my waist and lifted me way up into the air before doing a half-turn and setting me down on the concrete. As he reached for Mai Ling, I was thinking he must be related to Superman...

But before I could follow up on that thought, Col. Fortescue strode into view and congratulated us on a superb operation before reciting all the bloody details: thirty-two traitors dead and one taken prisoner – against one French security agent killed in the gunfight, and sixteen wounded, mostly from ricochets and flying glass.

Horrified by the sudden recollection of Michelle's frontal assault on the enemy, I gasped. "Not Michelle..."

Turning to face me, Col. Fortescue shook his head. "*Capitaine* Gaston received multiple gunshots to her chest, but none penetrated her body armor." Then he shook his head again, and chuckled.

"Trust me, *Mademoiselle*...

"*Madame* has more lives than the proverbial cat!"

As I sighed with relief, the colonel handed out assignments. Alex and Nguyen were to follow him for an after-action review, while *Madame Docteur* was to report to the clinic to attend to the wounded. Feeling very much left out, I asked him what I was supposed to do. After pausing for a moment, Col. Fortescue smiled and informed me that we would be having a victory celebration in the lounge at 8:00. "So perhaps *Mademoiselle* will wish to attend to her hair."

At that, my eyes crossed and my hands flew to my head. Having returned Mai Ling's helmet in the APC, it was still covered with what was left of my knit hat. Mortified, I pulled it down as far as I could and winced. "Right."

So after informing me that he would summon the stylist, he gestured for Alex and Nguyen before turning on his heel and marching off.

Looking over at Mai Ling, I asked how bad it was. Grinning, she stood up on her toes and pushed my hat and hair back with both hands. "Bad hair day," she joked.

Then after hemming and hawing, she told me I should call a barber instead. "You make handsome young boy."

Oh, great! I thought. *First Michelle gets on my case, and now Mai Ling...*

But much to my surprise, it all worked out. After arriving at our suite an hour later, the stylist spent a good five minutes examining my hair from different angles before ordering me into the shower to shampoo. After I finished and pulled on some sweats, he got down to work. Lucky for me, the 'Boy Cut' was all the rage in Paris that year – and to tell you the truth, it really was cute. I loved the wispy sideburns, the way he layered it and, aside from the fact that it was way low-maintenance, it had the unexpected effect of accentuating my eyes.

Not bad, I thought as I turned in the mirror.

Having dealt with that particular crisis, I shook out my hair and plopped down on the couch. Curious, I picked up the remote and punched the buttons for CNN. It was still early back in the States, but I figured they'd have something about the shootout by then. After waiting impatiently through a car commercial, an image of unbelievable carnage appeared on the screen. According to the newsreader, a group of East German terrorists had been ambushed on a Paris backstreet and wiped out in a raging gun battle by a group of Arabs – who were then promptly wiped out by a French counterterrorist squad which happened to be conducting a drill less than two blocks away. Although the motive for the attack remained unclear, some obviously important guy from the anti-terrorist police appeared on the screen, to speculate that the East Germans had double-crossed the Arabs in a guns-for-drugs deal.

Dumbfounded, I stared at the screen. *You have got to be kidding!*

A moment later, the image of *La Résistance* appeared on the screen. Cordoned off by yellow police tape and surrounded by scores of street cops and anti-terrorist police, it was a mess – all the windows had been blown out and the body of someone – apparently a Bad Guy – lay draped over a windowsill.

Major yuk factor, I thought, as I stared at the brains spilling out of his shattered skull.

But I bet it pulls in the ratings…

According to the announcer, an entirely unrelated group of terrorists had picked the worst possible time to stop in at *La Résistance* for a cup of java – because by complete coincidence, a couple of senior police officials were there enjoying an early lunch when they walked in. Having recognized one of the terrorists, they called for backup and drew their guns. In the ensuing melee, one police officer and six terrorists were killed.

Wow! I thought. *What a koinkydink!*

Then I chortled, because nobody was ever gonna buy that!

But they did…

As a matter of fact, it's in all the history books now, along with glowing accounts of the courageous French police who shattered two – that's *TWO* – major terrorist organizations in a single morning!

Shaking my head in disbelief, I flipped off the TV and got down to serious business. Which included the late lunch/early dinner the chef sent up, wondering what to wear to the party, and – naturally – awaiting the day's episode of *The Lies of the Heart*.

Mai Ling turned up halfway through the show, which we watched with rapt attention. Then after filling her in on what she'd missed – Mayor Douey's heated confrontation with Commissioner Rayneaud, Sophie-the-Spying-Slut deciphering a secret message from Moscow, and Madame Blanc retrieving a handgun from the safe hidden behind a painting in her bedroom – we began working our way through our dress collections. Mai Ling eventually settled on this really sexy black floor-length number with spaghetti straps, while I agonized over an even sexier red one I'd picked up one afternoon when I was feeling particularly bold.

Now of course, the whole point of wearing a dress like that is to send a message. But since I still didn't know Alex all that well, I was thinking something a bit more subtle might be in order.

But after Mai Ling assured me for the hundredth time that Alex would love it, I decided to throw caution to the wind. Thinking it was about time he noticed I was a girl, I spent the better part of an hour applying my makeup – with extra eye shadow, of course – before retrieving a really sexy set of lingerie from my drawer. Then after pulling on my hose and stuffing myself into the matching push-up bra, I slipped into my dress and twirled before the mirror.

Feeling wondrously wicked, I ran my hand along the oh-so-daring neckline and grinned. *If this doesn't get that boy's attention, nuthin will...*

I had just pulled on my heels – which had cost me $200 bucks, thank you very much – when there was a sudden knock on the suite's outer doors. So after calling to Mai Ling to let her know I'd get it, I took one last look in the mirror before scurrying out in the parlor to answer. Thinking it was weird the Legionnaires standing guard outside hadn't announced the caller, I pulled open the door to find a familiar form dressed in an elegant tuxedo.

"Dr. MacLaughlin!" I screeched. Then I threw my arms around him, and gave him a huge hug.

After holding him tight for a long moment, I demanded to know what he was doing there.

Returning the hug, he told me how good it was to see me. Then he pointed down at what looked like a big mail sack sitting on the floor beside his feet, and informed me he was delivering my birthday presents.

Huh?

Suddenly aware of the fact that I'd forgotten all about it, I stammered. "You came all the way to Paris to bring me birthday presents?"

"That, and a few other odds and ends." Still smiling, he hoisted the sack over his shoulder and asked if he could come in.

Well, duh, I thought, as I stepped aside to welcome him.

After wrapping an arm around my shoulder, we walked back into the parlor. Setting the sack down on the couch, he complimented me on both my dress and my hair. "You look lovely, Lass."

Thrilled that he liked the look, I thanked him. Then suddenly insistent, I asked him what he was doing at the *Palais* again.

"Top secret, Lassie...

"So if you want an answer you'll have to either torture me, or pour me a Scotch."

Laughing, I led him over to the bar and told him to help himself. After turning a crystal glass right side up, he began rooting through the assembled bottles. After checking several of the whiskies, he frowned and held one up. "Single malt, but I suppose it will have to do."

Then after pouring two fingers, he downed the glass before shaking his head and muttering. "And the damn French call themselves civilized!"

Remembering the French weren't exactly Dr. MacLaughlin's favorite people, I had just started snickering when all the pieces fell into place.

"Bloody hell!" I exclaimed. Then after taking a step back, I pointed an accusing finger at him.

"You set this whole thing up, didn't you?"

Chuckling, Dr. MacLaughlin poured another shot into his glass and swirled it, before dismissing my accusation. "You give me far too much credit, Lass."

Then after draining it, he winked and told me all would be revealed in good time. But in the meanwhile, we had a party to attend.

I was just about to protest when the doors to Mai Ling's bedroom suddenly opened. Stunningly beautiful in the black gown and diamonds, with her hair piled on her head, she glided across the floor like an Oriental Goddess. Stopping just short of Dr. MacLaughlin, she smiled before placing her hands together and making a little bow.

"Happy see you, *Professeur*."

After returning the greeting with a sweeping bow, Dr. MacLaughlin extended one arm to Mai Ling and another to me. "Shall we, ladies?"

So after snatching up my birthday loot and making a mad dash to deposit it in my bedroom, I scurried back and accepted his outstretched arm. Forgetting all about my suspicious outburst, I happily accompanied him to the Lounge.

The place was already packed with Legionnaires when we got there, resplendent in their dress uniforms, interspersed with surprisingly well-dressed security officers. As we made our way through the crowded half-lit room to the bar, I noticed Lt. Jollie off to my right. Wearing a maroon micro-mini skirt and tights, and a rather flimsy white silk blouse, she was flirting with one of the Foreign Legion officers I'd seen around the *Palais* but never met. A bit beyond lay a series of tables laid end to end, packed with goodies – shrimp, caviar, escargot, deviled eggs, little tiny sandwiches stuffed with a variety of exotically seasoned meats – and a half-dozen other things the French, for some mysterious reason, consider culinary delights.

After spending the better part of five minutes wending our way through the sea of sashes and epaulettes – stopping every couple of steps to exchange handshakes, hugs and high-fives with the exuberant Legionnaires – we finally made it to the bar. After obtaining glasses of champagne for Mai Ling and me, Dr. MacLaughlin ordered his version of a "Scotch and Water" – which turned out to be four fingers of Scotch, and an ice cube. Delighted to find a triple malt of unimpeachable integrity, he complimented the bartender before raising his glass. "Ladies – to a successful operation!" So after whispering a silent "Amen," I clinked my glass against theirs and echoed the toast.

Looking over as I took a sip, Mai Ling grinned and whispered a conspiratorial warning. "Be careful wit dis stuff," she said. "Too much Champagne make head explode."

Chuckling at the imagery, I took another sip as I glanced around. "So where are Alex and Nguyen?"

Smiling as he led us away from the bar, Dr. MacLaughlin informed me that they had arrived in Paris without any formal wear. "They had to go out and get fitted. But I expect they'll be here any minute."

The thought of seeing Alex in a tux again made me growl under my breath – at least, that's what I thought I'd done. But it apparently came out a bit louder than intended because Dr. MacLaughlin chuckled and Mai Ling cracked up. But lucky for me, Legionnaire Pierre appeared just in time to save what was left of my dignity. Setting my glass down on the table behind me, I turned back to greet him.

Taking both of his hands in mine, I eyed him up and down. "Rather handsome in that uniform, Pierre!"

Flushing, he looked down and mumbled his thanks before looking up again with a pained expression. "*Mademoiselle,* I must beg your forgiveness," he said. "I did not know he was your lover."

Huh???

Confused, I looked up at him as a puzzled expression spread across my face. "My lover?"

Private Pierre nodded his head. "The man I shot today..."

"He had raised a gun, and it was my duty to protect you."

Oh...

"You mean James?"

"*Oui, Mademoiselle.*"

Chuckling, I told him not to worry about it. That schmuck of an ex-boyfriend had not only tried to kill me, he'd trashed my shoes – which in my book, is definitely a capital offense.

But since I knew it would be expecting too much for a guy to understand that, I told him that James had it coming and earnestly thanked him for saving my life. Standing up on my tiptoes, I kissed him – which was well deserved, but probably ill-advised given the teen-aged hormones involved. Suddenly concerned I might light the wrong boy's fire, I dropped my hands to his dress tunic – just below his parachute wings and the single row of medals – and gently pushed him away.

"Thank you, Pierre."

But it seems that Legionnaire Pierre had already been around the block once or twice, so rather than protest the loss of a kiss that had lingered a bit too long, he straightened instead. Then grinning mischievously, he leaned down and whispered in my ear. "You kiss much better than Lt. Jollie!"

Caught completely off-guard by that one, I took a step back and looked up at the under-aged Legionnaire in shocked disbelief.

"*Pierre!*" I exclaimed. "Shame on you!"

Chuckling, Legionnaire Pierre gave me a sly wink and disappeared into the crowd.

Sheesh! I thought. *What are they teaching kids these days?*

Dr. MacLaughlin turned and asked me what that had been all about. Shaking my head, I explained Pierre was the Legionnaire who'd sent my schmuck of an ex-boyfriend to the Promised Land. "But someone apparently told him James was my lover, and he wanted to apologize."

"That," Dr. MacLaughlin chuckled, "Or steal a kiss."

As my mouth opened and my eyes crossed, I looked up at Dr. MacLaughlin incredulously. "He *played* me?"

Shrugging as he swished his drink in his glass, Dr. MacLaughlin smiled. "You can hardly blame a young lad, now can you?"

More than a little bit chagrined, I shook my head slowly. But on the bright side, as I hurriedly explained to Dr. MacLaughlin, Legionnaire Pierre had saved my life, so I figured he deserved it.

Smiling, Dr. MacLaughlin nodded. "He'll remember that kiss for the rest of his life, so don't feel badly."

"Ya think?"

Nodding again, Dr. MacLaughlin assured me he would. "That's the stuff of memories, Lass."

"Well, good!"

Then suddenly buoyant, I leaned over and warned Mai Ling not to rat on me.

Grinning wickedly, Mai Ling said it was gonna cost me. But then she chuckled, and promised not to tell.

I was about to make her swear on it, when I glimpsed Michelle out of the corner of my eye. Dressed in a loose-fitting running suit, she was hobbling over on a cane.

"Michelle!"

My first instinct was to throw my arms around her, but the pained expression on her face warned me against it. Then smiling bravely, she made her way through a group of Legionnaires before stopping in front of us.

Deeply concerned, I asked her if she was OK.

"Ees nothing, *Mademoiselle*. A few cracked reebs, but *Madame Docteur* has taped zem for me." Then smiling at Mai Ling, she expressed her appreciation. *"Merci, Madame."*

Mai Ling smiled back over her champagne glass. "Not worry," she said. "Fix ribs, piece of pie."

Huh?

It took me a moment to work my way through the figure of speech she'd just massacred. "You mean 'piece of cake'."

Grinning again, Mai Ling took another sip. "Pie, cake, same differen."

Laughing, I took a sip from my own glass before realizing how upset I was with *Madame Capitaine*. Pointing my finger at her chest, I demanded that she be more careful. "Don't you ever do that again, Michelle!

"You could have been killed!"

Michelle sighed softly and shrugged. "Zees ees zee war we fight, *Mademoiselle*...

"Our governments prefer eet remain secret, so we fight in zee shadows and zee back alleys, so our people may remain safe...

"And we mourn our losses and celebrate our veectories in private, like zees, faithful to our word."

Trying hard to grasp what she was saying, I nodded without truly understanding. It took a while for that to sink in.

"Now, *Mademoiselle*, let me introduce my good-looking friend." Then reaching behind her, she took the hand of a tall and ruggedly handsome officer. *"Mademoiselle, Madame Docteur, Monsieur Professeur*...

"Zees ees Lieutenant-Colonel Jacint Dubois, of our special forces."

So after craning my head back to smile – because the colonel was like, way tall – I shook his hand and told him what a pleasure it was to meet him. Smiling back, he replied in excellent English. "The pleasure is mine, *Mademoiselle*. You've become something of a legend, you know."

Me???

But by the time I'd recovered my wits, he'd already turned to thank Mai Ling for taking care of his love. Slaughtering another figure of speech, Mai Ling assured him that it had been her privilege. Stepping forward, and slipping easily into French, Dr. MacLaughlin offered his hand to Michelle's beau, before asking if he could get them a drink.

Then after a brief exchange, Dr. MacLaughlin excused himself and went in search of refreshments.

By that time, Mai Ling was engaged in an animated conversation with the colonel, so I glanced over at Michelle and winked. "He's a hottie," I whispered. Blushing ever so slightly, Michelle smiled and raised her eyebrows.

I was still chuckling about the look on her face when Alex and Nguyen suddenly appeared. Devastatingly handsome in their tuxedos, they introduced themselves to *Madame Capitaine* and her handsome colonel.

After greetings all around, I grinned as Nguyen sidled up to Mai Ling. "Got a date tonight, Darlin'?"

After chuckling, she gave him a dismissive look. "Get loss, Cowboy...

"You late, we find hansome young men take place."

Feigning a disappointed look, Nguyen shook his head. "Now that's cold, Darlin'..."

Then he looked over at Alex and told him they'd better move on. "Maybe we can find a couple of French girls."

Laughing, Mai Ling whacked him before reaching out and pulling him close. "Change mind," she said. "Woman perogi..."

Then seemingly confused, she knit her eyebrows together and looked at Nguyen. "What dat word?"

Nguyen smiled. "Prerogative."

"Dat right, woman prerogative!"

It was only then that I realized Alex was smiling at me. Which was like, totally unfair – because his smile could make me melt, and he knew it. As a flush came over my face I looked down at the floor, hoping he liked my dress and my hair. Laying one hand over the other in front of me, I crossed my fingers and held my breath.

"You look lovely, Ms. McAllister."

Delighted by the flattering tease, I tilted my head over to the side and looked up a little. "And you look very handsome, Dr. de Vris."

Then he reached out and stroked the side of my head. "I like your hair – it brings out your eyes."

YES!

"And the dress is stunning."

Suddenly excited, I looked up and beamed. "So, will you dance with me tonight?"

Alex smiled and nodded. "That's why I'm here."

As my jaw dropped and my eyes bulged, I became breathless. "You came all the way to Paris to dance with me?"

CHAPTER FIFTY-TWO

OK, so I got wrapped up in the moment...

While Alex was trying to choke back the laughter, the lights suddenly dimmed and off in a far corner Col. Fortescue stood up on a chair and called for everyone's attention. After congratulating us on a near perfect operation, he informed us that it had not been won without cost. Commandant Yves Rannay had died for France, leaving behind a wife and three young children. Then after saying a collection would be taken up for his family the following day – and telling the assembled security officers and Legionnaires that he expected them to contribute generously – he asked for a minute of silence to honor their fallen comrade.

Dead silence descended on the lounge, and as the Legionnaires and the security officers bowed their heads, I suddenly got it. *These guys fight and die every day, and no one even knows...*

Suddenly shaken, I bowed my head and offered a little prayer. *Dear God*, I pleaded. *Watch over them and protect them...*

They're heroes.

Then I whispered a special prayer for Commandant Rannay, and his wife and children.

I had just finished when Col. Fortescue cleared his throat. Life is for the living, he declared, and urged us to celebrate. Monsieur Rannay would want that, just as we would if we had fallen in his place. Then all of a sudden, disco poured from the speakers, and the sparkling ball Michelle had hung from the ceiling so many months before began to slowly turn.

Turning back toward Alex, I placed my hand on my neckline, bowed my head, and did a modified curtsy. Then after raising myself back into an erect posture – rather relieved that I hadn't fallen out of my dress – I took the initiative by extending my arm. "*Monsieur?*"

Smiling at my jest, Alex took my arm and escorted me out to the makeshift dance floor. So after finally remembering to thank him for my Unicorn, we danced at least a dozen times – including, naturally, to *Unchained Melody* right at the end. And in between, I danced with Nguyen, Dr. MacLaughlin and, at Michelle's insistence, her beau. In fact, I even danced with Legionnaire Pierre a couple of times after he promised to behave himself. Not quite sure I should believe him, I warned the under-aged scoundrel I had a brown belt in Tae Kwon Do.

"So watch the hands, Mister!"

As it turned out, all the guys were good dancers – but I have to tell you, I was just totally astounded by Dr. MacLaughlin. I had no idea a guy that big could be so exquisitely graceful on the dance floor. But as I admitted to myself, there was more to it than just his elegant dancing. Over the past year he'd become something of a father to me, and in some indescribable way, dancing with him helped make up for the fact that I'd never dance with my Dad.

Mai Ling and Nguyen snuck out early, to no one's surprise. But the fact that the injured Michelle and her beau disappeared shortly thereafter was something of a shock. Snickering, I pointed out both absences to Alex in the hope that he might take the hint. But he could be thick as a brick sometimes – especially, as I later learned, when he was playing for higher stakes.

But as disappointing as his feigned stupidity may have been, I still had a blast. Watching a thoroughly inebriated Dr. MacLaughlin get up on a chair and sing *Louie, Louie* in French with a group of totally trashed Legionnaires was priceless – and the snake dance through the *Palais* that Lt. Jollie organized to close out the night was even better.

Somebody had come up with a portable boom box, and by the time the chain of sixty or so Legionnaires, security officers, and miscellaneous spooks, spies, and other mysterious types dropped me off at the door to our suite, we were belting out that old calypso song about the workers loading a banana boat. With my left hand on the shoulder of the Legionnaire in front of me, and my right index finger pointed high in the air, I was dancing along, laughing and singing:

Day-O, Day-Ay-Ay-O...
Daylight come and me wanna go home...

Which wasn't actually the case...

But it was altogether appropriate, because after what seemed like about five minutes of sleep that night, an unusually buoyant *Madame Capitaine* marched in and dragged me out of bed for "breakfast and a debriefing." Having hurriedly scarfed down a baguette and two cups of coffee, Mai Ling and I dutifully followed her downstairs to a conference room, where we found a panel of intelligence experts waiting: two Americans, a Canadian, a Frenchman, a Belgian, a West German and, to my surprise, a

Brit. As the French guy seated in the middle explained the procedure and the projected time frame, I wondered what Her Majesty's Secret Service was doing there.

Debriefings would begin each morning at 9:00 sharp, and run through noon. We would have an hour off for lunch before resuming at 1:00, and would wrap up no later than 5:00. We would sometimes be questioned together, but for the most part separately. Mai Ling's debriefing was expected to take three to four days, while mine was expected to run two and a half weeks.

Bummer...

Then after telling the panel we understood, the French guy told us to take our seats at the table covered by a green baize cloth, and to speak clearly and precisely into the microphones in front of us so our testimony could be properly recorded. Then after pointing out the glasses and the pitcher of water that had been placed on a tray between us, they got down to business.

Now for those who've never suffered through a debriefing, it might not sound so bad. But after the first day or so, it became so boring I thought my brain was gonna melt and run out of my ears. Making it worse, they kept asking the same stupid questions in different ways over and over, apparently on the theory I was too dumb to realize what they were up to.

Must think I'm a blonde, I glumly concluded.

But what really got my goat was they wouldn't let us out to watch *Lies of the Heart* with the rest of the crowd. Michelle taped it for me and we watched it every night after dinner. But by then I'd grown so accustomed to crowding into the Lounge with all the Legionnaires and security agents that I missed their raucous company.

And to make a really irritating situation even worse, Alex had disappeared again and even Nguyen didn't know where he'd gone. But on the bright side, I finally found out why the Bad Guys had been after me. It seems that the management-consulting firm my schmuck of an ex-boyfriend joined after he graduated wasn't a commercial firm after all, but a front for one of the CIA's Black Budget operations instead – quite specifically, the one that had planned and organized the assassination attempt against President Reagan. James had told them about me, and just before I left Glen Meadows he'd very stupidly suggested they bring me on board.

Concerned that he might run his mouth, they transferred him to LA on short notice, and sent a surveillance team to the bus station to observe my arrival. When they saw Big Minh bring me the cheeseburger Alex had bought for me, they got worried – and when I left with Nguyen and Mai Ling for the hotel that night, they completely freaked. Fearing their little *coup d'etat* might have been compromised — a suspicion that only increased when Dr. MacLaughlin hired me as his assistant — they'd opted for close-in surveillance and harassment.

But when they found out I'd been selected to audit the Black Budget, they decided I had to go. Having tried and failed to kill me at the office, they ordered James to do it in Paris. Dark suspicions aroused by my seemingly miraculous escape from the CSS rooftop persuaded them that he was a security risk, so if he got killed in the process, then so much the better.

So after the French guy who was running the debriefing explained it all me on the last day, I felt bad for James for, oh...

A good ten or fifteen milliseconds...

But then I remembered he'd trashed my shoes, so I shrugged it off.

Stupid jerk!

But the best part was finding out my encounter with Alex at the bus station hadn't been some sort of set up after all. The fact that he'd been moving that day was purely coincidental, and the route he had chosen past the bus station was the shortest possible way to get from the warehouse where he'd stored his stuff to the new house he'd bought with Nguyen and Mai Ling.

Cheered by the fact that Alex hadn't been using me all this time — and finally convinced I could really trust him — I waited for the whole panel of spooks to assemble after lunch on the sixteenth day, before graciously accepting their thanks for my cooperation. The moment they dismissed me, I bolted for the door.

Things got even better when I returned to the suite. Finding Dr. MacLaughlin there with Mai Ling, I was delighted to learn we'd been given ten days of paid vacation in Paris, courtesy of Uncle Sam. Thinking we'd finally caught a break, I did a little Happy Dance in the parlor before grabbing Mai Ling by the shoulders.

"Paris Opera House," I whispered excitedly. "And a really elegant restaurant."

After she grinned and nodded, we raced for our closets to find something to wear.

It was really fun. After drafting Dr. MacLaughlin as my date, Mai Ling and I dragged the guys to fashion shows and art museums during the days, and operas, plays, and really fancy restaurants almost every night, with only Michelle or Lt. Jollie, and one of the Legionnaires, riding shotgun. Much to my surprise, the guys actually enjoyed some of it – and the rest, they dutifully endured.

But if that was cool, what followed was even better. On our second-to-the-last day in Paris, Michelle turned up early one morning in her dress uniform, followed by a tailor carrying two rather small sized Foreign Legion outfits. After *Madame Capitane* ordered us into our rooms to put them on, the tailor made all kinds of little alteration marks when we returned, before telling us to go back and change into our civvies. Disappearing out the door with the uniforms draped over his arm, the tailor reappeared just after we had put away our morning *soupe* – which is Legion slang for just about anything edible.

So after having us try the uniforms on to make sure they fit, Michelle ordered us into the regulation shoes she'd brought and placed white kepis on our uncomprehending heads. "Now, follow me," she said. "We have zee parade to attend."

By now totally confused, Mai Ling and I followed her down the stairs and out into the courtyard where the Legionnaires were drawn up in formation. Stopping midway in front of the troops, Michelle pivoted on her heel, came to attention, and saluted a much older officer who had a ton of medals pinned on his chest.

"Mon General! Capitaine Gaston and Honorary-Recruit Legionnaires McAllister and Tranh reporting as ordered, *Monsieur!"*

After returning her salute, the general smiled at us before opening a scroll and reading the proclamation contained within – stating that in recognition of our valiant service with the *Légion étrangère*, he was appointing us Honorary Legionnaires, First Class. Then he rolled up the scroll and exchanged it with his aide for two thin, leather-bound binders before marching over to us. Stopping in front of me, he saluted as I tried to come to some semblance of 'attention' and handed me the top binder – which contained my official appointment papers as an Honorary Legionnaire. Then after kissing me on both cheeks, he saluted me again. After I returned his salute, he turned on his heel and marched over to Mai Ling to repeat the process.

Which I thought was like, way cool – because I was pretty sure we were the first Legionnaire-girls in history!

Returning to his position in front, the general reminded us of the Legion's glorious tradition and admonished us to wear our uniforms proudly. Thinking that just wasn't going to be a problem – because I was already planning my first Bastille Day Party back in Washington – I remained at attention until the general saluted the formation and dismissed us.

Not quite sure what to do, I just sort of stood there taking it all in as the Legionnaires gathered around to congratulate us. Then after barking at the men to make way, Michelle marched up and smiled warmly. Congratulating us, she kissed each of us on both cheeks.

Then pretending to be suddenly stern, she informed us that our useless butts belonged to her now. "So you weel do as I command, or I weel make you do push-ups for zee rest of your meeserable lives!"

Snickering, I came to attention again and saluted. "Yes, Ma'am, *Capitaine*!"

Chuckling, Michelle castigated my salute as an affront to France and St. Martin – the patron saint of French soldiers, you know – before ordering me to fix it. Finally persuaded that my best effort was passably acceptable for a new recruit, she ordered us up to our suite to change into our best business suits.

"*Monsieur le Président* expects us at zee *Elysée Palais* een one hour!"

Huh?

Suddenly excited that I'd get to see President Mitterrand again – and visit the French White House – I raced Mai Ling to the elevator.

Exactly fifty-eight minutes later, the black Citroen limousine that *Monsieur le Président* had dispatched to the *Palais* pulled to a halt outside his official residence. Located just off what is now the Champs-Élysées, it had been built as a suburban retreat by a famous French count. The house had changed hands a number of times over the centuries, and had been owned by King Louis XV – who had bought it for his mistress, Madame Pompadour – then a rich Parisian banker, and after that King Louis XVI, followed by a succession of French governments. Along the way, it had been employed as a private art museum, a warehouse, a barracks for Russian Cossacks and – briefly – home to an orangutan which escaped from a nearby menagerie, before becoming the official residence of the presidents of France. Modified and remodeled by each of the early occupants – except for the Cossacks and the orangutan, of course – it's considered one of the finest examples of classical French architecture ever built.

Too ostentatious for his socialist inclinations, President Mitterrand preferred to remain in his own home on the Left Bank, but he still used the official residence for state functions. As we were escorted to his private office by a group of soldiers from the *Garde républicaine*, clad in old-fashioned dress uniforms topped off by shiny metal helmets with plumes, I marveled at the incredible beauty of the place. The hallway was huge, elegant and ornate, with unbelievably high ceilings and illuminated with huge – and beautiful – crystal chandeliers. Along the walls, what looked like gold-plated sconces were spaced at regular intervals, and between them original paintings, sculptures and *objets d'art*.

If the White House in Washington was dignified, stately and imposing, *Elysée Palais* was overwhelming. An unmatched blend of art and architecture, it was a monument to the glory of France. Glancing over at Michelle, I started to say something but thought better of it – ever the soldier, she was marching in lockstep with our escort. With her shoulders squared and her eyes fixed and level, she was almost as impressive as the Palace.

After what seemed like forever, we arrived at a set of huge open doors that ran almost from floor to ceiling. Saluting the two guards standing there at attention as we passed by, our escort marched into a huge room with fantastically high ceilings to an oversized table-like desk that stood in the center. Seemingly oblivious to our entrance, President Mitterrand, Dr. MacLaughlin, and another man I didn't recognize were chatting amiably alongside it. Turning as our escort came to a halt, saluted and announced our presence, President Mitterrand smiled and walked forward.

Not quite sure what to do when Michelle snapped to attention and saluted – being an Honorary Legionnaire, First-Class and all – I kind of came to attention, too, and hoped I got it right. But it apparently didn't matter, because after acknowledging Michelle's salute with a nod he extended his hand to welcome each of us in turn. Then after introducing us to the American Ambassador – the other guy, the one I hadn't recognized – he commended Michelle for her courageous actions at the café, and thanked Mai Ling for her assistance with the wounded. Turning to me, he smiled and told me what a pleasure it was to see me safe and then thanked me for my study. After good-naturedly cursing his own economists as dolts, he told me it had saved him – and France – a great deal of trouble. Then he winked and told me that the job offer he'd made at the White House still stood.

"When you become bored with Washington, *Mademoiselle*, I will have a position waiting for you here in Paris."

As Dr. MacLaughlin took his place beside me, President Mitterrand shifted gears and apologized. An urgent matter of state had arisen, so he had no choice but to abbreviate our meeting. Nonetheless, it was his great pleasure to award us the *Croix de guerre* with Bronze Palm – a French military decoration that meant we had been honorably mentioned "in dispatches."

And appoint us to the *Ordre national de la Légion d'honneur.*
Which was like, *way* cool.

So after two aides magically appeared carrying purple velvet pillows, President Mitterrand removed a scroll from one and cleared his throat. Unrolling it, he read a brief citation describing Dr. MacLaughlin's role in planning the operation, and then our separate actions at *La Résistance* before rolling it back up and returning it to the first aide. Then he lifted a cross-shaped medal off the pillow held by the second aide and pinned it on Dr. MacLaughlin's chest.

After commending him for his effort and thanking him for his service to France, he kissed him on both cheeks before repeating the process – with slightly different words, of course – with me, Michelle, and Mai Ling. Then as the Ambassador applauded, President Mitterrand picked up the second scroll and read another commendation, before appointing us as *Chevaliers* of the Legion of Honor – making us, technically, Knights of France.

So I was thinking that was really cool – because I was going to make everyone call me "Sir Alicia" when we got back to Washington – when *Monsieur le Président* interrupted my little fantasy to explain that since the entire operation would remain forever secret, our names would be entered onto the rolls without fanfare or publicity. We would be publicly recognized as members of the Legion of Honor, of course, and we could list our decorations and even wear them if we liked. But if asked, we were expected to explain that we had been honored for "Service to France," and then change the subject.

Oh well, I thought. *It's still gonna look good on the ole resume.*

After that, President Mitterrand apologized again for cutting short our meeting, and escorted us to the huge doors. Then he shook each of our hands warmly, and congratulated us again before we were escorted back to our limousine. As we descended down the steps of the Palace, Michelle was walking on air – well, marching, actually – as the rest of us joked and teased. Suddenly curious, I turned to Dr. MacLaughlin.

"Sir Charles," I joked. "What about Alex and Nguyen?"

Whereupon Dr. MacLaughlin laughed, and Michelle giggled. Pointing to the *Croix de guerre* pinned on his chest, Sir Charles informed me that Alex and Nguyen had already received their "Moron Buttons," as he called them. And since both of them were already members of the *Légion d'honneur*, they'd been promoted to the rank of Commander.

Oh, rats!

"Does that mean Alex outranks me?"

Laughing as the chauffeur opened the doors for us, Michelle informed me with mock seriousness that *everyone* outranked me.

But at least she addressed me as "Madame" – which is the proper form of address for a Lady Knight, you know.

But unfortunately, all good things must come to an end. So after being made Honorary Foreign Legionnaires, decorated for bravery under fire, and inducted in the Legion of Honor, we spent our last and final day trying to figure out how we were going to con the dogs into their travel cages, and packing up all the stuff we'd bought in Paris so it could be shipped back to the States.

So as it happened, Mai Ling and I were each in our own bedrooms packing up our gear and conducting a long distance conversation – well, shouting, actually – as we wrapped our loot up in tissue and stuffed it into heavy cardboard shipping boxes. I was in the process of carefully laying my sexy French lingerie into one when for some weird reason I started thinking about Alex.

"So where do you think he went?" I shouted across the way. "The big dummy hasn't even called me!"

Mai Ling was in the process of shouting back, telling me for the millionth time to relax because everything was fine, when I heard a knock on the open door behind me.

Uh-oh.

Forgetting all about the really sexy black lace bra I was holding in my hand, I slowly turned around to see Alex leaning against the doorjamb with a mischievous smile on his face. Then as his eyes drifted to the bra hanging from my hand, my face turned crimson.

Oh, my God...

Wheeling around as fast as I could, I stuffed it in the box and slammed the top shut. Realizing I'd been busted big time, I slowly turned back and forced a thin smile. "Hi, Alex!"

Chuckling, he apologized for the unannounced intrusion. "Like the bra, by the way."

Jerk!

By now horribly embarrassed, I closed my eyes and pressed my balled-up fists against my sides. Uncertain as to whether I should deck him for that, or accept it as a compliment, I hesitated. Finally deciding to split the difference, I opened my eyes and addressed him in my *Seriously Irritated Voice*.

"Well I'm *a girl*, in case you hadn't noticed."

"Really?" he said as he pushed himself off the doorframe. "I thought there was something strange and wonderful about you!"

With that, my anger collapsed. So rather than yell at him, I raced over and pretended to bang my fists on his chest. "Where've you been?" I demanded to know.

"And why didn't you call me?"

Wrapping his hands around my fists, he apologized. "Some more secret stuff — and I would have called, but it was one of those 'no contact with the real world' deals."

Looking up, I told him I'd let him off the hook if he told me what he was doing back at the *Palais*.

"Oh..."

"Well, I hired a genealogist to research my family, and he thinks they may have originated in Gascony way back when...

"So I'm headed down the coast tomorrow to see if I can come up with some documentation, and I was wondering if you'd like to come along."

Huh?

Stunned, I looked up at him with eyes the size of saucers. "You want me to go to Gascony with you?"

Seemingly surprised by my reaction, Alex nodded. "If you want to..."

By then on the verge of shock, I stood there for at least a full minute before gathering up the wit to nod my head. "If Dr. MacLaughlin will let me," I said in an almost pleading whisper.

Alex smiled, and said it wasn't a problem. "I've already talked to him, and he said he can get by without you for a couple more weeks.

"A couple of weeks?" I asked breathlessly.

Alex nodded again. "Yeah, there's some serious historical research involved, so it'll take a while."

"What should I pack?"

"Just some casual stuff...

"Jeans, shorts, running shoes, maybe a sun dress..."

Excited, I told him that would be great. "Just tell me when to be ready."

Smiling, Alex asked me to tell the stewards he'd join us for breakfast the next morning. "We can leave right after that."

So after I told him I would, he tousled my hair before thanking me. "I appreciate the company."

Then without another word, he turned on his heel and marched out the door.

Forcing my fist into my mouth, I held back the scream until I was sure he was safely down the hallway.

Then I screeched for Mai Ling.

CHAPTER FIFTY-THREE

Which is the short explanation for how I found myself in a little, tiny Gascon village by the name of *Ville de Jardin*, some ten days later. But what it doesn't explain is the foul mood that fell upon me as we pulled to a stop beside a quaint little inn.

We'd been traipsing from pillar to post for almost two weeks by then, searching the musty old registers of one village church after another for a mention of anyone named "de Vris." Which would have been fine, of course, except for the galling fact that Alex hadn't shown the slightest interest in me the whole time.

Well...

Not as a girl anyway.

Having spent four long years in a tempestuous relationship with Christine at Georgetown, I knew he wasn't entirely immune to feminine charms. But I'd tried every trick in the book during the course of our road trip, with no result – including pinning my blouse dangerously low, pretending to fall asleep on his bed and a couple of others best left to your imagination.

But so far at least, nothing...

Nada...

By that time the separate rooms thing in the little inns we'd been staying in had worn thin, and so had my patience.

It's time for THE TALK, I thought grimly...

You know – the one where you tell the guy to lay his cards on the table or hit the road?

So after Alex opened the passenger-side door of the brand new Mercedes convertible he'd rented for the trip, I didn't say a word as I climbed out. While he went inside to see about our rooms, I leaned against the rear fender and plotted my ambush instead.

From where I stood, I could see the inn had once been a fairly large residence. But having been converted to commercial use a century or so before, the front consisted of two small rooms: one holding the proprietor's desk, several old but well upholstered chairs and a coffee table and the other seemed to be arranged more like a sun-room. After Alex banged on the bell a couple of times, I heard an old door creak open in the back and someone greet him in French. Then after a brief discussion, Alex returned to the dimly lit aside where we'd parked and popped open the trunk. Smiling, he told me we were in luck – there were four rooms upstairs, and we'd gotten the two with the morning sun. After an indifferent shrug, I hauled the military backpack I'd borrowed from Michelle out of the trunk, and trudged inside.

As Alex followed a few steps behind with the other two suitcases, I hiked up the steps to the landing. "So, which one's mine?"

Pointing to the front left, he said it probably had the better view.

Shrugging again, I marched down the narrow hallway and pushed the door open. After heaving the backpack across the tiny room and onto the bed, I turned around and took my suitcase from his hands. "This place have a bath?"

Pointing to the two doors just past the landing at the rear of the building, Alex nodded and told me the toilet was on the right, supposedly, and the bath on the left. Then with a look of concern, he asked me if I was OK.

Thinking that just wasn't the time to confront him, I shook my head instead. "I'm fine."

Which in Girl-Speak means something *entirely* different...

So after curtly informing him that I was going to take a bath and go to bed, I pushed the door shut in his face.

A little harsh, I thought. *But fair warning...*

Then I opened my suitcase on the bed, and pulled out my robe and slippers and the Foreign Legion T-shirt I'd bummed off Legionnaire Pierre back at the *Palais*. After pulling off my clothes and wrapping myself in the robe, I stuffed my feet into my furry footwear and headed down the hall.

The bath was pretty much what I'd come to expect – a quaint turn of the century steel tub lined with copper, I thought, but maybe brass, with hot and cold water spigots. There were a couple of towels piled on a stool by the door, and a miniscule bar of soap wrapped in waxed paper. After turning both taps and carefully adjusting them to get the temperature just right, I crawled in the tub. Having spent the last five hours bouncing along irregularly paved country roads, it was a welcome luxury.

I returned to my room an hour later, squeaky clean and far more relaxed. After bolting the door, I looked around before realizing it was a lot nicer than I'd thought. The room itself was small, but the ancient wooden floor was polished and the brass bed a bit bigger than the ones I'd been sleeping in for the past two weeks. Two big pillows sat at the head on top of fresh white sheets, and there was a big fluffy quilt folded at the foot. So after arranging the pillows and laying out the quilt, I climbed out of my robe and pulled on my T-shirt. Turning off the overhead light, I pulled back the drapes and opened the window. From where I stood, I could see a half-dozen ancient stone buildings to either side, set in a half-circle along the road. And across the way and to the left, I could see a little stone church at the edge of a forest.

Just below and across the road there was a fountain, and everywhere I looked there were flowers.

So beautiful, I thought.

Lost in the moment, I stood at the window for the better part of ten minutes before suddenly realizing I was tired. Deciding to leave it open so the sunlight could wake me, I crawled into bed and fell fast asleep.

I must have dreamt that night, because when I awoke I remembered being a little girl again. Alex was there, and for some reason, I was tugging on his hand, and insisting that he had to come with me. But by the time I sat up, I'd forgotten most of it. Even so, I couldn't shake the feeling that for some mysterious reason, we were supposed to be together – like it was somehow preordained, as though the Universe wanted it that way.

Suspecting that some part of my mind was trying to derail my plan to confront Alex, I shook it off and got dressed. Reminded of the fact that I desperately needed to do some laundry, I pulled on a pair of cutoffs and my only once-worn top before putting on a bare minimum of makeup. Then after running a comb through my hair, I set off in search of Alex.

He wasn't in his room, and there was no one at the desk, so I went out on the cobblestone street. Shielding my eyes from the bright morning sun, I looked around. Relieved to find the car where he'd parked it, I looked down the street to my left and then to my right. Astonished by the lush green grass interspersed by carpets of flowers, I walked over to the fountain and sat down on the edge. Marveling at the physical beauty that surrounded me, I didn't even notice as Alex approached.

"Morning," he said cheerfully. "Ready for some breakfast?"

Startled, I almost fell into the fountain.

Taking his outstretched hand to right myself, I demanded to know where he'd been. Pointing up the street to the third stone structure with the small French flag hanging from an angled pole attached to the wall next to the door, he told me he'd gone to the mayor's office to borrow his phone. "Had to call Paris."

"That's City Hall?"

Alex smiled and nodded. "City Hall, post office, and part-time police station – on those rare occasions when the cops stop by."

Thinking that *Ville de Jardin* made Glen Meadows look like a major metropolis, I looked around for a restaurant. "I'm hungry," I announced.

Releasing my hand, Alex pointed to the building next to City Hall. "The inn keeper's sister has a little café."

Not quite a lie, but definitely a wild exaggeration, because the café, so-called, had one reasonably sized table with three chairs outside on cobblestones by the street, and three smaller ones inside. But the coffee turned out to be great, and the freshly baked French bread even better. Not to mention the cheese – made in a backyard a few hundred feet down the road – and the hardboiled eggs freshly gathered from the henhouse out back. All in all, it was one of the better breakfasts I'd had in France.

Happily content, I had just settled back into my chair at the roadside table when I suddenly realized that I'd way overslept – because Alex had not only taken care of whatever was going on with Paris, but been down to the church to see the Priest as well. Lighting a cigarette after he finished off a piece of bread piled with fresh churned butter, he explained that the Priest had gone to the neighboring village for a sunrise baptism and wasn't expected back for another half-hour or so.

That was fine with me, because I was enjoying the sunlight, the flowers, and the tree-covered hills that loomed in the background beyond the forest. Nodding absently before taking another sip of coffee, I was wishing we could stay in *Ville de Jardin* forever, when a VW minibus with German plates bounced past. After pulling to a halt in front of the inn, a scruffy-looking guy with a beard got out and walked into the inn, followed by a really sleazy-looking girl with stringy blonde hair.

Thinking that just didn't look good, I was relieved to see two Gendarmes roar by on motorcycles.

After pulling a hundred franc note from his pocket and laying it next to his plate, Alex pushed his chair back and stood up. "Good thing I called," he said. "They must have gotten lost."

Then after telling me to wait for him, he walked back down the road to the inn.

Thoroughly confused, I watched as the Gendarmes re-emerged from the little hotel and greeted Alex as he arrived. After saluting, one of them handed him a large manila envelope. Then after he opened it and looked inside, Alex said something or another to the motorcycle cops. Apparently satisfied, they saluted again before climbing back on their machines and roaring off down the road.

Thinking that whole thing had been totally weird, I finished off the last of my coffee and stood up as he returned. "So, what's that?" I asked as he rifled through the contents of the envelope.

"Marriage license."

Unable to comprehend what he'd said, I stood there in shocked silence before finally repeating his words in a whisper. *"A marriage license?"*

Nodding as he extracted it from the big envelope, he handed it to me. "Signed by President Mitterrand himself."

As my hopes and dreams crashed down around me, tears welled in my eyes. Trembling so hard I could barely extend my hand, I took the document from him – but I couldn't look at it.

Thrusting it back at him, I whispered in disbelief. "You're getting married?"

After pursing his lips together, Alex nodded. "I hope so."

Shocked, I stood there and stared at him.

Then on the verge of coming completely unglued, I asked him when in a dejected whisper.

"Well, I was thinking about this afternoon…

"Unless there's something else you'd rather do."

Since my brain was already in the Major Malfunction Mode, I couldn't make sense of what he'd just said. Then as it finally began to sink in, I closed my eyes tight and pressed my lips together, and swung my head back and forth a couple of times before finally looking back up again.

"Alex, are you asking me to marry you?"

After he nodded sheepishly, I continued.

"This afternoon?"

Alex nodded again. "Unless you have something else planned."

As my brain rebooted, I shook my head. *"Oh, no,"* I said a bit too quickly. "I can work it in…"

Smiling, Alex reached into his shirt pocket and pulled out a diamond engagement ring. "Mai Ling insisted on this one…

"She said you'd like it."

Somewhere between shock and hysteria, I gasped as he slipped the exquisitely cut stone on my ring finger.

"Alex, it's beautiful!"

Smiling, he told me he was glad I liked it. "Let's go find the Priest."

Thinking this just had to be a dream, I began worrying that I'd wake up before the wedding.

"Right."

The walk to the church took five or six minutes, and we arrived just as the priest bounced up the road in a battered Peugeot. Looking to be in his mid-50s, he was fairly short for a Frenchman and portly. But he seemed to be in good humor as he climbed out of the car and welcomed us to the Church of St. Genevieve. "I am Father Tomas," he said in French. "What may I do for you?"

I was still having problems with spoken French, and in any event, Alex spoke too quickly for me to follow. But I could understand enough to catch the drift. So, roughly translated, he explained to Father Tomas that we wanted to get married that afternoon – before adding as an afterthought that we were Americans, and I wasn't fully fluent in French.

Switching to English, Father Tomas smiled as he gently questioned us. "You wish to marry so suddenly?"

Alex nodded his head and explained that we'd known one another for over a year, but that things had been so hectic that we'd never found the time for the ceremony.

Thinking that was the understatement of the century, I nodded emphatically. "We just got the marriage license today, Father."

Taking the envelope from Alex's outstretched hand, Father Tomas asked if we were Catholic. Shaking his head to the contrary, Alex explained that while I was Catholic, he was of Huguenot descent – meaning French Protestant – which came as something of a surprise to both the Father and me.

For me, because I'd never really thought about it.

And for Father Tomas, because there just weren't many Huguenots left after the Religious Wars.

Shaking his head sadly, Father Tomas apologized. "*Monsieur*, I cannot begin to express the depths of my sorrow for those terrible times...

"But you must understand that I cannot marry a Protestant. My Bishop has forbidden it."

Seemingly resigned, Alex nodded and I could tell he was about to fall back to Plan B. But since my Mother was going to go completely postal if she found out I'd been married by a Justice of the Peace, I grabbed the envelope from his hands and pulled out the marriage license.

"Can't you make an exception, Father? This is signed by President Mitterrand!"

Then I looked him straight in the eye and pleaded. "And if I don't get married in a Catholic church, my Mom is gonna kill me!"

Taken aback, Father Tomas looked down at the document I'd held up. "*Monsieur le Président* signed this?"

"Yes, Sir" I said, and pointed to the signature.

After studying it for a long moment, Father Tomas shook his head. "*Mademoiselle*, you have placed me in a terrible quandary…

"You see, as a young boy I was a courier for the Resistance…

"And aside from God," he explained, "*La belle France* is my greatest love!"

Then after a moment of thoughtful silence, he articulated his dilemma.

"So who shall I obey? The *Président of the République?*

"Or that fat fool of a bishop?

"Hmmmm…"

Then stretching out his hands, Father Tomas opened one palm, then the other. "*Monsieur le Président* on the one hand…

"The fat fool on the other."

After going back and forth like that three or four times, Father Tomas grinned and threw his hands up in the air.

"*Viva la France!*" he exclaimed.

Then turning to me with a big smile, he said he'd marry us now and repent his insurrection later.

"But there are two conditions, *Mademoiselle…*

"I will perform the ceremony, but not the mass, and it will be outside in the garden rather than inside the church itself."

Anxiously, I pressed the point. "But the garden is still technically the church, right?"

"But of course, *Mademoiselle*. It is consecrated ground."

Works for me, I thought. Because there's no way Mom could complain about that!

So after doing a little Happy Dance, I threw my arms around Father Tomas' neck and kissed him on the cheek. Then after agreeing on one o'clock, I grabbed Alex's hand and tugged.

Forgetting all about the unsavory pair who had just checked into the inn, I told Alex we had to hurry. "I have to find something to wear!"

Which turned out to be easier said than done – because except for the cutoffs and the top I was wearing, everything I'd brought with me was either grimy from riding in the convertible Mercedes, or just plain dirty from weeks of pouring over dusty Mediaeval church records.

And the one sundress I'd brought was like, totally trashed.

Thinking there was just no way I could get married in a twice-worn top, I bummed a light blue button-down shirt from Alex.

Which explains how I ended up standing in front of the altar Father Tomas set up in the Church garden, with Alex's shirt tied just above my navel. Thinking I looked like the New England version of Daisy Mae, I turned to him and joked. "Like my dress?"

Looking down at me, Alex smiled and told me I'd never looked more beautiful.

Now that was a big lie, of course – but at that particular moment I wasn't about to quibble. Thrilled by the compliment, I looked away as the crimson crept across my cheeks.

Astonished by the beauty of the little garden, I surveyed my surroundings for the first time. Butting up against the south wall of the church, the garden contained a stone bench for contemplation, a statue of St. Genevieve standing before a little fountain, and row upon row of beautiful flowers that ran along the ancient stone boundary line that marked the other three sides. Broken only by an incredibly graceful stone archway that opened into the field that led to the village, it was breathtaking.

Thinking there just couldn't be a more perfect place to be married, I was about to thank Alex for picking *Ville de Jardin* when I suddenly remembered how harsh I'd been the night before. Feeling suddenly guilty – and more than a bit uncertain – I started worrying that my tantrum had forced his hand.

As my eyes crossed and my knees went suddenly weak, I looked down in horror. Then after pondering the awful prospect for what seemed like a century or more, I summoned up my courage.

Only one thing to do, I thought. *Give him an out before it's too late...*

But after glancing around, I realized that was going to be a problem.

Father Tomas was busy at the altar, with his back to us – but in the hour and a half that elapsed between the time the priest agreed to marry us, and our return to the Church, the whole village had heard about the wedding and turned up with a table load of wine and pastries and little French delicacies wrapped in wafer thin breads. The Mayor, who had insisted that it was his duty to stand in for *Monsieur le Président*, was standing beside and slightly to the rear of Alex, while Suzette – the darling little 9-year-old who'd woven a garland of flowers for my hair – stood next to me holding a beautiful bouquet.

Oh, well, I thought. *Now or never…*

So with Father Tomas still busy doing something or another, I took a deep breath before whispering out of the side of my mouth.

"Alex – you don't have to do this if you don't want to."

There was an unbearably long silence, and for a minute I thought he was going to bail on me. But instead, he leaned over and whispered back.

"Yeah, I know…

"But I really want my dogs back."

That took a moment to sink in. But when it did, I gave him my *Most Evil Glare.*

Then I slammed my right elbow into his ribs just like Master Lee taught me in Tae Kwon Do class.

Alex gasped, Suzette giggled, and some of the villagers snickered.

"Forget it, Mister – *they're mine!*"

Turning around, Father Tomas asked if something was the matter. Shaking his head, Alex straightened up and told the priest his allergies were acting up. "Must be all the flowers, Father."

Satisfied by his explanation, Father Tomas asked us if we were ready. After we both nodded, he spread his arms and launched into a little talk that, I surmised, was for the benefit of the assembled villagers. Then he switched into English, and asked me if I would take Alex as my lawfully wedded husband according to the rite of our Holy Mother, the Church.

Thinking that was a complete no-brainer, I quickly nodded and agreed.

Then turning to Alex he asked if he would take me as his lawfully wedded wife, in the *spirit* of the Holy Church.

Impressed by the way Farther Tomas had covered his backside – just in case the Bishop found out about the wedding – I smiled as Alex agreed.

Then after the priest joined our hands together and wrapped his stole around them, we repeated the eight short lines of vows he read to us "In the presence of God, and the assembled community…"

But since Father Tomas was performing the old fashioned rite rather than the updated version common in America, I kinda modified the part where I promised to "obey" my husband by muttering under my breath.

"Like that's gonna happen…"

That flew right past Father Tomas, but for a moment there I thought Alex was going to double over and die laughing.

But lucky for me, he didn't. So when the Priest asked him if he had the ring, Alex somehow managed to nod, before turning to the mayor, who held it on a silken pillow.

After he retrieved it from its resting place, Father Tomas instructed Alex to place it on my finger as a symbol of our eternal bond.

Having finally regained his composure, Alex turned back to me and smiled. Then after taking my hand, he whispered he loved me as he slipped the golden band on my ring finger.

Works for me! I thought happily.

But wouldn't you just know it...

The very instant Father Tomas pronounced us man and wife, the little inn where we'd been staying went up in a spectacular explosion.

Taken completely off-guard by that one, I looked over my shoulder just in time to see a cloud of bricks, beams, and roof tiles arcing skyward, with the second-story bathtub following not far behind.

Uh oh...

So after one quick kiss, we took off and ran like hell...

EPILOGUE

Having come to the end of the story, I grinned. "You've gotta hand it to Alex," I said. "He knew how to show a girl a good time!"

Staring at me with her mouth agape, it took Ms. Hernandez a moment to recover. "So that's how you saved the world?" she asked breathlessly.

Smiling sweetly, I nodded. "The first time."

Ms. Hernandez gasped as she raised her hand to her chest. "There were others?"

Seeing that she had taken the bait, I smiled indulgently. "Five or six," I said, "Depending on how you slice 'em...

"But unfortunately, they're still classified – so I can't discuss them without written authorization from the President."

Then after measuring the shocked look of surprise that appeared on her face, I stood and peered directly into the camera. After thanking the audience for joining me in my home and listening so patiently as I told the story of how I'd met and married my husband, I told them that I looked forward to telling them more about our fifty-year adventure...

Just as soon as it's declassified...

Then after a sly wink to Special Agent Robert M. Jordan, III – who was standing along the far wall, desperately trying not to laugh at the way I'd just ambushed the President – I told the audience that if they wanted to hear the rest of our story, they'd have to write or call the White House and persuade him to authorize the disclosure.

Then smiling sweetly, I assured them that A. J. – my eldest son, Alexander, Junior – would love to hear from them. "It's an election year, you know."

As the room exploded in deafening applause, I smiled at the still shell-shocked Ms. Hernandez, and then at the cheering media crew and my Secret Service detail. Then with the cameras still rolling, I placed my hand on my neckline and performed the modified curtsy Christine had taught me so many years before.

It's all show biz, you know...

JUST BEFORE MIDNIGHT

ACKNOWLEDGEMENTS

The origins of this book date to the fall of 2001, a few months after the terrorist attacks against New York and Washington. Due to an increased workload that followed from 9-11, I'd labored unusually late one night at the end of October, or perhaps early November. On the way home from my office in Alexandria, Virginia, I decided to stop for a beer before turning in for the night. It was a spur of the moment decision, and one that seemed inconsequential at the time.

I stopped at the first familiar establishment, and was surprised to find it packed with young, college-age women. After making my way to the bar, I found an open cranny and squeezed in. The bartender took my order, and after I paid him, I looked around. I had just turned back to the bar when the girl next to me spilled her beer, and splashed me with a few insignificant drops. After apologizing profusely, she began talking to me either from embarrassment or boredom. Being at least twenty-five years her senior, and more than a bit disheveled by a long and hard day's work, I was quite sure her interest wasn't romantic.

In the course of time she asked me what I did for a living, and I explained to her that I worked for the Center for Intelligence Studies, a public policy organization that specialized in the intelligence dimension of national security. Surprised and needlessly impressed, she began peppering me with questions about the recently begun War on Terror. Within a matter of minutes, three or four of her friends joined in, and before I knew it, I found myself in the enviable situation of being surrounded by attractive young women.

They were deeply anxious, and like a great many Americans at the time, fearful that Al Qaeda would mount a devastating follow-on attack to 9-11. As I listened to them pour out their concerns, it became increasingly apparent that they had only a fleeting acquaintance with national security issues. Their lack of knowledge surprised me, as they were all seniors at one of Washington's most prestigious universities. Surely, they had at least taken an introductory course in international relations.

Most had, and several had aced the course. But the focus had been on international economic integration, and in any event, they seemed to feel that national security was for men. That surprised me even more, because even though the field was still dominated by males, there had been prominent exceptions throughout the 30 years or so that I'd spent in and about the national security apparatus. There were several women strategists at the Pentagon, and more than a few accomplished female intelligence analysts at the CIA. In fact, there were even a handful of women intelligence officers operating in the field.

Over the course of the next several hours, I did my best to explain to them basic geopolitical and strategic concepts, American foreign and defense policies, and why I so vehemently disagreed with the Bush Administration's decision to militarize what was fundamentally an intelligence and security problem. The decision to invade Iraq had not been publicly announced at the time, but for those of us with access or insight, it was clear that a larger conflict was just over the horizon.

The young ladies listened with rapt attention, but growing unease. Despite the rapid expansion of women in uniform, their unstated belief – clearly visible beneath a thin veneer – was that national security, international conflict, and war were issues for men.

Closing time eventually rolled around, and I thanked the girls for the beers they had so generously exchanged for my analysis and insights. But as I walked out into the cool night air, I was taken by a sense of unease. The young women with whom I had shared the past two or three hours were exceptionally bright and well educated, and would doubtless describe themselves as feminists. Yet, they clearly preferred to leave questions of war and peace to the male half of the species. They seemed to share an implicit belief that there is a natural division of political labor, in which women looked after feminine and family issues, and men attended to the problems of the larger world.

I found that deeply troubling – women comprise slightly more than half the electorate, and for that reason alone I felt they should have a working knowledge of national security issues, much as men should have a working knowledge of traditionally feminine or family issues. That the girls I'd met in the bar did not, made me ill at ease.

I thought about that problem on and off for several years, and in the process talked to – interrogated might be a better word – any number of women, covering the full spectrum of age, education, and social status. Although the sentiment I'd stumbled across in the bar was by no means universal, it was unusually common. In my investigation, at least, most women shied away from national security issues. When pressed, most of those I questioned shrugged uneasily and said something to the effect that national security wasn't an issue they were especially interested in. Very often, they followed by saying they felt unqualified to hold or express an opinion on the subject.

It eventually occurred to me that one reason for their reticence was the lack of well-known female role models in the military services and the intelligence community, and I wondered if I could create a fictional character to serve that purpose. Perhaps I could write a novel that centered on an ingénue to whom female readers could relate, a young woman who by chance and circumstance had found herself cast into the shadowy world of national security policy. That way, the readers could learn the ins and outs of this important, but poorly understood, area along with her.

After mulling it over, I concluded it was possible – but obviously, not a simple task for one who has spent his entire life as a male.

I began by reviewing the handful of popular female action heroes of the time, i.e., women engaged in traditionally male endeavors such as war, espionage, or simple survival – or in the case of the phenomenally popular *Buffy the Vampire Slayer*, the never-ending fight against the Vampires, the Demons, and The Forces of Darkness in Sunnydale.

Since the framework for national security – that is, National Policy and Grand Strategy – is determined at the political level, I began wondering in jest who the political equivalent of *Buffy the Vampire Slayer* might be in Washington. She might be a staffer on Capitol Hill, or work in the Executive Office of the President. But given her age and lack of experience, it seemed far more likely that she would be toiling in one of Washington's many "think tanks."

After settling on that, I began by considering a half-dozen real and imaginary figures. *Buffy* was among the fictional characters, as was "Evy Carnahan" from Stephen Sommers' 1999 remake of *The Mummy*. A third was Melanie Griffith's character in *Shining Through* who, like the character I envisioned, had accidentally stumbled into the murky world of spies and counter-spies. Among the actual women I called upon in this process was one of the half-dozen or so female OSS officers who had served in World War II. Although properly circumspect in recounting her wartime career, I was impressed by her ability to adapt, after having been suddenly cast into a deadly game of cat and mouse. While her college friends at home were absorbed by the latest fashions, or obsessing over their marriage prospects, she was on the run in Occupied Europe.

It was through this process that "Alicia" finally emerged from the shadows of my mind.

I liked her immediately. I liked her adventurous spirit, I liked her independence, and I liked her buoyant optimism. Most of all, I liked her quirky personality.

The endless hours I spent with her while writing this book were among the happiest and most fulfilling of my life.

Once Alicia had fully formed, the book wrote itself. I imagined her in the twilight of her life, telling the story of how she had saved the world to a rapt audience, in the *Global News Network* interview recounted in the Prologue. Placing myself in the audience, I took careful notes. And in my mind, I occasionally interrupted with questions. She was invariably gracious in reply, and generous with her time.

Despite certain similarities, Alicia is not *Buffy* – a subject to which we will later return. Those of you who have studied psychology will recognize her as my "Anima" – that is, my feminine potentiality now manifest as an Inner Object. She is a part of me that has found expression through this book.

So too are the other characters who appear in these chapters: Alex and his lifelong friend Nguyen; Nguyen's wife, Dr. Mai Ling Tranh; Professor MacLaughlin; Christine; Jennifer; Julia; and even Alicia's nemesis, Jennifer "Two."

Also a part of me, in a different and perhaps more biological sense, are Col. Fortescue and Capitaine Michelle Gaston – the latter of whom Alicia irreverently refers to as "*Madame Capitaine.*"

I know where Alex and Nguyen came from. Alex is my idealized self-image, living a better life in a better world, and Nguyen is precisely the sort of man I'd choose for my best friend. But where the hell Mai Ling came from is a total mystery.

Although I can trace her to a youthful character I encountered in a film as a young boy, I cannot account for her personality or her wacky sense of humor. Somehow, she popped out of my subconscious fully formed – and I'm grateful for it.

Now for the acknowledgments.

First of all, I have to acknowledge – as opposed to thank – a certain section of the U.S. Intelligence Community. They're complete bastards, but without them this book would never have been written. They know who they are, and any further description would probably get me 20 years' worth of free room and board in a federal prison.

'Nuff said…

Next, I'd like to thank Joss Whedon for his character, *Buffy*, and for the endless hours I spent cheering on the Scooby Gang in their courageous battle against The Forces of Darkness. Despite my passing acquaintance with Greek and Roman mythology, my more substantial knowledge of history and my actual acquaintance with several brave women, I had never really thought of the fair sex as combatants – and still less, as heroes – until *Buffy the Vampire Slayer* came along.

T.S. Eliott once said something to the effect that young poets imitate, while experienced poets steal. The same can be said of writers, so with Eliot's observation in mind, I'd like to acknowledge the occasional overlaps between *Buffy* and Alicia. In Chapter 10, for example, Alicia described Tom Andrews as a nerd before finally deciding he was a geek instead. It seems the nerds had been picking on him in the canteen, and geeks wouldn't do that because of "Union rules and all that."

As *Buffy* fans may recall, she said something very much like that in one of her episodes.

In Chapter 16, Alicia finds Tom Andrews trying to drag his desk out in the hallway after being booted out of his office, and gives him a ration of light-hearted grief. As she walks away, she justifies the put-down by saying "You have to smack geeks around every now and then, just to keep them in line. Otherwise, they'd take over the world and we'd all have to wear pocket protectors and big thick glasses held together with scotch tape..."

Long after writing this scene, I recalled *Buffy* saying something to this effect. It lodged in subconscious memory somehow, and despite a diligent effort to find the quote in my collection of *Buffy* DVDs, I was unable to track it down for proper attribution.

Finally, in Chapter 17, Alicia is teasing Two about the paper hat she had fashioned to keep the dust from collapsed ceiling tiles from getting in her hair. Irritated, Two asks Alicia if she doesn't have an "elsewhere to be." That is a verbatim quote from "Cordelia Chase," in the first *Buffy* episode, and I stole it fair and square.

In addition to these three overlaps, there may be others – but despite a diligent effort that included an immensely pleasant review of all six seasons of *Buffy the Vampire Slayer*, these were all I found.

So to the charge of Grand Theft, Literary, I plead guilty, with extenuating circumstances – as with so many millions of other fans, *Buffy* made a huge and enduring impression upon me.

Readers might also detect a certain similarity between "Two" and "Cordelia Chase," but that is purely coincidental. Two is based on a young secretary I encountered many years ago, when the Center for Intelligence Studies' predecessor organization was located on Vermont Avenue in downtown Washington, DC. But since I'm a dead man if I mention her name, she shall remain forever anonymous.

I'd also like to thank the many young women who helped me write this book. As I stated earlier, writing a female character was a daunting prospect for one with no experience as such. To compensate for that deficiency, I recruited groups of young women for a series of focus groups. In exchange for beer and pizza, they read each chapter as written, and provided me with detailed commentary and criticism. Composed of coeds drawn from the local universities, their feedback was invaluable. Each chapter was re-written at least twice, and often more, until the young women were satisfied that I had fairly portrayed the feminine experience.

Finally, I'd like to thank the late Betty Wolfe for her encouragement and support; my friend Tony Ryan for reading, proofing and commenting on the manuscript; and my friend and former colleague, Dr. Joseph D. Douglass, Jr., for his path-breaking research of Soviet involvement in illegal drug and weapons sales, and for his patient tutoring of me in this subject.

I'd also like to thank my editor, Janet Ruegg Wynne, for reading, proofing, editing, and criticizing the manuscript through its final re-write. A journalist with magazine, newspaper and public relations experience, Janet's input and hard work were both invaluable. Without it, the tale of Alicia and The Gang would not have come out nearly as well.

I'd also like to take this opportunity to apologize to her for my "serial abuse of English grammar," as she so delicately put it. Despite the fact that my mother was an English teacher, I never learned to spell – and as for grammar, let's just say English class was so boring that I made up my own rules for speech and writing. I call it "Viarinese," and under no circumstances should it be construed as a reflection on Janet's skills as an editor. It drove her up the wall – and after this experience, she may need years and years of therapy.

In closing, I would be remiss if I didn't mention my former superior and mentor, the late James J. Angleton. The CIA's legendary former Chief of Counterintelligence, it was Mr. Angleton who instructed me in The Dark Art so many years ago.

I would also like to thank the late Raymond G. Rocca, the CIA's former Deputy Chief of Counterintelligence (Analysis). Mr. Angleton's exposition in Chapter 33 was taken almost verbatim from a research paper on *Operatsia Trist* that Ray prepared for the Counterintelligence Staff, which Mr. Angleton sometimes used in instructional seminars. According to Ray, it was pilfered from his locked office by the late Newton "Scotty" Miler, the Agency's former Deputy Chief of Counterintelligence (Operations), and thereby saved from the shredder when they left the Agency.

Sorry, Scotty – didn't mean to rat you out, but I know you'd want me to establish the essential authenticity of Mr. Angleton's talk at the CSS.

And now for my readers – thank you for picking up this book. I hope you enjoy reading it as much as I enjoyed writing it.

If nothing else, I hope it will make clear that things are not always what they seem to be in the shadows of power.

Charles S. Viar
Washington, DC.
September 2012

Post Script: The attempt to overthrow the U.S. Government presented in these pages may or may not be based upon actual events. I'll leave it to the readers to decide for themselves.

MUSICAL ACKNOWLEGEMENTS

Because music provides an important backdrop to the events chronicled in *Just Before Midnight*, I would like to express my deep and lasting appreciation to the individuals and organizations which generously permitted me to reproduce copyrighted lyrics within the text.

In order of appearance, I would like to thank Mr. Isidro Otis, President of the Clyde Otis Music Group of Englewood, New Jersey, for permission to reprint *Lover Please, Please Come Back* in Chapter 30. As I told Mr. Otis in an e-mail, this is one of my favorite songs, and I hope this reproduction will help introduce *Lover Please* to a whole new generation of music aficionados.

Next, I would like to thank Ms. Maura Sullivan for permission to reproduce *Christmas Eve in Washington* in Chapter 38. Sung by Ms. Sullivan, this is one of the most beautiful Christmas songs ever written or produced, and I encourage the readers of *Just Before Midnight* to visit her website, where they may obtain a copy. The address is:

http://www.christmaseveinwashington.net/

At the time of this writing, *Christmas Eve in Washington* is also available on Amazon.com

Finally, I would like to thank the Hal Leonard Corporation of Milwaukee, Wisconsin, for permission to reproduce *Bad Moon Rising* in Chapter 43. In accordance with the reproduction agreement, I am presenting the following information:

Bad Moon Rising
Words and Music by John Fogerty
Copyright ©1969 Jondora Music
Copyright Renewed
International Copyright Secured. All Rights Reserved.
Reprinted by Permission of Hal Leonard Corporation

In the course of the text, several other songs are prominently mentioned, but not reproduced. In Chapter 52 a version of Harry Belafonte's *Day-O* appears (often referred to as the *Banana Boat Song*).

In order to comply with my best understanding of the "Fair Use" provision of U.S. copyright laws, only two lines have been quoted.

Charles S. Viar

JUST BEFORE MIDNIGHT

ABOUT THE AUTHOR

Charles S. Viar is Chairman of the Center for Intelligence Studies in Washington, DC.

Readers are invited to e-mail their comments on *Just Before Midnight* to Mr. Viar at CFISPress@aol.com.

JUST BEFORE MIDNIGHT

CHARLES S. VIAR

Made in the USA
Charleston, SC
24 June 2013